✳ INDOCHINE ✳

W9-BEM-096

Christie Dickason

BANTAM BOOKS
TORONTO · NEW YORK · LONDON · SYDNEY · AUCKLAND

For Robert and Tess,
without whom this would never
have been written

INDOCHINE

A Bantam Book / published by arrangement with
Villard Books

PRINTING HISTORY

Originally published in Great Britain in different form under the
title The Dragon Riders by Century Hutchinson Ltd. Copyright ©
1986 by Christie Dickason.

Villard Books edition published September 1987

Bantam edition / October 1988

SAIGON, 1954....

Nina slept. Her long, fifteen-year-old arms and legs were spread as if to embrace the world. The next second, the room came alive. The framed photograph of her French grandparents fell off the wall. The sound of its glass breaking was lost in the belching crump of the explosion which blew out the front wall of the drawing room on the floor below. It also blew out a Louis Seize settee, three crystal wall sconces, half of the grand piano, and the body of Ariane, Nina's mother.

Still only half awake, Nina ran onto the landing. The great teak staircase to the ground floor was already blazing. She went back into her room and slammed the door on the flames.

Ever since the first Vietminh *plastique* had wrecked a Saigon café, she had rehearsed over and over exactly what she would take with her in an emergency. Now, from a shoe box at the back of her closet, she grabbed her secret money box, her journal, the photograph of her father, the velvet bag holding her grandmother's earrings and the carved ivory dragon bird seal her father had given her.

She sprinted to the veranda at the back above the servants' quarters. Heat rushed past her. Flames had reached the top of the stairs and were nosing down the corridor. Nina swung herself over the wooden railing of the veranda and launched herself toward the ground through the ancient bougainvillea trained against the wall of the house. She half climbed, half fell in a crash of branches, and hit the ground bleeding from gashes.

Where were her parents? She started to run round to the front of the house to see if her parents were there. Then she saw the back gate of the compound gaping open into the street. It was never left open at night.

Suddenly one gatepost flared bright in the headlamps of a car in the street. She ran to the open gate. Inside the rear window of the disappearing car, she saw the heads of two men; between them lolled a third. The third man was her father. . . .

My wish is to ride the tempest, tame the waves, kill the sharks. I want to drive out the enemy and save our people. I will not resign myself to the usual woman's lot, bowing my head to become a concubine.

—**Dame Trieu**
A.D. 238, age twenty-three

Abbreviations Used

ARVN	Army of the Republic of (South) Vietnam
DMZ	Demilitarized Zone
FBN	Federal Bureau of Narcotics (United States)
JUSPAO	Joint United States Public Affairs Office
MAAG	(US) Military Assistance Advisory Group
MACV	(US) Military Assistance Command, Vietnam
SDECE	Service de Documentation Extérieure et du Contre-Espionage
USAID	United States Agency for International Development
USIS	United States Information Service
USOM	United States Operations Missions

PART ONE

INTRODUCTION:
Vietnam, 1965—Nina

The young woman was an incongruous passenger for the Huey Transport headed north into the combat zone. Her hair was drawn back into a chignon; her skin and nails had the sheen of constant professional attention. Her linen suit had been cut in Paris and her shoes were Italian. The manicured hands were folded lightly over a crocodile handbag, the slim wrists were celebrated with the faint tinkling of gold bracelets shaken by the rotors.

Several of the grunts who made up the rest of the passenger list eyed her with covert speculation. Special passengers weren't unusual among the daily loads of crumpled marines, ammunition and supplies, and body bags, both empty and filled. The men had become used to Vietnamese officials and their wives, press, whores, and observers of one kind or another. They had learned to ignore the men escorting special, undefined cargo from upland hamlets near the Laotian border for distribution to various syndicates in Saigon.

But this passenger had been escorted to the helicopter by the CO himself and handed into the uncomfortable metal-framed seat as if it were the backseat of an Eldorado Cadillac. On top of that, she was a looker. Not pure-blooded dink; she was too big in the bosom, too wide in the shoulder; her feet were too long and narrow. But she had the native cheekbones, the skin like old ivory, the heavy, straight hair which she disdained to curl.

Her eyes were dark and repulsed investigation as she gazed straight ahead, over the shadowy shapes of the men on the floor. The edges of her painted lips were sweetly curved enough to twist a man's gut, but she had set them into an expressionless, forbidding line.

One of the marines sighed from within his private thoughts. She was one of those women who make men want to mess them

1

up a little. Her composure challenged them to unstring her with desire. At the same time, they would be sorry to see her lose her mystery and become like all the others, proof yet again that life was only ordinary when it wasn't awful. The marine shifted the stirring in his groin into a more comfortable position.

She was set down near a remote hamlet just south of the DMZ. The men watched her figure bend and run in its high heels through the dry golden grass which heaved and bowed in the down-draft from the rotors. A figure came out of the treeline to meet her. It bowed and took from her the leather carryall that she had kept by her feet throughout the flight. Then the elegantly dressed woman and the man in dark peasant's clothes disappeared into the scarred and tattered jungle of the mountain foothills.

As soon as she was out of sight in the trees, the woman stopped. While her escort kept watch along the trail from a discreet distance, his back turned, she quickly stripped off her linen suit and Italian shoes, her French silk underwear and her gold bracelets. She stretched unselfconsciously and sighed with pleasure as the air hit her hot, damp skin. Her young body was as smooth and golden as her face, like that of her native father, while the heavy breasts and thick dark pubic bush spoke of her French mother.

From the carryall she took a black cotton jacket and a pair of loose trousers with a drawstring waist. She put on the jacket and, with hands that shook slightly from excitement, pulled the drawstring so that the trousers rested lightly on her hips. Then she slipped her feet into a pair of rough sandals with soles cut from a Goodyear rubber tire. In a few moments she had transformed herself from one of the polished women usually seen on the arms of gangsters or Air Force officers at American receptions and cocktail parties in Saigon into a handsome peasant with an air of authority beyond her years.

Her escort took up the bag again and they set off along the narrow trail through the scrub. He ignored the deserted hamlet, where a few chickens still scratched in the dust around the burned-out huts. After crossing the blackened scar of a napalm drop, he turned back into the rough grassland beyond the trees, bent, and lifted a section of turf by one edge. The trapdoor opened cleanly. The young woman moved forward, climbed down the lashed wooden ladder, and disappeared into the earth. Her escort followed her. After a last look around, he lowered the trapdoor. The hot evening breezes stirred the ends of the dry grass, the only sign of life in the dead landscape.

1
Tonkin, 1926—Luoc

In Tonkin, the northernmost province of French Indochina, a boy lay on a limestone outcrop which gave him a clear view of the mountain gorge while hiding him from eyes below. He saw no movement yet on the trail, which played hide-and-seek through the rocks and scrub until it wound downward, out of sight below his ledge. Chin resting on folded arms, he closed his eyes to let his ears read the evening, but no unusual sound disturbed the clear, thin air.

He opened his eyes again and swung one slim gold-brown hand in the dizzy space in front of him, then stretched carefully so as not to dislodge a stone to patter and bounce down the narrow steps of the cliff face. The evening was cooling now that the sun had dropped behind the jagged fingers of the mountain range which scraped the sky like a broken comb.

In spite of his fear, his young body felt good; he was fifteen and just beginning to trust the new male strength the gods had given him. Filial respect would keep him from ever testing the fact, but he knew secretly that he was nearly as strong now as his own father, who was the headman of their village and the head of their family. The same respect made him quickly put out of his mind the anger and confusion he always felt when he remembered how the Round Eye, the year before, had dared to speak to his father, and the meek way that his father, the headman, had replied.

On that earlier visit, the headman had read his son's face. Instead of becoming angry at such impudence, he had said quietly, "Fate sent the Round Eyes to us. The Heavens keep them here. We watch constantly for omens of change, but they have not yet been shown to us."

All the same, the headman sent the boy, his oldest son, Luoc, down into the delta to a Round Eye school to see if he could learn the secret magic of the Round Eyes' power, which had brought to heel the ancient kingdoms of Tonkin, Annam, Laos, Cambodia, and Cochin China.

It was known that their magic had to be potent. For centuries, the Mandarins at the court of the Supreme Father had kept life more or less in order. They interpreted Heaven's will through the correct rituals, then, by their own example, had taught the people how to behave in harmony with this will. Then these others came. Four generations ago. First round-eyed men in long black skirts and then the ones in trousers. It was clear that they had powerful sorcerers who could interpret Heaven more clearly than the Mandarins, for Heaven turned its favor toward them. Even the Supreme Father and his court paid homage. The old kingdoms became the French Union of Indochina. The ancient Viet civilization began a painful sea change into *la civilisation*, which the French exported to their colonies with as much fervor as the priests who had carried the Catholic faith.

Luoc understood his father's purpose and worked hard at the Jesuit school. He learned French easily, and French literature. In history class, he chanted from French textbooks with other golden-skinned boys, *"Nos ancêtres, les Gaulois...."* He had learned to eat the white bread made of wheat which was the flesh of one of their gods. But he had not learned how any of this helped keep the French strong, nor had he learned what spells or sacrifices might loosen their grip and shake their terrifying confidence.

On his ledge, he stretched again, enjoying the smooth slide of his body inside his rough cotton tunic, rejoicing in his freedom from his hated uniform, left folded on his sleeping mat at school for the entire holiday. He allowed himself to think about the discoveries he had recently shared in the scrub with a montagnard girl from a higher village. He could not help smiling; his entire body vibrated at the memory. Much as he dreaded the evening ahead, it seemed a small darkness beyond which his life shone ahead of him, marvelous because yet to be fully imagined.

Metal struck against metal, only once and so faintly that he almost missed it. He eased back from his lookout, down onto the steep track to his village, which lay in the elbow of the curving ridge. Even in his urgency, he enjoyed the spring of his strong young muscles as he dropped from boulder to boulder to carry the warning.

By the time the Frenchman's mule train broke out of the gorge onto the narrow plateau, the huts lining the track were nearly deserted. Before Luoc arrived, children had been playing. There had been adolescent girls, and boys grown just large and strong enough for impressment into military service or road-building gangs.

Now, one old man squatted in the dust. Three old women peered from the porches of huts. The girl who had been born with the split muzzle of a civet cat continued plaiting her basket of rattan and bamboo. The headman stood motionless in front of his own hut where his wives and two sons lay hidden.

Luoc pulled back a torn corner of the matting that formed the wall of the hut. The Round Eye was the same height as his father but not so thin, with a stooped back and narrow jaw like a dog. His eyes and the top of his face were hidden in the dusk by the beak of a filthy Legionnaire's kepi; its sunflap hung in shreds around his shoulders like lank hair.

"We'll stay the night," said the Frenchman through an interpreter. "It's too dark to move on."

The headman made a gesture of welcome. The old women disappeared to fetch rice for their visitors. The six guards with the mule train tethered their animals and began to spread their sleeping mats on the ground. The mules pulled against their ropes as they looked for grass on the dry dust, but the rains had spent themselves farther up on the slopes that year; the grass, like the villagers' crops, had withered and died, high out of reach of the life-giving canals of the Red River delta.

Luoc's father stood politely while the Frenchman ate. The guards chewed in the shadows of the mules.

"Where is everyone?" The interpreter passed the question on while the Frenchman looked up and down the village.

"Had an epidemic?" The Frenchman grinned and shoveled in another mouthful.

The headman said nothing.

"I hope you aren't going to make me a problem," said the Frenchman. "Like the bunch over at Ha Giang."

There was a moment of silence when the interpreter finished. Word had traveled fast from Ha Giang.

"I don't enjoy talking to myself."

"I too hope there is no difficulty," said the headman.

"Then where's the rest of it?" The Frenchman pointed to the three small bales wrapped in dark blue cloth that sat in the porch of the headman's hut. He held the accusing finger steady while his interpreter repeated his words.

"There is no more, monsieur."

"Headman, I know you are lying!"

In his hiding place, Luoc wanted to seize his father's *coupe-coupe,* which lay concealed along a beam in the roof, and slice the Frenchman's arrogant head from his body.

"All the crops were bad, monsieur," he heard his father say. "And the landlord must be paid. We had to put the ground to maize and three-month rice, or starve. We will make it up next season. The sorcerer says there will be good rains."

"Poppies are highland crop," said the Frenchman shortly. "Grow like weeds. I think you've decided to go into business for yourself."

"That is our entire crop." The headman's voice was calm. A listener would not have guessed that his uncle had been one of the "bunch over at Ha Giang."

"It's not your crop!" said the Frenchman. "It belongs to the government of the Union of French Indochina. Stealing from the government is treason!"

"That is all we ever had this season."

"I have a nose for it, and I smell more."

"There is no more."

Passed through a third party, the exchange seemed calm enough, but the headman, too, had begun to consider the hidden blade. He looked at the men by the mules; there were too many of them. He was frightened.

"A pity to have wasted words," said the Frenchman. He shouted an order. The interpreter stood silent, his head down.

The headman started for his weapon. Two men caught him and knocked him to the ground. A third helped to drag him clear of the foraging mules. One, a Moroccan, kicked him in the stomach. The headman curled up as if embracing the Moroccan's boot. Then all three jumped clear while two Tonkinese guards fired their rifles. The headman flung himself akimbo when the bullets hit, raising puffs of dust with his scrabbling feet.

A long silence followed the shots. The early night noises from the scrub were shocked into stillness. The flapping and squawking of a startled jungle fowl died into the distance. Dust hovered in a sheer veil around the body.

The Frenchman strolled over and bent down. "Well done," he said. "No need for a coup."

"Tell them," he said to the interpreter, "to put more ground to poppies."

The man hesitated, looked around the empty village, then raised his voice and called the instruction into the growing darkness of the night.

Coldness shriveled Luoc's flesh, and sickness rose from his stomach. In his imagination, he ran from his hiding place and tore the Frenchman's face from his skull with his bare fingers. Then he imagined the bullets tearing into his own young muscles. He felt for a moment the glory of his action. Then, more clearly, he saw its futility. In a confusion of dream and reality, he saw his mother's face in the shadows beside him, pleading silently with him not to move and give away their position. His father's young second wife looked at him with terrified eyes, hands pressed to her mouth. She was the one they would drag into the scrub.

Luoc looked through the hole in the matting at the dark heap of cloth and hair and strangely angled limbs, barely visible in the heavy dusk. It had been his father, the most respected man in the village. As his uncle had been in Ha Giang. When the mercenaries moved the bales of raw opium from the porch, he strained his eyes to remember the faces of the Tonkinese who had fired the shots. Those of the Frenchman and the Moroccan were already burned into his mind.

The coldness now possessed him completely. With the coldness came the first shape of an idea—too huge to see clearly, too complicated to be understood totally. But he felt it take up residence within him like a possessing spirit. It filled his fifteen-year-old body with the strength of a demon.

2
Cap Ferret, Gascony, 1927—Ariane

Long before she became the wife of one of Saigon's most acceptable natives, sixteen-year-old Ariane Cellier, daughter of a chemist in provincial France, lay on her back in a field. Her blue eyes were closed, the lids red-hot. Her chin was lifted and her legs spread to the heat of the sun like a young Danäe waiting for her god. Every centimeter of her young body pressed heavily against the ground. The bones bit through the fleshy mounds of her newly widened hips, and the weight of her fair head, usually balanced unthinkingly, dug a hollow in the matted grass.

The new hay bent beneath her palms; a dry stalk from the last year's growth trailed its bent tip like a pen across her left wrist, pushed by the light and erratic breeze. She imagined that it wrote a message which she could not read. She was waiting for something and feared she would not recognize it when it came. She did not know how to ease the new restlessness that possessed her. She knew only that what she saw in her daily life was not enough.

When she could escape from studies and housework, she trudged across the dunes to the open Atlantic on the west side of the peninsula. There she would stand with her arms spread, letting herself be buffeted by the winds. She walked for hours along the sand, aimlessly, pulling up clumps of blue-green sea holly and mortifying her flesh on its thorns like one of the Blessed Saints. After she had carried each clump a few meters, she would toss it aside.

Some days she went down to the estuary, on the landward side, where the men worked. She would sit on a shoulder of rock above the mudflats which bristled with clumps of poles marking the oyster beds. A rivulet of fresh water trickled past her feet. For some reason it annoyed her; it took so long to join the main channel on its wide curve around a high mudbank toward the open sea. It twisted and etched a devious path across the mud, past boats that lay on their sides, crippled by the retreat of the tide.

The oyster fishermen annoyed her too. And frightened her. Their voices were loud and rough as they sorted the crusted shells into buckets according to size, mended their trays and crab traps, and threw broken bits of light back at the afternoon sun off the blades of their oyster knives.

Jules Martin annoyed her most of all. The whole village seemed to believe they had an understanding. Although Ariane's father was a professional man and Jules's father only a fisherman, the Martins had just bought a seafood restaurant out on the point of the Cape. There they could sell their catch directly to the summer holidaymakers who rented the higgledy-piggledy clusters of villas behind the dunes. Jules, therefore, had prospects. Ariane agreed with her mother that Jules was good-looking. She could not argue that he would not offer her a comfortable, if hardworking, life. But as she watched him from her rock, in his work clothes and heavy rubber boots, laughing with the other men, she knew that he would never touch the source of the yearning within her.

She would flee from the fishermen to the stillness of the meadows north of the village, beyond the plantations of young pines that had been set out to hold down the wandering sands of the peninsula. There she would listen to the stillness inside her, waiting to be filled with an answer.

Lying in the meadow one day, she suddenly sat bolt upright, heart pounding, dried grass caught in her fair short curls. What if she were falling into a state of sin? What if this lassitude and restlessness, this internal waiting, were preparation for possession by Satan? It was hard to know. The nuns at school were most unclear in their descriptions of evil. Ariane had noticed that Soeur Marie des Anges became quite flushed when she talked about Temptation, as if it had excitements she dared not mention. Ariane said a quick Hail Mary, cross-legged in the meadow grass, stockings dotted with bristled seed pods, heavy cotton work shirt creased and damp.

Another thought occurred. Perhaps she was waiting to be called to the Vocation. To become a nun. She considered the possibility. She wasn't at all sure she wanted to be called, but the idea had dignity, and it was grand enough to explain the sensation inside her like a bud that had swollen but was unable to break. The more she thought, the more she liked it. It should please her parents. It took care of Jules Martin. She picked two red poppies and laid herself down like a crucifix, a flower on each open palm, as a signal to heavenly watchers of her willingness.

She had misjudged her parents' reaction. They weren't pleased; they were horrified. Their first child and only son had died for the glory of France in 1917. Ariane was the late and unexpected pet of their middle age. They wanted grandchildren, someone to justify the nights spent over books, the middle-of-the-night awakenings to prepare emergency prescriptions. If Ariane locked herself away from the world, there was no point in having acquired stocks, a little something in the Crédit Lyonnais, and a solid reputation for the next generation to build on.

Her father eyed her over his bowl of breakfast coffee. "I mean no disrespect to Our Lord," he said. "But surely He would be happy to leave the ripest and loveliest fruits for His sons on earth . . . to inspire them to procreate in His image, as He had directed them."

It was a canny attempt, but he underestimated his daughter's newly acquired religious fervor. She did not question the implied compliment, but she was outraged. She felt that the Lord deserved the best once in a while. In her opinion, considering the sisters at the school, He took far too many brides who turned to Him in desperation because they couldn't find earthly husbands.

An educated man who had chosen peace in this small fishing village, her father recognized his daughter's restlessness from his own youth. It frightened him to open his protective hand and let her go. But he knew that unless he did so, he would lose her forever, one way or another. Before supper that night he had spoken to a business acquaintance, who promised to have a word with someone else.

Two months later, Monsieur Cellier made a pact with his daughter over dinner.

"Saigon!" cried Ariane.

"Alone?" cried her mother.

"It's common practice," said Cellier calmly, just as others had reassured him during the two months. "Garine is a highly placed *fonctionnaire* and his wife is a cousin of the Huberts in Toulon. . . . They have a large house in Saigon and a full domestic staff."

He wiped his mouth and smiled at his wife. "Far more than I could ever afford for you, I'm afraid. It just so happens that the wife asked her cousin—that's Paul Hubert—to find them a *vraie française* to be companion to their little girl, Paulette. There's a younger boy as well. But it seems that little Paulette is acquiring the most dreadful French accent from the servants. . . ."

"I won't dream of letting her go all that way by ship, alone," said Mme. Cellier. From her husband's determination and the radiance of her daughter's face, she knew that she faced a terrible loss. "To go so far. . . ."

"Don't worry," said Cellier. His wife's misery angered him because his own was so thinly walled away. "People are going out there all the time. Others like Ariane. Priests. Soldiers. Diplomats. It's not as if Indochina were really a foreign country. Think of it as a piece of France that broke off and drifted a little way out to sea."

"It is a *little* different, isn't it?" asked Ariane anxiously.

Her father smiled again. He had the smooth, kind, square face and silver head of a storybook family doctor; his ability to reassure had done more for his business than his pharmaceutical talents.

"I think you will find it quite different enough from Cap Ferret," he said. "I'm just trying to make your mother feel better." He winked at Ariane. "It's not easy, you know, to think of doing without you for a year or more."

"Saigon . . ." said Ariane to herself.

"The Sisters of the Presentation send out some of their members each autumn," continued Cellier. "Ariane can travel with them. Chaperoned by nuns . . . what more can you ask?"

His wife was cutting her braised duck so savagely that her floral-covered bosom, the mother mountains of Ariane's own, trembled beneath the rayon fabric of her dress.

He turned back to his daughter. "You must promise me two things. You must give up the idea of taking the veil for at least five years. . . ."

That time should see her safely married and, with luck, a mother more than once.

10

"You must also finish your final year of studies. To qualify for this employment, if nothing else."

"So far away...!" said her mother.

"Of course I will," said Ariane. "Of course! I promise!"

In bed that night, Cellier tried to comfort his weeping wife. "It's not as if she's going off to be among savages. I promise you, she might as well be going to Bordeaux. They have French society out there...French culture....Even better, perhaps. They say it's like France as it was before the war."

"Poor, poor Jules," sobbed Mme. Cellier. "How can we face his parents?"

Cellier said reasonably, "Jules was out in the cold, in any case. I have no doubt that our daughter will replace him with a young officer or diplomat....All the up-and-coming ones do a tour of duty in Indochina. I don't know about you, but I think our daughter can do better than a fisherman...."

He heard a pause for consideration in his wife's sobs and decided that it was safe to leave her to prepare a bedtime glass of hot water and cognac.

In her own bed, Ariane spoke the word *Saigon* aloud again and again, feeling it resonate in her facial bones. Against the white plaster wall, she saw jewels and tigers and dark-eyed princes and young lieutenants in glittering uniforms bowing over her hand.

"Sai...gon." On the exhaled breath of those two syllables, she finally slid into sleep.

3
Tonkin, 1926—Luoc

By the time the Frenchman had finished eating his rice, the guards had set up his camp and rigged a small canopy of mosquito netting over it. Then they laid out their own sleeping mats inside the ring of tethered mules.

The body in the dust already twitched and quivered under the minute jaws of armies of insects. In the hut, Luoc could hear the buzzing of a few wakeful flies who explored the puddled blood. He reached up and took his father's *coupe-coupe* down from its hiding place on top of a beam. When he tucked the wooden sheath into his belt, his mother grabbed his arm.

"Where are you going?" Her whisper was hoarse with anguish.

"I must go for the elder," said Luoc. "Then tell the area chief

11

of his death. The horoscope must be read. And the genealogy book inscribed with the hour."

Her fingers clung to his wrist. "You can't go!"

"Who else should go?" he whispered fiercely. "I am the eldest son! It's enough that I let him die like that. At least I can see that the rites are properly done. Or would you rather he suffered eternal misfortune?"

She recoiled from his anger. He saw her eyes and stopped pulling against her hand.

"Forgive me, Mother. I did not mean to criticize you, or hurt you. But I *must* go . . . or I shall explode with rage at my own helplessness. Allow me to go!"

"They took your cousin for road building. I will die if they take you too. Your brother will go for the elder; he's too little to be of use to them."

She turned quickly to Dinh, who was watching them both, wide-eyed and tear-streaked.

"Run and find Uncle and bring him quickly," she said to him before Luoc could speak. "Tell him to bring joss . . . and why."

Luoc clenched his fists as his younger brother, only eight years old, slipped away into the heavy dusk. A child was doing a man's work . . . his work. He was the man of the family now. His mother should be ruled by him, not the other way round. However, he remained silent. He knew that he was going to hurt her very soon; he would put it off just a little longer. He went back to his peephole, *coupe-coupe* still in his belt.

Squatting beside the body, his grandmother and two old aunts had begun to keen quietly, under their breath so as not to disturb the sleeping Frenchman. They rocked on their haunches and tore at their headcloths.

A movement from the surrounding shadows made Luoc put his hand on the hilt of the *coupe-coupe*. The old women froze in mid-sway. A sentry was walking toward them. Luoc heard each step of the man's feet distinct in the night. His muscles gathered themselves in preparation for attack. No matter what it cost, he could not accept more deaths, or a further outrage to his father.

Then he sighed and relaxed. The sentry walked past the old women. He fumbled in his waistband and bent to place several tiny objects in the dust beside the shattered head. He had made a blood gift. To pay for a life with money was not the custom of Luoc's village; it was a practice of the montagnards who lived and hunted in the mountain slopes above the villagers' foothills. A good omen, thought the boy. It is well to appease the *ma*, or spirits of the dead, in all possible ways—they are so unpredict-

12

able. He himself had already decided to make an offering to the spirit of the Virgin Mary, according to the rites of the priests in the valley. It was best to be safe.

The elder arrived with Dinh at his heels looking important. Luoc watched from the hut while the elder and the old women struggled to carry the headman's body inside.

"I can't even help with that!" he raged. But his mother was watching him anxiously.

When the body was finally inside the hut, the elder ordered the women to wash it immediately. "The hour is propitious for calming the spirit," he said. "You can keep him if you hurry. That is why I ran here so fast, in spite of my years!"

He sank onto his heels and stroked his heart as if soothing a struggling animal. Except for the brown spots on his hands and the loose cords of his neck, he looked younger than his age of seventy-seven.

The women began to wash the body. They wiped the blood from its eyes. They tied the broken plates of the skull into place with the headman's best turban. By the time they began to dress the body carefully in the headman's best tunic, the elder had recovered. He lit joss sticks before the ancestral altar which dominated the main room of the hut and read their smoke.

"Good news," he said briskly. "Tomorrow night is auspicious for the burial. A short time to make preparations—but best, considering the weather." He glanced at the body.

Luoc felt a stab of excitement and fear. The short wait was essential for his own new purposes. Omens continued to be good. He crossed cautiously to the door of the hut.

The Frenchman still seemed to sleep under his veiling; the sentry was visible only when his cheroot flared in the blackness under a clump of banana trees.

Luoc, his mother, and the elder lifted his father into his coffin. Bought in a season of good harvest, it had stood ever since in a corner of the main room, to reassure the headman that he would be properly housed when it was time to move on. The coffin was heavy, made of carved and painted wood. It took all of them—Luoc, his mother, the elder, his grandmother, aunts, and Dinh—to lift it onto blocks in front of the altar. They watched, panting, while his grandmother placed a smoking oil lamp on the floor beneath the coffin.

"Why did you do that?" asked Dinh. His grief had been slightly allayed by the excitement of the preparations.

"His spirit can ride up to the altar on the smoke," said the grandmother. "Or maybe to stop the smell." She snapped her

13

mouth closed briskly; its line was lopsided because she had lost all her teeth on one side but not the other. After a moment, she concluded, "One does it."

Luoc's mother put a few grains of rice in her dead husband's mouth.

"I know!" cried Dinh eagerly. "That's for the Celestial Dog To keep it from getting hungry and eating Father's stomach!"

Luoc glared at his younger brother. His mother caught his eyes and smiled sadly, drawing him into an adult complicity. Luoc was somehow consoled, though his hand still itched to smack his brother to teach him propriety.

Under the elder's watchful eye, the women placed three bowls of rice and three bowls of tea on the altar of the Ancestors, to entice the headman's spirit to take up residence there, along with the spirits of his own father and his father's father. They needed him to be there. They needed him to watch over them from that vantage point and to advise them by means of signs and omens.

The headman needed them to do it for his own sake. If he were not enticed into residence, he might escape to join the errant, angry spirits who were unappeased by rites. Like them, he might haunt the roads, ponds, and fields to drown children, ruin crops, weaken livestock, send diseases, and disrupt delicate negotiations among the living.

The mule train left in the pale light before true dawn, the three bales of raw opium from the village lashed onto other bales from other villages. Luoc slipped through the trees to watch it disappear into the defile that led from the plateau down into the valley of the Black River. He noted the slow rhythm of the mules. If he traveled fast, once his father was safely buried that night, he might be able to catch them before their escorts and cargo floated downriver, where he could no longer track them. He ached to follow them now, but his father's spirit needed him to stay.

The day was not long enough for what there was to do. The women were already making the flimsy, torn garments for the mourners to wear, to show their disregard for anything except their grief. There was the paper money to make, and the paper house and clothing, which would be burned to equip the headman with practical necessities in the spirit world. Before he returned to the village to help, as was his duty as the oldest son, Luoc had a rite to perform for himself alone.

In one hand he carried three sticks of joss he had begged from the elder, in the other was rice he had stolen from the cooking pot. He moved cautiously along the shadowy track that led from

14

the village to the graves of the Ancestors; these were sited in a small clearing among some lemon and banana trees where good energy flowed from the rocky ridge the villagers called the Dragon's Back. When he knelt before the cluster of painted stone markers, he could feel spirits stirring in the surrounding grove. He hoped they were his ancestors, but he knew they might just as easily be angry wanderers or the spirits of pigs and dogs. The breeze that suddenly shook the top of a young papaya on his right could even be the breath of the Celestial Dog.

In spite of himself, he found that his hands were shaking as he laid the rice on the ground on a piece of banana leaf and thrust the ends of the joss sticks into the earth. Steadying himself, he lit the joss and settled back to watch which way the smoke moved. The ghostly threads rose true and direct in the morning air; he knew now for certain that the movement in the trees was caused by spirits, for the air around the tombs was still. Though he lived with the knowledge of spirits around him, he had never before gone to the boundary where the daily world of men meets the unseen, to call across it. He felt fear as if he had to step off a cliff edge into space. The top of the smoke threads curved slightly, coiled into a knot, then spread like the fingers of an opening hand toward the mounds of the graves. This was his sign to speak.

"Father..." he said. His voice was hoarse with fear and sounded very loud in his ears.

"...Father, I do not know yet where you are, so I address you through my grandfather. Please listen, both of you...I need your blessing...and your forgiveness, for what I am about to ask."

He paused, but the smoke of the joss sticks still trailed toward the tombs, directing his words.

"I ask for permission to leave our family land and village."

He would not admit to fear, but something seemed to push his heart up in his chest so that it choked him.

"You must allow me to leave you with only the care of women, and my little brother. I ask you to let me cut the threads that tie us all, into eternity. I will return to tie them up again. I swear it! I will not leave you adrift. I will return to lie beside you and bring *my* son to carry on after me. Will you trust me?"

He waited. The dawn was unnaturally silent.

"Will you let me go? With your protection, not your curses...?" He waited again for a sign.

There was nothing. The singers and rustlers of the night had

15

ceased; the ones of the day still slept. But he felt the presence of spirits in the grove, waiting, watching him, listening.

He tried again. "I do not ask so that I may pursue glory in the world . . . it is for your sakes and for all our descendants. I tell you, I have recognized evil spirits who will destroy us all unless they can be destroyed first! I must go to learn more about them and discover where they are weak."

Still no sign. Cold despair leaked into his gut. He knew he would leave, with or without permission. He had recognized his fate the minute the rifles had cracked. He knew that a strong man should face his fate steadily and undertake it with resolution, but he had hoped for some assistance, some sharing of his overwhelming load, some encouragement. He felt cold as the stone of the grave markers.

They would not answer. He was alone. So be it! Nevertheless, he felt compelled to try one last time to explain himself.

"Father," he said. "In your wisdom and virtue, you accepted your fate and did not challenge the will of the Celestial Father. . . ." He faltered, dangerously close to disrespect.

"I am not yet so wise, nor so accepting." He drew a deep breath and exploded out the whole presumptuous truth.

"I believe I am a change-fate!"

He kowtowed immediately to hide his face.

A *cache-muong* or change-fate is a dangerous thing to be. Such a man dares to interfere with the great, smooth-working engine of the universe, to send jolts and vibrations into all the interlocking and interdependent parts. He dares to assume that he, a puny mortal imprisoned in his temporary husk, can anticipate or even guide the divine will that orders things. If he is right, he takes on powers that are nearly divine; if wrong, it is as if he has pulled a piece of wood from the bottom of a pile, and the whole structure could fall and crush him.

The silence around him should by now have been filled with the scratchings, coughs, and insect chatter of the new day. He raised his head at the flutter of wings, but the bird flew on and did not alight with a message. The rising sun laid its first hesitant mark on the dust at the edge of the clearing. Luoc felt the spirits leaving, but he would remain until all hope was gone.

He heard the slow passage of a jungle fowl foraging through the bushes. Then a fly began to buzz around his head.

I must not allow myself to read things where nothing is written, he told himself.

An ant crawled across the upturned sole of his left foot. Still he waited. He had said all he could. The sun crept farther across the clearing.

Perhaps I missed the sign after all, he thought.

Then he stiffened. A mouse had darted from the grass on his grandfather's mound toward the rice on the banana leaf. It stopped, moved a little to the right, and ate something it found in the dust.

Sitting rigid on his heels, Luoc willed it toward the offering of rice. Obediently, it moved toward the banana leaf. Then it stopped again, sniffed, and looked around.

Why, oh why doesn't my grandfather's spirit tell it to forget mouse business for the moment? he raged silently.

The mouse turned and darted back into the grass.

Luoc felt as if he had been hit above the heart. They had refused his offering. Even worse than ignoring it! Then he saw what had frightened the mouse.

A large cock pheasant walked toward the graves from under a lemon tree. It placed each scaly foot with regal certainty, thrusting its golden head forward with every step and drawing its body up behind. It came to within a few inches of his knee, took up several grains of rice in its beak, and moved on into the bushes with the same jerky dignity. In the dust, its track lay like two columns of Chinese characters, pointing at the rising sun.

He tried to contain his exaltation. How could he have thought a mouse was fitting? They had sent the perfect messenger, a Fire Pheasant, the earthly cousin of the divine Dragon-Phoenix of his people, the Viets. It was reborn from the fire that destroyed it. The message could not be clearer. The scale of this answer was beyond his expectations. He could now dare to attempt even more than he had yet imagined.

"You will be so pleased with me!" he cried, forgetting modesty in his excitement. "The Guardian of the Hearth will tell such good reports of me to the Divine Father! I swear it to you by my sons not yet born!"

He kowtowed quickly and scrambled to his feet. Only as he reentered the village did the reality of what he had undertaken begin to slow his steps.

4

Ariane went to Indochina determined to be charmed—and so, of course, she was. She was excited even by the long delay in midstream in the hot, lax river while the *Perpignan* waited for the tide to turn. Even though the French carried out constant dredging, the channel upstream to Saigon was too shallow for oceangoing ships when the tide was slack.

Under the tiny shade of her wide-brimmed hat, Ariane leaned her elbows cautiously on the hot varnish of the railing and gazed at the gold and mauve haze that blurred the distant meeting of mangrove swamp and water, incandescent compared to the mist that rolled in to mask the mudflats at home. The hot, muddy, metallic water was so unlike the pounding Atlantic.

She was alone at the railing. The previous afternoon, the rails had been crowded with excited white and brown faces. Two native ayahs had been dandling their charges on the small deck in front of the main stack when they had spied the three hills that marked Cap Saint-Jacques and the mouth of the Bay of Gan Raie. At their call, passengers raised parasols and donned hats to peer at these signs that they were nearly home after long, hot weeks at sea.

The hills meant home for many of the French as much as it did for their servants. France might be the model of all they aspired to, but while they were actually there they felt uncomfortable, foreign, and out of step. Safely back in Indochina, where many of them had been born, they could feel their own Frenchness again. And realize how fortunate they were. Ariane had heard them saying often how the Great War had changed France.

In their cabins, they might have cases full of the latest French books and fashions. They might be anxious that they were falling a little behind the times. But they were willing to admit, if they were completely honest, that they were delighted to return to a land where they were luxuriously housed and could afford a full complement of servants, and where the peasants still swept off their hats and bowed to the car of a passing official. Even for the less well-off, Indochina still offered the freedom and opportunity to make a fortune by hard work, unhindered by the petty bureaucracies of France.

At dinner, in the *grand salon,* Ariane listened to men in evening clothes rejoice in their country's prewar abundance. Rubber flowed from slashed trees. Opium wept from the scored pods of poppies. Cinnamon trees flourished. Coal and minerals detached themselves from mountains on the backs of a cheap and plentiful work force.

There were shadows, it was true. The price of rubber was falling. Some of the younger, French-educated native Annamites— as the French called all Indochinese, whether they came from

Annam, Cochin China, or Tonkin—were turning on their educators and stirring up trouble among the peasants. Nevertheless, there was much to be grateful for.

"There you are! You're mad to be up here in this heat!" Sister St. Georges's round face, tightly encircled by her white wimple, was dotted with moisture like a cheese left out in the sun.

"You must come below and lie down for a little," she said to Ariane. "Then be sure that your cases are all prepared for tomorrow morning."

Ariane peeled the skin of her elbows from the rail and followed the nun reluctantly down to the cabin she shared with another girl. She consoled herself with the thought that tomorrow morning she would say good-bye to the sisters, and, with them, to the last of her schoolgirl self.

The morning found her at the railing again, before breakfast. She had to admit that she was a little disconcerted by the flatness on either side of the twisting channel, which did not change as they steamed slowly closer to Saigon. She was enchanted, however, by the clusters of thatched huts which clung to the riverbanks and the tiny golden people who bathed and swam and propelled their tiny boats under the mighty nose of the *Perpignan*.

One minute chip, with a single oarsman, drove straight across the liner's path. The *Perpignan* gave an indignant bellow. Ariane dashed across to the opposite rail in terror, to see the craft rolling on the bow waves, unsplintered, the oarsman looking straight ahead as if the ship were not there.

Ariane saw boats with painted eyes on their bows, and red sails. There were others like Venetian gondolas, with high prows and sterns. Whole villages of boats were moored around the mouths of canals that opened into the Saigon River. They sailed so close to one cluster, at the mouth of a large canal that cut a silver swathe through a shantytown south of the city, that Ariane could see plants growing on the decks and children running from one boat to another across planks as freely as if they were on solid ground. Miniature ducks swam on the end of tethers, and cooking fires sent up tendrils of smoke from under woven palm-leaf awnings. A small boy, tethered like the ducks, stood on one deck pissing into the river. As they approached the Quai de L'Ysère, the river surface became crowded. Fishing junks, cargo junks, sampans, and pirogues wove and jostled with French frigates, customs launches, and yachts.

It took the *Perpignan* a very long time to dock. By the time the passengers began to shuffle down the gangplanks under the blue and white awnings, the dockside was deserted in the midday sun. The cranes were stationary; nothing moved in the shadows of the warehouse. The stevedores, whom Ariane had seen earlier running about in shorts and singlets and pointed straw hats, had disappeared. Only a three-legged dog sniffed around a stack of straw-wrapped bales that sat baking on the quay.

All visible activity was in the huge customs shed. A line of passengers had built up behind the customs desk. Other passengers wandered about looking for the coolies who had carried their luggage off the ship. In her confusion, Ariane nearly walked into a wall of large Algerian women draped in black silk. On the other side of this wall, a man's voice argued ferociously in accented French about the size of fee two coolies had demanded before they would hand over a pile of bags and parcels.

Ariane had no idea where her own cases were. A large, loud planter and his equally large but quiet wife had wedged her away from Sister St. Georges and the other nuns. She had just begun to feel very young and very alone when she heard someone call her name. She craned her head to see over a moving wall of parcels carried by two coolies and looked into the face of a tall, lean, elegant man in his fifties.

"Henri Garine," he said. His voice stopped while the last and largest of the parcels passed between them.

"I'm Henri Garine," he said again when the space between them was clear. "You must be Mlle. Cellier. Welcome. Welcome to Indochina!" He shook her hand warmly. "My wife asked me to give you her apologies for not coming to meet you herself . . . the time of day, you know . . . the heat. . . . She's waiting eagerly to see you at home."

He snapped his long fingers suddenly and a coolie appeared with Ariane's two bags. They marched straight past the customs desk and the ill-looking young man with bloodshot eyes who sat behind it and with whom M. Garine seemed to have an understanding. Outside the shed, M. Garine had two pedal cabs waiting. He installed Ariane in one and her luggage in another. When he climbed in beside her, the tiny man on the bicycle seat behind them heaved at his pedals to roll them slowly into motion.

Hot and sweaty as she was, Ariane was in ecstasy. She had arrived! Everywhere she looked, she saw something to feed the hunger inside her. M. Garine seemed a suave genie who had appeared to conduct her on a tour of marvels. Best of all, these marvels were to become part of her own daily life for at least the next year. She gaped at pails of tuberoses, orchids, and gardenias that were lined up casually along the street, at food stalls selling unrecognizable delicacies, at vendors of cold drinks who displayed rows and rows of amazing colored syrups—puce, bright green, orange, vivid yellow, and saffron. Instead of hiding away in shops as they did at home, dentists, barbers, and doctors all practiced their trades right on the street. A half-shaved man leaned back in a chair while a tiny boy held up a minute cracked mirror for him to inspect the progress of his chin. A tea seller fanned her charcoal stove in the center of a ring of customers. A fortune-teller—or so said M. Garine—squatted before a board covered with bits of brightly colored paper.

Ariane thought the people were beautiful. The men were slim; the women delicate in strange split dresses. Even the old and ugly, who no longer had teeth, had slim, graceful hands and tiny feet. They made her feel excessively damp and fleshy. What amazed her most about them, however, was the open way they carried on their lives in the street. They ate there, drank, dressed, washed, brushed their teeth, slept—all the things which were carefully hidden behind window curtains at home. She felt she had entered a fairy-tale world, where things were turned upside down and inside out. This was confirmed when an enormously fat woman being wheeled toward them in another *cyclo-pousse*—as M. Garine said they were called—turned out to be a trussed pig propped up in the seat.

The wonder of the narrow native streets gradually gave way to another, slightly more familiar, wonder. They turned into an area of wide avenues and open spaces. M. Garine pointed with his ebony cane.

"Down that avenue is the Chamber of Commerce, where I do business from time to time. And back that way . . . you can just see . . ."

Ariane craned her neck under the canopy of the *cycle-pousse*.

". . . the Central Market and the railway station."

The wide streets were lined with tamarinds and lime trees. A vista reminded her of pictures she had seen of the Universal Exhibition of 1900 in Paris. Then, just as she had a dislocated sense of being back in France, she saw a large stucco building with a pierced Chinese-style fretwork facade.

"This is the Avenue Charnier," said M. Garine. He was enjoying himself. He had expected a dumpy little provincial; this girl would be a pleasure to have around the house. For observation only, of course, but those sapphire eyes and great soft breasts would make even observation a pure delight.

21

"That building at the end," he said, "is the Town Hall. To the left of it is the Palace of the Governor-General of Cochin China. You will no doubt go there with us soon to some function or other. Well-brought-up French girls are in rather short supply out here. You'll dance your feet off."

Ariane was past speaking. As she imagined a ball in the Palace of the Governor-General, she could hardly take in its double turrets, its rows of arches, the balustrades, the baroque pediments, the small central dome topped by a minaret. A small boy began to run alongside their cyclo, imploring her for something in incomprehensible French. Ariane hardly noticed him as she wondered in despair what she would wear as a ball gown. She had one home-sewn party frock in her case.

"Our Cathedral is there." M. Garine indicated two red-bricked spires rising beyond the Town Hall. The boy gave up and went to pursue another cyclo.

"And this is where my wife spends much of her time . . . and my money." He laughed; his thin mustache flicked up at the ends in a most delightful way.

They had turned into a tree-lined street full of shops, boutiques, and cafés, where sun umbrellas hung closed and limp over empty bentwood and wrought-iron chairs. Ariane stared hungrily at the boutiques. The ball gowns were there; all she needed was the money.

"Come back here in three hours," said M. Garine. "In those chairs at those cafés, you will see everyone in Saigon who is anyone at all."

She stared in reverence at the empty café chairs, trying to imagine the glitter of the hour of aperitif. Her eyes passed blindly over an expensive *parfumerie* and a florist's shop with a sheet of water running down its plate-glass window, like a fishmonger's at home. She nodded at the bookshop, which stocked any French newspaper you could ask for! She was beginning to feel a little numb. She thought she could take in nothing more, but she was wrong.

The Garines' house completed Ariane's enchantment. Red-orange hibiscus sprawled over the thick stucco walls of the compound, whose gate was opened by a bowing servant. Inside the walls, huge palms and other trees she could not name cast a green coolness over the white stucco walls of the house and its encircling verandas.

She climbed stiffly down from the cyclo under the huge porte cochère and mounted the sweeping flight of steps to the marble-floored entrance hall where Mme. Garine was waiting to greet her.

To an older and more sophisticated eye, Mme. Garine might have seemed overdressed, with too much attention paid to detail, like a fashion model who does not actually have to do anything in what she is wearing—which was more or less the case. Ariane, however, fell into instant adoration of the vision who embraced her and cried, "Welcome to our family!"

The woman wore a peach-colored silk afternoon dress, which Ariane was afraid of crumpling, with a lime-green chiffon scarf pinned at the neck by a jeweled brooch. Her hair was cropped and waved in the latest fashion; her lips were painted; her brows thinly arched. Her lids were shiny with lanolin, while her nose was miraculously matte with powder. She smelled deliciously of gardenias. Ariane was too awed to notice that, because of the heat, Mme. Garine was not wearing stockings. Ariane felt sticky and smelly and very aware of the unfashionable high waist, low hem, and long sleeves of her best traveling dress.

"This is Paulette. And Willy."

Both children stared sullenly at Ariane.

"Shake hands nicely with Mlle. Cellier," said their mother. "She is going to be your new friend."

Paulette was about eleven, an unformed blob of child-flesh, uncomfortable in her white dress with a dropped waist, ankle socks, white slippers, and large bow in uncertain contact with her short, straight hair.

Willy was nine, in a blazer and short trousers. His palm was as sticky as Ariane's.

Their ayah stood unintroduced a few feet behind them.

Mme. Garine dismissed the children and ushered Ariane into the drawing room for a *citron pressé* to refresh her after the journey from the docks. Ariane gaped at the room, her senses finally overwhelmed.

Mme. Garine had modeled the room on the Salon des Saisons at the Hôtel de Beauharnais in Paris. The carved, gilded, and padded chairs had come from France by ship. She had had the carpet specially made by local Chinese craftsmen. Local painters had reproduced the Grecian ladies of the painted wall panels and approximated the effect of gilded, Roman-style carving. Only a careful look showed that the swans, with their arched necks and spread wings, looked more like dragons than European birds. Or that the candles in the wall sconces were supported by flying creatures that started as cherubs but tapered into scaly legs with birdlike claws instead of feet. Large fans replaced the chandeliers of the Hôtel de Beauharnais and slowly churned the hot air below the painted ceiling. The wall panels were sliced with shadows from the louvered wooden shutters that protected all the windows from the ferocity of the midday sun, or from the equal ferocity of the rains in the monsoon season.

Ariane was not yet looking closely. She grasped the carved sphinx that formed the arm of her chair; she was to share in this splendor for a time at least. She tried not to gulp the lemonade which had been served to her by a beautiful Annamite girl with cast-down eyes whom Mme. Garine called the *boyesse*. Ariane filed the word away in her memory. She had so much to learn, and she was determined to learn quickly.

Mme. Garine took one look at Ariane's clothes and sighed. The girl would be useless at providing the details of fashion in France for which the older woman hungered. Nor was she likely to know much interesting gossip. She was what should have been expected—a convent-educated provincial.

On the other hand, the girl was lovely and had only just begun to realize it. It might be rewarding to help her along. Paulette was still at the age best kept away from society, all elbows and no shape. Without looking again in her ebony-framed cheval glass, Mme. Garine knew that there was no more room for effort in her own image. She was like a garden brought to perfection by years of hard labor, which now needed only routine maintenance, leaving the gardener with idle energies. This girl would repay effort. With proper underthings to tame that excessive bust, makeup to set off the azure eyes, a proper haircut, and decent clothes. . . . She would enjoy seeing what she could make of her governess in Saigon society. It would be an amusing way to pass the time and to practice for Paulette. She smiled dazzlingly at Ariane; the project had been decided.

5

The mules were easy to follow, though their piles of dung had already begun to vanish in the busy jaws of beetles. The men left their own careless trail of ordure, fruit peelings, dead fires, and cooked bones. Luoc assessed the density of flies, the seething of ants, and the coolness of ashes to calculate how far he had dropped behind.

He slipped around the edge of the village where he knew the caravan always stopped after visiting his own. They were long gone. He watched briefly from the shelter of some wild banana trees; the villagers were tending to daily life—no signs of death here. He swallowed down a surge of rage and despair that the fates could be so random and unfair. He knew it was wicked to think like that, but could not help himself.

His trail dropped along the edge of a rocky hillside where the villagers had planted one of their poppy fields. The gray-green globes of the poppy heads balanced on long stems high above their deeply cut leaves, waiting for the seeds to ripen. The white petals had dropped long before; only a few remained on the dry earth like the fragments of cases of exploded fireworks. On the nearest pods, Luoc could see the dried scars where the women had scored them with their double-bladed knives, then scraped away the sap that oozed from the wounds.

Once again, he questioned the workings of the Heavens. His father had been killed because his village had not produced enough of that dried sap to suit Round Eyes in a faraway city of a distant province. His own people did not even use the opium they produced; chewing betel was far healthier and more enjoyable. He knew one or two old men and women who drank infusions of the sap or mixed dried scrapings into their tobacco, but everyone knew that true lust for the poppy was a vice of the Chinese. They were notorious for their enslavement to opium. His father used to say that the poppies brought little money to the village, but at least one had the satisfaction of knowing that the crop went to weaken the Chinese, who had once been the conquerors and rulers of the Viets but were now reduced to being mere merchants in the service of the French. His father said that the French wanted the opium to feed to the Chinese in order to keep them under control.

Luoc was lightly burdened: a little raw rice tied at his neck, a small amount of cooked rice and some fruit tied up in a piece of cloth, a few piastres tucked into his waistband, and his father's *coupe-coupe* in its wooden case bound with cane. His loping walk soon made up the distance between himself and the mule train. By the second nightfall he sighted them below him, crossing a stretch of rough open ground. His heart quickened. All day, as he walked, he had planned what he would do when he finally caught up with them, how to pit his own small resources against the visible might of their guns and swords. He had counted on darkness and surprising them in their sleep.

The rough ground where the mules threaded their way among the stones and tufts of coarse grass rose gradually to a ridge of rock where several low, thatched, stucco buildings stood, enclosed in a stockade. Their roofs and the stockade walls were of the same beige and gold as the dried land around them. Only their formal geometry separated them from the rock and vegetation of the plateau. They were strong and solid—visible proof of the power of the warlord who had built them.

Luoc watched in despair as the mule train climbed the rise to this fortress. The tiny, distant gate opened and the dark specks of mules and men filed inside, safe beyond his reach. He had prepared himself for action. Now he could not act; he felt cheated and empty. He wondered if he would be able later to recapture the rage that would give him the courage to do as he knew he must.

He followed the trail down to the edge of the trees and looked up the open slope toward the stockade; he had to wait for dark before he could move closer. Gazing up at the walls, he felt helpless and overwhelmed. He told himself that it was only because he was tired and hungry after traveling fast all day. He reminded himself that his hero, the warrior Sun Tsu, had said that patience was often more valuable to a general than heroism. In spite of his mood, crouched behind a fallen tree he ate the cooked rice, and fruit called dragon eyes, with all the normal gusto of a hungry fifteen-year-old boy.

When it was dark, before the moon rose, he worked his way up the slope to the base of the stockade. The walls were only ten feet high, but made of bamboo as thick as his waist. The smooth, shiny posts sloped outward and were sharpened at the top. There was no way he could climb over. He prowled the perimeter, looking for a gap or gate he might attack more easily than the slippery, leaning walls. He found a narrow slit where the joints of two bamboo posts butted against each other like gnarled knuckles, too narrow to wriggle through but offering a glimpse into the stockade.

He saw the back of the main building. Brightly lit openings in the walls showed servants moving back and forth with jugs and trays of food, as if across a stage. He heard laughter and the surge of men's voices as they pressed through to the climax of stories. The Frenchman was inside that light and laughter, while Luoc's father was hardly settled in the spirit world. An armed man crossed his line of vision. He looked behind him in case they also were patrolling outside the stockade. He listened. The normal night sounds hummed, whirred, whickered, and chortled undisturbed around him.

Suddenly a din like the battle cry of a demon tore the night apart. He whirled back to face the stockade. Cold ran up his spine and clamped itself around the back of his head, holding him rigid and helpless. His brain said "Draw the *coupe-coupe*," but his body refused to obey. Inside the stockade, a guard dog raged and snarled and heaved itself in an ecstasy of frustration against the bamboo posts, unable to get at the prey whose scent so tantalized its nostrils. Even when he became aware that it was not a demon but only a dog, Luoc still could not move. The sound of the sentry's returning footsteps unrooted him; he ran downhill toward the trees.

After a few strides he regained control of himself. If the dog were let out of the gate, he would never reach the trees in time. He flung himself into a stand of tall grass and turned, panting, *coupe-coupe* in his hand. He saw the glow of lights moving inside the walls near where he had been, but the main gate remained closed. He had to go back; he did not yet know whether there was another gate through which the caravan might slip away in the morning while he sat with his gaze fixed on the main gate. They would reach the Black River sometime the next day. If he missed them in the morning, they would escape him for good.

As he drew near the stockage again, his body trembled. Though he knew that it had been only a dog, he could not shake off his brief conviction that a demonic spirit had been clawing for him through the barricade. If I weaken now, he told himself, I am pitiful . . . a child who had the folly to imagine himself to be a man, and a *cache-muong,* then ran away at the first bark of a dog. How the Celestial Father must be laughing now! And my father and grandfather! His face burned in the darkness. He listened for the laughter of the spirits around him in the shadows, but heard only crickets, beetles, frogs, night birds, and a distant gibbon.

Luoc found a second, smaller gate on the far side of the stockade, which opened onto the stables and grain storage huts. Again, he found a slit between the joints of the bamboo posts, and peered through. His breath was tight; his ears strained for sounds of the dog. At one side of his line of vision, the rear end of a mule stirred in the shadows under the corner of a thatched roof. Directly ahead, two sentries stood watch over the caravan's cargo. Their single lantern cast enough light for Luoc to see that the number of bales had been multiplied by ten. They stood like a small, dark mountain range on a wooden platform under a shed roof.

This warlord, like the others in Tonkin and like those called *kaitong* in Laos, had been permitted by the conquering French to keep absolute control of his local fiefdom. He could collect taxes, extract corvee labor, sell offices and favors, collect fees for favorable judgments in legal cases, and exercise droit du seigneur as and when he chose. In return, he collected taxes for the French, including the opium needed by the government-controlled Opium Monopoly. He forced the peasants to give him the opium as tax, then sold it to the French for a handsome profit, which was part of his inducement to remain cooperative.

Luoc stared at the bales, all taken from villages like his own. Faintly, he still heard the voices of the men in the main building. Anger shifted inside him like a tiger moving in its sleep. It gave him strength to contemplate challenging the might of men who had been elected by Heaven to be his superiors. He returned to the trees along the shoulder of the ridge where the stockade stood and found a position on a wooded rise from which he could see the trails leading from both gates. A tree had half fallen out away from the slope, overhanging the slide of broken boulders that had unpinned its roots. He wriggled out a thick horizontal trunk, carefully shaking the branches free of possible vermin. He braced himself into position and stared, unsleeping, through the night at the stockade, while the moon rose and vanished again behind the teeth of the mountains.

The caravan left just after sunrise by the small rear gate. The seven mules and their escort of six men filed out; more mules and men continued to appear. When the gate finally closed, eighteen mules and twelve men followed the track that disappeared behind the far end of the ridge.

Luoc had to make a long detour around the ridge, staying inside the treeline in order to reach the trail unseen. By the time he reached the descending cleft, the caravan had disappeared back into the jungle. Tracking it was easy, however. The Frenchman seemed to be in no hurry to reach the river—Luoc had to stop frequently to avoid overtaking the end of the train. Their leisurely pace, he prayed, meant that they planned to sleep the night at the river and board boats downstream the following morning.

He rejoiced when he saw that this was so. The mules were led away to stables in the small settlement on the riverbanks, while the Frenchman climbed up rough stone steps bordered by pines to the inn which clung to the side of the gorge. The hamlet was a way station for river traffic, located at the point where the chasms and rapids of the higher reaches opened out into a long stretch of navigable waters. The near bank was a clutter of shanties which offered sleeping mats to the oarsmen and coolies, of drinking houses, and of open thatched shelters with benches, where charcoal burned in clay-pot stoves to barbecue bits of meat and fish and to steam great cauldrons of rice. A sampan tied to a rough wooden pier offered local women to travelers in need.

The inn perched high above the commerce of the riverbank. Open verandas caught the airs of the gorge to cool the rooms, which were reserved for wealthy merchants, warlords, and French officials. The proprietress also welcomed the occasional Chinese who escorted shipments of opium from Yunnan. In fact, her ability to guarantee a constant flow of Chinese opium southward to eke out the inadequate local supplies kept her in excellent odor with the provincial French administration. This was why she could run a hotel of comfort and elegance unexpected in such a remote place. Hidden among the cannas, in the garden that tumbled down the hillside around the inn, Luoc was awed by what he saw through the open windows. He had never seen such heavy carved wooden furniture in rosewood and mahogany, such huge porcelain vases, such amazing pictures of dragons and tigers constructed from bits of feather and shells.

On the hill behind the inn, the servants' quarters clattered and bustled like those of a lord at Tet. Luoc crouched among the dark, leathery leaves until he saw the Frenchman come out of a room to lean against the veranda railing, where he lit a cigarette and gazed out at the river below. The Round Eye was still in no hurry. The boy studied his pointed features and sandy hair which had been hidden before by the kepi. Most of all, he studied the man's neck—each muscle and tendon, the distance between his doglike jaw and his collarbone. At last the man returned to his room. Sometime later he left the inn and descended the stone steps toward the bustle of the waterfront.

Luoc scaled one of the pilings supporting the veranda and dropped softly onto the weathered teak floor. The Frenchman's room was open. Luoc paused just inside the door. The bed was simply carved and narrow, the mosquito netting patched. He peered curiously at the razor that lay folded on a table, and the funny brush that stood up by itself next to the razor. His nostrils wrinkled over whiskey left standing in a glass beside a nearly empty bottle. He could also smell the man's dirty tunic, which had been left flung over a chair, and his kepi, which had rolled across the floor into a corner. He had expected something much more grand for a man with the power to bestow death. This disorder reassured him, as did the ease with which he had invaded the man's private world. The priests at the school were

29

terrifyingly remote by comparison. This man was within reach, Round Eye or not.

At the sound of voices, he slipped back onto the veranda. The Frenchman had brought a woman with him. This was a possibility the boy had not considered. He squatted in the shadow of a heavy rattan armchair and rocked in frustration; he understood how the dog in the stockade had felt, so close to his prey but unable to reach it.

He tried not to listen to the sounds from the room. The woman made no sound except for one early exclamation of pain or protest. The Frenchman grunted and snorted like a rutting pig. He suddenly cried "Haii!" and then was silent. In the long silence that followed, Luoc was afraid they had both fallen asleep and that the woman would not leave until morning.

Then he heard rustling and stirring. The Frenchman muttered something and the woman thanked him with polite elaboration. The door into the passageway opened and closed again. Luoc waited. He heard the man moving around in the room, the chink of the bottle against the glass, and the creak of the bed as a body dropped heavily onto it. At last, he heard what he listened for—the even, steady flutter of the man's soft palate as he exhaled in sleep. Luoc stood up and pulled the *coupe-coupe* from its wooden scabbard.

This time, the double shuttered doors to the room were locked. Luoc pushed lightly against them once again, to be sure. He paused, then squatted and began very carefully to saw at the wooden pivot of a louver with the tip of his blade. The Frenchman inhaled with a snort and turned in his bed. Luoc waited until the man's breathing steadied again, then resumed his cutting. At last the blade broke through. Luoc pulled back on the narrow slat of wood until the other pivot snapped with a tiny crack.

The second louver was easier to get at now that the first was gone. When that one was gone, Luoc could peer through the narrow gap at the shadow under the mosquito netting. Whenever the shadow stirred, he stopped cutting. He watched the moon arc between the dark silhouetted tops of two trees that towered over the inn. Time was passing too fast. He pressed down harder on his blade. Twice he had to stop and hide again behind the armchair when other guests came out onto the veranda for a final breath of air. At last the hole was large enough. He wriggled through into the bedroom, fast as a lizard.

He did not allow himself to think. The blood pounded in his head and drowned the man's snores. Luoc's hand shook; he felt his gut open to spill down his legs. He crossed the room, parted the netting with a slice of the blade, and struck the man's head from his body just as he turned and opened his eyes.

Luoc jumped back away from the darkness that pulsed in jets from the neck, spreading over the pillow and staining the netting at the head of the bed. His heart hammered; his breath refused to return. His knees were shaking in a most peculiar way. He waited, paralyzed, for the spirit he had just released to seize him by the throat. He felt himself begin to choke under the ghostly hands.

Slowly, the fountains of black blood eased, the body stopped jerking. Luoc felt the blood slowing in his own veins. He realized that he had drawn several breaths, unhindered. His loose trousers clung, damp and sticky, to the backs of his legs.

He took two steps toward the bed and forced himself to peer closely. He saw emptiness. He was looking at a lump of meat in a bloodstained singlet. There was no life nor spirit in the bed.

Perhaps the French had no spirits, he thought. But that was not possible. Even trees and stones had spirits. Though powerful, the French were of this world; therefore they must be made like all other life. Slowly, he was filled with a sense of his own power. If his own spirit was so much stronger than that of the Frenchman, he had been meant to kill him. It was now confirmed. He must never let himself doubt again that he was a change-fate. What more proof could he ask than the acquiescent stillness of the murdered man's room?

Later, he could barely remember going down the hill to the stables where the mules were kept. He remembered only the act of striking off the head of the Moroccan who had kicked his father. He could not remember how he entered the wharfside dosshouse where the two Tonkinese mercenaries were sleeping. He moved in an exultation of all-powerful energy. He was unable to make a mistake. He killed the first Tonkinese, then the second. He did not return to himself until the head of the second man leaped off the sleeping platform with the force of his blow and rolled across the floor to stop with a feather of hair lying across his bare toes.

The light brush of touch from the dead man's head filled Luoc with cold horror. He stared around him like a man just wakened. The other two men in the room were restless. One turned on his mat and half raised his head before letting it fall heavily again. Luoc knew that the magic that had protected him had gone. He jerked his foot from under the hair as if breaking a noose of vine and ran from the room. He did not even stop to wash the filth

31

from his trousers but ran from the hamlet, back up the trail into the mountains. He ran and scrambled until he collapsed in exhaustion. He forced himself to his feet long enough to find a tree where he could spend the night.

He clung to his branch while his thoughts whirled. He had begun. He had succeeded beyond his expectations. His father was completely avenged. He had tested his strength and found it even greater than he had thought. Yet he was troubled. The physical horror was passing, even as his trousers dried in the night air. He was troubled by a sense of something insufficient. He believed that he was destined to destroy the French and their power in Indochina. To that end, he had just killed four men. But what had he achieved, beyond vengeance?

The opium would continue downstream into the hands of men more powerful than the ones he had killed. These men would continue to make their demands, through other agents. And he would be unable to stop them. He could chop and chop and chop at heads. He could return and attempt to kill the warlord in his stockade. He could ambush other caravans. But he would be killing only the visible men, leaving untouched the ones who ordained it all.

Killing was not the answer. His father had been right to send him to the Round Eye school. He must understand his enemies before he attacked them. There was more to learn about them than their spells and rituals, he was now sure. It was like stalking a jungle buck; before you could kill him, you had to learn the times and places he made himself vulnerable, then try to drive him there. Once again, the magnitude of his task overwhelmed him. His exaltation died like a watered fire.

Remember, he told himself, that what you have just done seemed impossible two days ago. He tied himself to the fork with his sash and fell asleep in the middle of a thought.

He did not wake until noon, when a jungle fowl landed on his branch to complain noisily about the wild pig that had disturbed its scratching on the forest floor. The bird's loud *rak-rak!* cut through a dream; he groped back into its shadows for more of its wondrous, undefined comfort. His limbs slowly came awake. He was sore, and his trousers had dried stiff against his thighs; his nose twitched unhappily. His food supply was finished. He had much to do.

He descended the trail toward the hamlet, then made a swing around it to the north, upstream. He scrambled down the rocky banks, through scrub and over fallen trees whose feet had been swept from under them by monsoon floods, to a flat shelf of rock

32

that glimmered out from the shore under a few feet of water. Here, he carefully scrubbed all traces of blood from the *coupe-coupe*, digging with his thumbnail at smears trapped in the rattan binding of the handle.

Then he used handfuls of grit to scrub the backs of his thighs nearly raw. He pounded his trousers against a boulder as he had seen his mother do, and spread them in the sun on a rock to dry. On impulse, he dived off the shelf into deeper water and struck off upstream against the push of the current. When it became too strong, he pulled himself from rock to rock, then turned and let the water sweep him downstream to fetch up against a silvered tree trunk lying half in the water, its broken branches polished down to smooth knobs by the constant washing. Sleek and glistening with water drops, thick hair plastered to his head, he stretched himself naked along the trunk and let the sun lighten his bones. For the moment, its heat crowded all thoughts out of his head as it seeped in through his red, closed eyelids.

At last he sat up reluctantly. He wanted to stay just where he was. He wished he were a water rat and could spend the rest of his life diving through the water or nibbling weed along the banks, with a dark hole in a fallen tree for sleep.

He worked his way slowly back upstream to where he had left his trousers. He hoped they might still be wet, but they had dried in minutes under the fierce beating of the sun. He shook them to loosen the rough fibers and put them on, along with his tunic. Each piece of clothing was another weight he hung on himself. He dug the *coupe-coupe* from under the stones he had laid over it. For a moment, he stood looking upstream into the mountains of his childhood which poured their waters down into the flat world of the delta where he now had to go. He exhaled a long, heavy breath and turned downstream toward the hamlet.

Hidden above the settlement, munching on bananas he had found in a deserted garden, he watched tiny figures scuttling about the waterfront. All the boats were still there; they had been joined by a motor launch, carrying a French ensign. The police had already been called. Two white men descended the stone steps from the inn and crossed into the dosshouse by the wharf. They were accompanied by a flotilla of Tonkinese natives of the province, one of whom was in military uniform and another wearing tropical whites and a kepi like the two Frenchmen.

When the sun had dropped behind the mountains but the sky was still bright with reflected light, Luoc saw two men, arms bound behind them, being escorted to the motor launch. He watched helplessly while the bales of opium were also loaded onto the launch. Three boatmen splashed into the water to push the prow away from the dock, and the launch roared away downstream. He had lost the scent.

At dusk he ventured down into the hamlet where he bought some rice, fish sauce, and steamed vegetables from a stall near th dosshouse. There was much talk of the murders; he wished he had left the *coupe-coupe* hidden back up at his watchpoint. But he did not want to leave. No answers waited for him in the solitude of the jungle; they were here, in the world of men.

After eating, he squatted in the shadows watching four coolies gambling at *tam cuc* on a mat outside the dosshouse.

"Three generals," said the man who the night before had raised his head and dropped it again while Luoc stood feeling the lock of dead hair across his foot. The man showed the three long, narrow cards. "Red!" he added triumphantly.

The others swore and revealed inferior hands of elephants, cannons, and horses.

"I wonder if the next lot will have the same problems," said one of the losers.

"If they do, we'll all be out of work," said another. The wiry muscles of his bare arms proclaimed him to be a boatman. "I don't mind waiting, as long as I get downstream again."

"Well, I'm not sleeping in there again!" said the man who had won the round. "The lice are too bloodthirsty for me."

They all laughed nervously.

Luoc stopped listening for a moment, to think. It didn't matter that he had lost contact with this shipment of opium. Other shipments came through. Any one of them would lead him to the same superiors, or others like them. He rocked slightly on his heels. Last night, he had accepted the limitations of his *coupe-coupe;* he had not yet worked out how to replace it. His mind kept returning to the Tonkinese in tropical whites who had accompanied the two Frenchmen down from the hotel. The way forward lay somewhere in that image.

He waited until the game of *tam cuc* became raucous, with the help of a rice-wine seller who rested his yoke against the dosshouse walls to sell the gamblers cup after cup from his tall jug. The owner of the dosshouse was so delighted to find a stranger willing to sleep in her ill-fated establishment that Luoc was able to beat her down substantially in price. He deliberately chose a bed where one of the two mercenaries had slept. Tonight, he feared no spirits. If he were stronger than the Frenchman, the *ma* of two underlings offered him no threat. He curled on his side, the *coupe-coupe* under him. He needed sleep; he had much traveling to do the next day.

6

Father St. Vincent jumped at the sound of the voice and peered across the protective width of his desk at the young man who had appeared unannounced in the door of his study. The school was closed for the holidays; his students should all be gone. He could not see the face clearly. Dusk had fallen and the priest preferred the soft light of oil lamps to electricity from the erratic local generator. He noted with irritation that his heart has speeded up and his mouth gone slightly dry.

Over the last few days, the district policeman had brought several pieces of disturbing news. The first had been the murder of the chiefs of two upland villages; one had been the father of one of his pupils. Then came word that a French mercenary and three of his men had been butchered at the Black River. Finally, at luncheon that same day, the district policeman had arrived to say that although two men had been arrested for killing the Frenchman, their guilt was in doubt after interrogation. It seemed that the dead Frenchman had ordered the death of the two chiefs, and that the son of one chief, Father St. Vincent's pupil, had disappeared. The police wanted to talk to the boy and asked the priest to notify them if he showed up at the school.

Here he was.

"Come in, my son." Father St. Vincent was angry to be put in a moral dilemma. He knew what the Frenchman's business had been, and deplored it. He didn't mind the smoking of opium; it was said to be excellent for wet-season colds and influenza. He had used it in that way himself. However, the trade had always been a violent business—first for the British in China and now for the French. Too many people, including governments, wanted the high returns and fought for them in ways he could not approve.

On the other hand, he knew that money from the Opium Monopoly paid the wages of the soldiers in the local garrison and bought peace with the local warlords. Therefore, it allowed the French to protect the peasants of the district from the brutal feudalism of these warlords. Before the French had taken power, the warlords had demanded up to a third of the peasants' crops each year as rent for the land they farmed. They had extorted

35

tolls from any farmers with enough produce to wish to carry it to market by road or by river. Even now, some still tried to wring rice and raw opium from the peasants, but it was believed that the worst abuses had been stopped.

Father St. Vincent was aware that money from opium sales bought not only soldiers, guns, and the loyalty of native allies, it also bought the medicine and books he needed in his own battle to claim a small part of Tonkin for France. It had financed his considerable success in molding French citizens from the superstitious pagans who lived here.

The boy sitting across his desk was one of his successes. Or had been, until now. The priest prided himself on his ability to read other people. He felt a change in the boy that disturbed him. The policeman's message clamored loudly in his brain. He opened his desk drawer slowly and put away his pen, then left the drawer open, as if carelessly. His revolver lay in the drawer under a folded baize bag made to hold candlesticks.

The boy's eyes glinted with sardonic amusement. Father St. Vincent felt his own eyes drawn helplessly to the rest of his pens, which were ranged neatly in their ebony stand on the front of his desk and from which one was missing.

The priest was rattled by his mistake. "How can I help you?" he asked.

"I am in need of a letter from you. To find employment. It is necessary for my family now that my father is dead. We have no rain and no rice. I must work."

The boy's tone was respectful, his eyes level, but the priest had been given an order, not a request. Suddenly, he knew that the boy had murdered the four men at the Black River. Moral dilemma took second place to personal fear. He could smell it on himself and wondered if the boy could smell it too.

"If you feel I am worthy..." The boy bowed his head with disarming humility.

You're a fool, the priest told himself. He's not threatening you. He's not even armed. What had frightened him, he decided, was the force of will he felt flowing across the desk from the boy's slight frame.

"One of my best students..." he said aloud. The compliment was offered in part as compensation for the betrayal he was considering. "I will be happy to write you a letter," he heard himself say.

The act of writing would buy time while he thought things through. He took a sheet of paper from the center drawer of his

36

desk, placed his ink bottle deliberately, and shifted the bottle of blotting sand a few centimeters to his left.

Automatically, he wrote the opening salutation to the Bishop of Hué. He had written so many similar letters. It was a thousand pities that so few positions were open to natives. Sometimes he felt secretly that he educated his boys to take their place in a society that did not want them. It wanted young men to build roads, dig tin, or serve up dinner. It had no use for those who qualified for the Civil Service or government posts. He had written several times, personally, to the Governor-General to argue that the French must stop ignoring their responsibilities.

Responsibility for this boy's future was now in his own hands. His revolver lay within a second's grasp; his servants were within shouting distance. He had clear instructions from the police. And yet, in spite of the fear, he was having second thoughts. As he wrote, he asked himself whether seeing your father shot down in cold blood might not cause a change in manner. The boy seemed open about his father's death and unaware that he was wanted by the police. Surely, both things indicated his innocence.

Father St. Vincent wanted to believe he was innocent. The boy had always been attentive, receptive to teaching. He had gained excellent French, impeccable manners, and a reading knowledge of Latin, and had recently asked to be allowed to take Mass. The priest had spent his life trying to create young men like this. He needed to believe in the power of his own influence and effect. If God, working through him, had been unable to make a lasting mark on such promising material, if a soul that had seemed so safe were to be so quickly lost, then Father St. Vincent might as well admit he had lived for nothing.

The boy watched calmly. The priest wished that God would whisper whether the level gaze of those large dark eyes held a plea or a challenge. He signed the letter. He moved from behind his desk to hand over the envelope.

The boy scrambled to his feet and bowed his head. "Father, thank you. I realize fully how much I owe you."

The priest felt a flutter of gratification in spite of himself. He floated on a current of action where his own will was suspended. He made one last try.

"Do you wish to make a final confession before you go?"

The triumph and amusement in the boy's eyes made him uneasy again.

"Thank you, Father, but no. Thank you." The boy tucked the letter into his tunic, bowed respectfully, and turned to go.

"Remember, my son," said Father St. Vincent, "that humility and forgiveness are both treasured Christian virtues." He could still call his servants.

The boy flung up the shutters that had veiled his eyes and struck the priest with the full blazing force of his personality. "Father, I will *never* forget the lessons I have been taught."

Father St. Vincent closed the study door and leaned his forehead against the teak panel.

"Please, God, let me have done right!"

7

Ariane saw the speculative interest in Mme. Garine's eyes. She knew at that moment, as she had known in her field on Cap Ferret, that life held more for her than she could imagine. The wonders she had seen so far were only the beginning. She floated up the wide double staircase to her new room behind the silk-clad rump of Mme. Garine. The room was just one more confirmation.

It was spacious and white-plastered, with a wonderful bed of knuckled brass swathed with white netting like a bridal veil falling from a tiara on the ceiling.

"I generally lie down for an hour or two," said Mme. Garine. "You will learn that it's the best way to get through the heat of the early afternoon."

She hesitated, then stretched usual practice for the sake of her new project. "We have aperitifs around five, if you would like to come down and join us. Do eat with us as well tonight. Don't concern yourself with the children until you've had a night to settle in. We usually dress." With that last enigmatic instruction, she left Ariane to prowl her new territory like a happy cat.

It was a corner room. One window opened onto the veranda, which ran the length of the house; it was screened but had no glass. The other window had a heavy shutter propped up like an eyelid against the sun, and looked out from the back of the house onto the roofs of the servants' quarters. Ariane heard voices arguing and singing in the strange language, and a wet, slapping sound from the washhouse. As she looked out, Willy and Paulette darted across the compound into the cookhouse, where they were greeted noisily. Willy had taken off his blazer and Paulette had lost her bow.

There was no sign of Ariane's cases in the room. Her

hairbrush and toilet things had been laid out on a little carved table beside the bed. She opened the Biedermeier armoire. Her few dresses hung neatly in its cavern. Her slippers and her everyday shoes huddled together on the scented paper that lined the bottom. Her writing set, which her parents had given her as a farewell present, lay in the drawer of a little writing table with porcelain plaques set into its top. She was glad her bags had disappeared; the scuffed leather must have looked dreadful in this lovely room.

Ariane took off her damp, wrinkled traveling dress and lay down on the bed in her chemise and knickers. She stretched in sensuous delight, and felt like a princess. A hot princess, but a princess nevertheless. She imagined herself again at a ball in the Governor-General's Palace. How did I ever imagine that I wanted to become a nun? she asked herself. How wise my father was to send me out into the world and not let me retreat from it!

Mme. Garine went to work on Ariane the next day. She took her to her own hairdresser to have the messy curls cropped into a neat, chic cap. Together at Mme. Garine's dressmaker they ordered two light silk shifts, one in blue and one in watery green *eau de nil* to set off her fair skin and hair. Then Mme. Garine took her to a *corsetière* on the Rue Catinat and insisted that Ariane buy an uncomfortable *bustier*, which strapped her full breasts sideways toward her armpits in order to flatten her silhouette as the new shifts demanded. Mme. Garine said reassuringly that they would come to an arrangement about her wages to pay for all the lovely new things. The haircut was her own gift of welcome.

Ariane joined the adult Garines for dinner three nights a week. Mme. Garine gave her an old, long gown of her own to wear as long as the meals were only *en famille*. At table, Ariane watched carefully; she had never seen so many knives and forks at one meal. Or crystal glasses. At first, she was embarrassed to have another person serve her, but she copied Mme. Garine's casual indifference, which allowed her to carry on chatting while the number one boy or *boyesse* spooned wilting soufflé onto her plate.

In a recut gown of Mme. Garine's and a liberal splash of her Joy perfume, Ariane attended the first function the Garines gave after she arrived. Beforehand, she was terrified. By the end of the evening she was delirious with pleasure and relief. Other men shared Henri Garine's appreciation of her luxurious looks and eager, unspoiled shyness. All the younger men wanted to

39

appraise the new face in town. She danced, laughed, chattered, and accepted champagne from three different hands at once. She was too excited to notice or care about the wry looks she got from some of the women. In any case, Mme. Garine's obvious pleasure in her success was cushion enough from jealousy.

It was well after midnight when she fell through the mosquito netting onto her bed. She had met delightful tanned young men of mixed blood, French boys her own age, and older men with elegant mustaches. She had danced with a Japanese who was a second cousin of the Emperor of Japan, with a colonel from Sécurité whose eyes made the pit of her stomach feel delightfully peculiar, and with a tall, handsome bachelor called Raoul Costals who made her feel as if she had done the fox-trot all her life. She wanted nothing more from any of them, for the moment, than this evening's intoxicating conviction that she was desirable. One day, when the time came, she knew that any one of them would make a better husband for her than Jules Martin in his rubber boots.

In the midst of these more important concerns, Ariane maintained a state of reasonable truce with Paulette and Willy. She spent one hour every morning reading the plays of Corneille and Racine aloud with Paulette. Paulette twitched and fidgeted while Ariane closed her eyes and recited the words which the nuns at home had said were the most beautiful in the French language.

"Ariane, ma soeur, de quel amour blessée. . . ."

Mme. Garine occasionally included Paulette as well as Ariane in educational visits to the theater or the opera. Once a month, Paulette came down to dinner in the big dining room to practice the table manners that Ariane was supposed to be teaching her in the nursery. Otherwise, the children were quite happy to carry on as they had before she arrived, playing with the servants and their school friends.

The one duty that Ariane adored was taking the children out on expeditions. The ayah always accompanied them, but Ariane didn't mind.

"What does that sign say?" she would ask the woman. "What is that man doing to the tree? Who are those women in white robes and headdresses like flat bakers' hats folded over at the top?"

She loved to take them to Mass in the Cathedral; Mme. Garine slept on Sunday mornings and M. Garine was uninterested. Through half-closed eyes, over folded hands, she would study the rich collection of worshipers—half-breeds of all colors,

Annamite Catholics, North Africans, elderly Corsican women in black dresses, as well as the ranks of elegantly dressed *françaises* who tinkled with gold. Their perfumes were a fugue of honeysuckle, patchouli, musk, sandalwood, gardenia, and violet around the deep bass theme of the incense.

She loved to take the children on a late afternoon promenade in the park near the waterfront at the end of the Rue Catinat. She loved to take them to the Central Market near the railway station, and to the Pet Market where monkeys and cockatoos were sold on the street, beside iron baths full of lizards and turtles and tanks of fish. She loved the Flower Market. She loved the windows of the Rue Catinat. She was happy to bribe the children into patience with ice cream and strange, forbidden sweets from vendors. Without them, the ayah, and their small procession of two cyclos, she knew she could not have explored so freely. Each time they went out, she grasped at new experiences as if plucking handfuls of marguerites in her field. It seemed only fitting that one of the most exciting marguerites was found in her favorite place of all, the zoological gardens.

8

Father St. Vincent was a thin, ascetic-looking man. With dark hair and long, fine bones, he looked like the ideal of an unworldly priest. The fact gave him pleasure, which he managed, most of the time, to quell. He knew that physical vanity was a regular marcher in his personal parade of sins; he had wrestled with it for years. The vanity of spirit he now confronted was far more deadly.

He knew both newspaper cuttings by heart. He had himself cut out the one from *La France-Indochine* when the paper arrived at the mission school a week late. A fellow priest had sent the clipping from *Le Courrier d'Haiphong,* thinking it might have local interest for his colleague. Father St. Vincent pushed the cuttings away across the top of his desk and bent his high forehead against his folded hands.

They were both accounts of what had been dubbed the "Black River Massacre." Both named only the Frenchman and lumped the other victims together as "three accompanying natives." *La France-Indochine* reported that the Frenchman had died in the service of his country. The same paper suggested that the radical left wing in France was to blame for such atrocities:

41

Those men who encourage the spread of cankers, like the so-called "nationalism" of the Young Annamite movement, must acknowledge their culpability when their native disciples distort French ideals of democracy and republicanism in order to stir up revolution—like that which has so recently destroyed China!

Though not a left-wing radical, Father St. Vincent had been accused of creating dissatisfied "quasi-Frenchmen" who would end up only making trouble for their benefactors. But he was secure in his belief in the right of every human soul to aspire toward perfection, and he continued to educate his boys. This belief was all that he now had to weigh in his favor against the enormity of his guilt.

Second thoughts had quickly followed the writing of his letter. Once the strength of the boy's presence had faded from the study, Father St. Vincent realized how much he had been swayed. The newspaper accounts increased his torment; the date and place of the murders were too apt. He knew himself that the motive was strong.

He pressed himself back into his chair; the edge of his desk cut furrows in his palms. The oil lamp on his desk left most of the study in warm shadow. Father St. Vincent closed his eyes yet again and imagined his meeting with the boy. He knew that he had believed the boy to be guilty, even as he was writing the letter to the Bishop of Hué, and that he had chosen to ignore his own inner voice for the worst of reasons. He had wanted the boy to think well of him. . . . He closed his eyes in pain. The boy had challenged his generosity and he had taken the bait, at the expense of truth. He could claim that he had acted out of compassion. The truth was that he had needed to confirm his own success as a shepherd gathering lost sheep. Faith, he noted ruefully, did not make it less painful to accept the humiliation of having made a terrible mistake.

He replaced the two cuttings in the drawer of his desk, to lie there like a knotted scourge. He needed to walk. Quickly, before anyone could run in with messages of fights in the dormitory, or a wet bed, or insects in the food stores, or a failing generator, or the disappearance of more textbooks, he slipped out of the school building and set off along a dirt path flanked by dark sheaves of cannas, toward the kitchen garden. In that stony patch he defied monsoon and dry season to suggest, if not re-create, the ordered geometry of a French cloister garden. Between finger and thumb he nipped a sprig of sweet basil and inhaled the fragrance for comfort. He was deaf to the noises of the night.

If I am utterly honest, he thought, I am less horrified, *au fond*, by the death of four men than by the fact that I could have been so wrong. It would be funny if it weren't so appalling. He marched fiercely past a patch of staked tomatoes, lumpy and fetid in the hot night air. The swinging skirt of his soutane released the animal smell of their bristling leaves.

I must accept full responsibility for the danger I have loosed on the world, he told himself. I cannot continue to protect either the boy or myself. I owe penance both for my self-delusion and for the pride that makes it so hard to admit.

He turned back toward the school. There was no one there to whom he could make confession; he would have to wait until his next visit to Hanoi. In the meantime, he must carry out a practical penance which would make him suffer more than any imposed by a fellow priest. He returned to his study, relit the oil lamp, and wrote another letter to the Bishop of Hué.

9

"Have you ever seen this man?" The tall Frenchman held up a grainy photograph of a young scholar in a Chinese tunic.

Luoc's eyes were still half blinded by the light on the ground floor of the prison after two days in darkness on the floor above. He shook his head humbly. The force with which his elbows had been bound, points touching each other, made his chest feel as if it were being torn in half. The pain in his shoulders had become unbearable; it had become the substance of his entire body.

"Look again," said the Frenchman, still holding the picture before Luoc's face. "I want you to be very sure." Unusually, for a Frenchman, he spoke Tonkinese. The fact made Luoc distrust and fear him even more. He wondered what other powers the man had.

"We know that you killed those men," the Frenchman went on. "That does not concern me. I wish to discuss your reasons. I'm certain they must have been good ones."

Luoc kept his eyes lowered. If this man were a sorcerer who could read what lay in men's minds, the eyes would open the soul far too much.

"Who are your assistants?" asked the Frenchman. "Who encouraged you to do it?"

Luoc flung his head up and stared at the Frenchman, half again as tall as himself, with a long head like a northern Chinese, hair dark as a Viet, but with white skin like a drowned man. This man was no sorcerer, or he would never have asked those two stupid questions. He was lying; he knew nothing. The boy felt a surge of triumph which quickly passed, but left a small residue of hope.

"Have you ever seen this man before?" the Frenchman repeated.

"Never," murmured the boy. "I swear it."

The Frenchman sighed and paced around the interrogation chamber. He paused to light a cigarette, one gleaming shoe placed carelessly on the raised dais where the examining Mandarin would once have sat. He wore tropical whites, immaculately tailored. He flicked a crumb of tobacco from his sleeve, looked at the boy perched, bound, on a stool, and sighed again. Then he ordered the two attending officers to leave the room.

"Now," he said, "we may speak frankly. I am not a mere policeman; I am an aide to the Chief Resident of Tonkin. I come from Hanoi. The local gendarmes are interested only in catching thieves and murderers who have the impudence to disrupt the local peace. I, and the men for whom I work, have larger interests."

He looked at the boy to see if he was following the line of thought. The dark eyes were regarding him with a steady gaze that startled him; the natives were seldom so direct.

"You are very young," he said. The boy had a perfectly heart-shaped face with high cheekbones and the eyes of a girl. "Much too young to suffer the tortures of *la question* and death before you have begun to live."

He saw intelligence in the dark, watching eyes, under the long lashes.

"Perhaps we can help each other."

The Frenchman lit another cigarette from the stub of his first; the boy was unnerving him with those large, dark eyes. The boy's slim strength and the way it was bound also distracted the older man from his task.

He stood squarely in front of the boy. "If you will tell me who encouraged you to kill the Frenchman—his bodyguards can be disregarded—I will get you out of here. Have your arms unbound."

Luoc wondered how they knew he had done the murders. He was certain no one had seen him at the time or they would have raised the alarm. And the two coolies would not have been arrested. This white devil Round Eye was no sorcerer, of that he was now quite sure, but he did have powers of knowledge which Luoc did not understand.

"I could arrange for you to go free."

Luoc stared up at the man's pallid face high above him; he suspected a trick. What did the White Devil mean by "who encouraged you"? His reasons were clear. He had needed no encouragement from another man.

"I have done nothing," the boy murmured again.

The man continued as if he had not spoken. "A young man with your excellent character references and education could be given a fresh start . . . once you have proved yourself worthy by offering help in exchange."

He saw the boy stiffen and his lips go white. The long lashes dropped to mask the eyes and the finely chiseled nostrils tightened.

The white devil priest! At the mention of character references, Luoc knew who his betrayer had been. At the same time, he realized with intense relief that they could not know; they merely suspected him. They had no power of magic over him, just that of ordinary human treachery. He kept his head lowered stubbornly.

The Frenchman knew he had lost. It was a shame, a waste of the boy himself, but there were other prisoners who would be more cooperative.

"Stand up," he ordered.

Luoc obeyed clumsily, his balance thrown by the binding of his arms. The White Devil reached down from his great height and touched the boy's lips with one clean, manicured hand.

"I can't bear the waste," he said. There was an odd look in his eyes.

When the man reached under his tunic for the top of the loose trousers, Luoc took a step backward and let out a scream of rage which transformed his heart-shaped face to a terrifying mask. The long-lashed eyes blazed with such force that the Frenchman stepped back in his turn, and raised both hands in protest.

The boy stood, head forward like a charging water buffalo, heart pounding, weaving slightly with the force of his fury. He did not know the words for what the man had meant to do, but he knew the meaning. If he touched him again, Luoc would kill him with only his teeth. All his rage, at all white devil Round Eyes, came together like a tidal wave. He growled in his throat and tears sprang to his eyes.

"Sit down!" said the Frenchman. He lit another cigarette with shaking hands and called the officers back into the room.

They looked inquisitively at the boy, who still stood shaking, back to the wall, watching the white man with a hatred that raised the hair on their necks.

"You can do what you like with him now," said the Frenchman. "He's too stupid to know how to help himself."

They returned him to darkness. His elbows were unbound, but his ankles were trapped again in wooden stocks bolted to the platform shelf that ran around the walls of the windowless cell. In the brief moment before the warder's lantern withdrew, he saw that all the other stocks were full. Watching eyes caught the lantern's orange glint as he was fastened into place.

When the door closed, the cell was darker than any jungle night. He could see nothing but dense, unvaried blackness, not even a shadow, which was as good as the substance when traveling at night on jungle trails. His ears became the rulers of his body.

When he was first brought to the cell, a voice had asked his name. He began to reply, but another voice stopped him.

"Brother, say nothing! There is a police informer in here with us."

So there was not even the consolation of conversation. He sat, more alone than he had ever been, listening to the groans and snores of the other men imprisoned with him. The first night, a man began to scream that the rats who visited the cell were eating him alive.

"They trap them and starve them," he screamed. "Then release them in here. . . . My foot. My foot . . . !" After a long time, the voice died into sobs, and then sleep.

Luoc remained sane only because the prisoners were taken down into the yard twice a day to evacuate their bowels into a trench. Locked back into the stocks in the dark cell, he would close his eyes to pretend that he had created the darkness himself and would try to hold in his mind the reality of the hot sun and fresh air until the next time they were taken down.

For two days he was numbed by the shock of his arrest. He had presented his letter at the residence of the bishop in Hué. One of the bishop's secretaries had read it, directed him to a Catholic hostel for young men, non-French only, and asked him to call back in a few days to see what kind of work might be available for him to do. He also gave him a few piastres to tide him over until he found employment.

The police had arrested him at the hostel. He was taken under armed guard by train to Hanoi and from Hanoi to the provincial capital by road, along with two other prisoners. He had been questioned briefly in Hué, in Hanoi, and twice here in the prison. When the door slammed on him after his latest interrogation, he was no longer numb. His mind was racing. They had not proved his guilt.

"Did they beat you, Brother?" murmured the man on his left.

"No," said Luoc shortly.

"You are lucky... do you hear him over there...?"

Luoc had been trying to close his ears to the whimpering that came from along the shelf to his right.

"*La question!*" breathed his neighbor. "The French do not forgive the refusal to confess. I am frightened, Brother. I admit it to you."

"I am innocent," said Luoc as steadily as he had to the Frenchman.

"It is sometimes easier to be guilty," said the man. "Much quicker. My turn is coming soon, I know it!"

Luoc shut his ears and tried to suppress fear so that he could think logically about escape.

"They break your fingers, joint by joint," said his neighbor. "They stuff clay into your nostrils, then into your mouth, so that you suffocate. They slice off your balls and make you eat them."

Luoc had been struck during his interrogation, and accused of insolence, but nothing more. The most difficult time was when a group of Round Eyes had questioned him here at the prison. They spoke from all directions about the opium raised by the village and tried to trick him into showing knowledge he would not possess if he had not followed the mule train. He had seen the danger and avoided it, but his body had been soaked with sweat and his hands cold as midnight on a mountaintop.

His neighbor subsided. Luoc slept, to escape the pain in his chest and shoulders and the sick feeling in his stomach from the prison food.

They woke him to move him to another cell. It was as dark as the first. At first, he was happy to get away from his nervous neighbor. Then he learned that the prisoners in his cell were not taken down to the yard but had to use a slop bucket that was emptied every other day. Someone in this new cell sang endlessly to himself under his breath. Luoc heard only an occasional surge of sound, as if the man had found an unexpected pocket of air in his lungs, and spasmodic tapping and clapping. Luoc began to feel he would go mad if he did not see daylight again soon. He slept more and more.

He was awakened once by a voice that shouted, "All of us in

this cesspit are going to die! But we should be proud—we die because they are afraid of us!''

He curled into himself away from the voice, as if from an evil dream. He tried to recapture sleep, but his back ached from leaning against the cell wall and the skin of his ankles was rubbed raw against the wood of the stocks.

There were other voices in this darkness; these men showed less caution because they had all been condemned to die already. Someone even exhorted him to die a hero's death by proclaiming the name of the Young Annamite movement as the blade fell toward his neck, but suspicion had sunk into the boy's bones and he kept silent.

Luoc did not understand how it was possible that he was here in this place when all the signs spoke so clearly of his success. He wondered how much longer the Heavens had in which to reveal their purpose, or whether the French would act first.

He woke knowing something was wrong. His eyes had not yet learned that they were useless. He strained them, searching for some faint variation in the blackness. As he turned his head, he imagined a rectangle on his left; it floated unexplained on the back of his eyes. It stayed, wavering. Then he imagined that he saw subtle shadings in its darkness. After some time, he realized that it was the door.

He was looking at the beautiful, varied darkness of night through the open door. His body jerked in excitement. He knew what had felt wrong in his sleep. He could move his feet. He nearly drowned in an overwhelming wash of terror that he had gone mad and entered the world of demons and things beyond speaking. Just as quickly, the terror was replaced by a blaze of excitement and knowledge that what he saw and felt was true in the world of mortal men.

He rose unsteadily to his feet and listened. He heard nothing except the almost forgotten sounds of insects, frogs, and birds that the heavy door had closed out. Inside the cell was also silent. He heard no breathing, no snoring, no restless shifting of bodies seeking impossible comfort.

As he began to climb off the shelf, his hand touched another man's foot. The man said nothing; he did not stir in his sleep. Luoc shook the foot, which was still in its stocks. Nothing. He felt his way up from the stocks along a mountain ridge of shin and thigh, across a plateau of rags and human flesh until he reached the wetness under the man's chin. He sniffed his finger.

The warm, acrid smell told him enough. He touched the hair; the head was still in place. The man's throat had been cut.

He climbed off the shelf and crossed to the door. The corridor was deserted. In the moonlight, through one of the small barred windows, he saw darkness on his fingertips. In a dream he trotted silently down the corridor, through the barred door at the top of the stairs, which stood open. So did the one at the bottom of the stairs. Dark offices lined the ground-floor corridor. He passed the room where the Frenchman had interrogated him and walked out, unbelieving, into the moonlit prison yard. He crossed the dusty yard and by the open gate found his first sign, since the man in his cell, that human hands had arranged this miracle.

The guard lay in the dust. A banner had been tied to the gate. A placard had been nailed to the guard's shoulders with the blade of a small rice-cutting sickle. In the moonlight Luoc read, "Drive out all colonialist exploiters, imperialists, and bourgeois, capitalist lackeys!" It was illustrated with a woodcut of angry peasants chasing skull-faced Round Eyes in top hats.

He stepped over the guard's body, back into the world. Outside the gate, he paused. There was a tiny irrigation ditch nearby. He slipped into the water to wash away the prison as well as the blood on his fingers. He inhaled the rich, warm smell of mud and listened in delight to the rustling of a clump of bamboo. He tilted his face back to peer up into the lacy, silhouetted tops of a stand of coconut palms.

He should never have doubted the will of Heaven! He nearly laughed aloud at the idea of the nationalist guerrillas who had thought they were rescuing some of their own members, when their greater purpose had been to set him free!

It took him a month to return to the hamlet on the Black River. First he collected his *coupe-coupe* from the village just outside Hué where he had hidden it rather than risk being caught with it in the city. No one in the hamlet recognized him, particularly since he now wore a stolen jacket and a pair of French trousers. He told people that he was trying to find his cousin, who had been a guard with the mule train down from the mountains. Four days passed fruitlessly. Luoc kept an anxious eye on boats from downriver, but no police arrived in search of an escaped prisoner. On the fifth day (five was an auspicious number for Luoc), he met two boatmen.

"What does your cousin look like?" asked one. "We carried men from such a mule train only a few weeks ago."

Luoc plunged. "He was with the Round Eye who was killed," he said. "Bigger than me. . . ." He tried to remember the other guards, who had not been involved with his father's death.

The boatmen looked at each other. They made a sign against bad fortune. Luoc's muscles tightened in excitement.

"We sat that unlucky party down in a village on the Red River, not far from Hanoi. . . ."

The man, a short, squat, mahogany-tanned southerner, began to turn away. "I want nothing more to do with that crowd!"

"Brother," said Luoc, "how unfortunate do you call it that there is one less Round Eye in Tonkin?"

The other man hissed between his teeth, which were black with betel. He peered at Luoc under the high ridges of his brows. "Noise . . . noise. The wind will blow such words away."

Luoc felt their tension. They looked about for eavesdroppers. One rolled a cigarette with Moroccan papers. They shifted their weight.

"Brothers," said Luoc carefully, "will you drink with me to all our good fortunes, however they are described?"

"Seems reasonable," said the short boatman.

They found the rice-wine seller. Within an hour, the boatmen had agreed to set him down in the village where they had left the opium and its guards.

"No more convoys come through this place," said the taller man. "But there may be one or two last ones from the highlands of Laos. We return downriver tomorrow. We'll leave you where you can pick up the scent."

The village where they left him was much larger than the one on the Black River. Fleets of rice sampans were moored alongside a huge warehouse. There was a small mechanical crane for heavy cargoes. A gasoline-powered generator hummed and thumped inside a locked wire cage to light up the waterside for nighttime loading and unloading.

Luoc haunted the quays. He watched every boat that arrived or left. Again on the fifth day, he saw a second Moroccan who had been with the mule train. The man did not get off a boat, but was leaning on a pile of baled rice straw beside his rifle, rolling himself a cigarette from a silver box stamped "Bambu." Like Luoc, he was waiting for a boat to arrive.

For Luoc, after that, it was a matter of time. Of tracking and of choosing which quarry to track. He followed the last of the season's crude opium from the quay, along irrigation canals, to a primitive workshop in a tiny farming village. Here he spied on two women, a Tonkinese and a half-Chinese *métisse,* while they boiled the raw opium gum in huge cooking pots with a small amount of water. They filtered the resulting solution and boiled the residue, which they called "dog," several more times. Then they stirred all the filtered liquid over a slow fire until only a thick, sticky paste remained in their pot. The sickly-sweet smell was lost in the miasma that floated from the nearby sugarcane mill.

A man dressed as a farmer collected the smoker's opium from the women. Luoc followed him and the opium to Hanoi, along with the man's load of stinking, squealing pigs, pinioned helplessly on the cart in woven wicker corsets. From the time he was able to name the broker in Hanoi who took over the opium, it took four more months of endless waiting and false trails before he stood in a broad Saigon street staring at the high walls and guarded gate of the house that belonged to a young Corsican businessman named Emile Carbone.

10

Luoc knew when he was admitted to the Corsican's house that he had arrived at the peak of the mountain. There was no one higher than this man. He could tell by the man's casual authority and by the way the other men stood around him, relaxed but alert for signs of his pleasure or displeasure.

The man was young to be head of clan. Carbone was no more than thirty-one—a young man though already shaped like an old one. He had begun to acquire flesh under his shoulders and across his paunch, flesh still hard but suggesting the bulk of age to come. His head was round, with hair as black and shining as Luoc's own. His skin was much paler than Luoc's and still flushed from recent barbering. The boy could smell sandalwood aftershave.

In spite of the heat, Carbone wore a necktie, loosened around his unbuttoned collar to show dark hairs curling at the base of his heavy throat, and the glint of a gold crucifix chain.

The sleeves of his white shirt—his third that day—were rolled up to his elbows, baring strong forearms in gloves of dark, thick hair. One large, stocky hand engulfed a delicate frosted glass; the other lay along the back of the wickerwork settee which he occupied alone, like a throne. His white-trousered legs, with their thickening thighs, lay loose and open in arrogant carelessness.

51

Luoc paused at the edge of the veranda, just inside the wooden arch that marched around the house, as the huge stone colonnades protected official buildings near the Palace of the Governor-General. The White Demon's legs were open like the jaws of a striking snake, attacking the space in which Luoc must stand.

The Corsican studied Luoc as the boy introduced himself respectfully. A provincial, to judge by his clothes. Trousers too large. Sandals instead of shoes. But nevertheless, not comic. Carbone sipped his drink. The boy was handsome in the feminine way of these people but still conveyed toughness. He had strong hands and arms, perhaps from working in the *paddi* fields. He also had impertinence, or courage, depending on how one looked at it.

"Where did you learn such excellent French?" asked the Corsican.

"In the same place I learned history, mathematics, dictation, to eat with a knife and fork, and to pray to the man in the sky who counts our sins." Luoc bowed again, in case he might appear boastful.

"A Catholic!" said Carbone. "Which school?"

Luoc replied steadily, "Jesuit school, monsieur. In a small village in..." His pulse quickened, but Carbone was not really interested in his answer.

The man lifted a darkly furred forearm to sip once more at his iced drink. "How old are you?"

"Seventeen, monsieur," he lied.

"So what do you want from me, seventeen-year-old Catholic?"

Luoc gazed into the intelligent eyes that met his across the width of the veranda and took a chance. "Work, monsieur, that will make better use of my education than waiting at table or digging tin."

The Corsican snorted. "Impudent little bastard, aren't you? How many others have you petitioned in this way?"

"You are the first." Luoc bowed again.

"I'm sure that I am," said Carbone. "Or you'd have had to crawl here to see me...crippled by a thrashing." His eyes, however, were amused. "And what do you suggest that work should be?"

"To do what you do, monsieur." Luoc kept his eyes lowered respectfully.

Carbone was taken aback. "Well, well." He laughed. "And what exactly is that?"

"You buy and sell important things. I have watched a little." Luoc raised his head and unveiled the depths of his eyes, looking deep into those of the Round Eye. He glanced quickly at the other men on the veranda to show that he was not certain of their discretion. "I know that you are Number One Boss. I want to work only for you, and to learn. I wish to become your follower."

This time the Corsican laughed aloud, startled by the sudden force of the boy's personality. He leaned forward. "How do you know that I am Number One Boss?"

Luoc allowed himself to sound slightly surprised at the question. "All the signs say so, monsieur." He took a step forward into the jaws of the snake. "And I feel it also, in your presence." He offered his profession of faith simply.

The flattery had been elegantly done. Both amused and pleased, Carbone settled his bulk firmly back into the cushions of the settee and studied the boy.

"There are times," he said, "when I wish more of my employees felt like that." It was his turn to glance around at the other men, provoking a tiny ripple of dutiful amusement.

He needed time to reflect. He was young enough to be still learning the management of his troops. His mind had not yet frozen into the automatic, habitual decisions of middle age. The boy was handsome and well-mannered, except for his surprising confidence. He spoke excellent French. With the new governmental fashion for *jaunissement,* he could prove to be very useful. If he could be controlled . . . that was the danger in his obvious intelligence.

"I could use another messenger," said Carbone. "To be on call night and day. You must go directly where you are sent. Once your task is completed, you must return without slipping into a cinema or gambling club. Do you understand?"

"Thank you! Thank you, monsieur!" Luoc bowed yet again. "I understand perfectly."

"I must point out," said the Corsican, "that it will not be much better than waiting at table."

"I know that, monsieur. But you will soon give me other things to do."

The boy met his eyes with a conviction that should have been impudent but somehow was not. He had stated a simple fact.

Carbone debated whether the time for a metaphorical thrashing had arrived, but it was an intellectual debate only. The boy had impressed, not angered, him.

"Don't count on that," he said. "It will depend on whether you please me or not."

"I will please you." Again, a simple fact.

Unlike some other Frenchmen, Carbone was not angered or made uncomfortable by signs of superiority in an Annamite. On the contrary, he had begun to search it out. Though he had been trained by a father who ruled his rubber plantation domain like a feudal warlord, Carbone was developing his own personal strategy. He had an inbuilt dislike of unnecessary bloodshed and had learned respect for the powers of negotiation and conciliation. So long as he was negotiating from a position of strength. As a result, he had developed an army not of soldiers, but of spies. He did not make enemies; he bought allies.

He also kept his nose in the wind. He had friends in the northern provinces. He listened with an open mind to reports of "local dissatisfaction." Through his spies he negotiated and he paid, not so much from foresight but as a way of covering his bets. He made business alliances with rebel groups in the north and south alike, which in later years would give him a *laissez-passer* for his opium trade and other dealings. His nose told him to bring more *jaunes* into his organization, as it had told him to send gifts of respect to sect generals and guerrilla leaders. Now his nose told him that this was an unusual *jaune* who stood before him. If pressure on the French from nationalist insurgents should increase, he could think of many ways to use the man this boy could become.

It was several years before Carbone regretted his choice of protégé. For the first few months of their acquaintance the boy constantly surprised him with the quickness of his understanding, his tact, his efficiency, and most of all his dogged loyalty to his chosen master. Sometimes Carbone was touched; sometimes he set small traps. Luoc never put a foot wrong. He never took money that was not his; he never used Carbone's time for his own purposes; he could never be caught taking bribes from Carbone's competitors in exchange for information; he never attended political meetings or showed any interest at all in discussions about the future of Indochina. His interests seemed to be only to serve and to learn.

Carbone's watchers reported only one odd piece of behavior in those first months. On three occasions, Luoc was followed to the zoological gardens where he stood for half an hour or more in front of one particular cage, staring at its inmate, a Fire Pheasant. As the bird was fairly common in the rain forests of the Col des Nuages, and relatively unafraid of men, Luoc's apparent fascination with it puzzled Carbone as much as it did the men who reported to him. Carbone sometimes worried that the boy did not drink much, gamble, go to the races, or seem to frequent prostitutes. His nose told him that the boy would impress others besides himself. He might well, in time, attract the attention of radicals looking for future leaders from the native ranks. In the meantime, Carbone did all he could to keep Luoc anchored to the service of French interests.

Six months after Luoc began serving Carbone he asked his employer for a loan of several thousand piastres. Carbone agreed; he was reassured to have Luc, as he called himself, in his debt. Carbone was curious about the purpose of the loan but asked no questions. Then he caught the young man in his first mistake.

Luoc asked permission to take leave for three weeks to visit his family in the delta south of Saigon. On the day after he left, the watchdog waited for Carbone outside the bookshop that sold French newspapers. Carbone saw him and asked his driver to drop him off for a stroll in the riverside park at the bottom of the Rue Catinat.

"Well . . . ?" Carbone didn't look at the young Annamite who trotted at his side, skipping occasionally to keep up with the Corsican's strides.

"He's gone, OK," said the young man. "Train to Hué."

"*Where?*" Carbone stopped walking. Hué was north. Not in the delta.

"Train to Hué." The man was positive.

Carbone passed over the folded note; it vanished with the speed of rehearsed sleight of hand. He walked on alone for a while. Either Luoc was not going home at all or he had lied about where he came from. It was curious, but one couldn't hang a man for either crime. Carbone assumed that every man was corrupt or corruptible in some way. He didn't hold that against anyone, as long as he could spot the form of corruption and didn't receive any nasty surprises himself. In this case something was subtly satisfied deep within him. He had caught Luoc out at last. The pattern of unnerving perfection was broken. Collated with other sniffs and snippets, this piece of information would one day emerge as the complete truth.

When Luoc returned from his leave, he continued to work just as hard and as well for Carbone. The unnerving pattern knitted itself back together in spite of the Corsican's renewed wariness.

Carbone began to use Luoc to spread grease in certain quarters which allowed Carbone's shipments of morphine base to sail freely from the port of Saigon to Marseilles without paying the government tax. It was a perfect opportunity for Luoc to line his own pockets, but he did not. Carbone checked and rechecked, but never found a discrepancy.

Just before the second Tet New Year after he joined Carbone, Luoc asked for permission to go home once again.

"Which village does your family come from?" asked Carbone casually.

"I must confess to you," said the young man. "I hope you will not be angry with me. My family lives in the north. In a small village upriver from Vinh."

Vinh was north of Hué.

"Why did you lie to me before?" asked Carbone.

Luoc looked embarrassed. "I wanted very much to work for you. I was young and inexperienced. I was afraid you might think I was a Vietminh if I said I was from the north. I did not know, as I do now, that I should have trusted your good sense and judgment."

Carbone suppressed a smile at the implication that the young man now felt old and experienced. He was relieved that Luoc had told him the truth before being faced with the lie. It seemed further proof of his trustworthiness.

He began to use Luoc more and more as a cut-out, the sensitive direct link between himself and others he did not wish to know his name. As the months continued to pass without a nasty surprise, Carbone found that instruction often merged gently into companionship. Because he felt sure that Luoc would never presume on moments of closeness, Carbone began to use his quiet, receptive, intelligent presence to test his own ideas aloud. Because he trusted this young *jaune* in spite of himself, Carbone even voiced anxieties to him that he did not want his own fellow Corsicans to hear. He also gave Luoc increased responsibility in administering the shipment of morphine base.

Luoc waited for the Customs officer to sign the manifest. In the pocket of his white linen jacket he held the thick white envelope steady while he regarded the top of the man's head. Dark blond hair, darkened further by sweat, stuck to his pink scalp in strands. The man was thin and stooped, made gawky by his great height. He glanced up from the sheaf of flimsy papers to Luoc's face. He turned over two more sheets and looked up again.

Luoc's heart began to thud against his ribs.

"I know you," the officer said.

Luoc said nothing, but his heart was pushing up into his throat so that he could not breathe. He had remembered how he knew this man.

"There you are." The man handed back the papers.

Luoc used all his will to control the shaking of his hands as he passed over the envelope from Carbone, which the man pocketed in a swift gesture, without looking.

"I remember the eyes," said the man reflectively. "Did we meet at one of the Rabbit's parties?"

Luoc didn't want to speak. His tongue was so dry that he was afraid the man would hear his fear. "Perhaps, monsieur," he replied cautiously.

"Are you a friend of old Rabin's then?" Luoc saw the man's mind continue to labor at his identity. He had heard of St. Clair Rabin and his parties.

"Oh no, monsieur. I do not presume to his friendship. I go to many parties."

This tack was tricky, but safer than the real scent.

"This is driving me mad," said the man, smiling. "Come, have a drink with me while I chew on it."

"M. Carbone expects me back immediately," said Luoc. That was what the man would expect him to say, the correct thing.

"I'll square with Emile for subverting his employee; leave that all to me. It's after hours, anyway. Come on."

Luoc knew he could not let the man out of his sight.

Assuming Luoc's obedience, the man took his jacket off a hanger behind the door and put it on over his damp shirt. He draped a tie loosely around his neck.

Luoc followed as the officer waved down a cyclo and gave the address of a club. The night was clear-skied. He forced himself to lean nonchalantly back against the leatherette seat of the cyclo, within the careless arc of the man's arm, which was draped along the top edge.

"What's your name?"

"Pierre," said Luoc quickly. "Pierre St. Vincent." Then he wanted to cut out his tongue. The association that brought the name into his mouth might also leap into the Customs officer's mind and remind him that this former student of a Father St. Vincent was wanted for murder.

"Sounds a little wrong-side-of-the-blanket to me." The man smiled. "Or are you a convert?"

"My family were . . . are Catholics, monsieur. From a small village southwest of Saigon."

"Lord! I wish I could remember. These things niggle at one

so. . . ." The man studied Luoc's profile against the moving backdrop of the crowded street.

"Here we are." He leaned back and snapped his fingers to signal to their driver.

The ground floor was the Palm Court Restaurant. Through the etched lace of the plate-glass window Luoc saw fragments of Round Eyes, seated at fragmented, pink-draped tables under fragmented chandeliers. A door beside the main entrance led down a flight of carpeted stairs, past a statue on the landing of a turbaned black boy holding an electrically wired torch of glass flames.

The door at the bottom was of heavy wood, carved and studded with bolts and iron straps. When the officer rang the bell, a tiny flap over a hole in the door was pushed aside. An eye studied them. A few seconds later the door swung open. A wave of sound hit them. Inside, the air was filled with body heat and the scent of orchids, jasmine, and patchouli. A jazz band played in a farther room.

Luoc gazed around, startled. The room was very like the room upstairs except that here were also a large number of Annamites—a few young men in evening clothes, but mostly women, drinking or dancing with French partners. All the women were beautiful, though most had cropped their hair like Frenchwomen, with curls like frogs' tongues pressed to their cheeks. Their brows were plucked and penciled, their lips made full and heavy with bloodred paint. A few wore the traditional *ao dai,* but most wore silk shifts or sheer gauze frocks, and silk stockings. What startled Luoc was that they were all men. He looked again to be sure. They had the heightened femininity of the actors in the Chinese opera who played the heroines; the observer was made more aware of the quality of the sexuality than of the person.

The officer was watching him. "You haven't been here before?"

Luoc shook his head. "But they are charming!" He let his eyes roam over the table while his mind raced over the problem of escape. And afterward.

"You're with me this evening, you naughty boy." The officer's tone had changed as he passed through the barricaded door. "Look, but don't touch!"

He led Luoc to a table against the wall and settled into the sea-green plush of his chair with a sigh of relief and pleasure.

"Two *pastis,*" he said to the waiter, who wore lipstick like the "women."

To Luoc, he added, "When I remember where we met, I'll order champagne."

Luoc watched the couples dancing the fox-trot on the tiny polished square in the middle of the room.

The young men dressed as Frenchwomen made him feel odd, even odder than those in the *ao dais*.

The officer was watching him again. "You know, I'm not at all sure that you're Rabbit's type." There was dangerous concentration in his eyes.

Luoc took the chance. "Rabbit is not *my* type," he said firmly. "He's much too fat."

The officer laughed with delight. "So much for poor old Rabbit! You're quite right, he's a pig! An overdressed porker hoping for a big bad wolf to gobble him up."

He smoothed his hair with a thin hand. "I don't care for fat, either."

One of the dancing couples touched the tips of their tongues together, delicately, before they slid into a slow, dignified tango.

"Do you dance?" the officer asked.

"No!" said Luoc quickly. Then he added, "I have not yet learned the art."

"I'm not much of a dancer either," said the officer. "My legs are too long. There's another room at the back where we could go, perhaps, a little later, for a quick pipe or two. . . . Excuse me a moment, I'll go have a quick word to arrange things."

He rose and trudged between the dancing couples, defiantly gawky. As he passed the bar, Luoc saw him touch the elbow of a slim young man in an evening suit, made up like the women. The young man smiled and nodded.

As the officer passed, the young man's smile dropped as if the corners of his mouth were weighted. His eyes flickered to some inward vision, then lighted again with animation as he turned back to his partner, an elderly Frenchman leaning on the bar.

Luoc rose from the table and moved swiftly to the door. It was easier to get out than in. In the shadows of the building across the street from the club, he stripped off his white jacket and shirt and rolled them into a bundle under his arm. While he waited, he smoked a cigarette. He was frightened. Not of the officer—he was not going to give the man a chance to remember that they had never met, but had looked at each other across a small interrogation room in a prison in Tonkin.

Clearly he had not been afraid enough of being recognized in Saigon. As he traveled south through Tonkin, Annam, and Cochin China, Indochina had seemed huge enough to swallow him without trace. Now he saw the French were merely a small village within this huge nation, although they pretended to be the nation itself.

What he feared was what he had to do. He had to find the strength of the change-fate within himself when the act did not merit it. His hands shook as he held match to cigarette tip, because killing this Frenchman would be no act of fatefulness or revenge powered by rage, but a petty act of self-protection. Unless this man died, he could finish all Luoc's plans to pull down the French woodpile, with one word to the police. Luoc tried to work up rage and hatred against the man to fuel himself for his task, but his heart remained empty.

At half past one in the morning, by the dial of his large, new wristwatch, the officer came out of the club with the young man from the bar. They took a cyclo which Luoc followed on foot through the shadows of balconies and of lime trees that overhung the streets. He watched them enter the building where the officer had his apartment, waited for a telltale window to light up, then turned and vanished toward his own home. Less than half an hour later, he returned. In the sports bag he carried lay his newly honed *coupe-coupe*.

The officer's window was now dark. Luoc slung the bag over his shoulder, embraced a lime tree, and a few seconds later hooked one leg over the iron railing of the officer's balcony. He listened to the murmur of voices in the dark and the breathing of the two men.

"Ahhh," said the officer's voice. "That's good. That's good."

A few moments later, the young man's voice begged to excuse its owner to go briefly into the washroom. Luoc took the *coupe-coupe* from the bag and pushed open the screen door into the balcony room.

The opium harvest that season was poor. Carbone decided to trust Luoc as his agent on a trip north to buy Yunnanese opium to eke out the local Indochinese supply. Once again, Carbone's faith in his protégé was confirmed. The young *jaune* negotiated excellent terms for the purchase and arranged trouble-free delivery of the crude opium to the military sect known as the Binh Xuyen, who refined the crude opium to morphine base before Carbone sold it abroad.

11

Ariane bribed Paulette and Willy with violet magenta drinks from a street vendor to visit the zoological gardens yet again. It was the fourth time in two months. The daily downpour of the new rainy season had just finished. Water dripped and splashed loudly from high trees onto the leaves of lower ones, then slid downward onto bushes and shrubs. For a short time the afternoon air was fresh. The unclouded sun was already hot enough to raise steam from the many puddles.

Ariane led the children past bo trees from India and arbutus from Indonesia straight to the cage of the Fire Pheasant. She sighed, in a gust of pure pleasure. As they arrived, the cock pheasant lifted, then shook down, his feathers. Yellow and crimson wrinkled like water before a wind, then fell back into smooth iridescence. Ariane looked around to share her pleasure with Paulette and Willy, but they had gone to sit limply on a bench; the only other spectator was a young native, dressed like a Frenchman.

Ariane moved on to the Peacock Pheasants. They were the same shape as their more sober European pheasant cousins, but had purple-eyed tails. So many of the names on the cages sounded familiar—robin, thrush, flycatcher—but the birds inside had impossibly long tails, and heads coiffed and hatted with tufts and topknots of every imaginable color. To Ariane, the birds were like Saigon—familiar, but better in every way than what they seemed to resemble. Every time a stretched wing flashed a patch of magenta or gold, it confirmed her belief in life's hidden treasures. One merely had to look for them.

She laughed aloud at a bird who reminded her of her grandmother, with its great rounded bosom held high over a froth of petticoat and tiny legs. The young native was still with her. She paused in front of a large cage of loriquets to watch them interweave their flights of rose, soft blue, green, and vivid yellow. The young man paused to watch them too. Ariane glanced sideways at him.

He stood with his hands in the pockets of his white linen suit, feet slightly apart as if balancing. Ariane could not yet make fine and instant distinctions like Mme. Garine, between Annamite, Cochin Chinese, Malay, Chinese, and *Tonkinois*. To her, he seemed just very foreign and quite lovely. He reminded her of a delicate bird of prey; he had light bones and springy hair which rose from his forehead and arched back across the top of his head. He was completely encased by his suit in the way a bird is contained in its feathers. She could see no fleshy bulges, no sweat patches. His limbs had made no wrinkles at the joints in the white linen.

"You find them beautiful, mademoiselle?" he asked without looking at her.

Ariane jumped and went red. "Oh yes!" she managed to stammer. "Much more so than at home."

"You are recently arrived from France, then?"

She nodded, feeling damp and fleshy beside him.

"I hope you would not mind if I address a few words of conversation to you. It would be most helpful for my French." He was meticulously polite.

Ariane wavered. She was sure that Mme. Garine would not approve, even with the ayah there as chaperone. And she was just as sure that the ayah would report back. But she wanted to talk to him; he was part of this new country she was exploring. He seemed to be a gentleman. Also, she found it difficult to be rude to someone wearing such an expensive-looking suit.

"I have been here only a few months," she said. "But I love your country already."

He turned his face toward her for the first time. "My country?"

She wasn't certain of his tone, but his eyes said that he was making a small joke. She smiled nervously. As she strolled on to the next cage she found that he walked beside her. She called sharply back to Paulette and Willy to make certain they understood that she was still in charge of this promenade.

If she were absolutely honest, she found their conversation rather boring. He asked her a string of polite social questions and fended off her own. He said he worked in a bureau, but never said which one. Ariane wondered if he might be a Viet agent. The Garines said that one never knew these days who might be a revolutionary, but you had to watch out for the young, educated ones.

She tried to detect a pattern in his questions. He asked about the Garines but seemed almost uninterested in her replies. She wondered then if perhaps he were part of a ring of burglars—the Garines said that this was common, too, among respectable-seeming natives. Had he been French, she would have thought that he was bored with her and merely going through the motions. But no one was forcing him to walk with her, so he must want to.

Though she was disappointed in their conversation, she was fascinated by him. She was able to study him; he gazed into the cages more often than he looked at her. On the rare occasions when he did meet her eyes, his own were dark brown and without depth, like the eyes in portraits of the saints at school.

He stopped and offered to buy them all some sticks of rice and coconut wrapped in banana leaf. Before Ariane could refuse, Willy, Paulette, and the ayah had accepted. As he handed her a small green parcel, she noticed his hands. They were fine but strong. His nails had been professionally manicured and were impossibly clean, like the rest of him. Once again, she felt damp, excessive, and awkward.

As they walked on, Paulette fell in beside them, eyeing the young man curiously and making Ariane even more uncomfortable. Willy and the ayah trailed behind, looking bored.

"There! You see," said Ariane to break the silence. They stood in front of a Scimitar Babbler. "That's what I meant earlier when I was talking about home. Everything is so ordinary in France; nothing is ordinary here. A normal bird wouldn't have that great red and yellow bill."

He studied the bird as if trying to see it from her point of view. "Forgive me, mademoiselle," he said. "You are mistaken. That is a normal bird. Very ordinary. In this country, you must redefine your terms. When you have done that, you will be ready to see what we Indochinese consider to be special."

With these words, he flung open the shutters over his eyes and honored Ariane with a look straight from the depths, which he had concealed earlier. She felt it like a physical blow. Her heart pounded; her palms were damp. It was utterly improper and totally exhilarating. It could not be allowed. She tried to organize a dignified exit in her mind.

"Come," he said. He led the little party back to the Fire Pheasant. "There is another. You might say he is ordinary. He is certainly very lovely. And in a cage."

For the first time, Ariane heard a note of more than casual conversation in his voice. It confirmed her sudden need to get away from this young man.

She fled more rudely than she would have liked, atwitter and aflutter like an entire flock of parakeets. When she refused his offer to escort them back to the gates and find them two cyclos, he bowed deeply, then turned back to contemplate the Fire Pheasant through the wire mesh.

Safe under her virginal veiling of mosquito net that night, she allowed herself to relive the meeting. There was no harm in that. He had entered her life briefly and left it again. There was no danger now in letting her unformed desires play over his image—desires her new life was feeding and bringing closer to the surface, day by day.

Though he had been delicate, he had given her an impression of strength far greater than that of most men she had met. It wasn't a brute, muscular strength like that of Jules Martin, but a wound-up springlike power. She began to imagine that he had frightened her. Perhaps he was Vietminh after all. Or a deposed prince biding his time.

She was not certain just what a demon lover was supposed to be or do, but this young man whose name she did not even know seemed to suit the term. Even as she shivered pleasurably, she laughed at herself. However had she arrived at such an idea from a most polite encounter with an exceedingly correct young *jaune*? She laughed at herself, but had trouble getting to sleep.

12

Raoul Costals had been a beautiful young man. Now he was on the boundary between young and not-so-young. He was tall and still slim, but a slight thickening had begun behind his white double-breasted waistcoats. The lashes were still dark around his cold blue eyes, but the temples of his smooth, pomaded hair were graying. His slim mustache was dyed. His pale skin, however, remained young, smoothly shaved, and moist with lotions. He had never allowed it to become cured by the sun, like jerky, as the provincial planters did.

For eight years, ever since he had arrived from France, fresh from the École Coloniale in Paris, Costals had been vital to Saigon society. He was blessed with the ability to succeed without too much apparent effort. He had a gift for languages and had progressed rapidly in those eight years from junior administrator servicing the permanent committee which serviced the elected Conseil Colonial to the position of aide to the Chief Resident in Hanoi. While there, he had studied the political situation and several local dialects.

When the Governor-General of Indochina, René Pasquier, made competence in native languages a qualification for government posts, he progressed even faster. He returned to Saigon to act as liaison between the native council for the Région Saigon-Cholon and the Resident. Recently, he had been tipped for an Assistant Residency, as the first step to an almost certain berth one day as the Resident of an Annamese province.

In addition to his professional talents, he could produce on demand an unbroken flow of amusing conversational trivialities. He could be relied on not to insert original ideas that might require his fellow conversationalists to pause for the effort of thought. He had, therefore, a reputation for easy wit and a good sense of humor. Recently, this humor had become more sardonic—which was one of the danger signs that his circle was discussing more and more.

They also noted that he had begun to smoke too much opium. Not the occasional, social three or four pipes after a good dinner, like everyone else with claims to style, but binges. He disappeared to Cholon with his valet for several days at a time. When he next appeared at a function, the whole of his circle would anxiously assess the tinge of his face for a clue to the degree of excess.

His looks, charm, and success had in the past made him irresistible to women. Moreover, he had been so discreet about his involvements that it was quite safe to be in love with him. At least four married women in the last three years had tried very hard to make each other believe that they were the one singled out for his bed. He flirted with all of them most delightfully and refused to satisfy curiosity about which one it really was. As a result, everyone watched everybody else and read clues so small as to be invisible. This passed much time most satisfactorily.

Recently, however, these games had become less fun. His flirtations had begun to take on undertones of irony. The women he flattered found themselves wondering privately whether it was possible that he was making fun of them. They no longer felt exhilaration when they met his eyes in frank flirtation across a dinner table or the pool at the Cercle Sportif; it was just possible that they might be making fools of themselves in a way they could not explain. From having been one of Saigon's prize bachelors, he was slowly becoming an object of concern and irritation.

Most of the women decided, over morning coffee, that he was seeing too much of the wrong company. Mme. de la Battre was told by her half-caste maid, Marie, who heard it from the Fléchiers' ayah, who walked out with Costals's driver, that he was spending more and more time with natives. It was feared around the pool at the Cercle Sportif that he might be getting seriously involved with an Annamite mistress.

No one minded such relationships in principle. One constantly entertained people of all races—the French prided themselves on their open-mindedness in this respect. But no matter how liberal you might be, as Mme. de la Battre said to Mme. Garine, you had to admit there might be a tiny *social* problem in certain cases. Imagine entertaining a mixed-married couple when the wife sat in silence all evening, had teeth black with betel, and kicked her shoes off under the table at dinner. Amusing in theory, perhaps, but nearly impossible in practice. Apart from anything else, you put the man in the difficult position of owing you a return invitation. In such cases, where the man had actually married his native mistress he would continue to drink with his friends at the club. The couple might appear occasionally at official functions. But the man was effectively lost to all but his closest male friends. Some men were no loss, but that would not be the case with Costals.

The most obvious solution, the women decided, was to get him to settle down with a French wife. She would take care of the sex, and the added responsibility should take care of the opium. It was worth trying anything to arrest his unfortunate "going-off."

The list of eligible possibilities was short. Celine Fléchier was already engaged to Marc Lesmoines. Constance Duprès, a widow, was far too old; Marie de la Battre was only fourteen. The two Simpson girls were still in boarding school in England; in any case, no one could visualize Costals falling in love with either of the *petites anglaises*. Michèle de Kuypers was far too shy ever to make a Resident's wife. Mme. Ray had already begun to suspect that Minou was pregnant, by one of two possible boyfriends whom she studied with the eyes of a circling buzzard. With unspoken, if sometimes reluctant, unanimity, Ariane was elected for the rescue mission.

Mme. Garine was delighted. She was herself involved in one of Costals's blameless, ambiguous flirtations. As commander in chief of Operation Marriage, she could maintain close contact with him while making it clear that she had no further personal intentions toward him. Paulette was far too young; he would never last until she was marriageable. It was June and the rains had just begun, cutting down on the range of entertainment available. She would enjoy rubbing a few noses in her protégée's continued and even more brilliant success. If she could make her governess into a Resident's Lady, her own daughter could aspire to anything. It was a perfect project with which to fill the next few months.

The truth dawned on Ariane when Costals was asked to take her in to dinner for the fourth time running in three weeks. She spent a hideous evening, heart thudding, hands shaking, unable to say anything more interesting than a five-year-old would have done. She even knocked over her wine.

The awfulness was made worse by the amusement in his eyes as, with his napkin, he helped her divert the burgundy from running off the table onto her new pale blue crepe-de-chine frock. She knew that he also knew, and was laughing at her. She prayed that she would get through the first course without bursting into tears.

She could not imagine herself with him. Like most of the other young girls she had pined for him, imagined being kissed by him and, even, the brush of his hand across her décolletage. But these fantasies were safe because he had been so clearly out of reach. He was an adult, grown-up male who lived daily with the secret final truths about life, politics, and love. Her proper mates were still growing into their dinner jackets. They roared past the cafés on the Rue Catinat on their motorcycles or in their new sports cars, hoping to catch young female eyes. They were more unsure socially than she, even though she knew from some of their sisters that many had passed the great barrier of first sex with a *boyesse* or prostitute. They might try to kiss her. A daring one might slide a timid hand toward her breast at the end of a long, wine-drenched evening. But she did not fear them as much as she had learned they feared her. She could always send them into red-faced, painful retreat if she wanted. She loved this growing sense of her own power.

She could not imagine having power over Raoul Costals. She almost disliked him for making her feel so helpless. One lift of his eyebrows, one ironic glance could destroy all the female confidence she had won since arriving in Saigon. At the same time, he did seem to like her in spite of her awkwardness and gaucheries. There he was, after all, carefully mopping at the spilled wine. As he met her eyes again, she realized with shock that he might be inviting her into complicity.

This thought sent her into another spin of confusion. He might want, after all, to be within reach. Filled with terror, she concentrated hard on the cutlery and crystal, moving with great deliberation to get through the meal without another accident. She wanted to hide away in her room and think. He made things easier for her by turning to his other partner once fresh napkins had been brought. Ariane then began to imagine that he was embarrassed by her and wished to disassociate himself.

A few days later, he disproved this by inviting her for a drive in his automobile. They took the road to Bien Hoa between showers, roof folded down behind them, uniformed driver in front.

Enraptured by speed, noise, the wind in her face, and the occasional pressure of his arm against hers, she decided that the uneasiness she had felt with him was really romantic turmoil.

There were other drives and other dinners. Her confidence increased. Slowly, it began to be taken for granted by the Garines' circle that he was her escort and that some sort of understanding existed between them. No one actually mentioned marriage, but he had fallen in so willingly with all the plans that their engagement was assumed to be a virtual *fait accompli* by everyone except Ariane and Costals. He never denied it, but he never confirmed it either.

He continued to take her for drives. He strolled with her on his arm on the Rue Catinat. He sat with her in cafés and on the terrace of the Hotel Continental. He escorted her to the opera. He bought her occasional bouquets of marguerites. When the rains cleared in early autumn, he joined the Garines on their staked-out patch of grass and table at the Cercle Sportif. Ariane would sneak shy looks at his white body in its belted bathing suit and try to imagine what it would be like to gaze on that flesh as a matter of marital course. Or to know it by touch. It was so much more real than when he wore his beautifully cut suits.

As everyone tacitly encouraged her, she began to fall in love with the idea of marriage to him. Uncertain as she was, there was no reason not to, either. It would be everything her parents wanted for her; she allowed herself to drop hints in her letters home. She imagined running a Resident's mansion. Like Mme. Garine, she would have both an ayah for her children and a French governess to talk to and keep her company. She would learn to control servants. She would choose which flowers the gardener should cut. She would buy a gibbon for her son and train it to pop almonds and dried fruit into her mouth as she sat on her veranda having afternoon *tisane*.

In time, she knew that she had fallen in love with him. His direct look made her tremble. His touch made her blush. She loved being seen with him, loved the constant public proof that he preferred her to all other women. Since they had become a recognized couple, he had not disappeared to Cholon. She allowed herself to take a little pride in that, which made her love him even more.

But still he said nothing about marriage. From time to time, when they were alone, his charm would drop and he would become thoughtful. Sometimes he seemed almost impatient with her chatter, which increased with her growing confidence. Ariane wished she had gained enough courage to ask him to share his troubles with her. He would learn that she could be a wifely support as well as a decorative escort. She also wished she had the courage to reassure him of her passion for him. He was still so careful and restrained after six months that she had begun to think he doubted it. He had hardly kissed her, and never on the mouth. She wanted him to know that, while she deeply appreciated the respect he showed for her inexperience, she would give herself over to his sexual tutelage with freedom and trust when the time came. Most of all, she wanted the courage to tell him that the time had come to formalize his courtship. Mme. Garine and her friends had made it clear that Ariane's uncertain position was becoming a little humiliating.

M. Garine had mentioned at dinner one night that Costals had finally been put forward for the Assistant Residency at Dalat, a plum posting north of Saigon. High in the mountains, it had long been a refuge from the heat and damp of the city. The Emperor had a hunting palace there, on the lake. When Garine finished this announcement, everyone had looked at Ariane. Mme. Garine had pinched her lips over her sorbet. Ariane stared down at her plate in a mixture of rage and embarrassment. If Costals loved her at all, he would put a stop to her suffering.

"Ariane, my flower. . . ." He had the tone of a man undertaking a substantial subject. Ariane went cold with terror and joy. She knew that the moment had arrived.

They sat on the deck of a picturesque junk anchored in the Saigon River a few miles upstream from the city. It was a favorite restaurant of many Saigon French. Fish and crabs were served fresh from bamboo traps hanging in the water. A pirogue ferried diners there, out of range of the coastal mosquitoes. A woven bamboo canopy sheltered them from the rains, and breezes cooled them. A smiling family of Cochin Chinese made them feel like private and privileged guests in their floating house. The family also served excellent French wines, as the real owner was a Tonkinese *fonctionnaire* from Hanoi with a house and business connections in Paris.

Ariane was wrestling with a steamed crab. The cook had not cracked the shell well enough, and she had just sent a claw sliding across the table, propelled from the jaws of her inadequate pincers. She let it go.

"As you may have heard," Costals went on, "I am being considered seriously for the Assistant Residency at Dalat. I believe my chances are excellent, if I may be immodest for a moment."

Ariane gave up on her crab and waited.

"It's a choice posting. Beautiful country, clear air, out of the lowland. Life there is simpler but no less comfortable. And you don't miss society because society comes to you. In season." He stared at the ring he wore on his right hand. "The appointment pays well and carries with it a very well-positioned house."

Ariane could not believe that he felt he had to persuade her of the advantages of being the wife of the Assistant Resident at Dalat.

"Most important . . . it is felt that the man chosen should be married, if at all possible, so that he and his wife can carry out the full complement of social responsibilities."

Ask, ask! thought Ariane. Her answer was so long prepared, the cue so long in coming.

When it finally came, she answered "Yes" with the absolute satisfaction felt when you know you are taking part in an act of destiny. There is no headier sensation in life.

"Ah, my darling. I'm grateful." With that slightly odd phrase, he leaned across the table and kissed her gently on the lips to confirm their betrothal. Then, with his main business settled, he seemed unusually at a loss for words. "I'll tell the Governor's office tonight," he said after a moment's thought. "He needs to know."

Ariane nodded mutely.

"And I must square with the Garines." A hint of irony returned to his voice. "I suspect that Madame may be prepared."

He leaned back in his chair and rearranged his linen napkin in his lap. As the big moment seemed to have passed, Ariane returned to struggle with her crab.

He pulled a piece of the meat from a claw on his plate and offered it. "No, no. Open your little mouth. I'll feed you."

Feeling absurdly self-conscious, Ariane opened her lips and took the morsel from his fork. It was not a disagreeable moment, however. She watched his long fingers continue to pull the legs from the crab, crack them expertly, and slide out the long, smooth cylinders of muscle on the end of his two-pronged fork. She admired the way he managed not to strew fragments across the cloth, and the way his wineglass remained unsmeared where his mouth had touched it. She looked quickly at the half-moon of grease on her own glass.

His concentration on the crab was absolute. It was one of his thoughtful moments again, but this time she felt safe. A waterbird took flight in the darkness, and her fiancé turned his head quickly toward the first crack of its wings. In a few more months, guerrilla terrorists would blow the restaurant up; there were isolated incidents elsewhere, even now.

Costals turned back to survey her in the light of the candles. Ariane found that she wanted to stroke the shadows under his cheekbones.

"I will insist that we learn to speak openly to each another," he said. "Too many husbands and wives never do. I see very little point, if you can't talk to each other."

Ariane nodded her agreement.

"Strange," he said, "how suddenly the rules change with the status of the players. Just as well, I suppose."

Ariane raged at her inability to understand and meet him on his own ground.

He smiled into her eyes and turned the anger into agreeable confusion. "What secrets of your lovely bosom can you bare to your husband-to-be?"

For some reason, Ariane thought fleetingly of the dark young man at the zoological gardens. She couldn't think why he had popped into her mind. She had been in such turmoil over so little. Costals's tone implied that he didn't expect much in the way of revelations.

"I don't have any dark secrets," she said, and tried to look as if she lied.

"A girl with your looks!" he teased her. "No brawny young farmer or fisherman wasting away for love back in *la belle France*?"

A blush scalded her face and she thanked the good Lord for the disguise of candlelight. If Paulette had blabbed, she would kill her!

"I'm sorry, little one. I'm making you uncomfortable. Forgive me." He kissed her hand lightly, but his contrition was tinged with weariness. He made no confessions of his own.

All the way back in the car, Ariane rehearsed the joy of telling the Garines and of writing the good news to her parents. They would have to come out to the wedding if they could. She would visit them at home whenever Raoul had leave. She would need many more clothes if she were to entertain in Dalat, and wondered if it would be proper for him to pay for them before they were actually married—she should begin to order them right away.

In the midst of this triumphant planning, she fought off a feeling that was to attack her many times later in her life—that the actual moment didn't live up to the way you imagined it. She did not allow herself to admit that, deep inside, she felt something was wrong.

A few weeks later, she was forced to admit that something

71

was indeed wrong. Just when he should have seemed happiest, Costals became irritable. He was even short-tempered with her in public. Once, when Ariane was trying to jolly him up, he told her to be quiet so sharply that she burst into tears right at their table on the terrace of the Hotel Continental. He apologized immediately and kissed her hand in contrition.

At the next table, Georges Breton pretended to gaze out through the arch of the terrace while he debated whether the time had come to say something to the Governor. He himself had always had reservations about Costals for Dalat. It was a highly sensitive posting, with the Emperor in residence so much of the time and his relationship with the French so finely balanced. His friendship was necessary to ensure the loyalty of his people, who still revered him as the Son of Heaven, in spite of his tiger hunts, gambling, and holidays in the south of France.

Breton had never liked Costals. He had held his tongue because he feared his own prejudice. He was one of the few men who knew the truth of the rumors about the man. He had tried to hope, like all the others, that his engagement would settle him, but that poor, silly, pretty provincial was no match. Anyone could see that she was terrified of him. Breton sighed and waved away the linen-draped trolley of pastries.

At Costals's table, Mme. Garine sipped angrily at her Picon punch. She was angry with Costals for cutting short her triumph, after the engagement was announced, by his strange behavior. She was angry with Ariane for not having managed to take more of an upper hand with her husband-to-be. After all, *she* had pulled off *her* part in the affair. In some ways, Raoul seemed in a worse state than before his engagement. He was more distracted and jittery than she remembered ever seeing him. She was afraid he might be smoking opium again. When Georges Breton glanced at their table with raised brows, she met his eyes defiantly. There was no other way—she would have to have a word in private with Raoul. Fortunately, Breton seemed to be the only one to have noticed the little scene at their table.

Three days later, Costals planned to take Ariane to the theater. A party of eight had been arranged; they would go on for dinner afterward to the Goldschmidts' house. At three o'clock that afternoon, Costals's driver appeared at the Garines' with a message that his master had succumbed to a migraine, probably as a result of overwork and the very high temperatures of the last few days. He was desolated to abandon his fiancée at such short notice and prayed that she would forgive him. He hoped she would be willing still to speak to him, let alone continue to contemplate marriage to such a scoundrel.

Ariane was disappointed; at the same time she was relieved to have an explanation for his behavior. Mme. Garine agreed, being prone to migraines herself, that they made you feel quite unlike yourself for several days in advance and served, like a summer storm, to clear the air. Ariane sent back an understanding and consoling note. Florent Dorléac was impressed into last-minute duty as Ariane's escort and the evening went well, until after the play.

As they climbed into their fleet of cyclos, Ariane suggested that she and Dorléac call by Costals's house to see how he was feeling. He might be recovered enough to need food; the Goldschmidts said they would be delighted to feed the invalid if he could drag himself out. One or two members of the party exchanged looks but said nothing. It was agreed that Ariane and Dorléac would meet the others *chez* Goldschmidt, with or without Costals in tow.

His house was not far out of their way. In a few minutes they were knocking at the gate. The gardener opened it.

"M. Costals is not here," he said.

"Don't be silly," said Ariane. "Of course he is!" The cyclo crunched over the gravel to the front door.

Costals's Cambodian number one boy opened it a crack and looked startled to see them standing in full evening finery.

"Yes," he agreed, "M. Costals is at home. The gardener is mistaken. But he is very ill. No one is to disturb him."

"He won't mind me," said Ariane. "I'm going to be your new mistress. I'll be very quiet." With less to drink in the interval of the play, she might have been less bold.

"Take me up," she ordered. How worldly I have become, she thought, to dare go into a man's bedroom, even if he is my fiancé.

The number one boy turned unhappily to lead them up the stairs. "Very ill," he muttered. "Very ill!"

Florent followed on exaggerated tiptoes. He looked so funny that she had to giggle. She copied him and they were both laughing when the number one boy stopped outside a closed door on the first floor.

"The master is not in here," he announced in a tone of surprise.

"Then take us where he is!" Dorléac began to snigger again.

The man opened another door and peered in. He closed it,

went to a farther door, and repeated his mime of searching. He looked more and more unhappy.

"Very sorry," he said. "I do not know where he is."

"The bathroom?" said Dorléac.

"Or maybe he went into the garden for some air," suggested Ariane.

They returned to the entrance hall while the servant trudged off obediently to look in both those places.

"Imagine," said Ariane. "Losing someone in his own house!" They had both stopped laughing.

Dorléac thrust his hands deep into his trouser pockets so that the sides of his jacket flared out like the tail of a bird.

"Yes," he said. "Listen, maybe we should leave him alone."

"Something might have happened to him," said Ariane. "He could have fallen."

The servant returned. "Very sorry. I am not able to find him." He stood waiting for their next instruction.

"Let's leave the man alone," said Dorléac. "Come on! The cyclo is waiting."

Ariane stood silent.

"Do come on!"

Ariane glanced at Dorléac, then away blindly at a Chinese landscape painting which hung over a console table. Florent didn't think Raoul was there at all!

She followed him down the steps and into the cycle. Florent was wrong! He had to be. Raoul would not have lied to her. Why would he need to? He had recovered and gone out for a stroll . . . but then, why had the number one boy said that he was in? In the cyclo she fought the sensation that she had been dreaming for the last several months and was about to wake up.

Florent Dorléac was embarrassed. He was also angry with himself for not having foreseen the problem. But he was an open-natured young man who tried always to see the best in people rather than the worst. Anyway, he thought, Ariane will have to learn what men are like—she might as well get it straight at the beginning. He tried to jolly her out of the black silence she had fallen into since they left Costals's house but she didn't hear a word he said. Finally he lost patience.

"Don't treat it as such a tragedy. There are lots of reasons why he might not be there."

"Like what?" asked Ariane dully.

"Oh . . . I don't know." He wished she would leave it alone.

Ariane wanted to go home to the Garines' and hide, but she knew she had to brazen it out through dinner. Dorléac made it a little easier by telling everyone that Costals had been asleep and they hadn't wanted to disturb him. Unjustly, Ariane hated him for being party to hiding her shame.

Alas, Dorléac could not resist telling one or two close friends how they had played *cache-cache* in an empty house. Word spread. Mme. Garine had her conversation with Costals. Costals therefore knew, when he came to see Ariane two days later, that she had tried to visit him.

She sat tensely opposite him in the Garines' drawing room, beside the huge bouquet he had sent from the florist's in the Rue Catinat. She had to decide whether to stop being angry with him, or not. She preferred to stop, but humiliation is hard to shake off. She really had no choice; if her world were not to fall apart, she would have to shake it off sooner or later. Besides, he looked so ill and so contrite as he sat in his chair with the sphinx-shaped arms that she felt moved by him in a new way.

He said that he still wanted her and was sorry that she had been hurt. The truth, if she could believe him, was less serious than she had feared. He had not been with another woman but in a *fumeur* in Cholon.

"I smoke much less now than before I met you," he said. "Just every now and again. When work is particularly heavy, it relaxes me. I didn't tell you because I was afraid you wouldn't understand. . . . I didn't think for a minute that it would be found out. I'm only sorry for your sake that it was."

It sounded so reasonable when he said it—a little thoughtless and perhaps self-centered, but nothing worse. To be honest, Ariane enjoyed seeing him apologize; so much of the time she felt at such a disadvantage with him. She glanced down at her gold and pearl betrothal ring for reassurance. It was her only concrete proof of his love and of her new adult status.

"*Can* you understand? It's not what you imagine. Very civilized." He looked at her reflectively. "It would be interesting to see whether the smoke likes you or not. It only gives its gift to some."

Ariane felt a sudden desire to be one of those who were thus privileged.

"Even Mme. Garine has a smoke now and again." He smiled at her look of shock. "For tropical colds and influenza," he said, with a trace of his original irony. "What do you think, little one? Would you like to share the experience with me? If it's dreadful as you fear, you will at least know what you are trying to save me from."

"I don't know," floundered Ariane. She touched her ring as if it could help her answer him.

"I won't force you," he said, with a touch of impatience. "But it would give me pleasure for us to share that. I invite you into my private life."

"I want to do that," she breathed. "Share your private life and thoughts, I mean. It's just that..."

"Don't rush at the idea," he said. "We have time. Years." There was an odd moment as they looked at each other and then away, Ariane at the betrothal ring on her finger, Costals through the open window at the palm tops in the garden.

"If you like," said Costals, "we could make a quick visit after the Governor's ball, in three weeks. That gives you plenty of time to decide whether or not you abhor the idea."

"I want to share everything with you," said Ariane. "I want you to take me with you."

13

As his name was called, Luoc faltered in the doorway. Carbone had arranged the invitation. Luoc was dressed as well as money could buy, in a faultlessly cut white dinner jacket made by Carbone's tailor. The creases of his trousers were as sharp as the edge of his *coupe-coupe*. He had paid a shocking number of piastres to have his hair cut and his forelock slicked back with pomade, his chin shaved of its sparse beard, and his fingernails rubbed and polished with perfumed wax. His uncomfortable evening slippers, with flat black bows, reflected the chandeliers from their toe tips.

He should have felt confident after his months with Carbone, but he was overwhelmed, as if he had dived into a current too great for his strength. He was overwhelmed by the sheer number of objects in the vast room—gold and white Louis XV console tables along the walls, rows of golden chairs, meters of silk draped at the windows, crystal chandeliers and wall sconces, silk carpets larger than three village huts together. At the far end of the room stood more tables, swathed in cloud-white linen, weighed down by silver trays of glasses, bottles, platters of food larger than a peasant's hat, pyramids of fruit, pastries like pagoda spires. It was richer than the most opulent Catholic altar he had seen. He had never seen so much all at once in one space.

Nor had he ever yet seen so many Round Eyes all together.

They made so much noise and gave off such sense of power and weight of lawful order. A band tightened around his chest under his white jacket. They were as tall as demons, imposing in uniforms encrusted with ribbons and medals. Swords swung by their sides in easy, unconsidered display. Or they wore evening dress, subtly different in detail from his own.

Their women were nearly as huge as the men, many made taller by hair still piled on top of their heads in the old style and by the heels on their shoes, in which they swirled and posed effortlessly through the dance steps he himself had been laboring to learn.

Wordlessly, he bowed to the Governor-General and his Lady. He could not remember how to speak. The clattering, clinking, laughing, and loud assured talk blended with the music of the orchestra into a nightmare of indistinguishable noise. The rapid French of the Governor's wife assaulted his ears nonsensically. He bowed again, murmured something equally nonsensical, and escaped to stand with his back against the wall, beside one of the console tables, in the illusory protection of a sheaf of orchids which arched from the crystal vase on its top. Cold sweat made a bright line on his brow.

None of the Round Eyes pointed at him and cried "Fraud! Criminal! Murderer!" He held steady the hand with which he accepted a glass of champagne from a uniformed Annamite servant; the man kept his eyes fixed on the reflected spots of the chandeliers on Luoc's polished black leather toes.

A young priest appeared at his side, black cassock at odds with the crystal glass he held and the sheen of social excitement on his pink forehead.

"I'm Father St. Sébastien," he said. "I don't think we've met before." He shifted his glass and offered an immaculate hand.

Luoc refound his French. Here, at last, was something familiar, to restore his sense of purpose. The plump young priest reminded him of the school where he had spent so many years, and of Father St. Vincent's betrayal.

"Please call me Luc," he said to the priest. "Luc Le."

Tonight, he told himself, you need only to be seen. To become familiar. Known in your own right, not just as Carbone's shadow. So that you will one day be trusted as nearly one of them. Over the priest's shoulder, his eyes began to pick out other brown faces in the melee. He promised Father St. Sébastien that he would attend Mass at the Cathedral. He allowed the priest to introduce him to a sword-hung Frenchman and his three companions. The Frenchman paused just long enough to acknowledge

77

the introduction before he continued his harangue on the growing disorder in provincial villages, which he felt the government was criminally negligent to ignore.

Luoc listened quietly, smiling when someone smiled at him. The Chinese ... always the Chinese. The conversation came back to them again and again. Without their provocation, said the Frenchman with the sword, the Nationalist movement in Indochina would never have been organized. Not that such ragged hit-and-run tactics could be called organized.

"The people here were perfectly satisfied before," said the man. "Except for the few malcontents who exist in any society!"

Luoc sipped at his glass and eyed the Frenchman from behind its rim. With every idiotic statement the man uttered so confidently, Luoc's own confidence grew a little more. Taken singly, the massed French were becoming less frightening. However, he did not make the mistake of thinking they were all fools. Fools did not hold a reluctant country captive for more than half a century.

The young priest also introduced him to two charming and intelligent women, and to a round-bellied man who was openly bored by the reception and keenly interested in the details of Luoc's small new import-export business. One of the charming women invited him to ask her to dance. He found it strange to hold an older, unfamiliar, white-skinned female so close to his own body, but gained the courage to ask others to dance.

In a rest break for the orchestra, in the midst of a chatting group, he paused, glass at his lips. Father St. Sébastien was arguing that awareness of physical beauty rather than denial of the senses could be a means of perceiving inner, spiritual beauty. Luoc was deaf to his words; his eyes were focused on a great distance; he had been sent a waking dream of enlightenment.

His eyes refocused on the glittering crowd around him but with an abstracted intensity that made Father St. Sébastien falter in his monologue. Luoc had just understood the thing he needed to learn. The strength of the French was not a gift from the gods, of an outside power that sustained them against their enemies. The force that had numbed him when he entered the ballroom was merely that of their cumulative assurance, of their belief in themselves and in their power to make and change the fate of others. By believing it so totally, they convinced others and made it truth.

"But of course," he murmured in response to a question from the priest. He was a change-fate. He could shake their woodpile until it began to fall.

"Monsieur!" said a voice at his elbow. "How amazing to see you here!"

A fair young woman with startling blue eyes and a heat flush staining her neck and shoulders smiled at him with arch shyness. Jewels swung from her ears and lay draped over the luxury of her bosom.

"Mademoiselle." He bowed to hide his bewilderment.

"I do believe you don't remember me." She paused as if suddenly uncertain. Father St. Sébastien dropped back a tactful step to swoop on a canapé from a passing platter. The rest of the group reformed a few feet away. The young woman smiled again.

"You must tell me the truth." Her eyes gleamed on the level of Luoc's own. He decided that she did not mean her abruptness to seem rude.

"I do not forget you," he blurted. He glanced at the others, who were watching them curiously.

The young woman glanced at the others as well. "Oh monsieur," she said. "Please *do* ask me to dance. Otherwise, I shall die of embarrassment, standing here like a ninny."

"My pleasure," he said formally. His hand met unexpected softness under the silk back of her gown, like a thin layer of duck down, but he knew it must be her flesh.

"You must stop pretending," she said after a few steps. "Or I shall think that you are trying to make it seem that I am mistaken . . . ooops! Sorry."

Their feet had tangled on the pivot of a waltz step.

"My fault entirely, mademoiselle . . ." he said. "I remember your eyes," he continued. "But not where I saw them. Is that more truthful?"

They were the color of sapphires he had once seen and made her resemble a female spirit. His heart thudded with his audacity, but she seemed to like it.

"It was in the zoological gardens," she said. "Looking at the bird-cages. I thought you looked like a bird yourself."

He glanced at her eyes once again to see if she intended to be insulting. Instead, she flushed as if she had embarrassed herself.

"You are the charming lady with the children!" he exclaimed.

"Yes!" She looked delighted and relieved.

He had thought the girl to be a sort of French ayah. But here she was, among the splendor, dressed in an indecently low-cut gown and glittering with jewels. He obviously still had much to learn about his enemies.

He didn't know how to phrase the question without risking offense.

"They are lovely children. Are you their mother?"

"Oh, heavens, no! I'm not married," she trilled in amusement. "I'm their governess . . . their companion."

"Like an ayah?" he asked cautiously.

"Not at all," she said firmly. "More like a teacher."

That made sense to him and explained her presence here tonight. The idea of a woman doing such things was strange to him, but at least he could now relate her to the scholars who won teaching posts as a reward for passing their examinations for the mandarinate. He gazed at her with new respect. She looked young to be a scholar. . . . She liked him, it was clear. Perhaps she would teach him some of the things he needed to know.

The waltz languidly stretched out its final bar. As they halted, he felt the soft flesh of her breast against his arm. He was startled to feel his organ stir within its prison of white wool garbardine. He had not thought of a woman since the girl in the neighboring village, before his father was shot. He willed his member back to quiescence as he bent in the formal handshake he had learned from Carbone. She sensed something. He felt her go still, as if she were waiting, or listening. Their eyes met quickly and slid away from each other. The soft round cushions of her cheeks acquired neat pink spots, like dots of icing on Chinese bean cakes.

An idea swelled suddenly like a bursting bud in his mind. Why had he not thought before of getting himself a Frenchwoman, to speed up the overwhelming task of understanding?

"Mademoiselle . . ." He had no idea how to go about it. "May I call on you?"

She fingered one earring nervously, still not looking at him. "Alas, monsieur, that wouldn't be proper. I'm engaged to be married, you see."

"Just to practice conversation," he begged winningly. "If you are a teacher, I wish to be your follower. How is that improper?"

She reached behind her, like a drowning swimmer clutching at the riverbank, for the man who had arrived with two glasses of fruit punch.

"Monsieur," she said to Luoc, "let me introduce my fiancé, M. Raoul Costals."

Luoc looked up into the thin white face high above him, its skin white as a drowned man's. His eyes went blank. He became still as a deer listening for a tiger's footfall. His hand, which he had begun to raise for a handshake, froze a few inches above his right thigh.

Ariane stared at him, wondering what had caused the great change she felt in him, far more than when she had said she was engaged. She could not believe that Raoul seemed not to notice.

Costals, for his part, in spite of the heart-shaped face looking up at him, did not recognize the elegant young Annamite as the dirty boy who had balanced on a stool in Tonkin with his bound elbows meeting behind his back.

When Luoc left the reception soon afterward, he went to the temple near his room. He bought joss sticks and placed them in a jar beside the smoldering ends and thin smoke trails of other offerings in front of a small altar. He knelt in his evening trousers for a few minutes, then rose again. His gift was not enough.

He went into the main chamber of the temple, where great red spirals of incense hung from the ceiling, thick as bats from the roof of a cave. By the flickering light of oil lamps he held the little flame up to the lowest end of a cone-shaped spiral. It caught quickly and cleanly, a good omen.

He knelt again and watched the slow progress of the fire upward, around and around, bit by bit a little closer to the heavens, while behind it spent gray ash fell away from the central wire core. His smoke rose straight and unwavering through the shadows of the carved ceiling beams and disappeared into darkness. The smoldering glow did not die until it reached the peak of the cone.

From the temple he went back to his room. He locked his outer door, closed the shutters, and took his father's *coupe-coupe* from its hiding place. In spite of careful oiling and the wrapping of rice paper, its blade had begun to rust. He balanced the weight with his arm outstretched, hand firm around the bamboo lashings of the handle. He had not held it like that since the death of the Customs officer.

He had hoped never to use it again. Not only was it futile to attack the enemy one by one, but he had learned how dangerous it was to be the hand that swung the blade. From Carbone's example of the last two and a half years, it was clear that it was safer to be the general who gave the order to attack than to be the pike bearer. And safer still, in battle, to be the ruler who ordered the general to order the attack.

This time, he had no choice. He wanted no one to be able to connect him with Costals. Therefore, no pike bearer. He did not think the Frenchman had recognized him. Their brief meeting had gone unnoticed by all but the girl with the sapphire eyes. He had excused himself quickly before a turn of movement or inflection of his voice could stir deep in the man's memory.

They must not meet again; he couldn't risk it. He had sworn to put aside petty personal satisfactions. Now his interest in the girl and necessity had come together in unarguable harmony... with an elegant harmony... which the spirits in the temple had not denied. He removed his white jacket and trousers, found his oil and whetstone, and began to sharpen the edge of the steel.

Ariane's agitation at their meeting was eclipsed by the prospect of going with Raoul to a *fumeur* at the end of the evening. They told the Garines that they were going to dinner with an American couple whom Costals knew from his Paris days, then slipped away like a pair of wicked schoolchildren. Ariane enjoyed being wicked with Raoul, because he seemed to enjoy it in the same way that she did. Normally his humor seemed distant and adult to her.

They dismissed his driver and went by cyclo into the heart of Cholon, Saigon's Chinese twin city. Though it was ten-thirty at night, the streets were bright and noisy. Ariane had never been there with the children, as Mme. Garine did not think it safe. They rolled slowly through narrow streets, under long banners and flags covered in Chinese characters, past open-fronted stores filled with shouting, laughing customers. Their cyclo had to weave and push through the bodies that crowded the streets.

The cyclo turned past the twelve-foot-tall face of a smiling woman with curling brown hair who was advertising dentifrice into a wider street with some shops and a few big houses set behind walls. The driver stopped in front of a round Chinese moon gate. After asking Costals's name through a slit, a guard opened the gate. They crossed a small paved courtyard filled with pots of trees and a tall boulder to the brightly painted door of the main building, where their host waited under the light of a candle lantern. An eight-sided mirror hung above the door. Ariane saw herself reflected in her ball gown and borrowed jewels.

"My dear Raoul! I *am* delighted . . . and relieved." Their host, a young Chinese-French half-cast, wore a silk kimono, loose silk trousers, and makeup. He seized Costals by the hands and kissed him on both cheeks.

"I heard dreadful rumors that you have been slumming lately," he said. "That's terribly naughty of you. I felt quite hurt . . . as well as worried for your health. I know what some of my competitors put in their pipes!"

Costals laughed and detached himself. "Ariane, this remarkable gentleman says he's the bastard of a French count...as often as you'll let him. Louis, let me introduce Mlle. Ariane Cellier, the French treasure I told you about all those months ago when I was being faithful to you."

Louis took Ariane by the hands and stepped back to look her up and down. "Delightful, absolutely delightful! You didn't exaggerate one bit. Those eyes...one could die for them!"

He beamed at her, then at Costals, and put his arm around her shoulders to usher her deeper into his house. She could feel him quivering with excitement or nerves; his hands had been cold when they took hers.

She had never seen anyone like him except in the Chinese opera. His face was powdered white, his brows plucked and penciled black, and his lips painted dark red. He looked beautiful and very strange—an appropriate guardian for the gates to mystery. He led them to a small reception chamber. Ariane felt she had entered a genie's cave. The room was dimly lit by gas jets which Louis had never replaced with electricity. Warm shadows lay over the swoopings and drapings of silk that concealed the shape of the room. Embroidered silk kimonos, like the one Louis wore, hung from folding Chinese lacquer screens. In the shadows of their silken sleeves Ariane saw glimpses on one screen of tiny, naked, lacquered women with minute stumps of feet being entered in a variety of ways by men in the winged headdress of ancient Chinese court officials. She averted her eyes quickly. On another screen, men and women lay on hard-looking wooden couches, drawing on tiny lacquered pipes.

Louis brushed his hand across several of the hanging robes, then went to the Chinese sandalwood chest that stood against the wall and lifted out a kimono of jade-colored silk that lay folded inside. He shook and swirled it through the air like a magician preparing a trick.

"Now we begin your transformation," he said to Ariane. "Take off your frock...lovely as it is...and put this on. No ordinary mortals are allowed further into the kingdom."

Ariane glanced at the first screen. "I think I'll keep my dress on," she said firmly. She looked toward Costals for help.

"Whatever you like, my dear," he said. "Just don't take all night about it." He selected a robe in rich peacock blue and moved toward the door. "Louis, I'll look after myself while you get Mlle. Cellier sorted out."

"I saved Xanadu for you," said Louis. "Can you remember where it is...after all this time?"

"Don't be a bitch," said Costals as he left.

When he had gone, Louis lowered the single brow which had shot upward at her refusal. He smiled forgivingly. "Many are nervous the first time. I promise you it won't last, not with Louis looking after you. Trust me. There's no better house in Cholon . . . or Saigon. Ask whom you like. And I mean *anyone*! To the very top. The answer will be the same—'Go and see Louis.'"

She could not help smiling back at him. He was so strange and childishly eager to please at the same time.

"Do at least slip this on over your dress, won't you?" he begged. "That green would be disaster against the cushions."

He held the kimono enticingly in front of her. His tone became confidential. "You may think I'm a fool, my dear, but these things are vital. If you stop caring about them, you have taken the first step toward becoming a barbarian."

Not wishing to be a fledgling barbarian, Ariane obliged. Louis produced a pair of embroidered slippers.

"I do hope you're not modest about baring your feet!"

He sat her down on a blue and white porcelain drum and knelt to unbuckle her evening slippers. Before she could protest, he reached up under her gown and expertly rolled down her stockings.

He smiled at her expression. "Come, come. You don't think you have anything to fear from me, do you?"

Still smiling to himself, he eased the slippers onto her cold feet. Her hands were now as cold as his had been, in spite of the hot night.

Louis appraised her with cool, level eyes. "Well, there we are," he said. "Let's go find Raoul and put him out of the misery he deserves to be in."

He spread his silken sleeves wide to usher her into the teak-paneled passageway.

Like the chamber, it was lit by gas jets. Religious and erotic statues stood in alcoves down its length. Incense burning at their feet cast a faint haze. In spite of her anxiety, Ariane felt transformed by the silk that brushed her bare wrists and by the slippers that made her walk in an unfamiliar way. She wished she had drunk a little more at the ball.

Xanadu was one of the many small rooms opening off the paneled passageway. Its walls were carved wooden grilles. Brass parraffin lamps burned on low tables while chips of candlelight escaped through the carving of the lantern hanging from the ceiling.

Costals lay on a pad of silk cushions on a large, ornate rosewood platform bed, his neck against a block-shaped cushion with silk tassels at either end. He had undressed and put on the peacock-blue robe. He was smoking a cigarette rapidly, but stubbed it out and sat up when they came into the room. He was more animated than Ariane had ever seen him.

"It *has* been a long time, Louis," he said. "I apologize. Am I forgiven?"

"To show you how much," replied Louis. "I shall look after you myself tonight. Then you will never want to desert me again. Not that you will anyway, after you try my new supply. None of your Yunnanese rubbish, like you get in other houses. I have a very special private source."

Ariane sat on the edge of the platform, inhaling the incense that burned in a dish on the small table beside the platform. She felt giddy at the thought of the enormous distance she had already traveled in her life, and gathered herself to cross yet another boundary.

When an old woman came in with a tray, Louis took it from her and set it on the table next to the incense. Ariane's heart pounded as she looked at the contents of the tray: a small lamp with a conical glass dome, open at the top to let out the heat, a porcelain container rather like an inkpot, an ivory-handled needle like a sawn-off crochet hook, and two bamboo pipes. These had silver caps at each end, one with a small hole in it. In the center of each length of bamboo was a tiny silver cup attached by a band of silver filigree.

Louis raised his hands like a magician to shake his sleeves back. With the needle tip, he carefully picked up a ball of smoker's opium from the inkpot. He heated the ball on the end of the needle over the lamp, spinning the needle in his fingers until the opium began to smoke slightly. He tucked the little ball of resin into the silver cup on one of the pipes, kneaded it with his thumb, and heated it again until it bubbled and smoked again. Then he handed the pipe to Costals.

Costals inhaled deeply three times, handed back the pipe, and lay back against the cushions. Louis watched him closely.

"Yes?" he asked. "Did I mislead you?"

"One more," said Costals. "One more, my friend. Then I will be able to say." They smiled at each other.

Louis repeated the process with another ball of opium. This time, Costals sighed happily and arched his head back against the rectangular cushion. Louis smiled with satisfaction, then prepared the other pipe for Ariane.

Her hand shook as she took the pipe from him. As soon as she inhaled she felt sick.

"You gulped too fast," said Louis. "Think of it as a friend

coming to visit. Welcome it. Don't rush it down like a nasty medicine.''

He poured her a tiny porcelain cup of tea from a pot on the tray. "This will settle your stomach."

The tea was fragrant with dried blossoms that floated on the pale golden surface. She sipped and watched the petals rock like tiny boats in the storm aroused by the tilt of her wrist. Her stomach unclenched and her heartbeat began to slow.

"Lie back. Lie back," ordered Louis. He filled the cup with tea again. Ariane let herself relax back beside Costals. She felt as if she were falling into the soft down of the cushions as they gave way beneath her weight. The little cup was a burning weight in her hand.

Costals held her second pipe for her. "Inhale just once this time. We're in no hurry." He finished off the pipe.

She no longer felt sick. Her anxiety had gone; a growing contentment took its place. Louis eased the cup from her hand. A delicious warmth began to spread out from her stomach. Cradled by the cushions, she felt once again the internal quiet she had felt, spread in the sun in her field at home. But this time, in place of the ache of waiting she felt acquiescence to the moment. Her mind soared upward toward a state of understanding that had escaped her in her field. At any moment, she knew she would comprehend at last that which had so far eluded her.

Costals's thigh was warm against hers. She watched his hand take another pipe from Louis's hand. Her mouth was dry. Miraculously, the tiny porcelain teacup blossomed in her own hand. Suddenly she was lost in wonder at the pattern of opposing movements—her mind traveled upward while the warm liquid slid delightfully down her throat. Opposite directions, yet connected in her understanding.

This sense of understanding became denser and richer as she felt Costals's hand come to rest on her breastbone; its weight connected through her body with the down cushions beneath her. The pattern of meaning was nearly in focus. She felt Costals pull at the top of her gown. The cloth cut into her chest; she turned slightly to allow him to unfasten it. She felt air on her breasts and sighed with pleasure at the freedom, rejoicing at the ease and tranquillity with which she occupied her flesh.

She was reconnected to Costals by his hand, which he was now moving rhythmically on her right breast, drawing warmth upward from her stomach. He lay on his side, eyes shut; only his hand moved, as if not part of him. She lost herself in the movement of his hand and in studying the shadows of tendons in

86

his throat. She could watch forever the way they shifted on the pale skin under the warm candlelight. Louis held a pipe to Costals's mouth, then drew on it himself.

For a moment, Ariane had to look away from the two men. Something in Louis's eyes when he smiled at her had sent a cold current through her warmth. She became aware that her legs felt tied, as if tangled in bedclothes. She decided that her dress was the problem and sat up to take it off. But it was underneath the silk kimono. She lost track of what she had intended to do and lay back against the cushions again. When she closed her eyes, she made Louis go away.

Something was missing; it was Costals's hand. She found it on the cushions and replaced it on her breast. She felt its weight and warmth. Then she went over the crest of a hill and began a long, gliding swoop downward as if on open wings, toes brushing the ground, headed for a warm darkness soft as down.

She opened her eyes drowsily, sometime later, to protest to Raoul that his violent movements had roused her too abruptly. Costals stared at her, teeth bared. His head lay at a sharp angle to his body on the dark silk cushions. A scream tried to rise in her throat but could not get past the vomit that choked her. The carved wooden grille of the wall at the end of the platform still dripped with the blood that had arced in a fountain from his cleanly sliced neck. Louis was gone. Ariane was sick onto the floor; then she began to scream. She hoped the first scream would wake her from the nightmare, but it did not.

On the night Costals was beheaded, Louis was twenty-seven years old and looked much older. He had not slept with man, woman, or boy for two and a half years, not since he had finished whoring for the French and opened the *fumeur*. Louis's mother had been the Chinese-Annamite *congaie* of a French officer in the Expeditionary Forces who had suffered the usual fate of being passed on with the house and furniture when the officer's period of service ended. The officer returned to his wife and family in France, leaving a *métis* son behind.

It might have been better for Louis if his mother's next master had been cruel or insensitive. However, the rubber manufacturer working for Michelin who took over the officer's house found the young bastard intelligent and charming. Partly to please Louis's mother—whom he enjoyed very much in bed—and partly from a sense of cultural responsibility, he had the boy educated. Sometimes, when the mood struck him, he would call young Louis into his library to sit the boy on his lap and give him a cake and a glass of wine, carefully explaining the merits of different vintages and the disintegration caused by the long sea voyage to Indochina. After one trip home, he brought back from Paris a tiny silk dressing gown which the boy wore day and night until the fabric disintegrated.

As long as Louis stayed in the big house, he was happy. The outside world was a different matter; there he was a bastard and a *métis*. His mother's people saw him as visible proof of French abuse, to be avoided and despised as a bad omen. The French boys at school equally scorned him, as a *jaune,* a primitive, a monkey in human clothing.

Given the run of the house by his indulgent master, he wiped out great chunks of otherwise intolerable time by poring over the illustrations in the manufacturer's books or by counting through and trying on the man's silk shirts, which draped around his slight frame like ceremonial robes. He played army with the mother-of-pearl and gold studs and cuff links from the velvet box in the top of the armoire, and was allowed to cover pages of delicious white paper with letters and drawings made with the man's jet and silver pen.

When Louis was eleven, the manufacturer was killed while on a tour of inspection to a supplier's rubber plantation south of Saigon. The overseer there laid on a disciplinary action to edify his visitor. As a protest against the flogging in question, the workers ran amok and butchered not only the overseer but his wife, child, and guest.

The next tenant brought his wife with him. The manager of the house told Louis's mother the bad news—the *congaie* had to go. But she was now too old to find a new protector easily. She gave Louis some of the piastres she had stolen from the house-keeping over the years and the studs and cuff links, which she took as soon as she heard of the manufacturer's death. She sent him off with vague directions about half-remembered roads to find her brother-in-law, who lived in a village west of Saigon, to ask him to come to fetch her.

It was Louis's bad luck to be picked up in a sweep for corvee labor to work on the great highway the French were pushing north toward the Chinese border. When they searched him before the medical examination, they found the studs and cuff links, clearly marked with the initials of the murdered Frenchman.

The Sécurité officer who interrogated him was not a cruel man, any more than the rubber manufacturer had been. He was moved by the boy's terrified, delicate face, the fawnlike lightness of his limbs, and his large eyes, which were a surprising dark hazel color. He shuddered to imagine the effect of road building on that young body, and even more to think what the *garotte* or blade would do to the set of the lips. He explained to Louis that he would normally be sentenced to death for his theft. However, as a police officer he was prepared to take Louis into private custody in his own household to give him a second chance. The boy's own behavior would determine how long this arrangement would last. Louis learned that night that "behavior" meant his willingness to bend over for the officer and be treated as his woman. His initial fury and humiliation were balanced by terror for his life. Then he found himself confused.

The officer, unlike later men, was gentle and showered him with tender caresses which stirred a warmth and gratitude in Louis. At times he wanted to kill the man who held him in his arms, but then he would remember how his mother had once held him in the same way. In spite of himself, he remembered the warm sanctuary of the manufacturer's solid and enclosing lap. If the Sécurité officer had raped rather than seduced him, Louis might have become a revolutionary. As it was, he gave himself to the only source of warmth and privilege available to him.

He learned to close his mind to what was being done to him and to accept the affection and the spoiling. He soon learned that he had very real power over the officer, that his moods mattered, that his acquiescence in small things was important. He learned to charm and wheedle, to sulk and to shine upon his master in order to get what he wanted from him. He acquired his own silk shirts and Chinese-tailored suits. He was given his own gold cuff links—which he saw as a delicate reminder of his own vulnerability in spite of his growing power.

On occasion he was taken to soirées, where he was allowed to listen to the gossip. He learned to serve wine and to prepare an opium pipe for smoking. He learned when to be discreet and when he was allowed to meet the eyes of other Frenchmen, where he saw the potential for exercising the same power that he held over his officer. He had at last found a world where he mattered. It was not the world he might have chosen, but the choice had never been his. It was a mark of his basic toughness and common sense that he wore the cuff links as a constant reminder to himself of the fragility of any state of existence.

When Louis was fifteen, this officer, too, was killed, shot by the brother of a bandit he had arrested. Louis became a male whore. For the next four years he survived by moving from one to another of the men he had met through the officer. They paid him and gave him gifts. He stole what he safely could. When he was eighteen, he considered killing himself after a particularly humiliating night. He stood by the river and watched the oily water flow past. Its heavy steadiness soothed and drew him. Then a drowned dog bobbed past, taut with gases, draped with weed, turning slowly in the current.

He went back to his tiny rented room and counted his savings. He contemplated the hand-painted scroll on the wall and the silk shirts neatly folded on a shelf. He unwrapped the two pieces of carved jade he had bought, and the ivory netsuke in the shape of a water buffalo which was a gift. He fondled their smooth surfaces. What did any of it matter, anyway? Given a choice, he preferred the cool jade to the damp rotting of flesh.

He lit a fire in the little charcoal stove, carefully made tea in a tiny porcelain pot, and set it out on a lacquer tray with a cup like a miniature lily, enjoying the scents of burning charcoal, of sulphur from the match, of the finest Green Dragon tea. Then he prepared himself a pipe of smoker's opium which he had stolen from a lover. He stretched out luxuriously. As long as he could create this peace and beauty for himself the rest of it truly did not matter.

Ambition came later in the form of a proposition, made under very unusual circumstances. He was stark naked at the time. He and the young Vietnamese stared at each other across the body of the Customs officer which Louis had recently relaxed with his hand and which the Vietnamese had just relaxed permanently with his blade.

Louis was aware of the accident of timing which had him out of the room when the murder was done. Otherwise his own head could have been lying with the Frenchman's in the ghastly puddling of scarlet that had disfigured the bed linen. He had caught the killer just after the moment of violence had passed; the urge to swing the blade had dissipated. He sensed that he might be allowed to live. All depended on the reason why it had happened. The Vietnamese regarded him through a moment of suspended time. Then he made a minute move with the hand that held the *coupe-coupe*, the merest start of flexing the muscles to raise the arm.

Louis finished wiping his hands on the towel he had left the room to fetch, the first movement he had made since freezing in the doorway.

"You might as well," he said. "They'll suspect me otherwise."

He told himself that it did not matter what happened, as it

never mattered, but the thudding of his heart contradicted him with the insistent reminder of life pumping through him. He wanted it to continue.

The Vietnamese relaxed his arm. The surprise in his eyes was replaced by speculation. Louis realized with a sense of irony that his indifference had been mistaken for courage.

The man sheathed his blade in a bamboo scabbard which he put into a leather sports bag.

"Get dressed," he ordered Louis. "I have a use for you." He assumed unquestioning obedience, even though he was younger than Louis.

Louis stood still for a moment, weighing the possibilities and what he was likely to lose in each case.

"Unless you with to remain *putain* until they throw you away." The young man spat out the French word for "whore."

Louis shrugged and dropped the towel. They both knew that the French were far more likely to execute him for the officer's murder. He dressed quickly in his evening clothes, collected his pocketwatch and walking stick, checked that he had not left his handkerchief or any other personal trace, and followed the Vietnamese from the room. A stranger seeing them together would have assumed that Louis was a wealthy *métis* and the other his driver or bodyguard. Louis was aware, once again, as with the manufacturer and then with the Sécurité officer, that he had encountered not just another man but a new direction in his fate.

Luoc's proposition to Louis was simple. Louis asked no questions but accepted gratefully. He would be provided with good-grade smokers' opium. He was to use his connections within the French community to build up a clientele for a *fumeur* in Cholon. It was not to be a sordid place where the French went slumming among Chinese addicts, but an establishment specially designed and reserved for *la crème de la crème* of French society. It would make opium smoking the new social rage.

Louis would furnish it to make Europeans feel comfortable. He would find a cook to cater to their secret longings; he would get hold of just the right wines and import the right cheeses and coffee. He would discreetly provide infection-free boys and women when required. In short, he would use all his acquired charm and social skills to draw the French to him to have their needs filled. There was to be one major difference from the past; he could withhold his own body. The profits would be turned over to the young Vietnamese, but Louis was allowed a generous cut for himself and enough to cover taxation by Chinese Chiu Chao syndicates in the district.

Louis waited for something to go wrong. But the house taken in his name by the young Vietnamese was exquisite, a villa in the Chinese style with a moon gate and internal courtyards. The opium arrived as promised. He was lent money to buy pipes and lamps. His new patron eliminated Louis as either witness or suspect by means of a little money in the right places and strong, though discreet, hints of possible damaging scandal if the case were pursued too far.

The *fumeur* thrived from the day it opened; Louis had at last found the world where he truly mattered. Relieved of the pressures of sexual bartering, he threw all his considerable seductive skills into winning and holding an ever-increasing clientele of smokers, and was nourished by their approval. He had a knack for keeping just the right balance between comfort and exoticism. He learned to appear colorful and just a little ridiculous in order to pose no threat to either the dignity or safety of the French who put themselves into his hands.

He learned to shut his eyes to any outside business that was carried out within his private chambers, before and between pipes. He always provided the best-quality opium, even when the French government claimed shortages of imports from Yunnan and were unable to supply their regular distributors with adequate stocks. He never again met personally with his young patron, although he regularly sent gifts of respect through his agents—until the night he had dismissed the guard and opened the moon gate himself to admit first Ariane with Costals, and then Luoc himself.

At the time Raoul Costals was beheaded in his *fumeur,* Louis was lucky enough to have several senior officers of the Garde Civile among his regular clients. This time, he did not need his patron to intervene but negotiated himself. Although the police were under pressure to produce the murderer, Louis's convenient availability for the role of guilty man was overlooked.

Unfortunately, gossip spread that Ariane had also been there that night. A native whore was one thing—a young, unmarried Frenchwoman quite another. For this matter the pressure demanded a penalty, and Louis was charged with hiring his house for immoral purposes without a license. Louis was relieved by the fine, which he could earn in four good nights at his house, but worried by other developments. Certain Corsican gangsters in Saigon had taken exception to his alleged foray into brothel-keeping, which was their exclusive province. Following the public announcement of his crime, he received a private visit.

Louis was tied up and forced to watch while his visitors sliced the silk robes with razors, then smashed the lacquer screens and the statuary in the alcoves. One of them defecated into the chest of robes and slippers. There was no other damage, although Louis kept an uneasy eye on the razors. His stock of opium had already been confiscated by the police for chemical assay.

Louis knew he had been lucky to retain his testicles. He did not notify the police of the visit. He knew better than to try to contact his patron. He smiled at the dealer who sold him back his supply of superior opium. He made as little disturbance as possible on the surface of life. Fate was on the move again, but he could not yet perceive his way forward.

After a month had passed quietly, he had his servants polish his collection of pipes and sent messengers to all of his favorite clients to invite them to a very special soirée. He personally arranged flowers in all the rooms and lit the incense. He had replaced the broken statues and had the grille in Costals's room torn out and burned, along with the cushions and drapery. He had given the bloodstained carpet to his *boyesse* to sell in the market. He felt he had driven out the evil and restored the atmosphere of peace. His cook had worked for two days making *bouchées* from recipes he had found in a French magazine.

Not one of his darlings came, and fewer than half bothered to send regrets. Louis sat in his little reception chamber, which was once again draped in silk, and cried. He had misjudged; he had lost the French after all. He would have expected mere Annamites to avoid anyone touched by bad luck, but hoped the French would be above such superstition.

He needed the French nearly as much as he had needed his mysterious patron. Without them, he was no longer useful to his patron. They were the source of the money which had allowed him to live in dignity for the last two and a half years. He had been happy. Carelessly, he had allowed himself to grow used to feeling that way. He was not ready for it to end. As long as he could obtain opium, he could probably survive with the Chinese for clients, but that would not make him happy. He had come to need gossip about *le jazz* and Charlot, about Patou and Chanel, and whether that delicious young bull of a Spanish painter was a potential genius or merely an *enfant terrible* who would burn himself out. He needed to pretend for a few hours every day that he could remember Paris and had the right to murmur how much the Rue Charnier resembled Vaux-le-Vicomte in April.

Most of all, he needed to be special to the French. He needed to be the one who provided what they could find nowhere else, who gave them that same peace he had once found for himself. He needed to be the magician who made life bearable. Without them he was nothing but an aging male whore, another *métis*, a man without a people. Without the French, he would become the equal of the sag-dugged Chinese grandmothers who helped coolies drug themselves into lifelong stupors in bug-ridden shacks along the canals. Or else he would become the servant of vicious, jumped-up Annamite peasants who swaggered and bullied, rich from crime and corruption.

He wiped his eyes on a silk handkerchief which had been made in Lyons. He must stop indulging himself in emotion. Memory needed longer to die. If people feared the place where a man had been killed, he could offer to arrange private parties in their own homes where they would feel safe. He would enjoy that, arranging his props, playing host as if the houses were his own.

He wandered into the garden to listen to the murmur of the mulberry leaves in the hot evening air. He moved lightly across the stepping-stones toward the ornamental pool to contemplate the moon's wavering image on the water. He gazed up at the hard porcelain presence in the sky which seemed so immutable.

"Change," he murmured to himself. Inevitable and unavoidable. The moon reminded him that it could be beautiful.

At the rim of the pool, he froze. Fear, clear as a mountain stream, washed his limbs. All his Ghost Carp floated on the dark surface, one in the center of the moon's reflection, white belly swollen like the beckoning finger of a drowned man. Music, fashion, gossip were suddenly nothing. He recognized a sign from fate.

"Pack, Louis," he told himself. "Don't fool yourself any longer. Move to Hanoi. Your patron will agree. There's French society there. You can still work for him. A new name and the old style. You've started from scratch here." He ran back into the house as if pursued from the shadows.

The consequences of Costals's murder were as serious for Ariane as they were for Louis. The Garines' servants saw her brought home by M. Garine and a senior police officer. They watched the doctor come and go at 2 A.M. They talked. They listened to the Garines and to a call M. Garine made to Georges Breton. And they talked. Word had reached every cookhouse in the French quarter before coffee was served the next morning.

Ariane woke up in her net-hung bed after fourteen hours of drugged sleep. Her mouth was dry. She climbed painfully up from darkness into the day. Her brain stirred uneasily with half-remembered horror. She had dreamed of voices and a journey. Of being naked in a group of people who were fully dressed. She struggled erect, eyes wide; she had remembered it all.

At that moment, since she had been spying for signs of life, a maid came in with a tray of coffee which she placed on the bed.

"Mademoiselle needs help to dress?" asked the maid. Ariane could tell from her eyes that she knew.

"No! Just go away," Ariane cried.

She reached for the cup with a trembling hand. She sipped the bitter fluid with her eyes shut.

If she tried hard enough, she could almost black out the image of Costals's teeth, bared as if he meant to bite her. She reran the evening over and over in her head as if it were a film and she might somehow be able to change the ending. Each time she reached the end, she still heard the quiet dripping of liquid and her own first scream.

The film cut back to the point where Costals was caressing her breast; she put the cup down hard on the tray and struggled through the netting to her feet. What else had happened in that darkness?

Her clothing had been neatly put away. She looked frantically for her underwear, which she finally found in the laundry basket. The crotch of her knickers was unstained. She sighed and sank down onto the edge of her bed. She observed the sensations in her body. She stood up again to walk a few experimental steps; she felt no pain or stiffness between her legs like Minou Ray had described after she had done it with her fiancé. Slowly, Ariane pulled up her nightdress; there was no blood on her thighs.

How did one know? She had thought it impossible not to know.

At that moment Mme. Garine came into her bedroom. Her face looked as if it had been taken apart and reassembled badly, the lines and contours all slightly askew. She stared at Ariane tragically, opened her mouth to speak, and burst into noisy tears. Ariane watched her numbly; she felt no desire to cry yet.

"Well," said Madame, surfacing after several minutes and rolling her waterlogged handkerchief into a tiny ball. "Well . . . now, what will we do with you? Whatever will we do?"

A cold grip seized the nape of Ariane's neck; coldness flowed like water into her arms and legs. Until those words, she had

been fighting only the horror of her memories. Now she understood that the horror would carry forward into her continuing
life. She was no longer the Ariane Cellier of Cap Ferret who had
arrived in Saigon what felt like years ago. If she were not now to
become Ariane Costals, wife of an Assistant Resident, who
would she be?

God was not fair! He simply was not fair! To offer so much.
To show her joys she had not known enough even to imagine, to
make her think they were hers, then to take them away! He was
malicious, hateful, wicked! The awful unfairness of it finally
brought tears, and she cried as hard as Mme. Garine had done.

Mme. Garine watched in turn, then rose and crossed to the
window, listening to the girl's sobs. She also had checked the
state of Ariane's underwear when the girl had been brought
home. The doctor had indicated that all was well, on that front at
least, but how on earth could one go about announcing that,
contrary to eager rumor, Ariane was still a virgin?

Mme. Garine shared Ariane's sense of unfairness. She had
planned to relax and enjoy well-earned plaudits for pulling off
the match. She was angry with Ariane for being so stupid and
silly as to become involved in something so messy, which would
reflect so badly on the Garines, to whom she owed so much.
Also, Mme. Garine was uneasy about her own role in it all,
though all her efforts had truly been for the girl's own good.

"I know that you have had a terrible experience," she said at
last. "And Raoul's death is unspeakable. Unbelievable! . . . But
you must try to pull yourself together. There's nothing we can do
for him, but as for yourself . . . people will be waiting to judge
how you carry yourself."

Ariane had curled up on her bed like a caterpillar fallen from a
leaf.

"A few days to mourn . . ." said Madame. "Then you must
show them all that you have nothing to be ashamed of. . . . You
have not, as far as I know. Have you?"

Ariane opened a startled eye. Could Madame read signs that
escaped herself?

The girl looked awful; it was reassuring to Madame that even
the young could look so dreadful at times.

Ariane was reading very clearly between Madame's lines. The
last year and a half had been a dream after all, and she was about
to wake into gray reality. Raoul's death had also killed the
Ariane she had begun to believe was the real one, leaving only
confusion and emptiness.

* * *

At the same hour, Georges Breton was asking his number one *boyesse* to bring cognac and strong coffee out to the garden. He led Henri Garine to an island of heavy rattan chairs on the lawn, out of earshot of the house and servants. The men sat in silence until the *boyesse* had poured the coffee and returned to the cookhouse. Only Breton, the elder by eleven years, showed signs that they had been up all night. He tested the unaccustomed stubble on his loose-skinned chin. For a few moments, both men enjoyed the freshness of the early morning garden as a respite from their problem.

"There's no use pretending," said Breton into the silence. "This will do us no good at all!" He poured cognac into the two cups that still stood on the wicker tray.

"To happen so soon after his appointment had been announced!" he continued. He handed one cup to Garine. "We look such fools. And so vulnerable, when such things are seen to be possible. A simple criminal coincidence? I wonder."

Garine rubbed his hand over his still-irritated, freshly shaved chin.

"Personally," he said, "I think you give the political hotheads too much credit. They're mostly peasants and students, after all. That young quasi-Frenchman in Hanoi—Quack . . . Quoc . . . whatever he calls himself—isn't able to mastermind everything they do. I do agree that the timing is lucky for them, if they want to make something of it."

The two men sipped in unconscious unison. They did not need to elaborate to each other on the damage that Costals's murder could do to the authority of the French—a man they had just seen fit to promote to higher office, executed like a common criminal, in an opium den. And it was unlikely from the style of death that a French hand had killed him. By making himself so vulnerable, Costals had put all the French in jeopardy; if one of the ruling French could be so easily killed, why not others? The only possible remedy was to demonstrate swift and accurate powers of retribution by punishing the true killer or killers.

This would not be easy. The head of Sûreté had told Breton frankly that they didn't know where to begin. There was no weapon in the *fumeur*. They had found no fingerprints that could not be explained. They had arrested Louis as the most available suspect, but he was no use unless they could extract a confession or otherwise prove his guilt. If they punished him without one or the other, they would merely confirm that they were finally losing their powers.

"I feel sorry for the poor, sodding Chinaman," said Breton. "Shouldn't think for a minute he did it."

"Not quite his style," agreed Garine.

They assumed that Louis was being questioned at the moment. Breton hoped it was by French rather than native methods. Such things were easier to supervise in Annam or Tonkin, where you had French police officers instead of natives.

"I had no idea Costals was in so deep," said Garine. "Fancy dress and all that. The occasional pipe is one thing . . . though I can't say I approve even of that. I would have thought his own sense of dignity . . ." He trailed off, leaving spaces for Breton to fill. The man had even taken his trousers off, in the company of a young, unmarried girl.

Breton said nothing. Unlike Garine, he had known about the native *fumeurs* down by the docks that had so outraged Louis. In fact, Breton had been the man discreetly delegated to get Costals back into line when the Governor feared that the man's language and administrative abilities were in danger of being lost to the Civil Service. Breton had also questioned the appointment as Assistant Resident, but his advice was disregarded in the face of Costals's apparent reform, and subsequent engagement to Ariane.

There was a pause while the two men watched Breton's gardener trudge past with a large basket full of weeds. Breton sighed and stared into his empty cup.

"I'm uneasy, Henri. Can't help feeling we're beginning to get some of the problems they're having up north again. I smell it." He tapped the sides of his strong, wide nose.

"Also," he added dryly, "several reliable informers tell me that the Revolutionary Youth League is having great success with its recruiting campaign down here. It wasn't so very long ago that the Vietnam Nationalist Party fell apart when it tried to move into the south."

"You do think it was political, don't you?" asked Garine. "The effect's the same either way," he added shortly, "whether it's a purely criminal act or a crime committed for the sake of ideals."

In his own case, the effect was to drag himself and his family into a particularly unsavory scandal. In spite of his debonair manner and elegant turnout, Garine was deeply conventional, with a conventional man's list of acceptable and unacceptable sins. Sex with an Annamite or Chinese woman was one thing, even when it involved refinements unthinkable with one's wife. But sex, or the appearance of it, between an older Frenchman and an unmarried French Catholic virgin was quite another. Then there was the opium and that grotesque half-caste who ran the pleasure palace.

"I have to say," said Garine, "that if it had to happen to anyone..."

Breton cut him off. "We shouldn't let it happen, ever!" His chair creaked with the energy of his disapproval.

Breton still felt badly shaken by what they had seen at Louis Wu's. During his younger days in Indochina he had represented the Governor at several executions and had never mastered his revulsion at beheadings. He had been relieved of the duty after he had finally disgraced the ruling French on one occasion in Hanoi by vomiting on the official dais. The story had hounded him for the next thirty years, but his secret relief made up for that fact. He was getting to be an old man, he thought, with too much on his mind already to sort and sift out before he died. He poured them each more coffee to justify another cognac.

As he drank, he let his mind rest on the faint sounds of the city outside his compound walls—a car klaxon, voices shouting, a single dog barking, and the constant murmur of the presence of thousands of people which was the voice of the city itself, never still, even in the middle of the night. In the neighboring garden, a coppersmith bird began its slow *"tonk, tonk"* in a minor key. He felt Henri Garine lean forward confidentially, and suppressed a sigh.

"Tell me, Georges..." Garine dropped his voice, though they were alone on the lawn. "Had you ever heard he was involved with boys? Could it have been anything to do with that? Considering that man Wu... if you can call him a man."

Breton shrugged. "You know what this city is like. Who knows what the women start, or the servants? Too much time to talk... all of them."

Garine leaned back, rebuffed.

Breton went on, "This will be hard on the girl. What will you do with her?"

"Lord, I don't know," said Garine. It angered him that people would think he had been unable to control Ariane, who had been as much in his care as his children had been in hers.

He stared at his left foot, which was waggling without his instruction. "I'd love to ship her back to her parents, but that doesn't seem right... not just yet. It would seem to be an admission."

"I would agree. Particularly in view of your wife's efforts toward the match," said Breton dryly.

Garine shot him a glance, but he seemed merely to be stating moral fact, not being malicious.

Breton went on. "I've already reminded our editor friend, Jumet, that Malraux's rag was closed down for troublemaking. He should take the hint. But there's not much we can do about the spread of news among the natives."

He was annoyed by the relief on Garine's face. He had thought the man understood that what the Vietnamese believed was far more important than some passing scandal around the swimming pool at the Cercle Sportif.

"I do have some funds available for emergencies," he continued. "Have you any thoughts on how best to deploy them to quash unnecessary rumor among the Vietnamese?"

The coppersmith bird was getting on his nerves with its inexorable, minor-keyed cries.

"I wish to marry a *française*. Can you advise me how I should go about it?"

Carbone stared at his protégé, startled and alarmed. "Any particular one?" he asked.

"Yes..." Luoc sounded ill at ease, which was unusual for him.

"Have you reason to think she will accept you?"

"Yes." The young man sounded once again like his decisive self.

Carbone paused in the darkened garden where they were strolling after dinner. His wife Angelica had stayed indoors to leave the men to talk business.

"May I ask who she is?"

"Mlle. Ariane Cellier."

Carbone laughed with relief. The young governess with the besmirched reputation. He would not have to protect his young friend from humiliating refusal. The Garines would fall over themselves to unload the girl just now.

"Well, my dear fellow," he said, "I'd say you're in with a chance. And I can see her appeal. Let's drink to your success while I consider my advice."

He asked Luoc to join him on the soft-cushioned rattan chairs on the veranda.

"Listen here, Luc, are you a virgin?" He had never been able to guess the answer to that question for himself by watching the young Annamite.

Luoc looked at the floor. "No."

"Splendid!" said Carbone. "That's a beginning." He motioned for Luoc to take a glass of cognac that the *boyesse* had poured.

"With a Frenchwoman you want to marry..." He sipped reflectively. "Treat her like the Virgin Mary but imply the charms of Lilith."

"I beg your pardon?"

"Never mind," said Carbone. "I'll tell you what. Why don't I buy us a couple of whores to practice on. . . . I wouldn't mind it myself. Take them out for dinner first, and all that. I know a club where I can get you in with no trouble. Then I can explain the ropes."

14

Mme. Garine stared at the small jeweler's box and the heavy cream envelope addressed to Ariane. The writing on the envelope was strong and flowing, a man's hand. Raoul had been dead only three weeks; the girl was impossibly lucky. Or else she had been behaving even more wickedly than Mme. Garine feared.

Ariane entered the drawing room nervously.

"What have you been up to now?" asked her employer. "A man is sending you presents. Might I ask who?"

"I don't know, madam, honestly. . . ."

Mme. Garine snorted her disbelief.

"I swear it," said the girl.

Mme. Garine studied her for a telltale flush or wavering of eye, but Ariane stood pale and puzzled, eyes on the little package that Mme. Garine had placed on the settee.

She is not recovering well, thought Mme. Garine. The circles under her eyes make her look like a marmoset.

"Well, open it!" she said.

Ariane obeyed, with dread. She could not imagine that the little box might hold something good. It was a small case of tooled leather, stamped with the name of the jeweler and his address on the Rue Catinat. Inside, on a white silk lining, lay a pair of sapphire eardrops.

Mme. Garine inhaled sharply. "You *must* know who has sent you something like that!"

Ariane opened the envelope. She knew that Mme. Garine could see the paper shaking in her fingers.

"A tribute to what I remembered," the card said, ". . . and

which I wish to study further." It was signed, "One who desires to become your student."

Heat masked Ariane's face and prickled in her hairline. She felt shock and surprising joy.

Mme. Garine took the card from the girl's fingers. "Who would have the ill breeding not to sign his name? What does he mean by 'student'?"

The shock of Raoul's death had made Ariane forget the young Annamite and the beam of intense purpose he had suddenly focused on her. When he had vanished as soon as she introduced him to Costals, she decided that she had imagined the quiver of awareness between them at the end of the waltz. She certainly never expected to hear from him again.

"I know who it is now," said Ariane evasively. "I danced with him at the Governor-General's ball. The night that . . . before . . ." She suddenly realized that the weight of horror had lightened a little.

"Only danced . . . ?" Mme. Garine's tone was acid. "What happened while you were dancing to make him presume like this? You were engaged to Raoul at the time, I believe. Or didn't you tell this man that fact?"

"Oh, I told him!" cried Ariane. "I even introduced them! He did ask if he could call on me, and I explained that it wouldn't be proper because I was engaged." Her knees began to wobble so much that she had to sit down on the settee.

"And that was the only time you've met?"

Ariane nodded, blushing. She did not dare mention the encounter at the zoo.

Mme. Garine had become thoughtful. She took the little box to the window and turned it in her hand to let the sun light little fires in the center of each stone.

"His intentions seem serious," she said, "in spite of the unfortunate gossip. You're a lucky young woman."

Ariane winced.

Mme. Garine continued. "Now the question is whether *he* can be taken seriously. What's his background . . . his prospects?"

Ariane twisted her hands in her lap. "I don't know, madame."

"Well, I shall get Henri to find out," said Mme. Garine briskly. "Under the circumstances, it would do no harm to get you settled as quickly as possible. Then let all the hateful stories die from starvation. What is his name?"

"I don't know, madame."

Mme. Garine turned incredulous eyes on the girl. "That's absurd! Quite beyond belief! Weren't you introduced?"

Ariane remembered how she had approached him, brazenly, it now seemed to her, secure in her role as future wife of an Assistant Resident.

Miserably, she said, "Yes, of course . . . it's only that I have forgotten."

Mme. Garine sighed. "Well then, perhaps you can manage to remember who made the introduction. I shall ask them at once to tell us everything they know about him. What did he do? Was he a planter, or a soldier . . . ? It's possible that Henri and I already know him."

Ariane could avoid the words no longer. "He was an Annamite."

Very slowly, Mme. Garine placed the little box on a console table, delicately, as if it might explode.

"An Annamite," she repeated, without expression. Just as slowly, her fingertips joined against her painted lips as if in prayer. After a moment, she added, "If you could remember who introduced him, it would be most helpful."

"I believe . . ." said Ariane, ". . . I . . . uhh . . . can't remember after all." She took a deep breath. "Actually, now that I think . . . I believe he introduced himself." She lifted her chin to meet Mme. Garine's eyes.

The older woman stared back. "I am beginning to lose all hope for you, my dear. You seem to have developed a penchant for getting into indefensible positions." She snapped shut the little box.

"What a shame. But that's how it is. We shall have to send this back to the jeweler. At least we know *his* name!"

Mme. Garine returned the earrings that afternoon. That night, she suggested to her husband that perhaps they should send Ariane back to her parents immediately, after all. It was one thing to stand by her through one tragedy. It was quite another to cope with an endless series of contretemps which she lacked the breeding to avoid.

Henri Garine nodded with absent agreement to all that his wife said. He was preoccupied with reports of rioting in the north.

The next morning, another box was delivered, this time to M. Garine's office. With it came a formal written request from a M. Luc Le to pay court to the Garines' governess, with the intent of marriage. This box held the same sapphire earrings and a matching necklace.

Garine studied the faultless setting of the stones. During the rest of the day, he made discreet inquiries among his colleagues, including a drinking friend in the Deuxième Bureau.

All the information was good. Through Emile Carbone, the young man held the licenses for two small import-export companies and worked for Emile Carbone as his regional liaison in Tonkin. He had been seen several times at Mass in the Cathedral. He dealt with French rather than Chinese banks, and had borrowed capital from the French-owned Sociètés Foncières. He had no record of political activities.

That night, Garine explained to his wife that this was not the time to be seen to rebuff an Indochinese who was pro-French. The security of French power in Indochina had always rested on the support of factions among the Indochinese themselves. For Garine, such a close connection between a native and his own family could well make him a logical choice for advancement in view of the delicate conversations that were constantly taking place.

"If the girl likes him, of course," said Garine. He observed the violence with which his wife was brushing her short hair, seated at her dressing table. He knew her well enough to read disappointment as well as disapproval in the stabbing flicks of ivory-back bristle.

"Come, my dear," he said. "It's not as if she were Paulette. . . . She's not even a relative. She's an employee."

"And what do you export, monsieur?" Mme. Garine gleamed brightly at Luoc over the demitasse.

"Buttons, madame. Among other things." His ease annoyed her.

"Buttons!" She thought she might begin to giggle hysterically. She hoped Henri was amused; this dinner was his idea.

"Silver, pearl, and polished horn." The young man was politely aware of her amusement. "French dressmakers find them most attractive. Most of my shipments are to France."

"Indeed?" She had struggled during dinner to talk to this arrogantly civil young Annamite. Ariane was no help at all. At this moment, she was sitting red and speechless like the awkward little provincial she really was *au fond,* under those good looks and the surface polish Mme. Garine herself had given her. The girl seemed stupefied by her Annamite, an indecently short time after Raoul's death.

"If you will permit me, madame. . . ." The young man reached into the pocket of his jacket, pulled out a small box, and offered it to Mme. Garine.

"I would be honored if, with your husband's permission, you would accept these modest samples of my wares."

Henri Garine nodded benevolently.

Madame opened the little box; inside were six hollow silver buttons, exquisitely hammered into a relief of birds, each one different from the others. In spite of herself, she was delighted.

"They're lovely, monsieur. I shall have to have a frock designed especially for them. Thank you."

"I thank you, madame, for the honor that that would do me."

Before the following pause in the conversation could grow too long, Mme. Garine said, "Ariane, my dear, who don't you sing M. Luc that charming setting of the Verlaine poem you have been teaching to Paulette? I'm sure he has never heard it before."

"No! Please, madame!" begged Ariane. "The piano is out of tune with damp."

"Then perhaps you could show him the garden." Her tone was impatient; the girl would just have to do her part in entertaining this bizarre suitor of hers. A stroll alone so soon was a little precipitous, but Mme. Garine had no intention of letting the courtship stretch out any longer than absolutely necessary. She had done her part for the girl once already. If her husband said that this Annamite was to be encouraged, very well. But that didn't mean that she had to have him hanging around her house for months. Quite frankly, she had lost interest in Ariane; she was not rewarding as a project.

Alone with Luoc in the moonlit garden, Ariane felt as awkward and clumsy as the little provincial who had first arrived in Saigon. Walking beside her, he seemed as clean and light as when she had first seen him at the zoological gardens. But this time she was also aware of the exact location of each of his limbs and their precise distance from her own flesh.

They strolled under the porte cochère, stones crunching under their shoes. She heard the light rush of his breath as he blew between open lips at a moth that dashed into the darkness and returned to fling itself at the light above the steps.

She felt a light pressure on her back. Then he touched her hair.

"In this light, you are all silver," he said. "At this rate, I will become a poor man, trying to buy all the precious things you resemble."

She tried to think of a light reply, but failed. The clamor of night insects filled her brain. She knew she was a different young woman from the one he had met at the ball. Then she had wanted nothing from him; now she was paralyzed by her need.

He touched her face. Her knees began to shake. M. Garine had told her of his stated intentions.

"Forgive me," he said, "if I do not know how things are done among your people. But I think we can speak together openly as a man and a woman. I feel it. Yes?"

She nodded mutely.

"I want to take you into my house as my wife. As a French wife. I want you to teach me how to behave like a French husband, and I will honor my teacher like a true Viet. Will you agree?"

His land lifted the hair from her ear, lightly brushing the skin of her cheek and earlobe.

His touch tightened the muscles above her kneecaps and spread through her chest like the thrill of a fall. This strange young man stirred up in her the physical passion for which she had mistaken her turmoil of uncertainty with Costals.

"Monsieur," she whispered, "among my people, it is not proper for me to accept so soon." She looked at his dark eyes, on the same level as her own. She felt the delicious certainty of knowing she was being stalked with the intensity of a hungry tiger.

"As soon as it is proper, then, what will you say?"

"When the times comes, I will tell you." She attempted an arch smile in the shadowy light.

"No," he said sternly. "That is not open. I do not accept it. You know now what you will say. Tell me."

It was no use pretending. He could read her thoughts. She did know.

"I will say yes." She waited in panic for his next move. She could not breathe.

He leaned toward her and laid his face against hers. He moved it slowly, lightly, brushing his cheek against hers, his mouth across her forehead and eyes. She stood still as a tree on a windless day, her entire being lost in those few inches of her skin. Her panic died and was replaced by a yearning for something more. When he pulled back, she leaned unthinkingly after him, then recovered herself.

"Good," he said. He saw her tiny movement toward him, and raised his hand to her face in a soothing caress and a promise. "Now, I think it is not proper among your people," he said, "if we don't go back into the house soon."

Reluctantly, she nodded. She wanted to stand all night feeling the brush of his face against hers. As they walked, she dared to take his arm. In spite of his appearance of lightness, she felt a strong and reassuring warmth of real flesh through the fabric of his jacket. She reflected how different her feelings of joy were from the flash of triumph, followed by anticlimax, of Costals's proposal.

Mme. Garine's pursed lips could not quench Ariane's excitement at her new betrothal. She did not care whether or not Mme. Garine could revel in telling her friends; she was too happy for herself this time.

"Thank you, Lord," she whispered at Mass. "Thank you for not taking away all that you seemed to have promised me. Thank you, Blessed Virgin, for interceding for me!"

Only another woman, she believed, would have understood.

She wrote the good news to her parents; they knew Costals had died, but not the details, and had written begging her to return home to France. Deep within herself Ariane felt a relief she could not admit—that the murder had saved her in some way from something oppressive that she did not understand.

She lived for her fiancé's visits, uncomfortable as they were, with Mme. Garine making visible efforts to sustain polite conversation. Ariane was happy just looking at him. She waited for his eyes to slide to hers in complicity against the older woman. He was everything she had come to Indochina to find—beautiful, powerful, and mysterious. As well as all those things, he was rich. With him, she knew that she would visit territory she could not yet even imagine, far stranger and more profound than anything in Raoul's petty self-delusion with opium. She felt sullied and uncomfortable even remembering her own cooperation.

The courtship was short. Against unseemly haste, Mme. Garine balanced the number of times she was willing to be seen at the opera with the young man in her party. She could not bear Henri's smug satisfaction at exactly the same thing. She had nothing against Annamites. But, as she told her closest friends, one could not get around the problem of feeling uncomfortable with someone whose background was so different. She was certain that M. Luc must feel exactly the same about her, and she would understand. The feeling had nothing to do with prejudice and everything to do with custom.

Ariane had no idea what she was getting herself into, said Mme. Garine. And no one could tell her anything, she was so infatuated. Mme. Garine would sigh and sip her cup of black coffee or her *pastis*. She just hoped the girl wouldn't come running back to her when her darling Annamite husband took a second wife. Or expected her to kowtow to his aging parents and aunts and uncles. Or asked her to serve that stinking fish sauce every day.

"On the bright side," she would say, "at least he seems to have enough money for a decent domestic staff."

Four months later, Ariane was married in defiant white in a side chapel of the Cathedral. The wedding Mass was followed by a small reception in the Garines' garden, under an awning with jasmine winding up its corner poles. Most of her new husband's guests were French.

She smiled with particular brightness on a large, heavy, well-dressed Corsican who winked at her and said, "That young man will be a member of the Conseil Général before he's thirty if he goes on making decisions as good as this one—choosing you!"

Ariane blushed and smiled again. M. Carbone had given them an apartment as a wedding present, in a residential hotel he owned.

"I hope I can help him, whatever he becomes."

"Just give him a son!" Carbone winked again. "Then you'll be set for life."

Carbone was pleased by the marriage of his protégé. The girl would be a pleasure to look at whenever wives were around. But more important, he had recently been uneasy about Luc. He had had him watched for the last few months, but without result. Carbone was relieved by his choice of a French wife. If Luc had any radical native friends, Ariane would make them hostile. Carbone was also pleased by her naïveté. She was not shrewd enough to be able to hide things of importance from someone like himself; she would be a useful, unwitting addition to the maid that Carbone had already placed in Luc's household, at the time he had handed over to the young Annamite the liaison with the Tonkinese opium brokers.

Alone that night with her new husband, Ariane's fear at finally confronting the sexual act was nearly overwhelmed by her pleasure in his beauty. His naked body, as he arranged things for the night, was finely muscled. His smooth skin was the color of a washed beach, but dry and smooth. He had none of the hairy coarseness that had disturbed her so much when Jules Martin and the other fishermen had stripped off their shirts in the afternoon sun at home. She watched him through the mosquito netting that draped their double bed while he locked the shutters into place with heavy bars and turned the key in the bedroom door. She thought he moved like a tiger, or a cheetah, pivoting lightly on the pads of his bare feet, reaching out with fluid strength.

Her mouth dried as he parted the netting and his weight bent the surface of the mattress; she felt her own weight shift toward him as if she were falling. He had left a small light burning beside the bed. In the dim, golden glow they studied each other silently.

This is my life, happening to me, thought Ariane. She was terrified.

"What should I do?" she asked finally, with a quaver.

His hand touched her mouth, as much in curiosity as to silence her. "Do not worry," he said. "For tonight, at least, I am the teacher. There is no hurry; we come together from a great distance."

His fingertips moved to examine the embroidered eyelets of their pillowcases, wedding presents from the Garines along with the embroidered linen sheets. After a moment, she lay back against her pillows. She watched his hand, then her eyes slid, in spite of herself, to the shadows at the base of his belly.

He picked up her left hand and opened the fist she did not know she had made. He ran his thumb across the scarlet enamel of her nails and turned her gold wedding band around the bone of her finger. Then he reached up and slipped the straps of her nightdress from her shoulders. Before she could protest, he pushed the embroidered lawn below the nipples of her heavy breasts. She felt his fingertips, light and exploring. She found it hard to breathe and heard her own heart beating in her ears. His hands brushed her neck and shoulders, always swooping down to draw out the dark startled points of her nipples. She wanted to say that he should not be doing such things, but knew that they were now his right.

She braced herself for his next move, but it did not come. He stroked and brushed, sometimes with his hand, sometimes with the smooth skin of his cheek and lips. Once in a while he inhaled lightly or touched her skin with his tongue, as if testing a strange new fruit. Her rigid expectation relaxed slowly into accepting warmth. Her nervous brain stopped trying to guess where his fingers might next touch and merely followed the delicious trails they drew across her skin.

To her surprise, he suddenly settled himself on the pillows beside her, with one hand cupping a breast.

"Now we sleep a little," he said.

Relief was immediately followed by a sensation of emptiness. This was surely not the normal behavior of a new bridegroom!

She had never heard of such a thing, unless the man was very drunk . . . in which case, she had surmised from giggling conversations among certain of her faster friends, a man is not capable of doing to his wife the thing he is supposed to do with that bit of himself which the shadows were hiding from her eyes. Her husband was not drunk.

She closed her eyes obediently, however, and tried to sleep. A line of heat from his leg burned through the thin fabric of her nightdress into her thigh. She lay awake for a long time in the shadows of the netting, thinking how strange it was . . . being married . . . being alive. The warmth of his hand on her breast became comforting rather than frightening. To erase the memory of Costals's hand on that same breast, she opened her eyes and turned her head to study her new husband's profile against the glow of the little light which he had not turned off. Eventually, she dozed.

When she woke later, the light was out. The touch of a body beside her jolted her into full consciousness. Stacks of pale lines in the darkness showed where the shuttered windows were. She remembered where she was, and the miasma of nightmare cleared like mist in a fresh breeze. He was awake beside her.

"Now," he said. "Now I will show you."

His hand did unmentionable things that left her gasping. She thought she felt pain but could not be sure in the sea of sensations that drowned her. His weight poised over her; she felt a brief butting sensation; and it was done.

Again, he stopped. She felt his hands on her face and smelled an odd, sweetish smell on them that she knew must be her own. He withdrew from her slowly and she cried out in unknowing protest. When he reentered her, she was waiting for him and wanting him.

She went with him for a long time. Just at the end, she suddenly became frightened by the force of his intensity, which distracted her from her own. She was both frightened and excited by the strength that he unleashed and the wildness with which she cried out in triumph in his own language at the moment just before he became quiet.

15

Luoc realized his miscalculation within weeks of marriage. Constant chaperones had made this impossible before. Besotted by him and overflowing with happy sexuality, Ariane chattered endlessly when they were alone together. He learned that she came from a village nearly as small as his own and was more nervous of many of the other French than he was. He learned that she was not a scholar. She could not teach him anything he did not already know about the reasons for the French power. She was herself a leaf on the current. His very first instinct to class her as an ayah had been reasonably accurate.

For several months, this realization made him angry with his own ignorance, but he did not turn his anger on Ariane. He could still learn much from her about French weaknesses. He still desired her.

He found something both pitiful and exciting in her pink dampness. Her abundance of flesh both repelled and attracted him. When he touched her, his hand sometimes seemed to penetrate her body, it sank so far. He felt that his body printed itself into her side-slipping flesh, which was so different from the taut skins of Vietnamese women. Each time he printed himself on her, he imagined he also planted a son. He imagined the joy and relief with which he would return to his village to fulfill his vow to his dead father and grandfather, with his tall, strong, respectful son at his side.

For those months, Ariane was happy. The freedom of her own home was intoxicating. Her small circle of friends was fascinated to hear all about life with an Annamite husband. The sense of expectancy returned to lodge in her belly. This time, unlike those hours in her French field, she knew exactly whom and what she was waiting for.

One night they gave their third small dinner party. The guests were business acquaintances of her husband, one couple that Ariane knew, and a small brown man who spoke little French but wore a general's uniform in an army unknown to Ariane.

When the last guest had gone and they were preparing for bed, Luoc asked her, "Are you doing something?"

"What on earth do you mean?" She stopped brushing her blond hair, which she was growing out into the new longer style. "I do lots of things." She prepared to smile secretly at some small linguistic confusion of his.

"So you won't conceive."

"But that would be a sin," she exclaimed. "Of course I'm not!" When she saw his intent expression, she went red. "No, of course not."

"Six months have passed," he said.

She began to feel angry, as if he were charging her unfairly with failure. "Well, I'm *not*!"

She was still angry and anxious when he made love to her that night. It was the first time she felt apart from him while they were joined together.

Two days later, he ordered her to accompany him in the chauffeur-driven car. Ariane was so upset by what followed that she could barely tell Minou Le Coultre, *née* Ray, who was her best friend since she had married. He had taken her to a medium who held office in the porch of a Buddhist temple.

"He told that witch doctor that I was barren," she wept to Minou. "The dirty old woman touched me.... They kept talking in Annamite and looking at me. I felt like I was on a market stall."

"Then what happened?" asked Minou breathlessly. Ariane was her only acquaintance who had actually been to bed with a *jaune*. Minou had heard that they were excellent lovers, but Ariane was not the kind of woman one could press too hard for sordid details. Minou tried to imagine André taking her to a witch doctor in order to get pregnant, but she couldn't. She herself already had two children, including the one she had carried under her wedding dress.

"Then the woman prayed for a while," said Ariane. "To one of those statues, all new gold paint and silk flowers. She started to twitch and dance about from one foot to the other. I was terrified. *He* just stood there watching her. And me."

Minou gave her another pink gin. It was early in the day, but circumstances warranted it.

"She started to write," said Ariane. "All over sheets of yellow paper. In those funny letters. Then you'll never guess what they made me do!"

"What?" Minou encouraged her.

"She burned some of the papers and made me drink the ashes in a glass of water!"

"No!" breathed Minou. "How barbaric!"

"I'll show you something," said Ariane confidentially. The gin was beginning to take effect. She leaned forward and pulled a tiny silver box from between her breasts.

"See that? There's one of the yellow papers inside. A spell. To make me conceive a boy. I have to wear it all the time."

"I'd never do it," said Minou.

"You don't know him," Ariane said. "Once he decided he wants something done, it happens. He frightens me sometimes.

112

He keeps checking to see if I still have it. I don't dare take it off!''

Minou sat back a little uncomfortably. Every so often, she felt the real distance between her world and the one her friend had entered.

The more time passed without her conceiving, the more Ariane felt her husband withdrawing from her. He turned the intensity of his energy to other things, and she felt as if the sun had been turned off. She tried to take an interest in his business life, as a wife should, but the little he said opened worlds so strange and alien to her that she gave up. His foreignness ceased to be exciting and became a source of deep loneliness before a year was gone. Even worse than her loneliness, eased only by a few casual female friends, was the loss of expectation. What she had now was what she would always have. There was nothing more to come. God had given what He had seemed to promise and it was less than she had imagined. Her soul began to die before her body had begun to age.

"Perhaps growing older," she would say to herself, "is accepting that such thoughts are possible."

The death of her husband's passion meant the end of even fleshly expectation. The stillness returned to her center, but she no longer hoped that it would be filled with an answer.

Searching, if no longer hoping, she returned to religion. Alone or less and less often with Minou Le Coultre, she began to go regularly to Mass. At worst, she enjoyed the company of other damp, warm bodies as she knelt in the nave of the red-brick Cathedral. She needed the familiarity of the Latin phrases which she had heard from birth, and the knowledge that this God, at least, understood French.

She shared one major activity with her husband: they entertained. Luoc, who had begun to use his proper name rather than the French version of it, continued to rise professionally. Although, as a *jaune*, he was not allowed to own a business or property directly, Ariane gathered that, through French holding companies, he in reality owned the hotel where they had lived as newlyweds, as well as others in Hué and Dalat. She knew he owned a fleet of sampans in the same way and that the export business of which he was the nominal manager now dealt with far more than buttons. She knew they must be rich, because he never put a limit on how much she could spend on clothes or on wine and food for their many guests. Buying became her chief pleasure.

If she could not give her husband a child, Ariane determined to give him the best dinner parties in Saigon. Her determination and his money led to soirées known for their lavishness, if not always for their chic. By sheer effort and expense in the next few years, Ariane nearly overcame the social disadvantages of her mixed marriage and her own humble origins as a provincial governess. She felt that she was making a real contribution to her husband's life. To try to please him, she fed Annamite politicians, Corsican entrepreneurs, including Carbone, French officials, and Chinese merchant bankers. To try to win his gratitude, she pretended interest in business conversations that excluded her. To please him, she kept in contact with any of the French society set who felt comfortable dining with a racially mixed couple. As he was a fair man, he said when her efforts pleased him, though his energy never turned back onto her. It was a dinner party, however, that drove them completely apart, five years after their marriage.

"Don't invite the general and his wife." Luoc tossed the guest list onto his wife's writing desk.

"Don't be absurd," she retorted. "You asked me to invite them weeks ago. We've owed him for that party in the restaurant for *months*."

"Please don't question what I ask," he said. "Are all French wives so impudent?"

Sullenly, she drew a line through the general's name. What a business! The man wasn't even a proper general, just one of those bandits who buys himself a uniform to strut in front of his gangster troops. She wondered what Luoc would do if she ever defied him. She had never dared, but she often imagined it.

Two days later, she heard that the general had been murdered by a group of his own men, along with his wife and four children. The self-proclaimed leader of the assassins had taken over the general's title. Her husband never referred to the matter.

She found herself watching him. She was now convinced that he was not just foreign but deliberately hiding from her important things about himself. She began to pry whenever she had a chance, which was not often, because she was sure the servants spied on her when he was away. Nevertheless, one day three months after the general's death, when Luoc had gone north to inspect property he had there and the servants were all in the cookhouse during the midmorning lull, she went into his library.

He never let her touch this room. She could fill the rest of their big new house with antiques and Limoges china, but this room was his private territory. She hated it. It reminded her beyond any self-delusion that she had married an alien being. A heathen, in spite of his original claim to be Catholic and his marriage vows. She glared at the portrait of an Annamite man which hung like an idol between the posts of a carved sandalwood frame, burned joss sticks before it.

Systematically, she began to go through the drawers of the two upright Chinese lacquer chests that stood against the walls. She found pieces of broken pottery, tiny carved jade figures, small bronze idols. In one drawer was an array of brushes with handles of tortoiseshell, bamboo, wrapped rattan, and lacquered wood. They varied in thickness from three hairs to the size of a cow's tail. In the bottom drawer, she found the *coupe-coupe*.

After a moment, she lifted it gingerly from its nest inside the long Japanese box. Compared to the other objects in the other drawers, it was coarse and very real. Not an artifact or artist's brush but a rough working tool. She pulled the blade from the bamboo scabbard. There were spots of rust on the blade which she imagined were dried blood. She shuddered and quickly thrust it back into the sheath. She slammed the drawer shut and turned in such agitation that she knocked over a porcelain vase on his writing table with her elbow.

"The *boyesse* must have done it while she was dusting," Ariane told her husband when he returned.

He called for the servant and made Ariane repeat her claim.

"Madame did it," the woman retorted.

Ariane inhaled with dramatic indignation while her face flamed scarlet. "How dare you say such a thing!" she cried.

"I will get another job," said the *boyesse,* "where they don't say I tell lies."

Luoc looked at the two women. "That is not necessary," he told the *boyesse.* "Please go continue with what you were doing before I sent for you."

"Why were you in my library?" Luoc asked his wife.

She started to deny it again, saw how certain he was, and turned the attack. "Why do you have that dreadful sword?"

His quietness alarmed her even further. After a moment, he said, "It was my father's."

"But why do you keep it? I want you to throw it away." Her voice rose. "It give me the horrors. I'm sure it could get you into trouble, having a thing like that!"

He looked at her from his chair for a few moments longer. Then he rose and left the room without speaking.

Ariane wondered whether he would return, and whether she wanted him to.

He came into the room with the naked blade in his hand.

Ariane tried to scream, but her throat had closed so that she could not draw breath. She curled tightly into the corner of the settee.

He raised his arm and sliced through the upholstered back of the nearest chair. Frame and upholstery parted cleanly like a split melon. Luoc glanced at his terrified wife with amusement and left the room, still without speaking.

A year later, Ariane finally conceived. Being Catholic, she had not tried to prevent it, but she had hoped that the infrequency of their now pragmatic matings would make a child unlikely. She was depressed for the first three months at the idea of bearing a half-alien creature. She tried to imagine loving something with black hair and slit eyes, more like her husband than herself. She didn't tell him until the bulge was obvious.

Her pregnancy brought a truce between them. She felt a renewal of his interest in her. At least he became solicitous for her health and comfort. He insisted on the best French obstetrician and allowed her to refuse a visit from a native midwife when the idea made her hysterical. She and he were no closer, but at least she felt she had regained some importance in his life.

She hated being pregnant, nevertheless. The heat made her ill; her ankles swelled alarmingly. Her full breasts became uncontrollable bags of jelly. She felt crippled, short of breath, and ugly. She prayed for the release of giving birth and for a son to make it all worthwhile.

The baby started to come early, in the heat of the rainy season, a little more than a year before war broke out in Europe. Ariane already had stomach pains from a mild case of tropical dysentery. She couldn't believe the intensity of the new pain which threatened to tear her abdomen apart. She screamed and swore at the nursing sisters who tried to hold her hand and soothe her. She gasped at the mask they held over her face, then pushed it away to scream again. Below her waist, her body took on a life of its own. It knotted and heaved and tore bits of her insides loose from each other, or so it seemed to her. As the contractions reached their peak, Ariane knew that with each next one her life would follow that itching, torturing lump down out of her body.

Her body contorted. She felt a searing heat between her legs. And stillness. She lay, panting, unable to believe that the pain

116

had stopped. From the bustle of women by her feet came a faint mewing sound.

The happy round face of a nun leaned over her. "Oh, my child! You have a beautiful little girl!"

PART TWO

❊   ❊

16
Dalat, 1950—Nina

"That beast goes outside at night. I've told you a hundred times!
You'll get fleas in your bed."

Ariane's voice stopped the twelve-year-old Nina in her tracks,
in the wood-paneled hallway of the family's holiday home in
Dalat in the highlands north of Saigon. The girl turned like a
startled fawn.

"*Maman*, please! I gave her a bath." Nina hugged Minou
tightly in her slim young arms. The little gibbon sensed that she
was the subject of the argument and locked her forepaws into
Nina's dark curls, which were the result of long, smelly hours at
her mother's hairdresser in Saigon.

"Look what she's doing now, to your hair!"

"Pleeese, *maman*!"

"Don't argue, mam'selle!" Ariane threw her eyes and manicured hands upward in appeal to the Good Lord. "How am I ever
going to teach her to be *gentille* when she wants to sleep with an
ape?"

"*Gentille*" was Ariane's word for all that was proper, desirable, and beyond questioning in her world.

"And put on your sandals before you go into the garden to
chain her up," Ariane added. "Sometimes I think you don't care
if you die of hookworm! Now go. Out!"

Nina stood in the hallway, pleading with her dark, hazel-
flecked eyes. Their wideness and the quivering of her long, thick
lashes were wasted on Ariane, however.

"Out!" said her mother. "Don't make me have to punish you
when there's company."

A cousin of her husband's had arrived late that afternoon,
while Nina was out boating on the lake with Annette Pluviez, the
daughter of a French family who had also come up to the
mountains during the lowland hot season. Ariane was not looking

119

forward to dinner with a Tonkinese thug who could barely speak French.

Nina obeyed, reluctantly. When safely out of earshot of her mother, she whispered, "Don't worry, Minou. I'll come for you when *maman* is asleep. I'll make myself stay awake until then."

Unhappily, she snapped the hook at the end of the traveling chain onto the gibbon's collar. The chain slid along a wire, strung like a clothesline between two posts under the tall pines that surrounded the bungalow. Here, high in the mountains around the lake, the evening air was chilly once the sun dropped. Nina buttoned the padded silk doll's jacket she had put on the gibbon.

"Hold still, my darling, Otherwise, you'll catch pneumonia. And *maman* wouldn't care a bit."

She kissed the little animal on the nose. "Don't worry. I will be back."

Minou hooted gently and set off along the taut wire in great swinging loops from hand to hand, her long furred wrists stretching comically from the short sleeves of the doll's jacket.

As she returned to her own room, Nina passed below the high veranda which faced out over the lake to catch the breezes. Above her, in the dark, she heard men's voices, not the words, but low, comfortable, stomach-tickling vibrations. One voice was her father's; the other was strange to her. They cut back and forth with the ease of men who knew each other well.

She climbed the short flight of wooden stairs at the corner and slipped into the shadows behind a hammock on an iron stand. Quite suddenly, she forgot Minou. Her father's back was to her. The stranger sat, half facing her, half looking out into the pines. He was slim and wore a Western-style suit. A dark forelock of hair fell to his eyebrows. His cheekbones were high, his mouth wide. He looked exactly like the picture of a Japanese movie star Nina had cut from one of her mother's journals and secreted in her wardrobe in Saigon. Nina fell in love.

Nina did not fall in love any more than most young girls, but when she did it was with total passion. Until she was six, her loves had included Doi, the gardener at the big house in Saigon, who carried her on his back to chase Simpoh Flower, the daughter of the family's cook, around the flowerbeds. The hair on the nape of his neck had tickled her nose and smelled deliciously of sunlight. She had also loved him because he did not laugh at her when she cried, "Me too!" and begged him to teach her the kicks and lunges he practiced every evening behind the washhouse. Instead, very seriously, he had taught the little girl the rudiments of karate. He never laughed, even when she pounded the side of her tiny hand against the corner of the washhouse as he did, to harden it.

"Are you a Vietminh, Doi? Are you?" she would whisper. "Are you?"

His mysterious smile made her heart beat even faster.

Other loves had been her old ayah, and Simpoh Flower. Then there was Minou, the gibbon, who still loved her, unlike the others. And now, there was this stranger.

The next day she was formally introduced to him, but she was too tongue-tied by passion to feel anything except agony in his presence. Her only comfort was that she learned he was a cousin of her father's. He left later that afternoon. Back in Saigon, when the hot season finished, she kissed the picture of the film star every night and imagined him saying her name in the voice she had heard in the dusk among the pines of Dalat.

It is possible that the intensity of Nina's attachments grew out of her need to love and be loved, which her parents left unfilled. When the nun told Ariane that the baby was a daughter, Ariane turned her face to the wall to hide tears of disappointment. It was only a girl who had distorted her waistline, swollen her ankles, and weighed her down all those months. Her chance to win back her husband was gone.

When she finally looked at the bundle the nun had placed willy-nilly in her arms, her despair deepened. The creature was bright orange. Not just yellow, as Ariane had secretly feared, but orange. Unfortunately, no one thought to explain to her about jaundice in newborn babies. The only glimmer of God's mercy was that the child did not have slit eyes. Even though her husband did not have them, Ariane had feared a throw-back. She could not stop crying. The sisters kept telling her that it was normal to feel depressed after giving birth. She didn't even try to make them understand that her grief was different. As soon as possible, she arranged for a wet nurse; she couldn't bear the painful tugging which seemed to drain her entire being.

When they told Luoc of the little girl's birth, he shrugged, French-fashion, and said, *"C'est la vie."* He didn't visit the hospital; he did not think he could bear to see his wife weep and look at him in supplication, wanting to be forgiven for what could not be helped by either of them. This birth simply made the other one, the secret one three and a half years ago, that much more precious to him.

* * *

As Nina grew out of babyhood, she did not realize that she was unhappy. She was too young to suppose that the stomachache she felt whenever she thought about her father might have anything to do with unhappiness.

Her first memory of him was of a pair of white-flanneled legs. It was shortly before war was declared in Europe, when she was not quite one year old. She bumped into the legs as she ricocheted off the black varnished leg of the damp-proofed piano in the formal drawing room. She remembered hitting her forehead on something hard inside the white flannel—his kneecap—and starting to cry in an automatic, unserious way to let her ayah know that she wanted comforting.

"Stop her making that stupid noise."

She hadn't understood the exact words, but the tone had stopped her abruptly. Mouth open, she stared up at the huge dark face so far above her. She had seen it before but never so close. It was brown, like her ayah's, and the cook's, and the gardener's, but unlike theirs, it did not bend down to her or smile or make comforting noises. She knew in some fashion that she had been brought into the drawing room for this face to look at. She also knew, from the eyes, that it did not much like what it saw.

Her ayah darted forward from her position by the door and scooped Nina up. Her father's face had already turned away to speak to her mother, who sat on the sofa and ignored Nina as well.

"You stupid child," hissed her ayah as they reached the safety of the hall. "Why did you make your father angry? You must show him that you are a worthy offspring. You'll never do that by bursting into tears over a tiny bump."

Nina continued to stare over the woman's shoulder at the closed door of the drawing room. Then she wriggled to get down.

"Go back," she said. She struggled harder. "Won't cry!"

"No, no, no. Never mind," soothed the ayah. "Let it be. You will see him another time. Come, let's go find Simpoh Flower and play *cache-cache*!"

Nina allowed herself to be distracted. But she felt the same sense of emptiness as when her mother told her she was a bad girl, and the same desire to prove her accuser wrong.

Besides her innocence the other reason Nina did not know she was unhappy was the servants—all of them, not just her ayah, and Doi, and Simpoh Flower, who was two years older than she. They adopted her, petted her, and kept her too busy to be aware of how much she missed the love and company of her parents.

When Nina was one year old, her mother gave her a pink and

blond doll, her father gave her a gold piece, and the servants gave her a "quitting the cradle" party. She was taken to Ariane to say good night as usual. Then, instead of putting her to bed, the ayah smuggled her out to her own hut in the servants' quarters. They were all there, with several of their friends and with the ayah's husband, who was a seaman, using the occasion as a pleasant excuse for eating and drinking.

After a few perfunctory prayers on her behalf, Nina was enthroned on the polished wood platform bed, ribbons in her hair, wearing the new silk tunic the cook had given her. As she sat steadily, regarding the laughing crowd in the little hut with interest, the women laid a series of objects in a circle around her.

She leaned forward.

"Wait. Wait, Little Rat," said the ayah. "Let them finish."

"Little Rat" was one of the nicknames her nurse had given her to distract marauding spirits, or *ma*, from the beauty that had already begun to show itself.

The women giggled as they positioned a flower, a pair of scissors, two pencils, a gold coin, a book, and a bowl of rice flour on the polished wood. When they finished, everyone was quiet. Nina felt their eyes on her.

"Now, Little Rat," said her ayah. "Choose one of these things." She stepped back from the bed.

"She'll take the pencils," said the cook. "She already wants me to tell her stories. She'll take the pencils and become a writer."

"You should have put a sword," said Doi, the gardener. "I think she'll be another Dame Trieu. A female warrior. You should see how she chases me." There was a general titter.

"That doesn't sound like a warrior to me," said the ayah's husband.

His wife cut in. "Poor Doi. He brags when he gets chased by a baby. Can't he do any better than that?"

Everyone roared. More rice wine was drunk.

"Come on, Little Rat," cried her friend Simpoh Flower. "You must choose!" Simpoh Flower was jumping up and down in gleeful expectation.

Nina reached out a chubby hand.

"It's the scissors!" someone cried. "A tailor!"

"Nonsense," said the ayah. "Look, she's already left them."

Young as she was, Nina felt their expectation and energy focused on her. It was warm as the morning sun, and she wanted more.

She stuck an experimental finger into the rice flour and put it in her mouth, looking around to see their reaction.

The circle of faces cried, "Oh, a cook!" and laughed again.

Nina laughed too, not certain why, but knowing that the laughter was comfortable. Then she reached out and firmly clutched the gold coin.

There was a sudden odd silence in the little room.

"Well," said someone. "She knows what's what. It's too bad she wasn't born a boy. Someone should tell her father about this."

"What difference would it make?" said her ayah. "He's got his boy. This one could be drowned like a kitten for all he cares."

Nina felt the change; the sunny warmth had cooled. Her tiny face began to look worried. She searched the faces for her ayah.

"Here I am, Piglet." The woman scooped her up from the bed. "Look, you're upsetting her. Don't make her cry, today of all days! It would be a dreadful omen!"

Doi jumped up on the bed and raised his glass. "Little Rat will become the wealthiest woman in Indochina!"

"In the world!" shrieked Simpoh Flower.

As more rice wine vanished, the original jollity returned. The cook disappeared to finish preparing the evening meal for the big house. Nina laughed along with the rest of them, and nodded as if she understood all the jokes, safe in her ayah's arms, still clutching the gold coin.

As Nina grew older, Simpoh Flower began to lug her around on her own small hip. The older girl taught her to feed the fish that were kept in the glazed tank by the cookhouse, and to race frogs in the garden. Simpoh Flower came into her room every morning with the ayah; she was allowed to carry Nina's cup of hot chocolate and sweet roll on a tiny lacquered tray, and to share the roll while her mother laid out the young mistress's clothes for the day.

Neither girl was aware that the Vichy regime now ruled both in France and in southern Indochina, where Saigon lay, through the Governor-General of Cochin China and the Chief Resident of Annam, the heads of the two southern provinces. Nor did they understand that the Japanese had annexed the third part of Indochina, the northern province of Tonkin, where Nina's father had been born.

Shortly before Nina's second birthday, in 1940, the Japanese marched south. The pro-Vichy French in Saigon prudently submitted to being occupied; in exchange, they were allowed to retain their own official positions. As a result, the French government appeared to roll on unchanged. The civilian French population entertained Japanese officers for aperitifs.

Far more important to Nina than these distant events, which took place outside the compound walls, was the special gift that the servants gave her for her third birthday. The cook, her ayah, and Simpoh Flower had accompanied her, like a procession, out of the gate of the big compound into the amazing noise and flashing movement of the city. They took her to the Pet Market.

Nina gazed in disbelief at tin bathtubs full of turtles and lizards, at cages of tiny birds, and at parrots tethered to perches. She peered at kittens and wide-eyed marmosets, unable to let herself hope what the reason might be for coming to such a marvelous place. She was still preparing herself for disappointment when the women paused beside a melee of monkeys and gibbons who twirled and flung themselves through demented arcs inside cages, while others looped along the wires to which they were chained.

"You must choose one to be yours," said her ayah.

Nina didn't move, afraid she had misheard.

"Go on, Little Rat, choose."

Without hesitation, Nina held out her arms to a small female gibbon who was hanging upside down, hooting gently at her through pursed lips and blinking long lashes over comical eyes. The gibbon dropped hand over hand down her chain and reached down one tiny, wrinkled, dark gray paw to Nina.

Nina held the little paw tightly while the cook shouted the vendor down several piastres. The gibbon's chain was unlocked from the perch. When the animal was placed into her arms—cautiously, as they could sometimes bite—Nina felt the softness of its fur against her skin and burst into tears of joy.

From that day, Minou was the third member of the trio, with Nina and Simpoh Flower. The girls dressed her in doll's clothes, pushed her in a wickerwork doll's perambulator, and stole treats for her from the cookhouse. Minou slept in Nina's bed every night, after she had finished scampering up and down the mosquito netting and dropping onto Nina's head. Ariane believed that the ape spent the night in the garden, tethered to her post as ordered. But Simpoh Flower smuggled her in, every night, under her tunic. The girls even smuggled Minou into the films the ayah took her charge and her daughter to see regularly when Ariane thought they were making a promenade.

In 1941, when Nina was three, the League for the Independence of Vietnam, popularly known as the Vietminh, was founded as a resistance movement against the Japanese. They were offered aid by the Americans, who helped them train their fighting men. By this time, the Japanese controlled the economy of Indochina and were redirecting all its international trade from France to Japan. They had seized the right, formerly held only by Frenchmen, to buy land and industries. Indochina had joined the Japanese "Greater Far Eastern Co-Prosperity Sphere." It was part of the French Empire in name only. Though the French still clung to the appearance of power, the ground quaked under their feet. After ruling for two hundred years, they had finally bowed their heads in submission—to an Asian people. This reality did not escape the notice of many Indochinese, including Nina's father.

By this time, Nina had become aware of the Japanese; they were too much part of the adult world to be completely invisible, even to a protected child. Her mother's friends talked about them and so did the servants. While Nina drank colored syrups poured over chipped ice which the servants bought her from passing vendors, she listened to the cook and her beloved Doi arguing hotly and often about who had the right to define the order in the world—the gods, the French, the Japanese, or the newly formed Vietminh. The cook upheld a coalition between the gods and the French. The gardener favored the Vietminh.

Nina learned many other things from the servants as well. They fed her sugarcane and sticky rice with coconut, and duck's eggs and *nuoc mam* with rice balls. They tied good-luck cords on her wrists. But most of all, they fed her intense curiosity, which was a combination of her father's intelligence and her mother's thirst for new experience.

"Why?" she asked. "How?" And, "Tell me another story!" she begged the cook as soon as she was able to talk.

As the woman chopped and sliced and prodded at pots with long wooden chopsticks, she told Nina wonderful tales of Vietnamese heroes and heroines, like Dame Trieu, and the warrior Trung sisters who had saved the Viet people from their deadly enemies, the Han Chinese.

"Show me!" urged Nina constantly, every day. And the servants would demonstrate the correct way to make offerings to the spirits which lived in every natural thing. They showed her how to explode firecrackers at the Tet New Year celebrations to frighten away Na Ong and Na Ba so they could not prevent good genii from getting to Heaven to report on the doings of their human charges. The cook explained that spirits can travel only in straight lines and that a mirror on your door will frighten away a demon by making it think another demon is already there. As the cook peeled and fried, she also instructed Nina that her first duty in life was filial reverence toward her parents, no matter how they treated her. This knowledge, which she drank in with all the rest, somehow made life seem a little clearer to Nina, in an area which was slightly confused.

As she grew older, the ayah and Simpoh Flower took her not only to see films but also to the native street theater. Nina was as happy pretending to be Ginger Rogers in a flowing gown as she was when Simpoh Flower bent her small hands into the correct Vietnamese dance positions. Everything she saw and learned was fascinating.

Distracted, petted, and instructed as she was, Nina still felt her stomach ache when she thought about her father. Though she was usually in bed when he came home, she crept out of her room to spy on him from the first-floor veranda as soon as she heard the sound of the gate opening and the big car in the drive. She would watch him unbend gracefully from the backseat, nod his thanks to the driver who held the door open for him with such obvious respect, and climb the front steps to disappear onto the veranda. She would then slip along the pale blue Chinese runner on the landing to the top of the stairs, to hear his voice greet the number one boy.

One night, she heard him compliment the man on his small son, who was being trained to help his father. In her hiding place, Nina felt a sickness and anger which she did not yet recognize as jealousy. The next day, she asked the cook to tell her again and again the tales of children who had gained honor by saving their parents, or by rescuing the family honor.

"Tell me again," she begged eagerly, climbing onto her special seat on the chopping block beside the brazier. "Tell me about the girl whose father was arrested by an invading Chinese general . . . you know . . . the one who went fearlessly to the enemy general and threw herself on his mercy and begged him to spare her father's life. And they stopped the execution! And gave her father lots of honors because he had such a brave girl!"

The cook smiled, repeated the story yet again, and watched the little girl sit with straight back, small pointed chin lifted, dark eyes alight with imagined glory, and small, already elegant limbs braced for imaginary battle.

* * *

One evening, when she was three and a half, she was playing in the garden just before her supper, helping the gardener between rides on his back. She stopped pulling weeds to watch a big black car slide up the drive. A yellow sun fluttered on its hood.

Doi too stopped working. "Come on, Little Rat." His voice was urgent. "Let's go see what cook has for you tonight."

"In a minute!" whispered Nina, her heart pounding. They had finally come for her father. Only generals and important men had flags on their cars. "You go, Doi. I'll come in a minute."

She ducked behind a row of cannas. "Go on!"

The gardener scooped her up and marched firmly toward the servants' quarters, but over his shoulder Nina saw the first Japanese place a polished boot on the driveway. Then she saw her mother on the veranda, smiling and extending her hand to the enemy.

Her father was in danger at last. She knew what her duty was. She was confused by her mother's role, but in any case, *she* was with the Japanese in the drawing room and would not be able to warn Nina's father, even if she wanted to.

Nina ate her coconut custard. She allowed her ayah to put her to bed, with Minou curled in the nest of mosquito netting at her side. But as soon as she heard the ayah's voice safely back in the servants' quarters, she was out of bed again.

"Stay here," she ordered Minou. "It will be too dangerous for you." The idea of danger for herself exhilarated her; but for Minou, it was unthinkable.

In her silk nightdress, she climbed down the vine trained against the side of the house. She had done it twice before. The second time her mother had caught her, sent her to bed without supper, and ordered the gardener to cut it down, to prevent thieves sending children up to steal her jewelry from the bedroom. Fortunately, Doi had not yet obeyed. Nina crawled below the drawing room windows, from which men's voices came, and through the garden from bush to bush to a hiding place in a thicket by the gate where the watchman could not see her.

Crouched among shielding branches, she permitted mosquitoes to bite her rather than betray herself by slapping at them. Stoically, she allowed a beetle to crawl across her foot. These things were trials of her courage, always encountered by the heroines in the cook's tales. She did wish her father would come soon, however. The evening was darkening; strange noises were beginning in the bushes around her which she had never noticed from the safety of her bed. And the brave children in the stories had all been older than three and a half.

128

At last the crack below the gate brightened. The watchman at the end of the drive leaped up from his doze to rattle the bolts and swing open the big gate. The big car turned as deliberately as an ocean liner into the Japanese trap. Nina sprang from the bushes into the beams of the headlamps. The car stalled as the driver slammed on the brakes.

There was a silence. Then her father opened his door.

"They are waiting for you," cried Nina. "You must flee!" She jumped up and down on her bare feet, her silk nightdress patched with flakes of dried leaves.

"Where the devil is her ayah? Who let her out at this time of night?" Her father's voice was angry.

"The Japanese are here," explained Nina urgently. "The foreign invaders! They are waiting for you!"

Her father strode past her up the drive. "Doi!" he called to the gardener, who had appeared around the house. "Take her back to her ayah and ask why she can't keep her under control."

Doi grabbed at Nina, who twisted away.

"No!" she screamed. "You must listen to me!" Her father hadn't understood. "The Japanese! They will arrest you. They will execute you!"

Her mother appeared at the top of the veranda steps; other faces peered from the drawing room windows.

"The Japanese!" wailed Nina, as Doi picked her up.

"Shut up, Little Rat!" begged Doi. "Shut up! You'll get everyone very angry! Please shut up!" He carried her, kicking and screaming with terror and frustration, to the cookhouse where he was met by the ayah.

"You're in a lot of trouble!" he said, and dropped the little girl into the woman's arms.

"I was going to save my f-f-father," Nina blubbed against the ayah's shoulder. "I would have saved him, but he didn't understand. He wouldn't listen!"

The woman looked helplessly at the other servants, who had come to see what was causing the furor. "He doesn't need saving, Little Rat. He's able to look after himself."

Nina was too much beside herself to listen.

"I'll show you," said the ayah. "You can see for yourself. . . . If you stop making that noise. Your father is safe. They are all going to eat dinner together. Be quiet now, and I'll show you that your father is perfectly safe."

"Here's a dried plum if you stop crying," wheedled the cook.

"Hush," said the ayah. "We'll go and see. But you must be quiet as a Vietminh!"

129

Nina gulped and was silent while the ayah carried her into the dark garden to the window of the dining room. They peered into the glittering light of the dining room, light broken and thrown from the walls by the glass jewels of the sconces. Her father stood at one end of the long table, waiting for his guests to find their places. The Japanese with the polished boots was smiling and speaking to him.

Nina began to shake with the even greater grief of humiliation. The ayah ran back with her to the other servants, who offered her tidbits, made Minou do tricks, and promised treats—a trip to the sea, to the zoological gardens, to the cinema to see *King Kong* yet again—in vain. Nina did not grow calm for a long time, and then only when the ayah pulled up her tunic and offered her a solid brown nipple to suckle, long dried up but still a source of comfort for the little girl in her moments of greatest need.

When Nina was six, Ariane decided that the servants were having far too much influence over her daughter. Her own loneliness grew as her husband disappeared more and more on mysterious business trips. At the same time, her marriage to a *jaune* no longer created curiosity among her friends but uneasiness. Because of the growing unrest among certain educated natives, the fashion for socializing with *les jaunes* was passing.

The child was bright and energetic. More important to Ariane, she showed signs of becoming a beauty. Her hair was thick and black; she had her father's elegant facial bones with a suggestion of her mother's lushness. Her eyes were large, with hazel glints in their darkness, and without an epicanthic fold, for which Ariane had never stopped thanking the Blessed Virgin. Ariane had failed to capture the elusive, ineffable joy that she believed was her destiny. She began to see her daughter as the raw material for another chance. She did not want to waste it.

She surprised and delighted the little girl one night by going to her room, not just for the usual swift brush of lips but for a serious talk. The next morning, as instructed, Nina marched down to the servants' quarters to earn her mother's love.

When she entered the shaded cookhouse, she was greeted by the usual flurry of delight. She swallowed the slice of mango which the cook popped into her mouth, then made her announcement.

"*Maman* says I am growing up and becoming a young lady now."

The cook and her cousin, Number One Wife, glanced at each other.

"She did?" said the cook politely as she went to loop an eel from the tank just outside the door.

"She said that you must call me 'mademoiselle' now and not 'Little Rat.' I must not be too familiar with you anymore." She waited importantly for their response to this proclamation. Secretly, she hoped that they might bow to her as she had seen peasants bow to the cars of passing French officials.

The two women said nothing. The cook handed the eel to Number One Wife, who slapped the squirming creature onto the slice of tree trunk that served as a chopping block. Doi put down the glass of tea he had been sipping and left the cookhouse.

Nina stared after him, confused.

"Number One Wife!" Nina tugged at her jacket. "Did you hear me?" The woman did not look at her.

"*Mais oui*, Mademoiselle Nina. I heard you clearly." She killed the eel with a blow of her chopper and, while it still writhed, began to skin it.

Nina watched them work. Still neither of them would look at her. Something terrible had happened and she did not know how to undo it. She decided to go and ask Doi to explain.

She found him clipping savagely at the grass along the drive and squatted beside him.

"Can I do that?" she asked. She would help him first, then he might stop being cross with her.

He stood up and turned to face her politely, as he would have done for her mother.

"I do not think it is fitting, mademoiselle."

"Please. You always let me." She cocked her head and gave him the winning smile that had won so many rides on his back, galloping around the bushes in pursuit of Simpoh Flower.

He looked at her for a minute without smiling back. "Your mother would not like it, mademoiselle." He continued to stand, eyes down, waiting politely for her to leave so he could resume clipping.

Nina was shocked by this turn of events. "You *must* let me!" she said, glaring up at him. She drew a deep breath. "I *order* you!" She held his eyes, looking as fierce as she could.

He looked back as if she were a strange child who had been trampling his flowers. "Madame has said that I must call you 'mademoiselle,' mademoiselle. She did not yet say that I must obey the orders of a six-year-old girl."

Nina felt short of breath from confusion and rage. She turned with as much dignity as she could muster and stumped off to find Simpoh Flower. Simpoh Flower was her best friend and she was older. She would be able to unravel the horrid tangle that Nina found herself in, and she would be able to explain it all to her mother, the cook, and to Number One Wife. And to Doi—if Nina decided ever to speak to him again.

She found Simpoh Flower behind the washhouse, threading gladiolus and jasmine blooms, pilfered from the garden, into long necklaces which the ayah would sell in the Flower Market. The girl smiled and Nina felt better. As she was considering how to begin, the cook called for Simpoh Flower to come and help prepare luncheon.

"Come," said the girl, and took Nina's hand. Together they entered the cookhouse.

"Go, cut me some lemon grass," said the cook sharply to her daughter. "Mademoiselle Nina must go back to the big house."

Puzzled at her mother's tone, Simpoh Flower turned to her aunt, who kept her eyes down as she wiped her cleaver against the edge of the chopping block. Simpoh Flower looked at Nina, then back to her mother.

"Why are you waiting?" asked the cook. "You will make luncheon late, dawdling like that. Get me the lemon grass."

Simpoh Flower went, unhappily.

"Mademoiselle Nina, you should go now. Your mother will be waiting."

Nina was appalled. She had not expected them to stop being familiar with *her*. Her mother had not told her that would happen! After a few minutes of horrid silence while the two women worked, she left, head held high. If they would not speak to her, she would not speak to them. She did not let herself cry until she was well away from the cookhouse.

The women watched her stop under the large bougainvillea by the back of the house to wipe her nose on her wrist. They glanced briefly at each other again. They did not need to speak. They had known this time would come, no matter how much they might have pretended she was one of their own. She was half French. What had happened was inevitable. The fierce thud of the cleaver as it chopped the eel into segments followed Nina back into the big house.

Around this time, at the age of six, Nina began to distinguish clearly between happiness and unhappiness. She was happy when her mother praised her table manners, or her appearance after endless unhappy hours of standing still for the dressmaker to adjust a hem when she would far rather have been climbing trees in the garden. She was happy when her mother talked to her about France and Cap Ferret, and her grandparents who loved her very much even though they had never seen her except in photographs. Nina was happy when her mother opened her jewel box and let the child trail her fingers among the slippery, waxy pearls, cup the blue sparks of sapphires in her hand, or try on a pair of amethyst earrings.

"Those were given to me by my mother," said Ariane. "They'll be yours when you grow up. Now, look at this ring . . . that shape is called a cabochon cut. See how it catches the light?"

And Nina would admire the slim white hand of her mother as much as the gem, while curling her own dirty nails into her fists.

She was happy, sometimes, when she played with Annette Pluviez, the daughter of a friend of her mother's, whom she was allowed to visit with Mlle. Berthe, her new French governess hired by Ariane as part of the reclamation plan. She was always happy in the company of Minou, who remained faithful to her while Simpoh Flower averted her face when she served Nina in the big dining room.

She was unhappy when Annette refused to kiss Minou because she was a "dirty ape." She was often unhappy with Mlle. Berthe, whose mouth was a tiny pink O painted on the center of a long, grim clamp of a crack. Nina was unhappy each time she disgraced herself, which was often. For instance, she forgot to put on her shoes when she ran out into the garden. She swore in Vietnamese when Mlle. Berthe combed out the curls of her permanent wave. She told Mlle. Berthe that she preferred the Trung sisters to *Lettres de Mon Moulin,* which bored her rigid. Unfortunately, all these offenses, reported by Mlle. Berthe, infuriated her mother, who wondered each time if the child were past rescuing. (Ariane was always alert for any overdone compliments from friends about her daughter's "lovely, wavy hair," or "fine eyes," but on the whole her looks were pleasing even if her manners were not.)

To expose the child to *de petits français,* Ariane sometimes took her along to tea or aperitifs with her friends. This stopped after Nina knocked out the two front teeth of one young host, a boy named Daniel Jouvet.

The horrified parents heard only Nina's scream of rage. "*Je suis française!*" Then a crash.

Ariane carried Nina away while the blubbering Daniel was comforted by his parents, and a maid wiped the blood from the floor. Icy silence filled the limousine on the way home; Mlle. Berthe made the pink O even smaller and looked out the window.

Ariane attacked in the privacy of Nina's room. "You're a barbarian! A disgrace! How can I hope to bring you up like a lady when you behave like an Annamite street arab?"

Nina protested that the two teeth had already been loose . . . that Daniel had been wobbling them shortly before.

"I'm not interested in excuses!" said Ariane. "You have embarrassed me beyond belief. The Jouvets will think I let you run wild with the servants."

She feared secretly that her friends were only waiting for Nina to do something uncouth like kick her shoes off at the table, or spit, and betray her "other side."

"I shall leave you to think about it. If you're lucky, I won't tell your father." She slammed Nina's door shut.

Nina glared at the door. It wasn't fair! No one understood her feelings. In this case, certainly not her mother!

Her young host had danced around her wobbling his teeth and calling, "*Jaune! Jaune! Jaune! Jaune!* Yellow monkey face!"

So she had hit him. But the act had not cured the sick feeling he gave her in the pit of her stomach.

In 1945, when Nina was seven, she was more alarmed than unhappy to learn that the Japanese had finally overthrown even the appearances of a French government in Indochina. Ariane's private preoccupations could not blur the panic in the French community when the Japanese interned all French soldiers, police, and civil servants, including Ariane's former employer, Henri Garine.

Then Mlle. Berthe told her that the new Independent Vietnam, as the Japanese now called it, was to be ruled by the Emperor Bao Dai. Since Bao Dai had already been the Emperor of the province of Annam under the French, Nina decided that, *au fond*, nothing much had changed after all. It was only when she learned that the family would not be going again to Dalat for a while that she began to understand the huge changes taking place in her country.

Later that year, she listened to the Allies bombarding Japanese planes at Saigon Airport. From her net-hung bed, safe behind the walls of the big house, the bombs were more distant and less frightening than the annual fireworks at Tet.

She eavesdropped on her mother and her friends to learn what they might be hiding from her. She heard talk of a place called Hiroshima, and much confusing speculation about the attitude of the Allies to the pro-Vichy Indochinese French once the Japanese surrendered. Then, one night, she eavesdropped on a party which turned out to be a jubilant celebration of the rearming of the French by the British General Gracie and the Americans. Once again, as with the Emperor, it seemed to her that the politics of the adult world moved in circles.

She was aware of the denials of the war, but they did not make her unhappy. The Allied blockades against Japanese shipping had meant no imported French footstuffs, but she was happy with Vietnamese food. She did miss the annual holiday at the bungalow in Dalat. She was kept inside the compound like other French children during the riots that followed the Japanese surrender, when many French were massacred by the Vietnamese. Most of the trouble was in the north, however, as the rice famine had been earlier in the year. It seemed unreal to her in the relative peace of Saigon. She observed that her mother was far more agitated when, in October 1945, General Leclerc arrived from France with his troops of the French Expeditionary Corps and set off a flurry of competition among the hostesses of Saigon.

It was a major triumph of Ariane's life that Leclerc accepted an invitation to a ball at her house. As usual during her parents' parties, Nina crouched in her nightdress at the top of the big staircase to spy on the sea of gowns and uniforms that washed through the front hall. The men led with medal-covered chests; the women glittered with prewar beading, though a few wore the wide, swirling skirts that were still fresh fashion news in France. She could not see "Uncle" Emile Carbone, who used to come regularly to their house when she was tiny but had recently disappeared from her life. She did recognize the famous General Leclerc from his photographs in the newspapers—a thin, romantically handsome man who satisfied her expectations completely. She did not recognize the ministers, members of important committees, military advisers, and wealthy businessmen, but she knew they were important by the way they walked and nodded to each other. She was happy to think that such people came to her house; such men bowed over her mother's hand and grasped that of her father with familiarity.

Her mother's golden hair was caught up in a twist; a complicated necklace of sapphires, which Nina had once been allowed to try on, draped itself across the soft hills and hollows of her nearly naked bosom. To Nina, she looked like a film star. Her father was small in the mass of white-skinned giants, but huge to her in his dignity. He wore old-fashioned tails and a white piqué waistcoat just like Fred Astaire's. She watched with pleasure as a

135

tall blond man in American naval uniform ducked his head politely to his host.

When the dancing began, Nina moved with practiced stealth into hiding behind a vast porcelain jar filled with peonies. Ariane had hired one of the big bands that had recently become fashionable in Saigon—Vietnamese musicians playing Western instruments. They struck up "Scarlet Sister Sadie" from a dais set up at one end of the dining room, now cleared of its furniture. Though they played trombones and clarinets, the musicians wandered off into native *gamelan*-style improvisation after a few bars. Nina listened, entranced, as they swept together toward a cadence like a flight of geese coming in to land, then swung up and off in separate directions. The dancers played safe and followed the drums.

Her mother was dancing with an elderly member of the Conseil Colonial. Her father was not dancing, but stood watching his guests with lazy attention. As he turned to speak to an elderly Chinese banker and his wife, who was wearing a long cheongsam and a mink stole, Nina's vision was blocked by two Frenchmen. They paused in front of the porcelain jar to bend their heads to the same cigarette lighter.

"Looks just like a waiter in that rig, doesn't he?" said one, gazing at Luoc.

"At home, dear fellow," said the other, "he would be a waiter. They have a natural talent for it, like niggers have rhythm."

They smoked reflectively for a few moments, watching Luoc greet the cousin of a powerful Laotian *kaitong*.

"Out here," the second man resumed, "they're all pirates, or in our pockets. I wonder which he is?"

"Or they're in American pockets," said the first man. "Like that Frenchman *manqué*—Ho Chi Minh—who's making trouble up north."

They ground out their cigarettes on the polished floor and strolled toward their host. As the three men chatted, a servant offered a tray of drinks. Nina saw the two Frenchmen glance at the servant, then at Luoc, lift an eyebrow each, and smile like conspirators. Without thinking, she left her hiding place and crossed the room in her nightdress to stand at her father's side. She couldn't let him continue to be polite to the two men who were laughing at him. Once there, she grasped his hand and glared up at the Frenchmen, trying to find words to strike them like a whip.

"Who's this, then?" one of them asked.

"My daughter, Nina," said Luoc stiffly, "who is about to go back to bed where she belongs."

She clung to his hand, suddenly aware of all the eyes watching them. Her father tried to withdraw his hand.

"She already knows how to hold on to a man," said a woman's voice, and there was a riffle of laughter.

Luoc flushed. "Go." He spoke quietly but his voice was tight. He knew if he tried again to detach her fingers it would appear comic.

Nina looked up, to explain that she had come to defend him, not to make him look foolish. He looked back with such distaste and anger that she flushed dark red in her turn. She dropped his hand and curtsied politely to him, with her back to the Frenchmen. Then she marched in her nightdress across the endless dance floor and up the stairs with her spine straight and her head high.

Back in her room, she flung herself into Minou's embrace in the safety of the net-hung bed. She did not cry; she felt worse than that. She had failed her father yet again. She was humiliated for him and humiliated by him. She was also angry. Under the anger, she felt something even more uncomfortable—the first thought of disloyalty.

Fortunately, for the next few years Nina was increasingly distracted from the problem of her father by the fascinating and terrifying process of becoming a young woman. First the points of her small, brown nipples became so tender that she had to stop wrestling with François Dorléac, Florent's son, when he came home during the holidays from boarding school in France. She began to enjoy the hours of former torture with Ariane's dressmaker, and poring over her mother's fashion journals. Unfortunately, her breast buds stopped growing as soon as they had become distractingly uncomfortable.

"*Mon pauvre, petit singe*," Ariane said, regarding her fourteen-and-a-half-year-old daughter who stood like a handbell, in a dress with a full, gathered skirt and crinoline petticoat—long skinny handle sticking stiffly out of the bell—while the dress-maker adjusted the hem.

"I sometimes wonder what God has against fashion; He always seems to design us to be out of it!" Ariane laid her polished fingertips on the soft mountains which she had tried to flatten under the crepe shifts of her own youth.

"Never mind, you have lovely eyes."

The child did have promise. Her thick hair curled in obedience to a recent perm. Her smooth skin was the color of *crème fraîche,* with a touch of gold. Her mixed parentage had given her the proportions of a large cat—a leopard or cheetah rather than a domestic tabby. A small, round head with a straight, blunt nose and pointed chin. Ears set neatly against her head. The length of her neck and limbs came from her mother's side and their catlike delicacy from her father's. Her eyes, also catlike, were sloed. Ariane was determined not to let her marry in Indochina. She was no longer impressed by colonial titles which disguised weary *fonctionnaires* and failed to placate their bored wives.

"I have a special reason for getting these new clothes," she said. Her gold bracelets clinked as she sipped her *citron pressé* to create a dramatic pause.

"I am going to take you back to France." She watched her daughter to enjoy her response.

"Maman!"

"Will the mademoiselle have the goodness to stand still just a moment longer?" said the dressmaker through a pinched lipful of pins.

"I don't believe for a minute any of those stories about the French being driven out of Indochina," said Ariane. "I simply want you to have a proper French education. With other French girls. I will take you back myself." Ariane shut her eyes as memories swept over her.

The dressmaker sat back on her heels to wait with resignation while Nina danced on the spot.

"You will see!" said Ariane, partly to herself. "It's lovely there. The sea is wonderful. Windy and rough. You can't imagine what it's like to be cool most of the time!" She smiled at her daughter. "I have only just written to schools. It will take a few months to arrange. In the meantime, you must work very hard for Mlle. Berthe, to become good enough for a place in France. They don't want ignorant colonials there. And I must speak to your father to obtain his permission."

For Nina's fifteenth birthday, Ariane gave her the amethyst earrings that had belonged to her dead French grandmother whom Nina knew only from a photograph on her bedroom wall. For Nina, the earrings were a magic link with the unreal land across the sea which, through her mother, now claimed her as its own. Nina claimed France for herself in an act of faith, rather like the act of faith required of her by the Catholic Church.

In honesty, the two beliefs were slightly muddled in her mind. Like the colonial French and some Vietnamese, she accepted that a kind of holy French spirit had descended on Indochina in the eighteenth century, in very much the same way that Christ took up residence in the Communion wafers and made them into his own substance. In fact, it was even easier to believe in the French than in Christ, because they were so much more in evidence. Each time she shook her head to make the amethyst droplets strike against the soft flesh at the corners of her jaw, she felt in mystic contact with the country that had sent that French spirit. I am coming, she would call silently. Once things are arranged!

For her part, Ariane put off speaking to her husband. However little attention he seemed to pay his daughter, she had noticed his recent speculative glances at the girl after years of neglect. She was certain he would have a view on the project and feared his reply. In addition, Ariane had just begun a new affair with an officer in the French Expeditionary Corps, who had arrived with Leclerc. She was in no hurry to leave, even though the French were now virtually at war with some of their rebellious subjects. A few of her alarmist acquaintances, like the Jouvets and the Pluviezes, parents of Annette, had begun to ship their most valuable paintings and pieces of furniture to France. A few more, like Henri Garine, were moving their money out of Indochina into Hong Kong or Swiss accounts. Most, like Ariane, believed that the troubles would shortly be settled and the hotheads punished, and that life would return to the ease and prosperity that had been temporarily interrupted by the world economic slump of the thirties and by the war.

The troubles were mainly in the north, in any case, near the inciting presence of postrevolutionary China. Like many others, Ariane believed that without Chinese shelter and encouragement, the Vietnamese rebels would be too weak to stand up to the French military might. She thanked the Blessed Virgin for the troubles that had brought André to her, and kept his wife in France. Fighting in the remote north and the terrorist activities in the south, carried out by a few students and the peasants whom they recruited, seemed a small price to pay for the renewed sense of purpose the affair gave to her own life. There was plenty of time to plan her return to France.

In the meantime, she saw that Nina learned to dance. The large number of single men and shortage of single girls guaranteed the girl plenty of practice at parties and balls.

A few weeks before her sixteenth birthday, Nina was in the garden feeding Minou some cashews when her old ayah ran out of the house.

"*Vite! Vite, mademoiselle!* Your father wants to speak to you. In the library."

Nina stood up from the grass so suddenly that the gibbon leaped from her arms into great swinging arcs down her wire. Frantically, Nina brushed at the creases in her full skirt and shook out her petticoats which had twisted around her legs. From old habit, the ayah smoothed her hair and refastened the barrettes that held her heavy dark curls back from her face. Tidy and panic-stricken, Nina knocked at the door of the room which her mother called the library, although it held no books.

Her father sat at a lacquered writing table framed by the window, through which came cool light filtered through the leaves of the simpoh tree just outside. By his right hand stood a cup filled with bamboo-handled brushes; by his left a bronze figure of a birdlike dragon stretched up from its base as if about to take off in flight. In place of books, scrolls hung on the wall. Their vertical columns of Chinese characters looked fierce and male to Nina, compared to the soft, rolling roundness of the Vietnamese script. Two upright lacquered chests stood against one wall. A single peach branch leaned from a heavy vase on a low carved table. The room was an Asian island in a sea of French brocade.

Her father surveyed her curiously as if he had never looked closely at her before. Nina went hot; her mouth went infuriatingly dry.

"Please sit down." He waved her to the carved drum stool by the writing table.

The five paces across the tiled floor felt like five kilometers. She sat, crossed her legs, then hastily uncrossed them again.

"Times are changing," said her father. "We should discuss your future."

"Do you mean the French school?" she said eagerly.

"French school?" His voice was cool but he felt sudden anger. His wife was clearly planning behind his back.

"What *do* you mean, then?" asked Nina, uneasy. Her future had never before needed discussion.

His eyebrows lifted imperceptibly. "Do you never discuss politics with your mother? Or listen to her friends talking about such matters?"

"Oh. That. . . . Sometimes." She stopped, uncomfortably. Her father was, after all, one of the "Annamites" they mentioned in different ways, none of which would be easy to repeat to him.

"Have these friends of your mother's ever said that the French are finished here in Indochina?"

"*Maman* says that all that kind of talk is nonsense."

"She knows nothing." His tone was flat. "Not after all these years. What do you know, yourself? Do you speak Annamese?"

"You know I do!" she exclaimed. He must have seen her in the servants' quarters.

His eyes narrowed slightly.

"Perhaps you didn't realize," she added hastily. "*Maman* doesn't like me talking to the servants anymore. So you might not have noticed...." She froze under his gaze.

"If you had listened more to the gossip in the servants' quarters and less to that in the drawing room, you would not have challenged what I said about the French in such an ill-bred, barbaric fashion."

He did not raise his voice, but Nina felt the power of his anger just as many others had, in equally quiet but equally frightening moments.

"I try to make allowances for your disastrous bringing up," he continued. "In case you do not know, it is ill-mannered to question an elder. When you are ignorant, it is also extremely foolish; you cut yourself off from the source of any wisdom you might hope to acquire."

Nina sensed that he was about to send her away again. "I'm sorry," she said. She lowered her eyes as the servants did, but her voice was firm. "I will try to learn." She raised her eyes to him. "You must forgive me. I did not choose the fashion of my bringing up. Please do not stop talking to me. I need more practice, it seems, in listening to wise people."

Her heart pounded at her impudence. The silence lengthened.

"I should beat you," he said at last. "Only the fact that you are half barbarian and know no better saves you. And the fact that there is some truth in your words. Perhaps I should have begun talking to you sooner." He leaned back and continued to study her again.

She felt the warmth of triumph and a rush of emotion toward him. She knew she had become real in his awareness, not just an inconvenient shadow.

"I must decide what to do with you," he said at last. "And it's not simple. Changes have begun in this country. When the wind becomes great, the little people must become like the grass, and bend. Can you think of yourself as grass? Or have you been convinced that you are a tree towering above the storm? Like all those other French trees."

Though he spoke in riddles, she knew that he was asking the question she had so far managed to avoid asking herself.

"Do you mean which side am I on? Because I'm half French and half Annamite?"

He looked startled. "I wasn't being quite so brutal . . . such directness is alarming. Rather like a stampeding buffalo. I'm afraid I may indeed have left it until too late to talk to you." Nevertheless, he regarded her with interest.

"What is your answer?" he asked.

"Which side has the most right to claim my loyalty?" she asked him in return.

"That's enough!" He stood up, white around the nostrils. "You go too far!"

She ducked her head under his rage and dug her elbows into her lap. If she fled now, it was the end.

"I want more than anything in the world to say whatever would please you!" she said desperately. "But I have to be honest. And I know that you wouldn't be fooled if I lied and said I choose you and your people. Until I know as much from you as I know from *maman*, I cannot choose, because my choice would be an ignorant one."

She felt his energy, like the heat of a fire in the silent room. At last he made a small, dry noise which was not quite a laugh.

"Yes. You are honest. It may kill you one day. But you are honest. And brave, if a little foolhardy. I suppose it could be worse. It's a fair answer."

She raised her head and met his eyes, which were now clear and direct. She imagined she saw approval in them.

He opened the doors of one of the lacquered chests and took two objects from a small drawer behind them. He laid these on the table. One was a photograph of himself, formally posed in white suit and dark tie, against a white backdrop.

"Oh!" she cried, reaching eagerly.

"It's not a sentimental keepsake," he cut her off dryly. "It's for after my death."

She followed his glance toward the other lacquered chest where a crudely painted portrait of a man hung in a carved frame, like a gate between two posts. A bowl of fruit and joss sticks stood before the picture.

"You want me to . . . perform ancestor worship for you?" The words sounded uncomfortable and foreign as she said them. It had been years since she had set out offerings to the spirits with the servants.

His voice remained dry. "I'm glad that your expensive French governess has taught you about the quaint native practices. Don't look so uncomfortable; I don't find it reassuring."

142

He handed her the other object. "Please take this one more seriously."

It was a carved ivory seal. The flat bottom was a circle on which twisted a flamelike dragon bird, like the figure on his desk but coiled on itself rather than reaching for flight. The ivory was clean; the seal had never been used.

"Keep it safe," he said. "The chances are you will need it."

"Why?"

He ignored her question. "It would be simpler if you were a boy, but things arranged themselves otherwise. *Tant pis!*"

He opened an embroidered silk box on his desk and lifted an ink stick from its slot. Then he poured a little water from a porcelain bottle onto his inkstone.

"We will talk again," he said. "I must now reflect on my choices."

"Must I go now?" she begged. "Please talk to me more!"

"Learn patience," he said. "Become less of a buffalo calf. Learn to hide your curiosity and frustration. To show them weakens you. Please go away now."

He was already intent on grinding his ink stick into the water on his stone.

Nina closed her fist on the carved seal. She opened her mouth, closed it again, and rose to go.

"Say '*Bonsoir, papa. Et merci.*'" The reprimand was gently spoken. He pulled the cap from a brush with a tiny pop.

She repeated his words, her voice heavy with frustration.

"You weren't listening to me," he said. "You still show too much . . . if you choose to be the grass."

"I promise to remember. Thank you, Father."

Their eyes met one last time before he bent to draw his first character.

Nina ran into the garden and snatched Minou off the post at one end of her traveling wire.

"Changes have begun, Minou! I think Papa may begin to love me. He said we will talk again!"

She hugged the gibbon so hard that Minou scrabbled furiously for freedom and launched herself from Nina's head back up onto her post.

Her father's final admonition returned to her; she looked around to see if anyone had witnessed the buffalo calf of the last few seconds.

"Right, Minou!" she said. "You are my witness . . . you and

the Blessed Virgin." She held the photograph and seal for the gibbon to see.

"I swear I will learn what he wants me to learn. I swear I will make the right choice. I swear, above all, that I will make him proud that I am his daughter! I will make him want to love me!"

Soberly, she returned to her room. She slipped the photograph between the pages of her diary and put the seal into the velvet bag with Grandmother's amethyst earrings. Then she sat on her bed, stretching the netting tight as the roots of a banyan tree, to practice composure. She thought of all the things she would say and ask when they talked again. She did not know how long she was going to have to wait.

In 1950, the Americans had given the French ten million dollars to fight Vietnamese nationalists who, the Americans believed, were pawns of the Communist Chinese: the Chinese advance into Southeast Asia had to be stopped. The Vietminh, who had once been trained by America to be guerrilla fighters against the Japanese, now fought the French. By 1951, the guerrilla war had become a standard war. The rebels called themselves an army. Their leader, Giap, called himself a general. They made threatening gestures in the north against French cities, with tanks borrowed from the Chinese.

In 1953, the American Vice-President Nixon visited Indochina to confirm American support for the French. In the spring of 1954, just before Nina's conversation with her father, General de Castris, the then commander of the French Expeditionary Forces, marched north to settle matters once and for all. The French dug themselves into the flat valley floor at Dien Bien Phu. American military advisers objected to the site. They said that it was too near the Laotian border and to the Vietminh supply trails that crisscrossed the Laotian jungle. They complained that it was too close for comfort to the opium fields in the surrounding mountains. These fields now financed Vietminh arms and intelligence, just as they had once financed French arms and intelligence before control of the area was lost. Worst of all, the surrounding hills would offer ideal sites for enemy artillery.

The French command replied that the Vietminh did not have artillery to take advantage of the hills. It was well known that no Viet gun could fire more than three rounds. Nor, they added, did the Vietminh have roads on which to bring in guns. Some French advisers agreed with the Americans that the site was a mistake. The Meo hill tribes around Dien Bien Phu felt bitter because for years the French had allowed the local warlords to cheat them out of a fair price for their opium crops. They would help the Vietminh against the French, said the advisers, and they knew the hills. But De Castris and his officers were confident. They had ten thousand troops in position—Vietnamese, Senegalese, Moroccan, French, and German mercenaries. They had reserves they could call in. The Americans were providing money and supplies. General Giap, the Vietminh leader, would need thirty battalions to surround the garrison, and wings to fly guns into position.

Morale remained high on the French side until March 11, 1954, when sentries thought they heard a faint, metallic chinking sound. Rumors spread that the Vietminh were digging their way up to the perimeter underground. No rumors warned the French that forty thousand Vietminh had taken up positions in the rim of hills overlooking the valley. Nor that many of these had ridden bicycles specially reinforced with bamboo in order to carry heavy loads along the mountain tracks. Nor that these heavy loads were the components of dismantled guns. During the night, Meos from the hill tribes helped the Vietminh haul the pieces of guns up cliffs, gullies, and steep mountain tracks into dugout positions on cliff tips and peaks. The guns were reassembled and trained on the French in the valley below.

The opening bombardment was so devastating that Colonel Piroth, the French artillery commander, committed suicide with a grenade when he realized how badly he had misjudged their enemy. The Vietminh guns kept the French from using their airstrips to land ammunition, supplies, or reinforcements. On March 13, Vietminh suicide squads blew their way through the first of the French barbed-wire defenses.

The French dropped in reinforcements and supplies by air, in showers of drifting canopies which the Vietminh watched from their encircling positions. In response, the Vietminh infiltrated the French airport at Haiphong, which was the base for these airdrops. By wading neck-deep through the sewage system, they avoided the guards and perimeter defenses. They blew up thirty-eight French planes on the ground.

Then came a lull. The Vietminh appealed to the Chinese for help. The French asked the Americans to launch an air strike against the Vietminh positions from U.S. carriers in the China Sea. Neither side got what it asked for. Unassisted, the French dropped a thousand gallons of napalm on the jungle north of their fortress, to try to burn out the enemy. In the meantime, the Vietminh quietly developed the system of trenches and earthworks they had already begun; the earlier rumors had been right.

At the end of March, the Vietminh attacked from these trenches, close to the French perimeter. They continued to bombard the French airstrips to keep planes from landing. Unable to evacuate their wounded, the French were nursing more than a thousand casualties under the surface of the plain. They were fighting in a sea of mud, vomit, and blood.

On the night of May 1, 1954, the French troops waited for the usual bombardment that came before each night's attack. They waited. There was only silence.

Death came in that silence. Ghostly figures rose out of trenches that had been dug right up to the French positions. The Vietminh used bayonets, then knives. The loudest sounds were the grenades thrown by the defenders. Four French strongpoints soon fell—Dominique, Eliane, Claudine, and Huguette. Only outpost Isabelle and the central command redoubt still stood. Supporting French aircraft bombarded the Viet trenches without effect. After more than twenty hours of continuous hand-to-hand fighting, a radio message came: "They are a few yards away...they have broken through everywhere...the Vietminh have reached the general's command post. Farewell." It was over, fifty-five days after the first attack.

The French had been defeated before in earlier conflicts, but this battle was the emotional turning point in the First Indochinese War. The Heavens had deserted the Round Eyes after two hundred years. Ho Chi Minh, the northern Vietnamese leader, Giap, their general, and the French went to the negotiating table in Geneva that summer. The Geneva Conference divided Indochina at the 17th parallel, across the thin waist of land separating the Red River delta in the north from the Mekong delta in the south. The French agreed to evacuate the North, which the Vietnamese already held. A temporary leader was chosen for the South—a Westernized Catholic named Diem—under the supreme leadership of the former Emperor of Annam, Bao Dai, who had also ruled under the Japanese. The Conference agreed that free elections would be held within two years to unite the North and South into one nation, under one leader. South Vietnam refused to sign the agreement, and was supported in this by the United States.

Diem, the new temporary President of South Vietnam, feared that a free election would sweep Ho into power. He kept refusing, therefore, to hold the promised elections. He won strong American support for his efforts to stay in power, because he had a record of avoiding corruption and a known aversion, as a Catholic, to communism. He began to buy himself allies. His brother Ngo Dinh Nhu became head of the secret police, the Can Lao, and set up huge networks of informers to sniff out enemies of the new regime. The Americans offered military advice and began to take over the training of South Vietnamese troops from the departing French. The Vietminh, now known as the Vietcong when they operated in the South, increased their activities. Officially, the North claimed that the Geneva Conference had been betrayed. The French were defeated, but the war continued.

Private wars also continued. Sudden, secret arrests by Nhu's Can Lao and guerrilla raids were perfect cover for the settling of old scores and the opening of new ones. It was neither the police nor the Vietcong who scaled the compound walls around Nina's house one evening in late 1954 and cut the night watchman's throat.

17
Saigon, 1954—The Year of the Horse
(Fixed Element: Fire)

Nina slept. Her long, fifteen-year-old arms and legs were spread as if to embrace the world. Her breathing was shallow and quick beneath the tent of mosquito net. The Paris street she walked in in her dream was lined with windows full of waterfalls. Curious, she placed her palm against one of the sheets of glass, which was obscured by water; her skin burned black, but she felt no pain. How hot the water must be! she thought. She heard the crash of breaking glass, whirled to brace herself against a rush of waves, and found herself breathing hard against her damp pillow.

The next second, her room came alive. It shivered and twitched. The framed photograph of her French grandparents fell off the wall. The sound of its glass breaking was lost in the belching crump of the explosion which blew out the front wall of the drawing room on the floor below, at the opposite corner of the house. It also blew out a Louis Seize settee, three crystal wall sconces, half of the grand piano, and the body of Ariane, her mother. The family's number one boy was later found crawling blinded in the street, and assorted fragments in the neighborhood of the piano were identified as the eight-year-old son he had been training to serve coffee.

Still only half awake, Nina ran onto the landing. The great teak staircase to the ground floor was already blazing. She went back into her room and slammed the door on the flames. Except for the roaring of the fire, the night was silent. The silence terrified her. I should hear the servants screaming, she thought. And my mother.

Ever since the first Vietminh *plastique* had wrecked a Saigon café, she had rehearsed over and over, like many other French children in Indochina, exactly what she would take with her in an emergency. Now, from a shoe box at the back of her closet, she grabbed her secret money box, her journal, the photograph of her father, the velvet bag holding her grandmother's earrings and the carved ivory seal her father had given her.

The first-floor veranda at the front of the house was blocked by a wall of flames. She sprinted to the veranda at the back, above the servants' quarters.

"Tranh!" Nina called. "Tranh! Doi! Number One Wife... Simpoh Flower!"

The huts below remained still.

Heat rushed past her. Flames had reached the top of the stairs and were nosing down the corridor; the edges of the Chinese runner had begun to blacken and curl. She inhaled sharply, then coughed as though she had drawn a lungful of water. The staircase leading down from the veranda into the back compound was blocked by heavy wooden gates at the bottom, locked each night to keep out intruders. She was trapped between the gates and the flame, which were now sliding along the Chinese runner as far as the door of her bedroom.

Nina swung herself over the wooden railing of the veranda and launched herself toward the ground through the ancient bougainvillea trained against the wall of the house. She half climbed, half fell in a crash of branches, and hit the ground bleeding from gashes on her hands, face, and legs.

She still expected someone to come looking for her, as they always did, to explain what had happened and tell her what to do next. She looked toward the servants' quarters for Cook and Doi the gardener, and the young wash ayah, Simpoh Flower. The huts were still, walls and corrugated iron roofs lit by the flames that advanced through the big house. Where were her parents? She remembered the explosion that had woken her; the idea that the fire might not be an accident settled into her brain. She started to run round to the front of the house to see if her parents were there.

Then she saw the back gate of the compound gaping open into the street. It was never left open at night. Now, it was a dark hole framed by flame-lit gateposts, a breach in the protecting walls. The sight made it hard for her to breathe or move her limbs: the reality of disaster flooded through that breach.

Suddenly one gatepost flared bright in the headlamps of a car in the street. She heard a door open, and then feet gritting across the narrow pavement. Then the car door closed again. She ran to the open gate. Inside the rear window of the disappearing car, she saw the heads of two men; between them lolled a third. The third man was her father.

She opened her mouth to scream, "Wait! I'm here. Take me with you!" Then she caught her breath. Something drew her attention from inside the compound. She flattened herself against the wall and slid into the deep shadows behind the giant water jars outside the cookhouse. Then she crouched down to listen.

For a few seconds, she heard only the rumble and crack of the flames and a growing outcry from the street in front of the house. The darkness around her was silent. The servants' quarters were deserted. The message was growing clear to Nina. Fortune was turning against her house. Though the servants had once loved her, they now abandoned her. Where the gods turn away, wise men follow suit. Even the Blessed Virgin could not change such things, no matter what the priests might say. The matter of Fortune was outside Her franchise in Indochina.

Then she heard feet moving across the packed earth inside the compound. It was not the heavy, confident tread of a rescuing *gendarme* or soldier, but stealthy and purposeful. She ducked farther down into the shadows of the water jars. At that moment, a pillow of smoke rolled out of the library window above a carpet of flames and spread among the huts of the servants' quarters. She gasped and choked.

"Who's that?"

A low startled voice spoke from the corner of the cookhouse. "Show yourself slowly," it said. "I have a gun."

Her white nightgown rose behind the water jars like a ghost. Blinded by smoke tears, she heard the footsteps grit closer.

"Mademoiselle Nina!"

She wiped her eyes on her sleeve and peered at the young familiar face of one of their drivers, which stared at her in the dancing light, its bones touched by red glints.

"Martell! Thank goodness it's you! What are you doing here?"

"There's someone over by the house," he whispered. "I thought you were him for a minute."

"Where's *maman*? And my father?"

149

"Don't know," he replied. "I had just dropped him off when I heard it."

The upper floor of the house was now ablaze; the back staircase was smoldering; feathers of flame had begun to brush at the carving of the wooden eaves of the roof. The heat stung their faces.

"I want to go and see who it is, over there by the house," he said. "Will you stay here for a minute?" He suddenly stepped into the shadows beside her. His fingers bruised the bones of her shoulder as his hand forced her down again.

She saw the man moving toward them, silhouetted against the flames. The orange light danced off high cheekbones in a lean face. The dark shadow of a long mustache outlined his mouth and chin. The shoulder strap of his carbine carved a deep groove of shadow into the jacket of his baggy, Western-style suit.

"That's the one I saw," breathed Martell. "I know him. A nasty piece of work!"

"Mademoiselle Nina?" the man called softly. "Are you there?"

Martell's fingers tightened on her collarbone.

"Mademoiselle Nina!" The man might have been coaxing a frightened animal. Nina held her breath.

He disappeared into the cookhouse; they heard him knocking the furniture as he searched. Then he crossed into the washhouse. After searching the washhouse, he prodded with his rifle at the shadows around the single ragged banana tree that grew against the compound wall. Then he went back toward the burning house and vanished from their line of sight.

"Wait!" instructed Martell.

The branch tips of the large trees above the house had begun to glow. Sparks died on the surface of the water jars with tiny hisses of protest.

"I'll bet," said Martell into her ear, "that he comes back this way. That he won't show himself to the crowd in front. You wait."

The man reappeared, suddenly and silently. This time, he moved swiftly past them and out into the dark street.

Martell kept his hand on Nina's collarbone for several minutes longer. Then he went to check the street.

"Right," he said from the gate. "Let's get out of here."

Nina brushed a spark from her sleeve and left a dark-edged hole.

"Come on," urged Martell. "Stick with me. There's too much bad company around tonight."

150

"I must find my parents," protested Nina. A thought struck her.

"Minou! Oh God!...Minou! *Maman* made me leave her on the chain tonight!" She began to run back toward the flame-lit garden.

Martell caught her by the arm, swinging her off-balance. She fell and the sleeve of her nightdress tore away in his hand.

"I have to get her!" cried Nina. "I can't leave her!"

Martell glanced over his shoulder toward the gap into the street.

"There's no time now. We've got to get out!"

She scrabbled away from him along the ground.

"Come on!" he cried, exasperated. "I'll come back for the damned beast. Just *move!*" His urgency reached her; she stopped fighting him.

"I swear it!" he said. "Dear God, will you come!"

She hesitated a second longer, then got to her feet and followed him out of the gate. As soon as they were in the narrow street, she stopped. "Tell me, what's wrong?"

"*What's wrong?*" He gaped at her.

"You're afraid of more than the fire. Tell me what!"

Martell danced like a boxer avoiding blows, scanning the faces which had begun to gather in the back street as well as the big street in front of the house.

"Would the idea of grenades or *plastique* get you moving?" he asked.

"Grenades? *Plastique?*" she repeated stupidly. But she suddenly knew he was right.

"I must find *maman* and let her know I'm safe," she said. "If she's safe...." She was quite certain that her father was gone.

"Others are looking for you too," Martell reminded her. "That man we saw was a montagnard mercenary. You know what that means. If he's not in French uniform, he's Vietminh. I want to get you away in case he's still around. *Then* I'll come back and find your mother. If he doesn't get to her first!"

Vietminh. They had been leaving Saigon alone since the ceasefire after Dien Bien Phu. But up north, where they were officially in control, they were said to be executing all the Catholics... and anyone they thought was a friend of the French. Her mother was French. Perhaps that was enough. For this....

She stared at the fire, numb and disbelieving.

The excited crowd jumped back as a burning branch dropped into the street; a woman screamed.

"Are you coming or not? I'm not going to hang around." Martell pulled at her arm.

Nina went. Once they were round the corner the air felt cool and the fire sounded like a distant waterfall. She had lived in that house all of her life. The girl who climbed onto the pillion of Martell's motor scooter seemed to be someone else.

Clutching her tiny parcel of belongings, Nina followed Martell up the damp, smelly staircase in a three-story apartment building in the native sector between the Cathedral and the Arroyo Chinois, the large canal that cut through the southern part of the city. She picked her footing carefully between the people who sat on the stairs and leaned in doorways, fanning themselves and chatting idly, unaware that her world had just been destroyed. She felt their eyes follow her up through the stink of urine and rotting fruit.

Martell's room was small, at the front of the building, with a balcony overlooking the street. He threw open the heavy shutters of the balcony and lit a paraffin lantern. In its soft yellow light the room looked clean and surprisingly inviting. Its closed door shut out the evil perfume of the staircase.

He had a native wooden platform bed, covered with a thick cotton pad. At its foot squatted a small, voluptuously rounded electric refrigerator. The wood floor was partly covered by a tattered Chinese rug, cast off from a grander house. Around it, the floor had been polished into a complex pattern of highlights by generations of feet following private patterns of business.

Martell's dark eyes gleamed in the lantern light. "Not what you're used to." He shrugged. "But it will have to do for a few days."

"A few days . . . !" she cried. "You're going back to find my mother and tell her where I am!"

"Yes. Yes," he soothed her. "I am."

"What are you waiting for?"

He hesitated, then made a private decision. "I'll go now. But you stay here. Don't go out. Don't show yourself."

She nodded impatiently. Of course she would stay here until she heard his news.

She heard the lock click as he left.

She stood still for a long time, in the middle of the room. She shook her head in protest at what was happening to her. Then she went out onto the balcony.

Sleeping bodies covered the pavement in the street below. Refugees had been pouring in from the Communist North for the last few months, ever since the division of the country, bringing with them stories of mass executions of Catholics. They had soon overflowed the camps set up for them by international agencies and now squatted wherever they could find space. She could pick out the family groups, and huddles of dirty, ragged brats with lice and running sores. Her mother had complained that you couldn't move through the streets anymore without one of them screaming after you for money. She raised her eyes and found herself meeting the level gaze of an old woman on the balcony across the street. The woman looked away and spat, deliberately.

Nina lifted her chin, but her hand unconsciously tried to cover the bare skin of her arm where her sleeve had torn away. She remembered that she was alone in a man's room, wearing only her nightdress, and went back into the room to wait for Martell. How funny, considering everything that was happening, that she should mind what a prurient old ayah might think.

She jumped when his key turned in the lock. When he entered the room he saw her standing on the Chinese rug, expectant as a grenade with a pulled pin.

"No luck," he said quickly, to get it over with. "It's a shambles! People running around in circles. The fire brigade late as usual. The fire's too hot to get into the house. Nobody's seen either of your parents. Tranh's been taken to hospital, but his family's disappeared."

She took one small step forward, then stopped, like a sleep-walker who has lost her way. "What do I do now?" she asked.

"Stay here for the night. I should be able to learn more in the morning when everything has settled down a little."

She considered. "I don't think I should stay here."

"Where else?" he asked.

While international diplomats were arguing in Geneva about the fate of Indochina, the defeated French were sending their women and children home. Nina's friend Annette Pluviez had been one of the first, gone back "home" to Amiens, which she had never seen. Most of her mother's friends whom Nina actually knew had also gone—the elder Jouvets, the Montherlants.

She didn't know the names of her father's important friends; they were a blur of faces to whom she had curtsied politely when introduced, if she was introduced at all.

"The sisters at the orphanage," she suggested.

Martell gestured toward the street. "Full up!"

She studied him. At least he was white-skinned and familiar. He was a family servant. She could argue that he should be allowed to continue to serve her until the family was together again and life returned to normal. It was up to her to make sure he kept his place.

"I will stay. Thank you, Martell. Just for tonight."

He grinned suddenly. His teeth were white in the lamplight. "Whatever you say, Miss Nina."

Before she could be certain whether or not she had heard an edge in his voice, her knees began to shake violently.

"Martell, I think I need to sit down."

His grin changed to concern. He took her arm and sat her on the edge of the bed.

"You need a drink."

She tried to tell him not to be ridiculous—she had never touched any alcohol except the occasional sip Ariane had given her to educate her palate—but she was distracted by how far her head seemed to be above the rest of her body. She lay back gratefully against whatever he placed behind her head.

He squatted in front of the little fridge, then brought her a thick, chipped glass. He sat on the edge of the bed and slipped his arm behind her shoulders to lift her up.

She jerked violently away from him, nearly knocking the glass out of his hand.

"Don't touch me!"

"OK, OK," he said soothingly. "I won't hurt you. Take it easy... you're in shock. I just thought you could use a little help. Can you hold it by yourself?"

Her wrist was too weak to hold the heavy glass; liquid slopped over the rim onto her nightdress. Carefully, he placed his hand over hers and held the glass to her lips. The drink was sweet and tasted of limes.

"All of it," he ordered.

She drained the glass and lay back again. The drink had made a warm path through her chest to her stomach. The rest of her body was cold, in spite of the hot night air. Her last awareness was of the light cover that Martell laid over her.

Martell had been born Andrew Martelli, by a Corsican mining engineer out of an English secretary working for Lloyds in Saigon. His parents were engaged, but his father was killed during an uprising at a copper mine in Tonkin before they could be married, and five months before Andrew was born.

His mother was a shy woman who had been grateful for her fiancé's warmth and affection. His death left her with a life purpose—to prove to the tight-knit, censorious, gossiping European society in Saigon that she was beyond all further moral criticism. At work she became obsessive about detail. Outside work she was soon established as one of those women found in the colonies who sit alone in good cafés, dressed immaculately, years out of fashion, smiling nervously to themselves lest anyone think that anything might be wrong.

She kept as tight a rein on Andrew as she did on herself. As a result, he began to leave home by the age of eleven. After four false alarms, when his mother called the police because he did not come home at night, she accepted defeat. He seemed always to survive. She could not face the dreadful embarrassment of the police again.

Andrew loved the streets of Saigon and Cholon; he could entertain himself in them for a lifetime. By the age of thirteen, he had learned not only Vietnamese but the Chiu Chao Chinese dialect spoken in parts of Cholon. He was an expert shoplifter and never paid to get into a cinema. By fourteen he had lost his virginity and was friendly with several fences and black market dealers, for whom he carried packages to earn money. By sixteen, he knew the street price of different grades of opium and which major officials— French, Japanese, and Annamite—preferred boys to women.

Short and slim, he had his father's dark good looks and smiling charm. Using these advantages, he became friends with many of the small number of young single white women who worked, or just lived, in Saigon. From time to time he arranged an introduction between one of them and a wealthy Chinese or Vietnamese with a penchant for white whores. Being short and dark, he could move inconspicuously among the Vietnamese and often acted as go-between for them with Europeans. He gained the reputation in certain circles as a useful sort to have around. He also became convinced that the men who had the fun in life were the ones with money.

Money was power. He saw that equation acted out every day of his life. At eighteen, he accepted the loss of face as a white man working for a *jaune* and took the job of driver for a young Vietnamese businessman. He had heard how the Vietnamese had used his Corsican patron as a stepping-stone and decided to follow his example. He assessed the money and power the man had quietly amassed. He set about making himself too useful to remain just a chauffeur. Then all of his plans seemed to blow apart. Literally.

Now he stared down at his employer's daughter, Miss Hoity-Toity Half-Breed, asleep on his bed. His plans might not have blown up after all.

Nina woke with the sun on her face through the open shutters. She sat up with her usual pleasure at the prospect of a whole new day. Then she remembered. She swung her feet swiftly over the edge of the wooden bed; her bare foot kicked a fat, dirty, padded basket which held a pot of tea from a stall in the street. Beside it, two plantains and a mangosteen sat on a chipped enamel plate. Under the plate was a note which said, ''Sit tight. I've gone for news. Cheers. A.M.''

She sat back on the bed and drew her knees tight against her chest. Her slim arms squeezed the long bones of her shins; her dark eyes stared blindly at a tear in the cover of the cotton pad. Everything may turn out all right, she told herself. Don't imagine things and make it worse. Wait until Martell comes back. She knew she was fooling herself.

She reached for the solidity of the little refrigerator. The yellowing enamel was smooth and cool under her fingertips, except where it had chipped away, leaving black, sharp edges. To distract herself from waiting, she stared around the little room. She had never seen the room of a white man who lived like a native. Daylight showed the dirt and the wear. The rug was stained by tea and food, with a large scorched spot in its center. The walls were dirty pale blue plaster, studded with evenly spaced flies. Other flies buzzed angrily, like tiny telephones, from a sticky gold ringlet of flypaper hanging from the frame of the balcony door. Behind the rattan screen that masked one corner, an expensive suit hung on a padded hanger from a peg in the wall, next to a black, native-style tunic. On a vegetable crate below were piled shirts, native trousers, American jeans, and underpants. Beside the crate was a pair of gleaming alligator shoes and some native sandals.

She went into the tiny, white-tiled washroom. An explosion of movement greeted her as pale little chinchook lizards scattered across the floor and up the walls. Two of them left their tails wriggling on the tile floor to distract their attacker. Besides the lizards, the room held a chamber pot and a large water jar as high as her waist, with a long-handled dipper resting across its mouth. A single tap was poised above the jar; a drain was set in one corner of the floor.

She returned to the main room with an increasing sense of purpose. She opened the refrigerator and regarded four bottles of Tiger Beer and half a lime. After listening at the door for footsteps on the stairs, she knelt to feel in the space under the bed.

Her hand met cool glass. She pulled out three unopened

bottles of Scotch, another of Suntory whiskey, and a liter of Polish gin. Behind the bottles was a rolled-up, tufted cotton quilt. From behind the quilt she pulled out a large, heavy plastic bag. Faded letters on the bag said "American Farm Bureau." Inside she found five bundles of piastre notes, four of French francs, and two of U.S. dollar bills. She didn't recognize the opium pipe she unwrapped from a piece of dirty cloth, nor the lamp. At the bottom of the bag she found eight empty plastic sachets, like the ones buttons or spices were sold in, and a half-empty packet of rice flour in a bright pink and gold wrapper. His gun was not there, the one he had been holding the night before.

She searched between his piled trousers and underpants, then behind the water jar. Suddenly she thought she heard him on the stairs. She stuffed the plastic bag back under the bed, then the quilt, and jammed the bottles after it. She was sitting on the bed as the footsteps continued up to the top floor.

She let out her breath and wondered why he needed a gun to go after information. All at once, waiting became impossible. She went out onto the balcony to see if he were coming and tried to ignore the trickle of fear under her ribs.

Unfiltered by trees and a garden, and unscreened by a compound wall, the noises from the street were raucous and sharpedged. The crowded bodies in the street depressed her. She went back inside and examined the pile of papers on top of the fridge. Under several copies of *Le Figaro* and a three-month-old *International Herald Tribune* she found a magazine, printed on cheap paper, in Chinese. Inside the back cover, which was the beginning, was a photo of a woman in white theatrical makeup, wearing a headdress of silver and feathers and carrying a spear. Apart from that she was naked. Nina turned the pages with shaking fingers and stopped again at a picture of two naked slave girls with chains around their wrists, begging for mercy from a huge man in Tartar costume who was brandishing a whip. She was breathless from shock, temporarily distracted from her fears. She had never seen anything like this before in her life. She couldn't believe that a normal young man like Martell would look at such things. In spite of herself, she turned another page. In the center of a bright blue-green lake, two water nymphs floated above the smudgy surface, holding each other's nipples between finger and thumb. The traveler whom they enticed was shown in silhouette at the side of the page.

The door opened. She slammed the magazine down and whirled, red-cheeked and wide-eyed, to face Martell.

He didn't notice her confusion. He put down the basket of food he carried and began to strip off his sweat-stained shirt without looking at her. From behind the screen, he asked, "Did you sleep well?"

"Yes, thank you." Her pulse slowed slightly. She slipped the magazine back between the papers, started to sit on the bed, changed her mind, and leaned against the fridge.

"What did you find out?" she asked.

"Just a minute . . . till I change my shirt."

A pair of cold pincers crimped the edge of her stomach.

Water splashed on the tiled floor of the washroom.

When she heard him moving behind the screen again, she repeated, "What did you find out?" She felt as if she were sinking down and down into icy water.

He stepped from behind the screen, bare-chested, combing his wet hair. She read his news before he opened his mouth.

"Tell me!" The words came out in a dry whisper.

"Your mother was in the drawing room when the grenades exploded." He crossed to her and reached for her hands. "She was killed instantly."

Nina jerked one hand free and hit him. "Liar!"

Anger flashed in his eyes but was quickly extinguished. "I wish I were."

"Not just badly hurt?" She begged him to change the facts.

"Don't make it harder for me," he said roughly. "I've just been to the morgue. She was DOA . . . dead on arrival."

Nina sat heavily on the bed. Ice water filled her limbs.

"And Tranh's in hospital," he added. "He's blind."

I can make it not be true, she told herself. If I try hard enough. She shut her eyes. But no matter how hard she tried, the new reality remained unchanged. Her mother dead. Her father gone.

She turned onto her side with her back to the room, and curled into a tight ball on the bed. It was too much. Martell waited for her to start to cry, but she didn't. She couldn't. She felt that she had turned to stone. Her back remained still except for the finest movement of shallow breathing under the silk of her nightdress.

After watching the movement of her ribs for a few moments, Martell opened two bottles of Tiger Beer and put one on the bed beside her head. Then he sat on the foot of the bed while he drank his own beer.

After a while, her muffled voice asked, "What about Minou?"

He debated with himself. Finally, he said, "I couldn't find her. Someone must have set her free." It was true in a way.

She sighed and was silent again.

He got up and walked out onto the balcony. When he had finished his beer, he set out food from the basket on two chipped enamel plates from a pile on the floor beside the fridge.

"You'd better eat something. It will make you feel better."

When she didn't move or answer, he squatted down and spooned rice into his mouth.

After half an hour, she rolled over and sat up. The skin of her face was tight over her cheekbones and around the sharp little point of her chin. Her eyes were hot but dry. Her voice was deceptively matter-of-fact. If she let herself feel anything she knew she would start to scream and be unable to stop.

"What do I do now?"

"First of all, you carry on staying here." He cut off her protest. "Nothing's changed since last night, except to get worse."

"Any news of my father?"

Martell shook his head. "Not yet. They still can't search the remains of the house . . . too hot. . . ." His voice trailed off as he watched her take his meaning. "He may be hiding," he added. "Like you should do."

"I just don't understand," she said.

"Think about it." He looked down at his plate. "About who . . . what . . . you are. And what it means in the 'New Vietnam.' "

A rush of heat invaded her coldness.

He still did not look at her. "Stay here."

"I'll think of somewhere else," she said. There were so many new ideas to deal with. The family was not going to return to normal. Her new relationship with Martell was not merely temporary. And she could still see the blue nipples of the water nymphs pinched delicately between another woman's finger and thumb for a man to see.

"It will be safest here," he said.

"It's not right." She met his eyes firmly. "I can't."

Martell blew out his breath like a man who has made a decision. "Nina . . ."

"Mademoiselle Nina!" She corrected him sharply.

He shook off her interruption. "I found Minou last night."

Nina went very still.

"In pieces. They meant her to be found like that. As a warning. It could have been you, if they had found you. Now will you believe me and lie low?"

"No!" she whispered. It was not an answer to his question. "Oh . . . Minou!"

"Stay here. Keep your head down."

"It was nothing to do with her!"

"It's nothing to do with you either," he said grimly. "And a fat lot of difference that makes."

"It's not fair." She didn't hear him. "It's not fair!" Her voice was still quiet, but fierce.

"Huh!" His lips twisted. "You'd better get over worrying about fairness . . . fast."

He put a piece of fish on her plate. "Now, eat."

"No!" she said again. She began to shake her head from side to side. "No! No! No!" She shook her head harder. "It's not fair! Not fair!

No!" The first scream came, at last.

"Nina! Shut up!"

She shook her head in a blind fury as if killing a truth held between her clenched teeth. "*No!*" She screamed the word again. And again.

Martell looked past her to the curious face of the widow on the balcony across the narrow street.

"Stop it!" He tried to hold her.

"*No!*" She hit at his arms and face. He put his hand over her mouth, but she shook it off and screamed again, a long, rising shriek of despair.

He shoved her onto the bed and pinned her with his weight. "For fuck's sake, stop it! You'll have the police in here!"

He jammed one corner of the cotton pad into her open mouth as she prepared to scream again. Her eyes stared at him in shock across the dirty calico that covered the cotton wadding. Then she gagged. He sat up quickly. She threw up onto the wooden floor, then began to cry. Tears fell unhindered to make dark spots on her nightdress.

"It'll be OK," he said. "Come on. . . ." He patted her arm; it was the one that was bare.

She continued to sob.

At last, he thought to himself. At bloody last. If it takes an ape to make her cry, I wonder what it takes to get her to screw.

18
Hanoi and Saigon, September 1954

A small boy of nine or ten years stood rigidly at the rail of the American White Devil ship and watched the city where he had been born disappear around a bend in the Red River. Once it reached the open sea, the troop carrier, commandeered for Operation Exodus, would swing southward to follow the North Vietnamese coastline from Hanoi to Saigon.

The boy refused to cry anymore; he had already dishonored his manliness too often in the last few days. He blinked and rubbed the ache in his head which would not go away. White Devils in uniforms were moving through the crowds on the deck, checking papers and asking questions. Chinchook shrank further into the shadow of a life-boat gantry. He had no papers, and no clear memories of the past week. Instead, he had torn images like half-remembered dreams and the knowledge that he must get to Saigon where he would be safe. If the White Devils found he had no papers, they might send him back.

He gripped the stanchion below the railing, lest he fall down in terror, into the blackness that had veiled his mind like a fallen sail on clear water. For days he had been moving carefully around that blackness, knowing that he must not break through and let out the things hidden behind it. He could not tell whether the churning now in his stomach was hunger or memory. The black veil shifted slightly, and he clung more tightly to the stanchion.

He remembered that he had betrayed his father; he had been too frightened to acknowledge him when he saw him being marched from their house by soldiers of the People's Army. But his father had also pretended not to know him, his son . . . perhaps he had done the right thing after all.

A hot breeze stirred the stubby shock of hair that rose like a cockade from his wide, flat brow. He dropped his forehead against the varnished railing and watched lines of white water fan out from the sides of the ship.

He remembered more. His mother had screamed, "Get out! Go away!" Then she had screamed again, not at him but at the four soldiers who remained in the house. First Sister had screamed also.

He could not run. He stood and gawped like a fool.

His mother turned her head, he remembered, to look directly into his eyes, ignoring the man who lay on top of her.

"Go! By the head of the Holy Virgin Mary and all the saints, will you run!"

And he had obeyed. The soldiers hardly noticed; they were too intent on the two women. When he had stopped running to catch his breath, his knees shook so much that he had to sit in the dust of the alley. He had wet himself like a baby.

161

"Ho will kill all the Catholics when the French leave," his uncle had said. Many others had said it also. It was coming true after all. His father had been wrong. The female White Devil priests who had tried to teach him in school had already fled for their cowardly lives. His uncle had already run with his family to Saigon, in the South.

"They will look after us there," his uncle said. "Their ruler is a Catholic like us. And the American White Devils have promised us land and new homes."

In the alley, Chinchook took off his cheap gilt crucifix. Because of this cross, his family was being punished. He was filled with sudden rage. He threw the crucifix into a drainage ditch. As he did so, he heard gunshots. He froze. In his mind, the sound and his action became the same. He had caused the sounds by throwing away the White Devil magic talisman.

Drawn against his will, he followed the sounds to a public park and joined the crowds which lined it to watch the executions. Chinchook wriggled through to the front. His father waited in the lines of men and women with bound hands who shuffled forward, orderly as petitioners before a lord of the mandarinate. When his father advanced with five other men to face the firing squad, Chinchook fell unconscious among the feet of the watching crowd.

A huge banner was stretched high in the air above the dock in Saigon. In Vietnamese it said, "Good Luck on Your Journey to Freedom." Another refugee ship had docked near theirs. Chinchook had never seen so many people. Exhausted, hungry, and bewildered, he let himself be herded into lines, into groups, from one place to another. He saw people being loaded into open-backed trucks and driven off. Some were waving and smiling, some weeping.

None of the White Devils he saw rushing around shouting to each other had come near the group where he had been crushed for the last hour. He squatted lower, trying to shelter from the pounding sun in the shade of a large basket carried by another refugee. He watched more trucks leave, full of people. There would be no room left for him in the city if he sat there much longer.

Followed by curses, he shoved and wriggled his way forward to where several White Devils talked importantly to one another, making marks on the boards they carried. Chinchook grabbed the nearest uniform sleeve.

"Hey, monsieur! Hi, mister."

"Wait your turn, sonny," said the man.

Chinchook didn't understand the words but the meaning was plain. "Hail Mary, Full of Grace. Blessed art Thou among women..." Chinchook rattled off the prayer in Latin and grinned winningly while his knees knocked against each other.

The American looked startled. "Whadiddysay?"

Desperately, Chinchook tried again. "Our Father Which are in Heaven..." Terror made him forget the rest.

"*Dieu, Qui nourrissait le dernier desmoineau...*" he sang, wildly off key from nerves. God, Who nourished the least sparrow...

That was all he could remember of the grace the nuns had taught him. He could hear the White Devils laughing.

"Go on! Let him through," someone called.

Numbly, not daring to believe that he was safe, he followed a pointing hand to a large shed, where a White Devil stuck a large pin into his arm and then had the effrontery to smile. Then handed him a bar of chocolate. He gobbled it ravenously; it was the first food he had eaten for thirty-six hours. He noticed that everyone who got stuck with the pin received chocolate. Without hesitation, he slipped away from the group of people where he was waiting, and went round to be stuck again.

He had hardly finished his second bar of chocolate when his group was moved on. Before he had time to adjust to the sudden activity after a day of waiting, he found himself in the back of a truck, clutching a parcel labeled "From the people of America to the people of Vietnam—a gift." A red, white, and blue shield on the parcel showed two hands cut off at the wrist, holding each other.

A wonderful full-throated roar of engines echoed Chinchook's silent shout of triumph. Hugging his welcome kit of soap, towel, toothpaste, and evaporated milk, he watched his new city begin to roll past. For the time being, the black veil in his mind was firmly in place.

It was near the end of the monsoon season. When Chinchook's truck arrived, the refugee camp was a vast sea of mud striped by disciplined rows of canvas shelters and edged with disorderly clumps of improvised shacks. Chinchook followed a White Demon in a Windbreaker across a series of planks laid in the mud to a canvas tent where he was assigned the top bunk in a stack of three.

He climbed up onto his bed and looked down on the heaving sea of heads and bodies, all intent on arranging their few belongings into the cramped space. His high bunk felt like an island. He shivered, although the afternoon was hot and humid. He was feeling most odd, and his arm was hot and swollen where he had been stuck twice with the pin.

He sat in a semidoze until someone told him to come for food. He followed the others in his tent to stand in line for a bowl of rice and a piece of fish. Then a female White Devil made him stand in another line with other children to be given a tin cup of milk.

The man who gave him the milk said in Vietnamese, "This is a gift from the American people."

After milk, he was taken to a shed where two White Demons touched and prodded at him and put pieces of metal on his chest and in his ears and made him open his mouth.

He protested when one of them felt the swollen lump on his arm, but the Vietnamese translator told him sharply to stand still or they would not help him anymore. Feeling dizzy, he followed the lines of planks in the mud back to his tent, where he curled up on his bunk, muddy feet tucked against his thin buttocks, and fell into a deep sleep, his first for three days.

The young man in the bunk below woke him the next morning to go and stand in line for rice again. As Chinchook headed back to his tent to eat, two larger boys ambushed him and took his bowl.

When he had gone through the line once again, the Vietnamese nun who was serving asked him, "Where is your bowl?"

"I don't have one," he replied.

"You were given one," she said severely. "Please go and find it. Otherwise I cannot give you any rice."

The woman behind gave him a push between the shoulder blades, and he moved on.

At this rate, he told himself, I will starve to death! He went in search of another food distribution point. He found another line and shuffled through. Instead of food, a White Demon handed him a cotton T-shirt and said, "This is a present from the people of America."

As his own shirt was still damp from the previous day's rain, he put the T-shirt on and felt cheered, though still hungry. It was very clean and white, like the shirt of a rich Chinese businessman. He allowed himself to strut for a while, until he found that he was lost. He trudged up and down the lines of tents, but could discover no landmark to guide him. Every bit of dry space was crowded with the bodies of people who sat or squatted, staring into space or fussing over babies. He found a standpipe where a line of women waited to fill up jugs with clean water. The mud was so deep here that the planks had sunk beneath the surface.

The sun was climbing. The mud began to steam. He decided to find one corner of the camp, then walk methodically up and down each row of tents; he would be certain to find his own eventually. He abandoned the track of planks and struck off on a diagonal through the mud and feces which piled up around the tents. Unexpectedly, he suddenly came across the place where his own food was given out. They were just finishing.

"Please, I am very hungry!" he said to the nun. "My bowl was stolen."

The nun gave him another bowl with some rice, which he ate standing beside her. He was taking no chances this time.

From there, he found his own tent easily. For two hours he sat on his bunk, waiting for something to happen. Once in a while, a White Demon or group of them would walk past, but none of them so much as looked in his direction.

At last it was time to stand in line again for lunch. After lunch he took a walk to see what was happening, but the sun was too hot and there was no shade over the avenues between the tents. He returned to his bunk and slept for an hour.

When he woke, he went for another sortie; this time, he found a sprouting of shacks where families lived together and cooked their own meals over tiny fires in tin cans set in the mud. The people floated on the mud on rafts of broken packing cases, under makeshift roofs of pieces of metal, scraps of canvas, and patches of cardboard.

Chinchook stared from a distance at one family where the mother sat with a tiny boy on her lap, carefully searching his head for lice. An older child, a little girl, was poking scraps of tinder into the minute blaze in a cut-down oil tin, which flickered against the bottom of a teapot. Chinchook swallowed hard and walked away; the sight tugged at the black veil which he fought to keep firmly in place.

To divert his discomfort into action, he stopped a White Demon who was balancing his way along the muddy planks.

"Please," asked Chinchook, "where is my new house?"

The man smiled and squatted down to Chinchook's level. "Sorry," he said in English. "Could you say that again?"

Chinchook stared into the strange blue eyes so close to his

own, and at the red hairs which curled out of the man's chin. The White Demon even had red eyelashes; Chinchook forced himself to stand his ground and not step back.

When he repeated his question, the White Demon raised his voice and called to another, who spoke Vietnamese. The second man asked Chinchook to repeat his question yet again.

"Please, where is my new house?"

"This is your home now," the man said. "We will resettle you as soon as we can." He smiled, as Chinchook had been taught to smile, to cover necessary social falsehoods or embarrassment.

"My uncle said you would give us all a new house and a *paddi* field." Chinchook was testing now.

The second man translated this into English and both men laughed.

Chinchook felt humiliated and angry; it was clear now to him that the promise had been a lie.

"By God, kid, I wish we could!" the American White Demon was saying. "I wish we could." They were both still laughing, but not as if they thought it was really funny.

They are laughing at how gullible my uncle was, thought Chinchook. And me.

"Would you settle for a Hershey bar?"

Chinchook nodded guardedly; he didn't know what a Hershey bar was. He nearly refused, but curiosity got the better of wounded pride.

"Come on, then."

He followed the second man, at a distance, to show his disdain.

The man disappeared into a breeze-block storage shed and reappeared with a bar of chocolate wrapped in silver and brown paper.

"Keep quiet about this, won't you?" he said to Chinchook. "We're running low on stocks."

He patted Chinchook on the head and gave him the chocolate. "This is American chocolate."

Chinchook snatched the bar and ran. He had the measure of the tactics now—first bribery, then humiliation. Angrily, he smoothed his hair where the White Demon had presumed to rumple it.

He crouched in the mud at the side of the nearest tent to unwrap his prize. Suddenly, a blow on his back knocked him forward onto his face in the mud. The mud filled his eyes and blocked his nostrils. He struggled up in a panic and tried to clear his eyes and nose with mud-covered hands. Another blow knocked him sideways against the canvas, but he managed this time to keep his face off the ground.

He lashed out blindly but hit only empty air. By the time he had wiped his eyes, spat, and blown his nose, his attackers had vanished, along with the chocolate.

This is only my second day here, thought Chinchook glumly.

The mud began to dry into a heavy fringe on his lashes and to pull at the skin of his face. The front of his new T-shirt was caked and stinking. After searching for ten minutes he found a standpipe, with its line of waiting women. He joined at the end and inched forward through the sucking mud.

At last it was his turn. He splashed the wonderful clean water on his face and head. The women behind him began to protest.

"If we all wished to bathe, there would be no water to drink!"

"Hurry up, you miniature spawn of a crocodile!"

Quickly, he sucked water from his cupped hands and threw a final refreshing splash over his neck. He would have to wait for the rains later in the day to clean himself properly. Meanwhile, the inescapable stink of his shirtfront made him want to cry. He peeled off the ruined American shirt and dropped it into the mud. He trudged back toward his tent and the safety of his bunk, glaring as he went into the shadows of the other tents. He had had enough of this place. He had to get out.

19

For the next two days Nina hid in Martell's room, buffeted by grief. It would hit her between lifting a glass and swallowing, making her set the glass down again and wonder why it was in her hand. It hit her as she tried to sleep, and left her staring at the shallow moon craters in the plaster of the ceiling, where she could see only flames. When she shut her eyes against the flames, they were replaced by unbearable images of what her mother might have looked like after the grenade had blown her apart. When she did manage to sleep, she dreamed that the lake in Dalat became a sea of fire, from which charring fish leaped and twisted in futile efforts to escape being roasted. And it was her mother in the boat with her, not her friend Annette, as the keel began to smoke and crumble beneath their bare feet. She also dreamed of finding, among the flowers in the garden, a small gray-furred arm, neatly sliced off, still wearing the sleeve of the doll's silk jacket.

When she floundered back toward the imagined safety of consciousness, she found it even more desolate than her dreams.

At least my father escaped . . . I'm sure of that! she would reassure herself, then find that tears were running down her face at the full horror of what she was reassuring herself against.

At Martell's urging, she would sit on the little balcony to breathe fresh air in the evening, but she no longer noticed the crowds in the street below, or their noise and their smells. She was oblivious to the curious scrutiny of the widow on the opposite balcony. She would hug her legs tightly and weep against her knees, or stare unseeing into the leaves of the trees in the street. She didn't even notice the distant bursts of gunfire which brought temporary hush among the crowds below her.

Inside the room she cried uncontrollably—for her mother, for Minou, and for herself. Sometimes she became angry and cried in helpless rage that she could do nothing to alter the truth.

Martell put food in front of her which she did not eat. He offered her drinks which she sipped once, then misplaced, in a room almost too small for the two of them. Martell controlled his impatience. He slept on a mat on the floor by the open balcony shutters. He called her "Mademoiselle Nina," as she had asked. And he waited.

On the third day she startled him by asking, as he served their supper, "Do you know who any of my father's advisers are? People he worked with . . . ?"

He sat back on his heels and rested his forearms on his knees. "Feeling better?"

She shrugged. "Do you know?"

"Why?" he asked.

"I suppose I have to start thinking about what to do now," she said. "You can't look after me forever. Someone must be able to help. . . . We weren't poor. . . ."

He drew a breath. "Don't let anyone know yet that you're alive. That Luoc's daughter is still alive. Don't take that risk yet."

There was a long silence while he watched her push her food around on her plate.

"Hang on," he said. "Be patient. We don't know yet exactly what happened. Or why. Or who . . . but they aren't playing games. If you lie low, I'll help you contact people when I think it's safe. In the meantime, you're not the only one at risk—I'm hiding you, remember. If you do something stupid, you risk my neck too."

There was another silence before she said, "Yes, I see that." Her voice was dull and she would not look at him. She wrapped her arms around her legs and dropped her forehead against her knees.

"I can't bear not doing anything!" she said to her lap; wet tear spots stained the cloth over her kneecaps. "I hate feeling so . . . helpless."

"Would you like to go out?" he asked. "Out of this room? You've been cooped up here too long. I can take you where no one will recognize you. How about it?"

"If you like." She sounded exhausted. It didn't matter one way or the other; the room was not her problem.

"We'll go north," he said decisively. "There's fighting to the south . . . you've probably heard it. The Hoa Hao are giving Diem some problems again. Put on the *ao dai* I brought you yesterday."

She hadn't realized he had brought it. He gave it to her again and waited on the balcony while she put on the high-necked split tunic over full, loose cotton trousers.

"Hold tight! Don't be shy," he cried. The scooter leaped forward into the torrent of bicycles, scooters, and taxis that poured through his street. As he weaved through the little encampments of refugees, she grabbed at his waist to keep from being thrown off. The back panel of her *ao dai* escaped and snapped like a flag in a gale. He braked to avoid a water seller's yoke; the warmth of his shoulder hit her cheek and she couldn't help letting her breasts touch his back. She pushed away quickly and clung stiffly to his belt as he swung between cars and around corners in a smooth, confident rhythm.

Fast as they were going, her mother's death still followed her through the streets. Then a butcher's stall made her imagine Minou, neatly laid out among the cutlets and scrag bones.

They jolted briefly over tram tracks and darted through the obstacle course of taxis outside the Central Station. As they circled Dien Hong Park, he raced a U.S. Army truck to a crossroads but accepted defeat gracefully, in a precisely calculated stop before the upraised, gloved hand of a White Mouse traffic policeman, safe in his ice cream cone pedestal above the wayward traffic. Nina fell gasping against Martell's shoulder again.

By the time they turned down the Rue Catinat, which had just been given a new Vietnamese name by the government, the warm air had dried the dampness on her neck and ribs. They turned north by the park at the bottom of the street where it met the riverfront, and soon left behind the passenger boats on the upper reaches of the Quai le Myre de Vilers, the naval docks on the Quai de l'Argonne, and the Arroyo de l'Avalanche which defined the northern edge of the city.

As they roared and muttered up the road to Bien Hoa, Nina settled more and more into the rhythm of the scooter; it soothed her, eased the pain a little. Enclosed by the sound of the engine, she gazed absently at passing *paddis* and roadside villages. She tried not to remember, among other things, that she should not be out alone at night with a young man, particularly one who happened to be her father's chauffeur. Then a curious thought struck her—there was no one left to care.

Except God and the Blessed Virgin, she reminded herself. Allow me this, she prayed. Both of You. Just this once. I need it. You can trust me.

Martell revved up the scooter even faster; for a brief while Nina felt that they were outrunning reality, leaving grief a short way behind. Martell turned down a dirt track through a small village. Nina fought to stay on the bucking, slithering scooter. Hysterical chickens fled from their path and dogs rioted alongside in delirium. A pack of shouting children accumulated in their wake. When the track ended abruptly at the river, Martell drove straight out onto a wooden wharf, slammed on the brakes, gunned the engine impressively one last time, and cut it. The night was suddenly still.

Martell paid the largest boy among their followers a few centimes to keep the scooter from being stripped of its parts. Then he led Nina down a sagging flight of wooden stairs, across a line of planks resting on floats, to a sampan moored offshore. Ducks clamored for their attention as they passed.

Full with recent rains, the river twitched like a pot coming to a simmer. Nina breathed in the curious odor that comes off the surface of water and stretched her eyes across the openness to the low line of the opposite shore. The distance made her giddy after the small room. In the failing light, a fishing sampan in midstream was poking its long, lashed bamboo snout into the air as it hoisted its *carrelet*. Two smaller boats were rushing out to collect the fish that jumped and danced in the great net.

"Come, sit down," said Martell. "I'm starving."

A woman in an *ao dai* brought a paraffin lantern to the low table where he was already sitting. Then she brought a rough clay jar and two cups. Nina sat on the deck beside Martell and swallowed the rice wine he poured for her. Their lantern threw a path of glints across the surface of the river. Fish sucked little pits in the water from below; moths and mosquitoes had already begun to fling themselves against the lantern, overwhelmed by their passion for brightness. After Nina's third cup of wine, a pleasant numbness took up residence within her, beside her grief which had caught up with her again. She would not have believed there would be room, but there was.

The woman brought them steamed crayfish and crabs with garlic. She brought a squirrel fish, fried so that it curled up to bite its own tail. She brought rice and another jar of wine. As they ate and drank, they heard talk and laughter from the rear deck of the sampan where another lantern threw a strip of light across the water. The diners were Vietnamese, not French.

Martell grinned. "That's why the *ao dai*! The village is government territory by day, guerrilla land by night . . . like that shore over there."

He leaned back against the rail in satisfaction. With his straight dark hair and slim build he could pass as a Vietnamese from a distance.

"It suits you, you know," he said. "You could be a real little *VC-esse*." His eyes were knowing, as they had once been in the rearview mirror of the car he drove for them.

She looked down and smoothed the silk of the front panel over her lap. She was too drunk by now to mind his familiarity.

His sharp white teeth cracked the last crab leg and his lips closed round it to suck out the flesh. She looked away, across the black band of water pricked by isolated lights of boats.

Martell followed her eyes with his own.

"Don't be frightened by what I said. The VC won't bother us as long as we mind our own business. And the scooter's too light to trigger mines. That's why I use it."

He leaned over to pour the last of the rice wine into her cup. "On this road, tonight, the mines are set for lorries and jeeps—full of American 'advisers.'" His eyes gleamed in the lantern light. "Trust me."

She nodded. She felt no fear, only the pleasant warm numbness. She burrowed into it, away from reality, like a sleeper into a morning bed.

On the way home, she leaned her head against his back and closed her eyes. Though not afraid, she preferred not to stare into the darkness beside the road, perhaps filled with the watching eyes of men like the ones who had killed her mother and butchered Minou. Drowsy with wine, she half dreamed that they flew high above the ground, high over the traps and mines which were buried uselessly far below their spinning wheels.

She snapped wide awake and cold sober when Martell climbed onto the wooden bed beside her. "No! Go away!" She couldn't bear for him to ruin her fragile new sense of comfort and safety; it would end soon enough when the wine wore off.

"Take it easy," he said. "I'm just fed up with the hard floor."

She lay stiffly until she heard his breathing steady into sleep. Then she began to feel guilty for having thought so badly of him, after all he had done for her. Balanced on the farthest edge of the bed, she finally let herself fall back into the comforting warmth of the rice wine. She did wake up the next morning, however, determined to start sorting out the pieces of her new real life.

Martell had left a padded teapot again. Under it were tucked some piastre notes. Nina didn't touch them; men gave money only to their wives or to whores. Mlle. Berthe had told her so, along with warnings never to take taxis alone and never to speak to strange men, and along with the assurance that she would suffer unspeakable torment if she ever gave in to temptation.

She dressed quickly in a wrinkled sundress Martell had found in the ruins of the washhouse and went downstairs to the street, without giving herself time to think of his warnings. Outside, the noise and stench were overwhelming. She stood for a time among the colors, in the blinding sunlight, as if she had been ill for a long time and had just begun to recover. This time she heard the distant gunfire above the noise of traffic and shouting voices. Faint as it was, it was enough to poise the crowds in silence for a moment. Then voices began to call again, engines were restarted, saws and hammers resumed.

"The Hoa Hao," Martell had said last night. One of the sect armies. Sniping at government troops south of the city. As she was going northeast toward the European sector, they would have no effect on her plans.

A name had come to her last night, released from the shadows of her brain by the rice liquor. She should have thought of him before. Though she had not seen him for several years, she was certain that Uncle Emile would help her.

She raised her hand automatically to stop a taxi, in spite of Mlle. Berthe's warning, then let it fall. She had no money, and she had left Martell's under the teapot. All she possessed were the amethyst earrings, her father's photograph, five French francs that had been a Christmas present from her grandfather in Cap Ferret, and her father's seal which she had hung around her neck on a piece of string. She began to walk toward the European sector.

"M. Carbone is not at home." The number one boy stared suspiciously at the *métisse* in the wrinkled sundress. "Sorry," he said, and began to shut the door.

"Who is it?" asked a man's voice inside the house.

"Nina Luoc," she called, through the narrowing opening of the door.

"Who?" A European face appeared in place of the number one boy. He was a middle-aged Corsican, of middle height, medium weight, and no outstanding features. His name was Paul Buonaparte and he was Carbone's arranger.

Nina stepped backward toward the stairs down from the veranda. The vehemence of his question startled her. Then he smiled.

"Luoc's daughter?"

"Yes, monsieur. I need to see M. Carbone. But I hear he's away."

The man still peered at her as if in surprise, his lips set in a friendly curve. "Yes," he said, thinking. "He's away. How unfortunate!" He stepped out onto the colonnaded veranda. "Do you have an address where he could reach you when he gets back?"

Nina retreated another step. Something felt wrong. "I'll come back," she said.

"No!" said the man. "I mean, that shouldn't be necessary. Why don't you come in and talk to Mme. Carbone. She's here...." He seemed oddly poised to leap.

She had met Angelica Carbone only a few times, when she was much younger, before Carbone and her father had "argued," as Ariane had put it.

Nina hesitated. "I don't really know her," she said. "It's best if I come back. When is he expected?"

The man looked at her while he thought. "I don't know. I'll have to ask his wife. Step inside while I go and ask." He turned back to the door, then nodded for her to follow. "Do come in. It won't take a minute. And she might want to say hello, in any case."

Nina stood, still undecided. He no longer seemed ready to leap. And it might be rude not to speak to Carbone's wife, now that she was here.

"She won't bite you," the man said. He held the door for her.

Nina crossed the veranda and went into the house. Buonaparte put a hand under her elbow and guided her into a small reception chamber on the right of the hall.

173

"Please sit down," he said. "I'll just go upstairs to get her." He closed the door gently behind her.

Nina looked around. There were two comfortable chairs under the one small window, two bentwood chairs, and a row of hooks on the doorway wall for coats. It was part waiting room and part closet. It seemed odd that he had shut the door of so small a space. She tried the handle. The door was locked.

Disbelief hit her again, but it was mixed with panic. All of Martell's warnings now clamored in her brain. Somehow, in spite of Minou, she hadn't believed him. She had thought that he was exaggerating, or talking of some distant male world that had nothing to do with her. She tried the door again.

It remained firmly locked. She backed off mentally. Pretended that nothing was wrong and that she had merely misjudged how the door should be opened. She turned the handle experimentally in the other direction. The door remained locked. She rattled the handle harder. Through the wood, she could hear someone in the hall. But they did not respond to her rattling. What are the unfrightening reasons why I might have been locked in? she asked herself. But there weren't any.

At that point, she stopped thinking and began merely to act. She ran to the window, returned to put on a thick linen jacket from one of the hooks to protect her chest and arms, forced up the bottom of the little window, and dropped from the window twelve feet into the rose bed below. A gardener squatted a few meters away, with his back to her. He turned and stared, mouth open, as she struggled free from the clutches of two large bushes of Cuisses de Nymphe Emue. Then he recovered enough to shout angrily at the damage she was doing to his plants.

She sprinted toward the front gate. There was a shout from the house behind her. The Corsican's voice. Another man appeared in the driveway, holding the chamois skin with which he had been polishing Carbone's big Citroën at the side of the house. The Corsican shouted again; the driver began to run after her.

The fastening on the gate was a simple hasp and loop; the padlock itself hung open during the day. Now both the gardener and the driver were chasing her. She reached the gate, hauled the lock out of the loop, heaved at the gate, and squeezed through into the street.

Then she ran as she had never run in her life. She was hardly aware of physical effort. She kicked off her sandals and flew on bare feet, darting and dodging through the pedestrians on the residential street, around three corners until she was at last back in the turmoil of a large boulevard.

A traffic light was about to change. She forced herself to a halt and proceeded across the wide street in a dense mass of secretaries, schoolchildren, beggars, vendors, and businessmen. She did not allow herself to look back as she walked sedately across the street; from behind, her heaving chest would not be noticeable.

She did not stop to catch her breath until she reached the Arroyo Chinois. There she sat on some water steps, where she could keep an eye on the street without turning her head unnaturally. She should go straight back to the little room and wait for Martell. He had been right; she should lie low. She should go back and hide. She continued to pant, and let her eyes turn from the street to watch the heavy commercial sampans and high-tailed pirogues slide past each other on the greasy water of the canal. Her nostrils were assaulted by stench from the drainage ditches of shacks in the open spaces between godowns and quays.

The little room held news of deaths and endings. She was trying to reorganize life. After thinking she would die of grief, she had decided that she would survive. She couldn't go back to the waiting, in the hot little room. She would not go backward.

Frightened as she now was, common sense told her that not everyone in Saigon could wish her ill. If she were careful enough, she might somewhere find someone who would lend her money enough to survive until she learned who her enemies were, or found her father, or life in some way returned to normal. It was just a question of remembering Martell's warnings and being careful. Of thinking things through and eliminating risk as much as possible. She decided to consider all her father's acquaintances as risks for the moment.

Twenty minutes later, she had still seen no sign of the Corsican, the gardener, or the driver. She had also thought of the perfect man to ask for help. Annette's father was still in Saigon—he had sent his wife and daughter ahead and remained behind to sell their house and tidy up his affairs. She had been with Annette once to his office and believed she could find it again. The Pluviezes were friends of her mother's, not her father's; they were leaving Indochina. Who better?

She walked close to the walls of the godowns that lined the wharfs in order to stay in the thin line of their shade. In the sun, the pavement burned her feet. She began to wish she had at least borrowed Martell's piastres so she could take a taxi.

Money would not have helped, however; the traffic in the street was jammed solid, horns blaring. She wondered why people had not begun to disappear into the coolness of their homes, now that the worst of the heat was nearly upon them.

The driver of a large truck loaded with wheelbarrows reversed and hit the taxi behind him. The taxi driver opened his door, shouting curses. Nina missed the next stage of the row because a motorbike suddenly roared down the sidewalk, scattering pedestrians and knocking over two pails of flowers that were for sale. No sooner had she dodged the bike than a government army jeep advanced up the sidewalk in the other direction, straight toward the heart of the melee. The three ARVN soldiers gazed down from the jeep at the crowds which parted in silence to let them pass.

Nina followed the jeep. Three streets farther on it stopped a short distance from a barrier of sandbags and barrels blocking the main street. The soldiers in the ARVN jeep regarded six armed men in black uniforms, with the snarling tiger badge of the Binh Xuyen on their berets, who were manning the roadblock between Saigon and Cholon.

20

Vietnam had been plagued for years by fighting between the private armies of the three major sects. The Hoa Hao and the Cao Dai were both religious in their origins. The Binh Xuyen, on the other hand, who were the largest and most powerful of the three sects, began as pirates on the Saigon River. Early recruits were coolies escaped from forced labor on rubber plantations and convicts escaped from Poulo Condore, or Con Son, the Indochinese Devil's Island. They took refuge in the mangrove swamps of the Rung Sat, a vast, swampy area southeast of Saigon. From there, they raided river traffic and collected protection money from boats on the canals serving Saigon. In their early days, the Binh Xuyen were popular heroes among the peasants because, like Robin Hood, they were believed to give to the poor what they took from the rich.

Like the warlords in Tonkin, the sects built up their own private armies of trained fighting men. As they grew in strength, they began to control more and more of the southern delta. Their support was the key to the power and survival of any ruling government. The French and the Japanese both courted them. Different factions of the three sects fought, at different times, for the French, for the Japanese, and for the Vietminh.

In 1955, Diem tried to strengthen his position as President of South Vietnam by buying the loyalty of the Cao Dai. He also bought some of the Hoa Hao. He could not, however, buy the Binh Xuyen. The problem was that the Binh Xuyen could have bought him.

Seven years earlier, in 1948, after the Binh Xuyen had fallen out with their former allies, the Vietminh, the French bought their loyalty and inside knowledge of the Vietminh by making the sect the police force in Saigon. In 1950, the French improved on the deal, and on Binh Xuyen cooperation, by also giving the River Pirates control of all gambling franchises in Saigon-Cholon. Control of prostitution followed. The French also used the Binh Xuyen for important and lucrative roles in their own clandestine opium trade after World War II.

With all these sources of income, the Binh Xuyen had no need of Diem's money; they could not be bought. Diem then asked the Americans for help in cleaning up corruption in Saigon. By corruption, of course, he meant Binh Xuyen gambling clubs, whorehouses, and opium dens. To the U.S.A., it seemed a commendable campaign, worthy of support.

Unfortunately, the Binh Xuyen had grown used to living in Saigon rather than the swamps. They enjoyed their enormous wealth and nearly total control over a major Southeast Asian city. They saw no reason to give up either wealth or power just because their former patrons, the French, had been defeated. They did not see why they should bow to a ruler who was sure, in any case, to be thrown out once the elections were held to unify North and South Vietnam. They turned to the remaining French presence in the Deuxième Bureau to back them up against Diem and the Americans. Certain French officers and former colleagues of the Binh Xuyen in the Service de Documentation Extérieure et du Contre-Espionage, or SDECE, were more than happy to help.

Hostilities began with government attacks on Binh Xuyen clubs; the River Pirates counterattacked. The rifle fire Nina had heard from Martell's room had come from pockets of continued fighting around the city. The Binh Xuyen at the roadblock were letting pedestrians through. They let pass several motor scooters, some cars, and most bicycles. They turned back a taxi with four Americans, several irate Chinese businessmen, and all official government transport. The soldiers in the jeep watched with stony faces but made no move. As Nina watched, a second ARVN jeep crawled up to join the first.

She was searched sketchily and waved through to trudge on toward the office of the distillery where Annette's father worked. As she walked, the cacophony at the roadblock faded into the normal blaring of horns, street sounds, barking dogs, clanking of machinery, and thumping of private electricity generators in the godowns.

"Sit down, mademoiselle. Please sit down."

Pluviez was small, round, bald, and very damp. Anxiety was making the damp patches in the armpits of his shirt even larger. He had a dreadful feeling that this girl, a *métisse* whom he hardly knew, was going to make him feel responsible for her—and he had too much to worry about as it was. Like everyone else, he had assumed until now that she had disappeared with her father.

Nina sat on the bentwood chair by his desk and hid her bare feet under it.

Pluviez called for cold drinks, then went to stand by the window as if looking out for rescuers. Light reflected from his wet, bald forehead and from the end of his pink nose. He took a lavender-rimmed handkerchief from his pocket and wiped his face and head.

"How can I help?" he asked nervously. "Not with lodgings, I'm afraid. You know that Annette and her mother have gone home. It would be most improper for you to stay with a temporary bachelor!" He laughed slightly to underline his levity.

Nina flushed with guilt. "I'm staying with a friend," she said. "Thank you all the same."

"Is it money, then?" He punched the handkerchief back into his trouser pocket with his thumb.

Nina flushed even darker and nodded. This was harder than she had imagined.

"I could manage a small loan," said Pluviez. "Though speaking realistically, it would really have to be a gift. I won't be here much longer myself."

He sat at his desk and folded his plump hands into a wall between them.

"Forgive me, mademoiselle, but I must ask . . . why have you come to me? I hardly knew your father."

That was exactly why she had picked him. "I can't think of anyone else," she said simply.

He pulled out the handkerchief again. "Surely there must be some . . ." he searched for the delicate phrase ". . . some of your father's people who are better placed to help you than any of the French community . . . just now. With things as they are."

He wiped his head again, avoiding her eyes.

Nina sat back in her chair as if he had hit her. She felt an unexpected burning of rage around the edges of her ears and down her neck.

"It is possible," she said, "that some of my father's people burned our house and killed my mother." She swallowed hard against the cold lump of truth in her throat.

"Of course. Of course," Pluviez said quickly. He unlocked a drawer in his desk and pulled out a cash box. "Dreadful! Dreadful business."

He counted out a small bundle of piastre notes. "Here you are," he said. "Will this help? I can't spare much more, I'm afraid. It's expensive closing up a house and moving halfway around the world."

Nina mumbled her thanks and put the money quickly into the pocket of her sundress without counting it.

"Well!" said Pluviez with relief. "I hope things go better for you."

Before he could stand up to end their meeting, Nina spoke hurriedly.

"Monsieur, I wondered if I could trouble you to help in one other way. I need information."

"What kind?"

"I'm trying to find my father."

"Phaugh!" He blew and exploded an imaginary bubble with considerable force. "I'm not a detective, my dear!"

"No, no," she protested. "I don't mean like that. I just need to know things like where he kept his money... what bank. Or the name of someone who might know about his affairs. And where he might have gone."

Pluviez looked at her with a strange expression. "I should go slowly if I were you. I'm not sure that your father's affairs are in a very helpful state."

"What do you mean?"

Pluviez spoke carefully. "It's rumor, of course, like all information these days. But I believe that quite a few other people are also trying to find your father. So far, without success."

He eyed her; she clearly had heard nothing about it.

"Who?" she asked. "The Vietminh? Surely my father has enough friends to... This is Saigon, not Hanoi. Surely..." She saw his expression.

"Not any longer... the friends." Pluviez wiped his head again, hard. "I'm afraid the people looking for him are French. The ones I know about, anyway. But of course, the whole situation is impossible now. With our new President seeing enemies under his bed every night... even if your father were French, it would be difficult."

He leaned forward across his desk. "As it is . . . Are you aware that in the last twenty-four hours there have been at least thirty-two known arrests for political reasons, and God knows how many more besides those? The day before, there were as many. I myself tried to trace an employee who was accused of being Vietminh. No one could show me any records of arrests. The man has simply vanished. How can anyone hope to trace your father in such circumstances?"

"My father wasn't involved in politics," protested Nina.

"My dear, he was a Tonkinese! A Northerner! That would be enough excuse for anyone who was already angry with him. A lot of personal scores are being settled this very minute in the name of national security! Believe me!" He gulped the last of his *citron pressé*. "Why the Americans let the man continue to make enemies like that, I cannot comprehend. The Yanks will soon be the only friends the government has left, at this rate."

"What am I to do?"

Pluviez's tone softened at the sound of despair in her voice.

"Well, *I'm* getting out," he said. "After thirty-five years . . . You must have *some* family in France . . . on your mother's side. . . ."

"Grandfather," said Nina. Eighty-seven and living in a hospice for retired professional men. . . .

"Couldn't I get a job," she asked, "in the meantime?" Whatever the "meantime" might be.

Pluviez performed a despairing laugh. "Do you have any idea how many refugees are looking for work? We have half the populations of Hanoi and Haiphong pounding on our doors every five minutes. They claim to be Catholics, or distant cousins of the President, and think that gives them special rights.

"Furthermore," he continued, "no one is taking on new staff. Not till after those damned elections Ho was promised in Geneva . . . not till we find out what he'll do when he gets his hand on the South. Which he will. It will be sad to see. I put up with it once under the Japanese . . . not again, thank you. Twice in a lifetime is too much for any man!"

With his forefinger, he made a sunburst out of the sticky circle left on his desk top by his glass.

"The British and Americans are welcome to the mess here," he said. "Of course, if they had helped us when we asked— *begged* them—during Dien Bien Phu, there wouldn't be any mess! An air strike was all we needed to send those peasants back into the jungle. The U.S.A. even had carriers in position."

"I'd be willing to try anything," cried Nina. "I must live somehow!"

Pluviez wiped away the sunburst with his handkerchief and studied her while he replaced the cloth in his pocket yet again.

"I wish I could help," he said. "Really I do. There is one name, perhaps, that I could give you. A *jaune*—Chinese. Has a high turnover of casual labor, and uses women . . . though it won't be what you're used to. I expect he's covered himself both ways against the coming elections, like the lot of them. The Jews of the East, the Chinese!"

He wrote a name and address for her on a scrap of paper, and a note on a piece of headed stationery, which he addressed to "Mr. Ma."

Then he stood up and escorted her firmly to the door, one hand on her elbow.

"Try your luck with Ma—you never know. Is your taxi still waiting?"

"I walked," said Nina.

"My God!" He was horrified. His eyes slid to her feet. "You mustn't do things like that. Here!"

He dug under the handkerchief and produced some coins. "Take these as well. Promise me you'll take a taxi. It's not safe for you to walk around the city alone—a girl of your age!"

He opened the office door. "Give me a few days," he said. "I'll try to make some inquiries, about banks and such. *Au revoir, mademoiselle.*"

She couldn't walk anymore. Pluviez's money, when she counted it, was enough to live on, if she were careful, for one or two weeks if she stayed with Martell. She flagged a cyclo, which was cheaper than a taxi, and gave Ma's address. She leaned back against the cracked leatherette of the lumpy seat, listening to the wheezing grunts of the driver behind her; she felt very, very tired.

They stopped by a large, peeling godown which leaned its top floors over the Arroyo as if admiring its raddled reflection among the oil slicks. Mr. Ma reflected his premises. He wore the jacket of a badly tailored suit over a dirty net singlet and a black *longyi*. Tight eyes in his pockmarked face moved from Pluviez's note to Nina, from her head to her feet, then into the middle distance as he refolded the note precisely on its original foldlines.

"What does M. Pluviez wish me to do? I have no openings for anyone of your distinguished background."

Nina looked at the green plastic plaque proclaiming "Chaussures de Qualité" and tried not to inhale more than absolutely necessary the stink of hides that filled the tiny office.

"I am willing to do whatever work is necessary."

"It would not be fitting for you to sit beside the daughters of whores and peasants," Ma said politely.

"It would be less fitting for me to starve to death," she retorted. She saw her mistake immediately; she would never have said it if she had not been exhausted by the heat nor fighting the beginnings of panic.

Hostility replaced ennui in Ma's eyes.

"May I most respectfully suggest," he said, "that the French look after their own." He handed her back the note.

Desolation sucked at her like the rising tide as she limped away from the godown. By accident, she wandered into a maze of small dry docks and moorings which had been carved out of the canal-side. The sun, now directly overhead, burned into the top of her skull. She turned up a pathway of planks over the mud, which promised to become a lane just beyond a tattered stand of fishtail palms. The lane was empty. All sensible people were indoors, having a siesta until the worst of the heat had passed. She leaned into the shadow of a doorway and found her forehead resting against a faded decal of the Michelin man. The building around the door was solid and three floors high. On impulse she hammered at the door, thereby waking the doorman, and demanded to be taken immediately to the number one White Demon Boss.

Number One White Demon Boss was French, as she had hoped, but also extremely curt. The *métisse* had interrupted his post-lunch hour of peace, and also the large glass of chilled beer which he had not yet even tasted.

"I don't care how badly you want work," he said. "Some things are simply not possible."

"I am a French speaker by birth," she said stubbornly. "I read and write perfectly; I plan to take my baccalaureate."

"How old are you?" he asked suddenly, looking at her closely.

"Seventeen," she lied, and blushed.

"Mademoiselle, I have no doubt that you are educated, but you are untrained to do useful work. There it is—it may be harsh, but it's the truth." He glanced at his beer. "I'm not refusing you out of malice or ill will. But I have more workers now than I can afford to pay. The price of rubber is disastrously low. And as if that weren't enough—if M. Ho wins these cursed elections dreamed up by politicians and theorists in Geneva, he will undoubtedly nationalize French industry in the South. Which

182

we have been building up for more than a century. I can't offer you a job—I'll be needing one soon myself."

He leaned to one side and took a notecase from his pocket. "Would a little cash help?"

Nina started to refuse indignantly, then stopped herself. She wasn't sure that she was any longer in a position to afford too much pride on the question of money.

"Thank you," she murmured, and blushed purple as a mangosteen.

She thought he touched her hand more than necessary to give her the money, but she couldn't be sure because she already had her head down and was running from his office.

Andrew Martell met her at the door of his room. "Where the hell have you been? I thought something had happened to you!" His hair was tousled and he held a half-empty bottle of Tiger Beer.

"I went to see Uncle Emile . . ." she began.

"You *what*? You went *where*?"

"I can't stay here forever," she said tiredly. "You can't think I mean to. . . . Anyway, he wasn't there." Considering his reaction so far, she didn't think she should tell him the rest.

"Are you sure? You didn't see him?" Martell's relief nearly made him drop his beer.

"I just said so," she retorted.

"So what happened? Did you leave a message? Your address?"

"I'm not that stupid," she said. "Not after everything you've said. I wasn't going to leave a message with just anyone."

"Thank God you had that much sense!"

She didn't have the energy to fight, and she needed to think. She crossed to sit heavily on the foot of the bed.

"Did you go anywhere else? Who else saw you?"

She considered, then she met his eyes defiantly. She would not be bullied by their chauffeur, no matter how helpful he was trying to be.

"I looked for a job."

He hit his forehead with his palm in exasperated disbelief. "I don't believe it! First you pretend to listen when I tell you to be careful. The next thing I know, you're out announcing yourself all over Saigon!"

He leaned over and glared at her. "If I'm going to take you on, you have to get a few things straight."

"You're not going to 'take me on,'" Nina replied icily. "As I

183

understood it, the offer was temporary. Which is why I went out today... to try to fix it so you don't have to 'take me on.'"

"You? Fix it?" He snorted his disbelief. "You'd last about three days without me to 'take you on.' You're a spoiled brat who drops her panties on the floor for someone else to pick up. *Fix it!* Don't make me laugh."

He slammed the beer bottle down on the fridge and stomped out onto the balcony. "I'll just have a little look to see who might have followed you home. To *my* apartment."

"If you're that worried about your own neck," said Nina, "I'll leave. Now. Then you won't have to worry about getting into trouble for helping me." She collected her tiny bundle of belongings and marched toward the door.

Martell grabbed her arm. "Don't be stupid."

"Oh, but I *am* stupid. That's what you obviously think. . . . Let me go!"

"Hold on a minute—I didn't mean to shout at you."

"It felt like you meant it." She struggled against his hand.

"I yelled because I was mad, because I was worried. About you. Nina, do you understand what I'm saying?" He tried to make her meet his eyes, but she turned her head away.

She yanked her arm out of the grip of his fingers. "It's 'Mademoiselle Nina,' if you don't mind!"

"Oh, Jesus!" He beat her to the door and slammed it behind him.

She started to follow, then sat slowly back down on the end of the bed. She inhaled deeply and eased the breath out through pursed lips. A few weeks ago she would have thought him presumptuous to imply that he cared for her personally. She explored the raw patches on her toe pads. The world was turned upside down and, after today, seemed likely to stay that way longer than she had expected. She was a fool, an absolute idiot, to rebuff the only person who seemed to want to help her. In fact, she felt ashamed. She wasn't really "Mademoiselle Nina" anymore. Martell had worked for her father; her own authority had been only borrowed, at best. She owed him so much. . . .

When he came back—if he came back after the way she had spoken to him—she would apologize. With that decided she began to feel better.

By the evening he had still not returned. The room was airless and hot, even with the shutters thrown wide. Flies crawled torpidly across her legs, refusing to fly away when she brushed at

184

them. She went to the balcony railing to watch for him. By ten o'clock he still had not returned.

She went down to the street to buy a bowl of noodle soup from a vendor, then lay on the hard wooden bed and slapped at the mosquitoes which had changed shift with the flies. She felt lonely and a little irritated that he was making her wait so long to play her reconciliation scene.

Suddenly she sat upright. What if he didn't come back at all?

She lay down again. Of course he would come; it was his room. She became angrier with the arrogance that had made her say such rude, ungrateful things to him. At last she drifted into sleep.

In her nightmare, her mother's blond hair swirled like waterweed in a rushing current. Then her face exploded. Drops of red liquid began to run along the strands of golden hair, turning them scarlet. The drops flew off the ends of the strands, faster and faster until the air was thick with a scarlet rain. Nina tried to fight off the falling drops but they soaked her, turning her arms and body red. Her mother screamed and screamed from a hole in the red sponge of her face as she fell away, shrinking smaller and smaller. Nina stretched after her with red arms, but the screams grew fainter and fainter; Nina was tied into place and could not follow. She moaned and struggled, then woke to find Martell's arms tight around her.

"There, there." He kissed her face. "It's all right. I'm back. I've got you. Everything's OK. Come on, wake up."

He kissed her face again and her hands, then her shoulders. When he kissed her mouth, she shivered and locked her arms tight around his neck to hold his warmth close.

"Oh," she sighed. "I was covered in blood."

"It's all over now. I've got you," he said soothingly. He kissed her mouth again. She felt his hands move down her body and welcomed the sensations they aroused. These sensations startled and distracted her. Her dream was forced into the darkness at the back of her brain where grief also lived.

His hand reached the meeting of her thighs, under the sundress which she still wore. For the first time in her life, she felt that urgent warmth that overruled reason and good intent. She sighed and raised her arms above her head, abandoning herself to whatever he wished to do. She did not let herself think. She would think in the morning. Now she kept her eyes and mind closed and let her nerves and skin decide her fate.

He unzipped her sundress and pushed the top of the bodice

185

aside. When his lips closed over her nipple, she quivered and lay very still, lost in sensation. When he began to enter her, she had a brief flash of clarity. She tried to protest that she had not meant things to go so far, that what they were doing was a sin. But it was too late. After the quick stab of pain, she relaxed and accepted the new, unimagined feeling of fullness.

He was patient and gentle. In order to be certain of his self-control, he had made love earlier that evening to a secretary from the British Embassy whom he saw from time to time. His forethought paid off. Although it took some time, Nina had the unusual experience of losing her virginity and having her first orgasm on the same occasion.

21

The next morning Nina was appalled. They lay naked together on the cotton pad. Martell's left arm was thrown across her chest. She stared down at the peculiar sight of a man's arm pressing into the flesh of her bare breast. The gamy smell of his dark armpit filled her nostrils and she felt the slide of sweat between their skins as she carefully pulled herself free.

Knees drawn up to her chin, she huddled against the wall and closed her eyes. When she opened them, the bloodstain still smeared the dingy cotton covering of the thin mattress. It had not seemed real at the time; she had hoped that somehow she would wake unchanged. In the faint light that sifted through the closed shutters she stared at the inescapable reality of Martell's naked body.

The damp skin of his arms and legs was lightly flecked with dark, curling hairs. The top of his chest was marked by a dark V-shape drawn by the sun through the open collars of his shirts, which pointed like an arrow down to an echoing V of thick, curly hair that spread up toward his navel from his groin. Nina's eyes moved downward to the strange, damp configuration of flesh which lay softly over his thigh. She looked away guiltily, then back again. It was so different from the tight, pert arrangement of the native toddlers who were the only males she had seen naked until now. Somehow that red and wrinkled object had entered and created the sensations of the night before. The memory of this made her scramble hastily, but carefully, from the bed and put as much distance as she could between herself and the sleeping Martell.

She put on the wrinkled sundress which she found on the floor and slipped out onto the little balcony. She stared down into the already busy street and tried to think, away from the disturbing effect of the body on the bed.

She knew what she had done; a large part of her education had been devoted to making certain of that. She had sinned in the eyes of God and the Blessed Virgin. She had made herself cheap in the eyes of Martell. She had made herself unworthy of the love of a good husband. And she might have made herself pregnant. Worst of all, she had liked it.

She stared blindly at the lower branches of the lime tree growing up from the pavement. The scale of her offense was far beyond any past mischief she had previously had to confront in herself and to confess. She was terrified—of pregnancy and of having become someone different. Someone wicked. Too much had changed too suddenly in her life. She had lost her parents, her home, her pet, her virginity, her self. She no longer knew who she was. She stared at a pair of wrangling sparrows in sheer terror.

She had enjoyed sinning; she could not avoid that truth. The memories rippled up her spine like snakes in the sun. There wasn't room inside herself both for repenting her crime and for the memory of its pleasures. Only one thing was clear; she had to move out. Now.

She went back into the darkened room. Quickly and quietly she collected her few belongings. She avoided looking at Martell.

"Nina?" His voice was warm and husky with sleep. "Where the devil are you?"

In spite of herself she looked at him, raised on one elbow while, with the other hand, he pushed back the front of his dark hair.

"Come back, love. It's much too early."

She could see that he was half erect. He peered more closely at her and sat up abruptly.

"What are you up to?" he asked, his voice suddenly hard.

"I'm going," she said, clutching her small bundle with shaking hands.

He swung both legs over the front of the bed; he was limp again. She avoided his gaze.

"It's my fault," he said glumly. "If I thought it would make you want to run away, I wouldn't have done anything. . . . What can I say? You were crying in your sleep. I only meant to comfort you . . . then you put your arms around my neck and kissed me back. I suppose I wanted to think you wanted me and

I persuaded myself. Do you have any idea how much I've wanted you?''

He stared at her challengingly.

''Andrew, I can't stay. Not now. Not anymore!'' There was a note of pleading in her voice. She accepted that it was her fault—all the more reason to go.

He found his underpants, slipped them on, and stood up. ''Of course you can stay.'' He crossed to her and reached for her hand. ''Are you afraid I can't control myself?''

She pulled away in panic.

''If you had anywhere else to go,'' he continued, ''I'd let you. For your own peace of mind. Believe me, I understand. But as things are, I can't let you.''

She backed away from his bare chest and warm, wicked smell.

''Do you think I put my pleasure ahead of your safety?'' he asked. He went to open the shutters and let the hot morning sun flood into the room.

Nina saw it glint off the tiny hairs on his thighs before she dropped her eyes to the bundle in her hands.

''You've nowhere to go,'' he said. ''You have to stay here. I'll behave myself. Don't run away.''

She shook her head helplessly. ''It's not just *you* I'm afraid of.''

He lowered his own eyes to hide his satisfaction.

''I'll be strong for both of us.'' He crossed to her again. ''As I should have been from the beginning. I'm older and more experienced . . . will you forgive me? And trust me again?''

''Let go of my hand and put some clothes on,'' said Nina weakly.

He disappeared into the little washroom and she sat down on the edge of the bed.

''Stay!'' His voice carried on over the sound of splashing. ''There's no other choice.''

He reemerged, towel around his waist, hair slicked tight to his head, water drops gleaming from his shoulders and arms. ''Give me that stupid bundle.'' He took it from her unresisting hands. ''The question is, can I trust you not to run out on me again, like you did yesterday?''

He replaced the bundle on the fridge and tossed her a plantain. ''I'm worried about more than just your personal problems. Things have started to get hot in the city. The Binh Xuyen closed off Cholon yesterday. The Hoa Hao have been deserting en masse from the Army in the last two days. Rumor says that they're talking to the Binh Xuyen in spite of old feuds. Diem could be in big trouble, unless the Yanks bail him out. I'm going to sniff around a little. I may want to get us both out of Saigon if things really start blowing up."

He sounds so confident and in control of life, thought Nina.

"I haven't heard you promise to sit tight till I get back," he said. He tossed his plantain skin over the balcony into the street. "Promise," he insisted.

"I promise," she said faintly. "Just for today."

He put on a fresh white shirt and tight chino trousers that followed the fine curve of his thighs. Then he placed one hand under her pointed chin and kissed her gently on the mouth.

"Don't panic," he said when she reared back. "No point pretending last night didn't happen. I won't pretend that I regret it, except for your sake. I care for you and I won't let it happen again, until you want it to."

After he left, she sat still for a long time. His kiss had set off another wave of turmoil. She sighed deeply. At least he didn't act as if he had lost all respect for her. Her mother and Mlle. Berthe had been wrong about that. She thought of another reason to stay. If she should be pregnant . . . she swallowed hard against a knife-thrust of panic. What would she do without him then?

She curled up on the bed, carefully avoiding the bloody smear. After an hour she fell into a deep sleep.

The explosion woke her just as the afternoon tipped into the daily monsoon deluge. She lay rigid, heart pounding, not breathing, waiting for the smell of smoke and roar of flames. When nothing further happened, she ran to the balcony door to see if she could locate the source of the explosion. Sheets of water fell from the sky; the spray soaked her ankles as it rebounded from the concrete balcony floor.

Her body began to shake violently. Her brain observed with detached interest but had no power to stop it. She had to sit down on the floor, just out of range of the bouncing raindrops. She felt disjointed, literally, as if bits of herself were swimming apart in space. As if she had exploded, like her mother's face in the nightmare, because there was not enough room inside her to contain everything: her mother's death, her father's disappearance, the fire, her sin with Andrew, the sound of another explosion, and the enormous question of what would happen now.

She held out one shaking arm. The bones seemed impossibly long and fragile, as did those of her legs. She found Andrew's small, blotchy mirror and held it up with shaking hands to seek reassurance in her reflection, but her face looked like that of a stranger. Dark, terrified eyes like a cow buffalo about to be slaughtered. The narrow, pointed chin, like her father's, and the long, slim neck seemed weak, too weak for what she would have to do, sooner or later.

She touched one still-growing breast through the fabric of the sundress; it did not yet feel like a natural part of herself. My body is not yet my own, she thought. How can I give it to a man? How can I make room for him in the midst of everything else? Her shaking lasted as long as the rain. In the stillness that followed the downpour Nina continued to sit on the floor, unable to move, listening to drips from the eaves onto the balcony. I will sit here forever, she thought. Sit here until I die.

After a while, when the drips had ceased and the balcony had begun to steam in the late afternoon sun, that idea began to seem ridiculous. It was clear, when she tried to think, that something else would probably happen. Then it became clear that something else must happen. After a while longer, when her ears began again to hear the voices in the street and sparrows in the eaves, it became possible that she could be the one to make something happen. Slowly, she stood up.

Once she had decided to act, she began to feel more like herself again. More recognizable, less like the terrified buffalo cow. She began by going out to find the source of the explosion, to make it a physical fact and not part of her nightmare. Three streets away she came to a gaping hole in a first-floor facade above a row of shops. The broken railing of the balcony twisted backward down toward the street. One upright bar had embedded itself like an arrow in a tree across the street. An ARVN jeep was parked inside the plastic ribbons that fenced off the building.

"A grenade!" said an excited young man. "I saw it! From an Army truck, right over the balcony railing. Those rooms are a private brothel for Corsican officers of the Deuxième Bureau."

It was run, like all brothels, directly or indirectly by the Binh Xuyen.

"They took out three bodies," said the young man. "All Round Eyes!"

Andrew had been right to say that things were heating up in the city

Then she remembered her promise and rushed back to the apartment, frightened that he would return and find her gone.

* * *

That night, Emile Carbone returned to Saigon, earlier than planned, for an emergency meeting with an officer in the Binh Xuyen; they needed to discuss how the new crisis with Diem's government might interfere with the collection of raw opium. He was particularly afraid that Diem might close down the private charter airlines, owned chiefly by Corsicans, that were the vital link with the northern poppy fields. Carbone also wanted to pursue a possible new friend at court, who had let the Alliance Corse know that Diem was feeling a financial pinch.

The President needed money for grease, if he were to stay in power. And while it suited him to break the Binh Xuyen by cracking down on their opium trade, he—or in any case his brother—could see the potential of keeping at least an unofficial interest in the trade and its enormous profits. If the trade were to remain illegal, once the Binh Xuyen were humbled, the income from licenses was lost. Unless such things were arranged privately.

Carbone understood that the American position on drugs was punitive. It put Diem in a difficult position. There were always ways around such difficulties, however, and Carbone intended to be the one to suggest them to the new regime.

He did not learn at first that Nina had been to his house. Buonaparte hesitated to confess that he had had her and let her get away. Then he decided, correctly, that the danger of Carbone's learning from the servants was too great, and he confessed.

Carbone was polite to Buonaparte; the man didn't usually make such mistakes. "Now that we know she's here in the city, we can find her. You find her, Paul. If you do, I'll forgive you." He smiled to show it was a joke.

The bombing of the Corsican brothel three streets away had frightened Andrew even more than it had Nina. He began making plans to leave Saigon. As soon as he went out the next day, to start sorting out their travel plans, Nina went back to see Pluviez.

There was now a sandbagged machine-gun emplacement at the Binh Xuyen roadblock. Two Vietnamese in chinos and Windbreakers leaned with their hands high against a house while two Binh Xuyen patted their inner thighs and caressed their armpits.

Pluviez was uncertain how to begin. He gazed at the lethargic revolving fan on the ceiling. After they had both watched four revolutions, he sighed.

"Well, mademoiselle, I have done as you asked."

"I'm very grateful . . ." she began. Her heart began to thump.

"Wait before you thank me. It's not particularly good news."

In unison, they sipped from tiny cups of black coffee. Nina

placed hers back on the saucer very, very carefully so it would not rattle.

He gave her a piece of paper. "Here are the names of various associates of your father's, his lawyers, his accountant. All French. And all owed money by him. I wouldn't think they're feeling particularly helpful."

He changed his focus to the dirty windows. "Now, as for his banking arrangements. . . . He dealt mainly with the French-owned Banque d'Indochine, as far as I could discover. Also had a deposit account with the Hong Kong and Shanghai Banking Corporation. It seems . . . just before he disappeared—though they hate to tell you anything—he had begun to withdraw large sums. He virtually wiped out his formerly large deposits. He had also borrowed heavily from various private members of the Office Indochinois de Crédit Mutuel. Several loans were unsecured, which can be arranged if the borrower's credit is good. And his had been. . . ."

He looked at her for the first time since she had arrived. "He had also borrowed from two Sociétés Foncières which were funded directly by the Banque d'Indochine. In other words, when he disappeared he was badly in debt. What's worse, several of his creditors are trying to leave Indochina and need their money. The Court of Appeals has been asked to start urgent bankruptcy proceedings against him. Are you able to follow me so far?"

"Yes," said Nina unhappily. "There's no money left for me to live on."

"Practically speaking, yes," said Pluviez. "Though it's not quite that simple. What it really means is that there's no money *available*—to anyone. Unless he comes back to sort matters out. Or until the court comes to a conclusion on the bankruptcy proceedings. Or until he's proved dead and the disposal of his estate—or what's left of it—becomes legally possible."

"What about our house?" She corrected herself. "What about the property? Could someone sell it for me?"

"Absolutely not," replied Pluviez. "What's left is held as security against one of the loans. If the court rules for bankruptcy, it will be forfeit. Otherwise, it's still his property until he is proven dead."

She tried to drink again from her cup but it was empty. "I don't understand," she said numbly. "I just don't. We had so much . . . or so it seemed."

"It does seem odd," Pluviez agreed carefully. "Others are saying the same." He brushed impatiently at a drop of sweat sliding down from the dark ring of hair that encircled his head like a laurel wreath.

"Isn't there anything left at all?"

"Some capital tied up in his companies. But it's no use to you or anyone while the case is being heard. And even there, certain things coming to light don't bode well."

He looked at her, uncertain of just how much to explain.

"What do you mean?" She couldn't imagine.

"Certain . . . um . . . irregularities," said Pluviez. "Money not where it . . . should be."

"It doesn't feel right," she protested, "for my father to let his affairs get into such a mess!"

"I'm afraid he had the Annamite fault of being overly discreet," said Pluviez. "He chose not to trust his friends and colleagues with his problems, so we, alas, have no way of helping you now . . . not that I was actually a colleague, but some of my friends were." He leaned forward severely. "You must understand, mademoiselle, that there was a great deal of French money involved. A great deal, which possibly will never be reclaimed. I feel I must warn you that your father left much ill feeling behind in the French community."

He showed just a hint too much relish. He was making it sound as if her father had chosen to disappear as he had. She knew she must leave before she lost her temper. "Thank you, monsieur, for your time. I am grateful. You must be terribly busy with your own arrangements to leave." She stood up.

Pluviez was relieved. He had not been at all sure how she would take her news; he had been terrified that she would have hysterics in his office and throw herself on his charity again.

And he had warned her about the bad feeling; now things were up to her. He was glad, *au fond*, to be getting out of the stinking swamp that Indochina had become since between the wars, away from men like the father of this half-breed who had so much to learn.

"Could you use a little more cash?" he asked "I could probably manage a little more."

Nina looked at him levelly. This time, she would indulge her pride. Having Andrew to depend on allowed her that luxury.

"No, thank you," she replied. "I hope you have a good trip back to France."

Andrew was waiting when she stumbled, hot and breathless, back into the little room.

"Where have you been?" His dark brows met over his eyes; his bare feet were planted wide and firm on the wooden floor.

"What are you doing back so soon?" she countered guiltily.

"My appointment was canceled," he said. "I came back to check on you . . . see if you were all right. A unit of Binh Xuyen have dug in at the big laundry around the corner."

"I didn't know . . ." she said. She avoided his eyes and crossed toward the balcony, fanning herself. "I can't stay in here every day, day after day. I'm careful, just like you said. It was terrible in here this morning. The rain is late. Doesn't it feel as if something is being wound up tighter and tighter in the atmosphere?"

He caught her by the elbow. "Where did you go?" His fingers touched the nerve behind the bone.

"Ow!" she cried. "You're hurting!"

"Nina . . . !" His voice was ferocious.

She gave in. "I found out where my father banked."

"Jesus!" he said. "You're as bad as the rest of them . . . can't trust you an inch when you're out of sight!"

She didn't ask what he meant by "the rest of them." She did not want to know, and pushed the question out of her mind.

"What did you find out?" he asked.

"The Banque d'Indochine." The anger she didn't let herself feel stopped her tongue halfway to the whole truth.

"Where did you learn that?"

"The father of a friend of mine. His wife was *maman*'s friend. I'm sure he's safe to talk to . . . definitely not Vietminh. He can hardly wait to get back to France!" She met Martell's eyes defiantly.

"I suppose it could have been worse."

"I didn't breathe your name," she said. "Or he would have felt it his unfortunate moral duty to protect my virtue."

Her creamy skin colored slightly.

"A little late for that, eh?" He grinned at her, inviting complicity.

"It's not a joking matter," she said sharply.

"Sorry. Let me give you a beer and make friends again."

He sat beside her where she had perched on the edge of the bed. She drank the cold liquid gratefully.

"Learn anything else?" he asked, after a silence.

She told him. He sucked on his lower teeth. As if he were unaware of it, his hand began to draw a line of fire along her upper arm. "I guess that's that," he said.

"Not quite." She tried to ignore his trailing fingers. "You're not going to like this—I want to go to the bank to confirm that

194

things are as bad as Pluviez said. They might let me have a little money, just to eat. . . . Please stop that!''

"Stop what? This?" His hand had reached the soft inside of her elbow.

"Yes," she said. "Andrew, I can't hide forever. I might as well start with the bank. I would rather know who and what to fear. Anyway, there can't be too many Vietminh working at the bank.''

"You'd be surprised." He continued to stroke her arm. "Tell me the truth . . . for once . . . if I don't agree to let you go, you'll go anyway, won't you?"

"Yes." They both knew it was true.

He kissed the lobe of her ear.

"That's not fair!" She stood up and leaned against the folded shutter by the door. "Please don't tease me. You promised!"

He sighed in resignation. "I'll come with you, then. At least I can protect your back!"

She gave him a grateful look; she had to be careful not to misjudge him. He really did want to help her, in spite of his manner. Her anger slid a little further out of her awareness.

He held her eyes. She went in a panic to lean on the balcony rail. She wanted him, even knowing it was wrong! She was shocked that she could feel such a thing so strongly. No one had warned her, in the midst of all the other warnings, that she would like it so much.

Below her, the family who ran the preserved egg shop on the ground floor had cleared a space among the refugees to set up their lunch table on the pavement under a lime tree. They were just finishing a large communal basin of rice. From an open window to her right came the clicking of mah-jong tiles and an uninterrupted stream of cheerful curses.

She would not give in, she told herself. No matter how unexpectedly pleasant, fornication was a mortal sin. She now understood why temptation frightened everyone so much, including tight-mouthed Mlle. Berthe—it was so real and so powerful!

She nodded guardedly at the old woman opposite. The woman gave a tight jerk of her head before she looked away.

I haven't confessed my sin yet, Nina thought suddenly. I could make love just once more, then confess both transgressions at the same time!

But she was too hard-headed to fool herself for more than a few seconds. You do it or you don't, she told herself firmly. Thank the Lord, Andrew was being so patient and understanding. She knew that men had a much harder time even than women restraining their carnal urges. She couldn't imagine it being harder; the idea was appalling.

Andrew waited in a tiny café in a side street while Nina presented herself at the grille that ran the length of the bank's vast counter. When she was ushered into an office, she knew that she was dealing with a very junior official. The walls were painted rather than paneled. The desk, a varnished utility model left over from the war, was covered by an untidy patience hand of papers.

The young man behind the desk was so slight and fair that his dark suit and gray face made him look like an ill child playing at being adult. His manner was comically pompous, as if to reassure her that he really was of professional weight in spite of his appearance.

"Mlle. Luoc, I don't know what you want me to say, if you know the facts already. The only thing I can add is that the Court of Appeals has now exercised a formal jurisdiction for discharging your father's bankruptcy." He rolled the phrases on his tongue.

"Is that as dreadful as it sounds? I can't really tell," said Nina.

"Absolutely dreadful!" said the young man, whose plastic name plaque said he was André Gidéon. He was relishing the interview. But his relish was excitement at the drama and at his part in it, not sly malice like Pluviez's.

"What does it all mean?" she asked.

Gidéon flipped the pages of the file on his desk, shaking his head. "As far as I can see, everything will go to his creditors. His liabilities were much greater than his assets at the time he disappeared. He still owes us much more than our securities are worth. Of course, we may not have all the information . . . people do tend to spread things around."

"Can you explain those words?" she asked. "Liabilities . . . assets . . . ?"

He did so, then repeated his summary of Luoc's financial position.

"It doesn't make sense!" cried Nina. "My father was too proud!"

"One never knows, with parents," said Gidéon.

"I do! About that, at least." She was emphatic. "He would never let himself be shamed like this."

She thought about something Gidéon had said a moment before. "You did say there might be more. There must be!"

"Ah!" He worried at the edge of his blotter with his thumb.

196

He had doodled a series of large-bosomed women across the dingy paper, and several stick men in boxes. "I only said *might*." He thought a little more, then dropped his voice and leaned forward across the stick men and the yellow varnish. "Anything's possible, of course. But if I were you, I wouldn't even talk about the possibility. I would keep very quiet about it. If something did turn up."

It took her a second or two to realize what he was saying.

"I'd be sacked if they knew I was advising you like this," he went on. "But honestly, you sound as though you need it. The others would manage; it's their business to manage." He was a little breathless at his own audacity. "I don't usually say things like that, but I don't think it matters anymore. Ho is going to nationalize business and industry and replace us all with his own people, if he wins the elections they promised him in Geneva this summer. . . . I can't imagine he'll lose, can you?"

"I don't know," said Nina. "I wish so much that I had paid more attention to these things!" She remembered her conversation with her father, in his library. "My father thought Ho would win, I'm sure of that."

"Did he?" said Gidéon with interest. "What a shame he ran into trouble when he did! A few more months and his debts might not have mattered—been written off as part of a negotiated settlement. I might have been asking him for a job." He smiled. "'Unless they shoot me." He seemed to relish even that. Sprigs stood up from the high tide line of his fair hair. His blue eyes had focused nobly on the far distance as if about to receive a blindfold.

He doesn't believe any of it, thought Nina. It's not real for him yet. It's just talk, like in the drawing room after dinner. *His* home hasn't been hit by grenades

"You wouldn't like to meet sometime for coffee, would you?" he asked suddenly. "It's all right if you don't want to," he added quickly, when she began to shake her head.

"I'm sorry," she said. "I would enjoy it, but I . . ." She tried to think how to put it. "I'm engaged."

"Doesn't matter. Doesn't matter," he said, becoming pompous again. "I'm sorry I couldn't give you more cheerful tidings."

"Oh no, don't say that. You've been very helpful," she said.

"Yes, well . . . don't put it about too much, will you? I'd like to work for the last few months at least."

He unlocked the door to let her back out into the public part of the bank. Then he returned to his office, nodding gloomily to himself.

"That's it, then!" she said to Martell. "Pluviez was right. There is nothing." She cupped her hands over her mouth as if to push the words back and stared at the tabletop.

He ordered two Pernods. "Do you good to get sloshed. Cheers."

"I must keep a clear head," she protested, but she swallowed a warming gulp. "I have to decide what to do now."

"Marry me," said Martell.

She set down her drink so hard that it slopped onto the tabletop and the front of her dress. Her stomach jumped a foot and dropped again.

"What?"

"The right answer is, 'Yes, darling, of course.'"

"Are you serious?" Her voice sounded strange in her ears.

He was indignant. "Do you think I would joke about it?"

She met his eyes for a long look. "No," she said at last. The front of her dress was jumping slightly over her heart.

"I'll understand if you say no. 'Miss Nina' and an ex-servant."

"For God's sake, Andrew, do you think that still matters to me?" It was her turn to sound indignant. "You're the only decent human being I can count on in the whole world."

He closed a strong hand around her wrist like a bracelet. "I'd like you to carry on counting on me."

"I'd like it too," she said faintly.

He looked delighted. "Guess I'm stuck with you, then... daughter of a bankrupt. Without the foggiest idea how to cook or keep house. At least you can't say I'm after your money!"

"Do you love me?" She leaned forward urgently, cutting across his banter. "You haven't ever said."

"No, I'm just temporarily batty from lust. . . . Of course I love you!"

He dropped his voice and picked up both her hands. "More important, do you love me?"

Yes, she thought with surprise. I suppose I do. Yes. She nodded mutely.

That night, he kissed her tenderly and went to sleep on his usual mat on the floor. Her last suspicions died. She knew from Mlle. Berthe that men often promised marriage in order to be allowed to make love. A lot of babies had been born to fiancées.

* * *

They were married twice, once in a civil ceremony and a second time in a small chapel in Cholon by Father St. Matthew, a Vietnamese. Nina used her Viet name, Le Thuyet, and lied about her age.

For their honeymoon, Andrew had planned to stay in a bungalow in the countryside south of Saigon, near the sea. But the day before they were married, members of the Cao Dai sect murdered two Americans—agricultural advisers who had been studying the irrigation systems and fortifications of a village not far from the bungalow. The murders led to a nagging exchange of hostilities between the sect army and Diem's forces; the area became off-limits to visiting civilians. The peasants continued to transplant their rice seedlings while men in uniform shot at each other in neighboring *paddis*, but Nina and her new husband went back to his little apartment for their first legal lovemaking.

Suddenly, Nina's life had become regular again, though in a way she would never have imagined. At least she thought it was regular. She was unaware of Buonaparte, who was asking everywhere for traces of her. She was unaware of the montagnard, who was doing likewise. She was unaware, though Martell was not, that a lookout had been posted near the burned-out house in case she should return. She was also unaware of Louis Wu, though he had just been made aware of her.

Instead, she obeyed Andrew's emphatic instructions to stay near the little room and threw herself into being a wife. The hostilities between Diem and the Binh Xuyen hit a lull. Andrew postponed their departure from Saigon.

She cleaned the little room, even sweeping the dried tails of the little chinchook lizards from the tiled washroom. She washed the cotton pad on the bed. She threw away the newspapers and the magazine with the blue nymphs. Tired of food from street stalls, she tackled the mysteries of the unused charcoal brazier on Martell's balcony. The old woman on the opposite balcony watched her efforts to get the thing going and began to shout instructions across the street. When Nina completed her first successful red-cooked casserole, she took a bowl to the old woman in thanks.

Her neighbor, a widow, was living alone; her two sons were both away fighting. Nina could not quite gather who they were fighting for; the old woman was far more interested in the progress of her eldest son's wife's first pregnancy. The younger son already had two sons, she told Nina proudly.

"The *bac si* downstairs gave me some medicine for her," the widow said. "Right away, she falls pregnant. You need some?" Her eyes swiveled to study Nina's flat young belly.

"Too soon. Too soon," protested Nina. The idea appalled her. Though she knew it was wrong, she didn't object when Andrew used those dreadful balloon things. He wasn't really Catholic; so perhaps it was all right for him . . . and therefore not her fault. She hoped God would see it that way. But in any case, she was finding less and less time these days to worry about His opinion on things.

She kept herself as busy as she could; the little room grew lonely during the days and frequent evenings when Andrew had to be away on his mysterious business affairs, which he never discussed with her. When she was alone too much, she began to think about her mother and Minou. She would find herself once again sitting, unable to move, feeling cold in spite of the heat in the room. Then she would force herself to go out, as she had after the rain when the brothel had been hit by a grenade. She tried to escape the ghosts that clamored in the silence of the room by spending hours in the noisy markets selecting pieces of fruit or haggling over the price of small fish to grill on the brazier. She couldn't buy meat, but rushed past the meat stalls with her head down. She knew that she would not see small, gray-furred joints laid out on the wooden planks, but still could not force herself to look.

Sometimes she enjoyed the shouting and cheerful rowing of the markets, and the fact that she could move unnoticed through the crowds, just another slim, dark girl in a worn *ao dai*. She had grown used to the flowing native garment; it was cooler and gave her more freedom than the tight waists and layered nylon petticoats her mother had bought for her. She would imagine herself with her father after they were reunited, walking through the same street together, but not unnoticed—people would ask each other the names of the distinguished-looking man and his charming daughter. Then, every so often, in the midst of imagining or of relishing a pungent smell or dazzle of color, she would be overwhelmed by the truth of her loss. Her mother was dead; she did not even know whether her father was still alive.

Nina was balanced uncomfortably between past and present. The past held her because, in spite of what reason told her, she was waiting for her father to return and sort things out. She could not believe what she had been told about his business affairs. He had always seemed too much in control of life. The level eyes she had met in his study were those of an honorable man, she was certain. She could not believe that he had fled in terror and abandoned her. He was not a man who would run away from trouble. His life had just begun to include her. She had seen the interest in his eyes. She could not stop believing that he would be back to find her and make things right.

She was kept anchored in the present by Andrew and their nights on the hard wooden bed. She spent her days waiting for him, watching from the balcony when she could find nothing further to occupy her slowly increasing energies. Her heart would pound, her thighs would warm when she saw his head among the crowds. She had never, even in her wickedest moments, imagined how wonderful it would be when temptation became OK. Sex with Andrew was a gift in part return for what had been taken away.

But even sex could not use up all her energy once she began to recover from her grief. To escape the empty silence of the little room she began to go stealthily to the center of Saigon, to buy an occasional magazine or book in French. She allowed herself to drift past familiar shops, which had already begun to change from smart French boutiques to servicemen's clubs and fast food restaurants.

One day she allowed herself to wander farther north toward the European sector where their house had been. Secure in her *ao dai*, she drifted closer and closer to her old home, looking up at the trees behind compound walls, peering through open gates at the neatly weeded beds and lawns short as American military haircuts.

Suddenly, with open purpose, she turned into her own street. She admitted to herself that she had been coming here all along. Her breathing quickened. Her palms grew damp. Known, familiar objects filled her with a grateful passion, like a loved face that suddenly appears in a crowd of strangers. She touched the crack in a neighbor's compound wall, knowing the elephant shape of bare stucco left where the paint had peeled. She gazed at a small tree, sprung from the base of its parent, like an old friend. She stepped over an often-jumped gap in the pavement, known from promenades and private rituals with Simpoh Flower for as long as she could remember. She raised her eyes; even the overhanging trees were familiar, though their swags and billows were singed. She might have burst into tears of happiness and loss if she had not looked again and seen the man.

The big gate was padlocked. The man was standing beside it, watching her. He continued to watch her as she approached. His eyes were cold and his face scarred. He was smoking American Camels; a crumpled pack and dead butts lay at his feet. He wore an expensive-looking watch. She lowered her eyes and walked quickly past him and away down the street. When she looked

201

back from the next corner he was still watching her, but he did not follow.

She should not have come. Andrew would tell her she was an idiot, and she knew he would be right. The man had frightened her. She walked for a long time along the river, all the way to the mouth of the Arroyo Chinois, looking behind her for the man's face. Then she followed the big canal toward Cholon. When she was certain she wasn't being followed, she became depressed as well as frightened by the episode. It had reminded her who she was and who she might still become again. Her short period of regularity was over. She had to accept that she would never be satisfied merely to be Andrew's half-breed wife, who waited for him in the little room. She could not forget what she knew; she had been pretending to forget.

She turned in the direction of the Banque d'Indochine. She almost hoped M. Gidéon would be absent from work, but he wasn't. His gray face warmed to a muddy beige when he saw her.

"Mlle. Luoc, what can I do for you?"

"It's Mme. Martell now," she explained quickly. "I just got married."

"My bad luck," he said. "But the offer of help still stands." He smiled.

"I feel ignorant," she said. "I want to understand more about what my father did. I still can't believe he let everything fall apart as everyone claims! I thought, perhaps, if I understood better how it all works, I might either be able to accept it, or find the real reason."

"Find out how all what works?"

"Money," she said simply. "Bank accounts, business, Sociétés Foncières. Debts. Discharging bankruptcy. All those terms you used last time. I felt I understood when you explained before."

Gidéon laughed. "That's a tall order. And not really what I'm supposed to be doing here."

She started to stand up, embarrassed.

"No, no!" he exclaimed quickly. "You misunderstand. I'd love to explain, but it will take time."

His face darkened further. "Why don't we meet for lunch tomorrow? That would give me time to organize some documents to show you as examples...to say nothing of my thoughts. And we wouldn't risk having my superiors breathing down our necks."

"If you're quite sure..."

"Do you know the Café Max? It's not far from here."

"The Café Max?" Andrew would kill her for going somewhere so public and so French.

Gidéon's beige darkened a little more still. "I'm afraid I can't afford the sort of place you're probably used to."

"The Café Max would be lovely," said Nina. No one would be looking for a girl in an *ao dai*; Mademoiselle Nina wore crinoline petticoats and French pumps.

Gidéon looked both flushed and shifty when he arrived at the café the next day.

"What have you been up to?" she asked.

He blinked rapidly several times and his color deepened to mahogany. He sat down and pushed a large document folder across the table at her.

"Look in there!" he said. "I reckon that if it's just a question of time before I get sacked by Ho, I might as well take the plunge. . . . I don't know how criminals do it! I'm a nervous wreck!" He raised a trembling hand to call a waiter. "Those are from your father's safe-deposit box," he said. "I borrowed them to show you . . . and I made a list of his assets. Among other things, he owns three hotels and some warehouses which are let to import-export firms. The rent from those is being held pending the court's decision."

He fell dramatically silent as a waiter arrived to take their order. Then, as they ate their sandwiches, he began to explain that money is only a symbol, represented not just by notes and coins but by certain documents such as banker's drafts. He told her that it could also be represented by assets—things which would have worth if bought or sold, like buildings or machinery, and by debts which you are owed.

She made notes and asked a stream of questions as he took her through the processes of simple bookkeeping and described types of bank transactions.

"Oh, Lord," he said suddenly. "I'm awfully late. We'll have to continue tomorrow."

They agreed on the same time and place.

The next day he brought her a copy of *Accounting for Small Businesses* and the flimsy pages of *The International Wall Street Journal* and *Financial Times*, from which he translated and explained for two hours.

"What are you going to do with all this information?" he asked over a cognac.

"Manage my father's secret fortune when I find it," she replied. They both laughed.

"Hire me instead," he suggested. "Then you won't need to know all this."

"But it's fun," she protested.

Since he thought it was fun to teach her, he did not disagree. "May I walk you home?" he asked. "I'm so late it won't make any difference."

"No, thank you," she said hastily. "I have to shop first. Why don't I walk part of the way back with you?"

Neither of them noticed that they were followed from the café.

Emile Carbone had been enjoying a quiet luncheon of grilled fish with coriander, and a cold beer, when the young man had entered the café. Carbone liked watching people; it amused him during life's inevitable *longueurs*. He also believed that such watching added to those tiny fragments of knowledge that settle unexpectedly into what is called intuition. The young man was clearly up to something. Carbone sat back to enjoy guessing what it was.

Over coconut ice, he thought that he recognized the girl sitting with the young man. By coffee, he was certain he did, but still could not place her. He studied the graceful line of her neck and the neat set of her ears against her head. He was distracted by the arrival of his driver at his elbow.

"What is it?" he asked in alarm. The man never interrupted his meals

"That's her," said the driver. "I'm sure, it is!"

"Who are you talking about?" Carbone was short. He was impatient with disorganized minds.

"The girl who came and ran away."

Carbone went rigid on his wrought-iron chair.

"Can you manage not to lose her this time?" Carbone asked.

"Yes, boss. I'm sure."

"Then follow her and find out where she lives. Don't let her see you. Don't frighten her. Do you understand?"

The driver nodded eagerly.

He wandered idly behind them as they drifted toward the bank, stopping to look into shops. He waited while Gidéon bought Nina a bunch of marguerites from the florist's shop. After they parted, he followed Nina's cyclo to the apartment and noted the address. When he saw her open the shutters onto the little balcony, he left his position in front of the *bac si*'s shop and disappeared into the crowded street.

22

Chinchook slipped out of the camp when the big wired gates were opened to let in more trucks.

"More fools, you!" he muttered to their passengers, all clutching bundles as he had once done. After a moment's thought, he trotted in the direction the trucks had come from. The street was straight and hot under the late morning sun, though a black line on the horizon promised more rain that day. Clumps of one-story houses, formerly separate villages, were linked by shacks like those at the edge of the refugee camp. Every bit of space not occupied by humans was under cultivation. Small patches of yams, melon vines, maize, and banana trees spilled through between flaking stucco walls or were tucked into their angles. The gardens reminded Chinchook of food. He swore at himself for leaving before the midday rice had been dished out.

He was not at all certain where the center of the city was. His stomach ached with anxiety as much as from hunger. As he walked, the buildings became taller, two or three stories, with balconies and arcades at the front. He was headed in the right direction, into the city. He passed shops as well as roadside stalls. Here and there, the smell of food made him pause thoughtfully before he trotted on. He stood so long by an open café terrace watching two men eat grilled fish and rice that the waiter shouted at him to move on. All the stall holders and street vendors seemed to read his mind and glared if he approached them. Since the Partition, homeless children had become a major nuisance, both as beggars and as thieves.

Then he saw his chance. A Vietnamese had left his table to greet two friends who had just entered the same café. While the man's back was turned, Chinchook hopped the little hedge of potted ivies, swooped, and ran, a bowl of noodles in one hand, sliced vegetables and sauce trailing from the other.

He heard shouts behind him and sprinted down a narrow side street, then ducked into an alley between two houses. He leaped over piles of debris, ducked around oil drums filled with rubbish, and finally paused, panting, among the carcasses of dismantled cars in a tiny yard behind a garage. He no longer heard the shouts but shoved the noodles into his mouth, just in case they caught up with him. By the time he was chewing what was left of the sliced vegetables, he had begun to relax. All he could hear was the hiss of an acetylene torch inside the garage and the occasional desultory clang of metal on metal.

After eating, he spent half an hour trying to find a main street toward the city center, but his flight had upset his bearings. Then the rain hit and he took shelter in another shed on the edge of a small canal. He curled up behind a solid mass of bicycles jostled together like bullocks in a pen and fell asleep immediately. He slept heavily until the early hours of the next morning when a dream and the rustling of snakes and rats in the darkness around him shocked him into confused and terrified awakening.

When Andrew came home early on the day of Nina's lunch with Gidéon, she thought at first he had seen her at the Café Max and was angry with her.

"You'll never believe what that stupid son of a bitch has done!" Martell sat on the bed and threw his sandals behind the screen. Nina sighed with relief and clattered the lid of the sand-colored pot as if busy cooking.

'What stupid son of a bitch?'

"Diem. The Little White Knight." Moving fast, he stripped off his sweaty clothes and walked naked into the little washroom.

"He closed the Grand Monde last night. The biggest Binh Xuyen casino. Sent the Army in. The town's buzzing with it! I hear it was a riot—all the gamblers marching out, fat cats next to coolies, trying not to be seen in such an undignified parade. . . . Come and rinse my back."

Water splashed onto the tiled floor as he poured it over himself from the large water jar. His voice continued. "I also hear that the expression on Bay Vien's face—he's the big cheese in the Binh Xuyen—wasn't so funny. He stood there by his Cadillac, eyes burning holes at forty paces, and watched his income going down the drain."

She prodded the charcoal a last time and went into the washroom. As always, the line of his back and buttocks made her catch her breath. He handed her the dipper and raised his arms so she could sluice water over his left side. It ran down his legs in a silvery coat and slid into the drain in the corner of the floor.

"It wasn't enough to take back the opium franchise!" He spoke fast and excitedly. "Now it's gambling profits. I tell you, it's going to be all-out war!"

She shivered. When she was to remember his words later, she would still see in her mind's eye the flick of the chinchook lizard that darted up the wall into the shadows behind the jar as he spoke.

"The Binh Xuyen can't really expect to control opium and gambling if they're also supposed to police them," she said.

"Don't be naïve, sweetie. That's got nothing to do with it." He turned so that she could rinse his other side. "Diem just wants it all back for his cronies. The French gave the franchises away, not him. He could buy back most of the Cao Dai and Hoa Hao with American money, but as long as the Binh Xuyen have opium and gambling they don't need Diem's grease. By taking back the franchises, he can cripple them and use the income himself to buy other allies against the Vietcong."

"He's already got the Americans," said Nina.

"Have we got a towel?" asked Martell. "Who knows? Maybe the Americans want opium. God knows, they're going to need every penny they can get their clutches on to sweeten all the people who would rather they went away!"

He dried himself vigorously. Nina admired the lack of self-consciousness with which he rubbed between his legs.

"And we're going to need every piastre I can lay my hands on to get out of town. There's a blazing battle going on right now across the Rue Catinat. The Binh Xuyen are actually in the Sécurité headquarters. There are roadblocks everywhere with French officers on the Binh Xuyen's barricades and American 'advisers' on the government ones." He threw the damp towel over the screen and began to dress hurriedly, in a pair of clean shorts and a patched shirt. "Damn! I've got to move!"

"There's been fighting for weeks," said Nina. "We were going to leave before."

Andrew pulled the plastic sack from under the bed. She waited while he got out the bundle of piastre notes and counted them silently.

"Fighting, yes," he said when he had finished. "But not like this. Diem can't keep slapping the face of a *grand fromage* like Bay Vien in public and expect to get away with it. Somebody gave him bad advice this time. They underestimated the clout that thug still has. And the friends." He grinned without humor and stuck the gun into his waistband inside his loose shirt.

"I want you to go see a man for me. I've spoken to him already today. At this mooring on the Arroyo." He wrote it down for her. "Think you can find it? Give him his first installment if he agrees to take us tonight. Here." He folded some piastre notes into a dirty piece of paper and handed them to her. "I'm going to collect some money someone owes me. I'll meet you back here in a couple of hours. You should be back first. Start packing . . . not too much. I don't want to look as if we're

207

moving house. Food and a change of clothes will do. If there are any problems, leave a message with the *bac si* across the street." He kissed her quickly and patted her bottom. "You won't go shopping on the Rue Catinat, will you? Tu Do street, I should say. See you later?" He disappeared down the dark stairs.

Nina stared at the line of rice sampans moored along the rickety wharf on the Arroyo. It was still midafternoon and both boats and wharf seemed deserted. She heard distant machine-gun fire again and wondered where Andrew had gone.

"Hello?" she called tentatively. Nothing moved except the rotting waterweed and oil slicks that lapped gently against the pilings of the wharf. She started to climb down a ladder of bamboo lashed to the deck of the nearest sampan.

"Hai!" The harsh shout froze her feet on the rungs. She looked up into the muzzle of an ancient French carbine.

"I'm looking for Mr. Two Boats Lu," she said.

The cold eyes considered her suspiciously. "What do you want with him?"

"Business matter," she replied. "Shall I come up?"

"I come down," he said. And did so, using one hand on the rungs and the other on the carbine.

In the shadow of the wharf, standing on the foredeck of the cargo sampan, she gave him Andrew's note and showed the money.

"You Mrs. Andrew?"

She nodded.

"OK. Come here, this boat, nine o'clock. I go upriver to bring load back tomorrow." He counted the notes Andrew had sent.

"Tell Mr. Andrew there's a new tax, very expensive. Now soldiers too. Not just VC. Very dangerous not to pay."

"I'll tell him. How much should I say?"

"I don't know. We have to talk when we get stopped on the river. Bring plenty."

She climbed the ladder, aware of his eyes watching her, and headed back toward their room. She was halfway over a wooden hump-backed bridge which crossed a large drainage ditch when the first shells were fired.

She heard the faint, distant crump of their launching and the louder explosions as they hit. She tried to tell herself that they were merely a few more of the random shots that the warring factions—Diem's army and his former police force, the Binh Xuyen—had been lobbing at each other for the last few weeks.

But the location of two of the black columns of smoke made her walk faster. Her breath fought through a tightness that threatened to close her throat.

She knew what she would see even before she turned the corner into their street. The sun had disappeared behind a shroud of smoke, ashes fell in heavy flakes, and sparks twisted through the air like lazy flies.

The entire end of their street had been flattened, not just the laundry where the Binh Xuyen had dug in. Their building had been at the edge of the destruction. She stared at a staircase which rose from the rubble to empty space where their room had been. A voice was screaming from under the rubble. People bumped and shouted in panic around her. A few darted at the flaming wreckage in an attempt to rescue family or belongings.

She ran toward the screaming voice, sure that it was Andrew. A veil of flames, transparent but fierce, flickered up from the broken chunks of concrete and twisted sheets of corrugated iron to engulf the remains of their staircase. She jumped back to avoid a burning beam that fell from a neighboring building and rolled into the street where it lay in broken, glowing fragments.

Then she remembered that Andrew had gone out. For a couple of hours, he said. She had been out for less than an hour. The voice, now silent, could not be his. For the second time she watched her home burn, unable to think what to do next. She turned suddenly and began to walk. There was no point in remaining, and she needed to breathe clean air. She was nearly knocked over by a wave of movement as the crowd surged away from another falling beam. As she elbowed her way clear, she searched the faces around her for Andrew's. But it was still too early for him to return.

She had only a few piastres in her bag, not even enough for a proper meal; she had planned to be out only a short time. Everything else had been in the room: her father's photograph, the amethyst earrings. She touched the seal hanging around her neck; thank God, she had started wearing it!

She walked and walked in a daze. Twice was too much; God must have singled her out personally for punishment. She threaded her way through people lying on untouched neighboring streets, and around piles of fruit peelings and human excrement. Sometimes, when the pavement was blocked with makeshift shelters of rags and broken packing crates, she walked in the street.

Suddenly, she turned back, afraid that Andrew's two hours were up and that she had missed him. Smoke was still heavy in their street but now the sun could be seen, weak and distant through the haze. She leaned against the wall under a balcony near the end of the street beyond the worst of the fire's heat and searched for his face among the churning crowd of the dispossessed, the rescuers, and the merely curious. She saw him twice; one man was a *métis*, the other Vietnamese.

She was still waiting for Andrew, squatting against the same wall, three and a half hours later when the sun had nearly vanished down its arc to the west. She fought cold stabs of fear. What if he had returned early and been in the room after all when the shell had hit? Or had been caught up in the fighting in another part of the city?

A truck had already collected the few bodies that had been pulled from the edges of the rubble. The rest of the dead would have to barbecue until the fires stopped flickering along broken beams or erupting suddenly from pockets in the wreckage. Her legs shook with fatigue and her throat was sore with heat and smoke.

Then she remembered Andrew's instructions about the *bac si*. The old man was standing beside his half-shuttered doorway, contemplating the ruins across from his shop. She asked him if her husband had left a message. There was no word.

There was one other chance. She walked back toward the Arroyo. Andrew was not waiting at the wharf either. Nor was the sampan of Mr. Two Boats Lu. She waited for a while by the dark gap of water where the sampan had been, then started to walk back toward their building again. After a few meters she collapsed onto the bench of a food stall. She was amazed that people could continue to eat and drink as though nothing had happened.

"Does the Honorable Madam wish to buy something? I have customers who wait." The stall owner's eyes were colder than his voice.

She rose to her feet and stumbled on. He had reminded her that she needed to count her money. She squatted near the water's edge and surreptitiously looked in her bag. She had so little that she might as well squander it all on the drink of water she needed to soothe her aching throat and to wash away the lump which had lodged in it.

The water seller dipped an enamel cup into one of the huge jerrycans he balanced on a yoke across his shoulders. She sipped slowly; the water was tepid, but cleaner than the sewage-filled canals. She felt suddenly how tired she was. And how alone. Without money, a hotel was out of the question. Every private spare room in Saigon was already filled with refugees. She stared blankly down into the dark, oily water of the Arroyo and tried desperately once again to remember the name of someone she could turn to.

Her eye was caught by a small boy of eleven or twelve, with protruding ears and a stiff cockade of hair rising from his broad forehead. He was removing a bun from the tray of a vendor across the street. Then he deftly rearranged the remaining buns to hide the gap. The vendor was busy examining some coins handed to him by a customer.

The need for one of those buns overwhelmed Nina. She followed the boy along the boulevard and down a side street. She overtook him, then stepped out into the opening of a narrow alley. As he passed, she reached out, seized the cockade of hair, and held out the last of her coins.

"This is for you if you'll get me one of those buns."

He twisted under her hand and glared at her.

"I saw you do it before."

"Bitch," he said, and stuffed the last crumbs of the evidence into his mouth.

"I wouldn't want to get you into trouble," she said. "But I'm very hungry." The sound of his chewing had given her a sharp pain in the stomach.

"Who isn't?" he replied around the remains of the bun

"Please," she begged. "With skill like yours, there's no risk." She offered the coin again.

He eyed her suspiciously and swallowed. She returned his gaze with no hint of mockery. Carefully, she let go of his hair.

"Money first," he said, reaching for the coin.

"You have to be joking," Nina replied.

Back among the glowing braziers of the waterfront he stole two red bean cakes, one each. They ducked into the shadows of another side street, where Nina handed over her last coin. The shadows were almost cool now, in the growing dusk.

"Where do you sleep?" she asked him conversationally.

"With friends."

"Comfortable?"

"Enough."

Nina chewed thoughtfully. In spite of everything, she was enjoying the bean cake.

"Have you any family?" she asked.

His face tightened in the shadows and he blinked several times. He did not reply.

Nina sighed. "My house was shelled today."

The boy looked at her as if he meant to speak, but changed his mind. Their jaws moved in unison for a few seconds while he watched her eyes regarding things he could not see. Then Nina took the plunge.

"I need a place to sleep. . . ."

"How much can you pay?"

"You've already had it."

He stared at the ground. In his experience, few favors were given or received. This lady was asking a big thing of him. He considered her suspiciously, trying to detect possible danger to himself in her request.

She smiled at him with a directness that had nothing to do with politeness or embarrassment; its warmth reached to his toe tips.

"Please help me," she said. "Only for a night. Until I find someone. I won't trouble you, I promise."

Chinchook inhaled; he felt the sweetness of power. He could either give or withhold. This pretty lady needed his help. On closer look, she wasn't so old, either—little more than First Sister would have been, if she were here. Quickly, he blotted out that thought. "OK, come with me," he said.

The wall of the houses closed in as they twisted and turned and ducked under the washing strung across the narrow streets. Many of the houses were damaged by the recent fighting. Stucco walls were pocked by bullets; wooden shutters hung splintered and askew. Some houses had lost entire walls; cooking fires smoked from behind woven mats hung across the gaps. One large family, eating by lantern light, was framed against the back wall of their home like exhibits in a museum.

The boy turned down a narrow passage between two houses. The one on the left had taken a direct hit from a mortar shell; its front had been blown out and its first floor slanted perilously, as if trying to slide into the street. Its slide was stopped only by a single beam which had jammed against the side of the house across the passage. Nina bent low under this beam and followed the boy through a gap in the side wall into what had once been the back room of the shelled house.

What he had called "comfortable enough" was an irregular space cleared in the rubble below the slanting floor above. Two other boys were feeding splinters of wood into a fire the size of a lighter flame, over which they were trying to roast a large rat or small cat. They glanced up briefly and returned to their task. A third, much smaller, boy, however, leaped into a crouch, a knife weaving in front of him like a cobra's head.

"Take it easy, Harvest Mouse," said Nina's guide soothingly. "It's me, Chinchook. And a friend of mine."

The boy froze, undecided, still in his posture of self-defense. The faint light of the tiny fire exaggerated the pouches under his eyes and glowed white where the skin was taut across the bone of his nose. His eyes looked like dark holes in an aged face.

"Put it away," said Chinchook gently. "No need. No need." Under his breath, he murmured to Nina, "Don't worry. I watch him for you."

Neither he nor Nina moved until Harvest Mouse finally sat down again against the rear wall. The dark holes continued to watch her.

Through all this, an adolescent girl sat stock-still, arms wrapped around her knees, staring into a dark corner.

Nina sank into a niche in the rubble.

"Not there!" exclaimed Chinchook. "That's Titi's place. See, there are her bags." He pointed out the shopping bags which Nina had missed in her exhaustion. "She works every night," explained Chinchook.

Lord help me, Nina said under her breath. She stood tiredly and began to clear broken bricks and mortar rubble from the only other space large enough to lie down in, while Chinchook and Harvest Mouse watched. Finally, she was able to lean against the rear wall and stretch her legs. Blood pounded and fibers twitched in the muscles of her thighs. She closed her eyes, not believing that she could now sleep.

The boys had divided up the cooked animal; she could hear them crunching the bones. She listened to the dry rustling of gecko lizards and chinchooks, to the skittering of mice and rats, and to the slower rhythms of house snakes in the rubble. A little farther away excited ducks exclaimed, voices passed, and a car engine was gunned. Even farther away were the sounds of gunfire. She noted them, but felt superstitiously safe in this ruin—it had already been hit. Andrew is alive, she promised herself in a final exhausted thought. He has to be!

She lay full length on the packed earth, slapped at three mosquitoes, and fell asleep.

Nina woke the next morning ravenous. She kept her eyes closed and imagined that Simpoh Flower was just entering her room with a tray of café au lait, croissants, and a slice of papaya with lime juice. The image brought her closer to tears than she liked.

"Good morning! Rise and shine."

She opened her eyes. A woman in her late twenties, no larger than a six-year-old, was perched on a pile of bricks near Nina's legs, swinging her own crossed legs; her tiny feet wore bright red Buster Brown children's sandals. She fanned the morning air with false lashes far too huge for her face. One hand held a plait of thick hair entwined with bougainvillea, in a winsome pose suggesting a mechanic's calendar. A khaki army-issue shirt draped the deformed mountain peak of her left shoulder and fell in an uneven hem around her short but shapely thighs.

"I'm Titi," she said. "Chinchook says you have no money. Do you want to come with me today?" She smoothed the rope of hair with scarlet talons.

"If so, you should wash that dress." She offered this as friendly advice, not criticism.

Nina's sleepy brain tried to digest Titi's invitation. From behind her Chinchook's voice announced, "No, the lady is coming with me today. See what I got already! I am blessed by Fortune. And I lined up two times."

He clutched in his arms two towels, two tubes of toothpaste, two toothbrushes, two bars of soap, and two tins of evaporated milk. He had one bar of chocolate in his shirt pocket.

Lord help me, thought Nina again. She looked around at where she found herself. By daylight, the rubble looked like an open wound. Her nose registered the faint sickly sweet smell of death buried under the chunks of concrete and twisted beams.

"I got these at the quay," said Chinchook. "Near the cannon boats. A gift from America!"

The adolescent girl seemed not to have moved all night. She still sat with her arms wrapped around her legs, looking at nothing. Nina felt something uncomfortably familiar in that stillness.

"We must all go back!" Chinchook deposited his loot and danced back to Nina. "Come on! Before it's all gone!"

Harvest Mouse slipped out through the gap in the wall and vanished.

"Why not?" said Nina. She could find out what was going on, with the gunfire. Then go back to see if Andrew had left a message yet with the *bac si*.

On the way, Chinchook darted ahead and back, like a puppy out for a run. The other two boys, Bulbul and Keelback, swam in convoy like remora around a shark. Nina led the silent girl; she couldn't bear to leave her sitting there alone. The child had come passively, without focusing.

"What's her name?" Nina asked Chinchook on one of his swings past.

"No One," he said. "She won't say who she is, so we call her No One." He dashed away, amused at his own wit.

At the quay, near the berths of the U.S.S. *Montrose* and the U.S.S. *Montrail*, a banner strung between two poles proclaimed, "The People of America Welcome Their Friends from North Vietnam." As if Saigon were their own city, thought Nina. ARVN soldiers distributed gifts, watched by two American advisers from the Foreign Operations Administration

They inched twice through the line of refugees; then Chinchook and Keelback lined up a third time. Arms full, they adjourned to the waterside park to take stock. They had collected twelve tins of evaporated milk labeled "A Gift from America," twelve toothbrushes, twelve towels, and twelve tubes of Colgate toothpaste. Nina saw possibilities here.

"I'm going to the market to try to sell my towels and toothpaste," said Nina. "Anyone else coming?"

"Me," said Chinchook.

Nina was already imagining the fish and rice she would buy when she had a little money. Another thought occurred to her. "I wonder what they're giving away at the refugee camps."

"I know." Chinchook smoothed the cockade of hair with a toothbrush, which he then tucked behind his ear. "Pills. There's no more chocolate at the camps, but they still have pills. To drive out the bad spirits that make your head ache. We can get some this afternoon."

With Bulbul's knife, they opened two tins of milk. Bulbul spat his onto the ground.

"Ptu! American piss! Tomorrow, I will go alone. I'll get *rice*."

Chinchook swallowed another gulp of the milk. "Big mouth," he said pleasantly.

The two boys eyed each other. Bulbul was the larger, already filling out in his chest and shoulders like a man.

"Big mouth means big bird," he retorted.

Chinchook snorted in derision.

"Shall I prove it, Shrimp?" Bulbul had the uneasy look of someone who has started more than he intended. He had gone red and avoided the eyes of the rest of his audience. He leaned against No One, who was ignoring the whole thing. When she did not react, he rubbed against her suggestively, emboldened.

"Wouldn't you like to see my bird?" he asked her. "I'll show

215

it to you. It's the only one in this crowd; the rest are chinchook tails.''

Chinchook had now gone red. No One moved away from Bulbul.

Bulbul pursued. "If you're good," he said, "tonight I'll show you how to make bang-bang. Cheer you up." He patted her tiny behind.

No One looked squarely at him. Encouraged, Bulbul pinched her miniature breast bud through her dirty dress.

No One opened her mouth and screamed. She screamed again, then again, and shoved Bulbul backward into a flowerbed. She screamed again. People in the park looked curiously.

Nina grabbed at No One. The girl struggled and scratched like a panic-stricken cat, calling in desperation for her mother. Nina's hands and arms were bleeding from scratches before she managed to pin the girl against her, and the screams dwindled to sobbing. Bulbul still lay in the flowerbed, confused and terrified by what he had done.

"Policeman coming," hissed Chinchook. "Quick!"

Bulbul scrambled out of the bedding begonias. He and Keelback vanished. Nina and Chinchook, with No One between them, merged with the crowds at a more dignified pace.

"Would you take these to market for me?" Nina proffered her toothpaste, toothbrushes, and towels. "I'll meet you back at the house; I have private things to do."

She saw Chinchook's expression.

" . . . if you would be so kind!" she added hastily.

She gave him the goods, then set off toward the apartment she had shared with Andrew. After a few meters she felt someone close behind her and turned in annoyance.

The girl, No One, stood, eyes down, feet firmly planted.

"Go back with Chinchook," said Nina. "I have things to do. You'll be all right."

She walked on. No One followed.

"Please go back!" she begged.

The girl stared into space, not hearing.

With No One on her heels, Nina found the shelled building. Five families had already camped where the ashes were cool enough, under makeshift tarpaulin roofs. Where the front door had been, a man squatted selling hubcaps from American cars, carefully arranged beside unrecognizable fragments of electrical equipment, old batteries, and three half-used tubes of Revlon lipstick.

All faces on the ruins were strange. The man selling hubcaps didn't know how many had been dug out of the wreckage. The *bac si* had no message for her. Nina waited in the shadow of the balcony for the widow who lived above the *bac si* to return.

When she came back, brandishing in triumph a live hen, Nina, still followed by No One, accepted an offer of tea and climbed up to the stuffy little room for the necessary polite gossip before the main business. She admired the hen; she offered congratulations on the birth of a third grandson. Finally, it was proper to ask about Andrew.

"He wasn't in the house," said the widow. "I saw him go out."

"Has he been back since?" asked Nina, trying to hide her elation.

"I don't watch all the time!" said the widow tartly.

"Then I am grateful for that one accident," said Nina.

The old woman grinned, acknowledging an even score. Then she looked grave again. "Many do not come back at all, these days."

Nina woke that night, in her niche in the rubble, with a spasm of terror. She strained into the darkness, trying to hear, above her own heartbeat and rasping breaths, the sound that woke her.

Then it came again, faint but unmistakable—the crump of an explosion, like the one that had set her house on fire and killed her mother. She heard another and another. Her body began to shake while her brain struggled to consider the sounds calmly. They came from the center of the city, near the Town Hall and the Presidential Palace.

She heard the others stirring in the darkness, but no one spoke. They were all listening, as she was. No One had come to sleep near her that night and was now sitting rigid against Nina's legs. She pulled the girl to lie close in the curve of her own body, as Minou had once done.

When the explosions finally stopped, Nina tried to sleep, but could not. She reminded herself that Andrew was probably still alive, and probably looking for her. Slowly, the gaps in the sloping floor above her head became sharper in outline with the increasing daylight.

In the cool of the next morning, Nina set off to the docks again with No One, Chinchook, and Keelback. Bulbul followed them, but at a distance. One of Nina's shoes had lost its heel. As she limped along, Nina had the sense of being a character in someone else's story, a disjointedness that was only partly the result of exhaustion. Near the Central Market they suddenly

217

heard the huge roar of an engine and the clattering of metal on stone; they scattered for safety into doorways.

A French tank rolled past like a legless elephant, snout extended stiffly in front, sniffing for its enemies. Though the tank was French, the gunner wore an ARVN uniform, the uniform of the government forces. People stared in alarm; a few averted their eyes from the unlucky omen.

At the next north-south boulevard, Nina saw an ARVN machine-gun position, three gunners waiting behind a wall of sandbags. There was another sandbag wall at each cross street in both directions.

Chinchook darted up. "Listen to me," he said importantly. "I have big news! The President is going to see the Emperor. Today." He waved toward a cluster of men who had regrouped, once the tank had passed, around an ancient wireless set on the pavement outside a café. "I heard it over there. Official!" He hopped up and down with excitement. "He must beg the Emperor to save him from the Binh Xuyen and the French! It is the end of Mr. Diem!"

Nina pushed her way into the group of men.

"I already told you the news," protested Chinchook at her elbow.

The radio now stuttered out martial music through a fog of static. The men shouted at each other

"I tell you," said one, "the ARVN and the Americans have recaptured Sécurité headquarters and kicked the Binh Xuyen bandits back into their swamp! You heard it as clearly as I did, just now!"

"Read between the lines, brother!" another retorted. "You can't expect the official radio station to admit that the government forces have met with defeat! It's obvious that the Binh Xuyen fought off the ARVN, the Americans, and their White Mice accomplices. They have chased the American puppet whimpering for protection to the Celestial Father, Bao Dai!"

"Well, *someone* threw fireworks at the Presidential Palace last night," said another man. "My cousin drove past it this morning with his cyclo. I can tell you, Mr. Diem was lucky to get out alive. And where one blow was landed, another can easily follow. I have already told my wife to leave her job with her American lieutenant. I locked her in the house."

Nina was not surprised to find that the truck dispensing gifts was not on the quay.

On Tu Do Street, four Vietnamese civilians leaned on their hands against a wall while American military police searched them for weapons. A fifth had already been bundled, handcuffed, into the back of the jeep where a young ARVN soldier with an automatic rifle was nervously watching the crowds in the street. Passersby averted their eyes and hurried on.

"We should go back," said Nina. "Too many soldiers around!"

Bulbul and Keelback had already vanished. Before Nina reached the next corner she heard a woman scream. She whirled, expecting carnage and disaster.

The woman screamed again. "My rice! Stop him!"

Bulbul soared over the bodies on the pavement with the agility of a young goat. He passed her and disappeared around the corner; people sleeping on the street roused themselves half curiously onto an elbow and lay down again. Nina thought she saw Keelback round the corner as well. Chinchook sauntered up to walk beside her with elaborate casualness. Nina said nothing, but resolved to have a share of the rice.

I should berate Bulbul, she thought. Or report him to the police. Instead, I want to cheer. It made her feel odd. As did the realization that the rice seemed more important than the soldiers.

On the way back she stopped at the burned apartment building. Now that she knew from the widow that Andrew was probably still alive, she would not give up. No One followed her again, still without speaking. The widow was out. The man selling hubcaps had disappeared and been replaced by a low-stakes-only card game. Nina approached a woman nursing her baby under the tarpaulin by the staircase and asked if a Round Eye who spoke fluent Vietnamese had been there asking for his wife. The woman looked her up and down, then turned away. Nina checked again with the *bac si* for a message, and settled against the wall beneath the balcony to wait a little longer for the widow. No One squatted beside her.

Though the streets were busy, they flowed with the aimless energy of people who had lost interest in their usual daily pursuits. Nina felt a tension under the talking, the spitting, the coughing, the calling, the car horns. Today, events were gathering momentum; everyone sensed it. They listened and waited.

Nina wanted more information, nearly as much as she wanted to see Andrew's face suddenly bob toward her in the street. If the Presidential Palace had really been bombed during the night, President Diem would have to crush his attackers completely, in an immediate show of power, if he had any hope of keeping his position.

She crossed the street to a young man in shorts, bare feet, and a ragged white French dress-uniform jacket, who was prodding the entrails of a motorbike as he listened to a transistor radio.

"Any news worth knowing?" She nodded at the radio.

The young man spat through the gap where his front teeth had been knocked out. "The President is dead," he said with satisfaction. "Last night. Didn't you hear? The Air Force attacked the Palace and flattened it. The Americans' man is dead." He glanced sideways to see her reaction

"So who is our new leader?" she asked.

"They haven't said." Whoever "they" might be.

"Come on," Nina said to No One. "Let's see what else we can learn."

The situation was confusing. Diem was the Americans' man, but the Air Force also counted the Americans as allies. And they had bombed the Palace. The Binh Xuyen had asked the French for help. If Diem fell, perhaps the French might return to power after all. They had returned after their defeat by the Japanese. Many Vietnamese who had opposed them before Dien Bien Phu already preferred them to the American newcomers.

"If it's Ho, on the other hand," she said to No One, thinking aloud, "I'm in trouble. You too." She looked at the girl's crucifix.

"Just watch me forget my 'Hail Mary's,' " she said, then cast an involuntary glance of apology upward. Forgive me, she thought. But You must admit You're not doing very well by me at the moment!

A noisy group had gathered around a tea vendor on the corner. In the circle of people who looked on, exclaiming and sipping from tiny chipped cups of tea, an old woman rocked on her heels and tore her hair in grief. Two younger women and an old man tried to comfort her.

"It is the end!" cried the old woman. "We are finished. Tell me how an American can speak properly to the Celestial One. Tell me how!"

"What's going on?" asked Nina.

"She heard some nonsense that an American colonel has proclaimed himself the new Emperor," said a young man. "In place of the Celestial Father, Bao Dai. But I don't think a barbarian would dare . . . even in these days." He chewed his gum twice. "Still . . . you never know. He already lives in the Presidential Palace."

Nina wished again that she had paid more attention to political gossip among her mother's friends. She couldn't remember what she had heard about the man probably in question—an American called Lansdale—except that the elder M. Jouvet had raged about him all through one dinner party.

Pretense that this was a normal work day was dropped altogether when the sounds of gunfire intensified suddenly in the center of the city. Everyone began talking about what had happened, was happening, or was going to happen any minute now. One man assured Nina that the French had reoccupied the Palace, and were planning to kick out the Americans and restore the country to normality. A woman wearing a crucifix had heard that Diem was planning a miracle to take place in the Cathedral, to demonstrate that he still had total support of the Heavens, both French and Vietnamese. A group of women washing clothes in a small canal told her in hushed tones that Bay Vien, the general of the Binh Xuyen, had already executed President Diem and declared himself the ruler chosen by Heaven. A few refused to acknowledge that anything out of the ordinary was happening.

"A speck of dust is blowing," said one old man. "If the *Chinese* were attacking us again, I might be concerned." "Again" referred to events four hundred years earlier.

Nina turned toward the Presidential Palace, to see the truth of things for herself. But she didn't have to go that far.

As she followed the large boulevard that ran beside the Arroyo Chinois, she came to a machine-gun emplacement like the ones they had seen earlier that morning. It guarded the Y Bridge, which connected a large island in midstream to both banks of the canal. The man behind the sandbags wore the snarling tiger badge of the Binh Xuyen. More emplacements guarded the other bridge approaches. The island was now obviously a fortified headquarters for the sect. Armored vehicles were rolling slowly across the bridge toward the center of Saigon. A jeep led the way. As it passed her, Nina saw the bulky form of the Binh Xuyen general. Beside him sat a much smaller man in the uniform of the Hoa Hao. Former enemies in the same jeep!

The sects were joining together against Diem, as Andrew had said. Even the Americans might not be able to help the President. Nina turned in the direction of the sporadic gunfire which came from the direction of Tu Do Street. She cut through the narrow back streets where there were no soldiers and turned left by the Cau Muoi Market near the Linh Son Pagoda. The gunfire was louder by the time she neared the Central Station. She thought for a moment, then waved down a *pousse-pousse*.

When she told the driver where she wanted to go, he laughed. "You crazy? You walk there, lady! Nobody takes you to the Rue Catinat! The Binh Xuyen are in Sécurité headquarters and the

221

ARVN are in the Ministry of Defense, across the street! Shooting at each other. Bad for the café business!"

He wheeled away, still laughing at her foolishness.

Nina made a decision. "We're going to Dalat," she told No One. "Now. If the trains are running. My family has a house there, for the hot season. If it's still there. . . . With my record, it won't be." That's not funny, she thought.

No One did not appear to register what she had said.

"We'll get away from the fighting, if we can," said Nina. "I'm not going to sit around waiting for it this time!" It was useful to think aloud, even to a blank face. "I hate to leave Chinchook and Titi without telling them, but I think we should go now. As soon as I do just one more thing."

She led the way back, for the last time, toward the burned apartment building.

As they passed the crowded houseboats and skiffs jammed along the banks of the canal, she wanted to shout to the people who lived there, "Get out! Can't you see what's going to happen? There's a military headquarters just a few meters downstream! Get out while you can!"

The widow was at her balcony rail. When she saw Nina, she called down, *"Bac si."*

She made a jabbing movement downward with her fingertips. *"Bac si!"*

"Andrew!" cried Nina with joy. "Did he come back?" She couldn't hide the unseemly emotion in her face.

"Bac si," said the old woman with finality.

Nina went into the apothecary's shop once more.

As was often the case, the *bac si* had placed his money both ways, medically speaking. On one side of the narrow, dark alcove of his shop stood two huge wooden chests with hundreds of tiny drawers filled with traditional remedies. Nina smelled the dried herbs and the undercurrent of less pleasant substances. On the other side of the shop four shelves were laden with Western-style drugs, the magical sight of which was often enough to effect a cure.

The old man sat in a dirty singlet, shorts, and plastic sandals behind a small table which held only a mortar and pestle and an abacus. Behind him, a six-foot-high chart in once lurid but now faded colors showed in diagram the intricate relationships between the five major organs, the five juices, the five tastes, the five colors, the five types of weather, and most important of all, the five natural elements whose influences constantly work on man's body.

"Lady, I still have no word from your husband." His tone was polite but disinterested.

"But the reverend old mother upstairs said I should speak with you."

"I find cures, not people," the old man said. "There is no cure I know for your condition. Many suffer from it these days."

"The foreign devil who lives like a Viet," insisted Nina stubbornly. "He lived in the building that once stood across from your nose."

"What do you want me to do?" The old man sighed with mock resignation and reached for a book on the lower shelf.

"Let me see what the Venerable Hai-Thuong-Lan-Ong has to say. Let's see . . . loss of hair . . . loss of teeth . . . No. No. Nothing for loss of foreign-devil-who-lives-beneath-his-dignity."

He slapped the book shut. "Sorry, missee. Bad joss for you." He slipped into Cholon pidjin. After replacing the book, he crossed his thin shanks and stared into space over Nina's shoulder.

She gritted her teeth in frustration; the old woman had been emphatic. He began to chew absentmindedly on an ivory pick.

Nina placed on his table the proceeds from selling three bars of American soap. "I am also called Luoc Nina or Le Thuyet," she said desperately

The old man shot a glance at the money. "Humpf," he breathed, and shuffled to one of the chests.

Her pulse began to bang in her ear as he opened and closed the lower drawers.

"I'm not a *poste restante*," he muttered. "People seem to be confused. I cannot do these things for charity."

Nina pulled her pocket linings into wings at her hips. The old man shrugged.

"Aha!" From a second-tier drawer he pulled a small rectangle of white cardboard. He dusted it and peered at the writing on it. Finally, he handed it to her.

It was not from Andrew.

It was addressed to "Luoc Nina." The engraved letterhead said "Louis Wu. Imports and Exports of Quality. Fine Art Objects. Hanoi and Paris." There was a telex number but no address.

The old man was watching her curiously. She thanked him and went into the street.

Away from his gaze, she read: *"Chère mademoiselle, Voudriez-vous avoir la bonté de m'attendre à cinq heures, le mercredi prochain, à la terrasse du Café Verlaine?"*

223

"What day is today?" she asked No One. The girl did not respond. Monday. It was Monday, as far as she knew.

The card was a ludicrous echo of her former life. She ran her thumb across the silky surface. Engraved, not printed, on expensive cream-colored stock. The message was handwritten in flowing italics.

"Who on earth is Louis Wu?" She did not expect No One to answer. What could he want from her? And how had he known where to leave the message? In two days, she could find out. If she stayed in Saigon.

"We'll go to Dalat on Wednesday night," she said to No One. "Can you bear the fighting for two more nights?" The question was addressed to herself as much as to the girl.

She stroked the silky card again; her fingers left dark smudges. In an unbroken window next to the *bac si* she saw two grimy Annamite urchins gazing at her. She could not meet Wu looking like this. If he were a friend, she must appear worthy of the world she had once belonged to. If he were an enemy, she must seem a foe worthy of respect.

"Come," she said to No One. "I must ask Titi for help."

The next night, Titi hauled a bulging shopping bag through the gap behind her. With considerable sense of drama, she slowly pulled out of the bag a bottle of Jack Daniel's, three cellophane-wrapped packets of Twinkies, a carton of Camels, four envelopes of condoms, and an open bottle of Wind Song toilet water. Finally she unfurled a sundress in pale blue gingham, with a matching jacket.

She shook the dress and laid it reverently across the rubble. "Very, very hard to get," she crowed triumphantly. "I was laughing all the time. My john wanted to get me another one. He said this one too big for me. It's 'Bobbie Brooks.' Number One!" She stroked the cotton and rubbed it between her red-taloned fingertips. "Number One!" She looked wistful, then brightened and handed Nina the Wind Song. "You can use this too. Before I sell it." She also lent Nina a few piastres to eke out the market proceeds.

That night, Nina could not sleep. She lay restlessly, listening to the now-constant sound of mortars. She imagined that the shells were landing closer than they had been in the afternoon. The others slept, except for Keelback, who had not returned. Forty-eight hours before, Nina would have been anxious for him. Now she felt that she was merely waiting to leave her borrowed refuge and its inhabitants.

She woke on what was to be her last morning in Saigon to the sound of almost constant mortars and gunfire from the city center. She stroked No One, who was curled tight against her belly. "Just one more day. We'll go tonight. After I meet someone. We'll walk north, to Bien Hoa. Then get a ride on a boat. Or a lorry."

She stopped to listen. The last shell sounded closer than the others had been. Quickly, she slipped on the Number One Bobby Brooks; it was too large and she had to hold her shoulders back to keep the straps in place. She tucked her father's seal inside the blue gingham bodice.

"I'm going out, just for a few minutes," she told No One. "To see what's going on."

She crawled out through the path in the rubble into the street, No One behind her. Nina stood watching the frantic energy in the street for a few minutes, then put out a hand to steady herself on the fallen beam.

People pushed and shoved, hauling huge, hastily tied bundles of possessions. A man wheeled past on a bicycle piled high, pots dangling from its axles, woven mats and clothing waving like flags. An entire family was trying to drag its two-wheeled cart toward the main boulevard; the grandmother was perched on top of a crate of hens, holding the youngest child tightly to her, while the mother, father, and the two youngest sons pushed and swore at those in their way. On the opposite corner, a *tay phap* had set up his board of brightly colored papers and tried to control the mob who shouted and waved money at him, pleading to be told the most auspicious sectors of the city to flee to for safety.

Still followed by No One, Nina climbed up the rubble, across the slanting beam onto the still-intact roof of the neighboring house. From that height she could see a grove of smoke trees which had sprouted and blossomed, far too close to their own sector. A sound like strings of firecrackers at Tet came from the northwest, in the direction of Tu Do Street.

She climbed back down, suddenly undecided.

"I'm not sure we dare wait until after five o'clock," she said to her shadow. "It may be too late already." Neither the girl nor she herself knew the answer.

Titi had returned to the burrow. "Everybody's on active duty today," she said. "No time for funny business."

She started repacking her several bags of black market goods and scavenging into two smaller ones, sorting, choosing or rejecting from piles in the dust of the rubble. "Or they're using their birds to piss themselves like babies," she added contemptuously.

There was a lull at midday; even fighting respected the ferocious heat. Sometime during the lull, Bulbul appeared briefly to announce that all roads from the city were closed. He collected something from a cache under a fragment of concrete and vanished again. Harvest Mouse had been gone when Nina woke up. Chinchook was curled up as if asleep, on the pile of rags he had collected for a bed.

The lull ended when a shell whined in and struck so close that the broken floor above their heads shrieked and shifted. Dust and rubble rained down. Nina, who had been frozen by the crump and sudden rising pitch of the shell as it approached, covered her head with her arms and waited for the entire floor to fall on them. It held. The shower of dust eased and then stopped.

Nina decided that she would rather be shot than crushed, and climbed back up onto the neighboring roof. No One followed her. They stood by the broken fretwork parapet of the roof and sniffed the air like young dogs. Behind the house, across the landscape of roofs, across drying laundry and roof gardens in oil cans, across chicken coops, rolls of barbed wire, and wrought-iron fans of spike railing, beyond some newly dyed trousers and a dismembered bicycle, delicate tips of flame probed up through a black umbrella of smoke where the shell had landed. It was too close. Nina's dilemma was resolved. They had to leave the house now.

In the street just below the front parapet a woman screamed. Nina ran to look down. A few doors to the left, in the street, a squad of Binh Xuyen were pushing the protesting occupier and his wife before them into a house. The woman in the street screamed again. She seemed mesmerized by more soldiers, in government uniforms, who had grouped near the corner. She stared at them while other people bumped and shoved past her, stumbling over bags and bundles they were dropping in their panic to get clear. Nina watched one man splash blindly through a pool of burning paraffin from a stove which had been kicked over. Another dragged a screaming toddler by one arm, while a baby shrieked on his other arm. A hen, feet tied together, squawked and flapped until someone stepped on her. Two dogs dashed in a frenzy, snapping at running legs.

The government ARVN troops separated into different doorways. The door of the house the Binh Xuyen had entered burst open. The owner stumbled out, hands above his head. His wife followed, weeping, hands also raised. The grandmother and

226

eldest son came next, pushed out by the muzzle of an automatic rifle.

"Don't shoot! Don't shoot!" screamed the man to the ARVN soldiers.

Behind them, the Binh Xuyen slipped out of the door and began to run up the street. The soldiers opened fire; the wife and grandmother staggered back as if hit by an uppercut to the chin, then fell bleeding. The son ducked into a zigzag run but went down when a bullet knocked off the back of his head. Two Binh Xuyen also fell.

Nina stared in disbelief at the brightness and quantity of blood on the dusty street. Then the father seemed to jump in the air and fall down, like an acrobat.

The Binh Xuyen forced their way into another house farther along the street. As their comrades gave covering fire, half the soldiers ran forward to shelter in new doorways. Then the rest ran up to new positions below the children's house.

Nina heard a scrabbling in the rubble. It was Chinchook, crying. She shook herself out of her horrified trance.

"Big trouble! Big trouble!" he gasped. "We must go. I don't like this. I don't like it at all!"

He turned and raced for the back of the roof.

"Where's Titi?" Nina called after him, then heard the woman scuffling and scratching up the pile of rubble below. Nina helped her up and across the beam. A grenade exploded in the street. Nina looked down again at the bodies in the street. Her tongue had glued itself to the roof of her mouth. She could not draw breath. Then she forced her feet to move.

They clambered down a narrow width of broken wall and back up onto the roof of the house behind. Below them, they heard scrabbling and bumping as the occupants gathered up belongings. They ducked under a drying saffron cloth and raced across the two adjoining roofs, then climbed some steps up onto a higher roof, crossed it, and slid down a rickety ladder. The gap of a narrow street, filled with milling bodies, brought them to a halt.

Nina swung herself down the iron fan that guarded the front corner of that house and dropped into the melee. Chinchook followed. Straight ahead, directly in their path, a block of houses had begun to burn. Nina checked her directions. The ARVN were closing in from behind and to their right. The squad of Binh Xuyen were fleeing to their left. On balance, after what she had just seen, Nina preferred their chances with the Binh Xuyen—just.

"We'll go left," she said to Chinchook. "Until we can get around the fire."

Before she could move, a mortar fired from the ARVN position to her right. The shell arched overhead with the sinking pitch of an outgoing one. It hit far to the left, deep in the heart of Cholon, well beyond the present position of the Binh Xuyen they had seen. Then she heard an incoming shell, from the other direction. It passed over but exploded far too close; a cloud of orange smoke belched upward and debris rattled down into their street.

Nina held up her arms for No One to follow her down the fan. The girl had already begun to drop down hand over hand like a young gibbon; she let go before Nina was prepared to catch her. No One hit the ground with a thud and hopped up and down on her stinging feet while Nina turned her attention to Titi.

"I can't come down," wailed Titi in despair. "I will fall!"

Another outgoing shell screamed overhead.

"Yes, you can," said Nina, "or you'll be blown up." She could hear herself talking, as if from a distance.

Titi looked round for another escape route, then resigned herself. She clambered onto the parapet and stepped out onto the most horizontal bar of the fan, clutching a higher bar with both tiny hands. Then she froze.

Nina kept her voice calm. "Now just step down onto the next one."

Grenades exploded in a neighboring house.

Titi started to step down, but hesitated when she felt the bar slope away under her to the street. Someone bumped into Nina.

"One more!" begged Nina. "Just come down one more!" She looked along the narrow street, praying she would not see soldiers.

Titi stepped down one more rung, then let go. She crashed onto Nina, taking them both to the ground. Tears stood in Nina's eyes as she tried to draw a breath but could not. She was going to die; the pain made her want to vomit. Then, at last, she managed to inhale. The pain slowly uncurled from her stomach and began to slide away like a snake.

Titi was crying. "Leave me. Please leave me! I will get you all killed. I will be all right!"

"Don't be an idiot," snapped Nina, more harshly than she would have done if it had been easier to draw breath. "I'll carry you if I have to."

They set off down an alley which led to their left, ducking among the crowds. Chinchook ran at Nina's side; he had recovered from his earlier shock and had begun to look excited. No One sprinted behind him like a terrified fawn, while Titi stumbled and galloped at the rear. They were knocked to one side by a large family who were dragging their household past on a two-wheeled cart in the opposite direction, toward the ARVN. Nina had wondered, with a thump of terror, what they were running away from that she did not know about. But she could not bring herself to turn back toward the sound of grenades. The dirty awnings over the alley had begun to trap the black smoke. Her lungs were stinging. She stepped across an old woman asleep in the street, saw that the woman was dead, not sleeping, and halted in horror as a sheet of flame blocked the alley. From an open window in a house just ahead a tongue of flame darted, light and quick as a frog catching a fly.

Titi's breathing was choked and hoarse, her face white. Nina ran them back to the last corner, turned back into their original path of flight, and stopped by the open door of a deserted house.

"Wait in there!" She shepherded the three others through a bead curtain at the back of the room, which hid only a broken charcoal stove and some scattered ash.

"There's a fire this way too. I must find a way to run," she said.

"I'm coming with you," said Chinchook. "I can help!"

Titi sank to the ground, eyes closed. She pulled at the front of the khaki shirt as if to tear it open and let more air into her struggling lungs.

They left No One and Titi and reemerged into the smoke-filled street.

"We must go around the Arroyo if we can," said Chinchook. "We will be safe in the water."

To do that, they would have to cross back over the Binh Xuyen's line of flight. But the fire frightened Nina more than bullets. She felt as if she could run forever to escape the flames. They chose a narrow street leading north from the house. The big fire was close by on their right, but the street was so far free of smoke or signs of burning. They would go a little farther that way, then circle back toward the big canal.

The shell passed overhead so close that Nina knew they would be hit. They dropped to the street and flung their arms uselessly over their heads. The explosion lifted her from the ground and dropped her again. A hail of debris pounded her back. She stood up dazed, but alive. Some of the debris was human flesh. She brushed something gray and granular from the side of her skirt.

People poured from houses, shouted, wailed, bumped against

229

each other in panic. Above the din, she heard the roar of flames. She and Chinchook ran back toward the house where they had left Titi and No One. Nina felt the fire suck the oxygen from her lungs as it flung its gases in a great rushing draft up into the hot blue sky, which was rapidly being blotted out by black. The shell had made a direct hit on the empty house; the heart of the flames beat there. Nina stared in disbelief. She took a futile step forward. It was her fault they had been there.

"No!" she cried and began to shake her head.

Chinchook danced at her side and pulled at her arm. "Let's go! Let's go! They're finished." He dashed back the way they had come. She followed him; there was nothing else to do.

Chinchook led them now. They stumbled and coughed, unable to see clearly where they were going, dependent on his knowledge of the network of streets. Two rats overtook them, dark streaks against the house wall.

We are running the same way, thought Nina, and gained heart.

After that, she noticed other rats and mice on the run. The lizards and house snakes would curl themselves deeper and deeper into crevices until they could go no farther and the rising heat of their blood sent them into permanent sleep.

She noticed with disproportionate horror a caged songbird, abandoned out of her reach on a balcony, beating in terror against the bars, its feathers already smoldering from the sparks. She was unable to take in the people who were no longer able to run. She could hear some, trapped like the snakes and lizards under the ruins of their homes. Others crawled on the pavement, looking for missing pieces of themselves. Or sat against walls, contemplating in a daze the wounds that were bleeding them to death.

Nina and Chinchook were nearly blinded by the dense, sticky smoke from an oil refinery that had begun to burn. They kept losing their way as streets disappeared in the bombardments or were blocked by flames. Their hands and legs bled from climbing over broken masonry. Their skin blistered from touching wood that still smoldered or was about to flare into flames. As she ran, Nina beat out sparks that landed on the blue gingham dress. She smelled burning hair.

Blindly, they followed the straight bank of a small canal which they hoped would lead them to the Arroyo. On the water, men and women clambered about in overloaded, sinking pirogues. Bows and oars tangled; swimmers grabbed onto the gunwales, begging to be taken to the Big River. Nina was nearly knocked into the water by a fat man carrying a crate of quacking ducks.

She saw one oarsman swing his blade into the head of a swimmer who clutched his boat. The swimmer sank and the water reddened above him. They ran on, past white bellies of fish already killed by the rising temperature of the water. Ash rained down.

"Beyond the Arroyo..." gasped Chinchook. "Rice fields. Between the Arroyo and... the Canal de la Dérivation. *Paddis*."

She knew them. Tucked into the triangle between Saigon's two major canals and the Quai de l'Ysère. She had passed them with her mother on the way to meet acquaintances off passenger liners. A piece of countryside tucked into the edge of the city. And said to be controlled at night by the Vietcong.

"Take us there," she said. Then remembered. "We can't follow the Arroyo. Too dangerous... Binh Xuyen headquarters are on Y Bridge... middle of the fighting."

They stared at each other for a long moment.

"OK," said Chinchook. "I know another way."

He doubled back to the west. They loped across the canal on a splintered plank bridge that rested on a single, half-submerged pontoon boat in midstream. Their crossing rocked surface debris so thick that it seemed solid until it moved.

The terrain they entered on the far side of the canal was an unfamiliar desert, so flat that Nina could not believe that houses had ever stood there, densely packed together, filled with people engaged in the comfortable, petty actions of daily life. Some of the people were still there. They dug in the hot rubble for possessions of their families. Or keened over corpses. Or they sat listlessly staring at what their lives had so suddenly become. One old woman was building a tiny wall of stones. Nina stepped around a twisted bicycle wheel projecting from a mass of broken masonry. The foot of the buried rider still wore its sandal.

By one of those small, eccentric miracles of hurricanes and war, in the middle of a flatness where a house has been erased two water jars stood intact, still filled with water. A third jar lay beside them, broken into shards with bright raw edges. Nina and Chinchook gulped at the water and splashed it over their faces and necks.

They had reached the backwater of the battle. The air was still thick with smoke, but the sound of shells and firing had receded into the distance. Fires flickered here and there, reluctant to give up territory once gained, but the raging flames had died. Once or twice, faint voices called from the rubble where people were digging.

They squatted for a moment of rest. Chinchook watched her; she looked very different from the lady who had caught his hair

231

in the alley. Her face was black from soot, with light, bright trails where the water had splashed it. The dark hair on the left-hand side was singed short; she had lost one shoe. Her hands, arms, legs, and unshod foot were bleeding. The dirty garment she wore was unidentifiable as Number One Bobbie Brooks. As he watched, she dropped her head against her folded arms which she rested on her knees.

He wanted to say something to her, about their shared flight and about Titi and No One, but he was no good with serious words. And though she had never told him so, he knew she was a *métisse;* you had to be careful with them. Misunderstandings were easy.

"We're nearly to the Arroyo," he said encouragingly.

She lifted her head, then looked past him as if he had not spoken. "It's our visitor!" she exclaimed.

He decided that their recent experience had driven her mad. He turned and saw the heads of two soldiers showing above the bank of the canal. Nina scrambled to her feet and limped toward the water. Chinchook followed anxiously. The soldiers waded shoulder-deep, pulling a pirogue toward the bank.

"I'm certain that's him," cried Nina.

She stared at the man who stood by the water's edge. The left leg of his uniform was bright with blood and his face was smeared with blood and dirt. But she was sure she recognized those high cheekbones and the dark forelock of hair from the dusk beneath the pines in Dalat.

"Thu!" Nina called. Her voice croaked with smoke and exhaustion.

The man turned. His eyes passed blankly over Nina and Chinchook, who were unarmed, not in uniform, and posed no apparent threat.

"Come, Colonel!" The men in the water called to him.

He faltered, clutched for support at a broken clump of bamboo, and half jumped, half fell toward the boat. He fell short and nearly capsized it, but his men caught him and heaved him on board. Then they climbed in and the pirogue headed rapidly downstream, threading through the wreckage toward the Saigon River.

"He knows my father! He's my cousin!" said Nina despairingly. "We need a boat to follow them!"

Chinchook was not much reassured about her sanity.

They limped to the edge of the bank. A single pirogue lay splintered in the water under some collapsed pilings and a woman lay dead, half on the bank. The back panel of her *ao dai* floated on the water like the petal of a large peach blossom; the mud was red under her chest.

"No more boats. Bad luck," said Chinchook soothingly.

"I've lost him," said Nina. "Did you see what uniform they wore?"

"Very hard to tell when they are so dirty," he said. "But I think Binh Xuyen."

"He was a cousin of my father's," said Nina more calmly. She remembered clearly the last time she had seen him: with her father in the dusk on the veranda of their house in Dalat, looking out at the pines and drinking local beer. She could still remember the sound of their low voices, rambling on with the intimacy of men who knew each other well. And she remembered how she had fallen in love with him.

She was positive it was the same man, although he looked smaller than she remembered. He was also younger than she would have thought; he must have been much younger than her father. The forelock, however, was the same, though now held in place by a worker's headband which sat oddly above his officer's uniform. In Dalat he had been wearing a well-cut suit. She wondered if he had already been a Binh Xuyen.

She suddenly stood very still; that question was like the tail of a snake. If you picked it up, you found that you had taken hold of more than you might have wished. Several questions about her father now occurred to her. And about her father and Thu. She would have to go carefully until things were clearer in her mind. But at least she had a fresh lead to her father, however slight. With determination and discretion, she should be able to locate an officer in the Binh Xuyen. She would do it, even if it took her months. She drew a deep breath. She reminded herself that she had just succeeded in doing exactly what she had planned; she had survived the fighting. The Binh Xuyen were in retreat, it seemed. The fighting was dying down. And she had survived.

Then she realized that she had missed her appointment with Louis Wu. And lost his card.

23

That night, after all fighting had stopped, Nina and Chinchook slept beside the water jars. Nina woke in the early haze that comes before the heat. Even then, in the early morning coolness, she smelled the thick sweetness of rotting flesh, more pungent and disturbing than the usual daily stink of excreta and rotting weed from the canals. Smoke and death overlaid the scents of mud, gasoline fumes, sewage, wood shavings, and cooking fires. The cyclist's foot wore a black, buzzing sock of flies. Ants and beetles probed at a nearby body which had already been gnawed by rats and dogs. The voices in the wreckage had stopped.

Nina stood up stiffly; she felt as if she had been severely beaten. Through a headache, she stared at the dried blood and scabs on her arms and legs. Her right foot refused to take her weight. When she raised her head, she was shocked to see the distant spires of the Cathedral towering above improbable stretches of wreckage where city streets had once run.

Here and there stood pieces of wall and half houses. She looked at the shining metal ribs of a beached whale for some time before she perceived that it was a ruined shed, twisting its girders up from the rubble. Two purposeful groups of men and women worked busily on the ruins; they shifted the rubble and flung unearthed corpses into open-backed trucks. Her brain struggled to digest what she saw, to encompass the magnitude of what had happened. She tried to locate herself in what her world had become. She had difficulty recognizing corpses as former people, like herself. Her mind kept returning to her hunger. Hunger seduced her; she could understand hunger.

Hunger, Thu, and Louis Wu. She seized on the little rhyme to give herself purpose. Otherwise, she was afraid she would merely sit blankly beside the water jars forever, unwilling to move. She could also locate points of pain inside herself—her mother, her father, Andrew, Titi, and No One—but she did not know what to do with them.

Chinchook was still sleeping, flat on his back, one hand on his chest, the other flung out to the side. The tuft of hair she had grabbed at their first meeting reared back from his broad, bony forehead as if surprised. He snored gently but firmly, even while he swiped at a fly which had landed on the rim of one protruding ear. Nina found his presence beside her the most cheering fact in her life.

While she waited for him to wake, she washed with water from one of the jars and smoothed down the short ends of her singed-off hair. Then she stripped off the remains of the Number One Bobbie Brooks and limped to the canal to wash it, moving upstream to avoid the decomposing bodies of a Binh Xuyen soldier and the woman in the pink *ao dai*.

As she stood in the water to her waist, in her brassiere and pants, she saw two duck eggs in a nest concealed in the bamboo at the water's edge. Her heart began to beat faster. She abandoned the dress on a piling, waded to the nest, and cracked the first egg. The embryonic duckling inside had begun to develop. She hesitated for one moment, then tipped the contents of the egg down her throat. The second egg she collected carefully for Chinchook. She was beginning to feel better; the series of small actions had broken through her early paralysis.

Chinchook was awake when she returned to the jars, curled on his side with his hands between his knees, staring at nothing.

"There you are," he said. "I thought you were gone."

"You are my brother now," said Nina. "I wouldn't leave you. Look, I brought you an egg."

He swallowed it instantly and licked out the pieces of shell. "OK, Big Sister." He grinned. "I won't think bad thoughts about you anymore."

It took them a long time to find the house where their burrow had been. Nina was limping badly, and the streets were changed. Once they thought they had found it and that it had burned; then they saw an unfamiliar barber's shop on the corner. Finally, they found the remains of the garage that had been two streets away, picked their way from there, past a distinctive Chinese fretwork balcony that remained unbroken, to their own street. The "trash men" had not yet visited and the bodies of the neighboring family still lay in the dust, glinting with the green iridescence of flies amid dropped cooking pots, sandals, and a sewing machine. Grenades had blown out the fronts of most of the buildings but the mortars had missed and the fire turned its course.

The upper floor of their house, however, had completed its slide into the street. A family had already cleared a space in the rubble and roofed it with a piece of filthy cotton. The man and two children slept, piled one on the other; the woman, nursing an infant, watched suspiciously as Nina and Chinchook tried to find their former entrance through the side gap. When they found it was blocked, they went round the corner into the street behind. The house backing onto theirs had been badly damaged; they were able to crawl through a hole four feet from the ground and drop into the space where they had lived. It was smaller and new light flooded in where the floor above had once been. As Nina looked around for signs of the others, her eyes fell on a bulging shopping bag.

"Chinchook! Do you remember that? Was it there before?"

Her heart began to pound, as if with fear, and her breathing thickened.

She saw him stiffen and go pale under his soot. He stepped backward away from the bag.

They whirled toward the sound of scuffling at the hole in the back wall. Titi slid to the floor. Nina crossed herself automatically while Chinchook made a sign to ward off an evil omen. They stared, mouths open wide.

Titi was just as shocked to see them. The three of them stood staring; the hunchback recovered first.

"I left the house. Forgive me for disobeying you. But I could not keep up. I would have held you back. So I left." She picked her way around the broken concrete to touch each of them in turn. "I thought you were all dead. You're sure you aren't *ma?* I don't know. . . . Can *ma* feel warm like this?"

"You are the one that must be *ma*," said Nina, placing her hand on Titi's arm in turn. They grinned at each other; the touch felt strong as an embrace.

"This is a lucky day," exclaimed Titi. "A most lucky day! We must celebrate it! We must eat and talk about only good things now!"

She dug into her shopping bag for a bottle of Seven-Up, a bottle of rum, four C-rations, six Hershey bars, and a mango.

"I knew this morning, when I went out and all was quiet, that the day was auspicious!"

She laid out their feast, then dug into a pile of rubble against the wall. She returned proudly with a small piece of rock sugar on a square of red paper.

"I have saved this for a long time. Maybe to celebrate my homecoming back to my own house. We will have it now, for your homecoming today."

After they had eaten the C-rations, Titi carefully collected the tins. Then they drank toasts in Titi's rum and Seven-Up. They drank to survival, success, and long lives. Titi and Chinchook drank to many sons for Nina. Nina and Titi drank to high honors for Chinchook, and always winning at card games. Then they ate the mango and five Hershey bars.

"What do you want most of all?" Nina asked Titi. Her tongue had developed a will of its own, she noticed.

"A shop," said Titi. "Or my own hotel to run, with many soft French beds and white tablecloths." So they drank to that.

They drank to no more fighting and to the departure of all White Demons from Vietnam. Nina was too drunk by this time to consider taking it personally. They drank to no more invasions by anyone, including the Chinese.

Rashly, Nina burst out with the question that had been weighing on her. "What happened to No One?"

"Not now, not now!" cried Titi. "Today, we are talking only of lucky things. I am here. You are here. Leave the rest. Don't think of it; you will change the luck."

There was a moment of silence. Nina tried not to think of it. Chinchook and Titi listened, but they heard no child crying or gunfire. No cloud passed over the sun. All was still well. They talked about themselves, drunk in the late morning sun.

"I bring good luck," said Titi. "A rich man once gave me a house so he could always come touch my shoulder with a coin to make it grow into many. He even brought his baby son to me. Many men like to touch me." She recrossed her little ankles with unselfconscious languor. The red child's sandals were scuffed and one buckle had torn away. She had replaced it with a string of coconut fiber tied through a hole in the strap.

Nina looked again at the small, lumpy body. The woman's pleasure in her own being changed Nina's vision of it. She admitted to herself that she had once found the woman's vanity perverse. Now she acknowledged the long, thick hair, the eyelashes, the short nose with fine, taut nostrils, and the crimson talons at the end of the short fingers, which all helped her to survive.

"I made a lot of money," said Titi. "Very lucky." She began to probe with the balls of her fingertips beneath the projecting nails at the silver foil on the last Hershey bar.

"Many lovers. Then the man beat me up because he thought I was giving his luck away. He was drunk...I won't talk further of that today."

She divided the chocolate evenly. "American White Demons give me many gifts to show their respect. I am still lucky."

She held up the hem of the shirt she wore as a dress, an American cowboy-style shirt with a horse's head painted on the back and a V of blue rayon fringe across the front.

"The one this morning gave me this—and paid me too. Because the fighting has finished. Crazy. Americans throw everything away. A very rich country. I will go there if I don't have a hotel."

Nina stretched in the strip of shade cast by the rear wall. "My friends," she said, loving them at that moment as much as she had ever loved Simpoh Flower and Minou, "Little Sister and Brother, we must not waste such an auspicious day. I must make

237

some new beginnings and I feel you are destined to bring me luck if you will help me."

"Just ask, Big Sister," said Chinchook grandly, waving his chipped enamel cup in the air. "As always, I will do what I can."

"I knew, when I left that house, that it was for a reason," said Titi. "What can I do?" She smoothed and folded the silver paper from the last Hershey bar.

"I must find three people who are part of my fate," said Nina. She told them a little, though not all, of what had happened to her.

With the last of the rum and Seven-Up they drank to Andrew, Colonel Thu, and Louis Wu, who were at that very moment sure to be following paths destined to cross their own.

Then Chinchook fell asleep, overcome by alcohol and heat.

24

The Café Verlaine had reopened three days after the end of the fighting in 1955. Nina studied the clientele. As in all the former French watering places, there were now more Americans than French. Two Americans sat near Nina, wearing crumpled MACV uniforms, drinking gin and tonic.

At another table sat a *métisse* like herself—or as she had once been: a slim, dark girl with permed hair, wearing a puffy crinoline under her gathered skirt which was printed with roosters. A crucifix hung at her neck. Nina touched the seal that had replaced her own golden cross around her neck. The girl's drinking companion was the only Frenchman in the café, a thickset Corsican in tropical whites who gesticulated as he talked with hands covered by dark hair and gold rings. The girl nodded and smiled; Nina never saw her speak.

A tall, red-haired American in civilian clothes sat alone at a table near the edge of the terrace. The spindly legs of his metal chair, built for smaller races, bowed under his weight. He was scribbling in a stenographer's notebook with a ballpoint pen from a row standing to attention in the breast pocket of his sports shirt. Nina watched his huge, long-fingered hands swallow up the tiny cups of black coffee which he drank as a chain smoker consumes cigarettes. His forearms gleamed as if flecked with gold dust.

He noticed her watching him and smiled. His eyes were such

an extraordinary blue and his smile so warm and open that Nina began to smile back. Then she turned away in irritation and confusion. Women who smiled at strange men in cafés were usually whores. He undoubtedly thought she was one. That was the problem with looking for Louis Wu in a café. People would think she was looking for customers.

To her right, five Japanese businessmen were drinking whiskey. Just beyond them an elderly Chinese sat alone, sipping a Pernod, immaculate in tropical whites. In spite of the heat, he wore a silk cravat at his throat. A jade-topped walking stick leaned against the chair beside him. He was reading a French paperback entitled *Les Amitiés Particulières*.

Nina eyed him speculatively. Another Chinese sat alone on the other side of the terrace, doing sums on a small adding machine and drinking rum and coke. She watched them both for a while. There were thousands of Chinese in Saigon. If she still had Wu's card, she could simply have left it lying on the table for him to see, as he no doubt intended . . . if he were still looking for her. And if he were still alive.

She sighed and lifted her head to let a faint breeze, smelling of fish, gasoline fumes, and smoke, cool her sweaty neck. She hoped Chinchook and Titi were having better luck.

She was debating whether to use another precious coin from Titi's loan to buy another drink and a few more minutes at her table when she felt someone stop beside her.

He was American, in civilian clothes but reeking of military from his crew-cut hair to the set of his spine.

"Can I buy you a drink, miss?"

"No, thank you," she replied politely, in one of her few phrases of English. His meaning was clear.

"Come on, honey. You look like you could use a few bucks." He leaned on her table with both hands and winked. "Be nice to me. I just got paid, and now I want to get . . ."

Nina stood up and walked away.

In the week since the end of the fighting she had grown more and more frustrated and discouraged. She had to fight to hang on to her sense of purpose, which was all that kept her from simply sitting, as No One had done. She knew she had to find her father if her life were ever to become again what it had once been. But her life in the big house now seemed distant and implausible, her life with Andrew a little more believable as it was more recent. Both lives were less important than the problem of finding food. Already slim, she was growing scrawny with hunger.

Chinchook showed her alleys where certain restaurants placed their rubbish bins, filled with scraps which they could eat. He introduced her to roasted cat, though the cat population was fast disappearing, as were the frogs that lived in the canals.

Titi couldn't understand Nina's refusals to go with her to turn a few tricks on Tu Do Street. Nevertheless, she seemed happy to share the booty she collected along with her fees. Nina's objection to whoring was by this time not so much moral as superstitious. She knew that if she ever went that far from what she had once been, she would never get back. And she had not yet given up.

And so she continued to look for Louis Wu, whose white, silky card had brought her a message from her former life. She no longer cared much whether he was friend or foe, only that he was a connection. She had also gone back to the the *bac si* shop for word of Andrew, as much for something purposeful to do as from real hope. The *bac si*'s door was blocked up with a sheet of corrugated iron. The widow upstairs had been replaced by a strange couple. The card game in front of her old home had gone and in its place were five sleeping bodies and their bundles of possessions. More squatters had moved into the ruins under makeshift roofs of packing case and flattened metal. The street stank of excreta and rotting flesh, like many others. The trucks of the "trash men" still prowled, collecting the last corpses.

After leaving the café, Nina went home and soaked the label off an empty rum bottle from Titi's carefully sorted collection. Then she smoothed the paper onto a flat piece of concrete to dry.

The Number One Bobbie Brooks was gray with dirt, in spite of washing; fire had eaten brown-edged holes in the grimy gingham. Her shoes had been replaced by a pair of Ho Chi Minh sandals Chinchook had found; she didn't let herself think about the dead feet he had probably robbed to get them. The rubbish-filled canals would not remove the grime that accumulated in the fine wrinkles of her skin. Her nails were broken. Her arms and legs were covered with scabs where the cuts and bruises of their flight were healing; those that weren't healing oozed green matter. Titi had trimmed her singed hair to even its ends, but she had not been able to pick out all the lice which itched unbearably when Nina tried to sleep.

She folded the dried rum label to the size and shape of the lost business card and put it in the pocket of the Number One Bobbie Brooks.

"Did you have a good day?" she asked Chinchook when he dropped through the hole in the back wall.

His right ear was purple and twice its normal size; his face was also swollen.

"Number ten bastard fucking motherfuckers!" he muttered. She noted his new American swear words.

"Five of them jumped me behind the Ming Yuan. Bigger than me. That restaurant's no good anymore, anyway!" He went to curl up on his pile of rags.

She was so hungry that she had no energy to go looking for food. Light-headed, she chewed an entire packet of Juicy Fruit, all that was left from Titi's last care package. Then she curled up, like Chinchook. There was nothing left to do but sleep and wait for the next day and her next visit to the Café Verlaine.

Titi woke them both when she returned, late and bouncing with news.

"I work American MAAG headquarters today. Business is number ten! No one even buys rubbers!" She dropped with an explosive sigh onto a perch and removed the red Buster Brown sandals.

Nina knew they had to wait for the reason why she had woken them.

"But then . . . !" said Titi. "I make conversation with a White Devil driver. . . . He's waiting for his boss to finish his important talking inside."

" 'What do you know?' I ask him. 'You're only a driver. You don't even know who won the fighting last week. You don't even know who is the president!' "

She laughed delightedly. "I use that trick many times. Always works."

She paused for dramatic emphasis. She squeezed her eyes to glaring slits under the canopies of false eyelashes.

" 'I'll have you know,' he says, 'we whipped the asses off those fucking dink pirates, right back into the fucking swamp where they belong!' "

She waited for applause.

Nina looked at her tiredly, trying to understand the importance of what she had just heard.

"Rung Sat!" said Titi triumphantly. "The Binh Xuyen have gone back to the Rung Sat, like the old days. Like that Robin Hood in his forest in America, in the film."

Nina still looked blank.

"Now you know where to look for your Colonel Thu!" cried Titi.

* * *

Nina had known of the Rung Sat since childhood; they passed its edges on the way to the seashore. It was a vast area of mangrove swamp, too shallow for all but the smallest boats, inhabited by snakes, lizards, bloodsucking insects, and now once again by the Binh Xuyen, who called it the "forest of the Assassins."

"Thank you, Titi," said Nina. "That's wonderful news. I am grateful to you for finding this out."

Titi beamed, sniffed an armpit delicately, and began to unbraid her hair.

"Thank you," repeated Nina. She didn't know what else to say. Privately, she patted her pocket to check that the rum label was still there. Her money, such as it was, remained on Louis Wu.

"A coffee, please, with milk." She reached the Verlaine as soon as it opened the next afternoon. The waiter eyed her torn, dirty dress and sandals, then walked away to stand looking over her head as if she were not there.

She began to count some coins onto the table.

"Garçon!" It was the big, red-haired American who was there again, weighing down his chair at the edge of the terrace.

The waiter rushed to his side with alacrity. A few minutes later he slammed a coffee down on Nina's table, still without looking at her.

Nina stared at it. She raised her eyes and met the blue ones of the American. This time, she was ready for his smile; she returned it with a precisely measured curve of her own lips, polite but chilly.

"Thank you, monsieur," she said in French. Then she could no longer look at him. Her heart began to pound at her next thought. What if she were to ask him to buy her a *croque-monsieur?* Tears sprang to her eyes at the vision of hot ham and cheese fried in a delicate egg coating. I can't! That thought was equally fierce. She sipped the coffee; it made her feel slightly ill. Her head was spinning from hunger and one temple throbbed.

How easy to be Titi, she thought. How simple. In frantic opposition to such thoughts she heard in her head the voices of her dead mother and Mlle. Berthe which had been silent for many months. "You never know . . . be careful . . . ! And she was never seen again!"

Then she began to laugh at herself. If they could see her now! Their world and their teachings had nothing to do with her anymore. Just as her mother could no longer love and protect her, she could no longer guide her. Nina was on her own.

"... bend like the grass." This time it was her father's voice.

The alternative was to break. And she had no intention of breaking. She had nothing left but her father and his fight, whatever it might be. If she broke, she would never learn what his fight was, or be able to help him and to earn his gratitude and love.

She asked the American for the sandwich.

"Of course, mademoiselle!" The red-haired man turned to look for the waiter.

He was matter-of-fact about her request. The money was nothing to him, of course. Perhaps he was used to beggars. Expected them to approach him because he had a white face. She blushed dark red under her dirt. Her heart was pounding, partly at the imminence of the hot sandwich, partly in terror at how easy it had been and at the thought of how easy it would be to go further. She glanced at him sideways and was shocked into breathlessness by the thought that it might not be too unpleasant to go further with him. Unbidden, her mind imagined his hands doing to her what Andrew's had once done, on their hard little wooden bed.

Horrified with herself, she thrust her fists into her pockets and found the rum label. Gratefully, she fumbled it out and smoothed it on the table, blank side up. She was afraid to look at the American, whom she now hated unfairly for unsettling her and for seeing her desperation. Eyes down, she waited for the food and for his next move.

"Mlle. Luoc?"

For a second she didn't react. Then she realized what the voice had said. A manicured finger touched the rum label. Her eyes followed the arm up from the gold cuff link in the silk cuff, along the tussore jacket sleeve to the face of the elderly Chinese who had been reading the French novel the day before.

"I did wonder if it were you yesterday, but you look so little like your photograph. Of course, you were only twelve years old then."

"Monsieur Wu?" She clasped her hands in her lap to hide their shaking.

Oh God, she suddenly thought. What if he heard me begging from that American?

He leaned the jade-headed walking stick against the empty chair and sat opposite her. He studied her for a moment.

"*Zut alors!* You must have a tale to tell!"

243

His face was broad, his eyes intelligent but guarded. The pads of his high cheekbones appeared to have been touched with rouge. Silver hair flared into elegant, blue-rinsed wings above his ears. He continued to observe her as if she were an object in a shop that puzzled but did not displease him.

"Forgive me," he said suddenly and leaned across the table to pick the seal on its string from between her breasts. He peered at the carving on the base.

"A lovely piece, that. Worth a great deal already. By the time you're as old as I am it will be a museum piece. Do look after it!"

"Who are you, monsieur? How did you find the *bac si?*" She fought the swimming sensation in her head.

"I'm a former colleague of your father's, one might say. And you were followed to the house a few weeks ago . . . word gets around. I was only too happy to oblige when your father asked me to try to find you. . . ."

"He's still alive?"

His eyebrows, neat as two willow leaves, arched in surprise. "Of course, dear girl!"

Nina burst into tears of relief.

"Didn't you know? I suppose you couldn't have done. How silly and brutal of me!" He sounded genuinely upset.

After a moment he added, "Do stop. Please." He passed her a freshly ironed square of nearly transparent cotton. "Your father wouldn't like to see you do that, particularly in public." He glanced around. "Do stop!" he urged, *sotto voce.* "Or that dreadful American behind me will come rushing over to defend you. He's getting that concerned look."

She began to laugh through her tears. Wu didn't know half of it. She blew her nose and reduced the fine cotton to a limp wad.

"My father really asked you to look for me?" she asked.

Wu nodded.

Nina gave a long, shaking sigh of pleasure and relief.

At that moment, the waiter dropped the *croque-monsieur* onto the metal tabletop with a disdainful clang. She was going to have to cough up a sweetener if she wanted to use his café as a hunting ground.

Behind Wu's back, the American smiled to himself in resignation. Nina kept her focus short, on Wu's face, as she swallowed the sandwich in four bites. Wu watched her with faint horror.

"Where is my father?" asked Nina. She picked up and ate two crumbs from the table.

"North of the 17th parallel somewhere. Possibly Laos."

"In hiding?"

He looked at her closely, trying to judge her tone. "You could put it that way. Although I think he had already prepared his hiding place."

"When can I go and see him?"

"I'm afraid you can't. Not for a while."

"Why not?" she asked fiercely. Wu retreated slightly back into his chair.

"For your own safety. And his." After a moment he leaned forward again. "May I give you a little advice . . . which means that I'm going to, like it or not. Anyone watching us would know that you're disappointed about something. You shouldn't give away so much free information. It reduces your dignity and shows weakness. And weakness is an invitation to bullies."

He touched her hand with a finger, to soften the criticism. "As it happens, I'm a friendly sort, but if I were not . . ."

"Are you trying to frighten me? I have survived so far!" Then she remembered her father's advice. "Forgive me, monsieur. I wanted to praise myself rather than listen and grow wiser."

His eyebrows arched a second time. "What a funny mix you are!" His tone was gentle. "Would you like something else to eat?" he continued. "Before I carry you off for our main business?"

The *croque-monsieur* was an alien lump in her stomach. "I think I'd better take it slowly with food," she said.

"You can always eat again this evening."

She had forgotten that meals had once followed each other with reliable regularity.

The waiter was hovering for Wu's order.

"Come with me, then," said Wu. He looked for the waiter, to pay for her sandwich. The American signaled that it had been done. Wu was too much a gentleman to let his brows arch this time, but he couldn't help a quick glance at Nina.

Purple with humiliation at what Wu must think, she turned to the American and inclined her head with majestic grace as she had seen her mother do, in her other life. "You are too kind, monsieur."

He replied in accented but accurate French.

Then, watched by both the outraged waiter and the amused American, Nina managed to walk steadily, with a straight back, from the café into the street. Wu flagged down a red, white, and blue taxi with his walking stick. Still watched by the men in the café, he handed Nina, in her ragged sundress, into the backseat as if she were a princess.

* * *

Their taxi turned into Don Due Street, formerly the Avenue Foch, in the European quarter. Nina's palms grew damp. The sandwich had not stopped the swimming in her head. After two more turnings, Wu told the driver to stop outside a gate that hung askew on broken hinges. When the taxi had turned out of sight, blowing coils of smoke from its exhaust, he led her briskly up a weed-clogged drive, under a sagging porte cochère, around the corner of the house, past an overgrown ornamental pond, and through a small gateway in the rear compound wall. He crossed the narrow alleyway, looked both ways, and unlocked the rear gate of the neighboring house.

At first Nina did not recognize, through the sandbags piled around the veranda and the antigrenade mesh nailed across the windows, the house of the Garines where her mother had once worked as a governess. Crouched behind its sandbag fortress, it was now divided into apartments. A crude arrangement of six bells had been wired up beside the chipped paint of the huge, carved front door, although there were no names in the metal slots provided. Inside, a wooden plaque hanging vertically from a single screw announced that the former dining room had been used, or perhaps still was used, by an organization abbreviated to USAID.

Nina followed Wu up the broad double staircase that folded back on itself like the half-spread wings of a gull, stepping in her own ghostly footprints on the dusty teak. On the first floor Wu clicked and rattled at a series of elaborate locks and led her into what had once been the master bedroom.

"Frightful, isn't it?" he exclaimed. "Absolutely frightful."

The airy, high-ceilinged room was furnished with a combination of orange standing chairs, a mauve velvet chaise longue, a pair of fine Louis Quinze console tables, a heavy rattan sofa covered in faded chintz, a huge cocktail cabinet faced in split bamboo, and a lacquered mural made of feathers and shells.

"The bedroom is worse," said Wu. "But at least it's amusing." He indicated the door to the former dressing room.

Nina turned slowly, looking around her. "That used to hang in the dining room!" she exclaimed. "*Maman* used to laugh and say how Mme. Garine always found an excuse for pointing it out to new guests."

Louis Wu looked over her shoulder at the large painting by Géricault of a white horse in a storm-lit sky. "Yes, a pity, that. It's a good piece. I heard that their agent let them down badly. Some family silver went missing too, I believe. I confess, I rather have my eye on that picture.

"Anyway, here you are." He dangled the key ring before her, then dropped it with a gesture unexpectedly feminine.

Nina caught the keys. "You mean I'm to live here?"

"If you can bear it." Wu looked around again and shuddered dramatically. "I'm afraid it's the best available on short notice. The lease is in the name of a Miss Owen—a schoolmistress, I believe."

"Miss Owen?" repeated Nina. "Is that my name, then?"

"It might be best." Wu began to run his fingers along the top of one of the consoles, not looking at her. "Your father prefers you to stay inconspicuous for a while. I believe he was a little naughty in the eyes of some friends of the present government."

While Nina gaped at him, he examined a glass case that held a frozen scene of little figures from the Peking Opera, made of paper and quivering gold and silver wires. "At least they were friends before . . ."

"Friends of *Diem*!" She cut him off, shocked. "I thought the Vietminh burned our house!"

"Why on earth would they have done?" His astonishment seemed genuine.

"Andrew told me . . ." She stopped. "Well, we were Catholics. My father worked with the French. All his business affairs seemed to be with the French. My mother was French."

"Our President," said Wu dryly, "has so many friends and relations in his government that he can't begin to know what they all get up to."

Nina stood silent, trying to think. Trying to fit this new information into her already overcrowded brain.

"Can you tell me which friends?" she finally asked.

Wu brushed imaginary dust from his fingertips. "It's not my business, that side of things. I help when it's necessary. But I no longer get involved."

"I see," said Nina. Her head cleared slightly. In relief and joy she had embraced Wu as her rescuer as if he were a long-lost beloved uncle. In fact, she knew nothing about him whatsoever. Except that he said he was acting on instructions from her father. She didn't know what their relationship had been, nor what Wu had done when he was still "involved." She looked at his expensive suit, his silk shirt, his gold cuff links, the jade-headed walking stick, the suggestion of makeup on his skin. She had a lot to learn about the aging, moneyed dandy who read Peyrefitte in French.

"How long must I stay inconspicuous?" she asked him.

"The elections might change things. One never knows." He

pulled a large white envelope from an inside breast pocket. "One last thing. . . . He wanted me to give you this."

She held out her hand for the message from her father. Explanations and instructions at last. She held the envelope to her heart while Louis bowed over her other hand like a French courtier.

He studied her again, with the same objective interest as in the café; she was surprised that she still didn't mind.

"We must do something about your dressmaker and *coiffeuse,*" he said severely. "I stroll past the Verlaine most afternoons at about the same time."

"That sounds like possible involvement," she said somewhat tartly.

"Oh no!" he replied. "It's necessary help!"

In spite of herself, she laughed aloud.

After Wu's silver hair had vanished down the gull-wing stairs, Nina locked the door carefully behind him and tore open the envelope from her father. Eagerly, she flicked through the contents. Then she searched again in disbelief. There was no letter—just a slip of paper on which was written the name of a bank in Cholon and an account number. At the bottom of the envelope was a small key. She also found several large-denomination piastre notes and one American fifty-dollar bill.

She sank onto the rattan settee, fighting tears. Though she knew it was pointless, she searched the envelope one last time. There was no message. No words of love or even concern. No indication of how long she must be patient, or even of what she was waiting for. Just numbers and money. The writing on the paper wasn't even his.

Then she began to feel foolish. She had no right to expect her father to have an envelope smuggled all the way from Laos or wherever he was. Wu had prepared it on instruction, here in Saigon. She wiped her eyes. She would never win approval from her father with yet more tears. Still, whatever she had hoped for when Wu spoke her name in the café, this was not it. She looked at the three orange plastic stacking chairs and the shell and feather mural, then down again at the slip of paper with the account number. Then she shook her head at herself.

I'm too dizzy with hunger and the speed of change, she told herself. I'm not thinking straight. I'm not thinking at all. I have made contact with my old world, or what is left of it. I know that my father is alive. And concerned for me. He has arranged

248

somewhere for me to live, and M. Wu notwithstanding, I prefer orange plastic chairs to rubble anytime!

The real implications of the envelope finally began to reach her. Her father was alive and he cared enough to take what must have been great risks to have her found. Joy began to warm her, the first she had felt in a very long time. In that slip of paper and little key, her father had given her the means to survive, if she were clever enough to know how to use them. She had little doubt that the account number was the "something else" that André Gidéon had speculated might turn up. Her father was depending on her to make the most of what he was able to give her.

"I promise," she told him, wherever he might be, "to use it wisely, the way you would want me to. I will make you proud of me. And I will help you in return in any way I can." For the moment, she did not let herself think what the existence of this "something else" might mean about her father.

A sudden itching of her scalp made her think of having a bath, now that she probably had a bathroom. She opened the door to the former dressing room and laughed aloud for the second time.

"*Amusante*," Wu had said. It certainly was! She suddenly wondered what kind of lessons Miss Owen, the schoolmistress, had taught.

The huge wooden four-poster bed nearly filled the former dressing room. The four corners of the tester were held aloft on the arms of carved caryatids with highly polished, hemispherical breasts. The canopy was heavy, sea-green Hong Kong brocade, the mosquito netting sugar-pink. Best of all, the canopy top was lined with mirror. Nina craned up at the dirty urchin who craned back down at her. It was a bordello bed, perhaps a relic from one of Diem's first attacks on organized prostitution.

She sidled past the end of the bed toward the white-tiled washroom she could see through a half-open door on the far side of the bedroom. As she squeezed between the bed and a utility writing desk, on which stood a vase of feather flowers and a bronze statue of Ganesha, the Hindu elephant god, the knob on the door of what she had thought was a closet began to turn.

She grasped Ganesha's bronze head as the door swung open. The man who entered from the rear landing was the man who had been looking for her on the night of the fire. Andrew's "nasty piece of work."

She recognized the high cheekbones and long twigs of mustache on either side of his mouth. He was not carrying his carbine.

249

His eyes rested on her hand, which rested on the Ganesha. He lifted both of his own hands, open, to show they were empty. He bowed.

"Welcome, mademoiselle."

She noted the hard fighting calluses on the sides of his palms. His baggy, Western-style suit could have hidden any number of weapons. Her mouth was too dry to speak.

"I offer you my services."

"And what are those?"she asked. His feet reassured her, for some reason. He wore graying tennis shoes with the front tops cut away to make room for his splayed toes with thick, horny nails. They were the shoes of someone who would rather not be wearing any at all.

"I am a very good driver, mademoiselle. Also a majordomo, watchman, et cetera." He bowed again.

"How did you get in?" She had not released her grip on the heavy bronze.

"M. Wu gave me a key." He raised both hands soothingly again. "Before, I work for your father."

Another one! She had to decide quickly. She must decide to trust Wu and this man, or . . .

Or she threw the Ganesha at his head and ran. Out of the apartment. Without the account number or the keys. Back to the streets and the burrow in the rubble. Back to dirt and hunger.

"When did you last see my father?" she asked.

"The night of the fire. I took him to his plane."

"Then what did you do?" He was smaller and older than she had first thought in her fear. His neck was corded and wrinkled. Gray wisps sprang from his temples at right angles to his drooping mustaches. Long white eyebrows twirled like reaching tendrils of climbing vines, over eyes that squinted as if trying to penetrate a fog to see the truth.

"I looked for you. As your father asked. He was hurt badly and could not stay himself."

"Why did he say you should look for me?" She held her breath.

His tone was respectful. " 'She will be useful,' he said."

Nina exhaled hard. If he had claimed that her father had wept and begged him to save his beloved child, she would have thrown the statue at his head and run, whatever it cost. As with Wu's white envelope, she would have liked much more, but she believed "useful." She took her hands off Ganesha's head.

The old man bowed in acknowledgment of this declaration of trust.

"Do you know where he is now?" she asked.

He avoided the question. "It is dangerous to him for anyone to know."

"But he can still send messages."

"Messages?" he repeated politely.

"To you and M. Wu. . . ."

He made an indefinite movement of his head.

"Can I send him a message?"

"Maybe one day." He closed the subject politely but with finality.

She accepted defeat, for the moment. "What do they call you?"

His eyes disappeared in the laugh lines that spread back to his temples like rays of light. His teeth, when he smiled, were black from betel like an old woman's or a montagnard's.

"Because of my great size"—he beamed more widely to point the joke; he was shorter than she was—"I am called Eight Hand Horse. And there are other reasons for the name which I cannot tell a lady." He must have been in his late sixties.

"Well, Eight Hand Horse." Nina grinned in return. "I would be grateful if your first service were to arrange a bath. I cannot tell a gentleman how long it has been since I last washed."

As he sidled past her to the washroom, she saw that he was as scrawny and tough as an old jungle cock. She listened while he shooed the chinchook lizards from the tub.

"Any minute now," his voice assured her over the sound of running water, "bath and food. The *mama-san* is coming right now from the food stalls. I sent her right away when you arrived with M. Wu."

It felt odd to give orders again and to have them obeyed without question.

Two hours later she lay on the four-poster bed, staring up at the strange young woman reflected in the canopy. Clean, fed, deloused, medicated, and bandaged, she wore a lemon silk *ao dai* which the *mama-san* had brought. Her dark, straight hair was slicked back from her face into a short fat tail at her nape. The filthy street urchin had disappeared but Luoc Nina, daughter of a rich Viet businessman and his French wife, had not reappeared. At least she neither looked nor felt like that girl.

I'm like an old temple, she thought. Bits of original masonry with bright patches of restoration and whitewash. Almost more restoration than original building by now.

She sat up suddenly. She had remembered Titi and Chinchook.

* * *

"Where the hell have you been?" asked Chinchook angrily. "I was nearly killed for you today!" His mouth fell open when he saw her properly. He stepped back in fright.

"It's really me," she said. "What happened to you today?"

He approached cautiously. "Are you *ma*?"

"No more than you were last time." She gave him a basket filled with mangosteens, a melon, cold noodles, chicken, and three cans of Coca-Cola.

With one hand he took the basket, with the other he stroked the silk of her *ao dai*. "Oh, boy," he breathed. "Like a flower. You really have good luck! Number fucking one! Oh, boy!"

He was already stuffing noodles into his mouth with his fingers with an intensity that Nina remembered but knew was already behind her.

"What happened to you today?" she repeated.

He held up an important, restraining hand while he finished chewing.

"At Monkey Mountain . . ." He swallowed some chicken like a boa constrictor engulfing a piglet.

"Where?" she asked.

"Gambling club," she thought he said, though she wasn't sure.

He licked his fingers. "Very secret place. For students and Buddhists and Binh Xuyen. I asked for Colonel Thu, like you want me to. And *bif,* this man grabs me from behind. Like this!" He shoved his own arm up behind his shoulder blades.

" 'What does a baby like you want with a bad man like that?' he asks me. He says to the other, 'Let's make this baby's teeth into mah-jongg tiles!'

"So I twist like this." He demonstrated. "Then I kick like this." He shot his leg out sideways. "That man was going to be on the floor when I finished, believe me! But some coward grabs me from behind and shoves me out the door."

Nina didn't have to pretend to be riveted.

"In the alley, I feel his knife on my neck. You are going to die, I tell myself.

" 'Why do you want the colonel?' the man asks, very quiet. And I know he is the right man.

" 'I have a message for him,' I say. 'From Nina, in Dalat. . . .' He pushes his knife harder so I can't talk.

" 'I don't carry message from whores,' he says." Chinchook's eyes were wide with the memory.

"So I slip from his grasp like a water ghost. I have to run for an hour to get away. I'm sorry, Big Sister. I don't say everything you want." He rubbed his throat.

"Not at all!" exclaimed Nina. "You were brave to say so much!"

He accepted her applause graciously.

She hadn't expected much from Thu as a lead anyway. After today, she no longer needed to find him at all. Life had moved on and made him irrelevant.

"Now, Little Brother," she said. "Come see what happened to *me* today."

25

The next day she had no trouble finding the bank named on the slip of paper; it was on a main business street in the heart of Cholon. Except for the huge gold Chinese characters on the fascia, it might have been any European bank.

The polite Chinese submanager explained that a number written on a scrap of paper did not constitute authority to release funds from that account.

"Our regulations require you to prove your right to access," he said. "According to our instructions from the account holder. Before we are permitted to give you or anyone else access to that account. You will find that this is standard procedure."

Nothing in his manner implied that her ignorance was deeply shocking.

"I do realize that." She could see the problem, but she had assumed that her father's arrangements would become clear once she reached the bank.

"How can I prove my right to access?" she persevered, carefully using the man's own words back at him.

The manager allowed the faintest touch of disapproval into his voice. "That is what you must show us!" He leaned back and watched her with satisfaction.

She did not respond. She was in a quandary; Louis had said not to use her real name. Did that restriction include the bank? Until now, she had assumed that it did.

The manager resumed after the pause lengthened, convinced that he was nailing her. "To tell you would be strictly against regulations," he said severely.

"Then I suppose that's that." She rose from her chair. "I'm

sorry to have troubled you." There was something she had overlooked, if only she could think what it was.

The submanager raised his eyebrows to a colleague as she left. Brazen hussy! Some of them would try anything to get their hands on the money of husbands or lovers. At least most had more finesse than this one—a half-French mongrel bitch, he was certain. What a pity those good looks were wasted on such an ignoble character!

You stupid bitch! Nina raged at herself outside in the street. She began to walk fiercely, to burn away her frustration and anger with herself. She had stampeded like a buffalo calf again, from excitement, without enough thought, while still unbalanced by the continuing changes in her life. She might have ruined the one chance her father had been able to give her.

The next morning she lay glumly in her ridiculous bed and regarded the cross-looking face in the canopy mirror. She heard a giggle and saw the reflection of the top of Chinchook's head at the end of the bed.

"*Ptchew!*" He popped up and mimed the throwing of a dagger. "You're dead! Lucky it's only me."

He rose from his hands and knees, on which he had crawled unseen into her room from his nest on the chintz-covered settee in the sitting room.

"Quiet as a Vietcong." He climbed onto the front of the bed and stared reflectively up at himself.

Nina peeled a lychee from the bowl by her bed and handed it to him.

"Crazy," he said around the shiny brown pip, still staring up. "To want to see the arse bounce up and down!"

Nina smiled quickly down at the second lychee she was peeling. "How much you know, Little Brother!"

He looked at her sharply, not quite trusting her tone. She handed him the second lychee and he slipped off the bed.

She watched him explore the crowded little room like a monkey. She had to be so careful of his feelings; it was quite tiring to remember sometimes.

He peered into the glass case that held the little paper-and-wire actors from the Peking Opera, which she had brought in from the other room. Seen from behind, his flaring ears seemed to prick forward with interest. He jiggled the case so that the paper spears quivered and the tiny coils of gold and silver wire hanging from the headdresses shivered in unison.

"Yeouw!" he said softly to himself. "Do you surrender, you

offspring of a turtle? . . . Never, you pig's arse. I will die first. *Hai!* Take that! And that!'' He moved on to her ring, which lay on the writing desk. He tried it on his finger, then left it hooked over one of the multiple arms of the bronze Ganesha. He put the chain that bore her seal over his head.

"Now I'm Number One Boss!" He swaggered back to the bed.

"What do you mean?" laughed Nina.

"Off with your head. Bam!" He mimed thumping the seal onto a decree. "You pay me one million quintals of rice for tax. Bam!" He smacked his fist against his other palm again. "You bring me Queen of Champa for number three wife. Bam!"

His cowlick bristled and his chin jutted forward like the blade of a plow.

"Yessir, yessir!" said Nina hastily. "Right away, your Excellent Honorableness!"

Chinchook lifted the chain off over his head. "You see, I do know things. You mustn't laugh at me."

"What do you mean?" asked Nina carefully.

"You're Number One Boss Lady. Like prince when the enemy has taken the throne." He looked at her with great seriousness. "One day, you take off your disguise and be yourself again."

Nina felt a physical jolt in her chest. "Why do you think that, Little Brother?"

He looked reproachful. "I watch things . . . and I think." He gestured at the bed, at the huge bouquet of orchids that Eight Hand Horse had placed by the washroom door. He took off the seal and placed it in her hand.

It wasn't what he had concluded but why that made her grab him in an exuberant hug and kiss his cheek.

"Hey! Don't do that!" He pulled away and wiped his cheek in embarrassment and discomfort. He was too old even for his mother to take such liberties. If she had been alive. He blinked twice, hard.

"I've been stupid . . . it's so simple!" she cried. "My father couldn't have imagined I would be so stupid. Little Brother, will you do me the great service of going to the market and buying me an ink pad?"

He was delighted to have a distraction. "Right away! Quick as lightning!"

As soon as he had gone, she leaped from the bed and dressed quickly in a blue *ao dai* and slippers. She twisted her hair into a neat bun at the nape of her neck, then penciled her brows into two willow leaves, like Louis Wu. She wanted to look as little as possible like the gauche *métisse* who had blundered into the bank the day before.

She sat down at the desk and penned a brief request to withdraw money from her father's account. Then she shook the little key from the envelope into her palm.

It was a rectangle of silvered metal; its round hollow-ended shank would fit over a shaped pin in the matching lock. On it were stamped four Chinese numbers. It was too small for a door key and the wrong shape for a car engine. She threaded it onto the string with the seal.

When Chinchook came back with the ink pad, she practiced first on a scrap of paper, then set the inked seal firmly against the bottom of her letter. The image was a little blurred, but the twisting dragon bird could easily be identified.

I should have known, she told herself. I should have trusted my father to arrange a simple way! "Try to take this one more seriously," he had said. "You will need it."

And it was nearly as simple as that. She was asked to show the seal that she had used. She answered two questions—her middle name, in both French and Vietnamese, and the name of her pet gibbon. The catch in her voice as she answered the last question convinced the bank manager beyond any lingering doubt that this was the correct young woman.

He ordered tea to be sent in with the forms, and a damp cloth to refresh her neck and face. He arranged her chair so that she could write comfortably and offered an array of pens in an onyx holder, along with an open red ink pad.

In each space marked "signature" Nina firmly stamped the mark of the twisting dragon bird—one on the form that identified her as a joint holder of the account, one on a request for a statement of the balance of the account, and one on a request to open the safe-deposit box. On each formal document, the red bird twisted like flames within the confines of its enclosing circle.

Alone in a small side room, she unlocked the safe-deposit box and lifted the lid. The top layer was American dollars in packets of different denominations. Under the dollars were French francs. Buried in the currency was a sky-blue cylindrical tin which had once held cinnamon sticks. She prized off its top and emptied it carefully onto the table. The gems inside tumbled like a mountain stream in the sun, spread across the table and rocked gently to stillness. She reached automatically to catch a pearl as it rolled off the table edge.

Lights winked and flashed as she stirred the stones with her fingers. She let out an involuntary sigh at wonders greater even than the contents of her mother's jewel box. There were opals, zircons, and duller, uncut stones that she knew were probably rough diamonds. Under the loose gems was a plug of rice paper. She pulled it out and unwrapped two baguette-cut emeralds set into gold rings. Below the rings, wrapped in more rice paper, were seven heavy gold bracelets—three plain, three twisted, and one set with small diamonds. At the very bottom of the tin she found a scrap of velvet cradling four huge cabochon rubies. Burmese reds. They were bright and dark at the same time, like the fresh blood on the street. Even to her relatively ignorant eyes, somewhat tutored by her mother, they insisted on their true worth.

She repacked the gems in the cinnamon tin and returned to the main box. The bottom was covered with assorted documents, four account books, and a small book sewn up in a wrapper of faded red silk. She took the account books, the red book, and the documents. The rest she replaced.

Back in the street, she sat down at a noodle stall to collect herself and to open the statement the clerk had given her before he bowed her back out through the metal banana leaves. When she saw the amount written, she knocked over her bowl of noodles with her elbow.

She exchanged a flurry of apology with the stall holder while she reread in amazement the figures in the little boxes on the form.

We're still rich, she thought. My father is rich. *I'm* rich! Very, very rich. No wonder they all kept bowing and scraping.

She didn't notice the second bowl of noodles the stall holder put in front of her. She was too shaken by a new truth that had just insisted on presenting itself. They should not be rich. Officially, her father was a bankrupt. André Gidéon had taught her too much. There was no legitimate way to explain why an undischarged bankrupt was also a piastre multi-millionaire.

The noodles grew cold while she stared at the bleached wooden tabletop. Her father must be either a crook or else something other than what he seemed. She remembered Eight Hand Horse's suggestion that her father was an enemy of the present government.

The stall holder glanced at her anxiously when she shook her head ferociously and said something to herself aloud that he could not grasp. He thought perhaps she was mad; the distraught expression in her eyes and her forgetting that she was in a public place

257

reminded him of a crazy boy who lived in his street. He stood near her and began to count some coins, loudly, to remind her, just in case she had forgotten, that she owed him for two bowls of noodles.

Absently, she paid him and began to walk back to her new home which she had no right to occupy—or so it might now seem.

I don't know what to believe, she argued to herself. My father was too honorable.

Too honorable for what? another internal voice riposted. Or perhaps he had an honorable reason for appearing to behave dishonorably.

By the time she reached the sandbagged house, she was deeply confused and depressed. She didn't know whether she preferred him to be a criminal or Vietminh. She realized that she had always blamed the Vietminh for killing her mother only because of what Andrew had told her. If the old man was right, the Vietminh were blameless and someone connected with the present government was guilty.

She trudged up the gull-wing stairs, locked the door behind her, and spread the documents from the bank out on the bed to see what they might tell her. There were deeds to several properties, including godowns, all no doubt unknown to the liquidators of her father's estate. Whether this was right or wrong was rapidly becoming less and less clear rather than more.

She leafed through the accounts for two hotels and some for a company called Eighty-eight Transport. A clear voice in her head, remarkably like André Gidéon's, kept telling her that she had no right to her father's money or to what it could buy, any more than her father himself did. Another voice, more like her father's, suggested that she did not know enough to judge.

One thing her complex childhood had taught her was that there was nearly always more than one way of looking at things. The French and the Vietnamese nearly always differed, not only in their interpretation of facts, but even in what they saw the facts to be. Her father was Vietnamese; she was looking at the facts with French eyes. It was possible, just possible, that he had good reasons for what he had done and she simply could not see his version of the truth.

Please let it be so, she begged of the Lord, the Virgin, and any other deities who might be listening.

After further thought, and feeling calmer, she called Eight Hand Horse and sent him with a message to André Gidéon, asking him to meet her, if he was still alive, in Indochina, and employed by the bank. She would make certain that she understood matters accurately from the French point of view. She was sure she could trust Gidéon that far. Then she would try to learn to see with her father's eyes.

Before she began to go through the papers a second time, she sent the *mama-san* for some lemons to make *citron pressé*, to sweeten the sour taste in her mouth. While she waited for the woman to return, Nina cut the red silk wrapper from around the little book.

Its brittle pages were covered in a fine handwriting in French. *The Art of War,* said the title page, by Sun Tzu, translated into French in 1792 by a Father Amiot. This copy was dated 1847. Doi, the gardener, had quoted the work as he practiced martial arts behind the washhouse. Since Nina had no intention of waging war on anyone, she carefully replaced the red silk and put the book into the top drawer of the utility desk in the bedroom.

Wouldn't it be funny, she thought, unamused, if after all my father turns out to be not only a fraud but a Vietminh? She didn't want to believe either possibility.

The *mama-san* was taking unusually long to get her lemons. When she heard a door open, Nina went out to ask where the woman had been for so long. Three Vietnamese stood in her front room, with the unhappy *mama-san*.

One of the three men held the servant. A second held a pistol, relaxed in front of him. The third, the youngest and best dressed, looked Nina up and down in calculated arrogance.

"Go and look," he ordered the man with the gun. The second man went past Nina into the bedroom. She heard him open the doors to the washroom and to the servants' quarters.

"Sit down," said the youngest man to Nina.

"No one here," called the man from the bedroom. He took up a position in the bedroom door.

"Sit down," repeated the young man. "I want to talk to you."

His slacks were expensive, his black loafers mirrorlike. His open-necked shirt was as crisp as the peaked roofs of a pagoda and he wore a gold watch that was as heavy as a handcuff. Nina noted these things, then forgot them immediately as fear crowded them out of her brain.

"Go and make us all drinks," the young man ordered the *mama-san*. "Stay with her," he told his man.

This order seemed strange to Nina, out of keeping with the break-in and the gun. She tried to make sense of it. In some way, it seemed to reduce the danger. It was social.

She detached her tongue, centimeter by centimeter, from the roof of her mouth. Don't show weakness, she told herself. Don't show fear.

"How dare you order my servant around!" she said, her bravado undercut by the quaver in her voice. She waited for his rage.

He laughed and sat on the sofa. "I gave you an order too."

"Sit down when he tells you," said the man behind her, the one with the gun."

She did, on the mauve chaise longue. Because he had laughed, she felt a little less frightened. A very little less.

"Who are you?" demanded the young man.

Don't show weakness. Don't show fear. She clung to the words for support.

"What happens if I don't tell you?" He looked familiar to her, but she couldn't think why. She was certain she had not seen him at Carbone's. This reassured her a little further.

"What if I said I'd have you shot?"

Not "I'll have you shot," she noted. He was in his early twenties, she thought. About Andrew's age. But without Andrew's shouldering energy. Instead, he had a calm assumption that he would be obeyed. She studied his face, his manicured hands, his pomaded hair, as if for clues to his intentions. Tight lines around his mouth were the only flaw in his classically handsome Viet features. She swallowed.

"I wouldn't believe you." She swallowed again. "Who are you?"

"Bo!" ordered the young man. Bo, the man with the pistol, stepped into Nina's line of vision and raised the little gun. She had never looked at a gun from that end before; she stared at the tiny dark muzzle and swallowed again. A nerve twitched in her left shoulder, which was on the gun side. She could not remember what the young man had just said to her.

"What were you doing at the bank today?"

She kept staring at the small dark hole, unaware that he had spoken again. The tiny dark hole filled her entire consciousness. It stared back at her.

"What were you doing at the bank today?" he repeated.

The world was full of secret enemies who attacked without warning. The nerve still twitched in her shoulder. The dark hole did not move.

"Why were you at the bank?" His growing irritation finally reached her, as another danger. She dragged her eyes from the dark hole to his face. It became a little easier to think, then. He had ordered *citron pressé;* she tried to think about that fact and why it had reassured her before. She did not let herself look back at the gun but forced herself to focus on his face. The face that had laughed earlier when she challenged him.

The bravery that her father had called foolhardy showed itself.

"Why," she heard herself ask, "should I explain myself before you do?"

"That's why." He pointed at the gun. She kept her eyes on his face; a thought was trying to free itself from the stunned darkness in her brain. If she let herself look back at the gun, the thought would remain trapped where it was. She thought a little more, then found the flaw in his logic that she had been groping for.

"If you shoot me, I can't answer your questions. So you must go first. Then I'll answer you." She pushed back into the cushions behind her as if against a sandbagged wall. She wrapped her arms around herself in unconscious self-protection. Useless self-protection, if he were to carry out his threat.

They looked at each other. The dark spot of the muzzle stayed where it was, a few feet from her left temple

In the silence, she heard the minor-key *tonk! tonk!* of a gold-beater bird in a neighboring garden. *Tonk! tonk!* Much slower than her galloping pulse.

The silence continued.

"OK," said the young man suddenly, as if he had been counting silently in a game and the time was up. He waved a hand and the spot of the muzzle vanished from her peripheral vision.. He smiled and leaned forward.

"My name is Kim. I am an associate of your father's. An accountant. I look after many things for him while he is away."

After a moment of paralyzed disbelief Nina shocked them, herself most of all, by rising to her feet, shaking with uncontrollable rage. *"Get out!"*

The young man was so startled that he stood up to obey.

"Get out! How dare you frighten me like that unnecessarily?" she shouted. "I suppose you were about to say that you're really a friend."

"Nina . . ." he began to protest. She was too much beside herself to notice his use of her name.

"Get out!" she repeated, hysterical with rage and relief. "Did I just pass some sort of test? Did I? Did my father ask you to do it? Well, let me tell you, *I don't need it!*"

"Nina . . ."

"You . . . *pig's arse!*" She was past calming. Her eyes blazed and her shoulders were hunched as if she were a buffalo about to charge him

He glanced at the other man and moved toward the door. "When you calm down, you'll find that you need my advice," he said. He placed a business card on one of the console tables.

"Get out!"

When the *mama-san* reappeared, with a stunned expression and a tray holding four glasses of *citron pressé*, she found her young mistress alone in the room, fists clenched, panting as if she had just run up a mountain.

At that moment, Nina's bell rang, faintly and painfully as if clogged with rust.

"I can't see anyone," said Nina. "Send them away!"

She folded her arms tightly around herself, to hold the parts together. The *mama-san* went cautiously down the gull-wing stairs. Nina heard raised voices. Then Louis Wu stepped through her door hugging a large parcel. He looked at her sharply but carried on as if he had noticed nothing wrong.

"You're on my conscience," he said. "I couldn't sleep last night."

Nina tried to focus on him properly. "What's the matter? Must I move out again? I know I shouldn't be here."

He assessed her again. "I was absolutely right to worry," he exclaimed. "Look at you!"

She remembered her manners. "Please sit down, monsieur. And tell me, what's the matter." She drew a deep breath to calm herself.

"It's this apartment!" said Wu in a tone of despair, while his eyes watched her, sideways. *"C'est affreux!"* Your soul is being eaten away every day you live here." He lowered himself gracefully onto the sofa—parcel, walking stick, and all.

Nina gaped at him, then began to laugh with relief, without the rage. "Is that all? My soul . . . ?"

"Don't laugh, I'm saying something very profound and true." Wu began to untie the string of his parcel. "As the responsible party, my sense of honor will not let matters rest. Now . . ."

He raised his hands and shot his cuffs like a magician above the parcel on his knee. ". . . I want you to forget those louts who nearly knocked me down in the drive, and give me your undivided attention. I'm trying to give you a present!"

Nina could not stop laughing.

Wu turned to the *mama-san*, who was hovering in curiosity. "I seem to bring on hysterics in her."

He uncurled a Chinese scroll painting—a spray of apricot

blossom, a butterfly, and, in the corner, a tiny frog. He draped it over the sofa back and unrolled another of chrysanthemums and a small black fly.

Nina's hysteria dwindled. "How beautiful," she breathed, between gasps.

"That's getting better," encouraged Wu. "Now sit down and close your eyes."

She sank onto the mauve chaise longue. She felt him place a smooth, cool object on her lap, hard, hollow, and about fourteen inches high.

"Careful," he admonished. "She's an original, not a copy."

It was a porcelain figure of Guan Yin, the Goddess of Mercy.

"Ohhh," breathed Nina. She laid her fingertips on the goddess's glazed cream and pink face. Its smooth coolness settled her slightly.

"I attach a condition," said Wu. "You must let me take that away." He pointed at the shell and lacquer mural. "And those . . ." Words failed him as he pointed at the orange plastic stacking chairs. "And the cocktail cabinet. Thank God, you already have the Géricault!"

Nina began to laugh again, real warm laughter from deep in her stomach.

"M. Wu, I don't know how to thank you. But I can't accept these. It's too much for a gift. Even for the sake of my soul."

Wu was suddenly serious. "I'm not giving you the choice. You must accept them, then, for the sake of your father. He thinks we're quits, but I do not. Not yet."

"Monsieur, do you truly believe he is worth such honoring?" She held her breath, her hands touching the divine serenity of the Guan Yin.

Wu looked deeply shocked. "Oh, my dear . . ." he began, then peered at her with his original sharpness.

"Never question his worth!" he said. "He was a great man."

Nina let out her breath carefully. "That's what I always thought. Now, I'm not sure. . . ."

Wu seemed almost angry with her. His hands made a gesture of helpless protest. "Nothing in this world is absolutely pure," he said. "I only know that your father changed my life. And saved it, for what it's worth. These gifts are still far from enough. I was . . ."

The hands made the helpless gesture again.

". . . in a bad way." His voice closed the topic, flicking out the last four words with ironic lightness.

They sat in silence while Nina reflectively stroked the Guan

Yin, and Wu examined his memories. After a moment he brightened, as if he had pushed an internal switch.

"Let's get back to my original point," he said. "I'm aware that you may think me a frivolous old clown, but I do know more than most men about the need to look after one's soul."

"And you think mine is getting ragged? Is this . . ." She continued to stroke the goddess's cool green and terra-cotta flanks. ". . . necessary help?'

"Frankly, yes," said Wu.

Nina was silent again. Then she asked, "Isn't all this merely a few patches?"

"What else can I offer?" he asked. "Except a few assurances which you shouldn't need. Patches are all that we can control. As for the rest . . ." He indicated the world outside with a twitch of his head. "Ah, well . . ."

"And you want me to accept 'the rest'?"

"What else can one do?" He took a glass of *citron pressé* from the *mama-san*.

"After this, I'll be off and stop depressing you with an old man's preoccupations." He drank, and unfolded his elegant figure from the faded chintz.

"You are lovely," he said unexpectedly. "Now that you've had a bath. What a pity I'm not younger. And the right way inclined. I do hope your father has the sense to know what he's got! And that goes as well for whoever put that ring on your hand!"

As Nina locked and bolted the door behind him, she heard his voice raised in song in English, fading down the stairs.

"A wand'ring minstrel, I, a thing of shreds and patches. . . ."

She laughed again and felt strong enough to pick up Kim's card from the console table. The bank must have told him within ten minutes of her leaving. Angry as she was, she now knew she had to make her peace with him, to find out what he knew about her father. To help her try to see with her father's eyes.

26

"I wish to apologize for my childish behavior when you visited me," she said to Kim. They met the next day, at her request, on neutral ground, the waterfront park at the bottom of Tu Do Street. They strolled slowly through the early evening crowds,

Kim's men somewhere behind them, and Eight Hand Horse a little behind that.

"No, no!" protested Kim. "It is I who should apologize."

They spoke French.

"I misjudged the situation," he said, "and the nature of your past experiences. I should not have tried to frighten you." He seemed determined to match her at manners. They eyed each other warily as they walked.

"You must understand," he went on, "that the times are disordered. We must all be careful...even more than usual. People are hungry; young women now do things they would never have dreamed of once."

His eyes followed two young whores in shorts and high heels, one wearing a blond wig, both of them parting the air before them with the padded, pointed funnels of their breasts.

"The bank told me yesterday that a young woman tried to persuade them to give her access to the account. When I heard today that she, or perhaps a different one, had succeeded, I thought it best to see for myself who and what she was. And, if she were really the daughter, whether she could be used by enemies."

"I want someone to explain to me," said Nina, "about Papa's bankruptcy, and how there is so much money left. And where he is and what he's doing. And what he wants me to do."

They reached the water and gazed out across the busy surface of the river.

"Your father was successful," said Kim. "Success generates jealousy. And as I said, these are disordered times. Jealousy and disorder came together at a time when he happened to owe a great deal of money to many people; such times are a normal part of business, for reasons that usually sort themselves out— investing capital for a later return, for example; borrowing in order to invest more against an even greater return. It stays in balance, most of the time."

"That's a description," said Nina, "not an explanation. And it answers only part of my questions."

A fishing sampan slid downstream through the warships and tugs toward deeper waters for its night's work, two sails held wide to catch the faint breeze like a lopsided butterfly.

Kim watched the sampan slip out of sight behind a troop carrier. Then he turned back to Nina. "Your father has arranged things so that you have a house and a little money. I think he wished you to live quietly, with as little worry as possible.

Perhaps even to choose to go and live in France. I don't think he meant for you to ask questions."

"Then he misjudged me," said Nina

Kim watched the retreating sampan and said nothing.

"I am at least half his daughter," said Nina bitterly. "I thought perhaps he had begun to realize that."

Kim looked at her uneasily, as if afraid she might have another tantrum in public. "What would you rather do, instead of living quietly? Which is a chance that most other people in Saigon would envy you."

"I would start by repaying as many of his debts as possible," she said. "To restore his honor and reduce the number of his enemies. Who seem now to be mine. He left me enough money to make a start."

"I wouldn't do that!" said Kim quickly.

"Why not?" Her voice rose in protest.

He glanced around. "You're not going to shout at me again?" he asked with unexpected levity.

She smiled tightly and he continued. "Such action might not be in harmony with his purpose. You should not alter the effect of his actions until you understand why he made them."

"Do you mean to say he wants things to stay this way? That he wants the shame and ill will? *Why?* Is he a Vietminh? What other reason can there be?"

Kim shifted his weight uncomfortably and looked faintly scandalized at her bluntness. He searched the far shore for assistance.

"He is a great man who does not share all his thoughts with those who work for him. Though I am privileged with his trust in many matters . . ."

"Bullshit!" said Nina in frustration. "You know—you just don't want to tell me. But I *need* to know! I *need* to understand!"

She saw anger set the muscles of his handsome young face. His voice, however, was cool and level.

"I do not abuse his trust in me," he said. "For anyone."

Nina glared down at a crust of floating rubbish, including a fish's head, which dashed itself gently against the seawall. She was being held at a distance again—all her life by her father, now by her father's man. She turned her glare on him.

"Who are you, anyway? Your name means nothing to me."

The anger had not left his face; his eyes were assessing. She saw again the confidence and authority he had shown in her room. He was being polite to her because of her father, but he did not really *see* her. As her father had not, until their last meeting in his library.

"A cousin of a cousin," he replied shortly. Which could explain the slight familiarity of his looks. "Why did you wish to meet today?"

"For explanations, which you have declined to give me. And for advice, which I will seek elsewhere."

"You are acting like a spoiled child," he said. "Having a tantrum when someone denies you what you want. My job for your father is to help keep you safe and financially comfortable. You have no right to expect more. I am the best person to advise you. The only one."

"I'll keep that in mind," said Nina. She watched the anger in his face again, and marveled at the power in being her father's daughter, which kept him from slapping her face as he obviously wished. That power interested her. It could be useful. Borrowed or not, its effect was real. She must remember that.

"And one first word of advice," he said. "Stay away from the French."

"Yes, I know," she said. "Ill will, and all that!"

They parted with extreme formality.

She immediately disregarded his advice by meeting Gidéon as already arranged through Eight Hand Horse. They met away from the European sector in a small café run by a retired Zouave mercenary not far from the Arroyo Chinois.

He looked grayer and more ill than when she had seen him last, an eternity ago, before the fighting.

"André," she said. "I need your help again. I've had some good luck since I saw you last and need expert advice. You're my expert!"

She put two sets of accounts down on the bird droppings on the dirty iron table.

"An uncle died and left me a hotel and a transport company."

Gidéon stared at her for three seconds, then laughed with delight. "That's your story and you're sticking to it!"

"Honestly," she said, and blushed.

"This is me, André. Remember? Never mind, let's have a look."

He reached eagerly for the hotel accounts she handed him.

"I think there's something very wrong here. Will you make certain?"

He scanned the pages, then asked, "Could I take these away for a good look?"

She hesitated.

"Come on!" he said. "Who am I going to tell about a fleapit in Cholon that seems to be going down the drain? My boss in some international industrial espionage ring?" He narrowed his eyes as he considered the possibility in his imagination. Then he tapped the side of his nose with great meaning.

"They'll never break me," he said.

She laughed. She had become suspicious of everyone, even this nice young man who was still playing at life. "Take them, of course."

She touched the accounts for Eighty-eight Transport. "This is my real problem. I need to make money. . . ."

In spite of Kim's warning about her father's intentions, she was going ahead. She would try to make as much money as she could; then, when she finally learned to see with her father's eyes, she would decide what to do about the debts.

"This company seems to be making a little money," she continued. "And I wonder if it couldn't make more. There's so much building work going on around the city, and all the supplies arriving at the docks. I feel that I ought to be able to take advantage of all that, but I don't know where to start."

"Leave it with me," said Gidéon gravely.

They met again for dinner the following night.

"You're absolutely right about the hotel," he told her. "The manager, or someone, is robbing you blind. Those accounts are so crooked that it's hard to tell how the business would be otherwise."

"Can you show me an example?" she asked.

He showed her examples for an hour and a half. Then they talked about possible ways of putting matters right.

Finally over coffee they considered Eighty-eight Transport.

"The turnover's about right for the present size," he said. "And, as you said, it's making a reasonable profit. Why don't you reinvest to increase your stock of vehicles, so you can take on more work?"

He offered her brandy, which she refused. He held his own balloon glass up to the light for intense study before he continued.

"After that, it's a matter of where you see your market. For instance, you could gamble on the government building program that's been announced and go for tipper trucks and earth movers. Or you could think more generally, about forklift trucks, for example, for shifting supplies in and out of warehouses. On building sites . . . that sort of thing. They wouldn't be limited to building sites, though, which would give you more options."

He sat back expectantly. What he had said made sense to her.

"I like your idea of forklift trucks," she said. "But I don't suppose one just walks into the nearest shop and buys them."

"Ahh," said Gidéon reflectively. "Yes. Well, I'm sure we can find out. Would you like me to find out some dealers for you?"

"That would be lovely, but you've been so much help already. . . ."

"Yours to command." Somehow, he managed to click his heels together under the table, in a sitting position.

"Meanwhile, I suppose I ought to talk to Gold Pen Kim," said Nina.

Two days after this dinner, she had a terse but satisfactory meeting with Kim and his lawyer. Kim agreed, grudgingly, to humor her on both the hotel and Eighty-eight Transport.

"As long as you stay away from your father's creditors," he said.

"I promise." She had decided that he was much more cooperative when she minded her manners. And she wasn't planning immediate contact with the creditors. "Thank you. I have to occupy myself somehow." She smiled at him. "And you see, I did come to you for advice, just as you said I should."

He was placated, though suspicious of her change in manner. "No harm in playing, I suppose. You might even learn something useful."

She closed her lips firmly over her retort. Her father's honor was at stake. Furthermore, she intended this "playing" to make Kim see her when he looked at her. If he saw what she was, he might even tell her father And perhaps her father might begin to see her as his own blood, not just an inconvenience to be tucked safely out of the way.

A week and a half later, when Kim and his lawyer had brought her the necessary papers to sign, she sent for the manager of the hotel, a Mr. Nghe. Kim offered to carry out the interview himself, but she refused, politely.

When he arrived, Nghe hovered just on the polite side of effrontery. His rudeness made her angry enough to forget her nerves as she pointed out to him that certain running expenses for the hotel might be considered overlarge.

"It is a successful hotel, mademoiselle," he said to the wall behind her head. "Of course the laundry bills are large. You would hardly expect the guests to sleep on dirty sheets." He dropped his eyes to his gold watch. "One solution," he continued, "would be to encourage fewer guests." He looked up again. "If that is the way you wish to run a hotel."

He obviously considered her a nuisance who interfered with his own plans now that his former employer had disappeared.

She was prepared; she had been through the interview in her head as many times as she had been through the accounts with Gidéon.

"Please don't misunderstand me," she said politely. "I am most impressed by the way you run the hotel." She allowed him a second or two of perfunctory, modest demurral.

"It must be difficult," she continued, "to maintain quality of service when, according to the laundry costs, you must have eight fully booked beds in each room for nine nights a week!"

She gazed at him, as if in admiration, from the new chrome and leather armchair Louis had forced upon her. "You are far too good for my modest establishment. I wish to terminate your employment."

Nghe rolled with the blow. "You can't do that. I have a contract of employment."

"Not with me," said Nina. "I didn't inherit the hotel; I bought it." With Kim's help she had—from her father's money from the secret account. "I regret that you were not listed among the assets that I acquired."

Nghe was breathing fast.

"I am prepared, however," said Nina, "to make a small, non-negotiable severance payment to you. I will also agree, should you accept this payment, not to press charges of fraud and misappropriation of funds."

Nghe had now had time to think. "Someone has misled you about me," he said. "I have a thief on my staff and you have decided that it is myself. I must accept your decision, as my superior." His voice made mock of the last word. "In any case, I suppose it is my responsibility—I am the ruler of the staff, as the Celestial Father is the ruler of his people. I must guide them, and be chastised for their faults, which are a failure of my example and guidance." He bowed his head in resigned dignity. "I think you will find, however," he added, "that no one will wish to replace me in such an ill-favored establishment."

His eyes were malevolent and left no doubt that the ill favor lay in the new schoolgirl owner of the place, and in what he would say about her.

"The staff are loyal to me," he added.

"Thank you for the warning," she replied. "The door is behind you."

After Nghe left, Nina could not think why Kim had been so worried about the interview. She allowed herself to feel a little pleased with the way it had gone.

Unfortunately, Nghe was right; she did have trouble finding a new manager. And staff.

"The cook was his brother-in-law. He went, too, along with five others." Nina thought aloud in the battered Citroën that Eight Hand Horse drove like a souped-up limousine. "He's been putting it around that I'm ill-fated."

The old man beat a motor scooter to a bollard before he spoke. "May I presume to offer advice?" He ignored the driver of the scooter who was chasing them along the pavement, screaming after them in rage. The question was rhetorical. They both knew how necessary he was to her.

"If I were you," he said, "I would call in a *tay phap.*"

"A *sorcière?*" asked Nina. "But I don't believe in them."

"Others do," said the old man. "And that is much more important. They act as the *tay phap* advises, which may alter the course of events. Which may alter your lack of belief."

He ignored a traffic policeman's upraised glove, like the rest of the traffic. Nina thought for a minute.

"Can you find me one?"

The *tay phap,* who normally kept office hours in the porch of a temple near the northern edge of the city, agreed to visit the hotel. After a few questions and a cursory inspection of the premises, he said to Nina, "It's very simple. Your father's bad luck is still with you. Sell the place; the new owner will bring different luck. Apart from that, you must balance the mountain— represented by the front wall—with water. And use more lucky red in the furnishings."

He accepted a modest fee and returned to his temple.

When Kim inquired, as he often did, how things were going, Nina did not tell him. She could not bear to say that she had been advised to sell the place again. She was determined to make a success of it, herself. The balancing of mountain and water was much the easiest problem to solve. She ordered an ornamental pool to be dug in the balding yellow patch of a former bowling lawn. The pool was soon nearly finished, but she had not yet solved the ownership problem. Then one night, just as she was falling asleep, she remembered a drunken conversation of several months before. The next morning she woke Chinchook from his nest on the rattan sofa where he still slept regularly, though of late he had often been away for days at a time. He would appear for occasional meals, without explanation but full of street gossip.

"Do you know where we can find Titi?" she asked him.

"She's with a new man, every night the same," he said sleepily. "They go off on a motorbike. But I know where she is in the daytime. Just follow me!"

They found Titi on Tu Do Street, in front of a new go-go bar, perched daintily on top of a large television set with a smashed tube and no knobs. She was balancing a large tray on her lap.

They watched while she sold a pack of Trojans from the tray, and a bottle of Wind Song, to a large pink soldier who was clutching a small brown woman to his side with one arm. Titi rearranged the remaining Trojans, Black Shadows, and Rainbow Ticklers before she saw them.

"Hello!" she called happily. "Come over here. I can't move because she . . ." She jerked her chin toward a hovering food vendor. ". . . . wants to put her damn brazier under my feet if I don't watch out. To cash in on my good luck in this spot."

"Business is good, then?" asked Nina, as she sat in the space Titi made for her on the television.

"Number fucking one!" said Titi. "I can sell one bottle eight times a day if the girls are careful not to make it too dirty. . . ." She felt the silk of Nina's *ao dai*. "Business is pretty good for you too, I think. Nice stuff!"

She pushed gently at Nina's thigh. "Now we must find you a man."

"I have one," Nina reminded her. "I think. Somewhere." It bothered her how little she had been thinking about Andrew recently. She had stopped looking for him. Too much had been happening.

"Somewhere?" repeated Titi. "That's no use. Leave it to me. You're clean enough now." She patted Nina's silk-clad thigh to make sure she did not take offense.

Nina laughed. "Wait till I'm a widow. I'll let you know. . . . Titi, I came to talk business with you."

Titi said nothing, but her eyes sharpened.

"Would you like to buy a hotel?"

"Don't joke with me," said Titi.

"I'm not joking, Little Sister," said Nina. "I have a problem and need your help."

She explained. "You buy it from me, so that it is known as your hotel. But you pay me only a little money every month. I keep the deeds and financial control until it is paid off. But you have a free hand in the day-to-day business. From time to time, we will discuss how things are going."

Titi had gone very still.

"You said you would like a hotel," Nina said. "Remember that we are lucky for each other. I know people who can advise us if there is a problem."

Titi looked into her eyes. "You're really not joking? It is very cruel if you are."

"I'm not," said Nina.

Tears began to slide down Titi's face. She wiped them away with a delicate, scarlet-tipped finger while she sold a bottle of White Shoulders and some Trojans to another soldier.

"I still think it is a joke," she whispered when the man had moved on.

"Come see it," said Nina. "You do me a great service if you will agree to help me out."

Titi quickly stowed her bottles and packets into a basket beside the television. "A hotel with many rooms, and sheets and towels and Western beds?"

"And a restaurant," said Nina. "Only twelve rooms, but that's enough if one is clever. We will call it the Phoenix Tower."

Titi raised a radiant face toward Nina. "I will be clever. I promise. You will hear such good things of me. You wait."

27
1955

That autumn, in October, elections were finally held in South Vietnam. But not the ones promised by the Geneva Accords after Dien Bien Phu, which were to have united the North and South under one government. Diem, backed by the United States, which feared a Communist takeover, refused to allow those elections to take place. The elections were held merely to settle the question of who would rule in the South—Diem, or Bao Dai, the former Emperor of Annam and head of the Japanese "New Vietnam." When they were over, Bao Dai was out and President Diem confirmed as Premier, the first in the land.

His triumph was marred only by reports that he was voted in by a majority made up of the ballots of dead men, of men too ill to get to the polling boxes, and of a remarkable number of men bearing exactly the same names. It was also marred by rumors of men with clubs and knives, who inquired politely about each voter's intentions.

Nevertheless, many Vietnamese, particularly the younger ones, preferred Diem to Bao Dai, a former colonial emperor who spent most of his time in the south of France. To Nina, the elections meant chiefly that her father's enemies were still in power.

That autumn there was also a series of explosions in Saigon. A small group of Vietcong dynamited new MAAG and USIS installations. For several weeks Nina had nightmares again. Of her mother. Of disintegrations. She woke up night after night, crying and reaching blindly for Andrew's warmth in the empty darkness.

Then the explosions stopped. No one had been killed and only a few Americans were injured. Her nightmares eased. The Phoenix Tower began to make a small but steady profit.

Titi embraced the Phoenix Tower as a missionary would a nation of lost souls. She found staff almost immediately, from among her acquaintances, for lower wages than Nina had been prepared to pay after asking at the larger hotels. She suspected that some of the maids, at least, were supplementing their income by night, but she had promised to stay out of Titi's way in the day-to-day running of the place. Her books showed that the rooms were filled with paying guests. The income was greater than the costs. Best of all, Kim modified his usual tone of amusement after he examined the first quarterly accounts.

"You're lucky," he said.

Louis Wu continued to call at her new apartment unannounced, bearing small gifts. He rearranged her furniture and replaced the worst horrors with silk Chinese carpets and German steel and black leather easy chairs, murmuring reverently of "Le Corbu." He arranged antique Thai bronze Buddhas on French plate-glass shelving. He hung a small watercolor by Klee and a large Burmese temple painting.

"The best of both worlds, my dear. Just like the pair of us."

Once he held out for her to admire a set of tiny sea spirits in bronze, tucked into minute coiled bronze shells. "Opium weights...exquisite! Someone cared enough to take all that trouble. You see, everything has its lovely side, as well as the other."

She was unsure whether his words held the weight of extra meaning.

True to his word at their first meeting, he also did something about her dressmaker and *coiffeuse* by sending her to some "very dear friends"—a Vietnamese couturier and a French hairdresser.

"Presentation!" he declared. "Vital. It's like the theater; people believe what they see, even if *we* know it's all corsets, toupées, and papier-mâché! When you're destitute, wear expensive clothes even if you have to steal them. And if you want to be taken seriously as a businesswoman, you must buy a few good pieces of jewelry and find yourself an office at a reasonable address!"

She took his advice and asked Kim to rent an office for her. They found one on Cong Ly Street, above a ground-floor office occupied by Walking Elephants et Cie, Importers and Exporters, whose windows were permanently masked by fretwork hardboard screens and a litter of unidentifiable machine parts gathering dust behind the dirty glass. By Christmas, her first one since Andrew had disappeared, she had installed herself and Eighty-eight Transport in three rooms on the first floor—one for visitors, one for files and a secretary, and one for her private use as the managing director. She had moved the files and the secretary, an aging Malay who wore dyed-to-match blouses and skirts, from a dusty alcove in a Cholon warehouse. Louis said it would all do, for the time being. As far as the secretary and her other employees were concerned, she was merely a new broom sent in by powers above to keep an eye on things.

She then spent two months observing, and talking to as many building contractors as she could. She noticed, among other things, how impatient Americans were with the pace of most work, including loading and unloading. She also observed that one forklift truck could do the work of ten coolies. Unfortunately, Gidéon had left for France just after the autumn elections, before he had found her a supplier of heavy machinery. He did, however, leave her reams of carefully prepared notes on anything he could imagine she might need to know in the next year. She refused his invitation to accompany him, but saw him go with considerable regret.

In these two months, her relationship with Kim became almost friendly. They had lunch together twice. He approved of the idea of forklift trucks. Cordial as he had become, he never said what she most wanted to hear: "Well done. Your father would be proud." And she refused to ask for reassurance.

Once she had decided for certain on forklift trucks, she asked both Eight Hand Horse and Chinchook to start a trawl for intelligent men who would like to learn how to drive machinery.

Then, one evening, she went to see Louis for help in contacting a supplier; he seemed to be able to lay his hands on anything in the world if he wanted to. Following his own example, she chose to visit him unannounced.

She was curious to see how he lived. Eight Hand Horse knew exactly where to go, and within fifteen minutes dropped her outside a moon gate in a side street in Cholon. She gave her name to an eye behind a tiny wooden wicket. There was a long wait after the eye disappeared, before the gate swung open.

She had grown very fond of Louis in the last few months, once she had stopped protesting at his patches for her soul and allowed him to enjoy his own generosity. She enjoyed his company; he made her laugh. Apart from Chinchook and Titi, both of whom were now even more occupied with private business than she was, he was her only friend. In spite of that she had never visited his house, nor had he ever invited her.

As she followed his watchman through the moon gate, she looked around the courtyard, curious for clues to the private Louis. A contorted arrangement of boulders dominated one end of the courtyard; an invisible pump spewed a precisely calculated ribbon of water over the shoulders of the rocks into a tiny pool at their base. She heard a faint unfinished sound as a single vane of a wind chime gently nudged another. Then, behind that sound, she heard the surge of organ music, muffled inside the house. She looked up at the eight-sided mirror over the heavy carved door.

Louis is as mixed up as I am, she thought with amusement. A public cosmopolitan but a private Chinese. It was even more complicated than that.

The door opened. Louis's astonished face looked out. Nina forgot her manners and stared back.

His face was powdered dead white; his lips were expertly painted into a scarlet cupid's bow. The silver wings of hair were hidden under the quivering tinsel of the headdress of a Chinese opera heroine. Instead of a well-cut suit he wore a complex layering of silk—a woman's kimono, belts, a multipetaled collar embroidered with thousands of silk French knots.

He was at a loss; she had never before seen him miss a single beat.

"My dear...!" he exclaimed. His improbably red-taloned hands made vague loops in the air, unable to settle.

"I've come at a bad time," she began, now off balance herself.

Then they both began to laugh.

"Do come in," he said. "Come in. Don't try to be formal with an old queen in drag." He took her hands and pulled her in. The organ music was deafening. "I'm entertaining a few friends," he said. "You caught me doing my party piece." He looked at her sideways.

"You look beautiful," she said, meaning it. "Strange, but beautiful." She put a hand on his arm. "I won't stay and bother your friends," she said. "I just wanted to talk to you and wasn't polite enough to give you warning."

"Don't be silly," he replied. "Anyone who knows enough to flatter me has to stay for at least one glass of champagne."

He began to lead her down the paneled hallway. "Anyway, when you're in business, it never hurts to meet new people."

At first Nina thought there were three men and one woman in the room at the end of the hall from which the music came. One of the men, a Frenchman, was clearly male, in spite of a Veronica Lake wig and beaded evening dress. He touched the wig self-consciously before he took her hand. His firm grip and five o'clock shadow made the beaded dress look like a drunken Christmas caper. The other two men, a Chinese and a Vietnamese, wore formal men's evening clothes. The woman, a Chinese in a long cheongsam and fox fur stole, was on closer inspection also male.

They had been smoking; two silver filigree opium pipes sat on a large tray on a low chrome and glass table of a style that was *le dernier cri* in France. Veronica Lake sank back onto the sofa. After accepting introductions pleasantly, the other three closed their eyes and let their heads fall back against their down cushions.

The tiny coiled wires on Louis's headdress shivered brightly in the soft light of the gas lamps he still preferred to use. He poured her a glass of champagne.

"Shocked?" he asked her quietly under cover of the music.

She shook her head. "Surprised. Not shocked."

"We were listening to the Saint-Saëns Organ Concerto," he said, somewhat unnecessarily. "Trying to pretend that the real world doesn't exist. That's my real secret vice." He had recovered his composure. "I don't suppose you'd like to try a pipe?"

She shook her head again. "*Maman* made me swear once that I'd never touch it. So I won't until I have a good reason."

"She did, did she?" Louis looked thoughtful and a little distant.

She noticed his distance and said, "I really should go. I'm interrupting a private time."

277

He laid a hand on her wrist. "It's not an orgy, my dear. We're only listening to music. Stay. Let them get used to your face. She . . ." He nodded at Veronica Lake. . . . "is with what remains of the Deuxième Bureau. We're old friends. She could still be useful to you."

He led her to an armchair upholstered in white linen. "Stay," he murmured under a surge of organ solo. "The world runs on familiarity. Not on logic or reason. On familiarity . . . and money. You have money and ambitions but don't know a soul, and I intend to change that."

She sank back into the unexpected softness of down cushions.

"Funnily enough, that's why I came here tonight."

"Splendid!" said Louis. "We'll talk in a bit. Now hush and listen. This next section is quite sublime!"

He sat and closed his eyes like the others.

At five o'clock on the following Thursday, Louis's driver arrived to collect her without Louis. He drove to the docks where they picked up an American from outside the Customs shed.

The man was fat, sweaty, and cheerful, with a military haircut.

"Parlez-vous anglais?" he asked as he climbed in beside her in the backseat. "What the hell, never mind," he said when she shook her head. "You'll have to put up with my French then. Clinton Clay. Pleased to meet you, Miss Owen."

He stuck out a fist and looked her over. "Any friend of Louis's is a friend of mine." He winked. "Speaking strictly in a business sense, that is. If you know what I mean."

She knew she ought to loathe him, but she didn't. He looked too happy with life; you couldn't dislike someone who managed to look so happy, without also looking smug or self-satisfied.

His belly rolled like rising dough over the belt of his chino pants and strained the buttons of his short-sleeved shirt. Though the chinos were dirty and the shirt had large sweat stains under the arms, he wore a heavy gold Rolex watch, two gold rings, and expensive lizard-skin shoes. He followed her eyes.

"Had those made in Hong Kong. I get some made every time I fly up." His French accent was appalling but his grammar firm and colloquial. "Do you need any shoes?"

Nina told him what she wanted. He didn't blink.

"How many?" he asked.

"Six. To start with. I might be interested in other vehicles later."

"Well, now." He leaned back against the upholstery, crossed

an ankle over one plump knee, and flicked a bit of leaf off his shoe. "I might be able to put you in touch with the man you need to talk to. Probably the only one who won't skin you alive."

"Thank you. I'm grateful," she said.

There was a pause. He began to look less and less happy with life

"And," she added, "I would want to show my gratitude in some tangible way."

He grinned. "Now you're talking!"

"You speak very good French," she said.

"Have to," he said. "In my business, it doesn't pay to let some other guy tell you what some other guy is supposed to have said, if you see what I mean. Leads to misunderstandings. I don't like misunderstandings. If I want to do business out here, I learn to talk the lingo. I can talk a little *jaune* too. Not much yet, but I'm working on it."

His eyes looked suddenly sly. "You thinking of learning a little English, maybe?"

"Do you think I might need it?" she asked innocently.

"Do I? Do I ever!" He looked out the window and laughed an open, cheerful honk of pleasure. "Christ, I think you might!"

Delivery took three months. In that time, Nina had her eighteenth birthday and learned how many people needed sweetening in the process—for the import license, for handling, for "insurance," for agreeing to allow new operators on the docks and building sites. The license was fairly simple: the Vietnamese who had been at Louis's turned out to be a personal secretary in the background of Diem's cabinet. For the rest, Clay earned his generous percentage of the purchase price by guiding her gently through the financial and diplomatic thickets. Three weeks after delivery she had all six of her new trucks out on long-term hire contracts, drivers included.

She spent the next several months in relative peace. Nearly two years had passed since Andrew disappeared; they had gone by quickly. She sometimes found it hard to remember him clearly, as if the five days of fighting had become a wall in her mind between the old Nina and the new one. The problems and satisfactions of daily business had begun to seem more important than her reasons for going into business in the first place. She still intended to repay her father's debts. In the meantime, she needed all the spare cash to reinvest.

Though Eighty-eight Transport continued to make a profit, something bothered her about the next final accounts. She compared them with past accounts and picked out a sharp rise in the cost of servicing the nine haulage trucks the company had already owned. She sent Chinchook around the city on a survey of garages and checked with Eight Hand Horse what he paid for the Citroën. The trucks were each serviced individually by their drivers, who took them to their own mechanics, then put in expense claims for what they said the mechanics had charged. When both Chinchook and Eight Hand Horse confirmed that she was paying over the odds, she asked Eight Hand Horse to inquire whether the man who serviced the Citroën would be interested in a maintenance contract with the company. Kim suggested that she also invite bids from two garages Chinchook had visited.

The drivers wouldn't like it, but she worked out a face-saving formula of a small fee for the drivers to deliver the trucks for servicing. Even with this fee, she would save money. And be certain that all the trucks were actually serviced. From the looks of some of them, she had her doubts.

It was after the Tet New Year 1957, when the Year of the Rooster began, that she took a table in a restaurant patronized almost exclusively by Vietnamese, to meet the owner of the garage used by Eight Hand Horse. As she studied her notes of earlier meetings with two other garage owners, she felt how much her confidence had grown in the last few months. Even Kim had stopped making jokes about her two enterprises.

While she waited, she watched a noisy group of young Vietnamese seated around a large table in the far corner of the restaurant. They were drunk enough to feel self-satisfied and not to care who knew it. All were well dressed, brilliantined, and glinting with gold like Corsicans. They were sharing a bottle of Chivas Regal—worth a fortune even on the black market—and three women who cost considerably less. The one sitting with his back to her seemed familiar. When he turned to call for another bottle of whiskey she saw that he was not Vietnamese. He was Andrew.

She took a sip of her drink. She had not mistaken a stranger for Andrew for months.

The woman sitting on the lap of the man next to him leaned over and whispered in his ear. Nina stared at the dark hair, shaved high on the familiar nape. He placed his hand on the woman's arm, a temporary claim on her person. Nina knew that gesture.

She crossed to the jukebox which blinked and glowed on the far side of the room and pretended to study the typed list of songs glued to the glass front. Her eyes passed blindly over "Bernadine" by Pat Boone and a *gamelan* version of "The Little Brown Jug." She walked back to her table. There was no mistake.

She was suddenly terrified that he would look up and see her. It was too sudden. She had begun to assume he was dead. Or at least to act as if he might be. It had been so long without a word. Suddenly, she had to rearrange the pattern of her mind to readmit him.

At that moment, the garage owner arrived. She tried to remember why she had asked him to meet her here. She looked back at the corner table. Andrew was staring at her.

"I'm sorry," she stammered to the garage owner. "Forgive me...." What could she say to the man?

"I'm not well . . . I'll arrange another meeting . . . Forgive me."

Andrew excused himself to his table and crossed to her, followed by laughter and kiss-kiss noises from his friends. Nina did not see the garage owner go.

"Nina?" Andrew sat down in the chair opposite her, looking perplexed. "My God! It is!" He caught her hands as she half rose in panic.

She was surprised at her own reaction. She should fling herself into his arms. Instead, she shook her head helplessly.

He pressed one of her hands to his face as if to confirm its living warmth. "I can't believe it!" he said. He studied her. The chignon was new . . . made her look like a bloody Chinese matron. Apart from that, she looked wonderful. Older than her age. Less lost. All traces of puppy roundness gone. Along with a new wariness, her eyes held shadows of knowledge which he found exciting. She'd gone completely native in her dress as well as her hair. And he noted the carillon of gold bracelets on her right wrist. They had some catching up to do!

"I thought you were dead," he said. "After what happened to the building."

"That's what I thought about you . . . after a while. The woman across the street told me you had gone out, but eventually I gave up hoping."

It really was Andrew, not another of the ghosts she had followed, but he still felt like a ghost to her. He looked so delighted to have found her; she wished she could feel the same.

"You look great," he said.

She suddenly realized that she was the ghost. The Nina whose hand Andrew thought he was caressing was not really there. The woman at the table with him was someone quite different.

281

"I asked about you everywhere," he said. "No one knew."

"I asked too . . ." said Nina. Instead of strangers looking like Andrew, suddenly Andrew looked like a stranger.

What were they going to do now? This man was her husband, joined with her until death. How was she going to refind the earlier Nina who had desired him more than she had ever imagined possible? Who had needed his advice and depended on him for protection. It was not his fault that she had changed.

"We have a lot to tell each other," she said.

He blinked. "You're right!" he agreed enthusiastically. After a moment, he added, "Come on, let's get out of here. Hold on."

While he went to make his excuses at his table, she stood up and smoothed the front of her *ao dai*.

"Let's go." He grabbed her elbow and guided her to the door. On the street, he waved down a taxi and opened the door for her. "Your place or mine?' He grinned. "Actually, it'd better be yours. . . . I'm in the middle of moving. What address shall I give?"

Nina glanced over her shoulder at the astonished Eight Hand Horse, who was waiting by her car. She shook her head in quick warning. The old man let their taxi pull away before he got into the Citroën to follow them.

She gave Andrew her address; she could think of no reason not to. She was interested that she had even hesitated. She also noted that the old Nina was indeed returning, paralyzing her mind and will and following Andrew's lead like the helpless schoolgirl she had once been.

He gazed around her apartment with open assessment, his eyes passing speculatively over the Géricault, the Guan Yin, and Louis's two Chinese scrolls.

"It looks like you've done pretty well without me," he said. "Maybe I should disappear again." He laughed to underline the joke.

"You've done well too," she said. He wore a gold chain around his neck, a gold ID bracelet, and several heavy rings.

"Come on!" he said. "It doesn't take much to do well these days . . . all those dollars pouring in. All it takes is balls and a little hard work. You know me . . . I don't sit still." He broke off and held out his arms. "Come over here. You're way over there across the room! You haven't even given me a kiss of welcome yet. It's been a hell of a long time!"

The helpless Nina, schoolgirl Nina, his legal wife, crossed to him and allowed herself to be enfolded. He kissed her hard on the lips and pulled his head back without releasing her.

"That's better." He kissed her again. "We'll have an early night tonight. Unless you want me to go crazy!"

Nina pulled away and suppressed an automatic move to wipe her mouth.

"Andrew, I'm not used to your being back. I need time."

"Feeling shy?" He patted her bottom. "Still a little Catholic schoolgirl, in spite of your new hairdo! You'll get over it once I get to work on you. Just the way you did before."

She moved away from him. "Probably," she said. "But I do need time.... I don't mean a few minutes." She looked at him pleadingly. "I mean ... not tonight."

She saw anger flash across his face.

With his thumb, he turned the ring on his little finger.

"Of course, sweetheart," he said. "I understand. To tell you the truth, it's strange for me too. I'm not even used to living a normal life again yet."

She took the cue. "Why? What happened to you?"

He sank into the sofa. "Not to put too fine a point on it, I was in the nick ... no joking matter under the Little White Knight, let me tell you."

"In jail? What did you do?" Somehow, she wasn't surprised.

The ring was turning again.

"Hard as it is to believe," he said, "I never really found out." He looked up at her and smiled. "As I finally understood it, they suspected me of something vague and political. To do with your father's northern loyalties. 'Aiding and abetting a conspiracy against the security...' That kind of thing."

"But I thought you once said..." Nina stopped herself. "You mean they thought you were helping my father help the People's Republic?"

"That was the gist of the confession some goon in the Deuxième Bureau kept pressing me to sign." He snorted in disbelief. "At first I thought they thought I was really working a fiddle with francs and piastres. But that's hardly penal colony league, even now."

"You were on Poulo Condore? Con Son?" She was shocked briefly out of her internal questions about whether he had lied before or was lying now.

"Just for two weeks." He smiled grimly. "But it was long enough to scare the shit out of me. Then they let me go. Just like that. I still don't understand it, any more than why they picked me up in the first place. I finally decided that the CIA got one of *their* pigeons to coo out enough to make up for a dozen of the Sécurité's bag. Diem doesn't care where he gets Commie witches to burn as long as he gets enough to impress his friends across the Big Water.''

He looked at her candidly. "That's me. What about you?"

"Much less exciting," Nina said mendaciously. She poured them both a gin and tonic; she knew she needed one.

"Do you remember you sent me to pay Two Boats Lu? I was on the way home when the house was hit. Afterward, I just wandered about. Looking for you. Finally got in touch with some of my father's people, so to speak. A relative left me a little money. There was a lot to do. Things had begun to fall apart after he disappeared. But I'm still keeping my head down, just like you said.''

She glanced at him; he was listening very closely. He sipped his drink.

"As you say," she continued, "I have done quite well, considering. Not as well as my father, of course, but well enough. You're quite right about all the new money around. And I quite like it." She laughed.

He joined her laughter. "My little tycoon! God, it's good to see you again. I missed you, you know."

She smiled at him with the first real warmth she had felt. He did seem happy to have found her. Her unease with him would probably fade in time as she learned more. She wandered to the window and looked down; there was no sign of Eight Hand Horse or the car. The identity of the old man was one thing she had to clear up with Andrew before her mind could rest.

"By the way," inquired Andrew, "who was that man in the restaurant?"

"Just a mechanic," she replied. "He's going to save me a little money, I hope."

"I don't need to be jealous, then?" He grinned.

When she said nothing, he went on. "If you need good men for any reason, I might be able to help. Since I got sprung, I've been doing work for a few firms with clout."

"Thank you," she said. "That's kind of you."

There was an awkward pause.

"You're really not going to let me stay tonight?"

"I'm sorry. . . will you forgive me?"

"Sure, sure. Like you said. You need time." With resolution, he crossed to her and kissed her long and hard.

"That's just to speed things up," he said. "I'm too old to enjoy sleeping on the floor anymore."

The following night, after taking her out for an expensive dinner, he took her back to the apartment and raped her.

"What the hell's wrong? You're my wife!" Martell glared down at the averted face on the pillows of the big bed when it was over. "Have you got someone else? . . . Been dancing on my grave, maybe?" He turned her face with his hand. "Is that what you've been up to? An Annamite, like Daddy? Or a rich French protector?"

When she just looked at him, he dropped back onto the pillows. "Is that how you've done so well? Should have guessed something when I saw this bed. It's a joke!"

"That's exactly what it is," said Nina flatly. "A joke."

He snorted. "Don't expect me to clear out when whoever he is comes to call. You're still my wife, and you'd better not forget it!"

The last shreds of her guilt at not being able to love him again had vanished. To his reflection in the canopy, she said coldly, "Do you have any idea how stupid you're being?"

He rolled suddenly so that his face hung close over hers, blotting out the distant reflections.

"Stupid is one thing I'm not, baby! Or gullible. Every bone in your body tells me that you've changed. And not just your hairstyle. Every move you make gives you away. Don't talk to me about 'stupid.' "

Nina stared back at him with blank eyes, then rolled from under him, off the bed, and began to dress.

Martell watched her. "I don't know where you're going. All I know is that you had better come back!"

As she combed her hair back and began to stab pins into the coil on the nape of her neck, he rose and crossed to her. He put his hands on her shoulders; she stopped pinning up her hair and waited like a stone.

"Nina, I'm sorry."

She neither spoke nor moved.

"I don't know how to handle you anymore. You've changed. I don't understand you. You used to beg me for it. But I'm sorry if I upset you. Really." He sounded sincere. "Let's take more time. Like you said. I'll try not to mind that you need more time than I do. I take back what I said about another man. OK?" He bent his head to try to catch her eyes in the mirror. "After all, you married me. You must have meant something by it. You owe it to both of us to give it a chance."

She let out a shaky breath.

"I'll even sleep on the floor for a bit. Sofa, actually, but you know what I mean. OK?"

"OK," she said tiredly.

The next day, through Louis, she arranged a meeting with M. Frey, the officer of the Deuxième Bureau who had worn the Veronica Lake wig. At Louis's suggestion, she met him two days later on one of the little passenger launches that shuttled back and forth across the river.

"I remember you," said Frey. "You're part of Louis's collection; all his friends are either connoisseurs or collectibles." He paused to consider his own turn of phrase. "How can I help you?"

She explained. Frey said he would get back to her. He left the launch on the far side and his head moved away through the crowd on the quayside. Nina rode back across the river to Saigon. A week later, Louis's driver delivered a note from Frey. He regretted that he was unable to find any record of either the arrest or release of someone named Andrew Martell during the spring or summer of 1955. He also pointed out, however, that he did not have access to the files of either the special forces or the secret police, which were both controlled by Diem's brother.

Louis knew someone else she might find useful to talk to. Four days later Nina sat having lunch in a new, international-style restaurant off Nguyen Thai Hoc Boulevard, not far from the Cau Muoi Market, with a plump, elderly Japanese camera importer.

Taki Hashimoto had arrived in 1940 as an officer with the occupying Japanese troops. He had then remained after the Japanese surrender as part of the Japanese peacekeeping force which was rearmed by the British in order to fight native insurgents while the French military presence was being reestablished. He had married a Vietnamese and stayed in Saigon, selling expensive cameras and occasional information, mainly of a commercial nature. Officially, he had retired from both pursuits at the same time, two years before this lunch.

Over beef Stroganoff and a good Australian claret he expanded, delighted by a chance to dabble in old interests.

"Yes, I can believe there are no records," he said in answer to her question. "It doesn't prove a thing. You people are casual about records at the best of times. I often despair of you. Disorganized. . . . Such potential wealth in your country, and you let foreigners strip it from you! Have done for centuries—the

Japanese included. It wouldn't take much more than good organization to stop it all.''

He raised his glass in an ironic toast. "To the new Vietnam. Kick all of us out—except for the harmless old has-beens like myself." He inhaled deeply over his glass, sipped, chewed on the wine, and swallowed. "What rubbish to say these don't travel well!"

He followed the wine with a large forkful of rice and sour cream. "Now, back to your question about the possible arrest. It was a free-for-all two years ago. Diem was fighting for his life and trying not to let the Americans know it. There were a lot of frightened, dangerous people who didn't know which way to jump. The French were fighting to hold on to the little they had left, and undermining the American upstarts in the process. Their two intelligence services were at each other's throats . . . buying off each other's men . . . withholding information . . . hardly in a mood to be cooperative about a thing like records."

He poured them both more claret. "Yes, I can believe that your husband's story is possible. And that no one can prove it either way." He glanced at her under the grizzled, curling brows, which were the oldest thing in his smooth, unwrinkled round face. "I have a feeling I haven't said the thing you wanted to hear. I do apologize."

"I don't know what I want to hear," said Nina.

The morning after the rape, and their fragile peace agreement, she had offered Andrew a lift in the Citroën. She watched him control his shock when he recognized Eight Hand Horse; then she ignored him while he studied her for signs of having noticed his recognition.

He refused the ride. In the mirror, she saw him watching the car as it pulled out of the gate.

"Old Uncle," she said to Eight Hand Horse, "that is my husband."

He drove with great concentration. After a long pause, he said, "If you say so, mademoiselle."

"Do you know him, Old Uncle?" she asked.

"He was one of your father's drivers, mademoiselle." The old man's voice was curt. She noted the "mademoiselle," not "madame." She knew she had just lost much face in his eyes, but it couldn't be helped. She had to admit to herself that she too wished it were not so.

For the next eleven months, she and Andrew lived in a shaky truce. He slept for a few nights on the settee, then began to stay away most nights, when she did not change her mind about letting him back into her bed. She saw him once or twice around the city with white women. She accepted that she had driven him into other beds, but secretly would have liked the women to be less blond and pink, and a little more like herself. He continued, however, to appear with her on formal social occasions.

She kept busy with her work. The Phoenix Tower showed a little less profit than before in its six-monthly accounts that year, but she could find nothing out of order. She sorted out the maintenance contracts for Eighty-eight Transport and lost only one driver in the process. Through a Vietnamese importer whom she met through Louis's Vietnamese, Khan, she ordered three Poclain earth movers for use on building sites. Through a Chinese, who approached her at the Eighty-eight offices, she also bought a consignment of Chinese-made wheelbarrows, on the principle that any builder who couldn't afford to use her vehicles would be able to afford wheelbarrows and coolies. In fact, she contracted them almost immediately to a government minister who passed them on to an agency which was responsible for repairing *paddi* dikes damaged by the fighting.

Clinton Clay put her in touch with an American contractor who was involved in planning a government program to build fortified villages to protect peasants in the delta from the Vietcong. She approached the American about a possible long-term contract for Eighty-eight Transport, to carry building materials, workers, machinery, and the supplies that would be necessary once the peasants had been relocated away from their own villages and fields.

Kim no longer dealt with her directly. He had become too busy with new affairs of his own. He assigned her one of his assistants as accountant and checked in with her from time to time. Their relationship never improved past the formal cordiality of their two lunches. Though he had stopped making jokes, he still never paid her a compliment or gave her word from her father.

On Louis's advice and without Andrew, she entertained widely among the Vietnamese and Chinese communities, in restaurants away from the European sector. As Nina Owen, she began quietly to establish herself as a young businesswoman of modest resources and moderate ambition. She found that many of her acquaintances were other young women. Unlike the French, Vietnamese men were usually happy to leave to their women the mundane problems of money management while they themselves dealt with the more important questions of religion, politics, and war. Her daily absorption in her work gradually became as strong as her original reasons for doing it. Personal fear, once so strong, had less and less place in her new life. Except for the nagging emptiness she felt at the thought of her father, an emptiness that Kim refused to help her fill, she would have thought she was content.

Her shaky truce with Andrew ended the evening she came home from Cong Ly Street and found him at the little utility desk reading through the most recent draft accounts of Eighty-eight Transport. Other documents were scattered across the desktop.

"What the hell are you doing?" she asked. "Those are my private papers!"

He turned on her with equal ferocity. "And what the hell are you playing at, hiding all this from me? I have every right to look at them! I had no idea you were up to all this . . . !"

They glared at each other in the narrow space at the end of the bed, under the stretched arms and polished breasts of the naked caryatids.

"As a matter of fact," he said, "I think you've forgotten my rights altogether. It's time you started behaving a little more like a wife. You've had enough time to get used to me by now!"

She began to back away, as he moved forward. "No, Andrew. Please! Not like this."

Still he moved toward her.

"Andrew. *Stop!*"

He pushed her off balance, then seized her shoulders and threw her onto the bed. She clawed her way across the vast expanse of coverlet. He grabbed her ankle. Her nails broke on the cloth as he pulled her back. She kicked, felt her foot connect with something hard, and pulled free, off the end of the bed.

"You goddamn dink bitch!" He wiped the blood from his chin and split lip. What frightened her most was that his eyes were gleaming as much with enjoyment as with rage.

"You ungrateful, dirty little yellow whore . . . !" He started round the end of the bed; she was trapped between him and the little washroom.

"I'll bloody teach you the right way to behave with me!" He began to unbuckle his belt. "Someone should have beaten manners into you years ago." He yanked his belt free.

She grabbed up the bronze figure of Ganesha.

"I'll kill you," she said desperately. He stopped moving.

There was a long silence while they eyed each other.

"I think you bloody would too," he said at last. "I think you bloody would!"

He wiped his chin again. "Well, well. Now that's interesting. I think you would."

"Get out!" she said. She didn't know what she would do if he attacked again. Her fingers were weak around the Ganesha.

He picked up the corner of the coverlet and wiped the blood from his face. "Cut my tongue as well," he said. "I owe you one."

"Will you get out! Or shall I call for help?"

"No. Sorry!" he said. "As your husband I have as much right to be here as you do. No matter what sugar daddy is paying for it. So don't try to throw me out, or I'll call the police."

He stared reflectively at the bloody smear on the coverlet.

"I don't know what kind of case you think you could make against me. You're the one who hit me, denying conjugal rights. I'll sleep in this bed tonight. I don't give a shit where you sleep . . . in it with me or in the bath."

He began to undress. "Don't worry," he said. "I'll leave you alone. I wouldn't touch you now with a barge pole. I don't have to work that hard for yellow pussy. Save it for whoever you like!"

Nina watched him, paralyzed. She debated whether to call Eight Hand Horse, but pride decided against it. She had lost too much face over Andrew already with the old man. She couldn't bear to involve him in what would look like a bad marital farce. Finally, she gathered all the papers from the desk and went into the sitting room; she also took the Ganesha.

The next morning, she left a message for Chinchook with the bookmaker in Me Linh Park on the riverfront at the bottom of Tu Do Street, whom he used as his *poste restante*. Chinchook met her at the suggested rendezvous as soon as the bars reopened after the midday break.

"Hey, Little Brother," she said. "You look like an American!"

He grinned. "I've got good luck just now." He was clearly on other payrolls than hers. He wore a short-sleeved Hawaiian shirt printed with green palm trees, puce flamingos, and orange moons on a yellow ground. Under the shirt he wore U.S. army-issue trousers cut off at the knee and Ho Chi Minh sandals. A gold Rolex hung from his skinny wrist. The fuzz was thickening on his upper lip.

He stepped over a pail of orchids on the street and came to sit at her table. "What can I do for you?"

The smell of flowers from the street mingled with the Bar Bip's own disinfectant and ground coffee. Nina inhaled absently while she considered the most tactful way to learn what she needed to know.

When she had ordered drinks, she asked him, "If I were to hear of you as some lucky young fellow, who would I hear named? I don't know your proper name. Imagine, after all we've been through!"

He dropped his voice in case evil spirits were listening, but could not hide his pride in his official name. "Nguyen Binh Kiem," he murmured. "After a famous poet, so my grandfather said. The Nguyens, of course, were kings, but you know that."

He hooked a piece of ice out of his glass and crunched it between his teeth. "When I am old and rich enough I'll earn honor by retiring to a pavilion on a lake somewhere, like him, to write poems."

"A good ambition," said Nina. She glanced at his shirt, then at the shadow of anxiety that always lay on his face when he forgot to smile. Ghosts of old values apparently survived behind palm trees and flamingos.

"Can you write your name for me now?" she inquired.

His head jerked up indignantly.

"I didn't mean to question whether you can write," she added hastily. "I meant, would you be willing to sign some papers, as a great service for me?"

"What kind of papers?"

She proceeded carefully. "Bank papers. To say some money belongs to you."

"Does it?"

"Some . . . if you sign the papers."

Excitement and suspicion waged visible war in his eyes.

"Big Sister, what are you up to? Will I go to jail?"

"Not unless someone learns of it," she joked.

Sly comprehension filled his eyes. "The money is yours, eh? But you give me a sweetener to say it's mine. Are you that rich now?"

"Are you rejecting more good fortune?" she teased him. "Do you want to become a change-fate?"

He just looked at her. She had changed since the days in the bombed house. He could feel it, but not how much, or why. And ignorance was dangerous.

Nina leaned forward and turned the force of her energy on him. "You are like a brother," she said. "Do you think I would want to bring you anything but good luck? We survived together in the past.''

''Yes, we're both still here,'' he agreed. ''OK. I'll do it. But for friendship, not for money.''

She went to buy flowers while, with her own Parker fountain pen, he laboriously etched his name onto the papers she gave him, beside her penciled X's. She hoped she was being foolish, to think she needed to put her money out of Andrew's reach. What worried her was that while he might think she was a yellow dink bitch, he also took pains to remind her that she was his wife. He might go out screwing white whores, but he also took pains, by appearing with her socially, to keep reminding the world that he was still very much her husband. She had begun to let herself fear that he had gambled on sharing her father's wealth even when he was pulling her from the shadows of the water jars behind the burning house.

As a driver, he might well not have known of the mess her father's affairs were in; everyone else, even the businessmen, seemed to have been taken by surprise after he disappeared. When she thought of how Andrew might have been laughing to himself when he called her ''Miss Nina,'' during her first days in his apartment, she felt as sick in her stomach as when the eight-year-old Daniel Jouvet had called her a ''yellow monkey face.''

She transferred the contents of the safe-deposit box, her business papers, and most of her deposited capital from the Chinese bank in Cholon to a Portuguese-owned private bank, also in Cholon, under the name of Nguyen Binh Kiem, with Le Thuyet as an authorized user of the account. She never took off the carved ivory seal, even when bathing and even when Andrew was not in the little apartment. She sacked the chambermaid whom she had added to her small staff at his suggestion, and replaced her with the sister of the wash ayah of one of her female Vietnamese business acquaintances.

After his lapse when caught with her papers, Andrew's behavior became faultless, except that he continued to claim the big bed each night. He was civil, did not touch her, and even tried to be helpful from time to time. Nina continued for several months to sleep on the sofa and to question her own suspicions.

One evening he came in with his old gleam of enthusiasm, which she hadn't seen for over two years.

''Have I ever got a deal for you!'' he said. He dropped onto the sofa and threw his arms open along the back.

''I was at a bash tonight given by some Americans, up on Duy

Tan Street . . . Ministry of Foreign Affairs. Met a USOM adviser, name of Thompson, out here on a contract for the fortified hamlets project. He's overseeing four, down in My Tho province. I think I could get you a contract for Eighty-eight Transport, guaranteed for two years.''

"Two years?'' she asked. "Are they so sure they'll be here that long?''

"On the quiet,'' he said, "I think you can count on five.''

Her own negotiations with the other American contractor were not progressing: she felt that his expectations for grease exceeded what was reasonable. On the other hand, she lost money every time her trucks stood idle, as they were now doing.

"Would you want to handle the negotiations?'' she asked him carefully. The muscles set around his mouth and his eyelids flickered.

"You don't trust me, do you?'' he said. "You don't deserve a thing from me! I'm just trying to show there's no hard feelings on my part, but you're making it bloody hard!''

He sounded so reasonable. She reminded herself of his lies.

"Thanks,'' she said. "I do appreciate your efforts.''

"Interested, or not?''

"Depending on the terms, yes, of course.''

"Well,'' he said, "there's a cocktail party the day after tomorrow; my man Thompson is supposed to be coming. I thought I could take you along to meet him. You can sort out whatever you like with him.'' He couldn't keep the bitterness out of his voice.

"Is it safe?'' she asked. Then thought how foolish it was to ask him if she suspected as much as she did.

He showed his white teeth in an imitation of a smile. "I always said I'd tell you when it was safe. If you're prepared to take my word . . .''

He turned a ring around its finger with his thumb.

"All right,'' she said. "I'll go.'' She might at least learn whom he was running with these days.

She was alarmed to learn that the party was being held on a river launch which departed from the Quai le Myre de Vilars, just above the mouth of the Arroyo Chinois and directly across the riverside boulevard from the Customs Bureau. By choice, she would not have gone anywhere quite so central to what had been French territory.

She dressed as inconspicuously as possible in a dark blue *ao dai*, and left off the multiple gold bracelets and jeweled rings of a successful young businesswoman. The retiring, straight-haired *métisse* who walked up the gangplank with Martell should not remind anyone of the cocky young half-French mademoiselle who once wore crinolines, petticoats, and beauty salon curls.

When they arrived the two tiers of deck were already crowded. A small native band was playing Benny Goodman hits on the top deck and uniformed waiters edged through the massed bodies with trays of drinks and snacks on toothpicks. She noted the large number of white faces; she also spotted Taki Hashimoto, busily talking to a turbaned Sikh near the port rail on the top deck. Between two blond European heads she thought she also saw Khan, her friend in the cabinet. There were a number of Americans in safari suits or slacks and madras plaid sports jackets. A few had wives with them, indicating that they were either diplomatic or on long-term civilian contracts with agencies like USOM.

She lingered near the starboard rail while Andrew went in search of Thompson. She felt the deck begin to vibrate beneath her feet, though the band and chatter nearly drowned the sound of the engine. Slowly the launch reversed out into the mainstream through a litter of sampans and pirogues. As it swung its nose upstream into the current, Nina became aware of a young Frenchman who leaned on the rail beside her.

"Good evening," he said. "All alone?"

She couldn't help smiling. He had the most ridiculous mustaches she had ever seen, large rusty butterflies on either side of his mouth, combed and groomed into unnatural alertness. He resembled an old sepia photograph of some French patriarch of the Belle Epoque.

He smiled back. "Hope you don't mind if I chat. It's going to be one of those boring affairs . . . necessary for business but hard on the stomach and disposition."

"What's your business?" she asked politely.

"Company director," he said, preening slightly. "For an importer of pharmaceuticals. I'm their legal adviser. And I dabble in imports and exports of my own as a sideline."

There was something familiar about him behind those mustaches.

"Are you alone?" He leaned closer and let his gaze slip down over her bosom and hips. "We can't have that!"

"I'm with my husband," she said.

"And who's that?"

She hesitated, but there was no point in telling anything but the truth with Andrew likely to swim up at any moment with his American in tow.

"Andrew Martell."

"Good God!" exclaimed the young man. "Old Andrew never said he had a wife. Imagine keeping quiet about someone who looks like you. Then again, maybe he's smart." He smoothed one side of his mustache with the back of his hand. "How did you meet a blackguard like Martell?"

While she was considering what evasion Andrew was least likely to disprove, the man's face changed.

"You know, I think we have met before . . . my name's Jouvet. Daniel Jouvet."

Nina gave up the pretense and laughed. "I had the honor of knocking out your two top teeth when you were eight!"

"My God, Nina Luoc!" He stepped back for a full-length look. "Lord you've changed! I promised myself for years that I'd knock out at least two of your teeth in return. I must say, I'd settle for something more peaceable now."

She smiled thinly. Andrew must have known that members of the old French community would attend tonight.

Jouvet was back on the rail, his upper arm against hers. "I think we should kiss and make up after all these years," he said.

"I might knock out the bottom ones," said Nina.

"What a fool I was at eight," he said, "not to appreciate a woman of spirit!"

"Why didn't you go back with your family?" she asked.

"To what?" he retorted. "Paper-pushing with a bunch of provincials who've never been farther than Neuilly-sur-Mer?"

She thought she glimpsed Andrew through a momentary gap in the crowd.

"Anyway," continued Jouvet, "I have to salvage the family fortunes. I'm the generation of the dispossessed."

She heard nothing more of what he said. Andrew had shouldered his way through nearly to the rail. The fleshy, gray-haired man with him, in a raw silk suit, whose intelligent eyes locked onto her like a radar beam, was not an American named Thompson. He was Emile Carbone.

"Emile, I'd like to present my wife, Nina," said Andrew.

"That's your wife!" Carbone could not conceal his shock. Luoc's daughter. Instead of the bright European ex-spinster or docile *jaune* he had been expecting.

What the hell is Andrew doing? Nina asked herself wildly. He was serving her up on a platter to one of the people she had reason to know she most needed to avoid. And he clearly recognized her, even after so many years.

Carbone recovered first. "Madame Martell, I'm delighted. . . ."

His large hand was as cold as her own. He turned to Jouvet and shook his hand. Then turned back to Nina.

"We haven't met for many years," he said. "May I call you Ninette as I used to do?" She replied something pleasant and they all chatted about nothing.

Nina had no idea what they said. She suspected that perhaps no one except Jouvet did either. The real conversation was both silent and intense. The air vibrated with it in a three-way tension between Andrew, Carbone, and herself. She was sure that Andrew had wanted Carbone to see and recognize her for some particular reason, that he had brought her here for just that very reason. She felt him beside her, intent and humming with satisfaction, watching Carbone. And Carbone, very still, digesting the information. Jouvet was like an eager dog who had picked up a scent he couldn't quite identify.

She felt danger in the hair follicles on the back of her neck and along her spine. She felt it in the muscles just above her knees, and in the smooth muscle of her gut. A real, physical sensation as clear as heat or cold or wet. She felt wound tight, like she did just before a summer electrical storm. She could not see exactly what shape this danger took. She could identity the sources, but not the shape it would take in her life. She felt, suddenly, from the vibrating within the small triangle of Andrew, Carbone, and herself, that she was finally about to understand what had happened to her life. Truth was going to come through this danger. At last.

Through her fear, which weakened her fingers around her glass, she also felt excitement. As if all her senses had previously slept and were now fully awake. As in negotiating, but a hundred times more intense. She also had the sensation that she was floating on this danger, as in dreams of running on the surface of the sea. If you move fast enough, without looking down, you don't fall in.

And if it is not a dream, but reality, she told herself, the runner falls in and drowns.

Carbone was studying her now. She turned her heightened senses onto him.

"You're very like your father," he said. Her ears heard a roar of unspoken words inside his head.

"I'm not my father, monsieur," she said. "I am an entirely different person."

Their eyes met. The Corsican understood her. His ears, too, were receiving like a bat, in wave bands above normal hearing.

"That is true, Ninette. . . . I really should say Mme. Martell, shouldn't I? . . . Very true. Thank you for reminding me. I was in danger of forgetting that. I trust you will always remain your own woman. Aspiring to be someone else is a common failing.''

He held out his hand to her and she took it for the second time.

"May I think of you again as 'Uncle Emile'?" she asked, holding him in a farewell grasp. "I came to you once for help, but got the impression I was in the wrong place."

"I know," he said. "I heard, when I returned. I was angry with Paul. Very angry. The same misunderstanding will not happen again."

He squeezed her hand before he released it. Andrew's left arm made an involuntary twitch of protest.

"Andrew, my boy," Carbone said, "you're a slyer dog than I realized." The center of his tone was jovial, but the edge cut.

I don't know any more than before where I am in all this, thought Nina. But at least I have unsettled Andrew, just a little.

He was thoughtful in the taxi home as it raced along the straight way of Cong Ly Street.

"What happened to your American?" she asked.

"What?" He looked at her from the distance he had been occupying in his mind. "Thompson? I expect he couldn't make it. Sorry about that."

He looked at her again, then out of the window. "Imagine, meeting old Emile like that! . . . I didn't know you knew Daniel Jouvet."

"Daniel and I go back a long, long way," she said. She had to give Andrew full marks for effrontery.

But she had underestimated more than his effrontery. Three days later he suggested that she meet him and the American, Thompson, at a café just off Tu Do Street, around the corner from the National Assembly Hall. With her newly tuned ears, she heard too much casualness in his voice. She watched him push the ring on his little finger round and round the bone with his thumb.

"All right," she said, just as she had agreed to the party on the launch. Knowledge would come through danger, she was now convinced of it.

Nevertheless, she asked Eight Hand Horse to stay after he had dropped her at the meeting place. She was not surprised by the heavy bulge in the jacket of his baggy suit, nor did she mind his precaution. She was too preoccupied to notice the tight, unnatural grayness of his face.

She sat at a table on the terrace facing the street, tossing bits of bread stick through the wire mesh that screened the café from grenades. Sparrows converged from all directions into an angry melee of flying dust and feathers. She watched the victor surface triumphantly with a piece of bread far too big for him to swallow and beat his way up to land on the wire mesh roof above her head.

Two men at the table just behind her began to voice loud compliments intended for her to hear. She looked at her watch; Andrew and Thompson were three minutes late. She checked that Eight Hand Horse was still propped against the dented front right wing of the car. Nina noticed inconsequentially that one rear light had recently been smashed.

At a far table, she saw a woman who was a relief receptionist at the Phoenix Tower. She was drinking alone, possibly trawling for personal customers to eke out her salary.

"Millie!" Nina called softly.

The woman looked startled, then smiled and crossed to Nina's table.

"Keep me company while I wait for my husband?" asked Nina.

Millie glanced past her and took in the two businessmen at the next table. "OK. Nice to see you." She sat down, facing the two men. Like Nina, she still wore the native *ao dai*, in spite of the growing fashion for Western dress among young Saigonese women.

"How's the hotel?' asked Nina. "Business good?"

"Come on!" said Millie. "You should know. Rooms full every night." She winked. "Sometimes more than once. You know how it is."

Chinchook had confirmed her own suspicions long ago. However, Nina had promised to stay out of Titi's way. As long as the hotel itself flourished, the extras were Titi's business and not hers.

"What are you drinking?" she asked Millie.

"Rum and Coke," said the woman.

Nina looked for the waiter, but he remained obstinately out of sight inside the café itself, bustling between two tables of Americans.

Nina went inside to collect their drinks herself.

She had just laid several coins on the rectangular glass dish beside the big cash register, ornate as a cathedral altar, when she heard an automatic weapon open fire. Just outside the café. A woman began to scream. Nina knocked aside the plastic strips hanging at the café door to keep out the flies. The tabletop looked as if it had been ripped by monstrous claws. Millie had been cut in half. Her head and upper chest hung upside down from her hips by a strip of flesh and skin. The force of the volley had half knocked over her chair, which was wedged with her hips under the tabletop. Her dark, wet hair just brushed the spreading pool of blood on the terrace.

One of the two businessmen lay on the ground at the table behind hers and Millie's. The other sat with his hands cupped to his face as if trying to hold the blood that leaked through his fingers.

Other drinkers stared stupidly. The screaming woman was somewhere in the street.

"Mademoiselle!" Eight Hand Horse pulled her back into the café. "Come this way."

In shock, she followed him past the cash register and the hysterical manageress, out through the steam and grease of the café kitchen into the tiny alley behind. She stumbled against a metal rubbish bin and felt his hand steady under her arm.

He bundled her into the car and accelerated away from the café. Behind them, Nina heard sirens surge and die.

When her breathing slowed enough to speak, she asked, "Did you see it?"

He nodded. "A Chatellerault mounted in the back of a French jeep. The driver was Corsican."

She exhaled fiercely and gulped in more air; she felt she was suffocating.

"And the gunman?"

He spat through the window. "An iceman for Emile Carbone."

"Take me home," she said. One of Carbone's men, she thought.

"Forgive me, mademoiselle, but I do not think I should." He was as frightened as she was. She heard it in his voice.

"You're right," she agreed. "I'm a little confused. . . . Please drive, anywhere, for a few minutes while I try to think."

Thank God, she said to herself. Carbone's iceman. Thank God it wasn't Andrew. I couldn't bear it. And now I know what shape the danger will take.

She kept seeing the streams of red flowing along the locks of Millie's hair. Like her mother, in her nightmare.

"There is something I must tell you," said the old man.

"What is that?"

Instead of answering, he revved the Citroën around the corner onto Ham Nghi Boulevard, away from the river, then screamed left and right again onto the avenue that followed the Arroyo Chinois, now rechristened the Ben Nghe Canal.

"Tell me what you have to say!" Her teeth had begun to chatter.

"Your brother was killed a few hours ago."

Nina threw back her head and laughed hysterically. "I haven't got a brother!" The old man had finally gone senile. She welcomed the release of her laughter, began to embrace it.

He continued to race along the boulevard without speaking. She observed the set of his head and stopped laughing abruptly.

"Take the road to the south," she said. "Across the Ong Lanh Bridge. We need to talk when you are not also trying to kill *pousse-pousse* drivers and babies." She had control of herself again.

He turned obediently and crossed the canal.

"Now stop."

They had reached the edge of the *paddis* where she and Chinchook had tried to flee to escape the fire. Strips of water glinted pewter and steel in the growing dusk, crisscrossed with lines of light from lanterns and cars.

He stopped. "VC are here at night, mademoiselle. We shouldn't stay long."

"We stay until you answer my questions. Old Uncle, you have hidden things from me."

He looked unhappily out the window into the growing darkness of the *paddis;* he had turned off all the lights of the car.

"Your father thought it was safer for you not to know."

"Not on today's evidence!" said Nina. "Who was my brother?"

"You know him, mademoiselle."

She was standing on the deck of a boat that kept dropping and dropping down the side of a wave.

"Who?"

"Mr. Kim." He pinched his lips tightly together.

The boat kept falling and she could find no handhold, nothing solid to balance herself. She had known nothing about her father or his life. She had only imagined him.

After a silence which made the old man look anxiously at her in the mirror, through the dimness of the car, she repeated quietly, "Kim." After a another pause, she asked, "Did he know I was his sister?"

She could barely hear his muffled affirmative.

Anger burned along her jawbone and down her neck; it cut through her shock like cold water.

"I would like to have known," she said. She would have liked not to have been made to look a fool, yet again.

"Who was his mother? He was not *métis*."

Again, she had to strain to hear.

"Your father has a concubine. A Meo. A montagnarde from Tonkin, where he was born. A Meo, like myself."

Her new ears heard the extra information, the tiny note he could not keep out of his voice.

"A relative of yours?" she asked abruptly. A Meo. It had happened on business trips north.

She heard his intake of breath in the darkness. "My sister, mademoiselle. To the honor of my family, she was chosen by your father."

When she said nothing, he added, "She is many years younger than myself."

Nina hardly heard him. The existence of a brother—the son her father wanted—explained so much. Kim had taken the love and respect that Nina had pined for as a child. The fight had been rigged and she hadn't known it. She wondered if her mother had known and suffered. She was glad that he was dead! She glared out into the darkening *paddi* fields.

Then, suddenly, desperately, she wanted for him to be still alive, to give them a chance to know each other as kin. She would have made him accept and love her if she had been given the chance, she was sure of it. But she hadn't known enough to try. Instead, they had wasted their time together on bickering, when they could have brought together the two halves of her father's world.

"Who killed him?" she asked.

"I don't know," said Eight Hand Horse with venom. "I will find out!"

Nina thought for a moment. "Am I the only one left?"

He nodded. She watched him scan the *paddis* once again for signs of movement. A few people trudged past the parked car, but none even looked at it.

"If you wish to be," he said.

"Wish to be?" Her voice rose. "I don't see that I have much choice. Either I am or I'm not!"

"Mademoiselle, I'm not explaining well . . . you have a right to be angry with me. But in your case there is a choice to make. . . . Please may I drive on?" He interrupted himself suddenly. "There is movement ahead."

Without waiting for her reply, he turned the key and jumped the car into motion. Then he braked abruptly as a water buffalo lumbered up onto the road and crossed, udder swinging, tail flicking.

"Not VC," he said unnecessarily.

He did not stop again, and she did not ask him to do so.

"Mademoiselle, I am taking you somewhere," he said. "I hope you will not mind. But first, I must explain." He was struggling slightly with his new role as tutor and mentor.

They continued on toward the junction of the Arroyo Chinois with the Te Canal, and toward the Y Bridge, where the Binh Xuyen had made their headquarters during the fighting.

Eight Hand Horse shifted a betel gob which had been lurking neglected in his cheek. "You are still very young . . . and female. And half Round Eye. Your father wants you to be very clear about what you choose."

He had said as much to her himself, in their meeting in his library.

"On the other hand," said the old man, "there is a little money, a little property. Perhaps France."

Almost Kim's exact words. She wondered if they had all had a group briefing.

"And what is my other choice?" She had already begun to feel the shape of it, without the details. To taste the flavor. Salty and complex. The taste of secret bank accounts and undischarged bankruptcy.

"With his many other franchises from the French," said Eight Hand Horse, "your father also had a license to trade in opium. Like M. Carbone and others. Before World War II, he sold to the government Opium Monopoly like everyone else. Independent since then."

Of course, she thought. Of course! The beginnings of real truth at last.

"He had an agreement with the Japanese, when they banned official trade during the war. We're very careful since Diem's ban, but continue anyhow. Kim is—was—liaison for the Region Saigon-Cholon."

The catch in his voice reminded her that Kim had been his nephew.

"Then he was head of the whole show while your father is in exile."

She wasn't surprised, or even terribly shocked, by this part of the truth. Unlike an American or European child, she had grown up with the vague awareness of opium as a large and firmly established element in the history of her country's economy. The government-run Opium Monopoly had given the trade respectability. Like copper and rubber, opium had been the legitimate basis of the fortunes of many of the leading French families. The stories of the Chinese Opium Wars were distant romances. Abuses of the poppy-growing peasants in the north by the warlords did not find much place in French social gossip, while smoking opium was thought by the French to lie somewhere on a scale between chic and déclassé, depending on age and social set. Furthermore, there was still at this time a large legal trade with European pharmaceutical companies, and many French as well as natives thought that an occasional pipe was helpful against colds and influenza. And finally, although the general trade was now illegal under the present ban, it had not yet become the exclusive province of gangsters and organized crime, as seemed to be happening in Italy, France, and America since the end of the war. She found this truth easier to accept than that of fraud.

Eight Hand Horse accelerated. "One hundred and ten kilos of morphine base are due to go at high tide, early this morning, on the *Tripoli Belle*, to Istanbul. But there is a problem...."

She waited.

"The banker won't release cash without proper authorization," he said. "Without cash from the bank, certain Customs officers will make a special search of the *Tripoli Belle*. Then— trouble for everyone!"

Another buffalo was lying across the warm tarmac. Eight Hand Horse crushed two gourd plants in a roadside garden and knocked several leaves off a banana tree as he went around it.

Still Nina waited.

"Mr. Kim made the authorization."

"Was he the only one who could?" she asked.

"And your father. With special seals."

"A two-legged dragon?"

"The Celestial Bird," he corrected gently. "The Fire Phoenix of our people, the Viets."

"That's all that needs doing tonight?" she queried. "A stamp on a withdrawal request? And you can get the money? For sweeteners?"

"Yes, mademoiselle." She could hear him controlling his urgency.

"How much?"

Silence. Then: "I don't know. It varies."

"And what will happen if I don't do it?"

"Ahhhh." He exhaled as if in pain. "As I said—a special search on the ship. Arrests. Interrogations. More arrests. With

303

your father not here or Kim to sort things out, it will be the end."

"Have such things not happened in the past?"

"At times. But then, there were always arrangements . . . understandings. As in any business. But now, at this moment, the Premier must prove to his American allies that he is really fighting bad things. To the Americans, opium is number ten. The worst! No matter that the Premier's brother is in secret talks with dealers, Diem must be seen to be severe. Anyone caught now is finished."

"I really have a choice?" she asked.

"Yes." He held her eyes in the mirror until they nearly hit a cyclo which had no lights. He braked, swerved, and found her eyes again. "Your father said, 'She must make a true choice. No matter what the cost to others. They are not her problem. Otherwise she will choose wrong for her.'" He repeated the lines like a memorized script.

"He really said that?" Her breathing was tight again.

"Yes, mademoiselle."

Through her shock and anger she felt a rush of joy. Those words were the greatest statement of his real love and concern that she could have hoped for—that she be free to be true to herself.

"He would not mind if I chose a little money and a little property, and let his life work be destroyed? Truly?"

Eight Hand Horse struggled with himself again. At last, he said, "I don't know. I was given no answer to that." He paused, then burst out miserably, "A man cannot help minding . . . !"

"It's too big a decision," she said finally. The vision of Millie's body remained with her. But if she refused his request, she would already have decided; there would be no further choices to be made. It would all end, he said. Which left her with one alternative.

"I will authorize the money tonight as you ask," she said reluctantly. "Then we will see." She could give her father that much in exchange for having given her a choice. It committed her to nothing. Bought time to think.

"Yes, mademoiselle!" He could not hide his joy and relief. "We are here already."

He turned the car into the gates of a small factory near the Y Bridge. The night watchman who had unlocked the gates was bowing to the car. On the roof of the squat red-brick rectangle which was the main building, a pink neon bird flapped its wings up-down, up-down in jerky sequence. The glowing turquoise letters beneath said "Heron Confectionery" in mirror writing, as they pulled up to the back entrance. The general manager had stayed late to greet her.

In spite of his name, Raoul Duprès, the thirty-two-year-old general manager of Heron Confectionery, was pure Annamite, from a good southern Cochin Chinese Catholic family. He used a French name for business, which he had entered while the French still held the reins. Now, he made it clear to all who would listen that he was loyal to the Catholic leader, Diem. He kept his eyes and ears open, however, and his head down. He was ambitious.

He bowed reverently over Nina's hand while his mind clicked in assessment. Whoever she was, her arrival confirmed that the other one was really dead, as he had heard that afternoon. Against the slight debit in his mind of being female, she balanced the considerable credit of being half French.

Duprès was one of the many Vietnamese who kept a lingering awe for the departed French. Thanks to French patronage, his own family had for forty years controlled a profitable pineapple-growing fiefdom southwest of Saigon. It had been lost only through the stupidity of his oldest uncle, a militant Buddhist, who had not read the signs of change accurately and had publicly opposed the Americans' choice of the Catholic Diem to lead the country. As a result, the fiefdom was now controlled by a Catholic family who were distant cousins of the Premier.

This young woman's greatest strength for Duprès, however, was the simple fact that she was there, in a superior position in the hierarchy. The hierarchy had been badly shaken by the son's death, but not destroyed. This young woman's actions would decide whether the structure of power survived, and whether he would continue to serve and to profit from it. Eyes down, he led her to an office on the first floor of the brick building.

Nina marched to the large, leather-topped partner's desk and took her place in the swivel chair behind it. She folded her hands and waited in silence while Duprès flipped back the Chinese carpet, pulled at the knees of his trousers, and knelt to open a floor safe. He took some ledgers from the safe and placed them on the desk in front of her.

"Mr. Kim's books," he said. He stepped four paces backward and assumed the at-ease position, alligator-clad feet apart, hands clasped behind his suit jacket. He waited.

Nina looked at the ledgers. She might have the seal of authority now on a gold chain, but she did not have the least idea

305

where to begin or what she was looking for. She felt Duprès's eyes, voracious and assessing.

"Wait, outside, please," she ordered. "I will call you if I need you."

Reluctantly, he obeyed, bowing himself out past Eight Hand Horse, who was stationed just outside the office door.

She opened the first ledger to find page after page in French, noting purchases of raw sugar, coconuts, banana oil, red beans, emulsifiers, dried plums and dates, coffee beans, eggs, replacement parts for machinery, cleaning materials, wooden and cardboard boxes, staples, labels, and colored cellophane.

The second ledger was a record of sales. The third listed details of wages and salaries, against the names of employees. On first inspection she found nothing related in any way to the amount of grease money needed to ensure the safe departure of one hundred and ten kilos of morphine base to Istanbul, and the continuing of her father's trade in opium products.

Two possibilities occurred to her, neither cheering. One was that Duprès was being obstructive and had given her the wrong books. The other was that her brother had kept the information she needed inside his own head. She tackled the easier alternative first and crossed to the floor safe.

There were no more books in it, only a brass box roughly the size of a shoe box. She took it back to the desk. A small padlock had been fused to the interlocking brass loops on the box with a lump of hardened sealing wax. The box could not be opened without shattering the stamp of the Celestial Bird which was sunk deep in a miniature lake of brittle red lacquer.

She hit the sealing wax with the handle of a Malayan *kris* which lay on the desk for use as a paperknife. Small sharp red chips of lacquer flew through the air and lodged in her hair like drops of bright blood.

Inside the brass box were two more books, in her father's handwriting. She looked down the columns of writing and figures in the first book—a jumble of French, Vietnamese cursive, and Chinese characters—and forgot completely about her immediate problem.

In disbelief she went over the pages more slowly, working through the semicode of the mixed alphabets. She knew the Chinese characters for the numbers from one to ten. That, together with her knowledge of French and Vietnamese, was enough to make her place both hands on the desk to steady them before she turned to the second book. It was even harder to decipher than the first.

Both books were written largely in figures and abbreviations. In the first, she could pick out what she thought must be place names—Ist., Ank., PP. The *Tripoli Belle* was sailing for Istanbul. Istanbul, Ankara, and Phnom Penh.

The abbreviations in the second book defeated her. Unreadable Chinese ideograms made blanks that completely masked any pattern she might otherwise have detected.

> 25 times TR blank, blank, 5.
> 125 times blank, blank, blank 33
> AK blank (Ch.) HCM.

She was able to read enough of the figures, however, to set her hands trembling. The sheer scale of the totals was overwhelming. They made her father's secret piastre account look like a week's pocket money. The sums in the pages accumulated, then disappeared again, a great sea of money washing in, then out again.

She looked down at the two little books on the tooled leather desktop in a mixture of excitement and terror. She knew that her own life was nothing in the face of such numbers, any more than Kim's had been. Men did much more than murder a Vietnamese accountant and his *métisse* half sister, for much, much less. She also knew that the books held, even if she did not yet understand it, the secret of her father's power in the world, which was now hers to preserve, if she could, or to destroy. When she understood that secret, she would at last see with her father's eyes.

Then she remembered what she had come to the factory to do. If I can, she thought unhappily. There was a gentle tap at the door. Eight Hand Horse put his head in.

"Forgive my impertinence if I inquire how you progress. High tide is in four and a half hours. It will take me an hour to get the money. The banker will go to bed. They may search the ship anytime after midnight." His tone was deprecating but his urgency plain.

Sweat banded her forehead and a double line of dampness beaded her spine as she leaned once again over the details of salaries and wages. If Kim had kept the information she needed in his head, then it would be the end, no matter what choice she might make. Her wristwatch said 10:45 P.M.

She wondered in panic if she were searching the wrong ledger. But shortness of time forced her to choose. Surely payments to people, of any kind, would be with salaries rather than purchases of supplies. She compared entries at different times, looking for a pattern, anything to suggest an answer. She plowed down columns of drivers, packers, wrappers, inspectors, *chefs de confection, sous-chefs,* washers, janitors, watchmen, clerical staff, electricians, gardeners, technicians, Duprès, and chemists.

She paused briefly over chemists; there were more of them, on higher wages than she would have thought necessary to run purity tests on raw ingredients and supervise the temperatures of manufacturing processes. But she could not make this irregularity tell her anything about how to ensure the safe departure of the consignment on the *Tripoli Belle.* It was now 11:15 P.M.

Some of the employees were on salaries, some on weekly wages. Dotted here and there in the columns were occasional entries for "casual labor," without further detail. She kept returning to them; they were the only break in the otherwise regular pattern of figures. Then she noticed that the payment dates for casual labor did not correspond to the rest, which were at the ends of either weeks or months. She looked again at several pages to be certain she was right about that. Then, in excitement, she turned back to the final page on which entries had been made.

Sure enough, buried in the columns of salaries and wages to be paid at the end of the week were entries for "casual labor," marked with the present day's date. She had missed them in her first anxious search. She listed them and added up the total. Then she called Eight Hand Horse.

"What language did Kim write in?" she asked him.

"French." His face lighted up with relief. "The bank does the necessary forms tomorrow." Then she saw him realize his slip.

"Does this look approximately right?" She held out the draft.

He hesitated. "I never saw it. It was in an envelope."

She waited.

"Yes," he said. "That looks right." His eyes slid away from hers and his hands moved unconsciously into the same open position as when they first met.

She felt slightly chilled. Still, if Kim had watched her, someone had had to watch Kim.

There was no ink pad in the drawer, but there was a stick of sealing wax. Eight Hand Horse leaped forward with his lighter to melt it for her. The carved ivory column sank sensuously into the molten lacquer and came away with a faint tearing sound. Nina stared at the twisting beast left embedded in the irregular red splash on the bottom of the page. It was now an extension of herself, the symbol of her strength in the world. She was interested in the real sense of power she felt when she used it. She saw the old man staring at it as well.

She asked him to fetch Duprès. While she waited, with the brass box resealed and back in the safe, and the two books it had held hidden in her bag, she considered her choices. She spread her hands on the desktop and felt the chair back behind her head.

Does it fit? she asked herself. Is it comfortable? Once again she saw the red streams dripping from the ends of Millie's hair, beside the image of her father's face as she had seen it in his library, the eyes sparked with the beginnings of interest.

She let Duprès stand in silence in front of the desk for a few minutes after he bowed himself into the room.

"Monsieur," she said at last, "like my father, I have a nose for ability and a long memory for loyalty."

She felt him poised as a compass needle. He bowed slightly. At least he now knew that she was the daughter of the old man. He was also following her perfectly.

"Like him, I value trouble-free running of day-to-day affairs. I hope you look forward, as I do, to our continued, mutually profitable association." She had not found Duprès's own skimmings in her first examination of the books, but she had no doubt that closer study would reveal all.

"Madame!" He had not missed the slight edge in her voice on the word *profitable*. He would be careful for a while. On the other hand, nothing in her words suggested a possible purge of corruption in the style of the present government

He handed her ceremoniously into the backseat of the surprisingly battered car and bowed as Eight Hand Horse burned rubber in a turn. The watchman, imitating his general manager, bowed even lower than he had when they arrived.

In the car, Nina fingered the seal at her neck as if to renew the strength it had given her.

"Take me to the Phoenix Tower for tonight," she said. "Then go on to get the money. When you have finished, please let M. Martell know I want to talk to him." She also had to decide how to deal with Carbone.

He leaned forward to fiddle with the instrument panel, then wiped the steering wheel with his sleeve.

"Do you have something else to tell me?" she asked. "More surprises?"

Eight Hand Horse leaned viciously on his horn at a bicycle which was minding its own business near the curb.

"Go on," she said gently. Her stomach felt cold.

"Don't tell M. Martell of this evening," he said at last.

"Any particular reason?" Her voice was chilly, to avoid shaking.

"Mademoiselle... why were you sitting in that café?"

Life was outrunning her again.

Nina sat very still for a long, long time. When the body or spirit is offered more than it can handle, it tries to deny. It blows a fuse. Shuts down. Nina shut down. She believed that she continued to think. She continued to speak aloud, as if she were thinking; she even made logical sense. But she wasn't really there at all.

Eight Hand Horse watched her in the mirror and drove with great care, for him. For once motorbikes, cyclos, and market cars were safe in his path.

"Andrew...!" said Nina, not knowing she had spoken aloud. The word was a faint, torn wail, like the first sound in the throat of a cat preparing to howl.

After another silence, the apparently controlled, apparently present Nina asked, "Did he know about my brother... about Kim?"

"Yes, mademoiselle."

She shook her head in silent protest. Her thoughts were slow and tangled. After another moment, she asked, "How long has he... did he know?"

"Always."

She shook her head again, in conference with herself. The old man still watched her, prepared to stop quickly if necessary, to calm her if she became hysterical.

He worked for Carbone, she told herself. He planned this from the beginning. No, she corrected herself. I don't have to believe that. It's not right. . . . I had nothing when he took me in . . . nothing when we were married. But he knew about Kim. . . . And that the opium business survived. . . .

She didn't notice the old man look at his watch and step on the accelerator. It was nearly midnight.

I don't want to have to understand, she raged to herself. I want to be back in the big house! Safe. With Minou and Simpoh Flower and my mother!

The green glare of a neon sign flickered across the backseat of the car. Two charcoal braziers in the darkness beneath a balcony glowed like the eyes of a demon. Nina gazed back at those eyes and saw with total, terrifying clarity how futile that wish was;

310

she could never allow herself such wishes again. All that was gone. Her old world was completely gone. Her mother was dead. Her father had no magical power to give her confidence or to protect her. Andrew had just destroyed her last illusion that she could ever depend on anyone. People would use her, direct her for their own purposes. She was the only one who cared about her life.

She was hit by loneliness so devastating that she wanted to die. She was totally alone. Andrew had just cut the last tie and set her free into loneliness. She had never been so alone. Nor so free. That idea shocked her.

"Now I understand," she said suddenly, startling the old man. "How free I am to choose. My father must have foreseen it." Her voice rang with nervous exaltation.

"Yes, mademoiselle." His reply was more cautious than confirmatory.

She sighed, almost luxuriously. She felt light-headed. She was the only person who cared about her life and the only one who could destroy her own fear. She did not recognize in herself the euphoria of shock.

Titi saw immediately that something was badly wrong and put Nina into the management's personal quarters. Eight Hand Horse posted a guard on the rooms and drove off to the banker's house at a speed that should have required both siren and flashing lights.

Still in shock, Nina wandered distractedly around Titi's spare bedroom. The boat was still sliding down the side of the wave; she waited for it to steady itself. She knew she was alone but was less sure just who "she" was.

She pulled off her *ao dai*, stepped out of the silk trousers, and stared at her image in Titi's mirror, not knowing what she would see. She felt as much in fragments as she had when sitting on Andrew's balcony in the rain after her mother had died.

A slim, cream-colored young woman with heavy dark hair gazed back at her. All in one piece and looking amazingly composed. A *jaune*, not a French mademoiselle. With high cheekbones and a pointed chin. But full French breasts and pubic bush. The bones in her long limbs were a little heavier than in a pure Viet. The eyes were those of a woman, not a girl. The face looked too old for the French mademoiselle, too clean and well fed for the burrow rat, but with the burrow rat's memories in its eyes.

Yet the image of the intact young woman reassured her; its

wholeness was what the world would see, instead of the sliding darkness that filled her mind. If it could convince the world, perhaps it would also persuade her. She continued to gaze at the physical reality reflected back at her.

I have decisions to make, she told the reflection. And the reflection made the first decision for her, one which at first seemed oblique. You belong here in Saigon, it told her. You are not French, in spite of your mother's hopes. You must let go of any last fantasy of going to France; it will only confuse you. It was your mother's fantasy, in any case, not yours. Why should the French there in France accept you as one of themselves any more than the ones here?

She nodded to herself as she understood the significance of that decision. It was the beginning of her larger choice, which terrified her more than anything had done for years, even more than the gunshots in the café that afternoon. You're insane, she told her reflection. Even to think of it. A girl barely twenty, undertaking the control of her father's trade in opium products! You know nothing about it. You don't know the people. It's a dangerous, violent, sometimes nasty business!

Life is dangerous, violent, and sometimes nasty, replied the composed-looking young woman with old eyes. You didn't decide on the fire in the big house, or on your mother's death, or on the bodies the soldiers and the Binh Xuyen left in the streets, or the dead woman in the canal, or No One's burning to death. You didn't choose the shell that flattened the apartment. There will be much, much more besides that will be beyond your power to decide. Your only hope is to decide to control as much as you can. Your choices might be less dangerous, violent, and nasty than those of other people. Consider that!

While considering it, she opened a cupboard to look for a robe; she had to get away temporarily from that composed, persuasive young woman in the mirror. She found a blue and white, light cotton yukata, like a short kimono, which Titi used for a dressing gown, put it on, then opened the shutters onto the narrow balcony, which was dark under the overhanging limes in the garden.

"I can't...!" she said aloud, without knowing she had spoken.

The air was thick with heat and sound. Wrapped in the fresh-smelling, much-laundered robe, she listened to the car horns and the low background murmur of thousands of voices in the streets, and coming from hundreds of open windows. A distant siren wailed and carried her back to the alleyway behind the café and the urgency of Eight Hand Horse's grip on her arm. She was just now beginning to believe that it had really happened. She covered her eyes with her hands while the scene replayed itself over and over in her mind, the details as clear and unstable as sunlight on water.

Millie's rum and Coke beside her own milky *pastis*. The faint clinking of ice and the duller echo of her coins on the little glass dish beside the baroque cash register. The sudden, obscenely inappropriate racket of the submachine gun. The silence . . . and the first scream. The multicolored plastic ribbons in the doorway which had tangled in her frantic hands as she tried to knock them aside. Then Millie. Where she herself should have been.

She started to shake again. She couldn't stop. She gripped the iron railing and leaned against it for support. After a time, her brain reminded her that she had not been at that clawed table. She was here, in the Phoenix Tower, safe, with a choice to make. She tried to focus on the chatter and laughter below her where some of the staff, off duty and free of the guests, had set up a table in the garden to eat a late-night supper by the light of three paper lanterns. They laughed and called to someone inside the hotel. A motorbike coughed down the street behind the garden, carrying with it the surge and dying fall of a loud transistor radio strapped onto the passenger seat.

Leaning on the iron railing above the three glowing paper moons, she felt her thoughts begin to untangle themselves as the first shock started to wear off. She didn't like the resulting pain, but at least it was clear and straightforward.

Andrew had helped try to have her killed. That was fact. But he had not necessarily planned it from the beginning. He might have gambled that she would someday be worth something when he married her, but the young man who had held her hand to help her drink and made love to her on that awful wooden bed did not intend, then, to kill her. He had changed while he was in prison, during their separation. Perhaps Carbone had reached him in prison, perhaps even arranged to have him freed. This version of the facts steadied her further.

Perhaps it would be possible for me, after all, young as I am. She inhaled the marriage of jasmine and cigarette smoke from the table below her.

It's only another business, she told herself. I have made a modest success of this hotel and Eighty-eight Transport. I am not too proud to seek advice. Now, instead of Gidéon, I have the old man as my teacher—and I'm sure that he is very close to my father. I learn fast. I like to learn. Think about how much I have learned since I began! And I am stronger.

She almost laughed at the memory of the naïve young girl who had climbed the stairs to Martell's room and insisted on being called Mademoiselle Nina when her life had just been blown apart.

She stood on the balcony most of the night, long after the staff in the garden below had gone to bed. She considered the illegality of her father's business. The opium trade had been legal for far more of its history than it had been illegal, a proper trade for the government itself to carry out. She remembered Andrew's explanations of why Diem had banned it—to cut off his enemies' funds. She remembered Andrew's suggestion that Diem would restore the trade, keeping it secret only because he did not want to upset his American allies and bankrollers. Legality seemed to be a question of politics rather than morality.

Even when it had become illegal under the Japanese, she remembered seeing many of her mother's friends smoke opium openly at parties. And that doctors had prescribed it for rainy season colds and coughs. Opium was not considered a Vietnamese vice, she reminded herself, merely one of the pleasures that made life more tolerable. The fact that some people abused it was surely not reason enough to reject the entire trade. Against the image of Chinese coolies she had seen by the docks, shrunken and lethargic, she could balance the elegance of Louis Wu and his friends—except Frey, perhaps—with their silver filigree pipes, vintage wines, and classical music. Finally, and most inarguably, opium was her father's business. No matter what embittered Frenchmen like Pluviez might say, she knew that her father was a man of honor, even if she did not yet understand his terms. If it was proper for him, it was proper for her. He would not ask her to do something that would dishonor the family. Her choice was becoming clearer—to follow the course that her father had marked out, or to turn her back on him and his world in order to hide away in safety, with "a little money."

From time to time, her thoughts swung in spite of her to the question of what would happen next with Andrew and Carbone. Each time, her mind bolted like a terrified horse in the direction of more tolerable thoughts. She would breathe deeply and look down at the now-extinguished lanterns and deserted dining table, trying to imagine that she was sitting down there among friends, laughing and eating with nothing to consider but how soon to go to bed.

At one point, in a swing between memories of the dead Millie and imagining the dead Kim, she felt how much the city around

314

her was soothing her; it floated her on her boat of a balcony like a warm sea. It was her father's city. His people and her people. Her loneliness was warmed by realizing how much she loved the city, with a strong, clear-sighted love like that which comes after seeing a man truthfully with all his faults and still finding him desirable.

I think I am going to choose this, she thought. I will choose to preserve my father's place in it for him and for myself. In my own way. If I can.

Then fear and confusion raised their voices yet again. She was still at the railing, undecided, at 5:30 A.M., when Titi arrived to announce that Eight Hand Horse had returned.

The old man entered the room and dropped to the floor in the traditional kowtow which had been banned from official use. Nina nearly laughed aloud from nervous surprise, but permitted him to touch his forehead to the floor before she told him to get up. Oddly, she felt he would be upset if she didn't.

"The *Tripoli Belle* sailed," he said, "like clockwork. Somebody had heard we had problems. They came prepared to give us more. They even brought sniffer dogs!"

His relief and happiness were palpable. "But we're still in business!" He was too discreet to push her more than that, at the moment.

Nina was surprised by her own sense of triumph at his news. Sooner or later, her father would hear it too, and would know what she had done. Her problem was whether she could do more.

"Now, Old Uncle, there is time for you to explain things to me properly. You must stay and have breakfast with me."

He began to protest that it would not be fitting for him to join her, but she cut him off.

"Please don't pretend. You have to teach me; I have a choice to make but am too ignorant to make it. You must be my teacher and guide."

This time, she allowed him to make the ritual protestations of humility and service, and of how she honored him with her words. His eyes had first acknowledged the truth of what she said.

"Please sit," she invited him, as she rang for breakfast for both of them.

He did so, on the rattan settee in the anteroom that Titi used as her office. Nina settled on a hassock.

"I want you to begin at the beginning of my father's story."

Eight Hand Horse shifted his bony haunches on the rattan. Until the age of fifteen, he had squatted on the ground or sat comfortably cross-legged like any civilized man. With his good luck in serving Luoc and his family had also come expensive but uncomfortable suits, shoes with laces, and an excess of furniture.

"In 1862..." he began.

"I didn't mean..." She nearly said that she didn't mean quite so much from the beginning, but she bit her tongue and prepared to learn from an elder.

"In 1862," said Eight Hand Horse, "the French government in Indochina puts an official ten percent tax on all opium from India, the biggest supplier at that time. The French government then takes control of all sales and forms the Opium Monopoly—everyone in Indochina must sell only to them and buy only from merchants franchised by the French. By 1918, there are 1512 government-licensed *fumeurs* and 2098 official shops, selling Indian and Chinese opium... mainly from Yunnan."

He rattled off the facts like an overfamiliar lesson.

"For the French, this situation is number one. After the First World War, one third of total government tax revenues come from opium sales. With this money they buy guns for their soldiers, they buy informers, and they buy allies. The most important allies are the warlords of the northern mountains, and the *kaitongs* in Laos, like Touby Myfong, who control the areas that are now the most important for growing poppies."

Nina controlled her impatience; he was taking so long to get to her father.

"The French," continued Eight Hand Horse, "let these warlords collect the opium for them. When the local people become angry that the warlords also take their wives and daughters, their rice and their buffalo, the French use opium money to pay soldiers to put down the people's rebellions against the warlords."

He rearranged his feet on the floor; he was still wearing his tennis shoes with the cut-out toes.

"When the Japanese invade during the Second World War, they ban the opium trade in Indochina to cut off the income. But of course the occupied French need the money more than ever, so they carry on clandestine trade—Operation X, it's called. French intelligence—the SDECE—fly the crude opium from the mountains of Laos and Tonkin to Saigon. The Binh Xuyen refine it secretly to morphine base, and the Corsicans—the Alliance Corse—arrange shipment to France. In 1945, when the Japanese are kicked out, the French still need the money, this time to fight the Vietnamese people."

He shrugged unhappily. "Many Viets are very angry. For years they fight to get rid of the French. At last, the Japanese overthrow them. Then the English put them back in power again. That General Gracie!"

The whiskers at the corners of his mouth arched in amusement at the ironies of fate.

"My father..." prompted Nina, unable to help herself.

"The Second World War is his big chance. It lets him start to work for himself instead of M. Carbone."

"Ahhh," breathed Nina, just beginning to understand.

"First the war closes the Chinese border, so no more Chinese opium for anybody. Then come Allied blockades of Asian ports, against the Japanese—so no more Indian opium either. The French are now in big trouble, including Carbone. Even Indochinese opium is scarce for them. The northern warlords are in disarray because the occupied French can no longer protect them; the Viets are rising up against the French, against the warlords, and against the Japanese. The people want no more foreign powers on Vietnamese soil. It is very dangerous for white faces in the poppy-growing areas. But your father is from the northern mountains. He goes home and they see he is one of them. The people sell their opium to him instead of the warlords. He always pays fair value; he uses no force. He becomes very rich."

"He took Tonkinese opium away from Carbone and the Corsicans?"

Eight Hand Horse bared his blackened teeth briefly. "Yes. Their biggest source gone. To a former underling...an 'Annamite.'" His satisfaction was obvious. "After the war, even so, until Dien Bien Phu, Carbone still buys a little Meo opium...Colonel Trinquier's Meos...." His tone made it clear what he thought of his fellow montagnards who had served as mercenaries for the French.

"Until Dien Bien Phu, the French Air Force flew this opium south. But after the defeat in 1954..." He sighed with satisfaction once more. "The VC make transport difficult for Carbone and all the rest. They must use private charter airlines. And now they pay, they don't just take like before, even in Laos, where they still have a little influence. And finally, there is now growing competition for European markets, from Turkish opium. Carbone is like an old tiger; his teeth are loose but his claws are still sharp." The old man looked at her seriously. "Too sharp, I think."

Nina nodded. The facts and figures were suddenly invaded by an image of Millie's torso hanging from her chair. Where Nina

317

was meant to be. But hadn't been. She was here. Safe. Waiting for her breakfast.

"Have you any questions for me, so far?" He was watching her too carefully. She reeled herself back into their conversation by an act of will.

"How do my father...how did Kim...get their opium to Saigon?"

"A cousin of your father, also Tonkinese, brings it south."

"And you said that the Binh Xuyen refined the crude opium to morphine base for the French. Who does it for us?"

"Ourselves. It is your father's idea. It saves money by cutting out one level of brokers and is much safer."

"Where?"

"At Heron. The stink of burning sugar is the same as boiling gum."

That explained the heavy weighting of chemists in their books.

"Then," he continued, "we sell through regular brokers here in the city and in Cholon, to buyers from labs in Turkey, Hong Kong, and Bangkok."

"Not America?" she asked.

He was dismissive. "Americans want *ma thuy,* already refined. And buy from the European labs. They're crazy. Smoking is much more pleasant than sticking yourself. We still, also, make good sales of smoker's opium here in Saigon, to the Chinese and the French. Lower price but steady sales. Solid business, almost like the old times."

He shifted his shanks again and patted the cheroot in his breast pocket with open wistfulness.

"Please." She indicated the pocket. "Go ahead. Breakfast is taking a long time to come."

He protested politely while his fingers fumbled joyfully for his gold lighter. She waited while he sucked hungrily at the plantain-sized cheroot and exhaled politely to one side.

"Solid business..." She repeated his words reflectively, troubled. "Not everyone would agree with you, Old Uncle."

"Fish swim in many directions," he replied. "And even one fish..." He made zigzags with his hand. "Diem, for example. First he burns opium pipes in public and closes all the *fumeurs.* Now his brother Nhu is already talking around to brokers. He needs money to pay his secret police and informers. He sees how many men they must sweeten if they are to stay in power. So he will give secret licenses...secret but official." He looked at her under the waving tangles of his white eyebrows.

"Diem's problem is the Americans," he went on. "Opium is

318

bad joss for the American government," He spoke with absolute authority and considerable regret. "They need grease money worse than Diem, but they make the trade illegal in their own country and lose the money to private citizens. It's crazy!"

Breakfast arrived. While the *mama-san* set out their plates of mango and pomelo and poured the café au lait—a gift from Louis—Nina considered what he had just told her. His prodding on the subject of Diem's brother was blatant. As was his belief in the value of the trade.

His eyes studied her through the gun slit between the top of his cup and his eyebrows, then slid away when she noticed his attention.

"It's a violent trade," she said. "And I have seen the coolies around the docks. . . ."

"It is money that makes the violence, not the opium." He peeled a section of pomelo judiciously. "Hard work and no food make the coolies ill. Opium stops hunger pains and makes them happy. . . ."

"And *ma thuy?*" She had stopped pretending to eat.

"That is not our business," he said firmly. "If White Devils who have looted our country for centuries wish to poison themselves for fun, it is their business! I believe many of their doctors still prescribe *ma thuy* for pain. It's official poisoning." The whiskers on his lips arched again in amusement.

"Old Uncle," she said, after a long silence, "why did my father want so much money? He had no armies to pay. And where did it all go? I have seen his books . . . where did it go? How can he be bankrupt?"

He ate a slice of mango delicately, with his fingers, his eyes on his plate. Finally he said, "He did not honor me with so much of his confidence."

She doubted that, but could not insult him by saying so. Since Kim's death his pose of genial old family retainer, previously a polite, mutually sustained fiction, had slipped almost completely. By French standards he was an uneducated Meo, a *moi*, or savage. But she could feel him still holding his intelligence in polite check. His energy made her forget the runnels in his cheeks and the whiteness of his whiskers. She was certain he had been much more to her father than mere chauffeur and majordomo. She also suspected that both he and his sister, her father's concubine, were personages of standing in their own territory. Smoke from the reignited cheroot had caught in his whiskers like clouds among mountaintop pines. Instruction finished, he was waiting for her to respond.

She rose and went out onto the little balcony where she had spent so much of the night. The staff dining table was gone, but the three paper lanterns still swung, unlit, from bamboo poles planted in the flowerbeds. By daylight she could see lilies in the little ornamental pool she had made to restore the harmony and good fortune of the hotel. Such problems already seemed very simple compared to the ones she now faced. She went back inside.

"Where would I fit in? What must I do if I choose to follow my father and Kim in the business? Is it possible for me?"

He picked his way carefully, balanced between persuasion and honesty. "Yes, it is possible. If things go smoothly, you will have to do very little. Only if things go wrong . . . then you must act. You must be the ruler who holds things together from the top. You must detect disorder, put it right, and chastise the wrongdoers. Same as any business."

"You make it sound so simple," she said. "But we both know it is not."

"It is simple. If you have good men working for you. And you stay informed. Both are bought with money. . . ." He paused, then continued. "But good men are held through their belief that you will rule successfully."

His eyes searched hers. "Their belief grows out of your own. You must let them know you intend to go on. If you believe you can."   (

She swallowed, without dropping her eyes from his. "I believe it." She almost did.

He bowed his head and his body went slack as tension left it. "We're still in business, then?" he asked quietly.

She swallowed again. "With your help. And the help of all the good men we can find, and keep. Yes, we're still in business."

He raised his head. Under the tangled brows, his eyes blazed with satisfaction. Then he bowed his head again, formally.

"How much time do I have in which to learn?"

He rubbed the end of his burned-out cheroot in the side of his saucer. "Mademoiselle, if I am to advise you, I must always be open. . . ."

"I expect that," she replied.

"You might think you want the truth, but perhaps you would be happier . . ."

"You disappoint me," she said. "What use is false information?"

"OK." He looked for an ashtray, then put the cheroot stump into his jacket pocket.

"Before coming back here, I went to some drinking clubs by the docks to hear what I could hear. The word just now is very good. The right people know that Customs came to make a special search of the *Tripoli Belle* and went away again. Those who also know of your brother's death are already saying that you know more than you do. That you are in reality behind the business for many months. Many don't know exactly who you are, but they say that someone has stepped into Kim's shoes. They even say that you have a more powerful *tay phap* than Kim—that the gods deserted him in order to favor you. Best of all, it is the Year of the Dog—a good year for new leaders. A good year to stand firm and assert authority. So far, the signs and rumors are on your side. In short, you have a little time."

"Except for the matter of Carbone," she said.

"Yes." He looked grave.

"That is disorder that I must put right. Now."

"Yes," he said again. He was silent for a few moments. Then he spoke again.

"There is a *tay phap* who owes me a favor... Perhaps with a little sweetening we can shape more signs through him. He can discover portents. To buy a little more time. I hope you do not mind if I presume."

"I'm grateful," she said. "Let me know how much it will cost."

"I must be open again."

"Please!"

"If the *tay phap* is later seen to be wrong," he said with care, "if he says 'back that horse' and it loses, he loses his reputation... and his clients."

"I understand." She spoke with more confidence than she felt. "I will think about how to shape fortune myself. Meanwhile..." She stood up before her nerve went. "Could I ask you to learn where M. Carbone is eating his breakfast?"

Eight Hand Horse stood up quickly. He looked at her face to see that she was serious.

"Of course, mademoiselle. If you will allow me to come with you." She could feel his fright and his excitement at what he guessed she had just decided to do.

The buffalo calf is stampeding again, she told herself. But it doesn't know what else to do.

Emile Carbone was enthroned on the terrace of the Hotel Continental, just inside one of the great arches that screened the tables. His wife Angelica had gone back to Ajaccio in Corsica to nurse her sick mother. It suited him to have company for breakfast and do business at the same time. He had just said farewell to one of his agents, who was back from a visit to the northern poppy fields in Laos. Carbone made a practice of such private checking in advance of the harvest each year; it protected his dealings with northern agents. He was pleased. The report had been positive. The peasants had had a good rice harvest and were happy to put their fields to poppies as a cash crop. Business had been worse.

Carbone spread his bulk in his chair like a handsome, gray-haired frog, and called for more coffee and for the large trolley with its linen-covered shelves and baskets of sweet rolls and croissants. He paused, startled, his cup halfway to his mouth, when he saw Nina Martell come onto the terrace.

He was even more startled when she marched the length of the checkered floor to his table and asked to sit down. She reminded him of a lotus, bloom held high on a slender stalk.

"Of course, Ninette . . . Mme. Martell. What a surprise!"

"I'm sure it is," she replied tightly. "Unfortunately, your man missed."

"I'm sorry?" He was off guard and genuinely puzzled.

"Why did you need to try to kill me too?" Her voice was passionate. "Why didn't you try talking to me first? We agreed to be friends not long ago."

He wiped his wide mouth with the linen napkin. "Too?" He asked.

"Like my brother?"

"Ahhh." He began to understand. He pointed to her and waited for the uniformed waiter to pour her a cup of coffee and hot tinned milk. When the man moved away, Carbone resumed. "You seem to think I killed Kim."

She nodded.

"I did not," he said. "In fact, I was sorry to hear about it. And I offer you my condolences."

"I don't believe you! I think you're still angry with my father for outwitting you and taking away your Tonkinese opium. I think you burned our house and killed my mother. Then you killed Kim. And then you tried to kill me!"

He leaned back in his chair. "My quarrel with your father is in the past. And you yourself said that you are a very different person. Why should I want to kill his children, one of whom is little more than a schoolgirl?"

She clenched her fists on the tabletop, her eyes wide with shock at his mendacity. "I know more than you think! And they were your men!"

"My men . . . where?"

"In the jeep with the machine-gun."

"Dear God," he said. "I see why . . ."

He leaned forward again and laid a large, heavily ringed hand over one of her fists. "If you thought that, then you are brave to come looking for me. Are you also strong?"

"Don't patronize me, please. I didn't think—I *know*. They were recognized as two of your thugs. And I'm not a school-girl." She tried to withdraw her hand, but he held it tight.

"Listen to me, Ninette," he said. "My men don't always tell me everything they do, but I keep track. Someone I know also saw them. They were working free-lance, I swear it."

He sounded sincere.

"For whom?"

The quick spasm of unhappiness that passed over his face before he spoke convinced her he was telling the truth.

"Your husband."

"Andrew," she said quietly.

He could hardly hear her. He watched her face try to rearrange itself back into an imitation of its former self. She seemed to be fascinated by a crumb on the white linen cloth.

"I thought he was your stooge," she said finally. "Your errand boy . . . setting me up for you." She looked at him suspiciously, unsure whether this new truth too might turn out to be a lie.

Carbone tapped both their hands gently on the table, hers still enclosed in his, while he thought.

"So did I," he said. "Until the party on the boat. . . . Thought he was my errand boy, I mean."

He looked at her almost absently. "He's going to be a problem for both of us. Would you like me to take care of him?"

He looked at her steadily, her clenched fist still in his hand.

"Take care of him." She knew exactly what he meant. Her heart leaped like a fish against her ribs. "No!" she whispered. "Oh, no!"

Suddenly, she could remember only the kindness that Andrew had shown her, his ardor in bed before the separation, the food he had put before her. She forgot her anger at his arrogance. She forgot her unanswered questions. She forgot that he had lied to her, lies that had changed her life.

If he had not lied, Eight Hand Horse would have found her on that first, terrible night. If Andrew had not lied, she would never have stayed in that little room, or married him. She would have been spared the second burning of a home, and what she believed was a second grief. She might have been spared the horrors of the five-day battle for Saigon. She would have been spared begging, and the shame of considering the idea of selling herself to an American in return for food.

For a few minutes, looking across a white linen cloth into the intelligent eyes of an aging Corsican gangster, she forgot all the lies. She opened her mouth to protest again.

"He must try again," said Carbone, "now he has shown that he means to get you out of the way and take over your father's business as your widower."

She began to remember the lies. And the flame-lit emptiness of the servants' quarters and how men desert those who are abandoned by fate.

"Soon," prodded Carbone. "Before you can fight back." He glanced automatically around the terrace and gardens.

She remembered the choice she had made that night. She had not expected reality to bite so soon or in this way. This was not the disorder she had expected to have to put right. She had not expected to choose so brutally between Andrew and herself.

Carbone waited as if he had asked whether she wanted more coffee. After a long silence she said, "I'll find some other way...."

Carbone squeezed, then released her hand. "It's not up to you. After what you have told me, I have no choice," he said. "You must see that. You were only the intended victim. He was challenging *me*."

He smiled at her expression. "You'll be grateful to me in the end. As I'm grateful to you now for the information. I'll be doing you a favor." He patted her hand. "You'll see. I hope in time that we will even do business together. There's strength in unison with the country in its present state."

She shook her head helplessly.

"Come now," said Carbone. "I can't believe you had no suspicion at all when you came to me so bravely."

"No!" she exclaimed. Then her hand moved to her mouth as if to put back all the words she had said. She wondered with horror if he could possibly be right.

"Do you remember the thrush I once gave you?" asked Carbone, who had been watching her.

"Yes, I set it free. But I think a cat ate it." To his ears and her own she sounded unnaturally bright.

"I see," said Carbone, and looked amused. "Well, I won't eat you."

"I don't mean to let you," she retorted, still brittle.

Carbone's tone sharpened. "Don't misunderstand my offer of friendship," he said. "You will need my goodwill in the coming months much more than I'm going to need yours. Don't make the same mistake as your father, of setting yourself against me. I'm helping you, whether you agree to it or not, because by chance you have control for the moment of things that I want. I mean to have them, but peaceably, and in good time. And preferably with your agreement. Don't make a fight where there isn't one. And which you can't win. You haven't the stomach for a fight. You're young, and female. Take your time; think things through. I'm helping now, because I'm sure of the conclusions you will eventually come to. I believe that you are more sensible than your father, who was an arrogant man, a traitor, and a thief."

She bit her tongue. He was right to say that she was not yet ready to deal with him. She needed to take time, to think things through.

"I can't think of my father like that," she said at last, temporarily sidestepping the real challenge in his words.

"He came to me as an ignorant peasant with a thin veneer of Jesuit polish," said Carbone. "I made him a success in the real world."

She held her rising voice in check with difficulty. He had already demonstrated his power and her own helplessness. He didn't need to overstress his point. Her self-control was going. "I can't bear to lose belief in both a husband and a father in the same day. You must forgive me, monsieur, if I choose to see that as merely your version of the truth."

He was gratified that she had decided not to fight.

"I always forgive honesty," he said. "Only deceit angers me."

They shook hands. Then Nina went back to the Phoenix Tower to wait for her husband to be murdered because of something she had said.

28

Raoul Duprès was drinking his early morning glass of tea, made by his Catholic Vietnamese wife, when the driver from Heron arrived to give him the news. Duprès had already heard that the

Tripoli Belle had sailed without incident. The driver bowed sketchily and rushed into his story.

He had gone to the docks that morning to collect a crate of mixer parts just arrived from Tokyo. A Foreign Devil had been found dead the night before, in the water near the U.S. Navy docks. His hands were missing and his genitalia inserted into a slit in his abdomen. He had been carted to the military hospital morgue where he had been identified almost immediately by one of the orderlies. The driver told Duprès that the White Devil was named Andrew Martell and that he had been married to Luoc's daughter. He added that the identifying orderly was said to deal in black market drugs from the military dispensary. Duprès paid him a bonus, and he left to continue his rounds.

Duprès was in a quiet panic. Life was falling into disorder just as he had feared when he heard Kim had been killed. His new employer had managed to fix Customs successfully. He had not heard about the men in the jeep or her breakfast with Carbone. The death of her husband was clearly an organized, syndicate killing. But he did not know whether to read it as a further sign of her powers or a first symptom of vulnerability. He hated times of transition; it was so hard to judge what to do.

He decided, by the time he had finished his glass of tea, to send his wife and two young sons for a few weeks to her family in their village just north of Hanoi. Her parents had decided to stay after the Partition, in spite of Ho's hostility to Catholics. He could easily fix the transport. The journey would have its dangers, but he believed his family would still be safer than if they remained with him in Saigon.

Word also spread to certain military clubs. When it reached Clinton Clay, he whistled between his teeth and later called the hospital orderly, with whom he occasionally did business, to confirm the story. Clay had already heard about the Corsicans in the jeep. And about Nina's breakfast tête-à-tête. These dink babes might look like you could break them with one hand . . .

He thought he would give her a week or two, to let the dust settle. Then he would arrange a little meeting to talk about something more interesting than forklift trucks.

Word also passed from one of the cleaners at the military hospital to her husband, and from her husband to his brother, who operated a small fleet of four fishing boats on the Saigon River. From the brother it passed, along with other snippets of information, in the routine way, to one of the Binh Xuyen toll collectors with whom he guaranteed safe passage for his boats. From the toll collector it went to his superior officer in the Binh

Xuyen, and by means of the officer to the heart of the Rung Sat swamp.

When Eight Hand Horse returned, shortly before the previous midnight, with news that it was done, he wondered whether he should tell Nina the details of how Martell died; someone else inevitably would. He looked at the tightness of her young face and decided to wait. Then he decided, on the contrary, that she trusted him for honest information and that it was a false kindness to protect her now, when "a house and a little money" were still an alternative. Just.

She closed her eyes halfway through his carefully worded exposition. She sat so still that her body as well as her brain seemed to have shut down. Then, very quietly, she asked him to take her back to the apartment. She was past feeling. Every time she tried, carefully, to test what she would feel, if she did feel, the result was so horrible that she immediately slammed down every drawbridge, every window, barricaded every door, gate, and crevice that might let feeling in. She found that she couldn't sit still, because inaction left her with nothing to do but feel. So she looked for something to do.

She began to clear Andrew's things from the apartment. She gave his clothes to the *mama-san* and didn't want to know what the woman did with them. She kept her mind blank as she dropped his razor and spare, unused blades into a sack of rubbish. Her fingers were unconnected to her brain as they collected up books of matches from assorted nightclubs and restaurants where he had taken someone else. She was nearly undone once when she tugged open a drawer and released his scent—a mixture of citrus and his own musky secretions. She slammed the drawer shut. When she thought she had finished, she went through the rooms again. When she had done that, she had erased their second life together as completely as the exploding shell had erased their first.

She tried to lie down to sleep but feeling rushed at her as urgently as a tide across a flat beach. She got up again and took out the two little books from the brass box in the floor safe at Heron. The patterns of the different characters seemed completely unintelligible this time, so she put the books away and paced, hugging herself as if in physical pain.

In spite of the drawbridges and barricades, she imagined it happening. Then tried to rewrite it another way. And saw him in pieces, instead, like Minou. Or sliced in half like Millie. The image she found most bearable was of Andrew with a small, neat dark circle in the center of his forehead like gangsters in French and American films. She walked for most of the night, trying to get away from the images which sniffed at her like hungry dogs tracking a wounded sheep. At five in the morning, when the world was beginning to wake and Andrew was draining river slime onto the military dock and the coolie who had spotted him was explaining to yet another White Demon in uniform, Nina finally collapsed onto the huge joke of a bed and let unconsciousness claim her.

Nina slept on into the following night, refusing to reenter consciousness, until she woke suddenly in a sweat. There was someone in her room. Speaking to her.

"Who's that?" she asked with a dry tongue.

"Only me, Big Sister," said Chinchook's voice. His shadow eased onto the end of the big bed. "You scream in your sleep. I want to wake you."

She stared into the darkness, still not recognizing him.

"Big Sister, come back!" He was urgent with terror. "Come back!"

"Ahhhh, it's only you. . . ." She blew out a shaky breath. "I was dreaming."

"I know," he said gently. "It was a very bad journey."

She drank some water from her jug to moisten her dry mouth. "I dreamed . . ."

She stopped, eyes still wide. ". . . Andrew . . ." She swallowed. "Before that . . ." Again she stopped to remember, then hauled herself back on course. "Before that, I don't know why I was so frightened. . . . Someone who said he was my father wanted to take me swimming. I knew I mustn't go . . . something terrible would happen." She shivered. "It sounds silly. But I knew he wasn't my father, even though he said he was. He was a Round Eye, with a beard. White, white skin. He kept saying he was my father and I must not deny him. And he was so strong!"

She stared into the folds of the mosquito netting as if searching for the face there. Then she refocused on Chinchook. "How did you get here? Has something happened?"

"You leave the shutter open; it's very dangerous," he said severely. "Anyone can come in like I did, up the pipes, when the man in the garden isn't looking."

She turned on the light and looked at him for signs of injury to explain his sudden appearance. "Are you all right?"

"Fine. Fine." He waved his hand dismissively and his gold

328

watch caught the light. "I just want to sleep somewhere else tonight. Is it OK?"

"Of course." She hoped it really was OK. She suspected he was getting involved in things he should not.

"Are you OK now?" he asked, leaning closer to her.

"It was only a stupid dream."

"No! Not so!" he cried. "Your spirit is making dangerous journeys. One time, it might not come back. Believe me!"

"Thanks!" said Nina. She made her voice light, but he had frightened her. She still felt the pull of the dream, toward some unimaginable disaster, even now that she was wide awake.

"I'll fix it in the morning," he said. "Let's play cards now."

She nearly laughed, and protested that it was 4:30 in the morning. Then she saw how frightened he was for her. He did not want her to sleep again, until he could fix it. She wouldn't be able to sleep in any case.

"There are cards in that box on the table," she said.

"We play for money?" He began to shuffle the cards in an arc from hand to hand, like a conjurer. "Blackjack. I'm banker first."

"If you like."

By 6:30 she owed him seventy piastres. She was certain he had been cheating, but she couldn't catch him at it.

"I'll go now," he said suddenly. She paid him his winnings.

When he had gone, she found she was terrified of being alone; she endured solitude like pain, second by second.

An hour and twenty minutes later he was back. This time he rang the bell. He put into her hand a twist of newspaper filled with dust which looked like table salt and chopped hair. She peered at it while he filled a water glass from her bedside jug. He stirred the powder into the water with his right ring finger.

"Drink it."

"What is it?" she asked.

He looked shocked. "*Bac si* never tell. Just drink it."

He forgot his new dignity of young manhood and hopped from foot to foot as he had done when she first met him. His cockade of hair had been greased back, making his ears stand out even more prominently, but two rebellious strands had sprung free and arched over his forehead like the lures of an anglerfish. A faint, dark fuzz made it look as if he needed to wipe his upper lip.

"Come on!" he ordered, his eyes intent.

On such things do friendships hang, thought Nina, and she drank it. His relief both amused and comforted her.

She had no trouble persuading him to stay for breakfast.

329

After Chinchook left, midmorning, on what he said was "business," Nina looked for some distraction from her thoughts. She could not concentrate on any of her usual business matters. Finally, she got out her father's two books and began to copy out a list of the Chinese ideograms that hid his meaning. The work required concentration but very little thought, and kept her busy until the middle of the afternoon.

Louis arrived just after the end of the afternoon siesta, the following day, apologizing for his delay in coming to see her.

"I'm terribly sorry, my dear! I was out of town." He leaned his walking stick against the wall without looking at her.

"What a thing to happen!" he said, not specifying what event he referred to. Avoiding her eyes, he ferreted in the pocket of his light gray suit and produced a small packet tied up in a piece of gold shantung. He bowed slightly as he proffered it.

It was an ivory netsuke of a coiled tiger, ready to spring.

"Another patch for my soul?" she teased. "It's very lovely. Very small but very powerful." She held it out on the palm of her hand to admire the energy pent up in an object the size of a walnut.

"An appropriate gift of respect," said Louis. He still did not meet her eyes.

Nina looked at him across the little tiger. Her hand slowly dropped and she let the tiger fall to the floor.

"At least you didn't kowtow!" she said bitterly. *"Merci!"*

When he didn't reply, she added passionately, "I haven't changed, Louis. Only my circumstances have!"

"They are usually the same thing," he said to the carpet. "And I hate to see something lovely altered in any way."

She felt as if he had hit her. "How can you be so cruel?" she cried. In spite of herself, tears came to her eyes. "You! Of all people!"

She turned away so he couldn't see the tears.

He followed and seized both her hands. "Oh, my dear." He kissed her hands in remorse. "I'm sorry! You're right. It was unforgivable. And I've made you cry again! I was being unfair . . . making you responsible for my own ideas about how things should be. People have no right to do that to each other. Please forgive me."

"But you're right," she said. "I am changing. I can feel it. I am doing things . . ."

"As you must," he said. "As you must. It would be insane not to change. Dangerous. I really should have known better."

"I'm not sure I want to change."

"I know." Something in his tone made her look at him. "Believe me, I know," he went on. "How many different people do you imagine I've been in my life, in order to stay alive?"

The question was direct, devoid of any of his usual theatricality; through blurred eyes she saw a tired old man looking at her, patches of rouge hectic against his sallow skin.

"I don't judge," he said. "Me, of all people. The idea's amusing, really."

He bent to pick up the little ivory tiger from the carpet where she had let it fall. "The important thing is to decide that it's worth staying alive. After that, everything becomes simpler."

He set the tiger on one of the tables. "Forget the teeth and claws. It has your passion and energy. I knew it was you when I saw it in the case. Now come sit down and tell me why you sent for me. What do you need me to do?"

She gave him the list of Chinese ideograms she had copied from her father's book. "Can you translate these for me?"

"Oddly enough," he replied, "among my many roles I've never been a real Chinaman. But I can have it done for you by tomorrow."

He seemed to have dropped his theatricality almost with relief, as if it were a heavy overcoat.

The change in me is changing others, thought Nina. First Eight Hand Horse, now Louis. So many little truths were accompanying the new larger ones.

"I would also like to talk privately with someone who understands organic chemistry . . . my father's kind, but not one of my father's chemists. I want to learn more about what I'm doing. I'll pay for his time, of course."

Louis nodded. "I'll think. And let you know tomorrow when I bring the translations. Is there anything else?"

"What did you do for my father?"

Unconsciously, Louis pulled a little away from her and crossed his slim calf across his knee. "Whatever he needed me to do." He gave her the ghost of one of his arch smiles. She did not smile back but held his eyes.

". . . I was a broker, I suppose." Louis dropped the smile. "Sometimes a distributor . . . direct to users. I ran a *fumeur* for him, a special one, for the French." She watched him remembering and flirting with frankness.

"It sounds petty, but I had my place in his scheme of things.

And it was an improvement over what I had been doing before I met him. I worked for him here, then Hanoi, then here again. *Plus ça change*."

"What can you tell me about his organization—the men I must deal with?"

He shook his head with regret. "He and I had a direct personal arrangement, until he went north and I semiretired. It was unusual for him; he liked to keep buffers between himself and the people he paid—'cut-outs,' as I believe they say. I was kept apart from the rest. By my choice as well as his. He gave me a special role. Me and my *fumeur*. Besides, if you know nothing, no one tries to extract information from you. Being seen openly with you now is probably the stupidest thing I've done for a long time. . . ."

He stopped her protest with a smile. "A risk freely chosen, I assure you. I suppose I consider your father still to be slightly in credit . . . though in truth, he and I are past the ledger stage. Anyway, I like you."

He patted her hand. "No. I won't turn your head that much. You amuse me. That's all. So there, tigress! *Rowh!*" He growled like a very small, very apologetic tiger.

She couldn't help laughing. "Since we're being so honest with each other," she said, "I have to warn you that you have competition in looking after my soul."

She told him about her dreams, and Chinchook's potion and the early-morning blackjack game.

Louis looked very serious. "I'm afraid you have to make a choice!"

"It's not like you to be jealous."

"Oh no," said Louis. "I don't mean a choice between me and this urchin of yours. I mean that you must either make your peace with him or kill him off. One or the other—if you ever want to sleep peacefully again."

"What do you mean?" Nina tried to laugh, but a chill crimped the edges of her gut. "Kill off whom?"

"God, of course!" said Louis. "Who else? That man in your dream is an illustration right out of a children's picture Bible!"

Nina stared, the sense of doom lightening as understanding came. "You know, you're absolutely right!" Impulsively, she threw her arms around him. "Oh Louis, I need you so much!"

"There, there," he said, suffering her embrace a little uneasily. "We need each other, then." He detached her with gentleness. "You're trying to make me smudge my mascara, aren't you? You're never going to learn proper restraint. I should have bought an octopus, not the tiger."

As he was leaving, he became serious again. "They'll let you know who they are, you know . . . the men you'll be dealing with. Learn what you can about them. The old man will help. But they'll let you know."

Nina went down the gull-wing stairs with him. She had not been outside since she returned from the hotel two nights before. She watched his car leave, then turned to walk a little, along the pavement, past the compound walls of the big houses. The air was hot, but it felt fresh after forty-eight hours in the apartment. She inhaled a sweetness and reached up to touch the swag of jasmine that had escaped over a wall from the garden inside. She failed, as she did so, to notice a taxi that had been waiting opposite her gate and was now following her.

29

In squash court number two at the Cercle Sportif, Daniel Jouvet dived to return the hard black rubber ball and missed.

"*Merde!*" he said. "Shit! *Scheisse!*"

"Pax!" cried his partner. "I need a breather."

The two men wiped their sweaty faces with the towels hanging on the knob of the court door.

"Nasty about Martell," said his partner, like Jouvet, a Saigon-born French solicitor. The two had known each other from childhood. Both had stayed behind when their families fled to France.

"What about him?" Jouvet was just back from two weeks in Singapore, sorting out the legalities surrounding a delayed shipment of pharmaceuticals, among other things.

"You didn't know? Found dead in the river. Syndicate-style. The day after his wife was seen having breakfast with Emile Carbone. Poor bastard."

"You're joking!"

"Makes my ballocks hurt, just to think about it."

"Any ideas why?" Jouvet was remembering the curious scene on the river launch—Martell looking smug, Carbone thoughtful, and Nina afraid.

"The word is that he got in her way. Screwed around too much, then got ideas above his station . . . like most men who marry for money." Jouvet's partner pulled out the elastic of his shorts with his thumb to let in some air.

"*She* did it?" Jouvet sounded incredulous, but his fingers went unconsciously to his now-perfect front teeth.

"Or arranged it through Carbone."

"Never!" said Jouvet. "Carbone's setting her up. If the story's true. Whatever he's doing! He's setting her up. You wait. Unless she gets a little expert help and advice."

His partner knew him too well. "Be careful, Dani," he said seriously.

Under his surface bonhomie, Daniel Jouvet was an angry, disappointed young man. His family had once owned two copper-processing plants in Tonkin. After the country had been divided in 1955, the North Vietnamese Republic nationalized the plants without compensation. Jouvet still held a grudge against the secret French negotiators who had managed to protect some French interests in the North but not those of his family. He felt it was almost his duty to his family to amass whatever he could, by whatever means necessary, as fair compensation.

To his delight, he found after the withdrawal of the French that many Vietnamese were as sorry about it as he was himself. He played on this nostalgia, modeling his style on the between-the-wars; young as he was, his mustaches, his bearing, and even his clothes always managed to suggest the straight back, sepia whiskers, and confident sepia eye of a faded ancestral photograph.

Now he smiled knowingly at his squash partner. "Don't worry. She and I go back a long way. I know what she's capable of, and it doesn't scare me in the least. She doesn't know yet how much she needs me." He smoothed his mustaches back against his cheeks.

The driver of the taxi was a stocky, crew-cut Vietnamese in an American sports shirt, chewing gum. Just as Nina noticed that she was being followed, he blew a large pink bubble, sucked it back into his mouth, and turned to open the back door.

She swung around to run back to the house, into a man in uniform who had stepped in her way. He began to apologize. Before he had spoken five words, a second man seized her arms from behind and swung her toward the open taxi door. The uniformed man dived around into the far side of the taxi and pulled her in on top of him. The taxi pulled away while the second man was still wrestling with the open door and the other with Nina.

334

She managed to free one hand and tried to reach his eyes with her nails.

"Take it easy!" he said.

She missed his eyes but drew blood on the edge of his ear.

"Please!" he begged.

Near her left eye a snarling tiger badge of the Binh Xuyen convinced her that these were Carbone's hired thugs.

You idiot! she told herself, too late. She should have been prepared for something like this. She should have told Eight Hand Horse that she was going out.

The man embraced her tightly and pinned her arms to her sides. The man with the badge now seized her two little fingers. "Please, stop," he said again, gently bending back her fingers. If he bent harder they would break. "The colonel will shoot us if you are hurt."

"What colonel?" she demanded.

"Colonel Thu," he said, as if it were obvious. "He sent us to bring you to him."

"Colonel Thu?" she heard her voice repeat stupidly. She had forgotten about him, and about the message Chinchook had once tried to deliver for her.

Both men eased their hold on her. When she did not struggle, they released her cautiously.

"The colonel wishes to talk to you." The uniformed man's voice was stiff with respect.

Her heartbeat began to slow down. "Why the hell couldn't he just ask me?"

"He wished to make sure you would come." That seemed to make sense to both her kidnappers.

She straightened her back and did not deign to rub her burning wrists. "I'm sure he didn't want you to half kill me."

The man in uniform began to apologize.

Death cannot be preceded by a farce like this, she thought. Their story had to be true.

The Citroën followed the Arroyo Chinois to a small commercial wharf with a fence and a locked gate. Nina considered trying to bolt as she climbed out of the taxi, but the two men shouldered her forward like polite herd dogs. A third man unlocked the gate and relocked it behind them. There was no one else on the wharf, although crowds milled along the waterfront street as was usual in the early evening.

She edged carefully down a narrow ramp to the deck of a launch which was flying a Customs and Excise pennon. They backed off. Roaring and gargling, the launch turned downriver.

As they left behind the last of the large quays the uniformed man said, "Very sorry, you must go below now." He looked worried but resolute.

Nina decided against another physical battle in which she could only lose face and went down the three steep steps into the tiny cabin. The door was shut behind her and the portholes covered. Light leaked through a number of cracks, but none was large enough to give her a view out. She fumbled her way to a padded berth or banquette and settled down to wait.

After a long time, during which she finally dozed off, she felt the launch swing to the left. Sometime later, the note of the engine changed and their speed dropped. She reckoned they had turned into one of the thousands of channels that opened off the main stream into the Rung Sat. The cracks around the door and portholes were darkening.

She listened for a long time to the furious humming of a single mosquito trapped with her in the dark. The sound of the insect emerged from the throb of the engine, then faded again. Finally it buzzed near her ear and fell abruptly silent; she felt the tiny prick on the side of her neck and slapped viciously.

The boat was weaving and twisting now. At last she heard the engine die and felt the launch slide slowly in to bump gently alongside a mooring. She climbed up the three steps into the night, which was thick with damp and smelled like a giant's fart. A treble chorus of insects chittered above the countertenor of frogs. Somewhere, something was adding a regular basso thump.

She tried not to inhale the cloud of gnats that wrapped itself around her head as she followed the two men off the tiny wooden pier onto a wooden walkway raised on pilings above the mud of the swamp. They passed through a gate into a bamboo palisade whose curving walls merged with the thick growth of mangrove. Once inside, they crossed a short stretch of high, dry ground, then marched hollowly across a zigzag bridge over more muddy water to a large area of high ground.

Beyond the bridge, scattered lights pricked holes in the darkness. Smudge fires against the mosquitoes, cooking braziers, and Coleman lanterns showed fragments of men in uniform and a few women who were preparing the evening meal. Through the smell of swamp gas and rotting vegetation came the sharp tang of citronella and charring meat.

They passed living huts on stilts, two concrete-block storehouses, and an incongruous ornamental humpback bridge over what seemed to be a formal pool. Straight ahead, beyond a tiny parade ground, a long ramp of packed earth led up to the central pavilion.

It was as if a fugitive wing from the Imperial Palace in Hue were skulking in the swamp. Silhouetted dragons snaked along the angles of the roof, sliding down the swooping curves from the sky. Carved and painted beams rested on a colonnade of painted columns. Two carved stone lions guarded the top of the ramp; between them a huge gong hung suspended from a teak frame as large as a pair of gateposts. Directly above the entrance and the gong, between the two central supporting columns, a carved and gilded tiger snarled down.

A man waited in the main chamber of the pavilion; an electric, European-style chandelier glittered and flirted its crystal drops above his head. The deep hum-thump she had been hearing was the sound of a gasoline-powered generator.

The light from the chandelier showed that Thu was still slim and hard-muscled. The fine lines of his cheekbones were unblurred by middle age. The forelock, which still fell to touch his eyebrow, was as black as it had ever been and still held in place by a worker's headband. He wore the black uniform of a colonel in the Binh Xuyen.

Nina's escorts stiffened to attention and saluted in unison. Thu returned the salute and dismissed them formally. When their footsteps had receded outside the chamber, Nina walked forward into the mocking beam of his eyes.

"My men have made a mistake," said Thu. "I sent them to bring me a dragon lady, who eats husbands. Who is this schoolgirl?"

Nina turned on her heel and began to walk out of the pavilion. She was cursing her impulse even before he spoke again.

"Don't bluff if you can't follow through," he said softly.

She stopped. He was right, of course. But she was tired from the journey and tired of being pushed and tested.

"Let me see your face again. It might jog my memory."

He was easing away from confrontation. She turned back to him.

"Ah, it *is* you, Little Cousin. Now I can see it." He looked far too pleased at his first trivial victory.

"Why did you send for me after all these months?" she asked. "The journey was unpleasant and my reception is as rude as the invitation."

The self-satisfaction died in his eyes. "You are being very stupid." His voice was now colder than his eyes had become. "Sit down and let me tell you a few truths."

337

He crossed to a large wooden platform and seated himself against some cushions at one end. She watched him kick off his sandals and fold his slim legs under him. Slowly, she obeyed, seating herself at the far end of the platform.

"Number one truth..." he said when she had arranged herself at attention, "don't ever try to bluff me again. I see through such things!" He was watching to see his effect on her.

"Number two!" He slapped his hand against the platform with a crack like a gunshot. "I rule here. You are powerless. You must behave in harmony with that truth."

His hand slapped the platform again. Ropy scars twisted up his wrist and disappeared under the sleeve of his jacket.

"Number three...even though you are my cousin, I will punish disloyalty by death.

"Number four." He did not hit the platform but placed his hand upon it as if to press the weight of his words into the polished wood. "You need me, but act as if you do not. The truth is that you are an ignorant schoolgirl who has accidentally grasped the tail of a tiger and believes that she can tame it. But you are wrong. You have had some good fortune and are arrogant enough to think it is yours by right, because you are so clever."

Nina drew a breath to retort, then stopped herself.

He leaned back, his list ended. "Do you understand me?"

"Yes." Her voice was quiet. There was enough truth in his words to shake her.

"Good." He assessed her sincerity. "Now that your brother is dead, we must do business together. I cannot risk trusting an ignorant, arrogant schoolgirl!"

"Schoolgirl!" she exclaimed. "Stop calling me that! Would a schoolgirl do as I did? What must I do to prove that I know the tiger whose tail I hold? It was no accident that the *Tripoli Belle* sailed! Andrew's death was not 'fortune.' I did not intend it, but I am partly responsible!"

He smiled and she felt her spine crawl.

"Do you think that one unintended death brings knowledge? Or confers power? Death is nothing—a small truth of every day. Watch!"

He raised his voice to shout an order. Nina was already shaking her head in protest when two soldiers dragged a bound man up the ramp and dropped him under the chandelier.

"Kill him," said Thu.

Both soldiers fired at the same time. The man on the floor leaped like a hooked fish. The soldiers dragged the twitching

338

body back down the ramp into the darkness. It had taken twenty seconds.

Thu was watching her. "Again?" he asked.

"I'm not a slow learner," she said. "That will do."

He must have planned it beforehand, to impress her. It was possible that another man was waiting now, bound, in the darkness, braced for the second summons.

She clasped her hands between her knees to hide their shaking and glanced sideways at the ragged double line of dark blood on the polished wood, the only proof that the unimaginable event had taken place. Then she dropped her eyes to keep him from seeing what she felt.

"Little Cousin," he said, "from what I have heard rumored of you, I did not expect you to be so shocked. I have only blown away a grain of dust. As someone will one day blow me away. And you."

"Why did you bring me here?" she asked quietly. "Merely to teach me lessons?" She was not so certain now that farce ruled out the possibility of death.

She heard the satisfaction in his voice. "You are not such a schoolgirl. Now that I look closely, I can see how much you have grown since you spied on us from the hammock in Dalat."

His mood had switched again; now he was playful and teasing. She looked once more at the bloodstains on the floor. In spite of them, when she turned back, she saw him as she had when she first entered the pavilion, as the man who had sat drinking beer and talking to her father in the soft dusk under the pines.

That is the real face of the tiger, she told herself. And I am a goat in the jungle. He frightened her as Carbone did not. His truths were too different from her own.

"How are you my cousin?" she asked.

"Through an uncle of your father; his second wife was my mother. My family lived in Ha Giang. But your father and I were brothers in our anger. I was only a baby when *my* father was murdered by the French, but your father was nearly a man."

While Nina tried to digest the shocking fact that her grandfather had been killed by the French, Thu paused, then changed direction.

"Your father and I were partners. Then your brother in his turn. And now you."

"How were you partners?"

"You didn't know?"

She shook her head.

"I control supply routes," he said proudly. "I have the responsibility for moving goods, both north and south."

This, then, was the cousin whom Eight Hand Horse had mentioned. She digested his words for a moment.

"Both north and south?" she queried.

"Crude to Saigon. Base to labs in Yunnan and Hong Kong."

They sold to mainland Chinese labs; this was information Eight Hand Horse hadn't told her. He had mentioned only Hong Kong sales.

"Do you move it north by sea?" she asked.

"By sea *and* overland." Satisfaction tinged his voice once again.

"*Overland* routes into China? Across the border?" She couldn't hide her surprise. "Even now? Surely it's not possible. The North is hostile and the Chinese have outlawed the trade! The border has been closed since the war."

He made an admonitory noise with his tongue. "You must learn not to doubt me, Little Cousin. It's not a healthy practice, even for pretty little cousins."

"Oh, I do not doubt," she said quickly. "I am merely puzzled, and humbled with respect."

He slapped the platform suddenly again. "Truth number five! It is dangerous to mock me!"

She held his ferocious eye without expression and without breathing. Then he leaned back again and continued as if she had not spoken.

"I am a northerner like your father. As well as a Vietnamese. Do not forget that. In 1948, the man who was then the leader of the Binh Xuyen joined with the French and fought for that French policeman, Savani. The Binh Xuyen became enemies of the Vietminh, where they had once been allies. But I am a soldier, not a brothel keeper for the French. I left the Binh Xuyen and made my own peace with Ho."

"No," she said. "You fought on the side of the Binh Xuyen, and the French. I saw you myself in the battle against Diem."

"I was fighting *against* the Americans, who fought for Diem," he replied. "We forgive old scars to fight a new invader. That does not change my position with the North."

He made a sweep of his arm to embrace his fiefdom of swamp and *paddi* fields.

"My people here in the South do not pay taxes to the Vietcong. That is why they remain loyal to me, even though I am a northerner. How many other peasants can say they sleep secure at night when the soft-bellied army of the South is locked up safe in its Saigon barracks? And the VC steal chickens even from Diem's coop? This whole area is safe . . . rice field and canals alike."

He searched her eyes. He might be weighing her, but he also wanted her admiration. "Who else can say that?" he demanded. "Not the Corsican *seigneurs*. Not even Chiu Chao!"

"That's good. It's very good," she said cautiously. She digested his information. "So you have friends and safe passage in the North. What do you do about the Chinese border?"

"You tell me." He folded his arms and waited.

She thought back over Eight Hand Horse's account. "I would guess," she said slowly, "that the Yunnanese still grow poppies in their mountains, in spite of the government ban on the trade. For some, it may be less dangerous and more profitable to sell their crude opium on the capitalist market to the South than on their own black market. So the border door swings both ways."

"Very good, Schoolgirl." His tone was still mocking. "But it's even easier than you think. They don't sell to me to escape government agents . . . they are themselves government agents. The Chinese government. All rulers have the same need for secret funds—to buy intelligence and allies. Old friends become enemies, and enemies friends, as the need arises." He leaned forward and tapped her knee. "You must have heard yourself how Diem's brother and other ministers are beginning to feel the windy hole in their purses that opium used to fill."

She felt his eyes assessing how much she did know.

"It's a shame," she said, "that they must hide it from their American protectors."

"Yes," agreed Thu. "The French were more practical . . . it was their only virtue." He glanced down at the scars on his arms. "Life was simpler for everyone in some ways."

"What have you decided?" Nina asked suddenly. "About me?"

Thu paused, off balance for a second. Then he laughed aloud.

"I have decided," he said, "that since I am not going to kill you I must give you a new name. I can't do business with someone called Schoolgirl. What would you like?"

"Any name you choose," she murmured politely.

He tilted his head and his eyes gleamed in the shadow of his forelock. "I think perhaps . . . School Dragon."

Her alarming cousin leaned forward and brushed his scarred fingers up the sole of her bare foot. "Come now," he said, "I must feed my new pet dragon before she forgets herself and tries to bite me again."

He stood up from the platform and led her to a table set under

341

the carved beams of the pavilion's side colonnade, in the center of another sitting platform. Nina felt the sidelong glances of the woman who brought them a platter of tiny steamed mangrove crabs. She had no doubt that many other eyes were watching them as well.

"We must sort out the terms of our partnership," said Thu.

"Who will be in the greater danger of being bitten?" she asked lightly. She was beginning to find her balance with him. He needed to feel the effect of his power on others, and had developed a repertoire of terrifying tricks. She had begun to spot the pattern. If she were to survive this partnership, she must remain respectful, but never, ever show fear.

He stopped chewing while he decided how to react to her words.

". . . The dragon or the tiger?" she concluded.

Amusement won the skirmish for possession of his eyes.

30

When a second taxi finally dropped her back in front of her own gate at 4:30 in the morning, Eight Hand Horse was waiting for her, as close to hysteria as she was ever to see him.

She told him briefly what had happened. His anger, as terror for her safety gave way to relief, was nearly paternal.

"Don't *ever* go out without me!" he cried.

"I know, Old Uncle. Please forgive me. I have learned. It was stupid of me."

"You're lucky!" he said. "Thu is a crocodile!" He began to calm down. "Anyway, you're back. I guess you handled him OK." It was a statement of faith, not a question.

"I think he thinks I am a little inexperienced," said Nina. She laughed grimly, remembering. "In his terms, so do I."

"But you have more brains," said Eight Hand Horse quickly. "You will do OK."

She heard the sudden uncertainty in his voice; her own statement of insecurity had made him feel insecure as well. Just as her statement of belief in herself the night she had authorized the money had confirmed his belief in her. To him, as to others, she was the symbol of her father, just as Kim had been before her. I am the public face of a man I hardly know, she thought. In his name, I hold power whose limits I cannot imagine. I'm not sure it is possible for me.

But her fear of failure must never show. She would be allowed to be wanting in practical information, but not in courage, vision, or self-confidence. She must not be seen to question her own right to her new position. Those were the limits of her relationship with the old man.

"Wait one minute please." He disappeared and returned with a small revolver with an enclosed hammer.

He watched her look at it. "American, Smith and Wesson. Very good at close quarters. Because the hammer is enclosed, you can even fire it through a pocket or handbag. Also, there's nothing to remember before you fire—just pull the trigger."

Two days before, she would have laughed it away. Now she took it thoughtfully and let him demonstrate in mime its rather basic method of use.

"Tomorrow, I will take you out to the *paddi* fields to practice."

"Yes." She balanced its weight in her hand. It was yet another small truth accompanying the larger ones.

She lay later in the big carved bed, but could not sleep. The first dawn light had already begun to etch lines in the darkness through the louvers of the shutters. She turned her head on the damp pillow to look again at the little gun on the bedside table. She stared up into the shadows of the mirrored canopy, where she could see a dim, formless shape stirring, like a creature deep in a cave.

She kept hearing Thu's words, ". . . . accidentally grasped the tail of a tiger and believes that she can tame it."

And Carbone's words, "By accident, you control something I want."

Her mouth was dry and her muscles tight. She reached in the darkness for her glass of water. Somehow, she must be seen to tame the tiger. Or at least appear able to do so. In the shadows beside the washroom, she saw the bound man leap again like a fish under the bullets, and the bright trail of blood he left across the polished wooden floor.

Abruptly, she sat up and turned on the light to destroy the shadows. These were the hours of death, as the night was just beginning to turn. Not the time to seek for courage in oneself. "If a *tay phap* is seen to back the wrong horse . . ." She fought away the old man's words.

Only you have the power, she reminded herself. No one else. There is no one else. Only you. There had been Kim. . . . She suddenly realized that she did not know how Kim had been killed. She didn't know where he was now, what had happened

343

to his body. She threw herself back against the bed and stared up, her mind racing. The shadowy young woman stared back down with intense dark eyes. *Kim!*

"Yes," the two young women said to each other. "Of course!" They closed their eyes, in order to think more clearly. Then they looked at each other again. "It's the right way," they said. "And my father would say, 'It is harmonious.' "

The young woman above mirrored Nina's swift energy as she sat up and swung off the bed. Then she vanished when Nina crossed to the desk and counted piastres into an envelope.

Nina dressed in a fine silk *ao dai*—white for mourning— pulled her hair back into a knot, which she pierced with a gold ornament, and painted her nails fiery red. Then she went into the sitting room and paced the cloud border of the Chinese carpet until the time when she could reasonably wake the *mama-san* to bring Eight Hand Horse.

"I shall order the tiger to come to me!" she said aloud. *The buffalo calf is going to call the tiger. To let it know she's still in business.*

When he arrived at seven o'clock, Eight Hand Horse looked rumpled and weary. There were dark circles under his eyes.

His personal grief is as great as my own, Nina reminded herself.

"Please take me to Kim's house," she ordered him.

He nodded his head as if he had been waiting for this instruction for some time.

Kim's house was off a boulevard that led toward Cholon, well away from the European quarter in the northwest part of the city. In a walled garden, it was modestly luxurious, built of brick with a tiled roof. Hibiscus and carefully pruned roses lined the short, straight concrete drive, long enough to hold just four cars. A new, pierced breeze-block screen shielded part of the veranda, and more breeze blocks made a low parapet around a sitting area in the lawn, in the style of many French houses of the 1950s. Two strands of barbed wire ran around the top of the solid garden walls.

A servant in disheveled garments opened the door. From deeper in the house came the sound of loud weeping.

"I am Mr. Kim's sister," said Nina. "I have come to pay my respects."

"I will tell madame." So Kim had a wife.

While the servant went to announce her, Nina looked at the way her brother had lived. The interior of the house was less modest than the outside. The furniture was mainly Chinese, and antique. The table in the entrance hall was finely inlaid with mother of pearl. A collection of old Vietnamese lacquerware stood in the corner cabinet. The carpets were silk.

The servant returned and led Nina into the main room of the house. The woman who stared at her with damp eyes was very young and very pretty. Her long hair hung loose over her shoulders. Like the servant's, her dress was disarrayed to show disregard for anything but her grief.

For a long moment, the widow and the half sister sized each other up. Then the widow bowed her head. They were much the same age.

"Welcome, Big Sister. You honor me with your presence in this terrible time."

Nina acknowledged the welcome and moved farther into the room. Against the far wall stood the altar of the Ancestors; on it was a copy of the picture in her father's study—her paternal grandfather who had been killed by the French. To the right, also against the wall, was a side altar. On it were three bowls of rice, three cups of tea, burning joss, and lighted candles. In front of this smaller altar was Kim's coffin. He had already been placed in it, wrapped in spotless white silk. A knife lay on his stomach. His widow lifted the white silk from his face.

Heart thumping, Nina stared at her dead brother, as if she could learn all that she had missed when he was still alive. He looked as polished and buffed as she remembered him. But paler, and terribly still. With knowledge, she could now see the similarity of heart-shaped face between him, her father, and herself.

She shook her head and said, "No," quietly. "No," she said again more loudly. Then she stopped herself. The young widow replaced the white silk,

Nina gave her the envelope of money. "I wish to pay for one hundred days of offerings for his spirit," she said.

The young woman thanked her profusely, then invited her to sit down on the antique wooden platform bed to drink some tea and take refreshment. They sat on either side of the low wooden table on the platform, legs curled beneath them, while another servant poured tea and offered Nina candied fruit and sticky rice cakes.

"Have you planned his funeral yet?" Nina asked.

The widow dropped her head and tears ran down her cheeks. "I have no one to help me," she said. "The priest from the pagoda has arranged things so far. My family is in the North.

Like his. The priest arranged to have him brought from the morgue...."

"I will give him a funeral," said Nina. "One worthy of our family. One that will balance the curse of being murdered and dying away from home."

The widow looked uncertain for a moment, but she had accepted Nina's authority in those first minutes of their meeting. "If the priest will not be upset."

"I want only to guarantee my brother's spirit a comfortable rest and eternal ease," said Nina. "I will not upset the priest."

On the contrary, she suspected he would be very pleased by her donation to the pagoda funds.

"Has he cast the horoscope yet for the funeral date?" she asked.

The widow nodded. "In two days' time, at the Hour of the Tiger."

Nina nearly exclaimed aloud. The Hour of the Tiger! A time of boldness and venturing. A time of cleansing fire. A time of danger. The time when she was calling her tiger to come to her. Though she had once told Eight Hand Horse that she did not believe in the magic of the *tay phap*, she felt encouraged nevertheless by this further proof of harmony in her plans.

"Before I go," said Nina, "there is one last thing. I must have his papers. He wished me to take them."

She held her breath, gambling that he had never said anything to the contrary.

Again, the widow nodded. "I will show you. He kept them locked away from the servants."

She met Nina's eyes; the two young women exchanged their mutual understanding of what her life had been—as the gentle, protected wife of a man whose life included violence that he could not keep out of hers.

Kim's safe here, like the one in his office at Heron, was set into the floor. His widow folded back the carpet and knelt as if before an altar, while she lifted out and offered up to Nina the bundles of papers and loose-leaf notebooks.

Nina forced herself to accept this wealth of new information calmly.

"If you wish," she said to the widow, "after the funeral, I can arrange for you to travel back north to your home."

"Oh, Big Sister!" the young woman cried. "I wish it so much!" From her kneeling position, she bent forward until her forehead touched the folded carpet. "I wish it so much! I thank you!"

Back at her own house, Nina told Eight Hand Horse what arrangements she wanted made—which native papers the announcement was to be placed in, what paper funeral objects and banderoles she wanted made, how many wreaths should be ordered, how many musicians to hire, and how many professional mourners to engage.

She wrote personal notes to Emile Carbone, to M. Frey, and to Khan. She wrote a longer note to Louis Wu. She asked Eight Hand Horse how she could get a message to Thu. Half an hour later, the gum-chewing taxi driver appeared to take the letter away. Then she went to visit the priest at the pagoda who was handling things for her brother's widow. It was evening before she could be alone with Kim's papers.

She had been locked in her bedroom with his records of the business for only a short time before she leaned away from the desk and stretched her arms aloft in silent exultation. Here, without question, was the information she needed so badly. His records were very much more detailed than their father's had been. Kim may have been naturally more meticulous or he may have trusted less to his memory—and, of course, he had to be accountable to their father. Kim had noted the total number of kilos of crude opium delivered to Heron against the kilos of morphine base produced. He had listed purchases of lime and laboratory equipment. He had listed all sales with dates, quantities, and the names or initials of the brokers he had used. Some initials corresponded to those in the first of her father's books. Kim listed purchases likewise. He listed agents by province and region. He had made another, untitled list of names with addresses in Saigon, Cholon, Phnom Penh, and Singapore. Nina knew several of them; they were all prominent Chinese and Vietnamese businessmen. Daniel Jouvet's name was also on this list. Kim had even made notations against some of the listed names, like "getting greedy," and "reliable." Against others he had put exclamation marks, question marks, or stars. She guessed that these last might be information passed on from their father. Jouvet's name was followed by a question mark. Closer examination showed that all the stars whose names she recognized held positions of some sort in the government or civil service. To all the stars and several of the exclamation marks she wrote notes, like the one she had sent to Carbone. She did not write to Jouvet or any other question mark.

It was nearly midnight before she had finished. In restless

excitement she returned to the second of her father's books, the one she could not decipher, which seemed to say where the great sea of money had washed away to, and why. She selected one page at random and copied it out, leaving gaps in the place of the Chinese characters. Into the gaps she wrote the translations Louis had had made for her. But each character had several possible meanings; without knowing the context, the translator had given all the meanings, and Nina had no means of choosing. Two hours later, and no nearer to understanding the book's message, she was finally exhausted enough to fall into bed.

When she slept, she dreamed that she was swimming in a clear mountain pool. The pebbles beneath her feet caught the light, and she dived deep for a closer look. She found that she was picking up silver coins. Able now to breathe under the water she filled the front of her full-skirted dress, fuller and fuller, until she glided lazily above the bottom of the pool, round and balanced like a silvery pregnant fish.

While Nina was sleeping on into the afternoon, three Chiu Chao Chinese visited a modestly furnished office that was part of a comfortable private house in Cholon. Jonathan Hong, the twenty-five-year-old son of the family who lived there, watched in despair as the Grass Sandal methodically smashed the new calculator with the end of a heavy iron stevedore's hook. His despair did not show on his face, because two soldiers of the same Chiu Chao tong were also watching, standing on either side of his father and younger brother. Fortunately for Jonathan the expression in his eyes was screened by the lenses of his heavy spectacles.

"That is very foolish," said his father quietly, in observation rather than judgment. Mr. Hong was a thin, handsome Cantonese of sixty-three. Kind eyes and an unwavering belief in the fifth Cardinal Virtue of Good Faith had made him a popular money-lender in his district, though not the richest one. They also made him an unusual one.

"How can I pay more tax if you destroy one of the means by which I can raise my profits enough to meet your demands? And thereby show the greater respect your Red Sandal requests." His voice was reasonable.

"Shut your rice hole, old man," said the Grass Sandal, "or I'll give you worse problems."

Jonathan Hong's thin body trembled with contained rage. How dare that young thug speak to his father like that! Hong was having trouble with rage these days.

As a good eldest son, he tried to cling to the prescribed belief

348

that there was a greater order in the universe than could be perceived by the limitations of a single man. Recently, he had been tempted to wonder. The more he saw of the way the world ran, the more he suspected that the idea of Celestial Order was a deception, a con trick played by the gods on man to keep him in line—too hard at work to cause trouble for the Big Boys Up There.

Hong had always been drawn to the idea of order. Even as a teenage chemistry student, he had found reassurance in the orderly balance of the formulas and in the boundaries imposed by the discipline of experimental research. Something in him was deeply satisfied by symbols with one absolute meaning instead of the shimmering halo of alternatives that hovered around the classical Chinese characters. Chemistry offered him real order, unlike life.

Take the case of his father, a rare example of a perfect gentleman—wise, fair, with proper concern for others balanced by self-respect. He had worked hard all his life, raised two sons, and won the respect of other men, only to be humiliated by uneducated sons of sows who deserved to be licking out his chamber pot. Hong could not see the order in that. Nor could he see order in his own history.

Considered a bit of an odd fish, he had done very well academically, first at the University of Hong Kong, then at Lyons. He had returned home six months ago with two degrees as proof of his new status as a qualified scholar. After the family celebrations were finished, he began to seek employment suitable for an expert on alkaloid compounds. He found that the new economic boom, triggered by the arrival of the Americans, needed builders, engineers, waiters, translators, and pimps. It had small need for a pure scientist who spoke no English.

To make his failure to find proper work even more galling, he also learned that his father was not doing as well in his business as his letters had made it seem. The business was being ruined by taxes. The Chiu Chao had for a long time charged a protection tax. The Binh Xuyen were creeping back into Saigon-Cholon; a local cell now charged a tax. The police had always charged a tax. And recently the Vietcong had begun to charge a tax, even in the city itself.

In addition to the tax problem, several properties held by Mr. Hong as securities against large loans had been destroyed in the fighting. One rice exporter had been killed while still owing Hong a five-figure sum. Another trusted client had suddenly refused to pay up when his sister married an Air Force officer in the new regime; the officer had convinced Mr. Hong that it was better to forget all about the debt.

The Grass Sandal placed a kick into the calculator as precisely as if it were a human face.

"This is our first warning."

The three Chiu Chao left. Old Mr. Hong sat down in his heavy oak swivel chair.

"Ah . . . well." He placed his hands very carefully on each arm of the chair, unable to hide their shaking. "That's unfortunate."

His eyes rested in turn on his two most precious possessions, his sons. " 'Our first warning,' " he repeated. "I wonder what the second one will be."

He spoke as if to himself, but Jonathan knew that his duty was to help, if he only could.

31

Two days later, just before the Hour of the Tiger, the early morning was still very dark. While the preglow of the sun had just begun to light the sea from within, the oily water of the Saigon River was still thick and opaque. The streets of Saigon were already busy. Porters trotted with goods toward the Central Market, near the railway station. Early workers and returning night-shift laborers pumped at the pedals of their bicycles, whose battery-powered lamps crossed weak shafts of light in tangential, inconsequential duels. Dogs nosed at the piles of rubbish and ordure along the curbs. Occasionally one would sniff at a body lying asleep on the street, then move on when it smelled life.

Taxis were already honking their horns. On the river, boats hooted. In the godowns, electrical generators thumped. Somewhere an electrical saw was already whining, releasing the smell of rosewood into the street. From Kim's house, on the side street off a boulevard running toward Cholon, came the sound of music. The funeral procession had begun.

The priest from the pagoda was already outside the gate, carried in an elaborately embroidered sling by two uniformed bearers. Behind him walked the white-clothed professional mourners, women and men, who carried banners and wide ribbons printed with inscriptions extolling the virtues of the deceased. There were twenty-four mourners, all reciting prayers for and praises of Kim. Behind them, an altar was carried by two more mourners. A framed picture of Kim stood in its center, surrounded by candlesticks, flowers, incense burners, and two oil lamps. After the altar came not the usual one or two, but five tables of offerings—a roasted pig, sugar cakes, rice in several forms, gelatined fruit, and wine in urns.

Attracted by the music, a small crowd began to gather outside the gate of the house, oohing and aahing at the magnificence of the display. Only one, a pregnant woman, rushed away, to avoid causing bad fortune to the occasion. The crowd reached a new pitch of excitement when the catafalque rolled majestically out of the gate after the tables of offerings. In former times, and still now in rural areas, it would have been pulled by male members of the family or friends. This one, however, in witness to the exalted status of the deceased and his family, was motorized, like a hearse. Unlike a hearse, it was ten feet high, a gold and scarlet castle composed of twisting gilded dragons and clouds. On it were votive papers symbolizing the worldly goods that the dead man would wish to use in his future existence—a house, clothing, money, a horse, a sword, books.

At the end of the procession marched eight musicians followed by twenty more bearers and eight cyclos laden with wreaths and flowers; the flowers had been lined up outside the garden wall along the street and had reached to the far corner. The crowd exclaimed as not only wreaths and huge bouquets were carried past, but also intricate arrangements of flowers designed to look like bowls of fruit and animals. One cyclo carried nothing but a single, enormous dragon made of gold paper and roses.

But the crowd was most fascinated by the center of the procession where ahead of the musicians and flower bearers and close behind the catafalque the dead man's family walked. There were three—Kim's widow, Nina, and Eight Hand Horse. All three wore specially made official mourning clothes of tattered white gauze.

Eight Hand Horse leaned heavily on a twisted walking stick, to show how he was borne down by his grief. Like the widow, Nina wore her thick dark hair loose and ceremonially disarrayed. She walked at the front of the little family group, back straight, eyes looking ahead. She could hear the widow, Snow Peach, weeping aloud and bemoaning the chances she had missed to show her love for her dead husband. Though it would have been proper for her to make a similar public show of grief, Nina found that part of her stood aside from this show that she had herself created. She had already fought to control and bury her own grief. As she walked, she thought how odd it was that she should

351

upset a Vietnamese like her father by showing too much emotion in daily life, but be unable to show enough when it was proper to do so. Behind her, the large band of native musicians thumped and wailed. Ahead of her, the professional mourners chanted and cried. Behind her shoulder, Snow Peach sobbed. My voice won't be missed, she thought.

She turned to scatter a handful of paper money, signifying the wealth that would follow her brother to his new life, and was gratified to see how large the crowd was growing. Early though it was, parallel processions of the curious had begun to follow along the pavements. She could hear voices exclaiming in wonder, and was satisfied.

As the cortege entered the gates of the Vietnamese cemetery nearly an hour later, leaving the crowd outside, Nina's eyes leaped to the line of black cars parked along the road on the way to Kim's burial place. The passengers were waiting by the grave itself. Nina counted twelve . . . fifteen . . . twenty-one suited figures, and felt her heart beat faster with triumph and fear. They had come, almost every one of them!

The procession swept on toward the grave—mourners, altar, offerings, catafalque, family, musicians, flower bearers, and cyclos. Only when they were all in position by the grave and the priest had begun his prayers did Nina allow herself to study the faces of the guests. They were the men from Kim's lists. There was also Frey, from the Deuxième Bureau. There was an Air Force colonel. There were two bankers, a Chinese rice merchant, a rice mill owner, and the owner of a large abattoir. Khan was there. So were others, all in expensively cut suits, whom she did not yet know by sight. Several of them glanced curiously at her from time to time. She kept her back straight and her face calm as Kim was lowered into the earth on broad strips of white silk.

The priest fell silent. He bent to pick up a symbolic handful of earth to throw onto the coffin; if Kim had had a surviving father or brother, this act would have been his by right. But the priest did not throw the first handful of earth, in place of the father or brother, as the watchers expected. He turned and gave it to Nina.

She took it carefully, so as not to let the smallest crumb fall too soon. Then she stepped forward and scattered it onto her brother's coffin. She heard the intake of breath in the crowd around her at the same time as the gentle pattering of earth on hollow wood. She held her own breath, her hand still open above the grave, while she prayed as she had never before prayed that nothing might happen which would seem to be an ill omen for her presumption. And for the priest's acquiescence to it. Miraculously, the moment was still as if the Earth itself had paused. For at least three seconds no taxi honked, no boat sounded its horn, no dog barked, no child cried. Then the sun slid silently up above the far, flat land across the river. Nina let her hand fall to her side and stepped back from the grave, unchallenged by fortune as the new head of the family, whom she led aside while the rest of the grave was filled.

All the black cars followed her back to Kim's house for the funeral feast. At the house they were joined by the cars of others who had been unable to make the earlier time at the cemetery. Nina stood in the center of the main chamber, in front of the family altar where in three days' time Kim's spirit would be induced to take up residence with the spirit of his grandfather. No one challenged her right to accept the good wishes and condolences or to offer her guests hospitality in her brother's home.

"Thank you for your kindest thoughts," she repeated again and again. "You do my family too much honor with these gifts," she said as she accepted their tokens of respect—coins, bottles of liquor, pieces of silk woven with silver or gold, old books, a piece of fine porcelain.

She repeated the names to herself and memorized their faces. She smiled as she met the open assessment in their eyes. A thin man with a tight round ball of a belly and bad skin, whom she did not know, turned out to be Mr. Wang; he was an exclamation mark on Kim's list. As was a self-assured Vietnamese in an old-style Chinese long gown, with skin as yellow as an opium smoker's.

The guests from the graveside were slowly joined by others who had read the announcements in the newspapers and came to show their respects. An hour after their return from the cemetery, the house buzzed like a cocktail party rather than a wake. Nina watched her guests study one another as well as herself as they drank the good wine, whiskey punch, and fruit juice being served by six uniformed servants. She could see some of them counting openly who else had considered it worth his time to come; she hoped they were satisfied with their company.

Carbone arrived late, in a dark suit with a black armband. From her central position she watched him pause in the hall to take note of those paying their respects to her family—to the dead son and to the new heir. She saw several guests mutter to each other when they noticed the Corsican.

353

Watched by the other guests, the man who had murdered her husband approached and bowed over her hand.

"My condolences to the family," he said formally, for all to hear. Their eyes met. Quietly, he added, "My congratulations, Ninette."

He knew exactly what she was doing. His hand was as cold as her own. They had not met since the breakfast on the terrace of the Hotel Continental.

"You have the style, but have you the stomach?" he murmured, as she signaled to a passing waiter to bring him a cup of punch.

"Thanks to you, I am believed to have both," she replied. More loudly, she added, "We are all honored to see you here, monsieur."

Louis arrived not long after Carbone, bringing with him a strange Vietnamese in a long gown. Shortly after that she found herself accepting a ceremonial sword from the captain of a sampan fleet. Still more guests continued to arrive. When they had all left, many hours later, well after dusk, she was very weary but satisfied. The tiger had come, sniffed, and gone away again. She believed she had made her point; the family was still very much in business.

Back at her own house, she went over the guest list with Eight Hand Horse while her memory was still fresh, asking him what he knew about each of them. The old man also showed her a list of people who had sent wreaths to the cemetery, and the approximate cost of each wreath. The respect shown was considerable. And Eight Hand Horse knew the going prices very well—on her orders, he had bought all the wreaths and flowers that had lined the street before the funeral, purporting to be from well-wishers.

The next morning, three Vietnamese papers reported on the funeral; one even printed a grainy photograph of the catafalque. Even for those who had not attended, there could be no doubt that Luoc's family, through its new head, was still very much in business.

32

The days after Kim's funeral were frantically busy for Nina. She had not known how much there was to be done after a death, even without the special complications of this one.

She carried out all the formalities of registering the death with the civil authorities, and paid for a Catholic Mass for his soul in the Cathedral, for the benefit of those still unaware of the native ceremony. She met Kim's lawyer and his banker to discuss the settling of his personal estate, most of which went to guarantee future provision for Snow Peach. Kim had made modest investments, mainly through brokers in Hong Kong and Bangkok. He had an account in a Cholon bank, a numbered Swiss account, and the controlling interest in a small electronics company based in Singapore. In the four years of his regency he had not yet accumulated a personal fortune to compare with their father's apparent one in the past. Through intermediaries, she asked Thu to provide an armed escort and safe passage for Snow Peach back to her family in Tonkin. The young widow showed no ambitions or aspirations, but Nina was happier to get her out of the way, as a possible complication of her own position.

She spent two days discussing the funeral guests further with Eight Hand Horse. When she had picked his brain clean of every scrap of information, she began to entertain these men with lavish meals in restaurants. She avoided direct talk of business, but still managed to learn a few hard facts, and also a great deal more about the nature of the men who faced her across the crisp linen and crystal goblets. She began to trust more and more in the effect of her charm, her willpower, and her intuition.

After a little thought, she augmented her intuition by giving Chinchook expenses for a month, and a small Leica, to take pictures of everyone who entered Carbone's house during that time and to make note of how many times each one visited. She also asked him to find a trustworthy friend who would do exactly the same outside Carbone's office, which was tucked in behind the National Tourist Directorate around the corner from the Bureau of Customs, near the river.

She dined one night alone at the Hotel Continental and suggested to her solicitious young waiter that it would be worth his while to keep track of the people who shared a table with Carbone in the next few months. He tucked a long loose strand of hair back behind his ear and said he would be more than happy to help. When he said his nickname was Thin Pig, she understood the reasons for it. He had a round little nose in a thin face, and a kind of eager energy that could be interpreted as greed. She had a feeling he could be quite useful to whoever would pay him the most.

Three days after Kim's funeral she attended Millie's, where she made provision for special offerings to settle the woman's spirit. She also later made a large settlement on Millie's small son, to be administered by Millie's older brother, who was head of the family.

As well as entertaining, she was also entertained. Five days after Kim's funeral, Daniel Jouvet invited her to dinner. The evening both amused and annoyed her. It ended fairly quickly after she finally convinced him that she had no intention, then or ever, of going to bed with him. They did not discuss his presence as a question mark on Kim's list.

She received invitations to drinks or dinner from two of the funeral guests, both exclamation marks. A week after the funeral, she accepted an invitation from Taki Hashimoto and his Vietnamese wife. The retired camera dealer proved to be an invaluable source of cheerful gossip. He seemed to know the birthdays, sexual quirks, promotion expectations, and secret allies of half the population of Saigon. His other guest was the personal secretary of Diem's brother Nhu. She wasn't clear what Taki wanted from her in return, but time would no doubt tell. She suspected that she should merely see the invitation as flattering acknowledgement that she was now worth keeping track of.

Late in the day when Millie was buried, Louis Wu brought her the curriculum vitae of a man called Jonathan Hong. "B.Sc., Univ. of HK, M.Sc., Lyons."

"I know his family," said Louis. "You can trust him not to mix with Chiu Chao. The family are strictly Cholon-based . . . stick to the Chinese community. Don't mix with the rest of us much. He's as safe as you'll find."

He agreed to arrange a meeting between her and Hong as soon as possible.

Finally, she had to catch up with matters at Eighty-eight Transport. She was still unable to agree on terms with her contractor over the government's proposed fortified hamlets scheme. Andrew's Leo Thompson had written to the Eighty-eight office on Cong Ly Street, either ignorant of or unperturbed by the fate of his sponsor. She wrote back, agreeing to meet for a discussion on numbers of possible vehicles and length of contract. There had also been trouble with two of her drivers after Kim's death. She told her manager to fire them and replace them with two others. Meanwhile, she asked Titi and Chinchook to trawl for street whispers concerning any candidates for the jobs. Through the company, she also bought herself and Eight Hand Horse a larger, less battered car.

Apart from the two drivers, her only unpleasant surprise was the evening Eight Hand Horse arrived to introduce Snow Man and Tiny Albert Joyful.

"They go with you, everywhere. It's better that way," he said.

She regarded the two men unhappily. Snow Man, in his late thirties, had prematurely white hair. Tiny Albert Joyful explained his name by his mere presence. But his bright, cheerful eyes and smile lines were at odds with the bulge inside both his suit jacket and that of Snow Man, and with the fighting calluses on the sides of his hands.

Nina knew that Eight Hand Horse was right. She didn't like the idea of constant company, but she was resigned to it. She also knew the blow it must be to the old man's pride to admit the need for reinforcements.

Ten days after Kim's funeral, a small boy delivered a note to her office on Cong Ly Street.

"Well, well," she said aloud after reading it. Clinton Clay spoke *"jaune"* well enough to read the newspapers. Or else he had someone read them for him. He wanted to meet her for a drink at the Broadway Bar, near the docks. Of course, he might want just to discuss equipment for Eighty-eight Transport, but she suspected not. His timing was too fortuitous.

The bar girls eyed her viciously as she entered the Broadway. She acknowledged the circumspection of Clay's rendezvous; no one would look twice in a place like this at a half-breed woman and the fat, sweaty American who was waving to her from a corner booth. Similar couples were huddled together in every part of the room. It was a choice, however, that was below the demands of her new dignity, and she would not let it happen again. Snow Man and Tiny Albert, for a start, would not be impressed.

She edged through the dancing couples, plastered together, in spite of the heat, on the central rectangle of linoleum, and sat opposite the American. The pink shades on the lights made him look even more hot and flushed than usual.

He half stood in awkward greeting and shook her hand.

"Howdy-do," he said solemnly. "Sorry to hear about your brother." He remained downcast while she murmured thanks for his condolences. Then he called a waitress and ordered champagne.

"The real stuff," he said in Vietnamese. "For both of us. No cold tea." He slipped the woman a wad of piastre notes.

"Congratulations, ma'am," he said to Nina. "And all that.

Sad as the reasons are for it." He looked at her approvingly. "It always makes a great change to do business with you."

He was so cheerful that she couldn't take offense. "Thanks for the congratulations," she said. "But under the circumstances, I don't have the slightest idea what you're talking about."

He winked. "OK. I'll slow down. We'll have a drink first. I always feel better myself, talking business after a glass or two."

The waitress returned to their table with a bottle of nonvintage Veuve Cliquot and two glasses. She began to open the champagne.

"Hold on," said Clay. He fingered the twisted wires and peered at the foil around the cork.

"OK, go ahead," he agreed. In English, he added, "Pop your cork, baby."

She did not smile as she obeyed and poured two brimming glasses.

Clay lifted his to Nina. "Here's to English lessons."

"If you say so, Mr. Clay." She smiled and waited for him to tell her what he wanted.

"How are things with Eighty-eight Transport? Thinking of expanding some more?"

She had been, but the matter had been far back in her mind the last few days.

"Possibly," she said. He had come to her first. She didn't believe he had done it for the sake of more forklift trucks or earth movers.

"They will seek you out," Louis had said.

"How's business with you?" she asked.

"Never better," he chortled. "Never better . . . but worse than it's going to be."

He lifted his forearms from the Formica tabletop to lean closer to her; she heard his damp skin rip away from the plastic.

"I hear you've diversified," he said confidentially. "It just so happens I could maybe make some sizable sales for you. It might open up a new market."

"What were you thinking of selling for me?"

He shook his head in mock sorrow. "Come off it, Nina . . . you don't mind if I call you that, do you? You call me Clint. It makes it easier to talk."

He glanced at their nearest neighbors, both white men in intense negotiation with their respective bar girls.

"I can move Mary Jane for you in bulk."

"You mean *bhang*?"

He nodded.

"I wish I could help," she said. "But that's not my territory. Sorry."

His jovial gaze was suddenly cold and assessing.

"Smoker's opium," she explained.

"I see." He began to look friendly again. "I suppose I could shift a little of that, but it hasn't really caught on.... A few kilos a month, at most. *Bhang*, now, or *ma thuy*...horse...we'd start talking big numbers. And U.S. dollars."

"I really haven't diversified that way," she said.

"No bullshit?" he asked in English.

"Sorry...?"

"Sérieusement," he said in French. "You're not messing me around?"

"No bullshit, Clint," she imitated in English.

He guffawed. "I love it! Marry me, honey, so I can teach you to talk right."

He refilled both their glasses. "Just promise to keep me in mind if you happen to stumble across anything interesting."

They drank, and she left before he did. Apart from the moderate pleasures of the champagne it had been a pointless meeting.

However, she was thoughtful as Tiny Albert and Snow Man escorted her home. It would take more than a cooperative priest and a successful funeral to hold Fortune's favors in the eyes of the world. Eight Hand Horse had warned that she must act soon to shape the signs. She must be seen to be more fortunate, more successful than anyone would expect. It was not enough to shelter behind her father's name and achievements. Her father's name had not saved Kim and would not save her from the tiger whose tail she held. Until now, she had not seen what she could possibly do. Clay had just told her how she could shape the signs, but the means frightened her. She would have to step off her father's marked path.

What would he want me to do? She wished, as she had so many other times, that she could ask his advice. By the time they had reached the house, she had decided that Clay's opportunity would be harmonious with what she understood her father's will to be. If she went down, so did his empire. Much would depend, in any case, on her meeting with Louis's Chinese chemist.

"How much base does it take to make one kilo of *ma thuy*?" she asked Eight Hand Horse that evening.

"Ma thuy?" His expression grew guarded. "Direct dealing is bad joss. Steps on toes. Like those of the Chiu Chao."

She thought he looked tired. He had insisted on kowtowing when he came in, saying that she must get used to it, and his age had showed as he rose like a buffalo, hindquarters first.

"Do you know?" she persisted.

He shook his head. "We never do it. It's all imported from Hong Kong, and a little from Laos . . . a Chiu Chao sideline. And the Alliance, of course, but they mostly ship to France."

"How much crude opium, then, to make one kilo of the morphine base we sell?"

"Ten kilos, mademoiselle."

This confirmed her own calculations from Kim's records, allowing for losses of one kind or another.

"Why don't we refine to morphine base in the North and transport one tenth as much weight?"

He nodded his approval of her question. "Your father did try that once. For two years it was OK. The Vietminh—Vietcong—accept taxes to allow safe passage of goods through countryside they control, but a refinery in their territory is too much temptation. It becomes a fort which needs an army to defend it, and then it is too visible to everyone else."

She kept returning to her original thought. "What is the price of *ma thuy* to wholesalers, here in Saigon?"

His approval vanished and his eyes peered from under his wiry white brows as if trying to pierce through her to the truth of her thoughts.

"Very little is sold here," he said. "I don't know the men. . . ." He sighed. "I will find out for you." It was the first time he had obeyed her unwillingly.

"And also how many Americans are in Vietnam now. Real numbers, not the official ones."

She looked at his inclined head. "Old Uncle, I am only thinking of how I can shape the signs, as you advised me. To keep our good men and hold off the tiger."

"Yes," he said. "As you must. As you must. It is just that I am a silly old man who finds that the world changes too quickly. Never mind. . . ."

He stretched his callused toes in the cut-out tennis shoes. "I am not past it yet."

Five days after her meeting with Clay, Nina settled herself in the faint down draft of the slow-moving ceiling fan to wait for Jonathan Hong. Her two bodyguards waited outside. She had picked a café that she never planned to visit again, on a side street off Tu Do Street. Its high prices for a cup of coffee or a beer were partly explained by a large, hand-lettered sign in English announcing that U.S. currency would be accepted in settlement of bills.

On top of a glass-fronted drinks cooler, a table fan waved its grille languidly from side to side as if following a slow-motion tennis match. Fly-blown prints of Toulouse-Lautrec posters had been taped to the walls. On a glass shelf behind the bar a mirrored line of American beer bottles—Budweiser, Michelob, Schlitz—glowed luridly under a fluorescent tube. The proprietor, a Moroccan, was impaling bills on a spike as if destroying enemies by black magic.

There were two other women there; one was a hooker, pure Viet but wearing a tightly belted Western-style dress, seated on Nina's right. She had locked eyes with a middle-aged American in a crisp new safari suit at a table on Nina's left. Nina leaned back out of the crossfire, as the man's companions exchanged low-key ribaldries before they called to the whore to come and pose for a photograph with them. One dug into the leather camera bag slung on his chair and produced a camera and a selection of lenses.

Nina's eye caught that of a man sitting at the table just behind theirs, and she almost got up to leave again. It was the red-haired American from the Café Verlaine. He was watching as the coquettishly protesting whore perched on the American's knee and slid one delicate hand inside the jacket of the safari suit. He saw Nina look at him and smiled, inviting her into the complicity of the onlookers. She looked away in a panic. This man was haunting her. He invaded the moments when she least wanted to be seen—first as a beggar and now just as she was about to take a dangerous first step into new territory. When she glanced back, he was watching the other table again. Then he made a note in his stenographer's pad. She looked away from his hand holding the pen and flushed at what she had once imagined it doing to her. At least, he didn't seem to recognize her.

Small wonder, she thought. I don't look much like that begging urchin in the Café Verlaine. Nevertheless, she decided to wait for Hong outside and take him somewhere else for their meeting. She gathered up her bag, then put it back on the chair in annoyance. She was too late.

From the doorway a young man was peering into the café through heavy-rimmed spectacles. He saw her and began to cross to her table. To leave now would attract too much attention. She stayed where she was, but she would keep the meeting brief.

Hong looked freshly scrubbed. His black hair was slicked tight against his head. His beige chinos were crisp, his shoes new. He carried a light blue American-style Windbreaker arranged in immaculate folds over one forearm, discreetly exposing a gold Bulova watch on a thin wrist. He wore a starched, short-sleeved shirt and had honored the occasion with a tightly knotted red silk tie, for good luck. Above the spectacles, his wide brow was lined with a semipermanent scowl of impatience with the world at large.

He bowed and announced himself as Jonathan Hong. Then he shook her hand, with a force that jangled the bracelets on her wrist. After that, without speaking further, he arranged the Windbreaker carefully on the bentwood chairback, seated himself, folded his hands precisely in front of him, and regarded her through his lenses. Nina couldn't help smiling at his seriousness.

He was at least four years older than she was. The eyes behind the sheltering lenses were wary but intelligent. The wide brow tapered to a narrow jaw, hardly wider than the line of his neck, which was encircled by the tight red tie. The knuckles of his folded hands were white, and vertical grooves between his brows had joined the scowl lines.

"Thank you for coming," she said.

Still scowling, he said formally, "My father requested me to ask you to do him the great favor of giving Mr. Louis his very deepest respects."

"With pleasure," she said. "What would you like to drink?"

"Lemonade, please." He looked away before his own survey of her could become impertinent.

"Mr. Jonathan," she said, when the Moroccan had slapped his sandals across the tiles back to the bar with their order. "I understand you are an expert on alkaloids."

"I have only begun to learn, madame," he replied. "I will not yet call myself an expert . . . the subject is too large."

He waited with interest to see where she would lead. He was no fool. Louis had told his father exactly who she was and what she now did. He knew why his qualifications interested her and had done his homework before coming here to meet her.

"Are you expert enough to know how to refine heroin from morphine base?"

His head jerked in shock at her bluntness. The scowl lines shifted slightly in his surprise. Her haste to reach the nub was almost unseemly. They had hardly exchanged formalities.

"Do you mean do I know what must be done? Or whether I could do it in practice? The two questions are different." He enjoyed answering her with equal bluntness.

"Could you do it? Is it a feasible venture? Or does it need specialized technology unavailable here?"

He blew a tiny puff of air between pursed lips. "I have never actually done it, though I have carried out analogous processes. In properly fitted laboratories, of course. It is much more difficult than refining crude opium to morphine base—which, as you know, is merely a matter of boiling and filtering, with a precipitant if desired, to increase efficiency of extraction."

She didn't know; that was one of the things she had wanted to learn from him. "What precipitant?"

"Ordinary lime, the kind used for agricultural fertilizer."

"And what about heroin?"

He peered through his lenses at an invisible textbook in the air, the one he had studied the night before. "Transforming morphine base to heroin is a five-stage process that bonds the base with an equal amount of acetic anhydride." He touched one forefinger with the tip of the other. "In stage one, the morphine and acetic acid are chemically bonded through the application of heat, to form diacetylmorphine. In stage two, impurities are precipitated out through the addition of water and chloroform. In stage three, the crude heroin is precipitated out into particles by the addition of sodium carbonate. Stage four filters these particles from the sodium carbonate solution under pressure. Then comes purification, in a solution of activated charcoal and alcohol. Once the alcohol is evaporated by heat, the heroin can be sold as a low-grade powder."

He paused while the Moroccan placed two lemonades on the table. When the man had left, he resumed quietly.

"If you wish to achieve the purest form of heroin, of the kind known as number four, which is eighty to ninety percent pure, you must complete a fifth stage—further precipitation, using a solution of alcohol and ether and hydrochloric acid. Again, you filter under pressure and then dry the resulting flakes to powder."

He sipped the lemonade to moisten his mouth, which was slightly dry. "It is this final stage that can produce explosions if incorrectly carried out. Ether is extremely volatile."

"But like the other ingredients, it can be obtained fairly easily through legitimate suppliers of pharmaceuticals, agricultural chemicals, and so on?"

"Correct."

"Could you do it in practice? I still ask in principle." She lightened her question with a smile.

He knew what she was asking, and was dizzied by the speed with which they continued to advance.

"In the right circumstances, I believe I could."

He looked at her, trusting that his baldly stated confidence would not look like arrogance.

Nina liked him. She, too, felt the ease of their mutual understanding. Hong was what Eight Hand Horse meant by "a good man."

"What would be the right circumstances?" she asked.

"A properly equipped laboratory, with the equipment I specify, including an electrical suction pump. Two assistants, not necessarily chemists."

He hesitated, then decided to test her straightforwardness to the limit. "And no one breathing down my neck."

To his relief and pleasure, she laughed. "Agreed," she said. "In principle. Now you tell me whether the right circumstances would also include the following." She held up a red-nailed hand. "One," she said, touching her forefinger, "isolation. No taking advice. No consulting academic colleagues."

He scowled impatiently. "I prefer to work alone, madame."

"Two." She touched her middle finger. "You would be responsible to me alone. I would have to trust you not to become involved in any way with any other of my employees."

His scowl deepened. He hoped she didn't think he was afraid of responsibility. As for reporting only to her... if he could bring himself to work for a woman, she was as good as any. He felt he could trust what she said. She was clear as a chemical equation.

He nodded.

"Risk." She looked at him candidly. "And I don't mean ether gas explosions. You are very clearly not a fool, Mr. Jonathan. You will know exactly what I mean." She smiled. "Your salary would reflect all these circumstances harmoniously."

"Life is dangerous at all times," he said, thinking of his father and the smashed calculator.

"Yes," said Nina simply. She and Hong looked at each other openly, in a moment of balance. Complete strangers, they knew that they shared common experience.

"Is it worth talking further?" she asked.

He touched his father's watch on his wrist; its loan was a paternal blessing on this meeting. His family needed money badly. The only other job he had so far been offered was that of teaching in a Chinese school for young boys. He had no desire to spend his days cramming old texts down the throats of unwilling pupils, or coaching them at soccer. She was offering him possible escape from that prospect.

On the other hand, his mouth was dry and a tiny pool of fear lay in the bottom of his stomach. The risk she had mentioned was considerable. The local Chiu Chao, for example, would be most displeased with him if they learned he was in competition with their trade between Cholon and Hong Kong.

She saw him touch the watch and guessed the reason. Louis had told her a little about the family's problems. Unconsciously, her own hand went to the seal around her neck. "We would consider it an experiment for the first year. If I were to decide to cancel in that time, I would continue to pay your salary."

Still he hesitated.

"Say what you feel," she said. "If you're frightened now, you'll be more frightened later. Perhaps with good reason. I don't mind what you choose, but you must be clear in your own mind." She was offering him the same free choice her father had given her.

He allowed excitement to gleam through his spectacles. "I would be honored to discuss matters further with you." Personal fears were nothing against the prospect of restoring his knowledge, so painfully acquired, to its rightful position of power in the real world. That would count for even more than the money, with his father as much as with himself. If he could make this experiment work.

Nina exhaled a breath she hadn't realized she was holding. With Hong's agreement, her course was set. She hadn't expected to come away from this meeting with so much decided, so quickly. But it felt right—a good omen.

"Shall we drink to further discussion?" she asked. "And to our fathers? With another glass of lemonade . . . ?"

Hong's eyes widened behind his spectacles, then he actually smiled.

As Nina called for the drinks, she couldn't help looking again at the red-haired American. Though the other Americans had left with the hooker, he was still there, making notes with a ballpoint pen from the row in his shirt pocket. The front of his hair, worn longer than that of his military compatriots, had fallen forward and gleamed with a lavender highlight from the fluorescent light at the bar. He glanced up and caught her looking at him. She turned away quickly. He made her nervous. She wished he hadn't seen her with Hong, even if he didn't remember her. She was sure that he couldn't have overheard their conversation. She noticed the camera hanging over his chair.

She hurried Jonathan Hong through the second lemonade. He agreed to draw up a list of what he would need in the way of space, equipment, and supplies. They arranged a further meeting in two days' time. He stood up and took her extended hand. He bowed slightly as if he meant to kiss it, changed his mind, and shook it firmly again, setting her bracelets into tinkling motion once more.

She watched him weave his polished shoes and scowl through the tables to the street. A teenage hooker accosted him; Nina noted his vague, impatient scowl as he stepped around the girl. She was pleased with this first of her very own good men. She promised herself that he was only the first of many more.

"It is not our business," Eight Hand Horse had said, "if White Devils who have looted our country for centuries wish to poison themselves for fun." And would pay for this "fun." Enough to ensure her future and that of her father, if she made it her business.

She considered the dangers once more, now that they were becoming real ones. Carbone would be furious if he ever learned. Then there were the Chiu Chao, who imported what *ma thuy* was sold in Saigon from their labs in Hong Kong. They would be ruthless in punishing competition.

If I don't go ahead, she argued, I may not survive anyway. I could be blown up at any time by a VC mine. Or be hit by a shell meant for someone else. Or step between a sniper and his target. It's foolish to fear dangers that I can see and anticipate when there are so many already beyond my control. I have survived this far; I must trust in myself and in my duty to my father.

The inescapable certainties were her need to shape the signs and her danger if she could not prove to the world that she held the mandate of the Heavens.

The Moroccan was polishing coffee spoons with the corner of his dirty apron and refused to meet her eye. A shadow fell on her table. Nina turned to face a wide smile which exposed two blackened teeth and a gap in the lower jaw.

"I'm Dao," the man said. He was one of the runner-pimp-hustlers who floated on the streets of the European sector. He wore a Brooklyn Dodgers baseball cap and an open pack of Camels stretched the breast pocket of his shirt.

"A Yankee *bao chi* would like to meet you. Very, very much. But he's not really from a newspaper; he's making a book!"

His tone relegated newspapers to their rightful place in the gutters of respect and oozed awe toward the author-scholar.

"Get lost," said Nina, opening her bag.

"Nice man, number one," said Dao cheerfully, as if she had

not spoken. "I told him that you are a very important lady. He wishes to pay his respects." Dao waited for her to take in the full force of his salesmanship.

Nina stared at him venomously She should have followed her first instinct and used some excuse to hustle Hong to another bar. She wanted the meeting to be unnoticed, and this idiot points her out as a *personnage* to the American press!

"Tell him I'm busy." She began to count out the approximate cost of their drinks onto the tabletop.

Dao scuttled away to the red-haired American.

Who else? thought Nina. She felt the panic begin again. I wonder if he's remembered now and wants to collect for his sandwich.

From the corner of her eye she watched Dao's pantomime of deep regret. The American put money on his table. Dao's hand swooped in mid-gesture, like a swift scooping up a mosquito. He trotted back to Nina's table. He *has* decided that I'm a hooker, thought Nina. I wonder what he thinks I'm worth.

"Very, very nice man. He wants to take you to dinner."

Does he think I still need feeding? she wondered.

To Dao, she said, "You can tell him where there are lots of women he can take to dinner. . . . Your mother works there!"

"No, no!" Dao pursed his lips sadly at her misunderstanding. "I told him already that you don't want any monkey business."

She dropped two more piastres onto the table and walked out of the café, looking straight ahead. She would do her best to make sure that bright-blue-eyed American never crossed her path again.

Her second meeting with Hong two days later was as pleasing as the first. They agreed on terms quickly. Then he went away to buy equipment from the list she had approved, and Nina went looking for somewhere to locate his new laboratory. For two weeks she tramped around garages, godowns, vacant machine shops, and cellars. Then Snow Man suggested that she look at some buildings behind the factory of one of Heron's suppliers, a syrup-bottling plant.

The managing director of the plant unlocked the three dingy outbuildings for her inspection; one was used to park delivery trucks, one held wire baskets full of empty bottles, while the third was littered with a miscellany of half-repaired engines, baskets of rotting corks, a mattress now housing a commune of rats, fragments of neon sign tubing, broken bamboo mats, and bundled papers already crumbled halfway back to the earth where they had started.

Nina agreed to rent the third building, if the managing director would hire Jonathan Hong as a quality controller for his business—with Nina paying his actual salary, of course. Hong would spend two afternoons a week making himself publicly visible in the bottling plant, in an official white coat, before retiring to carry out the mysterious business of quality controllers in his private quarters. The managing director would receive a retainer to contain his curiosity.

Dirty as it was, the outbuilding had solid walls unpierced by windows, a heavy door, a ventilation fan, and a good supply of electricity. Hong was delighted when he saw it. With his two new assistants, his younger brother and a cousin, he cleaned and painted, hammered and assembled. His scowl disappeared. Though his manner was always businesslike and controlled, his entire demeanor became lightened and fresh as a garden newly washed by rain. The lenses of his spectacles beamed and flashed with reflections of the bare overhead bulbs as he was everywhere at once, creating a kingdom for his knowledge in the concrete garage with the rusting corrugated roof.

While Hong was setting up his laboratory, Chinchook delivered the first of his photographs. His perseverance was greater than his expertise; Nina studied the first three proof sheets—108 blurred humans. One or two she recognized as the expected visitors to a prominent member of the dwindling French community. There were half a dozen Corsican matrons, friends of Angelica, photographed leaving with her for Mass. Middle-aged European males in indistinct suits. One or two unfamiliar Chinese, a wide variety of Vietnamese, including several who were obviously deliverymen with flowers, crates of wine, etc. And there was Daniel Jouvet.

Nina peered at his blurred mustaches thoughtfully. So far, he was the only one from Kim's lists to appear at Carbone's house. Two days later Thin Pig told her he had had drinks with Carbone at the Hotel Continental.

In the meantime Nina also met Andrew's American, Leo Thompson. By the time they parted he had agreed, in his capacity as a USOM adviser, to recommend that she be given a government contract to supply twelve heavy trucks to move equipment, labor, and supplies to and from the sites of four strategic hamlets. These were shortly to be built south of Saigon in the Mekong delta, where guerrillas had killed or kidnapped at least three thousand people in the last year—mainly petty officials seen to be supportive of Diem's government. Much to her surprise, although she left him several openings to raise the matter, he did not ask personal remuneration for this favor. She made a note for Clinton Clay to get her a case of Jack Daniel's from PX stocks, as Thompson drank it throughout their meeting.

After the Tet New Year 1959, and shortly before the beginning of the opium harvest, Carbone contacted her. They had not met since Kim's funeral.

He leaned across the backseat of his limousine and invited her to join him as she stood on the pavement just outside her office on Cong Ly Street.

She nodded to Snow Man and Tiny Albert that it was all right, then slid in onto the gray leather upholstery.

"It's good to see you again." Carbone sounded as if he meant it. His bulk was encased in a white suit; his white silk shirt was open at the neck to release curling gray hairs.

"And you, Uncle Emile." She smiled sweetly, as if her heart had not begun to thud.

"Are things going well?" he asked, just like an indulgent uncle.

"As far as I can tell."

He locked the fingers of her left hand between his own strong stumpy ones and regarded their two hands joined together. "I'm very pleased that we are able to be friends, after all," he said. "I was very fond of your father, you know. In spite of what happened later."

Reflected in Carbone's dark brown eyes she saw her father's ghost, seated opposite him in the back of the car.

Carbone sighed. "Yes, I was very fond of him for a long time. He was unusual, *jaune* or no. Many of my men were jealous of my regard for him. They told me I could never trust an Annamite."

"I'm half Annamite," said Nina. She wondered what he wanted.

"And I half trust you." He laughed. "Which is why I want a little chat. To protect this trust."

"Half trust," she reminded him. "Go ahead."

"Have you learned which districts are your agreed trading areas for sales of smoker's opium?"

"Do you mean the boundaries that were drawn up while I was teething? Yes, I know those limits. And yours. And those of the Chiu Chao."

"Good. That saves a lot of explanation. Now, the other question is exports."

"Of rice?" she asked, eyes mock-wide. "Of sugar?"

"You're a terrible actress." He smiled nevertheless. "Were you aware that your father had approximately ten percent, more or less, of export sales from Laos and Indochina?"

"Ten percent of export sales to Europe, from Laos and Indochina?" she repeated carefully but inexactly, and waited for him to correct her. But he did not.

"That's right. I want you to agree to leave it that way. Once the harvest is in, we start to estimate the likely total. You agree not to go beyond ten percent, more or less. Assuming you reach even that much. It has to be approximate, of course, but we can reach a workable understanding."

"Why should I agree?" she asked.

"Because you owe me a favor," he replied. "And because I said I would help you find your feet. Because I am a peaceful man and hate cruelty to children." His voice was amiable. "And I would be forced to be cruel if I found you were repeating your father's mistake . . . becoming greedy and trying to take more than your share—even if only to prove yourself, which you will need to do. Sooner or later."

Anger began to burn dangerously around the edges of her ears, but she kept her temper. His last point was accurate.

"What am I supposed to do if that ten percent leaves me with surplus stock?" she asked.

"Sell it locally as smoker's opium, if you can. Sell it legitimately to pharmaceutical companies, if you can get a license. Or sell it to me, at a broker's price . . . it's not a problem for a girl with your enterprising mind. By the way . . ." His tone remained light and teasing. ". . . I was most impressed by Kim's funeral."

"Thank you," she replied. "It still fell short of his worth. . . . As for sales, I'm a peaceful child who hates to upset her elders. I will agree. For the moment. While I'm finding my feet, as you said. What else can I do?"

He squeezed her hand in his paw; both their hands were cold. "I'm delighted you're such a reasonable young lady. I could become quite fond of you too."

She didn't miss the warning.

"I'm glad for another reason," he went on. "We're going to need to cooperate. It seems that the FBN in America and Narcotics in the Deuxième are beginning to panic about the amount of refined heroin entering their countries. Particularly into America, where trade virtually stopped after the war. But since the U.S. let that Italian, Luciano, out of prison in exchange for Mafia help against the Nazis in Sicily, trade is up again. I'm told that investigators are already sniffing at the poppy fields of Turkey.''

Absently, he withdrew his hand to take a cigarette paper from a silver box.

''There are rumors of raids. One of my best buyers has had to move his lab out of Marseilles to Bangkok.'' With concentration, he sprinkled the tobacco shreds, then he looked at her as he rolled the dark brown cylinder back and forth between his thick, strong fingers.

''Sales of base to Europe could be hurt, of course,'' he said. ''But what really concerns me is that my Italian cousins too will begin to look farther eastward if the Middle East is closed. And, my dear, some of them are not gentlemen, like we are used to knowing.''

He licked the paper delicately with a beefy, purple tongue tip. ''We here in Indochina must agree on how we wish to handle such a move, if it happens. I believe we would profit from a unified position on the matter.''

Her nostrils flared at the acrid breath of his match. He looked at her through the smoke of ignition.

''I'm a much safer playmate than the Italians.''

Her ears, which had never lost their new range of hearing, picked up a real concern under his apparent ease. For the first time during this meeting, she looked at him without he veil of her own anxieties. He was an old man, in spite of his bulk and apparent vigor. She accepted his patronizing flirtation partly because he was old enough to have earned the right to it. He had reached the laissez-faire state of old age which has earned the right to behave outrageously by years of solemn adulthood.

His eyelids were crumpled hibiscus petals. There were deep lines from the sides of his nose to the top of his jowls. The skin of his neck hung in folds above the vigorous white hairs on his chest. The intelligent eyes were tired; in them, she had seen appreciation and envy of her own youth, which was quite separate from the business between them. He was old; he was tired. He no longer wanted new battles to fight.

''I expect you can count on my cooperation,'' she said lightly. ''I won't want to take on the Italian-American Mafia all by myself.''

He threw back his head and guffawed at the mere idea of her doing so.

He dropped her back on Cong Ly Street.

''You must come for dinner with us,'' he said through the

open window. "Angelica is back from Corsica now. Her mother died, unfortunately. It would cheer her up to see how you've grown."

Nina thanked him and said that she would be honored. As he was driven away, she gave a little wave and wondered why he insisted on the pose of friendship when his intentions were so clear. Her adulthood would mean nothing to Angelica Carbone; she hardly knew the woman. Perhaps he thought Nina would be fooled. Or perhaps he really thought that Nina would come one day and beg him to relieve her of her responsibilities.

She shrugged to herself as she climbed the stairs to her office. More important was the fact that she had limited her agreement to European sales only, and he hadn't questioned it. That left sales to Hong Kong unaffected. As well as anything that might result from Jonathan Hong's experiment, which would begin as soon as the poppy harvest finished. If Hong succeeded, she would have a way of shaping the signs in her favor and still be able to look Carbone straight in the eye, hand on her heart, swearing that she had kept to the letter of their agreement. And so Nina entered the Year of the Boar, in which the signs advised her to avoid high-risk investments and to beware of new associates.

33

In late February, a few weeks after Tet, high in the mountains of Laos and northern Vietnam the petals of the opium poppies began to fall. The women of the mountain villages prepared their double-bladed knives and containers for the raw sap. A few days after the last petals dropped to lie like scattered firework cases on the chalky soil, the women went to the fields and scored each gray-green seed pod from the top to the bottom in a pattern of parallel cuts. The next day they scraped off the brown gum which had oozed from the cuts during the night. Then they scored each pod again. The day after that, they repeated the entire process for one final time. The pods were now milked dry.

The brown gum was crude opium. The villagers kept a little for themselves in amounts too small to be missed. They boiled and filtered it to smoke or to drink in a solution. They believed that it reduced hunger pangs and cured colds. Sometimes, for a greater effect, they mixed it with a small quantity of local marijuana.

They prepared most of the crude opium for collection by Meo soldiers who had once been mercenaries for the French. The soldiers delivered the crude opium, for a price, to the first level of local brokers. These brokers might be warlords who had survived the defeat of the French and still operated the fiefdoms consolidated under French rule. They might be local government officials or military officers. They were always men who had the power to insist on an annual quota of crude opium as "tax," or at a price far less than they themselves charged to the Indochinese laboratories where the brown gum was refined to morphine base.

A small percentage of the crude opium, from an area of remote mountain valleys in Tonkin, went by a slightly different route. It was collected from the chalky upland ridges by other Meos and carried by backpack to a mountain stronghold, built by a warlord but now occupied by a unit of Binh Xuyen who had fled there after their defeat in 1955 by Diem's ARVN and the Americans.

The local farmers had expected yet another band of marauding thugs and were pleasantly surprised to find that these Binh Xuyen lived up to the sect's original reputation for fair play toward the peasantry. It was rumored that the unit's commanding officer in the South had executed two of his men for violence against the farmers.

From the mountain stronghold the crude opium was carried by mountain ponies and mules, under armed escort, to the top of the navigable section of the Black River. Binh Xuyen officers escorted the cargo downstream in small boats. Some opium then continued south disguised as a wide range of agricultural products. But as guerrilla activity increased the amount of fighting, more and more opium was loaded onto fishing junks which hopped down the coast to Cu My, a small coastal port near the eastern edge of the Rung Sat. From Cu My, shallow-draft sampans ferried the opium through the maze of the great swamp into the Saigon River. The sampan owners dropped their cargo at points along the river, or along the Nha Be Channel, which the river joined briefly before branching off westward to Saigon itself. Thu's men, dressed as farmers, fishermen, and delivery boys, collected the opium and transferred it to the Heron Confectionery, near the Arroyo Chinois in Saigon, where it was refined to morphine base by Luoc's own chemists.

All morphine base, whether refined at Heron or in other Indochinese labs, many of which were in Laos, was sold abroad, through brokers, to buyers from labs in France, Turkey, Switzerland, Germany, and Hong Kong. These establishments were far more sophisticated than those in Indochina, designed to refine the morphine base into heroin.

More brokers sold the heroin at wholesale prices to big foreign importers from the United States, France, and Italy. These wholesale prices were something in the region of eight hundred times the price paid to the poppy farmers for the crude opium. By the time it hit the streets of New York or Paris in "dime" packets, the heroin would have been cut several times with various fillers, and could bring profits more than ten thousand times the original price of the gum.

Very little reached the streets of Saigon. Among the Viets, smoker's opium and local *bhang* were still the fashionable forms of chemical escape. Those who did use *ma thuy* generally smoked it in the Chinese fashion. The habit of injecting heroin—and enjoyment of the brutal rush that it brought—was, like most of the heroin itself, a foreign import, from Hong Kong in the case of the drug and from America in the case of the habit.

Of the crude opium, a very small percentage went yet another route. Twenty kilos, collected from a drop near the Ong Cal Bridge by a Binh Xuyen soldier, never reached Luoc's chemist at Heron Confectionery. Instead, Snow Man delivered those twenty kilos to a garage behind a syrup bottling company half a mile away, into the hands of Jonathan Hong.

While Hong and his two assistants worked on the "experiment," Nina had a second meeting with her cousin and new colleague, Colonel Thu, to settle the terms of their associations. They met in a hut in a village across the river, in territory believed to be held by the VC.

Thu wore peasant's clothes, a black tunic with rolled sleeves and loose trousers and headband, instead of his colonel's uniform. His feet were bare. Nevertheless, his men saluted smartly when they escorted Nina into the hut.

"Greetings, Cousin Tiger." Nina was determined not to let him bully her this time, or to see how much he frightened her.

Thu chose to ignore her frivolity. "Greetings. Welcome. Let me offer you some refreshment after your dangerous trip into enemy country."

One of his men appeared on cue with a tray of tea and fruit.

"You sent for me," she began, after settling on the woven fiber mat which covered the dust of the floor.

"Not so fast," he chided gently. "I can see that if we are to do business together, I must teach you how to behave."

She had learned her lesson the last time. She lowered her eyes and murmured, "I am sure there is much I can learn from you, Cousin."

He didn't reply. She raised her eyes, afraid that he thought she had forgotten truth number five, and was mocking him. He was studying her curiously.

"You've changed," he said abruptly.

As her face went hot, she reminded herself wildly that he could not possibly know about the twenty kilos of crude opium or her agreement with Jonathan Hong. Even so, his awareness was alarming, even dangerous.

He leaned forward on the knuckles of his hands to look into her face. She kept her eyes steady on his for as long as she could, until they dropped in spite of her to the scars that twined around his bare arms.

Thu grunted and sat back. "We'll see," he said. "We'll see." There was silence while he peeled and offered her a lychee. "OK. Down to business," he said at last. "The harvest was good but it is growing harder to get south. Government patrols look for VC but instead, they keep finding my men." He invited her to join his amusement, but he had not lost his earlier speculative look.

"For the moment, you and I should leave things as they are. Your father and I divided responsibility, as I said. I pay my men to deliver. He paid his to make and sell. You should do the same. We divide net profits fifty-fifty."

This time, as he held her eyes, she wondered if he were lying. It was possible that her father had divided equally, but she doubted it. Without her father's chemists, brokers, and buyers, Thu's crude opium, however hard to transport, was almost valueless, worth only what he could get from sales to small, local Indochinese labs.

She didn't dare call him a liar, however. He smiled slightly, mocking her suspicion.

"Who else knew how things stood between you and my father?" she asked at last.

He followed her reasoning. "Only ourselves. And Kim. Only family."

She would lose no face in the world by agreeing. Only Thu would know her weakness, if her suspicions were correct. She was going to need her new venture with Hong more than ever, to mask a possible shortfall in income lost to her cousin.

"Of course, I must agree to any terms my father found acceptable. I must trust you." She kept any hint of irony out of her voice.

"And I must trust you of course," he said.

He leaned forward and stroked her bare neck. "I like to do business with you." His touch was familiar and possessive. "You are even prettier than your White Demon mother, and already better mannered."

Fear cut through her confusion. His drift was more dangerous than mere flirtation.

"I have been told, on the contrary, that I am very like my father."

"We shall see." His speculative look returned. "I will now explain how we organize things." He unrolled a map and spread it on the floor. "Come sit by me and I will describe our system of drops and collection."

Forty-five minutes later, she left.

"Don't trust your Saigon brokers too much, School Dragon," he said as they parted. "Southerners are all crocodiles."

Little about him that day reminded her of the man who had said "Kill him!" before offering her dinner under a crystal chandelier in a palace in a swamp.

Nina stayed away from the garage until Hong sent for her. The shortness of his breath gave his message away even before he spoke. He opened the plastic bag as delicately as if it were the petals of an unopened rose. They gazed at the fine white powder and sighed in unison. It was softer than snow but not so brilliant.

"No explosions," said Hong. "Eighty-five percent pure."

"Not bad," said Nina. If she said more, her voice would shake. Hong smiled, however, as if she had fired an eight-gun salute in his honor.

She picked up the bag carefully and held it directly under the bald glare of the overhead bulb.

"I still have one and half kilos of base left," said Hong. It was a question.

"The breath of the dragon," murmured Nina, as if she hadn't heard him. Now that it had happened, she realized that she had believed it never would.

If she wished, she could now give Clay what he wanted so badly. She turned the bag slightly and studied the shadows of the plastic edges on the white landscape they encircled.

One step past this crossroads was too far to come back. She was mesmerized by the white landscape. It was the only step she could see.

Fortune showed me the way, through Clinton Clay, she thought.

Will Fortune be more offended if I advance or if I retreat? Which would my father prefer?

"Go ahead," she said to Hong.

Their eyes met quickly across the miniature moonscape in the plastic bag, then looked away just as quickly, but not before each saw in the other the same mixture of excitement and fear.

The following day she called Clinton Clay. The military switchboard was more reliable than the civilian one; she reached him on the second try, at his quartermaster's desk at Tan Son Nhut, in one of the military cargo sheds.

"It's Nina," she said. "I thought you might like to invite me for another drink."

She could hear his brain click, even over the telephone wire.

"Why not make it dinner?" he asked. "Somewhere nice."

"I was thinking of something more private," she said. "Just you and me."

"How can I refuse an offer like that? Is tomorrow OK?"

"I'm busy tomorrow night," said Nina. "Perhaps next week, then."

"Wait a minute," said Clay. "Maybe I could rearrange things. . . ."

There was a pause in which Nina heard the rustling of papers over the wire, then muffled voices as he placed his hand over the receiver.

"How about a little drink out here with me, tonight?" he asked, suddenly loud in her ear. "I've got some really great hooch—just in. You could tell me what you think. If you come late enough, no one will bother us. And I could show you around."

Nina considered.

"I'll fix the gate," said Clay. "Just say who you want to see."

"There will be three of us," said Nina.

Clay paused for thought again. "OK," he agreed. "Half past nine?"

"D'accord!"

At twenty-five minutes past nine, Nina, Snow Man, and Tiny Albert Joyful presented themselves to the guard on duty at the gate, while Eight Hand Horse waited in the car. Nina wore a black tunic and trousers and no makeup. The two men were in shorts and singlets instead of their suits. Both carried large woven baskets filled with pineapples.

The young American on duty looked doubtful. He asked

several questions through his ARVN counterpart, then reached for the telephone on the table in the gatehouse. Nina saw him expostulate, listen, then nod his head several times in agreement with what was being said. He hung up and came back out.

"Through there." He pointed along the tarmac. The ARVN guard translated. "Turn left and follow round the perimeter. Clay's in the third shed after the two hangars. Don't leave the road until you're there or you might get shot."

He picked up and replaced two pineapples as a gesture toward searching the baskets. Then he let them pass.

Snow Man and Tiny Albert left the baskets in Clay's office and went to wait outside the prefabricated building. The office was a snug corner nest in a sea of loaded pallets that stretched away into the shadows of the shed. A soft drinks cooler stood in one corner; an air conditioner rattled in one window. There were bars over the windows even though the shed was actually inside the base.

Clay eyed her clothes with amusement. "No wonder the poor bastard at the gate didn't recognize my description of my guests!" He offered her a drink; she accepted a Coca-Cola from the cooler.

"Well, M. Clay . . ."

"Clint!" he said in smiling reproof.

"Clint," began Nina again. "I have kept you in mind, as you asked. An acquaintance, whose name I won't mention, came to me yesterday with a product that he would like to sell."

Clay's eyes were bright as a terrier's. She could practically see his tail begin to wag.

"I can't comment on the quality," said Nina. "But I thought I'd let you know about it all the same. You might find it of interest, you might not." She took a tea tin out of the cloth bundle she carried and put it on his desk.

"Ma thuy," she said.

Clay opened it and sighed just as she and Hong had done.

"White as the tit of a Georgia cheerleader," he said. "You've got interesting acquaintances!" He looked up at her.

"Do you mind if I check it out?" He licked the tip of a finger, dipped it delicately, sniffed, and licked again. He produced a small flat metal scoop and lifted a little powder out of the tin onto a piece of white paper. "Back in a minute."

He disappeared through a side door of his office into the shadows of the cargo shed. As she waited, Nina glanced over the bars on the windows, the antigrenade mesh over the glass panel of the door, the large pink udders of a naked blonde on his wall calendar. A series of clipboards on nails held shipping lists, invoices, flight schedules. In one corner, opposite the cooler, was a large heavy safe. On Clay's desk was an empty whiskey glass, a half-eaten bag of American potato chips, and two brown Hershey chocolate wrappers.

Clay came back into the office. He looked delighted.

"Well, it beats the number three shit I've been offered lately . . . . I couldn't sell that stuff for coffee sugar in the PX. How much more has your acquaintance got?"

"How much can you sell?"

She could see the excitement and ambition in his eyes.

"As much as there is." He also looked a little frightened, but not too much. His tongue made a tiny dry clicking sound against his palate.

"The best thing," said Nina, "is for you to talk with the agent for my acquaintance. He'll have all the facts and figures for you."

"Do you know where he gets it?" Clay licked his lips. "It doesn't look like Indian. Could be Chink. . . ."

"I really don't know," said Nina with regret. "But I'll let my acquaintance know you're interested. His agent will get in touch."

"Tell him, 'Pronto!' "

"Sorry, I don't understand."

"Vite. Fast. *Aussitôt que possible."*

"Pronto," Nina agreed.

"One more thing," said Clay. "Do you think this guy could undersell Thai grass? I've got a market you wouldn't believe!"

"Ask the agent," said Nina. She held out her hand. "Thanks for the drink."

His plump hand was damp with excitement. "Thank *you*! Just let me know if I can ever help you out. A seat on a flight. Hooch. . . ."

"I will." She smiled. "And the pineapples are on me."

After considerable thought, Nina invited Daniel Jouvet to her apartment for a drink. In her opinion, formed during their dinner together, he had changed little since she had knocked out his two front teeth. He was still arrogant and she suspected that he still blubbered when someone hit him back. In spite of the heat, he was wearing a three-piece suit and a tie when he arrived at seven. She wondered why he had left off the solar topee.

Nina had spread downward unofficially through the house into the empty apartments below hers. Her staff now occupied the back of the ground floor. The USAID sign no longer dangled from its single screw outside the door of the former drawing room. However, the sandbags remained around the veranda where she and Jouvet sat, to make the most of faint stirrings in the evening air. Below them, just out of earshot, Eight Hand Horse was polishing the new Citroën with a piece of chamois and chatting to Jouvet's chauffeur, who squatted nearby smoking a cigarette. Insects and night birds had already begun to warm up for the night. Nina could hear the frogs in the ornamental pond of the house across the alley sorting themselves out into sopranos, altos, tenors, and basses.

"To old times, Daniel." She raised her glass. She wore a French-designed dress and high-heeled pumps; she suspected that Jouvet's conditioned response to an *ao dai* was a rush of droit du seigneur.

He raised his glass back to her. "Old times. As the Yanks would say: 'Today sucks!'"

He was beginning to feel better already with a gin in his hand and Mlle. Hard-to-Get crossing her legs at him—he could see most of the way up. He had been feeling sulky after playing squash with a cousin of the former Emperor, Bao Dai, now a powerful officer in the Air Force. Jouvet had lost, and he disliked being beaten at anything by an Annamite, even when it was good politics.

"To the future, perhaps," said Nina. She recrossed her legs and watched Jouvet's eyes focus down the length of his glass, from which he was drinking, as if down a gun barrel.

"Daniel," she said, "how much would you like to put someone in his place and take his money at the same time?"

He smiled briefly; his teeth were now perfect. Above them sprang the astonished-seeming mustaches, flaring brushes of rusty red, just like his father's.

"Don't be a bitch," he said. "It spoils your looks." He recrossed his own slim ankles, touched his fine sandy hair, and smoothed his mustaches.

"Could you lower yourself to talk to an American?" she asked, ignoring his comment. He would be only too glad, she thought. So he could feel superior; Clay would be a sitting duck on that score. Jouvet played squash with a Vietnamese only in order to hear how the Annamites secretly preferred the French to these new barbarians who had begun to take over, and how they yearned for the good old days nearly as much as Jouvet did himself.

"I'll talk to anyone as long as I'm taking his money," said Jouvet.

"You'll take it," said Nina.

Jouvet opened his arms like wings along the back of the rattan settee.

"It's a sort of trial run," said Nina. "Testing the water." She told him what she wanted him to do.

"Naughty, naughty," said Jouvet. "You'll get your little bottom smacked one day, by a great big special policeman." His interest was palpable.

"You've missed my main point, Daniel," she said. "You're going to take that risk for me. You're the expert at being naughty—fiddling piastres, for example."

He folded his arms across his chest, noncommittally. "I'm expensive."

"I've never doubted the nature of your price."

They locked eyes for a moment. He lifted his smooth, slightly weak chin a fraction of an inch.

"I'll want fifteen percent."

"No way," said Nina. "Twelve and a half, top. That's good, and you know it. Considering the potential value of sales, many men would be happy with five."

"What volume are you guaranteeing?"

"I'm not making any guarantees. But it's a waste of everyone's time to think small." Her wicker chair creaked as she leaned forward. "I'm offering above the odds as it is," she said. "Because I'm investing in your discretion. You'll be a direct link to me, and I don't want that known. Ever!"

For a moment his mind flicked to the memory of Andrew Martell. He smoothed his mustaches with thumb and middle finger, as if wiping expression from his mouth.

"There aren't many I would trust in that position," she said.

His eyes became slightly vacant as he did mental arithmetic. "Just a thought," he said after a minute. "A fleeting query...what if Emile gets wind of it, and his lot...the Alliance?"

"He won't. They won't," said Nina. "That would be part of your job. He and I are friends; I'd hate anything to disturb our friendship."

Jouvet considered the styling of his shoes from several angles. "He could be a real problem, you know."

"Not if you go on peddling for him as usual."

He went very still, eyes glued to the brogued, butterscotch calfskin. Then he looked up at her with a reasonable imitation of incredulity. "What did you say?"

Nina shook her head in gentle reproof. "Dearest Daniel, you're hardly invisible. Eyes and ears everywhere, as they say."

She watched him digest the extent of her information about him, courtesy of Taki Hashimoto. She was pleased by a dawning wariness in his eyes.

After a long pause, he shrugged.

"Now Daniel," she said. "I don't expect you to do me any favors. Apart from your percentage from me, there are real possibilities in this situation for someone with your enterprise. This American is looking for a range of merchandise that I'm not interested in handling—grass, for example. Possibly pharmaceuticals. . . ."

She saw his eyes flicker. He was sweating lightly; even in the dusk she could see the glaze on his forehead.

"Imagine the efficiency," she said. "Negotiating for several clients at the same time—me . . . Carbone . . . anyone else you can rope in. No one ever need know how many sources you're tapping. If you're clever enough."

He shook his head. "A new source of *ma thuy* . . . a new brand . . . in a small local market. Your anonymity can't last."

"It's not a new brand," she corrected him. "The labels will say 'Vientiane.' With all the right trimmings. The American is already buying a little imported stuff. *He* won't know where it really comes from. Just you and me."

Jouvet shivered inside his three-piece suit. "One could weep," he said to the shadows of the overgrown garden. "One really could! Just think of my grandfather—*chef du département,* dispensing commercial franchises for the government, including those for sales of government opium! Then look at me—the last colonial blossom on the family tree—whispering the joys of illegal smack in counterfeit packaging, into the cauliflower ears of the new Huns. For a female Annamite half-breed! How can anyone talk of progress?"

"Well," said Nina reflectively, "in the good old days I suppose I might have been your grandfather's *congaie* . . . there's proof of progress for you. Your wages are so much higher."

His knuckles whitened around his glass. Then he relaxed and raised it once again. "To the future, I suppose." He had lost all desire to go to bed with her.

Nina was satisfied and relieved. She had gambled that dollars would be stronger than his pride, but she had needed to be sure.

She raised her now-empty glass to him. "To the future."

34

While Nina drank to the future, Premier Diem depended more and more on the United States to guarantee his own future. In the following year, 1960, the VC kidnapped or killed more than three thousand village officials, teachers, and others associated with the government.

To counter guerrilla attacks on villagers, Diem carried out his plans to build "Agrovilles," or fortified villages, with American advice, funds, and supplies. The villagers who were to be relocated were used as forced labor. All the Eighty-eight Transport vehicles were booked by Thompson on a two-year renewable contract. Nina also imported and resold a further thousand Chinese wheelbarrows.

In the early summer she arrived at an understanding with Khan, now a personal secretary of Nhu. For a consideration, Khan (no relation to the minister of the same name) agreed to arrange that her agents and brokers would not be bothered by Narcotics Division.

No sooner had she arrived at this understanding than it was threatened in November by an attempted coup against Diem. The coup failed, however, and all arrangements with his government still held good. On the other hand, the greater number of arrests by Nhu's secret police increased the already considerable resistance to the Premier and his family. In the following January, Radio Hanoi announced the formation in South Vietnam of the National Liberation Front to fight the oppression of the "American Puppet Regime." In May 1961, the American Vice President, Lyndon Johnson, visited Vietnam. After Johnson returned to the United States Dean Rusk, the Secretary of State, promised Diem "every available help" in this struggle to stay in power as the leader of "free" Vietnam. Nina continued to be grateful for Thu's private treaty with the People's Army of the North; both sides of her business proceeded smoothly that year.

The next Tet brought in 1962, the Year of the Tiger—a year with a traditional reputation for wars and disasters, for brittle alliances and hotheadedness. It was also considered a year for boldness and gambling against the odds. For the government, the wars had already begun sometime before.

Diem had announced in October, before the aborted coup, that the guerrilla campaign against him in the South had become a real war that required wartime measures. Two weeks later he had then declared a state of emergency and suspended all constitutional processes. The Vietnamese Air Force stepped up its bombing of reported guerrilla strongholds. On December 11, 1961, an American aircraft carrier had docked in Saigon with thirty-three U.S. Army helicopters on board, and four hundred air and ground crewmen. In February of the new year, rebel Air Force pilots bombed Diem's palace one breakfast time in the first move of another attempted coup d'état. This coup also failed, but the Saigonese were entertained by the sight of tanks circling the Presidential Palace.

Nina's own Year of the Tiger began well by comparison. The opium harvest in Tonkin was good, Thu's private treaty with the People's Army of the North still held, and all consignments of raw opium reached Saigon safely. Clinton Clay bought Hong's entire, increased output through Daniel Jouvet, in advance, for U.S. dollars. The profits from this sale were more than enough for Nina to make up the value of Thu's percentage of the raw opium she had diverted from Heron to the syrup bottling plant. Her father's regular buyers were still satisfied with the quantities of morphine base his daughter was able to sell. Her father's brokers were still satisfied with the percentages they were able to take. Carbone, after careful checking, was satisfied that she was keeping to the terms he had imposed.

With her increased profits, Nina began to shape the signs as she had planned, to guarantee her continued survival. She gave Eight Hand Horse money to buy a larger, newer car as a discreet message to the rest of the world that she was doing well. She gave a pay raise to each of her servants. She bought the lease on the big house and officially took over all the rooms, which she redecorated. She repaired and repainted the compound wall. Then she invited people for drinks and dinner, to observe the changes. Anyone who wished to look could be sure that the gods were still backing Luoc's daughter, and through her the father, just as the *tay phap* who owed Eight Hand Horse a favor had originally predicted they would.

For the first time since Kim had been killed, Nina allowed herself to relax a little. After nearly three and a half years of anxiety, she paused in her dream of running over water and did not sink. Her other businesses—the hotel and Eighty-eight Transport— were also thriving on the arrival of the promised American aid, both in dollars and in men. She saw balance and harmony in her business which she did not feel in herself. She was restless and dissatisfied.

I'm just overtired, she told herself. I'm very, very tired. That's why something feels so wrong.

"I shall go to Dalat," she said one day to Eight Hand Horse. "Would you enjoy a break from the heat of Saigon? We haven't had a holiday in years!"

The old man's eyes brightened. In spite of the addition of Snow Man and Tiny Albert, he was exhausted by the effort of keeping track of his young mistress. She never stayed in one place. She would dart off suddenly, on a harebrained scheme like that fancy-dress visit to Tan Son Nhut, and expect him to think of every contingency. In Dalat, he could rest. She would stay put, resting herself. There were fewer people to watch. Strangers would be obvious. Her father had been so much easier—and he himself had been younger, of course, in those days.

Nina and her maid packed padded silk jackets for the cool evenings in the mountains. She bought herself the latest French novels, a book of Vietnamese poetry, and a handbook of English phrases. She would read, eat, walk in the pines, and go boating on the lake as she had when she was a child. Above all, she would sleep, deep, soul-scouring sleep, in the fresh, pine-scented air. The night before she left, she went over her books to put together the financial summary for the harvest. As she worked, she thought with wistful amusement of all her tutorial sessions with André Gidéon. "It's fun," she had said, all those hundreds of years ago. Automatically, she checked the total of a column a second time, and all thoughts of fun vanished.

Nina went over the figures again and again—the compilation of reports from agents at all stages of the transfer and refining process. Ong Cal Bridge drop—fifty kilos of crude; the abattoir drop—thirty-seven kilos; Dong Nai Junction—seventy-five kilos. She couldn't make them add up with the final figures from the brokers.

She allowed for the opium she had diverted from Heron to Hong's lab. She allowed for the usual skimming off by agents, which Eight Hand Horse had explained was part of keeping the system harmonious. She allowed for Duprès to have become unusually greedy, or to have had debts with the Chiu Chao gambling syndicates which he needed to pay off. She made every acceptable allowance she could think of. It still didn't add up.

After calculating from Kim's meticulous records, she expected a rough ratio of ten kilos of crude opium to each kilo of base produced by the Heron chemists. Her own experience had confirmed these figures. Even with all her allowances, it now seemed to have taken nineteen to produce one. Only a little more than half the expected amount of base had reached the brokers in Cholon. If the harvest had not been so good, the discrepancy would have had the brokers screaming in outrage long before now.

She felt the hot breath of the tiger on her neck. At the very beginning, after Kim's death, Eight Hand Horse had said, "It is when things go wrong that you are most needed... you must hold matters in order from the top. You must see if things go wrong, put them right, and chastise the wrongdoers."

Something had gone wrong now; others would know that too and be waiting to see what she did about it. She went over the figures yet again. The deliveries were fine; the numbers there were consistent with what she had estimated from the number of villages, Kim's past reports, her own experience, and the reports of a good harvest. Fourteen to fifteen kilos per village. The brokers were each selling as much as they were delivered. The discrepancy lay between the amounts of crude opium delivered to Heron and the number of kilos of base delivered to the brokers after refining. That narrowed the problem, but still left an overwhelming number of alternatives to investigate. Including the alternative that the disorder was very near the top. And that the wrongdoer, whom she must chastise, was as strong as or stronger than herself. She invited herself to dinner at the Rung Sat.

35

They had finished eating. Nina turned her glass in her hand.

"I think," she said casually, "that we should consider replacing the chemists at Heron."

Thu crossed to his sleeping platform and settled back against the cushions. He wore a black cotton tunic and trousers, and his headband. "Come sit with me," he ordered. "And bring the bottle."

Nina knelt beside him on the platform and filled his glass with Scotch from the U.S. Army PX. This was going to be interesting— she had obviously touched a nerve if he had decided to be quite so indirect.

"Am I presuming to give such advice?" she asked wickedly.

He caught the hand that held the bottle, set the bottle down and spread her fingers so he could study her palm.

"This is not a stupid hand," he said, ignoring her question. "But it is a little mixed up. Many influences but few clear indications."

He brought it close to his mouth and blew gently on her palm, then traced the line of each finger with a column of warm air. Suddenly she could not meet his eyes.

"*I* am an influence. That, I can read clearly."

She couldn't tell how serious he was. She tried to withdraw her hand and regain her composure.

His grip tightened. "Perhaps it also says that you will be an influence on me. That is less clear. And what kind of influence is not clear at all."

She could not miss the note of threat, mixed though it was with sexual undertone.

His grip on her wrist tightened still further. "It says here that you must choose what to make of what already exists for you. Not change it."

He knows exactly why you came here, Nina told herself.

He looked at his own hand without releasing hers.

"As I must." He shook his head dolefully. "If I were wiser, I would probably throw you to my tiger."

They looked at each other for several seconds.

Be careful, said Nina to herself. Be very careful. You have let go of the tail and are staring the tiger in the eye.

"I would not presume to argue with what you read in my hand," she said at last.

He held her eyes, unsmiling, a little longer. "You have learned much in the last months. I'm glad. I would prefer to eat you myself—the tiger is getting too fat."

He slid his hand under her *ao dai,* and pulled on the cord tied at the waist of her trousers. "I read this in your hand also."

"And if I said I wished to consult another chiromancer?"

She said it lightly, although her voice shook a little in spite of herself. It was so long since she had been with a man. Since two nights after Andrew had reappeared in her life. She spoke to buy herself a few seconds. To consider what this would do to her purpose in coming here.

"That would be cowardly," he said. "You have already decided, have you not?"

She did not like him; she did not approve of him; but she was able to desire him, just as she had once pined for him in the shadows of Dalat. This was a very different man from that earlier one, but she was very different from that little girl.

If I see a tiger, she wondered, what does he see when he looks at me? I am no better than he is, and with less cause.

She touched the scars on his arm with two fingers, the scars from the French.

She feared him a little, but that was a separate issue. She untied the cord at her waist, which had made a knot, and slipped out of her trousers.

He laid her down on the platform and pulled the *ao dai* above her breasts. She expected the brutality of her own decision to be reflected in their lovemaking. She lay down like a goat expecting to be eaten by the tiger, half wanting it, and found that she was a flower being smelled and brushed and finally penetrated gently as if by a butterfly.

In their soft writhings, the warmth in her belly contracted into a knot, then uncoiled and spread through her chest and limbs like a monsoon river bursting its banks. To her horror, it also burst from her eyes in a flood of tears and her body shook with sobs. Only then did she feel his energy gather momentum and drive through to the finish.

Her energy ebbed into quietness. They lay peacefully, face to face, her leg across his hip, his hand on the nape of her neck.

Be careful, she tried to tell herself again. Don't trust this sense of peace and safety. Don't trust it! Don't trust him. Don't trust his warmth. You may allow yourself a few more minutes of warmth against your skin. But do not trust.

She sighed and fought her way back from the half dream to the cold present moment; it was a vantage point she must never abandon. She felt a slide of wetness against her thigh and a coolness as he began to contract and withdraw from her.

He propped himself up on his elbow and looked down at her with satisfaction. "It was good for you? I think it was."

She was grateful that it was so easy to agree. .

"You thought I would make love like I fight." He made the statement with pleasure at his own awareness. He grinned. "I don't fight all the time."

"I am honored to share a moment of peace with you," she murmured.

He dropped the grin abruptly. "Now am I going to teach you something else, School Dragon. . . . Don't bullshit with me, as the Americans say. You have learned a lot, but you don't bullshit well enough. It will make me angry. I know it was good. I can feel things."

He fixed her with his scaring-the-troops glare.

End of tranquillity. She was glad she had prepared herself.

"Fine," she said. "In that case, now that we have cemented our alliance, can we talk about those chemists at Heron?"

His mood switched yet again. "Oh! Oh! Now you're rushing off like a startled buffalo calf. Too fast. Too fast! You'll get it right eventually, I hope. Pour me some more Scotch now. Then you may rub the soles of my feet."

"You know," said Nina cheerfully, "I could get angry with you too."

"But you will not let me see it, because you do not have a stupid hand." It was a flat statement of fact, and an accurate one.

She forced herself to smile at him. Her entire business depended on his private treaty with the North, on his Meos, his mountain ponies, his sailors, his sampan owners.

"But you feel things," she said. "And you will know, in any case. So I have no protection against you."

"There you are," he said happily. "You are getting better at it already, as I said you would. See, I'm not angry all the time."

They lay back on the wooden platform, refilled glasses in hand. He seemed to have forgotten his order to rub his feet. He pushed the *ao dai* up again and idly weighed and pressed her left breast with his free hand. Once, he leaned over and nosed at it gently, pulling back to watch it fall into place.

"Very nice," he said. "Not a buffalo udder like some French-women, but more than one usually finds. Very pleasant."

He sipped while continuing to regard her body with detached but approving interest.

"Why do you think we should replace the chemists?" he asked suddenly.

Nina wanted to laugh. He was outrageous. He was willing to talk business now that he thought he had her stretched out naked and vulnerable, sexually satisfied, and full of good Scotch. It was going to be a dangerous game with him and she must never, never underestimate him.

"I think they are very careless," she said.

He looked politely interested and ran his hand down her breastbone, across her navel to the dark triangle of pubic hair which he tugged at curiously—few Vietnamese had so much.

"They seem to lose a lot of raw opium," she continued.

"Why do you say that?"

"I have checked the books. It takes ten kilos of crude to make one kilo of morphine base. We are not shipping in proportion to what you are bringing down."

She had his attention now. His hand stopped moving.

389

"For example," she went on, "the fifty kilos picked up from your Ong Cal Bridge drop. . . . It showed up as two kilos of base. Even allowing for the usual cuts and losses in the expected ways, the difference is far too great."

"How do you think they are losing it?" His hand was moving again, but she felt him make a conscious effort to do it.

"I think they sell it, either before or after refining."

She believed he knew what she was getting at.

"What do you think should be done with them, if they are guilty? The old penalty for theft was death."

She chose her words carefully. "It would depend entirely on the person they choose to sell it to."

They had reached the nub. He looked reflectively up at the carved and gilded dragons which undulated across the high ceiling to generate a good energy flow.

"They don't sell it," he said suddenly.

"I thought perhaps not," she said. There was a pause. His hand still lay on her body, but without awareness. All his energy was intent on watching her face.

"I shall give you a commission in my army," he said. "Then I can execute you if you are disloyal."

She sat up, first moving his hand with hers so she did not appear to be throwing it off. "My loyalty doesn't bend to threats," she said.

She looked closely at him in turn. She had no illusions about his emotions or his potential brutality. But the pupils of his eyes were wide as he gazed back at her, in spite of his neutral expression. For the moment, at least, she held a small advantage which his eyes betrayed. She blew gently into his palm.

"They give it back to you," she said quietly. "After they have refined it."

He sighed deeply, as if relieved of a weight, removed his hand from hers, and reached for his glass.

"For how long?" she pursued.

"Since your father went north." He drank without looking at her.

She fought down the anger of betrayal. This was her moment of greatest danger. She must not let him retreat back inside his loneliness to contemplate the threat she now posed to him.

She put his palm to her lips and moved them gently against its center, then bit gently, softly, at the callused mounds beneath each finger.

"I am not my father," she said at last. "I do not make the same claim on your loyalty."

The cold assessment in his eyes chilled her; she thought she had overestimated even her temporary power over him. She let his hand lie loosely on her thigh.

At last he made a small noise of assent, agreeing to the appearance of truce that she had offered him.

"Lie on your stomach," he said abruptly. "I have not seen your rump."

She obeyed, half from discretion, half from desire. She wondered what would happen when the day came that she did not want to offer her body to him when he demanded it. She believed she would be brave enough to refuse.

The future was too unsure; she chose to deal with the present only. The skin of her back and buttocks shivered under his fingers but her head felt clear. Then she let herself slide into the comfort of unthinking sensation as he lifted her hips off the hard wooden platform and entered her from behind. She knew she would live to return to Saigon. They would negotiate the terms of their truce another time.

She went to Dalat the next day, but did not find the tranquillity she had hoped for. They set off with Nina, Snow Man, and Eight Hand Horse in one car, followed by Tiny Albert, the *mama-san*, the cook, and the maid in another. As they drove north, Nina was shocked by the damage caused by the fighting. Saigon had been relatively untouched in the last two or three years. But in the countryside they passed entire villages that had been burned, though it was impossible to tell by whom—guerrillas meting out punishment to villagers who collaborated with the government, or government soldiers punishing Vietcong supporters. Here and there they passed the burned-out skeletons of trucks or armored personnel carriers, though the fabric of the vehicles had been stripped by the peasants to use in rebuilding their houses. Dike walls had been broken by Air Force bombings and the beginnings of the rains were already melting and washing away the geometry of the *paddi* fields.

Eight Hand Horse glanced morosely out the window at the undulating spine of peaks that curved up from the left.

"They are draining the life energy from the body of the Dragon," he said. "First they block his breath with roads and railways, then they cut open his veins. It's madness!"

Nina did not smile. The earth did indeed seem wounded.

Dalat itself was untouched. The Emperor's hunting palace still hung above the lake. The pines still sighed and murmured. But the garden of her family's house had returned to the wild. Where cannas had once grown, shrubs and vines stormed the veranda like assault troops. Bat droppings littered the veranda, and birds had nested in the carved beams.

The *mama-san* tut-tutted and scurried busily, mustering the staff to open the heavy shutters, scour the kitchen, bring charcoal, chase the mice from the upholstery in the main drawing room. While the house was readied, Nina walked on the cushion of pine needles below the veranda, where the underbrush had bowed to the greater might of the pines and crept with humility across the ground.

Minou's post still stood, the empty chain dangling above the pine needles. Thu's ghost sat on the veranda. Her mother's ghost lay with its novels, and the mice, in its room just above. Nina leaned on the little fretted stone parapet her father had had built on the hillside where a slice of blue lake showed between the pines. She did not know if she could hold matters together from the top. This disorder with Thu could prove too great for her strength. This time, his challenge was public, no longer private within the family. Betrayal at such a high level was a very bad sign which would not be missed. Her own show of increased wealth and prosperity would not balance it.

She tried to suppress her panic over Thu, but it reappeared as uneasiness at being so far from the center of affairs in Saigon, not knowing what was happening. She had Eight Hand Horse drive them all back after only four days. She was twenty-three, looked thirty, and felt three hundred years old.

36

She spent the rest of the year watching for another shift in the signs, or an indication that others imagined they had seen such a shift. She returned from Dalat to learn that, in her short absence, the United States had officially confirmed that American pilots were flying combat-training missions with the Vietnamese Air Force. She shrugged when she read the two-day-old news. Everyone who had paid any attention knew this already. What did everyone think was going on at Tan Son Nhut? Or at the new airstrips that had been built outside the city? Unlike the earlier troubles, this escalation seemed much less serious than the immediate problems of her own empire.

For a month she tried to distract herself with private English lessons, remembering Clay's original advice and feeling she needed every possible advantage she could marshal. Already bilingual, she had little difficulty with a third tongue, except her own edginess which made it hard for her to concentrate. She tried to involve herself in furnishing the big house, now redecorated and restored to its former turn-of-the-century elegance. She chose carefully, with an eye trained by Louis.

"The best of its kind or not at all," he would urge. Under his guidance, she invested in Chinese and Vietnamese antiques, good modern European furniture, and the wool tribal carpets of the Middle East which were newly fashionable in Europe. Louis made her buy a rough, vivid painting by a refugee American named Karel Appel though she preferred the serene geometry of an early Mondrian she had bought on the international art black market. The Mondrian suited the calm she wanted in her personal refuge. Louis's mixing of styles began to make sense to her, a reflection of coming to terms with her own mixed background.

Louis happily took her on expeditions to look at paintings, at sculpture, at designer furniture; however, he looked more at her than at the items on show. He noticed the troubled, distant expression that settled on her face whenever she forgot to remain animated. He thought she was becoming too thin; her delicacy was in danger of becoming gaunt if she lost much more weight and her generous bones began to show too much. The day he spotted a rogue white hair above her right ear he shrieked in horror, relieved to have found a concrete reason for voicing his concern. Since she would not take up his suggestion of going at last to Paris to buy clothes, he begged her to make at least a three-day trip to Singapore as a treat. They never went, however.

In May the Premier brought in a new set of restrictions in the interest of national security, including the prohibition of any meeting of any kind without prior government consent, granted seven days in advance. Then, egged on by his sister-in-law, Mme. Nhu, Diem outlawed all dancing, boxing, animal fights, and beauty contests, in the interests of national morality. Saigon society became jumpy about entertaining. Nina, like many other Saigonese who were within the reach of the secret police, stopped buying and stayed close to home.

Like other Saigonese, she heard the rumors about peasants in the north of the province who wanted to stay at home but could not. It was said that the South Vietnamese Army was burning its own people's villages to keep the farmers from fleeing home from the new fortified villages. Officially, the program of forced relocation was now called "Operation Sunrise"; on the streets and in clubs, many people called it "Operation Arson."

Careful as Nina was, she was nevertheless picked up by a U.S. patrol for a security check one evening as she came out of the office on Cong Ly Street. One moment she was strolling, lazily, waiting for Eight Hand Horse to arrive with the car to take her home. The next minute a jeep had stopped beside her and she found herself leaning against the wall of her own office building while an American ran his hands up her legs. The fact that she wore an *ao dai* and spoke French did not help; she forgot every one of her new English phrases in her fury and terror.

While she was being searched, another American emptied her briefcase. Then he began on her handbag.

"This dink says she's a businesswoman. Pretty good business... look at this purse!" He waved it in the air, spilling papers, makeup, pens, money.

The first soldier turned her round. "I'd like to try some of your business. When are office hours?"

She could not believe this was happening to her. She smiled politely. Behind the American was an attending ARVN officer.

In Vietnamese, she said to him, "Tell these two pigs that I have a luncheon date tomorrow, with M. Khan. *Vous comprenez?*"

He understood. It was even possible that she was not lying. He looked at her papers, which he was now holding as if they had begun to smoke at the edges. He turned to the two Americans and stiffened to attention. "It is possible," he said in English to the two soldiers, "that I recognize madame's name. I do not believe that she is a VC."

"Who the hell is?" asked one American.

They were looking at her speculatively. She fought her rage; she was too vulnerable. She had heard stories of women who had been raped by entire platoons of ARVN, and threatened with beatings or worse if they complained.

"You must persuade them that they would be making a mistake," she said to the Vietnamese. "That they *are* making a mistake. A bad one. You know how such misunderstandings can grow until *everyone* suffers."

The ARVN officer was looking more and more worried. The white soldiers were his superiors in rank, but this lady's threats, however indirect, might just have some foundation. *On ne sait jamais!* Life altered so quickly, one could never keep up.

"Madame is not a VC," he repeated, looking sideways at Nina.

"How the hell do you know?"

394

"I know," he reiterated flatly.

"What's she been saying to you?"

"Madame is not a VC," he repeated, as if prepared to keep repeating the phrase indefinitely.

"Ask her where she gets enough money to buy crocodile purses."

The Vietnamese did so, half sketching with his head the bow he dared not make.

"Business," she said curtly. "With M. Khan, among others."

While the Vietnamese translated, the Americans eyed Nina, who forced a diffident smile onto a face frozen with rage.

"How the hell are we supposed to tell, anyway?" said one. "They look like this, then they pull a grenade out of their powder compact."

To Nina, through the translator, he said, "You're on record now, so stay out of trouble. We won't let you go next time."

He tossed the empty handbag back to her. The three men watched her crawl on the pavement to collect the scattered contents. The Vietnamese started to kneel to help her, stopped himself, and straightened again, eyes on Nina. He was in an agony of indecision. If her threats had substance, he should be helping her, but with the American soldiers watching he didn't dare.

Once she stopped shaking, Nina's chief concern was who had witnessed this demonstration of her vulnerability. To her relief, all the passersby had rushed quickly on without stopping. She was standing again, apparently composed, by the entrance to her office building when Eight Hand Horse drove up at last with Snow Man.

That night she rang Louis and asked him to come and have dinner with her. She said very little to him generally and nothing at all about the evening's episode, but she found his presence comforting. He busied himself arranging and rearranging some of their recent purchases and watched her from the corner of his eye.

Finally, she said brusquely, "I need some Western-style clothes."

"What fun!" exclaimed Louis, but their eyes met in silent acknowledgment that "fun" was not the point.

The next day he accompanied her to a boutique where she bought two French suits and four silk cocktail dresses, with matching pumps and sandals. Then he took her to a dressmaker who specialized in making up Thai silks and Indian saris for Americans to take home to their wives. She still, said Louis, made formal ball gowns for the few remaining Frenchwomen in

Saigon and for a growing number of Vietnamese. To her surprise, Nina recognized her mother's old *couturière*, who had trained with Schiaparelli, as Ariane had been prone to mention casually and frequently.

The old woman watched critically as her assistant knelt at Nina's feet to adjust the band of beading that coiled around the hem of a silk chiffon dress. The girl held a row of pins clamped tight between her lips as her employer had done ten years before, while Louis perched on the edge of a cutting table, ankles crossed, assessing Nina.

When the assistant sat back on her heels, Nina turned on the spot, watching the flow of the fabric and feeling the odd angle of high-heeled shoes after the flat slippers she had worn with her *ao dais*. Familiarity and strangeness warred in her; she had worn clothes like these for just over half of her life. Now, after the first strangeness, they felt no more or less comfortable than those she had worn since. She wished she felt more strongly one way or the other.

"Stunning!" said Louis.

The previous day's episode had made clear to Nina something she had thought about before only in a vague way—Americans were interested in, and excited by, the exotic, but they did not trust it. They trusted Diem because he had been educated in Europe and was a Catholic. They had trusted Ho in his days as a French radical and ally against the Japanese; they distrusted him when he became an Asian Communist. There was considerable wisdom in Clay's suggestion that she should learn English; if she were to deal with the growing number of Americans in the marketplace, she must become a "safe" exotic.

As the *vendeuse* in another shop exclaimed over the merits of a stiffened silk bra which gave just the right silhouette to the jackets of her new suits, Nina had a further, uncomfortable, thought. How am I different, she asked herself, from the whores who are bleaching their hair and having operations on their eyes? They are only making themselves familiar to their new clientele, as I am doing.

In late summer, three and a half months after their last meeting, Thu sent a message that he wished them to meet immediately. He suggested a rendezvous in the same village east of Saigon, across the river in an area thought to be controlled by the VC, where they had met before.

Nina set out from the east bank of the river in a battered 2 CV driven by Eight Hand Horse. She wore a white collarless blouse, black trousers, and sandals. Eight Hand Horse wore an old singlet, cut-off shorts, and his cut-out tennis shoes. Tiny Albert followed separately on a motor scooter.

They were stopped on the outskirts of the hamlet by a man she recognized from her first taxi ride to the Rung Sat. He demanded politely that Eight Hand Horse stay where he was, with the car. Madame would be escorted safely to the colonel, and back again. This request was reinforced by an unsubtle pat on the bulge in his pocket.

"It's all right, Old Uncle," said Nina. "I don't fear the colonel."

She followed the Binh Xuyen along a track that led off at right angles from the road. As they rounded a clump of banana trees she looked back and saw Tiny Albert trotting after them.

She shook her head to herself in disbelief. If this is how we behave when we're friends, she said to herself, how will it be when we are enemies? It seemed likely that they would become enemies, sooner or later.

Thu was waiting in a ruined pagoda on a small rise behind the settlement, in the curving embrace of an irrigation channel. He, too, was dressed as a peasant, in black tunic and loose trousers.

Nina's breathing became shallow and quick. She had meant to be entirely businesslike with him, but her knees began to tremble and betrayed her.

He took her hand and led her past the stone lions and crumbling drum posts, under the tower for the smoke of offerings, into the main rear chamber of the ruined temple. A large woven bamboo mat was spread on the floor. A bottle of Scotch and two crystal glasses stood incongruously on the mat amid the crumbling plaster carvings and faded stucco dragons.

"Well, Cousin Thu," she said, "what is this urgent business of yours?"

"Sit down and show more manners," he said. He folded his legs under him and sank onto the mat. His eyes gleamed under the forelock.

She kicked off her sandals and sat down facing him from a safe distance. He pointed at the bottle of Scotch. "Pour two glasses."

She hesitated, wondering if the time had come to take a stand. Then a mixture of discretion and amusement led her to obey. She handed him his glass, then sat back again. "Is it polite yet to inquire what your business with me is?"

He treated her to a long, slow, but cheerful stare. He seemed

397

excited, and younger than he had appeared that night in the Rung Sat.

"Our joint enterprise needs the injection of more energy," he said. "It was drained when your father left and Kim died. Much bad energy remained. The White Tiger of the West must couple with the Azure Dragon of the East...." He looked at her mischievously to see if she followed his mythology. The male Tiger and the female Dragon.

"The dragon and the tiger...?" She looked at him under lowered lids, but put down her glass because her hand had begun to shake. She kept her voice light. "Is that the only reason you asked me to risk coming all this way?"

"Is there a better reason for risking danger than to enhance harmony and generate life energy?" He crossed his arms to strip his tunic off over his head. Then he unfastened his trouser top. His torso was finely muscled but crisscrossed with lines of scars, like his arms.

When she sat unmoving, the expression in his eyes began to harden. "Perhaps you laugh at such ideas, with your French teaching...."

"No," she said quietly, with a dry mouth. "No. I don't laugh at all...." She rose to her knees and moved across the mat to lie beside him.

He became as serious and intent as a child opening a gift. He carefully unbuttoned her blouse and undid her trousers. Then one by one he pulled the pins from her hair. Once again she felt the incongruity between the bloodthirsty public bully and this strange, temporarily gentle, private sexual man. Such observations stopped when he began to explore the surface of her skin, inch by inch, by touch, taste, and smell. She lay quietly, sometimes making a small intake of breath or exclamation. She set aside her caution and anger and fear and allowed her entire being to concentrate on following the slow, delightful progress of his fingers and mouth.

One clear thought flickered into life: This was not a gangster accustomed to using and discarding women in the same way that he consumed food and drink. She felt from his absorption that the experience was not usual for him either. Not one of the women who had waited on them, on either of her visits to the Rung Sat, had suggested by so much as a flickering of an eyelid that Nina was an unwelcome rival. She shook the thought out of her head without wanting to consider what it might mean.

He had reached the meeting of her legs. She opened her thighs to give him free access. His fingers stroked lightly, spreading fire, and tugged at the dark hair. Then he sat up and kicked off his own trousers.

"Now you make love to me," he said.

He lay full length on the mat and watched her with serious eyes. She had never thought of men as being beautiful before. Andrew had been handsome, but Thu was beautiful. She ran her fingers over the fine lines of his ribs and along the curved muscle from his hipbones to his groin. She circled his slim ankles and stroked his elegant toes. He was like a carving, hard and spare, and like an old carving he was chipped and damaged.

The old bullet wound in his leg, which had dyed the leg of his trousers red when she had seen him on the canal bank after the fighting, had left a white-tented gouge in the top of his thigh. Ropes of scars twisted around his chest.

She leaned forward and gently kissed one of the scars. He twisted from under her lips.

"Don't!" The cold fury in his voice shocked her like a blow. "They are vile scars, from vile acts. They need neither pity nor honoring."

"Where did you get them?"

"Con Son." Poulo Condore. The Devil's Island.

He rolled onto his side and stared out into the tower room of the temple. She felt his mind's departure and laid her hand on the smoothness of his shoulder tip.

"I'm sorry I made you think of such things right now." She was terrified that he would stand up and dress, and that she would have to return to Saigon still carrying the uneasy warmth that his mouth and fingers had stirred up in her belly.

He did not answer, but lay staring at nothing.

She bit the skin on the side of his hip, not too hard but sharply enough. "Come back, Cousin. I can't follow you into the past."

"Bring me back," he said. He rolled flat again and found her eyes. His own were wide and dark and distant. "If you can."

Meeting his challenge suddenly seemed the most important task of her life. With absorption as great as his own had been, she began her own exploitations. Slowly and carefully, she reeled him in. Not pushing too fast, nor rushing. She advanced and retreated, as he had just taught her how. She advanced farther and paused.

He had closed his eyes and begun to breathe in deep sighs through his open mouth. She brushed his belly with her hair, then trailed her fingers around his scrotum. When her hand closed on his penis, his hands suddenly reached for her hips and pulled her onto him.

All at once they were bucking and twisting. Her loose hair

swung and snapped with their motion. He pulled her down and they rolled on the mat. Over and over. She felt his weight pushing into her, shaping her flesh. Then she was in the air once more, twisting and flying.

"Mon dieu!" she cried. She shook her head from side to side till her hair was like a whirling blade. "Ahh, *mon dieu!"*

In the stillness that followed, she stared down at him with wide, astonished eyes. *"Mon dieu,"* she whispered again.

He opened his eyes and looked back at her with what seemed almost like fear.

He closed them again and cupped his hands over her knees. She knelt on his warm hips, feeling the moment of total peace, even as it was already passing.

Still without opening his eyes, he said, "Those scars brought me my northern friends on Con Son. They are a small price to pay."

She waited, considering possible ways further onto the delicate ground.

"And they are why I hate the French as much as your father does."

She slid sideways off the damp distraction of his groin. The peace was finished.

Thu opened his eyes and gave her a mock glare. "So one half of you must be very careful with me."

"All of me is very careful." She gave him a grin to match his glare. Then her breath caught and the effort of pretense was still too much, too soon. "But not careful enough, I'm afraid," she said quietly.

He dropped the mock glare as well and lay with his head turned toward her. "The dragon and the tiger, eh? It's good energy. Very good." His voice was as quiet as her own. His hand fastened tight on her knee again.

On the ride back, Nina imagined that Eight Hand Horse was self-conscious and uncomfortable with her. She had no doubt that Tiny Albert had reported in detail. At least, in the old man's eyes, Thu should be an improvement on her father's chauffeur. She wondered if she would ever again be able to make love without a committee in discreet attendance.

Thu sent for her again three weeks later, to the same place. As she had half expected, this meeting was unsatisfactory. Thu was jovial and bullying as if to prove to her and to himself that their closeness of the time before had been an accidental and temporary aberration. He made love to her and insisted on her pleasure, but she felt he was demanding it in submission to his powers. When she left him she was feeling physically eased but mentally unsettled.

Back in the car, she asked Eight Hand Horse, "Do you know his family?"

"He has none," said the old man. "His father was killed by the French when he was three."

He created squawking panic among three foraging hens who had been picking at a pile of dung in the road. "His mother was killed four years later." He added nothing further.

She almost wished she hadn't asked. She did not want to understand Thu. She didn't want to excuse him and grow fond of him. It was bad enough to ache at the elegant line of his arm as it lay across his forehead, or to become breathless when he reached out for her. Somehow, she was going to have to make a clear-sighted decision when their truce ended, as she was sure it must. He was stealing from her. She was hiding important dealings from him; as long as he had to remain in the Rung Sat, cut off from the city and its river of whispers, she could probably keep her secret from him. But she did not know what other secret alliances he might have formed besides that with the Vietcong, or whether he had a buried trump card that changes in the government might shuffle to the top.

In the meantime, she had the small advantage his eyes still betrayed. Even his behavior that day was testimony to her strength—that he had worked so hard to disprove it. She would hope, a little, that he might back off from another confrontation at the next harvest. She prayed that he would let his feelings for her triumph over his instincts for business. She also knew the real odds against that happening.

She closed her eyes and leaned her head against the seat. She already wanted him again. She wanted to relive the mating of the tiger and the dragon that had so frightened both of them. She wanted to put right the discord of this last meeting, by holding his warmth between her thighs again.

"Am I strong enough?" she asked under her breath.

37

In October of that year, the National Assembly voted to extend by one year Premier Diem's right to rule by decree. Students at the universities in Hue and Saigon began to join their voices to those of the Buddhists, who had long been protesting Diem's suppression of all groups who were opposed to the Catholic hierarchy of the government.

Rumors persisted of the farmers' resistance to being relocated in the fortified villages, now known as "New Life Hamlets." Nina became increasingly concerned about Eighty-eight Transport, which was still on contract to the government project. She asked Eight Hand Horse to drive her south into the delta to see for herself. They spent the day on the site of one nearly completed hamlet, located, on American advice, in the center of a large flat valley.

Over rice, at noon, one farmer who had been conscripted to work on the hamlet explained his objections. "It's a bad place," he said. "The energy is dead in such a spot. See . . . ?" He pointed to a new canal. "They made us dig that. It's too straight; it will merely carry away any good fortune that might accidentally wander this way."

She offered him a cigarette.

"Furthermore," he added, "the VC will know that anyone in this village is under protection of the government. We will be singled out for punishment by the guerrillas."

"Old Uncle," she said to Eight Hand Horse as they bumped back along the sandy track from the hamlet toward the highway, "this venture is ill-fated."

He nodded vigorously. He had heard Diem and the Americans compared to the French and their conscripted road gangs, and slave labor on rubber plantations. "It doesn't take a *tay phap* to see it!"

She looked out the window at a burned hut subsiding back into a lump of vegetable matter and mud beside the road. "Advise me. I don't think it's wise to share in this ill fortune."

"Do you want me to be open?"

"What is the use of false information?" she reminded him.

"OK," he said. "You survive. You are making money. People can see that. But there are problems." He hesitated delicately. "Your cousin Thu . . ."

Nina's face burned but she met his eyes in the mirror. "I can see the danger there. I am not in love with a crocodile. Not so much that I am blind. But I can't yet see how to deal with that particular danger."

"Then," said Eight Hand Horse, "it is wise to eliminate as many other dangers as possible."

She nodded. "I hear what you tell me. I think so too."

When she returned to Saigon, she went over the Eighty-eight

Transport contract to check the get-out clauses. There was no way to break the contract without financial loss. So she contacted Clinton Clay about finding a buyer for Eighty-eight Transport who would not be concerned with whether or not it was involved with an ill-fated venture.

It would be interesting to see whether the sale was seen as a crack in her strength, or whether future events would confirm it as further proof of her hot line to Fortune.

In the middle of all this, Titi asked to see her. Nina was curious. The Phoenix Tower had been doing well and Nina had stayed out of the woman's way.

They met in Titi's office. The shutters on the large window looking out over the walled garden were open to admit the faint stirring of breezes. A late season monsoon rain had just passed and everything in the garden gleamed and dripped in the afternoon sunlight. Titi wore custom-tailored Western clothes which fitted neatly around her irregular back and tiny frame. Her hair had been professionally coiffed, and her fingernails were longer than ever, immaculate and unchipped in scarlet enamel. Her elevated status had not changed her instincts to acquire; along one wall were stacked boxed bottles of scent, a pile of cotton net singlets, five cases of Jack Daniel's bourbon, twelve cartons of Lucky Strikes, and one pair of new combat boots. Blue velvet watch cases were stacked on top of the small freestanding safe.

"How's business?" asked Nina, amused.

"Number one!" said Titi happily. "And the hotel too!"

Nina's smile widened. "And your heart?"

Titi winked and placed one red talon alongside her tiny nose. "Something's cooking . . . which brings us to something I wished to discuss with you. I also have a new chef." She pushed an electric bell by the door.

In a few moments the door opened and a uniformed waiter entered with a tray.

Titi waved him out and lifted the metal covers over the dishes herself with a dramatic flourish. "For you to try! My new idea." She produced a bound and printed menu. "See. I made a special menu of Vietnamese treats, to introduce to my American guests. Here . . ." She pointed with a red talon. ". . . I explain what is in everything and how delectable it is."

Nina nibbled and approved. When she had tried everything, Titi offered her a cigarette from a Thai niello-ware silver box.

"No, thank you."

"How about this instead?" Titi took a box of rosewood and

403

brass from a table drawer and hooked out a hand-rolled cigarette with her nails.

"I don't smoke at all," said Nina.

Titi flicked a huge Zippo lighter with the side of her thumb and interwove lighter, talons, and cigarette to achieve ignition. Tendrils of smoke escaped from her nostrils like the breath of a miniature dragon

Nina sniffed. "What's that?"

Titi glanced mischievously under her long lashes. "*You* should know!"

"Titi!" Nina leaned forward in alarm. "You're not chasing the dragon?"

"Now and again," said Titi. "Among friends." She raised her plucked eyebrows slightly at Nina's seriousness.

"You don't?" she asked Nina in disbelief.

"It never crossed my mind," replied Nina. After that first experiment, she had never even seen what Hong produced. Since then she had left quality control to him. Jouvet and couriers handled the rest. She merely looked after the numbers. Her *ma thuy* vanished onto the military bases, via Clay, as if into outer space.

"Actually, I wanted to talk to you about that as well, if you don't mind my presumption," said Titi. She studied Nina as if quickly revising a prepared appeal. "Sometimes my friends want a little for themselves. But I only have what I can find by chance. I was wondering if you could recommend someone who could help my friends...."

"Why do you think I can help?" asked Nina calmly. Saigon's river of whispers was terrifying in the speed with which it carried news.

Titi swept a thick eyelash through another broad wink. "You are a very powerful lady now. A number one boss."

"Hardly," said Nina. She wondered where the leak had started.

"As you say," said Titi, polite but unconvinced. Then she laughed and tossed aside her assumed discretion. She leaned forward. "Pssss! Pssss! Pssss!" she whispered to Nina. "From ear to ear. Don't be modest. It's good news. Better than buying from the Chiu Chao!"

Denial seemed pointless. And she remembered Titi's free handouts of scavaged food and cheerful loans of cash.

"OK. I'll give you a name. But listen, Little Sister, it's nothing to do with me. And I can't protect you if you accidentally step on someone's toes. I don't even know what toes you should avoid. So this is just for your very close friends, OK?''

Titi looked at her skeptically. "Sure. Sure. I understand. Thank you. Thank you very much. It's just for my friends. Don't worry.''

Nina gave her Jouvet's name. It was a breach in security, but the damage seemed to have been done already.

"Speak to him in a month or two.''

"You are my best friend. My sister! I am so much in your debt,'' crowed Titi. She insisted Nina take home two large bottles of White Shoulders toilet water as a token of her respect and gratitude.

Titi's request troubled Nina. So did Thu's silence which followed their last meeting. It troubled her because she wanted to feel his fingers again on her skin, and the weight of his body. It also troubled her because she guessed that the silence might be a sign of his intentions toward the next stock of morphine base. She looked forward with uneasiness to the Year of the Cat, which should be a time to lick one's wounds and rest from battle.

In spite of her uneasiness, the year began well, yet again. Just after Tet 1963 she sold Eighty-eight Transport for an excellent price to a consortium of Americans based in Bangkok who were building airstrips in South Vietnam.

When the poppy harvest began, she could only wait to see what Thu would do. By the end of March she was richer than she had been before, but she also knew that Thu had no intention of backing off. The discrepancy was even greater than it had been the previous year. For two nights she didn't sleep.

In the early morning hours of the second sleepless night she realized where she could turn for help with Thu—her father. Thu owed the father respect which he could withhold from the daughter. Her father could mediate and help restore the balance. And she was ready to show him what she had done, and become, for him. She had a right to demand contact now, and to insist on the help of Eight Hand Horse, who she was certain had always known where her father was. With that decided she fell asleep for seven hours.

The next afternoon, her head cleared by untroubled sleep, she noticed what had escaped her before. Some of the missing base appeared to have vanished between Heron and one of her brokers. Not within Heron itself, like Thu's thieving. Fifteen kilos—too much to overlook. Someone had noticed what Thu was doing and decided to emulate him. As others would do unless she restored order and chastised the wrongdoer. Disorder was contagious unless cured.

There were two possible villains: the broker, or the courier who delivered the base to him. She started with the courier. Eight Hand Horse brought him to her in a deserted office in one of Heron's warehouses.

Nina expected an inconclusive interview which would leave her in a dilemma. Instead, faced with what he thought to be her supernatural powers of knowledge, the man crumbled immediately. He dropped to the office floor and begged for mercy.

"Get out," she ordered. She was white around the mouth with rage, not only at what he had done but at the terrible choice he was forcing on her. She delayed for twenty-four hours, hoping that an answer would present itself. Finally, she summoned Eight Hand Horse.

"Old Uncle, what can I do? I'm afraid this man is only the first." Her eyes passed unseeing over the bright cave of a café. She had asked the old man to drive around the streets of the city. The noise and bustle distracted her and somehow helped to clear her mind. They could also be sure of privacy in the car, away from the ears of the household servants.

He drew together the curling vines of his eyebrows. He had known the matter was serious as soon as she had climbed into the front beside him. "With respect, mademoiselle, you have only one choice—he must be severely punished, for the world to take note and learn."

"How severely?"

"The world has already forgotten M. Martell, it would seem."

She felt a jolt in her chest. Then she felt sick, remembering. She wanted to be anywhere except in this car, with this problem. Carbone was right; she did not have the stomach for the business.

"There must be another way!" she cried. "If I understand you."

"It is a matter of degree," he said carefully, watching her. "Fifteen kilos' worth of degree. The money value is less important than the degree of the challenge."

She closed her eyes and pressed the bridge of her nose with her finger as if her head ached. "I do understand you," she said. "But there must be different ways of dealing with the man."

After a moment, he replied stiffly. "The results will also be different. For you and for your father."

"I can't agree!" she said fiercely, still remembering the night

406

she had waited for the news of Andrew's death. "I won't agree!"

Eight Hand Horse pulled over to the curb without her instruction and parked the car. His hands shook as he turned off the ignition. "I'm sorry, mademoiselle. I can no longer drive while we speak of this. It is too great a matter. I might kill someone."

He was too upset to see the irony of what he had just said, but Nina nearly veered into hysterical laughter. Then the old man's obvious fear sobered her. He turned in his seat and dropped any remaining pretense of servility.

"After Kim was killed, you shaped the signs to show your strength and that of the family. Though I disagreed at first, you have even improved on the signs through your prosperity from your new American dealings. Fortune's visible favor has been shielding you. Until the last harvest."

He looked away. The subject of Thu made him very uncomfortable. He did not understand the relationship between that pirate and his young mistress. There was a silence in the car.

Then he continued, reluctantly. "This man is not the first. Thu challenged you and went unpunished. He is now seen, by those who know of it, as stronger than you. Some believe that the Heavens are shifting their favor to him, away from you, as they once left Kim. Two cobras have already struck. It is only a matter of time before the rest see that it is safe to follow."

Nina closed her eyes again as if blindness could also make her deaf to what he was trying to make her hear.

Eight Hand Horse swallowed audibly. "If you are killed, your father will have nothing left except an old man and a few errand boys. With no errands to run."

She recoiled. "How can you use my father against me like that?"

"Because I love him as much as you do," he replied with dignity. "And because I spoke the truth."

"I know, Old Uncle. I'm sorry. It's just that..."

"Mademoiselle," he said hoarsely, "I love you as I do your father. You cannot hurt me with words—only if you allow yourself to come to harm by refusing to face the truth and to act on it."

She shuddered. "If only it were enough to face the truth, without acting."

"You need do nothing," the old man said gently. "Leave it to me. Please say nothing more." Though he sounded reassuring, his expression was disturbed as he turned the key in the ignition.

The courier was found in the Arroyo Chinois the following

day. Nina gave his job to Thin Pig, the assiduous waiter from the Hotel Continental.

And that was that. Except that one night, suddenly, she said to Louis Wu, "I thought you said that once you have decided that it's worthwhile surviving, the rest becomes simple!"

They were walking around an empty exhibition, in a private house, of paintings by a new young Paris-educated Vietnamese painter who had just discovered Expressionism. Louis paused in front of the drawings which were studies for a large painting of the abattoir. He mimed a shiver of distaste, then looked at her.

"I said 'simple.' I didn't say 'easy.'"

On the way home, their car was caught up in a demonstration outside the National Assembly Hall. They sat trapped in a stream of shouting students, Buddhist monks and nuns, carrying banners that read, "Diem—Assassin of Buddhists" and "Murderer of Buddhist Rights."

Somewhere on the far side of the crowd they heard the snapping of gunshots. The car rocked in the surge of the crowd. A grenade exploded close by.

"I can't...!" said Nina.

"What did you say?" Louis leaned closer to her solicitously. His face was pale.

She shook her head as if to deny her words. Then she burst out, "It's all going to start again in Saigon. Like before!"

The bared teeth and pink gums of a furious, shouting face appeared at her side window. Fists drummed on the roof of the car. Then the crowd was running. The gunshots snapped closer.

"No!" Nina breathed. "No!" She began to tremble.

Louis's driver reversed hard. The car bumped over something in the street, but the crowd closed in front of the car and hid what it had been. The car went backward, faster and faster, until the driver reversed suddenly around a corner, did a U-turn, and accelerated down Nguyen Hue Boulevard.

Hypnotized with horror, Nina stared out the rear window, back toward the mist of smoke and the growing sound of police sirens. Then the buildings of the boulevard masked the snap of the gunshots.

The following day, Chinchook called at the house to tell her that soldiers had put barbed wire around all Saigon's Buddhist pagodas, and that several of the main Buddhist leaders had been arrested during the demonstration the day before. Others had been badly beaten, and arrests continued.

* * *

She felt the same waiting hush in Saigon as she had felt before the fighting in 1955, between the government and the Binh Xuyen—the same feverish unease, the mass inability to concentrate.

The hush ended eleven days later, when a Buddhist monk set fire to himself in protest in a main street in Saigon, surrounded by seven hundred other monks, while the traffic lights above him blinked from red to green and back again. More demonstrations were rumoured in Dalat, Nha Trang, Quon Nhon, and Hue. In the weeks that followed came more suicides of more Buddhist monks and nuns.

In August, Diem again declared martial law, thereby confirming to the people of Saigon the truth of any rumors of trouble they might have doubted before. He also imposed censorship of newspapers and radio stations, and a curfew between 9 P.M. and 5 A.M.

Nina could hear the distant explosions of grenades and tear gas bombs as government soldiers and police attacked the Xa Loi Pagoda, the main Buddhist headquarters in Saigon. She also heard Diem state in his broadcast, when he declared martial law, that government goodwill toward the Buddhists had been undermined by a few "political speculators" who had deliberately created confusion and discord.

She wished she knew what the Americans thought of the Premier's actions, but did not wish to contact Khan, who was her only reliable source of inside information. The other person who could have told her was the red-haired American, but she had so far managed to avoid him.

By the end of the month, Diem had closed Saigon University and all secondary schools in an effort to halt student unrest. Nina began to consider making arrangements to leave Saigon. Then, suddenly, curfew and martial law were lifted. It was said that the government and Buddhist leaders were in negotiation. The city settled back on its heels and sighed with cautious relief.

A week later she was returning from a dinner party in subdued celebration of the possibility of peace. Her host had been a Chinese merchant banker who might or might not be bankrolling one of her main Hong Kong buyers of morphine base. The party of eleven had met behind the closed shutters of a Chinese restaurant in Cholon, and left at intervals, in separate cars, fur coats hidden behind darkened glass, still cautious in spite of the relaxation of martial law and the lifting of the curfew.

As usual, Eight Hand Horse left the car in the driveway while he escorted her to the front door. He rang the bell. While he waited for the *mama-san* or the number two boy, something moved in the shadows of the sandbags. Eight Hand Horse produced a gun from his baggy garments with astonishing speed.

"Call off your watchdog, School Dragon." Thu stepped forward into the moonlight. Instead of his uniform or the peasant clothes, he was wearing an open-necked shirt and slacks. The headband was gone; strands of the dark forelock were stippled with light but his eyes were in shadow.

Eight Hand Horse lowered both gun and head with equally grudging inclination. Thu's head turned to measure the degree of respect being offered.

Nina ran her tongue over her dry lips and clasped her hands to steady them. She was shocked to see him here in the center of the city. Something had changed to let him take the risk.

"Aren't you going to offer me food and drink after my long, dangerous journey?" he chided.

"Of course, Cousin. Come in."

They stood in silence while the bolts grated open on the inside of the door. Eight Hand Horse went off to give hell to the night watchman who had let Thu take them by surprise.

Nina ordered a tray of coffee and cognac from the *mama-san*, then led Thu into the drawing room on the ground floor. She did not open the shutters.

"What a surprise!"

He ignored her and prowled the room, touching Louis's paintings, sculptures, and antique Chinese pots.

"You live like a *française*," he said abruptly. "I didn't know."

"And what's the maximum sentence for that?"

He tossed away her attempted frivolity with an impatient jerk of his head like a bullock, and completed his circuit of the room. He stopped in front of her and touched her as if she were the final object of his observation

"Come to bed, School Dragon. I must go away for a while. I want to sleep with you first."

And "sleep," she learned, was precisely what he meant.

The puzzled *mama-san* returned to an empty drawing room, searched the veranda, the dining room, listened at Nina's door, and drank the coffee herself.

Thu was both taciturn and intense. He curled his lip at the big bed, now back in the original bedroom, but said nothing. He stripped and arranged his clothes precisely on a chair, then climbed into the bed as if it were his own territory.

Nina followed more slowly, resisting his sense of haste, but not quite challenging him either.

Their lovemaking was quick but not unpleasing. He entered her as if resuming an act interrupted only a few moments before. Shocked once again by the intensity of her own response, she wrapped her legs around his waist and reflected that she was safe only when she was this close to him. Then he turned her face toward him and she stopped reflecting altogether.

"Where are you going?" she asked, when it was over and she lay in the taut circle of his left arm.

He shook his head.

"Will you see my father?" she persisted.

"I may, I may not. Now shut up, School Dragon. I want to sleep." He closed his eyes, held her tight to him with arms like iron, and slept.

She lay awake for a long time, constricted but not wanting to struggle free. There was something both frightening and desperate in his grip.

She woke up once in the night to find his arm bent around her neck as if he were about to break it. She turned toward him to relieve the pressure, and eventually slept again. When she woke in the morning he had gone to wherever he was going. His unexplained departure added another unease to those already troubling her. Warning of specific trouble, however, came from an unexpected quarter, one that she had nearly forgotten.

38

My dearest Nina,

It is more than time to renew our acquaintance. Would you be kind enough to join an old man for breakfast once more, in the same place, same time, on Wednesday the 3rd.

Until then,
Uncle Emile

She distrusted the tone of his note; it was too jovial. It had the same edge as his remarks about cruelty to children. Perhaps he wanted to make his takeover bid—it was long overdue.

When she entered the terrace of the Continental, Thin Pig was on duty and armed under his white jacket. Eight Hand Horse, also armed, was squatting in the garden smoking a cheroot like a resting gardener, in a direct line with Carbone's table.

She slipped into the chair that a waiter was holding for her. Carbone did not rise.

She laid both hands open on the table, palms upward. "Here I am, Uncle Emile."

"I don't usually make the same mistake twice," he said.

Nina turned her hands palm down on the white linen. Her stomach contracted and its edges went cold. Their long truce was over.

"I also know how dangerous it is to look like a fool."

Carbone paused while the waiter poured her a cup of *café au lait*. As the man left, Carbone leaned forward.

"I made the mistake of liking you. As I liked your father once. You told me you were different and I wanted to believe you. But I was a foolish old man. You are as much a liar and cheat as your father ever was."

Nina did not try to smile. "What is your accusation?"

Carbone's face reddened. "Stop selling number four heroin through *my* Saigon brokers. Is that specific enough?"

"It's specific enough," she said gently. "But I can't stop what I'm not doing."

He shook his head helplessly. "Nina . . . you don't understand how serious I am. Bluff won't work. Not now. Please don't rely on what I said about my preferences for peaceable dealings. My stomach will always be stronger than yours."

"I don't know what evidence you think you have. . . ." Her bat ears quivered to learn where his information had come from. She must have put too much trust in Jouvet's greed.

"I'm surprised that you are so stupid . . . to lie to me when your close associates are peddling *ma thuy* and barely bothering to hide their source."

She gaped at him in genuine astonishment. "*My* associates *peddling*. . . . What was that about *your* brokers, then?"

"Once upon a time," he said tiredly, "I might have believed that look of shocked innocence."

He cut a Cuban cigar with a tiny guillotine, licked it, and lighted it. The hovering waiter replaced his offered, unused lighter in his uniform pocket. Carbone's hands were shaking.

"Are you talking about street pushers?" She wanted to be very clear what he was saying.

"Not on the street, but direct to users." He stared at her through a cloud of aromatic smoke. "Interfering with our imports. What do you think you're doing? I'm amazed some of your Cholon rivals haven't taught you a lesson by now! So I'm going to."

It was odd that he had not mentioned the Americans, only the general term *users*. The leak was Jouvet or below.

"Would you believe me if I say that, if such a thing is happening, it is without my knowledge or approval?"

"No."

She shrugged in helpless acceptance. "You don't know what bad news you've just given me."

His fury mounted at what he saw as her continued deception.

"Get out of the market! I have no time or patience left."

Thin Pig turned his head toward the sound of Carbone's rising voice. Eight Hand Horse saw that small movement and strolled casually toward the hotel, tossing his cheroot into a flowerbed. But Nina was already standing and walking away from the table.

It was nearly midnight when Thin Pig knocked on the door of the big house. He bowed to Nina, then tucked back behind his ear the long strand of hair that had fallen forward.

"You'd better come to the hospital pretty quick, mademoiselle."

"Who is it?" asked Nina, surprised that he should have come for her rather than the family of whoever was involved.

"It's Mr. Louis," said the young man.

Nina moved fast, gathering up her bag, calling Eight Hand Horse.

"I come with you, back to the hospital," said Thin Pig.

When she didn't argue, he climbed into the front seat beside Eight Hand Horse and directed him to the Binh Danh Hospital on the northwest edge of the city.

Louis had been sedated.

"Who did this?" Nina was shaking with rage.

Wu shook his head fractionally and closed his eyes. "Don't know. Some young thugs. Probably didn't like my style. You know how it is."

He sighed and fell into a drugged sleep.

Black stitching held his right cheek together over the bone. His silver hair had been cut short and was matted with disinfectant around a shaved patch and more stitching on a scalp wound. All the fingers of his right hand were in splints.

"Mr. Louis is lying." Eight Hand Horse tapped his foot impatiently as a late-night convoy of U.S. Army supply trucks

413

carrying jerrycans of fuel crossed their path. "Thin Pig told me while I was waiting for you."

"And . . . ?"

"He knows who beat him; it was two of Carbone's Binh Xuyen. Mr. Louis wants to protect you . . . to stop a vendetta. But he is wrong. Ignorance is weakness. He would not yet realize that Carbone will make sure everyone knows who did it."

He accelerated under the tailgate of the last truck.

So this was Carbone's warning! Its victim was totally unexpected. Once again Nina had the sensation of standing on a boat that was falling down, down the side of a wave.

"Is Thu back yet, from wherever he went?" This was one request for help he might enjoy—dealing with renegade Binh Xuyen, who served the French.

"I will learn," said Eight Hand Horse.

The next morning she returned to the hospital.

Louis was awake, and unsedated enough to be in considerable pain. Without makeup, his skin was yellow as an onion.

"Thank you for trying to protect me," she said. "But I know the truth. Now, for both our sakes, you must tell me why."

"Why what?" Louis's eyes were distant, watching his pain.

"Why it was you."

He turned his head away, then winced from the movement.

"Louis, are you dealing in *ma thuy?*"

"Yes," he said.

"Why?" she cried.

He turned carefully back to her. "What a funny question to come from you."

"It's my business, my father's business." She brushed away his protest. "But you . . . !"

"I told you I was a dealer once. For your father. Leopard's spots, and all that. I like to give people what they need . . . I told you that." He closed his eyes. "I'm sorry if I have made trouble for you. Sorrier than I will ever be able to express."

"How do you know the stuff is mine?"

"That little woman of yours, at the hotel. She's very useful for getting things. She just happened to let slip something a few months ago. She assumed that we were friends, I suppose."

"Still are, as far as I am concerned," said Nina.

Louis smiled slightly, but did not open his eyes.

"Is there anything I can bring you . . . anything you need?" she asked as she stood up to leave him in peace.

"I don't suppose they'd let me have my opium pipe," he said. "It would do wonders for the pain."

From the hospital she went to the Phoenix Tower.

"Can we talk privately?" she asked Titi.

"You don't want breakfast?" Early as it was, Titi had been to the hairdresser or else had an expert maid.

Nina shook her head curtly. Titi hesitated, assessing, then unlocked the old ground-floor office which she was turning into a hotel shop. The chambermaid continued to push a dirty wet cloth around the hallway floor with a stick.

"You must have coffee, at least," Titi insisted. She ordered it on the new intercom.

"Was that name I gave you several months ago helpful for you?" asked Nina without ceremony.

"Very, very good. Number one," replied Titi cheerfully. "My friends are very grateful."

"Too many friends, I think," said Nina.

Titi waited for her to continue, as Nina had waited for Carbone.

"They gossip too much. There are whispers that I am a pusher... selling directly to users...."

"How terrible!" said Titi.

Nina knew the frustration Carbone must have felt. She held Titi's sympathetic gaze.

"It's not half as terrible as what I'm afraid might happen to anyone the rumormongers believe to be my dealers.... Who are operating outside the system of agreed franchises... underselling the Chinese and French imports."

"How foolish of them," said Titi.

"Not foolish. Insane!"

"Of course."

"I thought you should know," said Nina. She didn't know what more she could say in the face of bland ignorance. "Never mind the coffee. Thank you."

She returned home to learn from Eight Hand Horse that Thu was still absent from the Rung Sat and his second-in-command did not know, or would not say, when he would be back.

"What do you wish me to do?" asked Eight Hand Horse, as if he had not relieved her of the last decision like this.

Carbone might be right in the end about her stomach, but he underestimated her loyalty to her friends. This decision was easier than others she had faced.

"Exactly like Louis," she said. "No more, no less. You can

415

have as much money and men as it will take. Can you handle it?''

"I'm not completely past it yet," said the old man.

Emile Carbone allowed his wife to pull his ear to draw the skin beneath it taut. Angelica was the only person he would allow near him with the old-fashioned straight razor he preferred for his heavy grizzled beard. He watched her intent face and heavy, black-dressed figure in the mirror. He had deliberately, at the age of twenty-six, married someone on whom he knew it would always be safe to turn his back. He had taken Angelica from the slums of Ajaccio and made her into a wealthy matron. She owed him everything; even better, she was still at a loss in Indochina after all these years so far from home. She would always need him. When he was younger, Carbone had sometimes found this dependency constricting, even though he had created it. Now, at seventy-one, he was grateful to have one area of settled simplicity in his life.

As his wife wiped the razor on a crisp white towel, Carbone patted her broad thigh, and she smiled.

"Capu...?"

The head of Paul Buonaparte appeared through the door of a large dressing room. Buonaparte was the second half of Carbone's double right-hand man, not the legal adviser and counselor, but his ear to the ground and his arranger.

"What is it?"

"A delivery van dropped Bébé and Kif outside the gate sometime this morning. Early. The gardener found them trussed like pigs when he opened up to sweep. I took the liberty of calling Doc to come and stitch them up. They're in the poolhouse."

"Shit!" Carbone grabbed the towel from Angelica and wiped the half beard of shaving cream from his face. He left his face buried for a second too long in the towel, then threw the linen across the room.

"Oh shit!... Did they say anything?"

Buonaparte was regretful. "It was dark... they think there were a lot of them...."

"They would say that!" said Carbone. "What should they say, that they were overpowered by a one-armed midget?"

He put on his jacket. "How bad?" He pulled away from Angelica's busy tidying fingers.

"Right cheeks slashed... both of them. And the fingers of their right hand... a few other bruises but nothing to speak of."

Carbone bared his teeth. "Fucking beautiful! So poetic! So . . . just right. Does she think this is a game?"

Angelica looked at him anxiously. His face had become red again, as it had done recently when he was upset. Her recurring nightmare was that his heart would stop suddenly or a vein would explode in his head and he would leave her to cope alone in this place, with no family to go back to in Ajaccio.

Carbone stepped into his shoes and jammed down his heels. She had returned the problem to him. Now it would be his decision where to take things next. He was tired of making such decisions. He was old and rich; he wanted to enjoy what he had worked for so long and hard. He had survived the defeat and withdrawal of his fellow French. He deserved a little peace, but no one would allow it—not this little bitch of a *métisse*, nor, he had learned the day before, the American Mafia.

"Take me to see these idiots," he ordered Buonaparte. "Their story had better be good!"

39

While Nina waited for Carbone's next move and he considered what it should be, the swelling boil of political discontent finally burst.

Nina woke on November 1, 1963, thinking that a plane had just tried to blow her roof away in its slipstream. In the silence after the plane passed she heard the clanking of alien machinery in the streets. And gunfire and grenades. Then another plane. It *is* happening again, she said to herself. Then it stopped.

She learned later that rebel army units had blocked off the road to Tan Son Nhut and captured Nhu's special forces at their airport headquarters. Vietnamese marines had invaded the city and captured the Ministry of the Interior, with its communications systems, the Defense Ministry, the naval headquarters, and the police compound. The planes she heard had attacked the Presidential Palace.

The following day it was rumored that Diem and his brother Nhu were dead. Killed while trying to escape through a tunnel from the Palace. Then came an official statement that they had committed suicide in the back of an army truck.

Two days later, newspapers and radio stations announced the formation of a new government, the Military Revolutionary Council. Headed by the victorious military leaders, it contained many faces familiar from the preceding government. Two days after that the Council of Sages was formed, a body of advisory civilians. The following day the United States recognized the new government, which promptly enlisted American support not only against the Vietcong but also in the battle to wipe out Diem's legacy of corruption, persecution, and patronage.

Nina was told, with the rest of the Saigonese, that censorship was ended and they were now free to come and go with the lifting of the curfew. It all had a familiar ring.

When Louis was released from hospital he invited her to a party in honor of one of the new ministers. She could not help remembering the last "peace" party she had attended, and how short-lived the respite had been.

"Are you sure you should be doing this?" she asked him.

His new haircut, a short bristle to match the hair growing back around the scalp wound, gave him a curiously American military air.

"A guarded celebration," he said. "But everyone needs a party... needs something. I know I do."

"I don't feel like celebrating anything."

"Then come and watch journalists getting drunk in honor of the end of press censorship."

"What a revolting thought!"

"Then why not come let me spoil you a little?" He watched her anxiously. "I'm holding it down at the villa. Country air would do you good."

He's terrified that I'll refuse, thought Nina. He needs to know that I'm not angry with him. But it had been Titi, not Louis.

"How can I resist your spoiling?" she said, though she felt weary and distracted. A party right now, with Thu and Carbone on her mind, was the last thing she wanted.

On the night of the party, Eight Hand Horse had a night off. He offered to change his schedule, but Nina said she was perfectly happy with Snow Man and Tiny Albert. Snow Man could drive.

They crossed the Y Bridge and headed south into the Mekong delta. Louis had recently established his own personal strategic hamlet in the flat cultivated area between the Song Sirap River and the river port of My Tho on the Fleuve Antérieur, not far from the sand dunes of Pointe de Mirador. The *paddi* fields were polished sheets of pink and steel gray in the rays of the setting sun. Nina leaned back against the leather upholstery and told herself to try to enjoy the evening, for Louis's sake if not her own. She was wearing one of the silk cocktail dresses she had bought after being stopped by the American patrol. It was a dark jade green which made her skin creamy, but she felt uncomfortable and constrained by the bits of fabric, elastic, and nylon needed to shore up the well-dressed European female. She longed to change into an *ao dai*. She felt hot and unattractive in this dress, though a mirror would have disagreed.

Once across the Song Sirap, most of the villages they saw dotted on either side of the road were deserted. A little farther south Nina saw the stockaded walls of a fortified hamlet catching the low sun rays across the higgledy-piggledy seaming of *paddi* dikes.

She checked that the square of red paper Louis had given her was still taped to the inside of the windshield. The paper would tell night patrols of guerrillas that their toll had already been paid. It was not something she wanted to question Louis about too closely. She studied the occasional patches of scrub and *herbe à paillotte* for signs of guerrillas but saw no one except a few peasants bent double in the *paddi* lakes and the occasional small boy resting on the neck of a buffalo headed back to the animal stockades. It was still early evening; the guerrillas ruled at night.

The Citroën jolted and creaked over a crude patch in the road where a mine had been detonated. Nearby, the stripped and burned-out carcass of an American half-track lolled against a broken dike wall. Then Snow Man turned the car down a sandy track toward the coast, which was overlaid with heavy bamboo mats to improve traction. As they approached the stand of casuarinas and bamboo that masked the low walls of the villa, the track became surfaced with expanded metal mesh, like a landing strip.

Inside the heavy steel gates Snow Man parked the Citroën in a school of Cadillacs, Buicks and Studebakers, Peugeots and Citroëns, near two Datsuns as majestic as ocean liners. The drivers had already gathered into a noisy card game under a Coleman lantern at the side of the villa. A gasoline-powered generator thumped from somewhere behind the stuccoed building. Under the thumping, and the laughter and curses of the drivers, Nina heard a low sound like a swarm of bees, or the tumbling of shale on a beach; it was the sound of human voices. She nearly got back into the car and ordered Snow Man to drive her back to Saigon. Then she remembered the anxiety in Louis's eyes and braced herself to enter the villa.

Louis flung himself at her in a mixture of relief and the ecstasy that always overwhelmed him when a party was in full, successful swing.

"Thank God you came! I was beginning to wonder if you had decided to stay home and sulk, after all." He beamed and kissed her cheeks.

He wore a white smoking jacket and full warpaint. Somehow the gray bristle on his head had become chic and spare, a comment on the military style rather than a scrappy imitation. The black stitches in his scalp and cheek had been removed.

"They've all come," he whispered to her in delight. "I was afraid that for some reason they might not."

She thought she understood his relief that so many owners of so many big, expensive cars had thought it worth risking the journey down, in spite of the constant guerrilla activity in the area.

"Find me a drink, dear Louis, then don't worry about me. I'll get into the mood eventually. You go play with your other guests." She blew a kiss at his left ear.

Over his shoulder she surveyed the guests in the front courtyard of the villa. Several fur coats, in spite of the heat. Cheongsams and diamonds. The tall white back of an American naval uniform bent down toward an invisible miniature Vietnamese. Beyond the dress uniform was the red-haired American, talking to a blond woman in a sari. Nina took the champagne Louis offered and headed quickly on through the main salon of the house into the garden at the rear.

In spite of the guerrillas there were people everywhere, even on the little island in the middle of the artificial pond, under the single willow that trailed its locks in the water. Louis had been right—everyone needed a party. They leaned on the railings of the arched bridge and propped themselves against the fretwork pergola. Swags of colored electric bulbs looped from tree to tree tinged their faces and clothes pink, green, and yellow in the glowing dusk. She pushed through the crush of cocktail gowns, saris, *ao dais*, high-collared Mao jackets, and tuxedos to the railing of the terrace behind the villa. The voices became the chatter of insects. The clinking of glasses deafened her. She sighed and leaned the tops of her thighs against the parapet to feel the cool stone though the silk of her dress. She should never have come, even to save Louis's feelings. She felt cut off from the normal world and the pleasant minor concerns of that insect chatter.

"She's gone all Garbo on me tonight." She heard Louis's

voice behind her, among the other insects. He touched her elbow.

"My dear," he said in French, "this dreadful man wouldn't leave me alone until I promised to introduce him. . . ."

When Nina turned, Louis faltered at the unexpected shock in her eyes. Then he continued smoothly, "I'd like to present M. Will John Haines."

The red-haired American held out his hand. Nina hesitated, then allowed him to take her own.

"You're a hard lady to track down," he said. His hand had swallowed hers, as it had swallowed the coffee cups. It was warm and firm and did not let go, but continued to hold on lightly and companionably.

"The Yankee *bao chi* who is making a book!" she said. "You have bad taste in associates." She withdrew her hand. She should have known he'd turn up again.

Well, well, thought Louis curiously. He turned to Haines. "I hope she doesn't mean me!"

"I think she means a rat named Dao," said Haines in his accented but accurate French. He smiled at Nina, the blue eyes a long way above her own. "Don't be mad at Louis. He has no idea that I've been accosting you in restaurants."

Louis looked at Nina's flush, then at Haines's smile. His eyes lost their look of concern and his silver eyebrows quivered in anticipatory delight. "Please, *please,* one of you tell me what . . ."

He glanced past Haines at a silver-haired Vietnamese in a smoking jacket who was hovering impatiently at the door of the house.

"Merde! I knew his sense of timing was dreadful, from his speeches in the National Assembly. I'll be back. . . ." He rushed away with both hands extended in welcome to the newcomer.

Nina and Haines stood for a moment in silence.

"How much did you give Dao in the café?" asked Nina. "I can't help wondering."

"Less than you're worth."

"How could you possibly know?" she retorted.

"Come off it," he said in English.

"Sorry?" The phrase was unfamiliar in spite of her English practice.

"You understood me," he said cheerfully, in French again.

There was another pause. Nina felt too tired to flirt, if he was flirting. She was too distracted to decide how serious he was. He behaved as if he knew her. She wanted nothing less than for him to know her.

421

She looked around for rescue by Louis, or anyone else.

"If you need something to say," prompted Haines, "you could ask about my book."

He was unsettling her again, as he had from their first meeting. She did not let herself look at his hands this time. The dirty urchin who had considered soliciting him was dead, part of a past life.

"What is your book about?" she asked sweetly, with exaggerated politeness.

"I'm investigating the effect of the undeclared war on the lives of ordinary Vietnamese. Louis was introduced to me as an interesting character. He's helping me with others. That's the only reason I wanted to meet you . . . as a case history, I swear it. Scout's honor." He placed his right hand on his heart.

His face was rough-boned and smooth-skinned. Its whiteness was sunburned across the ridges of his brow and nose. His hair was the color of almond shells, and baby-fine. Nina lifted her head to meet his blue eyes. Their wicked gleam disproved his apparent earnestness.

" 'Ordinary Vietnamese' . . ." she repeated. "I suppose I shouldn't mind being called ordinary." She saw his eyes flicker. She had him there. He was afraid he might really have given offense. Americans were so vulnerable that way. "But God help you if Louis heard you call *him* ordinary! He'd have his bouncers chuck you out to the guerrillas for target practice."

"Would he mind being an 'interesting character' instead, do you think?" The gleam was still there. He wasn't worried. He was making fun of her. She was too weary to deal with it. She decided to counterattack.

"Your research is letting you down," she said. "You see, ordinary or not, I'm not really Vietnamese."

High above hers, his face looked deeply concerned. She didn't trust that look.

"Nor is Louis, for that matter. We're both 'mongrel dinks,' to use a current American phrase. I'm half French; Louis is half Chinese. If you look around, and can tell the difference between different kinds of dink, you'll notice quite a few Japanese. To say nothing of the recent spate of toddlers with blue eyes. Colonial souvenirs . . ."

Why don't I stop talking like this? she asked herself. What is it about him that makes me so gauche? He seemed both fascinated and abstracted as he watched her face. She had forgotten that he was a writer. Now she could practically see the phrases taking shape in his head.

"How was that for raw material?" she asked.

He shook his head. "Don't . . . please."

She couldn't stop herself. "Let me guess." She fixed her eyes on the perfunctory terra-cotta dragon on the corner of the roof above her head. "Beneath her calm, inscrutable Oriental exterior lay the vulnerability of a woman trapped between two worlds. Am I close?"

"You got the gist," he said pleasantly, "but I write better than that."

Her chin tilted up on her slim neck and the jade-green silk quivered with the force of her deep breath. He had no right to be so rude. Or to watch her with such proprietary interest.

"I know Americans are supposed to be ill-mannered, but you are insufferable!" She placed her still-full champagne glass on the stone parapet, careful not to spill it.

"Are you mad about being vulnerable? Or being a lousy writer?"

He was most definitely laughing at her and tonight she was in no mood to be laughed at. "Please excuse me, monsieur. I'm sure you can easily find other case histories to practice your research technique on." She turned away in a swirl of silk.

"There's no technique," he said. "I just keep my mouth shut and listen."

She stopped. She had set herself up for that one. She half turned back. He was not looking amused now.

"Or you just watch," she said. "The way you journalists stand around and watch men killing each other. Take a few notes. Maybe jostle each other out of the way for a better view of a burning monk."

"Calm down," he said quietly. "I don't want to fight with you. I don't want that at all. Come sit down somewhere with me and actually drink a glass of champagne. I promise not to pry into why you want to fight with me. I won't even talk, if you would rather be quiet."

"*Va te foutre!*" she said. It was childish, but she enjoyed saying it. She didn't dare say it to Carbone or Thu, but she could say it to Haines. She fled into the crowd in the garden under the swags of colored lights. The insect chatter deafened her. Her stomach hurt and her head ached.

There was a white flash in the night sky, brighter than the colored bulbs beyond Louis's garden wall. And an explosion. The explosion was followed by six seconds of absolute silence in the garden, except for one unconcerned cricket sounding its tiny ratchet. Into the silence came the crackle of distant rifle fire. Nina started to shake.

Someone near her let out his breath. Then someone else began to breathe again. For another three seconds she could hear nothing but breathing around her. Then a voice spoke, and another. Quietly testing the silence. Like skaters testing new ice. Like stepping out in her dream onto the surface of the water. She tried to stop the shaking of her legs and hands, but they remained fiercely independent of her brain. She had to leave.

The fabric of the night, torn by the explosion, knitted together again. The volume of conversation slowly rose once more. Nina plunged back toward the house. There was still the long dangerous drive back, little square of paper notwithstanding. She craned her head above the crowd to spot Louis to say farewell.

Then there was a polite spattering of applause. She looked to the terrace and saw the new Minister, his hands raised in acknowledgment. She couldn't leave now without causing offense. Someone rapped on a bottle with a spoon; into the silence that followed chattered more distant gunshots. Nina shut her eyes and bit hard on her lower lip.

An American in a smoking jacket stepped beside the Minister and raised his glass. "I'd like to propose a toast to your hew leaders," he said. "To the Military Revolutionary Council!" He drank, imitated by a choreography of upraised arms in the garden. The Minister accepted the toast on behalf of the Council and the new Premier.

Nina opened her eyes and spotted Haines as he raised his glass at the end of a long arm. He turned to look at her across the heads between them and she looked away. Why wouldn't he leave her alone?

"And to the Council of Sages!" cried a Vietnamese in a tunic. "A new voice for democracy! Who will carry out revolutionary policy in conformity with the people's aspirations!"

The guests drank again, and again there was applause, more scattered and jagged this time.

Haines began to move toward her in the crowd. She pushed and bumped past other guests in a panic to escape. He caught her when she had to stop again because the Minister had begun to make a speech. They stood side by side, watching the Minister. Nina tried again to control her knees and caught occasional references to the "fight against communism" and being "on the side of the West in this fight" and "the best weapons are democracy and liberty." She clapped perfunctorily when the man finished, and felt Haines's hand on her elbow as she turned to flee again.

"What *do* you want from me?" she said desperately.

"Why do you want to fight with *me*?" he asked.

To her horror, she heard herself say, "Because you once bought me a sandwich and don't find it worth remembering!"

She tore her elbow out of his grasp and fled to a corner where the terrace parapet met the house, in the shadow of a carved stone urn. She leaned her forehead against the stucco wall and tried to draw her breath past the band around her chest. That wasn't what she had meant to say to him at all. She had just regained the appearance of composure when Louis alighted beside her.

"Can I persuade you to stay the night? We can have a quiet drink when the mob has left. Only four are staying, though the fireworks may persuade a few more."

"No, thank you. I was just coming to find you to say good night. I'm sorry, Louis. I've been an appalling guest. I won't stay and make things worse."

"Quel dommage," said Louis. "But of course, you must do as you think best."

He shifted his thin buttocks on the parapet balustrade. The scar on his left cheek changed from pink to green. "In that case—I'm almost afraid to ask, in view of your earlier response to the man—but M. Haines is looking for a lift back into Saigon. The couple he came down with has decided to stay for breakfast. And daylight."

She couldn't see his eyes in the shadows. He sounded straightforward enough. She gave a single bark of a laugh. There was no escape from the man; he was her punishment.

Louis said curiously, "I didn't know you two had some kind of history. . . ."

"We don't," said Nina curtly. "I'll give him a lift, if he really needs it. I'd hate to land you with yet another guest for breakfast. Particularly one who's the size of two." She stood up. "He'll have to leave now if he wants to come with me."

"I'll have someone call your driver." Louis smiled to himself as he went back into the house. He had never seen her so on edge about a man before. He rather enjoyed the spectacle.

In the car she decided that she would survive the journey only through scrupulous, impersonal politeness. She would not let herself be drawn into a conversation about anything.

"I'm very grateful," said Haines, as they began bumping along the mesh pathway toward the main road.

"Not at all," said Nina. "It's my pleasure."

Haines smiled and looked out the window into the darkness. Part of her discomfort with him, she decided, was that he crowded her. Americans crowded everyone. He was too big, at least six feet two. The backseat fell down away from her toward his weight. His large hands rested loosely on long thighs as he looked out of the window. The back of his head was square. His almond-colored hair was thick and curled slightly above his collar. When he turned to face her in the reflected light inside the car, she saw that his nose was flat-bridged and straight, like the nose of a *kouros* Louis had once pointed out among a collection of early Greek sculpture of heroes and soldiers.

"Would you mind?" He touched his black tie.

She shook her head. The side of his neck was dark from the sun, against the white of his collar. She heard the rasping of silk against silk and a tiny snap. Then his hands rolled the tie. The seat heaved as he leaned sideways to put it in his pocket.

In the neck of his open shirt, fine gold wires curled up to catch tiny sparks of light. She looked away and studied the dark *paddi* fields. There was a red glow in the distance, behind them, where the explosion had been.

"I think I'd rather fight with you," said Haines.

"I beg your pardon!" she said blankly, but her heart pounded.

"It was more fun than this."

Once again she was speechless. How dare he speak to her like that! As if he had known her all his life. Didn't he know who she was?

He started to say something else, then glanced at Tiny Albert and Snow Man in the front and shook his head as if to say "later." She made the mistake of meeting his eyes and found that she had been trapped into intimacy.

He picked up her clenched fist from her lap, opened her fingers, and kissed the palm. Then he replaced her hand on her lap with a quick pat. She didn't know which made her more furious, the kiss or the condescending pat. The man was impossible. If he weren't a friend of Louis's she would be tempted to throw him out of the car and let him walk back to Saigon, unless a nice "ordinary" VC got him first. Screw politeness! She curled tightly into her corner, against the door, to endure the rest of the ride back to Saigon.

In the silence, Haines stared contentedly out through his open window at the shadows of the landscape, apparently unaware of her fury.

She could feel the skin of her hands, burning at every point that he had touched. The band around her chest was tighter even than it had been at Louis's; she sucked at the thick, viscous night air. She glared sideways at his hands, lying so relaxed and unconcerned on his thighs.

"Jesus!" he said. They rocked back across the mine crater, past the burned-out half-track.

"You know," he said, "I had managed to forget about all that for a few minutes, just now."

She had trouble concentrating on his words.

Snow Man suddenly stopped the car and got out to examine the road ahead of them in the light of the headlights. In silence, Nina and Haines watched him squat down and brush the dusty surface with his hands. The headlights turned his white hair into a halo of brightness around the concentration of his face. Then he got back into the car and drove on without comment.

When they reached the edge of the city the streets still seethed with people pushing, calling, staring, selling, and buying. Selling food, drink, haircuts, dental repairs, shoeshines, cheap jewelry, dope, themselves. Groups of soldiers prowled, buying, brown, white, and black, but rarely any two colors together.

Snow Man leaned on his horn and squeezed past two Cadillacs that were disgorging two men in business suits and two women in fur capes and silk *ao dais* at the door of an expensive club. On the other side of the car, nearest to Nina, a pair of women was waiting for customers. The neon sign above their heads blinked on and off; their faces showed green, like Louis's guests, then disappeared above the white ghosts of their blouses.

The car crept forward, abreast of a line of red neon arrows that chased themselves endlessly across a balcony and dived toward an open doorway. Beside the doorway, the crude outline of a woman flashed violent pink and then electric blue.

Snow Man wedged the car into a cross-tide of human bodies, motorbikes, and taxis. A girl in a long hairpiece and blue jeans, with tight, twitching buttocks, tilted past on high heels. She bent down to peer into the car; her eyes registered Haines, then Nina, and she moved on. A Vietnamese soldier leaned from a jeep that was also stuck in the traffic and lifted the girl on board.

Nina could not look at Haines. All she could think was how close she had come with him to being one of these women.

"Where can I drop you off?" Her throat was dry in the heat.

427

"You go wherever you need to go," he said. "I'll make my own way from there!"

She told Snow Man, in Vietnamese, to take her home.

When the car stopped in the driveway, Snow Man opened her door and Tiny Albert leaped out to open Haines's.

Haines followed her onto the veranda. "May I come in?" he asked.

Nina felt panic again. She didn't know how to get rid of him. No matter what she said, he still seemed to be there, unperturbed.

"You don't take no for an answer, do you?" Saying it made her feel better, a little more in control.

"Not when it's important," he replied.

Her pulse was pounding in her ears as the *mama-san* opened the heavy door. She led Haines into the drawing room and dismissed the *mama-san* after checking that the ice bucket was full.

Haines stood in the center of the carpet, beneath the slow-moving ceiling fan, while she crossed the room to open the shutters onto the veranda. One lock of the almond-colored hair stirred in the gentle down draft.

Nina fastened the shutter back, then crossed toward the lacquered Chinese chest with which Louis had replaced the bamboo-faced cocktail cabinet.

"What will you have to drink?" she asked.

Haines held open his arms. She stared in disbelief.

"Come here," he said. "You need comforting."

Years of self-protection made her start to protest angrily, but she couldn't speak. An unexplained rush of tears threatened her. The word *comforting* had made a dangerous lump in her throat. When she continued to stare at him, struggling for words, he crossed and gently closed around her, like a mountain or a wave. Her mind tumbled into free-fall. Thu vanished, Carbone vanished. Haines seemed to engulf her; she wasn't sure she liked it. It felt strange. Both Andrew and Thu were slight men. But she couldn't will herself to move a single centimeter away from him. He wrapped her in a blanket of warmth, like a child.

They stood like that for some time, Haines rocking very slightly on his feet. She kept her head down, buried in the safe darkness of his chest. She almost dreaded his next move, which would change the moment. He loosened his embrace by one notch. She lifted her eyes as far as his mouth.

He was watching her. When she raised her head, he raised it farther and bent to place his mouth on hers. It was warm and firm and as inescapable as its owner. She didn't want to escape.

Desire struck her like a blow, unforeseen. All the emotions that had been tearing at her twisted themselves together and were transformed into hunger. He had seen what she had not allowed herself to see. She had not realized her need until he had offered to fill it.

She was afraid to look at him now, because she knew her eyes would expose this newly acknowledged need and her newborn weakness. She wanted to cry. She wanted him to make love to her. She didn't know what she wanted. She was suddenly terrified that he might change his mind and leave her alone again, without comfort.

"Are you OK?" he asked quietly.

She nodded. "I think so." She was shocked to hear herself speak so openly.

"Am I rushing you?"

She shook her head. She couldn't speak, because his continued concern was going to make her cry in spite of herself.

"Hold on, then, Scarlett." He bent and scooped her up in his arms as if she were a length of silk. "Ever see *Gone with the Wind*?"

Confused by the change of direction, she looked into his blue eyes, which were now only a little above her own. Then she saw that he was inviting her to laugh. He wanted to make her laugh. It would make him happy to see her laugh. She had never laughed with either Andrew or Thu before making love. A warmth spread through her chest and stomach.

He kissed her again, then said, "Oh Lord, I don't know where the stairs are!"

She started to laugh, a rich deep laughter, holding on to his neck and leaning her head helplessly against his shoulder. She knew that what he had said wasn't really that funny, but it didn't matter. What mattered was how good it felt to let laughter shake and warm her limbs and body, to let it loosen her jaw and the skin of her scalp, and to see the pleasure this laughter was giving to him. She clung to him, the soft red-gold silk of his hair against her face, still laughing softly with the relief and pleasure of it all, as he carried her up the gull-wing stairs whistling "Dixie."

Later, safe in her ridiculous bed, she felt foolish for her earlier sensation in the car that he crowded her. In spite of his size, he hovered and balanced without settling heavily upon her. It was she who pulled him down in order to feel every square centimeter of his fair smooth skin against her own. Under his clothing, where the sun couldn't reach, his skin was white, lightly freckled, and smooth as a woman's. His long dry fingers delicately skated and probed, making of her hills and valleys a complete and absorbing geography where he lingered in fascination. She floated with him, happy to go where he would take her.

When he finally entered her, she was undone—she had happily been prepared for less. He seemed to feel the same, though she had done no more in this lovemaking than reveal her own undoing. They fell asleep still locked together. Even in sleep, he held her gently but firmly, as if she were fragile but might try to escape. This reminder of Thu troubled her. She stirred in his arms but could not move away without waking him. She settled her damp back against the sweat on his chest and flat belly, her mouth against the salty taste of his arm. It was like being caught in a monsoon downpour—you struggled for a few moments to stay dry, then stopped fighting and gave in, with a certain satisfaction.

She woke in the night to find him moving slowly inside her, stayed in a half dream until the gentle release, and slept again. At six, she woke, terrified that he would not be there. At 7:30 she woke again to find him propped on an elbow looking at her.

"You're lovely," he said. "I can't tell you how lovely you are!"

She turned her head away to hide the tears. It was ridiculous how everything he said made her want to cry. With all the advances men had made to her in her life, no one except Louis Wu had ever told her she was lovely.

"I'm afraid of you," she said. "I can't seem to lie to you." How did I dare say that? she asked herself.

"Me too. Scared of you, I mean." His arm encircled her, one hand warm on her breast. "I feel too comfortable."

She rubbed her head against his shoulder like a foal. They both looked at the pink and cream couple above them in the mirror of the bed's canopy.

"This is terrible," she said, thinking of Thu. "You have no idea."

"Yes I do. I'm married with two kids." He kissed the top of her head.

She felt a sweep of desolation, then it passed. "To hell with all of them," she said. "For now."

She waited for the desolation to sweep back with his reply. "Yes," he said again, and pulled her over on top of him to look into her face. The desolation rolled on toward the horizon and vanished.

* * *

On the principle, to which they both agreed, that life was short and the future uncertain, he stayed with her constantly for the next four days. Nina tried to feel caution with him and fear, but it wasn't possible.

"What's your greatest fault?" she asked him on the second morning, as they ate fruit and drank coffee under the Nina and Will John who were eating fruit and drinking coffee on the ceiling. "I want to get it over with." They spoke French together, with the occasional seasoning of English when Will's French failed him or Nina found the courage to practice what she had learned from books.

"I don't take no for an answer," he offered. He held his empty cup at arm's length and expertly spat a mangosteen pit into it. "Your turn."

Nina paused in her inquiries to spit a pit at the cup, which he moved at the critical moment so that she missed. She laughed, delighted but self-conscious in play; she had forgotten what it was like.

"I didn't ask for your virtues," she resumed, searching for her pit in the rumpled sheets. "What's *wrong* with you?"

He put on the serious face she remembered from Louis's party. "I can't tell jokes . . . or so friends tell me." He thought. "And I steal ballpoint pens."

She turned serious. Though he was joking, she could believe that those were his worst faults. She had never felt such palpable goodness in someone. It terrified her. She didn't know whether his confidence was because of his goodness, or the other way round.

"You're too good for me," she said. "I mean it."

"Crap," he said. "I'm rotten to the core. For example, I bought you a sandwich."

"I've forgiven you already for that," she said, moving to lean against him.

"Please," he said. "Please don't make up a false Will John. I couldn't bear it."

She saw thoughts of elsewhere in his eyes. Then he smiled.

"Take me as I am or leave me beeee . . . !" he suddenly sang. His voice was a rich baritone that she felt through his chest and in her bones.

She pushed away thoughts of saying the same to him. "I still don't know what I have to watch out for."

"If you really want to know, I suffer from the eighth deadly sin—ingratitude."

"Ingratitude!" she laughed. "How terrible!"

He stroked her bare stomach. "You're condescending to me . . . like you were so scared I was doing to you at Louis's party."

"You're right. Sorry." She moved his hand to rest in a friendly fashion on her pubic bush. "Go ahead and put the case for your wickedness. *J'écoute.*"

"OK. If you're interested." He moved his hand gently. "For a start, I had a great childhood—dogs, horses, swimming, boats, all that. I have a lovely wife and two kids in New Canaan. . . . I made football fullback in high school and my English prof at Harvard thought my poems had the flavor of early Robert Lowell. When I graduated I got a job . . . on a newspaper owned by a friend of my father's. I went to Korea as a paratrooper and survived."

"What's wicked in that?" she asked. "That's just luck."

"Hold on . . ." He kissed her. "Checking that you're still there, while you make me go somewhere else."

She couldn't breathe from happiness.

"The wickedness was in how I felt about all that," he continued. His hand forgot her. "For example, I was terrified of the jumps, in Korea, but felt peaceful during the most dangerous time, hanging there on the wind, waiting to be shot at from the ground. I would think, Never mind, you've had more than your fair share of good luck. I'd seen what some other kids had gone through to get to twenty-three. It seemed like my turn to suffer—there was no point in fighting it. And do you know, all that danger was a free gift. No charge. I went back home without even a Purple Heart."

He pulled back so he could see her face. "Isn't that obscene? To think of danger as a free gift?"

"It sounds peculiar," she said, "not obscene."

He remained propped up on his elbow. "Where's the biting edge? I asked myself. When do I start to pay like everyone else?" He searched her eyes for understanding. "It seemed like it had to happen and I wanted to get it over with, like a virgin who wants to be screwed to find out. End the tension. And the ignorance. But I graduated with honors, got a good job, and every goddamn sniper missed. By the time I left Korea I had had a good look at a lot of other people getting screwed and I began to go off the idea, but still felt left out."

She was suddenly frightened for him. "Is that why you're out here? Instead of back in New Canaan? Are you still chasing your bullet?"

He sighed as Thu had done when she had relieved him of the truth about the chemists. "I expect you may be right."

"Then you are wicked! I agree. The Viets would say you are challenging the workings of the Heavens, to have good fortune and wish to change it."

"If it's any consolation," he said, "I want to stay lucky now. Since the night before last. That's why I'm afraid of you. You make me afraid."

He kissed her gently. She fled into the comfort of his arms.

I've arrived, she thought. And it isn't going to be possible to stay.

"Now you know the worst," he said into her hair. "Let's talk about something else."

Will John fascinated Nina. She was fascinated by his soft white freckled skin with its patches of burn. She was fascinated by his improbably long limbs, the blueness of his eyes, and the pale line of lashes around them. She would pull his long curved toes straight and measure them against her own fingers in amazement. She explored the clean, rich-smelling pink and white complexities of his genitals and buttocks. She shut her eyes and ran her fingertips over the skin of his rough-looking face, which was unexpectedly smooth, like silk-upholstered rock. Most of all she was fascinated by his clear assumption of his absolute right to occupy space on the earth, his right to ask for what he wanted, and his polite expectation that it would be given to him. As with herself. Yet he wasn't arrogant in this assumption, but almost apologetic, deprecating the inevitability of his power.

She was also fascinated by his gentleness. It seemed to grow out of his confidence that he wouldn't have to fight for what he wanted, but could reach out quietly and pluck it. She also deduced, correctly, that his gentleness stemmed partly from his size.

"Doesn't it ever cause you problems, being so big?" she asked.

He laughed. "My size is relative; you should have seen the football fullbacks at Yale and Princeton. Or the basketball team! Anyway, it's an advantage to be big . . . if anybody gets aggressive, I just stand up, slowly."

He crouched and rose, by degrees, till he stood naked over her on the bed, imitating King Kong about to attack a skyscraper, as in the film she had once seen with her ayah and Simpoh Flower.

"And it's useful for bullying you titchy little things out here." He pounded his chest and roared.

She laughed, delighted by this silliness but still shy about joining in. She was out of practice.

"That makes you jiggle in the most peculiar places!" she said.

He wasn't at all offended.

She didn't mind what the servants thought. She preferred to have him naked. The chinos and short-sleeved plaid shirt he went home to exchange for his dinner jacket made her laugh, like his Windbreaker. In them, he reminded her of a lion dressed up in children's clothes for a tea party at the zoo. Nakedness showed his full dignity.

He preferred her naked too. He seemed delighted by everything about her—her hair, her breasts, her navel, her legs, her bossiness, and even her occasional awkward shyness. She had never experienced such a feast of frank admiration. The closest she had ever come were Louis's compliments, offered as solace in her moments of need. She drank in Will John's words and caresses. Whenever she could not help wondering what he would think of her if he knew what she really was, she hid her face in the safety of his warm chest and postponed the thought a little longer.

40

Will John broke their idyll first. On the fifth day he came back from the daily press briefing at the JUSPAO building and carried in the outside world instead of casting it off as he always had before.

"I have to go up north for a few days," he said. "To investigate some stories of more attacks on Catholics by Buddhist mobs. It's not official, but I ran into a colleague who's just back from Da Nang and says it's pretty bad up there. I'm sorry."

Nina nodded wordlessly. She had been preparing herself for the end of their impossibly wonderful, insulated time. Her own world, too, was beginning to clamor.

As she watched him crunch away down the drive, she was overwhelmed with terror. She would never see him again. She knew that if she were a sniper, she would never miss that bright square head in a crowd. As the gardener bowed him out of the gate, he turned and waved. She waved back as if for the last time. Then she dressed for the office, to get through his time away somehow.

The first thing she learned when she visited the office in Cong Ly Street was that the new government had suspended the building of all strategic hamlets and would no longer force the peasants to live in them. The news pleased her: she would gain credit for having sold Eighty-eight Transport and thereby disassociating herself. Her hot line to Fortune was confirmed.

Out of general curiosity she sent for Chinchook and asked him to spend the next two weeks organizing his unofficial network to watch military convoys and barracks; she wanted an approximation of the number of members of the U.S. military mission in the Saigon area. She asked him in particular to try to find out how many wounded Americans were in the military hospital.

She dined with Louis, who had moved back to the city from the villa because of the upsurge in guerrilla activity in the delta after the coup. She still had no word from Thu.

Will John was gone for a week. When he returned from Da Nang, she pulled him quickly into the relative safety of the four walls of her house. As a matter of course he moved his razor and toothbrush from his rented room into her bathroom, though he insisted on going back to his own room daily to change his clothes. While she would have preferred to have him with her totally, she needed the cracks of time his absences gave her to shore up the realities of her own real world.

He was with her, however, on the afternoon that Chinchook arrived unexpectedly. When he saw Will John sitting in the drawing room, he was nonplussed. At first Nina thought he had come to report the early results of his investigations for her and was just shy in front of the big American. Then she looked more closely at his face.

"What is it?" she demanded. He was subdued and anxious; she had not seen him like that since their days in the rubble.

She felt a quiver of fear like the first shiver of wind through the leaves of a bamboo before a storm.

"I think Titi is in trouble," he said, sliding his eyes sideways at Will John. "Men at the hotel. I went to eat there, like I sometimes do." He telegraphed urgency to her with his eyes.

"What kind of trouble?"

"Please go now! See her!"

"Little Brother, tell me!"

"I go get Eight Hand Horse!" He ducked from the room.

435

Will John stood up. "I'll come with you."

"No," said Nina fiercely. "You mustn't. I'll be all right." She stared at him wildly, trying to think how to explain. "I'll take some of the servants."

"And me." He was moving toward the door. He was in one of his moments of knowing he would get his way.

"No!" she cried. "You mustn't!" She grabbed his arm, and thought how silly it was even to try to stop him physically.

"If you're going somewhere there's trouble, I'm coming." And he did come.

He did not comment when Tiny Albert and Snow Man joined them in the car, with Eight Hand Horse at the wheel. If he noticed that all three Vietnamese were carrying guns, he did not comment on that either.

Nina was gripped by a sense of double disaster—what could have happened to Titi and what Will John might learn.

The main entrance to the hotel was locked. That was already not good. Nina rang the bell, but no one came. She rang again. Still no one came. There should be a porter on duty twenty-four hours a day.

She left Tiny Albert at the front and went around the corner of the compound wall, down the side alley, to the side gate of the garden behind the hotel. Snow Man and Will John followed. The gate was open, swinging on its hinges. Nina felt a jolt in her chest as an old terror woke. Her mind was suddenly filled with the dark gap of the gateway in the servants' quarters of her childhood home.

The garden around the lotus pool was deserted. The door onto the veranda stood open, like the gate. There was no staff or guests visible anywhere. Nothing had been disturbed on the ground floor. The new shop was locked. Chairs and tables still stood in comfortable, conversational groups in the lounge, on the veranda, and in the card room. The vases were filled with freshly cut flowers. In the kitchen, a pile of bamboo steamers on top of a burning brazier oozed steam from under its crowning lid. A cut melon lay like a pair of translucent bowls on a tabletop, beside the knife.

Nina sprinted up the stairs. The sound of a radio came from behind the closed door of one of the guest rooms. She went into the little room that Titi used as her office, next to her bedroom. At first her eyes tried to misread the little pile of battered flesh and matted hair on the carpet beside the low lacquer table that Titi used as a desk. The green carpet was stained black by fresh blood, which had also flecked the lacquer table and the wall beyond. The ends of Titi's broken bones had pushed through her skin; the side of her head had been caved in by a blow. One small hand stood out with startling clarity against the carpet as a recognizable human part, long red talons spread. Only one nail was broken, Nina noticed in a daze before she was sick.

As her retching subsided, terror gave her the strength to bend and extract a piece of clear wrinkled plastic from the hole that had been Titi's mouth. A small white tooth came with it. Bile rose again in Nina's throat, then she forced herself to smooth the plastic and wipe away the film of blood on it, to be certain that it was what she feared it was. It was a small, empty sachet, printed with a rough picture of a tiger suspended above a globe of the world. The words *Tiger* and *Globe* were written in both English and Chinese characters.

She nearly screamed when Will John knelt beside her; she had forgotten that he was there. He took the plastic bag from her shaking hands.

"It's for number four," he said.

Nina ran her hands over her face, as if washing it, or trying to wipe away the sight that filled her eyes. It was one of her counterfeit bags. She was certain. She couldn't think for a moment what it had been doing in Titi's ruined mouth. She stared at it in Will John's hands; Titi's scarlet lipstick had smeared the tiger's muzzle and part of the globe.

Something cut into her foot. She rocked back onto her feet and saw the litter of shards on the floor. Someone had smashed a large number of the plastic vials often used for street sales of heroin and ground them into the carpet.

Somewhere, far away, a bell rang. Then it rang again.

"Will, would you . . . ?" But Snow Man had already gone.

"Nina, what can I do to help?" He was regarding her with steady eyes, any shock or horror hidden by his concern for her.

That concern nearly undid her. She nearly broke down into sobs and told him everything. Then she shook her head violently to herself.

"It looks as if she might have been dealing," he said.

She looked away from his eyes and flung herself toward the window, toward fresh air, away from the little heap on the carpet. But the air was hot and thick as syrup.

"She always had a commercial instinct," Nina heard herself say in a strangely precise way. She gave two small, harsh barks which were part laughter, part hysteria.

437

Snow Man reappeared. "It's one of the guests, come back. What do you wish me to tell him?"

Nina didn't reply but stared at the battered heap of flesh which had been Titi.

After a moment, Will John said, "Tell him he'll have to go somewhere else . . . there's been an accident. And the hotel's short-staffed." His eyes remained on Nina. "Tell him he can get his money back later for anything he paid in advance."

The safe was still locked, its top still stacked with velvet jeweler's boxes. There was still one crate of Jack Daniel's by the wall. Titi had not been attacked by thieves.

"But I know that!" she said aloud. Though he didn't show it, Will John was frightened by the desperation in her eyes.

"It's happened," she said to him, from a vast distance, as if he weren't there. "I can stop waiting. . . ."

Then she buried her face in her hands and sobbed. "It's too much for me," she said. She let Will John hold her but there was no longer safety in his arms. Only much later was she calm enough to realize that he had never suggested calling the police.

She spent the next few days having the hotel cleaned and arranging for Titi's funeral, which the *tay phap* said must wait for ten days. Once all traces of the murder had been cleared she also arranged to sell the hotel, to an elderly but wealthy Chinese widow whom Louis knew. She had Titi's spirit, which had been disturbed by the murder, exorcised, and she called in a second *tay phap* to resite the kitchen in a more propitious relationship to the rest of the building. She built a spirit screen inside the garden and hung three mirrors at crucial points to deflect any evil spirits who slipped past the other defenses. As a result, she received a good price from the widow, and the widow had no trouble finding new staff. Most of the long-term American guests remained anyway, not being concerned with the malign workings of Fortune. They did not have her nightmares, nor become sick when they found an unexpected morsel of white cartilage in a dish of chicken.

She was running on water again; any minute, she felt she would fall through. She was filled with the certainty of disaster. Her attempt to shape the signs was curling back on her, like a snake. Disorder was spreading through her life and she was losing any power to control it. And suddenly, when walking the streets of Saigon, she began to see signs of *ma thuy*—groups of young men, still almost children, huddled around a matchbox cover, inhaling the smoke. She saw that the figures huddled along closed shop fronts were shaking with need and anticipation, not hunger or exhaustion. She saw that the eyes of the White Devils in uniform were not looking for women, but for one special man or woman, with supplies. She didn't know if these things had been there before Titi was killed, but whatever the reason, she had not seen them before, or had not let herself see them. She had fooled herself that they were nothing to do with her. She merely manufactured a product that disappeared though checkpoints, behind chain-link fences, out of the reach of her own people. Now, even if that were still true, she saw that she was feeding a lake that seeped like *paddi* water through the strongest dikes.

My father couldn't have wanted this for me, or for his people. That thought followed her into sleep and through her days.

I fought to save what I imagined was his reality for him. Now I fear that my reality is not what his used to be, she admitted to herself. I was blinded by my need for his acknowledgment. Now I see that my reality is no longer his.

She suffered most when she was with Will John. She knew how he would hate her if he knew the truth. Each time they touched each other, she felt it was for the last time. The better their lovemaking, the more she was reminded that it must end unhappily.

He said nothing, though he felt the change in her. He just stroked her and played the clown, perhaps a little more than he had before. She noticed, however, that from time to time he took a sleeping pill at night.

Then in January came another coup d'état. The Military Revolutionary Council was bloodlessly overthrown. The former junta leaders were arrested on a charge of conspiring with the French against the interests of South Vietnam. Major-General Khanh, the commander of the Army's First Corps, appointed himself the new Premier. A week later, the former chairman of the previous junta, General Minh, was released from prison and appointed an adviser to the new regime. The United States pledged over $31 million worth of surplus U.S. commodities as aid to the new regime. The following night, Will John proposed to Nina.

"I want to get you out of here," he said. "The country's in a mess and it's getting worse. I just heard that U.S. helicopters have been ordered to fire first. The number of VC in South Vietnam keeps increasing...."

"Why do you think that I should want to leave?" she asked. "It *is* my country."

"Is it?" She heard the darkness in his voice that she had noticed several times in the last few days. "Is it still the country you grew up in?"

"Almost exactly the same," she said. "One of my earliest memories is the sound of the Allies bombing Tan Son Nhut."

"I see what you mean...but do you really know what's going on now?"

"Do you?"

"I'm a journalist. It's my job to dig out the worst."

"I think we're having a fight," she said.

"Because you're scared. And I'm making you face it."

She stared at him as she had the first night they had met at Louis's party, speechless with rage and confusion. She wanted to hit him for daring to say such a thing to her, who had braved so many things and survived.

"I'm not scared," she said. "You just feel guilty that you Americans are making the mess worse."

He glared back for a minute. "Right! OK! But that doesn't make you less scared. I don't know what of, exactly, but you are. And I can't bear to see it."

"Are you going to rescue me? Is that it? Mess up that lovely life back home—to relieve your American guilt? I will tell you something—self-sacrifice is a luxury. Only possible if you have too much of everything. And you have it all. Like you said....Too much faith. Too much confidence. Too much future. I don't have any of that. You'd better stick to your own kind! All those good people, like you. Not some nasty little half-breed whom you like to screw but will screw you up in the end." She burst into tears. "Who takes pills at night to sleep? You or me?"

"Hey, where did all that come from?" He tried to embrace her, but she pulled away "I wasn't criticizing when I said you were scared. I would be, in your place."

"What do you know?" She whirled to look at him. "What do you know about me, really? And whether or not I should be afraid?"

"I know you're as crooked as a picket fence, like everyone else out here. But I still think you're wonderful. And I still want to marry you and take you back to the States with me. Though maybe not to New Canaan, Connecticut," he added dryly.

"Do you believe anything is possible?" she asked.

"Yes." His reply was matter-of-fact. "On a personal level. I don't think I could get the U.S. out of Vietnam right now. But on a personal level, yes, I do think that."

"I used to think so too," she said. She stopped to listen to what she had just said. "Can you say something to change what I know now?" she asked. "Can you make my world like yours?" She held out her hands as if pleading.

He pulled her close "I can change your world, but not with words. If you will let me."

"It's not possible," she said into his chest. "Not possible. My world and I are the same thing. That's one thing I have learned. I can't unbecome what I am. Nor can you."

Two nights later, she woke suddenly at 4 A.M. She stared straight up into the darkness for a few moments, then turned to study Will John's sleeping profile. In her head she heard him say again his first words after they discovered Titi's body.

"It's for number four." The matter-of-fact certainty to his voice kept her awake until dawn. That and his failure to suggest calling the police.

She didn't find the courage to tackle him until the following evening. "Just what kind of journalist are you?"

He looked up from the tissue paper pages of the *International Herald Tribune,* which he read faithfully. "I don't have my own byline, if that's what you mean." He gave the question his earnest concentration. "I suppose you could call me an investigative journalist. Like I said at Louis's party, I'm investigating the effects of the hostilities. And those include a lot of things. Not just personal tragedies, but other things that get thrown up, like weapons deals, drugs, the politics of insurrection."

It was a reasonable explanation for his knowledge.

"Why do you ask?"

Nina avoided his question. "Do you know a lot about these things?"

"I make a point of learning whatever seems relevant," he replied.

She went into the little dressing room to her desk, and brought back the copy of a page from her father's two books that she had found in the safe at Heron.

"Does any of this mean anything to you?" She watched his face closely.

"It's a list of arms," he said. "'Type 59' is a Chinese copy of the Russian Makarov pistol. PPSh 1941 is an old Russian submachine gun. There's some American stuff here too—USC M1, that's a carbine, goes back to the early days of the last war. It doesn't say which modification, but they're in use all over the world in one form or another. I used one in Korea. WPK is a German make. . . ." He looked at her curiously. "Where did you get this? Are you going into the business?"

His eyes were laughing, but she felt a stillness in him.

"I'd hardly show it to an investigative journalist if that were the case." She might not be going into business, but her father clearly had done so. Now she knew.

She decided that near-truth was safest. "It turned up in some old family papers," she said. "I had a feeling it wasn't just a stocktaking list for a sweets factory. It was driving me crazy, not knowing what it meant. Thank you."

She felt him waiting in friendly neutrality for her to say more, guessing that she half wanted to unburden herself. She took the paper back to her desk in the dressing room and put it away. It would be easy to tell him everything. Where she had found the list, and why. Where the money had come from to buy what was on the list. That she was suddenly afraid that her father might be supplying arms to the North, and that she had been helping him, unwittingly, for the last four years.

She went into the washroom to splash water on her face and neck. It would be all right to tell him. He would enfold her in his calm acceptance. She would tell him about Thu's betrayal, Carbone, and the reasons behind Titi's death. And that she had to respond, and why. In telling him, she would see it all more clearly herself and understand what she should do to hold matters together from the top.

She buried her face in a soft towel. What she missed in her life was someone to talk to frankly and openly, as she had done many years before to Simpoh Flower and then to Annette. Never since. Nearly with Louis, sometimes, but he always veered away from real exposures; she felt she would be placing an unendurable burden on him. She needed someone who cared enough for her both to accept her confidences and not to misuse them.

She had already said things to Will John that made her giddy with terror and delight at her own daring. No matter what she said to him, he seemed to take it as natural and undisturbing. The idea of going back into the other room and telling him the whole truth about her life made her light-headed with relief.

Then she threw the towel viciously into the corner of the white-tiled cubicle. He cared for her, more than any man she had ever known, she was sure of it. It was a self-evident truth. But he was also an American. How could she tell him about the opium? Or her sales to Clinton Clay? If she were to see rejection in his eyes, created by her own words, she would want to die.

442

For a moment, standing in the harsh white light of the bulb that bounced off the white tiles, she felt again as she had long ago in Andrew's little room. She was too small to contain within herself everything life was sending. Like her mother, she would explode, split into the different pieces of herself. Float apart in space.

41

Life did not ease up in its malevolent bounty. First, Chinchook brought her the whisper going around, about an American big cheese who had arrived in Saigon two days ago. He was said to be throwing a lot of money around, making a show, and talking to people in Nina's line of business. There was a rumor that he had even met some Chiu Chao leaders in Cholon.

In early August, the new government again declared martial law and a curfew, banned public meetings, and imposed internal press censorship. In late August, the government resigned. By late October, a former mayor of Saigon named Tranh van Huong had replaced Khanh as Premier, heading a government of civilians.

Then Thin Pig asked Nina to meet him in Me Linh Park, by the river, near the bottom of Tu Do Street. She saw him across the pool, bandylegged and alert as a little terrier. He dropped into step beside her as she walked past, and greeted her respectfully. His sandals scuffed the pavement as they walked up the boulevard that edged the river.

"You know I work at Maxim's now, madame?"

She nodded. Two U.S. destroyers were anchored in midstream. The sailors were washing the gray superstructure in spite of the heat.

"Last night, M. Carbone comes in with an American."

Thin Pig had an excellent sense of what information was valuable and what was not.

"New face in town,"he said. "I think he's the same one who is talking around."

"Did you get his name?"

He smiled proudly. "I listened very carefully. Bill Falci...."

"Falci!" An Italian name. Nina stopped walking and regarded the destroyers while she thought. She did not notice the flower seller offering a garland of freesias at her feet, or the passing police patrol.

"What did he want?" she asked Thin Pig.

Several people pushed past them and they began to walk again.

"This man is from a place called Tampa, Florida," said Thin Pig. "He is looking for suppliers in Vientiane and Saigon."

"What did Carbone say?"

Thin Pig tucked a long strand of hair behind his ear and sucked his teeth. "He drinks no wine. Just coffee. And says that there are many difficulties in Vietnam. Supply lines are broken by fighting. Mines in harbors. Navy patrols on rivers. Not like the old times. He says he just wants to save the American from counting on too much." He grinned. "Then the American says, 'Don't give me that bullshit. This country is golden, war or no war. Maybe you just don't want to talk business with me.'"

He skipped a step or two, to keep up with her stride. "Then M. Carbone says, No, no, he just likes to save people trouble. And he drinks more coffee. Which is good, because he needs me to stand close to fill his cup all the time."

"What do you think?" asked Nina. "How do you judge it? Will they come to terms?" She slowed down to let him reflect.

He rubbed his nonexistent chin. "Both want to come to terms. But Carbone is scared. Too many Americans coming."

She had noticed before his knack of hitting the center of things. That was why he was so useful to her; he grasped and remembered essentials. So many others passed on every tidbit and left her to do the sorting. After she had tried him out as a courier, she would consider other ways to use him. She paid him generously for the news, and walked on by herself.

Of course Carbone was scared. Thin Pig had hit it exactly. The government of his own kind had been thrown out. Now, after years of privilege, he was scrabbling for patronage like everyone else. He was right to fear invaders from that young country across the sea, which produced men with the self-confidence of Will John but without his gentleness. Invaders from a country that seemed to decide even who should or should not rule in Vietnam.

She waited for her own invitation from Falci, but it didn't come. She supposed that he didn't consider it worth his time to talk to small fish with only 10 percent of the market—more or less. Once the American brotherhood had sorted out the big opposition—the Alliance—if that was what they planned to do, the rest of the dealers would be child's play. Louis told her that Falci had asked an agent to find a *pied à terre* in Saigon, in spite of the political uneasiness that was driving more and more Europeans home again.

She had expected the next evil gift of Fortune. When the results of the new harvest began to come in, she found a shortfall once more, between the amounts of crude opium being delivered to Heron and the amounts of morphine base she was told had been produced. Thu's continued absence had made no difference.

"Old Uncle, can you advise me?" she asked him once again.

He shook his head listlessly. She thought he seemed to be shrinking in size in recent months, as if from the unpalatable truth of the developing signs.

Her only joy was her time with Will John. Their shared ease, which had felt odd and premature in their early days, now settled into a sense of comfort and rightness. Nina would watch him shaving or doubling his tall frame over to tie a shoelace and marvel that such a creature could have arrived in her life and settled there. All facts said that it was impossible, but it was unarguably happening. She sometimes thought that the only darkness he could not touch and lighten was the truth hidden as deep as she could thrust it, that one day it would all end. She was almost glad the fighting continued, because it kept him there. If the price of Will John was the presence of his country's army, she would accept it.

One evening Daniel Jouvet arrived unannounced and invited himself for a drink

"So you're the opposition," he said when he was introduced to Will John.

"Against whom?" inquired Nina sweetly, outraged that Will John should think this ridiculous man had ever had her favors.

Will John stood up very, very slowly. He crushed Jouvet's hand in a parody of a hearty American handshake.

"Pleased to meet you." He ignored Jouvet's flinch and continued to flail the Frenchman's elbow while he pounded him on the other shoulder and released him. He grinned past Jouvet at Nina.

"Any friend of Nina's is a friend of mine." He gave Jouvet a final bearlike thump on the shoulder and released him. The smaller Frenchman reeled to his seat. By now, Nina recognized the deadpan performance and suppressed a laugh.

Jouvet looked at her wildly, and then collected himself. He turned to smile at Haines, who had returned to the sofa. "I'm delighted to meet you too," Jouvet said. "It's high time that

445

Nina found herself an American. She's always had a nose for the latest fashion."

Will John put on his earnest interviewer's expression. "Now, that's an interesting way to look at international politics, M. Jouvet. As a question of fashion. Does that mean you think that the French just went out of fashion in Indochina? Could you link that up for me just a little more ... like with military strategy at Dien Bien Phu?"

He leaned his elbows on his knees and waited, as if enthralled, for Jouvet to speak.

Nina laughed in spite of herself. "Please don't start interviewing Daniel, darling. I think he has probably come to talk business with me."

Will John looked convincingly regretful. "Another time, maybe. I do find that concept of yours an interesting one. Worth developing. I'll leave you two to talk, then."

He rose from the sofa and offered Jouvet his hand in farewell. Jouvet grabbed his glass of gin and tonic and declined the offer. As he passed her, Will John gave Nina a quick, surreptitious pat on the bottom.

Nina was still smiling to herself when she sat down opposite Jouvet to hear why he had come to see her.

"You're not serious about that overgrown cowboy?" asked Jouvet.

"Don't ask impertinent questions," said Nina. "Now, Daniel, what's up? Is something wrong?"

"You tell me," he said. "All I know is that I could lose Clay if you're not careful."

"You've already lost me," she said.

"You're not the only one supplying him now. With all the Americans here, *ma thuy* is getting bigger on the local market. Other dealers are jumping on the bandwagon."

"Daniel," she said warningly, "slow down and start again. What is the precise problem?" She no longer felt like laughing.

"I couldn't deliver what I had promised him. He wants my balls."

"Why couldn't you?"

"You didn't produce it!"

Nina held on to her chair with hands that had gone cold. The tiger's breath was on her neck again.

"Are you still there?" Jouvet asked after she had been silent for several seconds. He leaned back in his chair, away from the rage in the look she turned on him.

"Are you sure you never received it?" she demanded. "If you're lying, I'll kill you!"

Jouvet pulled one mustache nervously. "I swear I'm not! What would be the point? I swear!"

"How much less was it?"

"Twenty kilos. Of number four, not base."

Nina brushed her forehead with one hand. If it wasn't Jouvet, who was it? Was Thu going for a confrontation, like Carbone? Or was that why he had gone away? To remove himself from suspicion.

Jouvet relaxed slightly. At least she was prepared to consider alternative offenders. He watched the rage ebb in her eyes, replaced by a focused thought.

Could it be Hong? Nina wondered. He was the best placed of anyone to expect to get away with it. He had sent the figures that had proved to be incorrect. He could say that base had been ruined and he had been afraid to tell her. And he might count on her open liking of him to protect him.

"What shall I tell Clay?" asked Jouvet.

"Nothing. He won't refuse to use you next time. Not with the figures I've seen recently for manpower on the U.S. bases. He won't turn his back on any supplier right now."

Then, of course, there was always Thin Pig—useful, perceptive Thin Pig, who delivered to Jouvet. She hardly saw Jouvet as she showed him to the door.

Will John watched her for the next hour.

"Can I help?" he asked finally.

"No, my darling. You can't. I'm sorry."

"Some men might be offended," said Will John cheerfully. "I can fix an electric plug, milk a cow, start a fire with two dry sticks. I can do one hundred push-ups. I even read Goethe in German. Why do you assume I can't help?"

"Please!" It was a cry for mercy.

"OK." He watched her a little longer. "How about going to a movie? A Chinese historical epic in Cholon, with magicians first? Or we could go out to Tan Son Nhut. They're showing a late-night Doris Day film on the base. I've got a pass."

He caught her hand. "Maybe you'd rather screw." He kissed her gently. "How about both?"

She shook her head helplessly but kissed him back. "Sure. Why not both?"

* * *

The following day, she was waiting in the parked car for Hong when he left the syrup factory and set off for home on his bicycle.

"Jonathan!" she called softly through her open window.

"Madame Nina!" He skidded to a stop and his thin mouth stretched into a smile. She listened carefully. He was neither nervous nor on guard.

"I just happened to be passing," she said. "And thought that it was time to talk and catch up a little. How are things going?"

"You must tell me, from the results," he said happily. "Excuse me for one moment."

He wheeled his bike around to the other side of the car, out of the traffic. She opened the door and invited him to sit.

"No problems with supplies?" she asked him. "Or the lab?"

"No more than usual. Young Cousin Ping is showing an aptitude; I'm encouraging him to apply for a university place...."

He left the words floating; she surmised correctly that he hoped she might offer some financial help to the aspiring scholar.

"We will discuss young Ping's affairs further," she said.

"Thank you, madame." He looked pleased and relieved to have the request over with.

"How's your father?" She could not believe that he was cold-blooded enough, or a good enough liar, to ask a favor if he had a guilty conscience. One thing she liked about him was his ineptitude at social politics.

"Very well, thank you." Hong's gaze was level and earnest. "I am very happy that I am able to relieve his former worries."

Neither too much sincerity, nor too little. Nina could not believe that Hong had stolen the heroin.

"Have you finished yet?" she asked, returning to business.

"Nearly. Some crude opium was delivered late because there was too much fighting near the pickup point. Or that's what I was told. Why? Don't you wish me to go ahead?"

"By all means. When will it be ready to go?"

"Tomorrow evening. Your man usually picks it up on his way to work." He had heard something in her voice. She saw a look of concern behind his thick spectacles, but he was too polite to inquire.

"I'm delighted to have seen you," said Nina. She was even more delighted to feel certain that Hong had nothing to do with the disappearing stock. That left Thin Pig and Thu. Unless, of course, it had been Daniel all along.

448

42

"Follow me," Nina said to Eight Hand Horse. "I'm going on foot."

The car slid into the traffic outside the syrup factory, with Tiny Albert and Snow Man slumped into the backseat.

Thin Pig had left the garage with a lumpy bag slung over one shoulder. She followed his head as it bounced through the evening crowds. At first she had to stay so close that she could just pick out the clopping of his sandals. When he turned into a side street, where the crowds were thinner, she let him gain several meters.

The bag Thin Pig was carrying was not the mailbag Jouvet usually collected from the back of a locked van on Ven Do Street. He did not walk north toward Ven Do Street, but west toward Cholon. When he looked behind him, once, she bent to examine a basket of lychees, prickly as sea urchins.

Because she was bending, she did not see him disappear through a gateway. She looked along the street in disbelief, then ran to where she had seen him last.

She nearly passed the gate without noticing, because it was closed again. Then she realized that she was standing outside the delivery entrance of one of Heron's wholesale distribution warehouses. She went on to the end of the street, turned left, then left again to the front entrance of the building. It was locked for the night. A nervous night watchman answered her ring. She noticed his first instinctive movement to close the door in her face when she identified herself.

"Take me to Thin Pig," she ordered.

"Who, madame?" That was his second mistake; he lied stupidly, out of panic.

Nina smiled, to share his little joke about not knowing the name, baring her teeth with fully threatening intent.

"Take me to him. Quietly, with no accidents to warn him. If you do, I will excuse your carelessness in not guarding the rear entrance."

"Yes, madame. Thank you, madame!" His jaw trembled. Such were the advantages of rumor about one's reputation, which in this case, she noted, had not yet been overtaken by rumors of her growing weakness.

"Leave the front door open."

He looked astonished but obeyed.

The man led her down to the basement storerooms, a series of small, lockable chambers that she had had built in the former open cellar to cut down loss of stock. He stopped in front of one of the heavy wooden doors which opened off the central corridor like a double row of cells.

"Open it," she said quietly. "And go in first."

Reluctantly, he took out his keys and unlocked the door. When he pushed it, it did not budge.

"Who's that?" called a frightened voice inside, muffled by the thickness of the door.

"Huong," he replied. "With an urgent message."

His eyes begged Nina to note down his cleverness to his credit, against the weight of his crime.

She heard the sound of a bar being lifted out of its socket. She had ordered locks only for the outsides of the doors; the bar had been added since the rooms were built, by someone who planned to use the room more than once.

She followed the watchman into the small, windowless room.

Thin Pig had frozen in panic. With him were another man and a woman. None of them had a gun. Nina relaxed slightly. Then she saw what was on the table in the center of the room, lit by a single bare bulb hanging from the ceiling.

At first, she thought it was a doll. The gray-blue skin made it look unreal. It lay on its back, abdomen slit open. She had interrupted them in the act of disemboweling it. Bright blue and yellow intestines lay in an untidy pile on the table beside it. One blue twisted cord swung from the table edge, still attached within the cavity and dropped in fright when Huong had unlocked the door. The scalpel they had been using also lay on the table, shiny and bright, looking far too clean.

"Oh, God," breathed Nina. She moved a step closer.

The dead child was still wrinkled like a newborn. The minute fingertips and palms of the hands which lay beside its shoulders were ivory white in the harsh light. The underside of the little body was stained deep purple with bruising where the blood had settled after circulation had stopped. It had feathery black hair, like a duckling, and large, fierce, heavily lashed black eyes which stared unfocused into the shadows of the ceiling. It was a little girl.

Nina looked down when her foot struck something on the floor beside the table. It was a tiny coffin, waiting open. The lid leaned against the far wall.

On the table was also one of Jonathan Hong's plastic bags, still full, an open bag of rice flour, a bowl of white powder, and a chemist's scoop. The woman still held a plastic bag she was filling before stuffing it into the baby's abdominal cavity.

"Where did you plan to bury her?" Nina could not recognize her own voice.

"Please, madame. I never took it before!"

"Where?" she repeated.

Thin Pig's terror increased.

"What graveyard? Which city? Tell me!"

Thin Pig gathered himself to dash past her out of the room, then reversed like a shying horse. Urine ran down his bare, bandy leg from under the wide hem of his loose shorts. His eyes focused on the air to her right.

She stepped left, to give Eight Hand Horse a clear field. Behind him, in the passageway, she glimpsed the white head of Snow Man.

"Whom were you going to cheat with the rice flour?" Nina's voice was quiet now, almost casual.

"Only Americans," volunteered the other man suddenly. "I will tell you everything you want to know, madame."

She turned a cold eye in his direction.

"It is only for Americans," he repeated eagerly. "For the soldiers. At Long Binh." He gave her a cunning look. "So they shoot only themselves."

She continued to look at him. "Which of you killed her?"

"Her mother didn't want her," said the man placatingly. "Too many babies. No food. Another daughter."

"*Who killed her?*" She wanted desperately to hear that they had found the baby dead.

"He did." The man pointed at Thin Pig.

Thin Pig seemed not to hear; he was staring at the gun in the hand of Eight Hand Horse. His mouth moved like a hooked carp.

The woman began to cry quietly.

"Take all their keys," said Nina to Eight Hand Horse. "Including his." She pointed to the watchman.

He lined them up against the wall. Thin Pig and the watchman had keys. Nina took them, and the other contents of their pockets. The man swore when Eight Hand Horse tossed her his fat, polished, calfskin wallet.

"Put the child into the coffin," Nina ordered the woman. "All of her. Then put the coffin by the door and go back to the wall."

The woman scooped up the pile of intestines and tucked it back into the abdominal cavity. Her hands were shaking. She put

451

the baby into the little coffin and put the coffin near the door. Eight Hand Horse backed into the corridor to block her escape.

"Break the light," said Nina to Eight Hand Horse.

He fired once. The bulb exploded and the room went dark. The woman screamed. As Eight Hand Horse slammed the door closed and turned the key, the woman screamed again, a long high wail. Someone clawed at the inside of the door.

Then a man's voice began to scream for them to open the door. The clawing turned to the thudding of fists and shoulders against the thick wood. The man begged and pleaded. The woman was still screaming.

"Unlock it in eight days," said Nina to Eight Hand Horse. "See that no one opens it before. I left them the scalpel. Fortune will decide."

As they retraced their steps down the basement corridor, the sounds from the locked room grew fainter. At the front entrance, where Tiny Albert was on guard, she turned again to Eight Hand Horse.

"I want to walk alone now. You stay and arrange a guard. No one is to go into the cellar. Then have the child buried properly, as if she were mine."

"But, mademoiselle. . . ."

"It should not be hard to arrange," she snapped. "Find a *tay phap* you can trust . . . how much can it cost?"

The old man regarded the floor. "I will arrange everything, of course. It is just that I am not happy to have you go out alone."

"I told you what I wanted. Go do it, now!" she said. "Don't fear for me. Nothing will touch me tonight. I know. I feel deadlier than a krait."

She set off down the street. The old man nodded to Tiny Albert to follow. As he watched from the door of the warehouse, he imagined that the evening crowds parted in front of her like leaves before the bow wave of a ship. He had seen her father move like that, carrying an energy which could be felt, like heat from a fire.

Nina walked fast, as if she could run away from the scene in the cellar storeroom. She felt raw, stripped of her skin. The hot night air burned like boiling water. She walked toward the river, needing the space of the water's edge and distance. She swung and pivoted among the night food stalls, the cooking braziers. She passed families at dinner, nursing mothers, entwined lovers, cyclo drivers touting for fares, a letter writer surrounded by eager customers. But she didn't see any of them; they were too much part of ordinary life from which she was exiled.

She hit the Arroyo Chinois and followed it toward the Saigon River. On her left, among the other blinking neon signs, she saw the pink heron above the confectionery factory flapping its wings in staccato rhythm. Up-down. Up-down. Up-down. It no longer looked silly to her, but frightening in its endless energy. Up-down. Up-down. Forever.

She walked on, almost at a run. When she reached the junction of the canal and the river, she stood with her back to the lights of the food stalls and charcoal stoves to look across the water. In midstream, a mysterious geometry of lights slid upstream toward the military docks.

No matter how she twisted and turned the facts, her heroin had killed the child. She held matters together from the top and was responsible for what happened below her. She had not set an example, as the leader should; she had merely ignored many truths, and left other people to sort them out as best they could. She had not looked beyond the problems of her own personal truths, to try to grasp the entire pattern. She had begun to grasp it now, and it appalled her.

It was not enough to consider her father's business and her own part in it, or even the part this business played in the life of her country. The pattern was now reaching out into the entire world, drawing in men like Clinton Clay, and Bill Falci from Tampa, Florida, U.S.A. It included men like the black American soldier she had passed, crying to himself on the ground under a blinking green neon palm tree. It included the line of young men, squatting a few meters back against closed shop fronts, dreamy-eyed and self-satisfied, or waiting and shivering in spite of the heat. It included the dead baby. And Titi. And Thin Pig, locked in the cellar on her orders. She could not contain it all.

I wonder what pattern my father sees? she asked herself. It cannot be the same as when he was holding matters together.

Suddenly she thought of Will John, outside the pattern. A cramping pain in her belly screwed her down into a crouch above the shadows of docks and piers. She rocked on her heels.

Will John was coming to the house later, after a dinner at the Press Club. She couldn't let him see her. He knew her too well, even without knowing the facts. He would see the dead baby in her eyes, and her fear. Suddenly she vomited into the street. She crouched, with her arms wrapped around her body to hold it together while it tried to turn itself inside out. She rocked on her heels and wept, and was sick again. She rocked and retched, again and again. Her eyes were glued shut and her ears were blocked by the force of the spasms. She gasped for breath between each attack.

The mysterious geometry of lights slid on upstream. Porters and coolies and revelers passed without noticing the woman doubled over, paralyzed, blind, and deaf with her body's need to reject.

At last she drew a breath that was not followed immediately by another knotting of her insides. She raised her head carefully and opened her eyes. The charcoal braziers still glowed around her. People passed, silhouetted against the light of stalls and the more distant signs across the street. She shook her head and wiped her eyes. She drew another breath and felt the continued quietness inside her. She stood, cautiously; her legs trembled under her, but held.

It was like waking from a heavy sleep. She heard talking and laughter from the roofed sampans moored in the river and around the mouth of the canal. On her left, meat sizzled over charcoal. She heard and smelled it all with amazing clarity. She felt lighter, as if she had vomited up a great weight. Her body told her what she had decided. She wanted to stop.

Once she gave the idea shape and admitted it to her mind, she knew that she had begun to reach for it after Titi had been killed. She wanted out. The idea was simple but enormous. Carbone was right; she didn't have the stomach. She no longer wanted to have it.

She stared across the water at the lights of the far shore; the idea remained with her. It did not vanish, but became stronger. She began to walk again, slowly this time.

This choice was truly for herself, but against her father. That part frightened her. After four years of working in his shadow, to maintain his world.

Carbone also frightened her. She had to be very, very careful and very clever. The buffalo calf must not stampede this time. Energy and daring had served her in the past; now they were not enough. She also needed vision, strategy, and complex planning. She needed help which she could not find here in Saigon. She had to go north to see her father. She would enlist Eight Hand Horse in the morning.

Nina hailed a taxi and gave the driver her address. She continued to feel eased; her body seemed to float through the streets on the patched leatherette seat. She would see Will John tonight after all. She would be careful not to shock him, but she would begin to tell him a little of the truth, at last. He would approve of what she wanted to do. He might even want to help. She could finally let him help her. It was even possible that what was between them might not have to end.

If I don't fall through the surface. If I survive. If I can figure out how to dismount from the tiger.

The thought interrupted the beginnings of euphoria.

Back at the house, she dismissed the *mama-san,* locked the bedroom door behind her, and undressed. She was back in balance now, neither elated nor terrified. She moved onto the more comfortable territory of practical thought.

She took some papers from the little desk in the dressing room, to begin to estimate, roughly, her total assets, and decided to work in bed while she waited for Will John, safe inside the netting from an insistent mosquito which had begun to fly in formation with her, just behind her left ear.

As she raised her hand to part the netting she saw a dark shadow against the white sheets. She felt the blood leave her head, to weight her legs and feet like stones.

"Don't be frightened, School Dragon."

Thu's eyes gleamed with enjoyment of her shock.

"Cousin Thu!"

She turned and scooped up a silk kimono from the chaise longue and put it over her nakedness before she returned to the bed.

"Take that off again!" he ordered. "I've been away for months, and then you hide yourself!"

"I am happy to see you," she said with a dry mouth. "I wish I did not have so much work to do." She had to get him out before Will John came!

"Come here and sit down," he said. "And let me see you when you talk to me."

She climbed inside the netting and turned on the lamp on the wall. Thu was fully dressed and still wore his gun belt.

"You are wicked to frighten me like this," she said lightly.

His hand closed on her wrist and he said reflectively, "You don't look at me. You don't let me see you. I ask myself why not."

"When did you get back?" she asked. "Has something happened to make you risk coming into the city?"

His hand remained on her wrist like a ring of iron. "It's easier to move a man than opium," he said.

"I'm glad you're back," she said. "I need to talk to you . . . ask your advice. About the American brotherhood. Have you heard? One of them was here, in Saigon. A man called Falci, looking for suppliers, in case Turkey is cleaned up. Or that is what he says. He could have gone to India if a source is all he wants. He has taken an apartment here. I think he is after more.''

She looked at him inquiringly. "What do you think?"

"Shall I kill Mr. Will John?" asked Thu. In the silence after his words, the mosquito flung itself against the netting like a minute buzz saw.

She was afraid to speak; the price of a wrong word was too great. But if she didn't say something, soon, he would realize how much he had terrified her. She wasn't stupid enough to ask "Who?"

"Why?" she asked at last, her voice nearly normal.

He hit her with the hand that was not holding her wrist. Lightly. Even in the shock, she felt him holding back. The cuff of a mother lion's paw.

They looked at each other, the truth out.

"The act wouldn't be worthy of you," she said. "As that blow was not."

Eyes narrowed, he was assessing his effect.

"He's already looking for his bullet," she said. "Let him find it by himself."

"Don't protect him," said Thu.

"Kill him, then," said Nina between her teeth. "And I will never speak to you again for being so uncivil to my friends. . . . Is that better?"

He said levelly, "I prefer you not to laugh at me. The man is the enemy of us both."

"He's not an enemy," she said. "An American, but not an enemy. They differ, as we do."

"He's an enemy," Thu repeated "You will see."

Her hand began to ache, beyond the tourniquet of his grip. He pulled her face close to his own.

"*Écoute bien*, School Dragon!" he said. "You do not belong to an . . . American." He made the word sound like an obscenity.

"I don't belong to any American! Or to you!" She tried to free her hand.

"We belong to each other," he said.

His words chilled her more than his threat to kill Will John. His pupils were wide, his voice intense. He believed what he said. He opened his fingers and blood burned back into the veins of her numb hand.

"Oh, Cousin!" she whispered. "You overwhelm me. We are partners. I have shared your bed . . . but belong . . . !"

And he had trusted her with pieces of his past.

"What more?" he asked.

She looked away from the blazing conviction on his face. This wasn't just a simple war of male ownership rights. He believed that he loved her. As far as possible, perhaps he did. Betrayal was clearly another matter altogether, for him.

She touched his face gently while her mind raced. He could never know the peace and comfort that Will John brought her so lavishly and unthinkingly from his golden life in America, even while he fought against that life. Any more than Will John could understand what it was never to have been loved and secure for one moment of your life, like Thu. Or understand what that did to your heart.

She bowed her head to hide her face. If he were to suspect that she pitied him, he would certainly kill her and Will John as well.

He pulled at the silk kimono.

"Wait," she whispered. "Wait a few seconds. I am neglecting my duty to you as hostess. Let me call for some drinks. And something for you to eat."

She reached for the bell before he could stop her and went to unlock the door.

"A drink tray with two glasses," she ordered the *mama-san*. "And some fruit. Then see that I am not disturbed."

The woman bowed. "Yes, madame. Except for M. . . ."

"Let *no one* come in! No one at all! Do you understand me?"

The puzzled woman hesitated outside the half-open door, then knowing comprehension flooded her eyes.

"Yes, madame. No one at all!" She bowed again and left.

Nina leaned against the door. She couldn't imagine how she would be able to explain it to Will John the next day. What if he were to arrive as Thu was leaving: Or decided that she was in trouble and came upstairs in spite of the *mama-san*, while Thu was still there?

She waited for the tray and carried it to the bed.

"Which of my servants did you bribe to get in?"

He laughed. "That's my secret. Now leave those stupid drinks. I'm tired of waiting. It has been many weeks!"

The dangerous edge had crept back into his voice. When she had thought, in the Rung Sat, that she would one day be brave enough to refuse him, she had not imagined that she might be protecting someone else.

She put the tray on a table and shrugged off the silk kimono before she slipped back through the mosquito netting.

Thu woke her at half past three in the morning.

"I'm going soon," he said. "I want to talk to you."

She struggled toward alertness.

"I've been in Laos, where I bought a villa. In the mountains. I want you to come there with me."

"I would be honored to be your guest," she said.

"You are to live there with me."

She woke as completely as if he had put a gun to her head. To live with him, in a remote mountain villa! Surrounded by his army, forced to treat his whims as law and to anticipate and read them constantly in order to stay alive. Without Will John.

She shivered. "My father needs me here in Saigon," she said. "The business needs me."

"I don't need you here."

She shook the last of sleep from her head; she couldn't deal with such things in the dead hours of the night, without warning.

"Why not?" she asked. "They still fear you too much to let you walk the streets openly. Who will handle things for you in the city if I have gone with you to Laos?"

He put on the light to see her better. "Things change."

This was what she had feared when coup followed coup. Diem replaced by Minh, then Minh by Khanh. Now, it would seem, the new government formed by Tran Van Huong had finally brought Thu's buried trump card to the top.

"I think you have a deep purpose that I can't perceive," she said.

"You're right." He gleamed with satisfaction and triumph. "I will tell you something that I will kill you for revealing. . . ."

His hand stroked her neck, half caressing, half measuring.

"In a few days' time—don't ask me how I know this—the People's Army will attack many American installations, all at once. It will be a major blow . . . as strong as Dien Bien Phu. A slap across the face for the Americans. They will have to strike back or leave. I don't think they will go home; I think they will fight. And in the fighting even my friends in the North cannot guarantee the safety of my men, as they once did. Things are already bad, with the Air Force bombing from American planes But they will soon become impossible. I will lose many kilos, couriers, mules, boats. I will not struggle to stop the change. The coins and sticks have told me what to do."

"And that is . . . ?" She did not have to pretend interest.

458

"We will make a new lab, at the villa. I will bring the crude opium over the mountains into Laos, a very short distance. You bring your chemists."

"And then . . . ?" she prompted.

He tickled the skin beneath her left ear. "Then I sell base to the White Devils and *they* take it to Saigon."

"The private Corsican airlines are not flying into combat zones."

"I didn't say *French* White Devils." He lay back to receive her applause.

"I don't understand," she said.

He assumed his tutorial tone. "Who are the only men now who can guarantee transport in and out of combat zones?"

"Dear God, Cousin!" She began to laugh from nerves and at the ridiculousness of it all. "You are outrageous!"

He looked pleased to be so.

"What does Uncle Ho think of this new alliance of yours?" She could not stop laughing. "The Americans!"

Thu grinned with delight. "He's very pleased to have American money to spend on more guns."

"I can't believe it." She lay back against the pillow and wiped her eyes on the corner of the pillowcase. "I just can't believe it all!"

His trump card wasn't in Huong's camp after all, but the American one. Perhaps he had come forward with evidence against Diem. Or offered information about the cell structure of the Vietcong, former allies, in the Saigon area. However he had done it, he was out of his swamp.

He caught the harsh note in her laughter and stopped smiling. "I still have not had your reply to my invitation, School Dragon."

She rolled onto her side and looked into his eyes.

"Why don't you want to come?" he asked. He netted his fingers into the hair at the nape and shook her head gently from side to side. "You want to stay with your American!"

"No, Cousin! As you said, we belong to each other."

She felt his warm breath as he sighed. "But I ask you to let me have one more season in Saigon. There is too much to finish so quickly. A year is no time at all to tie up loose ends. Ours is not a simple business."

She relied on the fact that for all his perceptions and quickness he was still a peasant and a soldier, not a city man. He still had to take her word for certain things, even though he was out of the Rung Sat.

"I think you are too clever to try to trick me," he said.

She smiled into his eyes and thought to herself that her safest act would be to kill him at this moment. If he left the room, she would not ever again be sure of her own safety or Will John's. But she had just turned her back on such solutions and had to face the new risks brought by this choice. Her father must help her find the alternative solution.

"I will take the chance," said Thu at last. He was not wholly sure.

She kissed him. "How long do I have to arrange things?" she asked. "And when does the People's Army attack?"

"No more information!" he said. "You'll learn nothing more with kisses."

She lay awake after he left. ". . . a few days," he had said. Whatever that meant. A few days before movement in the North became impossible. A few days in which to reach her father and return.

As soon as it was morning, even before she called Will John, she spoke to Eight Hand Horse. Then she rang Clinton Clay to ask him finally for the favor he had once offered her.

"Can you arrange passage for me, on military air transport?" she asked. "As far as the DMZ? As soon as possible."

It took five days, a lot of money, and all of Eight Hand Horse's organizing ability. Nina was already north of the 17th parallel when the VC attacked Pleiku.

* PART THREE *

43
Tonkin, March 1965

The explosion shook the field where the dry grass had bent beneath the helicopter's rotors. Nina awoke when a clod of earth hit her face. The wooden supports of the tunnel creaked and shifted. A dribble of fine earth followed the clod. Half awake, she tried to scramble to her feet in the darkness and hit her head against the bamboo struts that supported the three-foot ceiling.

The ground shook again, hard enough to throw her back to her hands and knees. More earth hit her back and shoulders. Her arm clawed sideways and hit the wall of the tunnel. She couldn't see. She couldn't breathe. The tiny chamber was her coffin. She sat and squeezed her arms around her pulled-up knees to stop herself screaming in panic.

The next explosion was closer. Her entire body began to tremble violently. She could hear her teeth knocking uncontrollably against each other. Somewhere in the darkness a voice was moaning. "No . . . no . . . no!"

Something touched her arm. Another voice said, "It is almost over. One way or another. Just a little longer."

The hand was holding her arm firmly. She realized that it was she who had been moaning.

"Air is still coming through the bamboo pipes," said the voice. "Breathe slowly."

She grasped the hand that was on her arm. Its fingers twined hard into her own; the palm was wet with sweat. She could hear the planes, even through the roof of earth and grass.

The next shell was almost a direct hit. The earth leaped and bucked as the street had done when No One had been killed. Nina heard a cracking of wood and a groan, far louder than her own. She ducked her head between her knees while earth drummed onto her back. The voice beside her screamed in fear at the same time she screamed. The earth fell and fell. Nina knew she was being buried.

461

She was at the bottom of a huge hourglass, beneath a cone of sand rising higher and higher until it would become a mountain on top of her.

The fall of earth slowed, then stopped. It had filled the space between her back and the wall of the tunnel so that she could only sit forward. She stretched a leg in the darkness and hit something solid which had not been there before.

Something creaked.

"Don't move," said the voice. "I think a support is broken." The hand she had been holding withdrew itself.

She heard a faint rustle of cloth as he moved in the darkness.

"One air pipe has been blocked, but the other still seems clear."

"How often does this happen?" asked Nina. All the circuits of her brain had been scrambled. She was surprised that her words appeared to be coherent.

"Every night, since the National Liberation Front attacked the marine base. Three nights now."

His voice died away at the growing sound of more aircraft engines. The noise swelled and passed directly overhead. The next explosion came four seconds later. The tunnel vibrated but it did not jump. More dirt pounded down on her head and shoulders.

The man beside her let out a long breath. "I think they have missed us, for the time being."

A faint, irregular shape glowed faintly in the darkness ahead of them. They heard scuffling and scraping. The light grew brighter and they could make out the sound of muttered instructions and curses. A moment later, a head appeared beyond the fallen strut.

"Just a few more minutes," it said. "We must shore up the roof before you can move."

The ground vibrated with another explosion. A fine rain of earth splattered onto Nina's legs. The floor of the little tunnel was an uneven terrain of fallen dirt. She pressed her shoulders back against the earth as if holding up the world.

The lantern light was blocked by the bodies and limbs of the two men as they struggled to insert a U-shaped frame of wood under the roots of the grass above them.

There was another explosion, farther away than the one before.

"That's the last one you will have to worry about," said one of the silhouetted men. "We're nearly finished"

462

They forced the wooden support into place and removed the fallen strut, as carefully and delicately as if playing jackstraws.

Nina crawled into the main tunnel. "When do we go out?" she asked. Dust and pebbles shifted inside her clothes and gritted in the cracks and folds of her skin.

"It's still four hours to dawn," said the man with the lantern. "We'll make room for you along there." He pointed down the tunnel where the other villagers lay.

"We can't go out now?" She hated herself for her weakness, but she had to get out into the air. She had to stand upright. She had to breathe fresh air.

"No," whispered the man. "Sometimes they send clean-up patrols from the dragonfly airships. They watch for us to open the tunnels after an attack and throw in grenades."

Using the last shreds of her self-control Nina curled up on the dirt floor, jammed between other bodies. The lantern was extinguished and no one spoke. The precautions might not be necessary but the risk was too great to ignore.

At 4 A.M. a villager woke Nina quietly, his face close to hers in the dark tunnel, a landscape of bone and flesh exaggerated by the quavering rays of the lantern.

"We will go soon. No more fire dragon airships until morning." He handed her a bowl of hot rice gruel flavored with bits of dried fish.

She shivered and swallowed the thick, glutinous soup. The earth was damp against her back; large clods had fallen onto her sleeping mat. She could hear rustling and coughing in the tunnel, but had no idea which of the dark shapes had been beside her during the air attack.

When one of the villagers opened the trap, Nina seized the lashed bamboo ladder and flung herself up into the hot night like a drowning swimmer against a shore. At the top she stood for a moment to get her bearings. The world had changed during the night; where she had run through the grass, she saw the humping shoulder of a ridge of earth. Smoke and the tang of chemicals prickled her nostrils. Half a kilometer away, the remains of the village still flickered against the darkness of the foothills.

She followed her guide away from the tunnel, along a zigzag of dike-top trails to the northwest. Soon after they left, the land began to rise away from the delta, up through clumps of scrub and bamboo to higher terraces of *paddi*. Before first real light they stopped briefly in a small settlement, tucked into a grove of bananas, lemons, and bamboo, to pick up two saddled mules.

Clay had arranged her a seat out of Tan Son Nhut on a military flight to Pleiku Base. From there she had continued by helicopter hops from base to base. It had taken a large sweetener to persuade the last CO to allow her to fly into a combat zone. She looked out to her right, across the land falling away from their track; the edge of the sea on the horizon had begun to glow as the sun nudged it from underneath. Closer fires burned here and there in the shadowy landscape.

She smiled to herself at the memory of Will John's expression when he had finally realized that he would not get his way this time; she was going alone and that was that.

Well, she thought. That's partly what he wants from this place—not to have things go his own way all the time. But for the price not to be too great.

The trail the mules were following led due north now, climbing along the spine of the Dragon, the Chaine Annamatique. Nina thoughtfully watched a group of coolies who exchanged muffled greetings with her guide and edged their shoulder yokes and baskets past the mules.

"Tell me," she asked her guide, "is this part of Uncle Ho's road?"

"I don't know, madame," he answered politely.

She settled back into the swaying of her mule. The man was being well paid to help her journey; there was no reason why he should trust her as well.

Once they had moved under cover of the jungle on the mountain slopes, she saw no further signs of the bombing raids. They continued traveling north for most of the day; much time was spent on slow descents into gorges and equally slow climbs back up the other side. Four times she had to dismount to let her mule scramble for footholds on the steep, rocky slopes. During the day they passed two patrols of armed men in the black pajamas of the guerrillas.

It was late afternoon, to judge by glimpses of the sun through the roof of vegetation, when they turned west and began to climb the fold of a small, steep gorge, higher and higher above the narrow stream that plunged down from the mountains to feed the Red River in the delta far below. They continued westward and upward until the sun rolled over the Dragon's back and fell into the west, leaving their side of the mountains in shadow.

Suddenly, their track climbed over the edge of a high plateau. The forest thinned and the river gorge swung away to their right. The mules climbed around the edge of a poppy field, an expanse of glaucous gray-green dusted with white blooms. The crumpled petals shivered in undetectable breezes. Nina drew a sharp breath. She had seen poppies before, but not like this, in a delicate sea.

She bent from her mule and picked a flower. The center of the fragile skirt of petals was a hard-ridged globe that would become the pod. She raised her head from the flower and saw the villa above them on the ridge above the field. It faced down the sloping plateau, the rising mountain slope to its right and the river gorge to its left. Between mountains and water. Her father observed such things too.

She kicked her mule forward, fighting down a mixture of excitement and terror.

The villa's enclosing walls, settled into the contours of the land, were the color of dried earth. The tops of small trees showed above the walls. The heavy wooden gate began to swing open; they had been seen. As the mules swished through the long grass beyond the poppy field, Nina waited for something to happen to prevent this meeting, which felt so implausible after all these years. Then they passed through the gate. They had arrived. A black-trousered watchman, with a carbine slung across his back, closed the gate behind them. A small boy ran out to take Nina's mule. She dismounted and looked around her.

She was facing a large courtyard. Behind her, just inside the gate, was a spirit screen. The center of the courtyard was filled by a lily pool, which was probably also the reservoir for the villa. Beyond the pool stood the main pavilion. Its wooden peak was ornately carved but the roof below was golden thatch. An outer row of wooden columns supported the roof of a wide porch; an inner row of columns opened into the shadows of the principal chamber, which had open walls whose panels were folded back during the day.

Two separate buildings formed right-angled wings to the main pavilion. From the building on the east, the women's side, a middle-aged woman was approaching. She wore a short black jacket and half a dozen heavy silver necklaces. Her hair was coiled around her head in the montagnard fashion.

"Welcome, First Daughter," she said, bowing. "We are honored by your presence."

Clearly, Nina's message had arrived. As she bowed in return, she wondered if this were the sister of Eight Hand Horse, the mother of Kim. She looked into the woman's eyes and caught a flicker of something quick and sly before the lids were lowered.

"Please follow me," the woman said. "Your father is waiting for you."

As they passed the main pavilion, Nina saw in the cool depths her father's sleeping platform and the altar of the Ancestors. A wide fillet of red cloth around the principal beam protected the pavilion from the genie of fire. An altar to the spirits stood in the corner of the courtyard on a carved and lacquered post under a half-grown banyan. Nina looked at the two altars and shook her head in bewilderment. Her father had been a man of white suits and attaché cases, constantly arriving in chauffeured cars from mysterious business meetings. His so-called library had shown his secret other self to have the dry edge of Confucian scholarship; it was a throwback to the intellectuals of the Chinese mandarinate, not this lush abandonment to the old popular Vietnam.

The woman led her between the main building and the eastern pavilion, through a garden of yams and herbs, to a small gate in the back wall of the compound. She went through the gate, onto a raised wooden bridge over the gully outside the wall, to a small pavilion set on an outcrop of rock directly above the main river gorge.

Nina followed with growing panic. She did not know what she felt. She had imagined him for too long; the idea of the real man was terrifying. At the end of the walkway, the woman bowed and turned back toward the villa. Nina climbed the five wooden steps into the little pavilion and looked into her father's eyes.

Her first thought was that he was too old and too small. His face was more deeply lined than the face she carried in her head. His hair was graying and thin, although the lock still swelled up over his forehead to fall back over his crown. His eyes, unchanged, were still those of a man accustomed to power.

She collected her wits and bowed. He was seated at the far end of the pavilion, leaning on pillows, in a traditional Chinese-style long gown and trousers. His feet rested in slippers on a rectangular silk cushion.

"I assume that this strange woman, whom I do not recognize, is my daughter?" His voice was as dry as she remembered it. "I must study this new acquisition. Please." He motioned her to a pile of silk cushions on a carved bench.

She sat self-consciously. She wished she had taken the time to change back into the polished young woman who had boarded the last helicopter instead of rushing out in the black pajamas. She looked covertly at the thick veins and liver spots on the backs of his hands.

"Did you have a pleasant journey?" he asked. "I imagine there were one or two surprises."

"The surprise is that I arrived at all." Her heartbeat was slowing. Now that their meeting was upon her, it was simpler than she had feared.

"So I would gather," he said. "That is why I live as far as possible from anything or anyone in the least way important."

The woman climbed the five steps with a lacquer tray of tea and coconut cakes. She served them both, bowed, and left again. Nina watched her go; she saw her father's eyes watch her own, then shift away.

"The rains are late this year." He sipped his tea. "The bombing starts many fires when the jungle is so dry. My own garden is sadly not what I would have liked you to see... and the pond is so low that I imagine at night I hear the carp praying for rain."

They were watching each other, seeking information about the last ten years.

"On the contrary," she said, "your garden is most beautiful." She smiled over her teacup, willing to play his game and compliment him on the felicity of his placement between mountains and water, and on the elegance of the villa.

She couldn't get used to the old-fashioned clothes, or to the style of the villa. She wanted to ask him why he had chosen this isolated, antique way of life instead of a villa in the south of France as the Emperor had done.

She wanted to ask him why their house had been bombed and whether it had been Carbone, as she had suspected. She wanted to ask him about the list of weaponry and the missing money. She wanted to ask him about his real relationship with Carbone. And with her mother. There were a hundred personal things she suddenly wanted to ask him. But she made herself wait until he decided to drop formalities. Now, even if never again, she would show him that she had learned a little patience and decorum, that the buffalo calf could restrain herself once in a while. She laughed at herself; she was a child wanting to be told how well she had done. The desire only showed how little she had achieved.

He took another sip of tea and said, "You insisted that we meet, and endangered several messengers to tell me that. Then you took not inconsiderable trouble to get here. Why?"

Proprieties were concluded.

"I want out," she said. "Out of the business. Unless you can

467

give me very good reasons for going on." She hadn't meant to blurt it out quite so bluntly.

"Ah," he said. He put his cup down very carefully. "You want reasons. Let me see. Position? Money? A little power? Men fight for all of them, I believe."

"I don't undervalue those," she said. "Believe me. I see what happens to men who have none of them. But they are not enough!"

"You made a choice," he said.

"Yes," she replied. "And I was grateful to be given a choice. At the beginning. But I was ignorant, and now I've learned things I would rather not know."

She couldn't judge his reaction; he was studying her so intently.

"Why did you make the choice you did?"

She hesitated only a second. "To earn the love and respect you refused me as a child. And had just, perhaps, begun to offer me when . . . it all happened."

His head jerked with shock at her bluntness.

"It's the same buffalo calf. . . . I recognize you very well now." He was silent then for some time.

At last he laid his hands, palms up, on his knees as if offering her his words. "You have done honor to me, and to our family. I am pleased with you." He leaned forward slightly. "You see how easy it is to give you what you wanted so badly. Is it enough? Now?"

There it was, at last. She tried to hold back her answer but it forced itself out between her teeth. "No!" She held his eyes. "Forgive me. But it is not enough. Not now. I know what I am saying to you. That there is no one left to carry on. That I am throwing away your life's work."

"And you wanted to come here to tell me that in person?"

"No," she said. "I came to ask you to help me get out."

He raised his eyebrows and gave a dry little bark of a laugh. "You want me to help you dismantle the empire, so to speak? To undo my own life's work?"

"You're the only one who can."

He shook his head in amused disbelief. "I've heard rumors over the years about how you sometimes triumphed by recklessness and bravado. . . ."

"Will you help me?"

He turned his head to look out over the gorge. In the silence, she heard a small rodent gnawing on the wood of the pavilion.

Then he turned back and clapped his hands twice.

468

"We will dine now. Then you must sleep, after your bad night last night."

Two servants began to climb the steps into the pavilion.

"Will you help me?" she begged.

"There is something I want you to see tomorrow," he replied. "Then it will be easier for us to talk about such a large subject."

The servants unrolled a woven sling from a pair of long poles and laid it on the floor. Then they lifted her father from his chair, set him in the sling, and hoisted the poles to their shoulders, supporting him in a hammock between them.

"My back was injured in the explosion," he explained, seeing her face. "I had no time for proper treatment that night and it went bad. The strength of my legs comes and goes. I didn't want it known."

His helplessness shocked her even more than his age had done. It made her feel giddy, as her sense of aloneness had done the night Kim was killed. She felt a jolting forward of her own being, the realization of aging, which accompanied the terror that her father would not, or could not, help her.

Her father was still sleeping when a servant woke her early the next morning. A saddled mule was waiting for her in the courtyard, where a second mule balanced a pair of woven panniers across its back. Two men also waited, one a middle-aged montagnard who was carrying an assault rifle. The montagnard led them around the walls outside the villa to a track that continued on up along the river gorge toward the ridge of the Dragon's spine. The second man drove the supply mule.

At first they picked their way far above the sound of water through the splintered light of the early sun, under overhanging trees and bamboo clumps. Then they began to make sudden lunges upward through narrow gaps between boulders, over rocky promontories. At the crest of each successive rise, Nina breathed deeply and looked up at the jagged ridges and high peaks above them, whose sides seemed clothed in yellowing green coral. As they climbed, the sound of water grew fainter and finally died away. The vegetation became drier and more sparse. Nina tucked her hands inside the long black sleeves of her tunic to protect them from the growing heat of the sun.

They rested once, briefly, in the shade of a small cave in the side wall of the gorge. At noon they stopped in the shade of a fall of boulders. Nina slid gratefully from her mule and removed the peasant's banana-leaf hat that had shaded her face. She lifted the neck of her tunic away from the sweat on her throat and shoulders. The mule driver laid out their midday meal from a tower of stacked baskets, then began to brew tea on a small U.S. Army solid-fuel stove.

The two men squatted at a respectful distance while she ate her cold rice and pickled vegetables and drank her tea. She leaned back against a boulder and stretched her legs in their black trousers, feeling an unexpected rush of well-being. The only sound was the buzzing of insects in the dry scrub. The height, the silence, and the solitude scoured her mind of all other concerns; she let it float. The montagnard was asleep in his corner of shade.

She heard her father's voice saying once again, "You have done honor to me, and to our family." Though not enough, the words nevertheless settled warmly inside her at last. She shut her eyes and listened to the insects. She did not want to continue this journey, to learn of more complications of life. She wanted to stay like this, warm from the sun and from her father's words.

The mule driver began to repack the panniers. She heard him move, sighed, opened her eyes, and drained her glass of tea. Then she picked her way around the boulders to find privacy to squat and relieve herself. Looking back down the deep gorge, feeling sun on her back, and smelling the acridness of her urine as it ran away over the hard, dry ground, she smiled at the idea that she wanted to remain frozen in that moment, but it was true.

As they emerged after lunch from the gorge onto a bare rock ridge, heat reflected up to burn the undersides of their chins. The sun pounded into their heads and backs, even through their protective hats. The occasional breezes were like gusts from an open oven; Nina's eyes burned with the strength of the light. Suddenly, as they crested the ridge, both men stiffened and turned their heads like dogs to listen. She turned her head and caught a faint, distant roar which rose in pitch and fell again.

"Overflight," said the montagnard. "Fire Dragon airships." He pointed toward the north, but Nina could not make out the jets which were already lost against the bulk of the distant peaks.

The montagnard moved noticeably faster down the far side of the ridge, until he had led them under the cover of some trees. Their rhythm settled again as they continued to descend farther and farther under the thickening canopy of forest. They acquired an escort of gibbons who swung along above their heads, shrieking and hooting their outrage at the interlopers.

Then their progress slowed while the montagnard hacked a clear passage through webs of lianas and bushes along the small watercourse they had begun to follow. They dropped slowly between steep walls of stone. Through gaps in the vegetation

470

Nina saw that these walls were hollow with caves, filled with green ferns and the sound of dripping water.

Suddenly, the montagnard attacked the vegetation on his left and led them into the mouth of a large, shallow cave. Then Nina saw that the cave was not shallow, but angled back behind the arch of its opening into the cliff and total blackness.

Almost immediately there was light again, far ahead and slightly above them. She clung to her mule while the animal stumbled and scrambled up along the stony floor. They emerged into a basin of rock which had once been a huge underground chamber before its roof fell and opened it to the sky. Rock walls opened away on either side like theater wings. Ahead, vision was blocked by a blanket of young jungle spread over the former cave floor. The montagnard stopped near the mouth of a small cave in one of the rocky walls of the open chamber, and turned to Nina with the finality of arrival.

44

The small cave smelled of bat droppings. Its floor was piled with shadowy boulders. As her eyes adjusted, she began to see that the boulders were unnaturally regular in shape. She touched one and felt rough wood; another was metal. Ranks of neatly stacked crates and boxes marched back into darkness.

The montagnard turned a torch on the closest pile of crates. Nina scraped away the mold and moss on the wood to read: "Sewing Machines. Made in China." Helped by the montagnard, she cleared cobwebs, mold, and bat droppings from other boxes and crates. Some labels were no longer legible. Others announced their contents as cash registers, nautical flares, spare parts for agricultural machinery, brake fluid, garden rakes, teapots, and glass chandeliers.

She asked the montagnard to open a crate of sewing machines and was not at all surprised, in principle, to find it full of Type 59 pistols, Chinese copies of the Russian Makarov, just as Will John had said. Each piece was individually wrapped in oiled paper, and they were interspersed with calcium silicate crystals to absorb moisture. The "teapots" were Chinese-made grenades; like the pistols, they were shiny and clean.

She took the torch deeper into the cave. As far as the dim beam could reach, she saw more crates and packing cases. Small ones were ranged on ledges or slung in nets from rocky projections in the walls, among the dark rags of sleeping bats.

The hair lifted on the back of her neck when the beam touched the shape of a man, wrapped in white, propped against the right-hand wall. He did not move. She touched him. Through the damp canvas she felt cold metal. More of these ghosts leaned on the wall in a line stretching beyond the reach of her light.

She went back to the cave mouth and began a systematic investigation. The cave held M2 and M31 mortars, Chinese mines, American Second World War bazooka launchers, and four RPG2 rocket launchers with German markings. There were crates of M1 rifles, more Type 59 copies of the Makarov, crates of Makarovs themselves, and AK33(Ch) rifles. Along the left-hand wall, she found a large consignment of light DPM machine guns, new and used U.S. flak jackets, flares, explosives, detonators, fuse wires, shovels, and picks. She found French, American, and Russian grenades.

Thoughtfully, she went back into the fresh air outside the cave and coughed bat dust out of her lungs. She wondered what her father was trying to tell her, by sending her to see this arsenal, that he couldn't have said. She had already half suspected him of sympathy for the North. The fact that he was supplying them with arms was a logical next step.

"Shall we start back?" she asked the montagnard. "It is growing late."

"But there is more." The man gestured toward the blanket of jungle.

She stared at the blanket of young trees battling up toward the light through the tangle of lianas. Then, as in the cave, she began to detect regularities which should not be there.

Certain hummocks were of exactly the same height; their lines were too straight and their angles too precise to be natural. She saw them clearly once her eyes had dismissed the green swags, frills, and arabesques of vegetation. She asked the montagnard to clear the growth from a nearby hummock. As he swung his *coupe-coupe* a family of wild pigs crashed away squealing. Under the growth was a moldy tarpaulin lashed with ropes. Under the tarpaulin were unassembled sections of an American armored personnel carrier. She pointed to other hummocks, now clearly visible against the jungle around them.

"Those are all the same as this one," the man said. "Over here is different." He hacked a path to another shrouded shape.

Without removing either growth or cover, she could see that it was a lightweight tank, its snout masquerading as a tree branch already hung with lianas and sheltering a large tree lizard who regarded them, insolent and unmoving. She clambered onto the tank to look at the jungle floor from a higher vantage point.

While the gibbons, or their cousins, abused her from overhead she identified four jeeps, their covers adrift and not replaced, and three more tanks. A gun carriage tilted, uncovered and rusting, at the foot of the tank. A mound she had thought to be boulders was a mountain of truck tires with wide treads. Away to her right stood twelve identical hummocks, larger than the jeeps. To her left, closer to the cave mouth, were three strange constructions like overgrown fairground wreckage. She climbed down over a pool of water caught in a depression in the canvas, which was filled with minute frogs and their spawn.

The three constructions were American Huey helicopters disguised under camouflage netting that guided the undergrowth upward like a huge garden trellis. Here and there metal glinted dully through. Beyond them she suddenly saw two more personnel carriers, almost consumed by the jungle.

She knew that the more she looked the more she could continue to find. But she had already seen enough outside the cave to comprehend what had escaped her among the crates and cases—this huge arms depot had been abandoned. Less than twenty kilometers away men were trying to kill each other with homemade rifles, sharpened bamboo stakes, bombs of tin cans and nails, and Coke bottles filled with gasoline and soap. Here in the caved-in chamber, helicopters were being strangled by vines and rust was nibbling at tanks. It made no sense at all.

A flight of bats suddenly detached itself from the mouth of the small cave. The air around her head fanned and boiled. A solid mass of high-pitched, barely audible sound pressed on her eardrums. The cave mouth danced before her eyes as if a mass of dark leaves were blowing upward in a gale. Then the cave emptied and they were gone.

The mules stood ready. The air was cooling.

As they reemerged from the other end of the entrance cave into the overgrown watercourse, Nina asked, "Is there another way in?"

"Yes," said the montagnard. "On the other side of the basin. But there's fighting there now. And it's too close to Uncle Ho's trail. Better this way."

"Not with a tank," said Nina dryly.

Most of the return journey to the villa was in darkness.

They had arrived back at 3 A.M. Nevertheless, Nina asked to be wakened in time to join her father for breakfast. When she emerged from the guest pavilion, in her dress and Italian shoes, he was looking out over the lily pool. He wore a silk jacket and trousers; his feet were propped on the rectangular silk cushion. The montagnard woman brought them tea and steamed rolls, then went to feed the carp in the pool.

"What did you make of it?" he asked casually.

"Is that where you've put all the money you have taken from the business?"

He nodded.

"Before I came," she said. "I had guessed that you had bought, or were buying, arms. I thought you were supplying the Vietcong. It made me uneasy, but at least I understood. But to waste all that money! And power...!" She shook her head.

He smiled. "I thought that would trouble your practical half-French soul." He became more serious. "Do you mean that you did not answer your own question to me, about whether I would help you?"

She shook her head again.

"You didn't see how we have become the same?" he asked. She waited.

"I will explain." He sipped his tea reflectively. "Once upon a time," he said wryly, "when I was very young, much younger than you are now, I knew my destiny with absolute clarity."

His eyes held a flicker of their former blaze. "I knew exactly why I did what I did. It was my destiny to destroy the French."

Nina felt something contract inside her.

"I was to destroy them as they had destroyed my father. I was to drive them from my country. The first few were simple. I killed a Frenchman with my *coupe-coupe* to avenge my father. Anger made it easy. Then I killed another. Then I grew up a little, and saw how many heads I would have to slice off to fulfill my destiny . . . more than I could manage in a lifetime of butchery."

She listened to his calm voice talk of killing while his eyes gazed out at the lotus blooms which held their heads high above the still water of the lily pond.

"I became crafty," he went on. "I studied the precepts of Sun Tzu. . . ." He interrupted himself to start to explain whom he meant.

"I know," said Nina. "I found the book."

"From the general, I learned to value strategy and planning. I learned to gather intelligence about my enemies before I attacked them. And I learned that, under their power and confidence, the French were weak men like any others. The gods might have

474

favored them for two hundred years, but would not necessarily do so forever."

He stretched an arm to the low table between them to select a tidbit. "I changed my methods, but my purpose remained clear, and beautiful in its clarity."

He bit into a slice of candied yam. "There is no ecstasy like that of faith in a purpose."

The bones in his heavily veined hands seemed too light to have swung an executioner's blade. But she saw the force in him that had frightened the servants when she was young.

"It seemed clear to me that only the gods, or the French themselves, could bring down the French. I decided to help the French destroy themselves. And chose opium as my weapon."

He lifted his head and smiled up into the sky; a chill ran up Nina's arm.

"As I was still very young," he said to the sky, "I took great pride in the harmonious nature of my plan—to use the tax to destroy the tax collector."

He turned to her suddenly. "You and your generation will never know how much blood the Viets paid to sustain that 'legitimate' business of the French government. You may think things have changed, that they grow worse, but you are wrong! Nothing has ever been good about our business except the money... and that had virtue only when properly used. I knew that, even then."

The montagnard woman had finished feeding the carp and came to pour them more tea. As she did so, Nina's father touched the woman's hand, lightly, but it told Nina what she wanted to know of their relationship.

"Yes," said Luoc, "I was very proud. And sure. My pride and sureness sustained me while I made myself a spy within the French camp. My pride had a little trouble now and again, when I forced myself to seem a 'good Annamite,' for the sake of destiny. The French government policy of *jaunissement* helped me. It may have been no more than a desperate attempt to pacify the Vietnamese people, but it was timed right for me. I was picked up by French society; I was useful as a token *jaune*."

"Was that why you married *maman*?" Nina cut in. "To infiltrate?"

"Of course." He looked at her without apology. "Though to be entirely fair, I desired her too. Does that make you feel better?"

Nina shook her head silently. A cold lump settled in her center.

"The marriage seemed harmonious," said her father. "Within my larger purpose. She loved me, and was a little stupid. A clever Frenchwoman would have found me out. Also I might have loved her too much."

Nina looked at him levelly. 'Was that why you did not want to love me? Because I might have made you soften your purpose?"

Anger flashed in his eyes. "You presume!" He stopped himself. "Perhaps. I can't remember now. Too much has changed since then . . . we wander from the track."

He used both hands to shift his right leg on the silk cushion. "I saw greed and corruption, and fed both with opium. I sold the French opium to smoke. Louis had a special talent there. I used the money from the sales to buy weapons to fight them. I fed their private wars with intrigue. It was satisfying. And successful."

"You drove them out," said Nina. "Just as you planned."

He raised an eyebrow at her tone. "Have you ever decided, by the way, which side you choose?"

"I'm both," she replied. "There's no escape from either."

He shook his head sadly. "Then you won't like anything I have to say. Yes, I helped drive them out. *We* drove them out—peasants, sects, students, bonzes, Vietminh—who were simply a mixture of all these. We drove them out, but it was too late."

Nina made a small noise of surprise.

"It was the end of my destiny, after all." He glanced at her. "I had not thought of what was to come next."

Anger began to enter his voice as it had not before. "I learned that we were just the scattered pieces of a nation. The French had always encouraged our divisions and factions, to keep us weak. They stamped on the Dragon's back and broke it . . . not just by force. In two hundred years of ruling they rearranged good and evil according to their own patterns; in doing so, they shattered the harmony of the Old World. Many Vietnamese—the ones who seemed the most favored at the time—tried to see by the French light and found themselves in darkness. That was the worst violation—to rearrange our understanding of the world."

He was becoming lost now in his own story. "As the French began to leave, I saw what chaos is. 'Where is the sage,' I asked myself, 'who will know how to make order again?' At first I had hopes for Ho and his plans to unify the country. Then he was prevented by a fellow countryman who wished to keep the country divided for his own sake. And the Americans helped him. And Ho turned for help to our ancient enemies, the

476

Chinese, whom we have fought for centuries. I thought, Such an alliance with old enemies can never be harmonious.

"I continued to wait for our new leader to show himself. I continued to sell opium in order to buy arms for the right man. I waited. And I waited. Each time I found a man I thought I could trust, he was destroyed by corruption, either his own or that of others.

"At last I came to a bitter conclusion—that we had gained nothing by defeating the French. I saw my own people continue to tax each other, just like the French. We continued to fight each other, to bombard and burn our own cities and villages, to execute our brothers, always in the name of the nation!

"Some Viets blame the Americans. The 'new barbarians' replacing the French. But the French came to loot. I believe the Americans came to help. Or that was what they intended. Unfortunately, in exchange for this help they too wanted to rearrange our understanding. And their truth was not ours, any more than the French truth had been.

"Now the Americans are another hammer driving wedges into cracks already there—a large hammer, I'll admit."

He smiled briefly, then added, "We must become the hammer, not the rocks."

He leaned forward to replace his teacup on the table. The cup rattled as he put it down.

"Now I will confess a folly to you, to show you the weakness as well as the wisdom of your elders. For many years, I believed I was a change-fate. I believed that I could throw my individual might behind a direction of fate and make it happen."

He looked at her directly. "After the French left, I lost that direction and could not find it again. When I accepted that failure, my life ended."

Nina knew that this gift of honesty cost him far more than any protestation of praise or affection. They sat in silence for a long time.

Finally he cleared his throat. "So you see, those arms are there because I don't know who deserves such means to kill his fellowmen."

"And the business existed in the end only in order to buy them?"

"Yes." He threw a piece of steamed roll to a bird that had landed beside one of the porch columns. "Shall I give them to you? Would that change your intentions? To have power like that?"

"The power to decide who deserves such means to kill his

fellowmen?" she asked. "You couldn't . . . why should I be better qualified?"

"You're more in the center of things," he said. "Perhaps you can see a leader now who is invisible from here."

"I live in the darkness you described earlier. I don't see any sages there, only wolves and crocodiles." She remembered Thin Pig and the darkness in which she had left him, for good as it turned out.

"I sometimes think I've become a crocodile now, myself." For the sake of arms rotting in the jungle.

He threw another piece of roll onto the floor.

"All life is good; only man makes it evil," he said. "That is why I choose to stay here. Once I had accepted that I was not a change-fate, I was free to desert purpose and seek only harmony. And that is not to be found among my fellows. Do you want to come and live here with me?"

The question caught her off guard.

"Two retired crocodiles together," he said lightly. He looked at her and said gently, "Yes, I know . . . half of you would like to." He laughed. What does the other half want to do?"

She told him about Will John. Then about Andrew, and Carbone, and Thin Pig. It tumbled out. Thu's betrayal—though not their relationship. The Americans . . . Hong . . . Falci. She talked for half an hour. "I can't fight their way. I don't want to."

He listened with few questions, nodding from time to time, and gazing out over the lily pool. When she finished he asked, "Are you angry that you have wasted your life becoming a crocodile, in a dead cause?"

She thought deeply. "Not angry. Sad, perhaps. But it gave me my own purpose."

He tipped the two remaining rolls onto the porch floor, and watched without speaking while a dozen sparrows tumbled from the sky and roof beams into a flapping melee. He was silent until the battle finished and the floor was clear again of every crumb.

"Now you want my help against all those sparrows who want to eat you up?"

"Bloodthirsty sparrows," she replied. "Yes, I want you to be my change-fate."

He laughed. "You have more faith than I do. But I will try."

He called for paper and ink. They cleared the little table and began to work.

"First," he said, "let's try to calculate what it will cost you to get away. Then to live, safely as well as in comfort, to an honorable old age." He laughed. "I've had practice, after all. I did this exercise once before, for myself."

As he began to write, he became as she remembered him, dry and decisive.

"I assume," he said, "that you wish to exclude the arms as realizable assets."

She nodded emphatically.

For another hour and a half he fired questions at her and she replied. Finally he laid down his pen.

"I'm getting tired," he said. "It's time for me to sleep for a while as I do each morning. We will continue after lunch. But there is some help I want to ask of you, as well."

"Of course," she replied.

"I am going to die soon."

He cut off her cry of protest with a gesture. "I assure you I'm not planning to hasten it, though I lack your Catholic abhorrence of the idea. My body has decided. It is very tired."

He glanced at his paralyzed legs. "I believe it will be very easy merely to stop."

She could think of nothing to say. He continued as if planning a trip to Dalat.

"As a boy, I swore to my dead father and grandfather that I would return to lie beside them and I would bring my son to look after our spirits, if they would grant me a favor. I wished to leave my native village, but promised to return to tie up the break and keep our spirits from wandering."

He looked at his spotted hands. "Now Kim is dead, I wish you to act in his place, and to bury me when the time comes, in a grave properly sited according to ritual."

He laughed to himself. "I don't see why the gods can't be a little flexible on the question of daughters. Who knows the truth, anyway? Seek harmony. Pursue propriety. Observe the rituals as best we can. What more can we do?"

He held out his hand to her. She felt the force of his will, as others had done all his life. She hesitated, her response confused. He had given her so much, yet still saw her as second best. Then her soul shrugged and said, Take what is offered.

She slid off her carved chair onto her knees and took his hand in hers. "I am honored that you ask me," she said. In his terms, after all, she was. "I will do it, of course."

He looked gratified but weary. The will ebbed like a dying wave. "I must sleep now. We will continue later."

The two servants came and lifted his chair between them. The woman followed behind.

They worked again in the afternoon. After supper, they went out to the little pavilion overlooking the gorge.

"I still have some questions," said Nina.

He smiled but looked weary. "If they are neither too long nor too difficult. Much as I have enjoyed today, my brain is not used to such exercise any longer."

"Why do you still grow poppies?"

He snorted. "I don't, but my people here need the money. I have no right to deny them the income and I still have the power to protect them a little from abuse by the agents. My woman still tries to persuade me to use opium as a painkiller!"

"Then there is the matter of Carbone."

"Ah . . . yes." She saw a flash of his earlier anger. "What is the question?"

"I know in general why he was angry with you. Did he bomb our house? Why did he choose to wait so long after he began to suspect you?"

Luoc spat onto the porch. "Yes, he did it—after he dared to ask me, in recompense for my alleged thefts from him, to arm a gang of River Pirates to fight the Son of Heaven . . . who in those days still remained in Vietnam to fight for his people. Carbone learned of the arms from my onetime friend and ally, Cousin Thu, who couldn't resist the temptation to swagger in front of a Round Eye. No malice intended, it was just stupidity. Carbone made an ultimatum which I refused."

"But I thought Thu had been working together with you . . . for you and now me," said Nina.

"A man who can't forgive one betrayal would have no allies at all. Yes, he works for me and for you. When he is not working for himself." His glance said clearly that he had heard what she had left out about herself and Thu.

"One last question." Nina turned her head away to hide her blush in the dusk. "I once wanted to pay your debts, but Kim would not let me. Now that I know your feelings about the French, I can begin to guess why."

"Oh, yes," he agreed. "It was quite deliberate. I knew the French were finished, and I was preparing to leave Saigon in any case. Carbone merely forced me before I was quite ready. I had been transferring as many assets as possible into offshore companies and foreign accounts—which I will tell you more about before you leave. I borrowed to the limits from French banks and Sociétés Foncières. I purchased to the limits of my credit from French companies. I wished to do the maximum damage when I left. I had also invested in gold, precious stones, and other commodities that are more useful up here.... I had to leave some behind...you have found some of them yourself."

She stayed that night and one more day. During the day her father introduced her to a group of Meos who worked as agents for the family. They kowtowed to her as well as to her father.

By that evening their planning was finished. Nina said good night to her father as if they were going to meet for breakfast, went to bed until the night bombing raids were over, and set off for Saigon shortly before dawn.

Before Will John could learn she was back, she wangled a visa and a seat on an Air Force flight to Los Angeles. She was there for exactly seven hours before she boarded a return flight. In those seven hours she opened a bank account in the name of Le Thuyet. For the rest of the time before her plane left she strolled the streets of downtown Los Angeles, trying to avoid the torrents of cars, as unruly as those in Saigon but much larger. She finally found an area of side streets where she tried to understand the fast American speech with its Spanish phrases. She bought spicy tacos from a street stall which reminded her of home. She also tried to decide how these Americans on their home ground differed from those in Vietnam. She tried to imagine how she would feel about them as a long-term prospect compared to, say, the French. She returned via Hong Kong, where she opened a second account with Barclays Bank.

Tired as she was from the two long flights, on her return she closeted herself with Eight Hand Horse.

They met in what had been the dining room of the house she now used as her home office. Louis had insisted the previous year that she buy two high-backed white chairs designed by a man called Saarinen, which a colleague of his had bought in Bangkok. Nina found them beautiful but formal; she always felt as if she were sitting on a throne, facing another enthroned member of royalty. Eight Hand Horse sat forward in his, hands on his knees as if ready to leap out at any moment.

"First, Old Uncle," she said, "I bring love and respects from your sister, who is as happy as can be expected when she has lost a child. But she is well. And my father cares for her. I could see that."

The old man's eyes lightened.

"My father, I regret to say, is not so well. I'm very glad to have seen him."

She watched him sag slightly against the white canvas upholstery and look down at his own knotted knuckles.

"Old Uncle," she said, "I have too much for you to do for
you to begin to feel old."

His sharp eyes leaped to her own. "Even I, who should know
better, sometimes think that you have special gifts of understanding."

She laughed. "It's just that we all understand different things."
She was pleased nevertheless. "Now, here is what I want you to
do for me. If we all succeed in the next few months, you will be
free to retire and feel as old as you like. Or to play with the new
grandson I heard rumors of from my father."

She instructed him for an hour. At the end, he looked both
excited and saddened.

When she finally allowed herself her reunion with Will John,
it almost overwhelmed her.

"Did you get what you went after?" he asked.

"Oh my darling Will . . . oh yes! Yes!"

"So when do I get let in on the secret?"

"Not yet. . . ." She paused to kiss him yet again. "Not yet.
When I know more. Have something definite to tell you."

They might be able to remain together if the plans she and her
father had made worked out. She might yet be able to join Will
John's world.

"Whatever happened took twenty years off you!" He was
delighted by her new high spirits.

"I can tell you one thing, in secret," she said, unable to hide
everything from him. "I saw my father."

"I didn't know you had a father."

"Neither did I," she said happily. "But it seems that I do. At
last."

The next evening, he asked, "Does any of what's going on
mean I might persuade you to change your mind about coming
back home with me?"

"Maybe, maybe," was all she would let herself reply.

Falci did not return to Saigon for six months. Thu was proved
right. After the bombings of the North that followed the attack
on Pleiku, the Americans and the South Vietnamese continued
the air strikes without specific provocation and brought the first
reported response from the North Vietnamese Air Force.

Waiting for Falci, on whom her plans depended, Nina became
afraid. Of the sound of planes and of the antiaircraft artillery on
the edges of Saigon. She was frightened by the wounded, who

began to be seen more and more in the streets, and by the growing number of homeless children who roamed in packs. She was alarmed by the fungus of shantytowns which continued to creep into every vacant space that the city didn't think it had. The river was full of American ships, the streets full of American uniforms. The war was intensifying; she was afraid it would overtake her, as she had been overtaken in the past. Thu also seemed likely to overtake her. In his new freedom of the city, he visited her again in June, unannounced and necessitating an unbearable lie to Will John.

Even before Falci returned she began to transfer money to her father's offshore companies and into her Hong Kong and California accounts. Louis took the cinnamon tin of gems to Hong Kong for her on a porcelain-buying trip. She bought an assortment of other small stones to use as emergency currency. She was running faster and faster on the surface of the water.

At last a baggage clerk at Tan Son Nhut, who was on her payroll, told her that Falci had flown in. The man had followed the American from the airport to his new apartment. Nina paid him generously for his enterprise in learning the address. Then she sent Falci a message that she wanted to see him.

45

The Phoenix Tower was now named the Happy Garden. Nina paused briefly on the wide, first-floor balcony. She could not see the guards placed by Snow Man among the ornamental trees beyond the lily pond, but she knew they were there. Eight Hand Horse was stationed in the corridor outside the room. Then she turned to the ornate mirror. Framed in the surround of broken mirror chips, she saw a young woman very different from the one who had first stared up at her reflection in the canopy of the bordello bed. This one looked rich and cool, diamonds in her ears, her hair knotted back to expose a long, smooth neck that rose like a lotus stem from the deep-water blue of her silk dress. The dress was a Patou copy, reassuringly European in its soft chic. She had chosen the color especially for the Catholic Falci, the blue of the Blessed Virgin, honest, virtuous, safe, and demanding respect.

Then she rechecked the labels on the three bottles of wine in the silver cooler. Val di Lupo Bianco. Their presence was a triumph of information and money over implausibility. They held a Sicilian wine, made from grapes from the center of the island where Falci's father had been born. Nina intended to treat the Mafia man to a piece of Oriental one-upmanship. It had taken Louis most of the last six months to find them for her.

She paced the room nervously, touching the immaculate ashtrays, the framed rubbings from temple carvings, and sank into one of the two silk-covered armchairs. Under her tension lay a deep exhaustion. It was now a question of hanging on, and of finding the will to succeed. She shut her eyes to think of Will John. She was making him carry too much for her; he bore the weight of her hopes; he stood for everything outside the pattern from which she was fighting free. Like a sailor on the open sea, she had to keep fixing her eyes on him, to hold her bearings.

The door from the corridor opened. A thin, dark man in a dark suit swept the room with his eyes, then stepped aside. A second man entered more slowly. He was in his early thirties and small by American standards—or at least those of Will John. However, though he was small-boned, broad shoulders and unnaturally heavy biceps pulled at the seams of his short-sleeved sport shirt like those of a weight lifter.

His dark eyes were the only sharp feature in his face, which was otherwise a landscape of little pillows. A soft hillock of chin rolled up into the shadow of a full, sullen lower lip. Two round cheeks propped up puffy lower lids, while the upper lids met his brow bones in curves tight as buttocks. Lax, fleshy ears unfolded from black sideburns which were edged as meticulously as the lawn around a flowerbed in a public park.

She watched his eyes, and the slight swagger of his disproportioned body. The eyes gave him away; they held a hint of uncertainty, of a stranger in a strange land. The swagger demanded that others confirm his power to him, because he did not trust it himself.

Nina forced her hands to relax the fists she had unconsciously made. She made an effort to place them, easy and open, along the arms of her chair. She positioned the muscles of her face into a smile of welcome. Then she lowered her lids to give the Italian a chance to find his bearings in the room without feeling observed.

"Please sit down, Monsieur Falci," she murmured. She raised her eyes to his, looked past him, and felt a rush of warmth on her chair as her bladder opened for a second in shock.

She had already started to offer her hand to the Italian but it fell back into her lap, ice-cold.

Falci followed her eyes and waved for Will John Haines to step forward.

"It's OK, Bill," said Will John. "Madame Martell and I have met before." He nodded toward Nina. "It's nice to see you again, ma'am."

"And you, monsieur..." she croaked. She started to use his name, then decided against it. She blinked to make him disappear, but he did not.

"Please sit down..." she said. She wrenched her attention back to the Italian.

"Welcome to Vietnam, Monsieur Falci," she said automatically in English, as she had rehearsed over and over again. She had her voice under control, but she was afraid he could see her pulse trying to escape from her neck. "I'm delighted to meet you at last. I heard much about your last visit to Saigon."

The Italian gave a perfunctory grin. "Since I got your invitation, I've heard a lot about you too."

Her head turned involuntarily toward Will John.

"Not from me." His blue eyes were steady. She looked away quickly and swallowed. His goodness had all been a sham. He had fooled her. He was a gangster after all. She was in deadly danger and had only imagined her safety with him. She locked her fingers together in her lap to steady them. She scrabbled after her thoughts. Tried to reconstruct Falci's last sentence. Grabbed at a shred of remembered meaning.

She smiled at Falci again. "At least what you heard was good enough to make you accept."

"I never refuse an invitation from a good-looking broad."

Nina held her smile fixed while Falci's eyes made the regulation sweep of her body in its blue silk dress. Mechanically, she rehearsed the points she had asked him there to make. Found a thread of logic and began to pull herself forward along it, hand over hand.

"Then you always buy?"

"It depends on what's on offer."

"Ah well..." said Nina. "It would be rude of me to start business talk without first offering you a drink.... Would you...?"

She turned to Will John with an effort. "Would you be kind enough to pour us all a glass of wine?" She could not stand up for fear she had stained the back of her dress.

"Of course, ma'am. My pleasure." He unfolded himself from the side chair where he had perched.

It gave her a slight satisfaction to see that his hands were trembling as he poured the wine. She could not meet his eyes when he passed her a glass.

Falci extended an arm to take his own glass. "I brought my friend here along in case you wanted to talk French instead of English, but you seem to talk English OK."

"As you wish," she said. She would have preferred to deal in French, in spite of the English teacher she had employed while waiting for Falci, but she didn't think she could survive having all their words reshaped by Will John's warm, dishonest lips. Fortunately, she had rehearsed her main points in English, night after night, before falling asleep.

Falci sipped his wine, looked at the bottle, did a double take, and took the bottle from Will John. "I can't even get this stuff in New York, let alone Tampa! Where the hell did you find it?"

He looked again at the label and shook his head; he seemed genuinely excited by it.

"To honor you, monsieur, nothing is beyond me." She smiled to make her words into a little Oriental joke, but she saw him nevertheless continuing to work through what it had taken to get those three bottles to Saigon. That much of her planning, at least, had succeeded.

"Salute," said Falci in Italian.

"Salut," she replied in French. Will John had not taken a glass himself. She turned in her chair to try to shut him out of her line of vision. He was no longer an ally. Without him, she had no chance of survival unless she won over Falci that evening.

"One of the things I hear, Monsieur Falci, is that your company wants to expand into Asia."

Falci jerked in his chair. He recrossed his legs involuntarily. "Somebody told you wrong! I'm looking for suppliers, that's all."

"You don't have to come all this way to talk to the Alliance Corse," she said. *"Les vrais gentilhommes* have representatives in Marseilles, I believe. To speak for their suppliers in Indochina."

Falci placed both feet on the floor as if braking a car. "What makes you think my company would want to move into Asia?"

"The closure of Turkey," said Nina. "The Middle East is going to dry up as a source of raw opium and stay dried up. Am I on the right track?"

"Keep going," said Falci. "I'll tell you."

"Like it or not, you'll have to buy direct from India, Burma, Thailand, and Indochina. Like everyone else will." She could feel Will John behind her, like an open stove. She wanted to weep, or scream.

"With Turkey cleaned up as a major world source," she said, "and production steady in the other places, the biggest undeveloped potential growing area is the Golden Triangle. Everyone has known how good it is for centuries. But it's still a cottage industry; there's a lot of land in the mountains not yet being used. Good limestone soil, at the right altitude, in areas difficult to police."

She looked at him. "One doesn't have to be too intelligent to see what could happen."

"You still haven't explained why I'm not just a potential wholesale buyer," said Falci.

"I think you want in at ground level. Apart from wanting to save on broker's cuts, you know what we all know—the established suppliers out here . . . the Alliance . . . aren't up to the potential. They set up in business when they had a government to back them. They survived a shift to clandestine dealings during the last war because they had their intelligence service to help them, and their sect army mercenaries to do the dirty work. Most of them are old men now; the young ones are getting restless. But I don't think any of them are thinking positively enough about what is happening here or abroad."

"What *is* going on here?" Falci was leaning forward now, listening intently. "Maybe I don't know either."

"The U.S. has gone from seventy-five thousand men to nearly a hundred and seventy thousand in the last year. Every soldier is a potential user, in spite of what your papers say . . . I've read them in the USIS library, so I know. Every user who survives will take this habit home with him. And how many more men will you commit before it's all over?"

"The market here's worth peanuts," said Falci. "And the papers *I* read are talking about peace negotiations."

"I know what I see," said Nina. "I would be happy to take you for a drive around the delta so you can see for yourself. I see new military installations being built. I see shipments of metal mesh for new landing strips. I see warehouses full of American whiskey and manufactured goods. Every day I see more Americans on the streets of Saigon in combat dress. I see increased staff at MACV headquarters, and new hangars at Tan Son Nhut. I see dollars being invested in the long term."

She paused. "What I do not see are signs that the South is winning the war. You must tell me if your government would allow Ho and the North to unify the country under their rule."

"Under a *Communist* government?" Falci's shock was answer enough.

"Then I rest my case," said Nina. She motioned for Will John to pour more wine.

"And where do you fit in this growing market?" asked Falci. She had made her first point.

"I'll come to that. First, you must understand that while the French may not be able to handle the future of the business, they will hate anyone who tries to take over. They can still do a lot of damage."

"Maybe, maybe not," said Falci.

"If you have family still in Italy," said Nina, "ask them whether a village would rather face an advancing army or a retreating one... which is the more vindictive. The French, including the Alliance, are still a powerful presence in Vietnam. A lot of deals were made with Ho, back in 1954, to protect French capital here. Certain French are here to stay. Defeated or not."

She had finally given him news he didn't know. He looked up from his nails when she mentioned the deals with Ho. She pressed her point.

"The French were here for two hundred years. They know the country; they know the hill tribes who grow the poppies; some of them still keep private armies of Meo and Lai and Lung. They have made and remade alliances with the *kaitongs* and *sabwas* in Laos and Burma who control vast areas of production. Where would a stranger start, if he wished to challenge them?"

"I have a feeling you're going to tell me," said Falci.

"In that stranger's place," said Nina, smiling to acknowledge his sarcastic sally, "I would be most interested in taking control of an existing network, which is not part of the French structure. The size would not matter so much as... how do you say it... getting a foot through the door."

"What kind of foot?" This wasn't what he had expected.

"Control of certain high-yield growing areas," she said. "A network of agents in the field, existing supply lines and means of transport, contacts to guarantee safe passage of goods in transit, labs, chemists, safe houses... and the information you need to make these assets work for you."

Falci's mouth was slightly open.

"Maps," she continued. "Names of brokers you can trust. Cooperative Customs officers. Introductions to helpful government officials. And a certain amount of legitimate cover." She could feel the intensity of Will John's listening behind her.

Falci closed his mouth and reset the pillows of his face. "What's to stop my company getting all that for themselves anyway?" he asked. "*If* we wanted it. I work for a big company."

His confidence was as absolute as Will John's. If the Mafia wanted something, he knew they would have it. She wasn't afraid of this oddly upholstered little man, but she was suddenly very much afraid of what he represented. She called on her will to fight his confidence.

"Of course, you would get what you want. In time. But it would take time and cost more than I'm asking for the network I'm offering you. And not only that, everyone would know about it by the time you had finished. Vietnam is a small village, monsieur, when it comes to gossip. And in the exclusion of outsiders—we've had so many."

She leaned back in her chair. "Then there's the language problem, of course. You'll have to trust someone sometime. Why not start with me?" She would never trust anyone again.

Falci fished a cigarette out of a pack in the pocket of his sports shirt. The bodyguard, who had been standing by the window, leaped forward with a platinum lighter. Falci sucked at the cigarette and examined the tip carefully to see that it was alight. He exhaled smoothly, and watched the smoke rising.

"You won't be popular," he said.

"I'm not popular now. Does your company worry about popularity?"

Falci's pupils had contracted to pinpoints of suspicion. "Would you agree to a limitation of trade? Not to deal for an agreed period? After a handover period, when your advice would be made available to us."

"Yes, I would agree," she said.

He moved restlessly. "Give me a good reason why you're selling if things are going as great as you say."

She hesitated. This was not how she had imagined telling Will John.

Falci had turned his body away from her in his chair. He was pulling back, preparing to spit out the hook he had so nearly swallowed. She had no choice. Will John was finished anyway.

"Would you believe me if I told you that I have recently learned that I am with child?"

Behind her, Will John made an inarticulate sound.

"It's probably the only reason that could induce me to sell out. I plan to leave Vietnam to have my baby and raise it peaceably in the south of France, where my mother was born.

Women and children don't do well in times of war. And war is what we have here, even if it has never been declared."

"Congratulations," said Falci roughly. "Well, well." His eyes went inevitably to her belly, still flat under the blue silk. "That's food for thought. What kind of terms were you looking for?"

"The value of the capital assets and something for the elements of surprise and goodwill. We can discuss a separate agreement for my services. It's all here." She offered him some papers. "These are for you. They'll give you a more precise idea. Please note that I have excluded all existing stocks of morphine base and next season's crop."

While he read, Nina concentrated on the sound, like two flints being struck together, of a lizard behind the balcony shutters. When he looked up, she added, "No names, of course. On that you have to trust me."

He tapped the ends of the paper together. "I don't know."

She shrank into herself. He was going to refuse her offer. She had ruined herself with Will John for nothing. She was going to remain in the darkness. She didn't understand; she had felt him bite.

Then Falci's eyes slid away with his earlier uncertainty.

"I'll have to talk it over with some people. It's a little premature, if you'll pardon the expression."

Her spirits shot up again. Now she understood; he was only a messenger boy, without the power to decide. His company had not expected things to move so quickly when they sent him out as a scout.

She smiled. "Of course. As long as you remember that the longer we wait . . ."

"I'm flying back Stateside in two days," he said. "If we're interested, I'll get in touch with you."

She had to wait, and pray to every god she could think of. She remembered to press the two remaining bottles of wine on him as he left.

Will John left with Falci, without looking at her again.

She was still awake at a little after midnight, pacing around and around the cloud borders of the Chinese carpet in her bedroom, hardly aware that she followed its predictable symmetry for comfort and in search of calm.

Someone knocked at her door.

"I said I'm not to be disturbed," she cried.

Eight Hand Horse peered through the half-opened door. "I

thought you should know . . . Mr. Will John is downstairs. He won't leave without seeing you, he says. He has a devil in him tonight. Shall I throw him out?"

Nina collapsed suddenly onto the chaise longue and wrapped her arms tightly around her exploding self.

"Yes," she said. She drew another breath. "No! Don't! I have a devil too." She rocked slightly, in her own tight embrace.

The old man looked at her. "Maybe better if he goes away."

She shook her head fiercely. "No, bring him up. Our two devils need to talk!"

Will John paused inside the door, alertly relaxed like a fighter feeling for his next move.

She couldn't look at him when she spoke. "Do all American journalists have friends like 'Bill'?" She was too distraught to attempt English. Her voice was high and tight in spite of her efforts at control.

"Why don't you just ask if I'm Mafia?"

"Are you?" It sounded absurd, even as she asked. But he had been there, in the room with them. With "Bill." As "my friend here"!

"I'm not Mafia. Nor connected with them in any way. I was there to translate, as Falci said."

"Why you?" Her eyes were angry. "I'm not a fool. How did he happen to pick you?"

"I volunteered." He took one step into the room. "Why didn't you tell me your father was a gangster?"

She stood up. "He was never a gangster! He was a patriot . . . if you can understand that. As an American, you should understand patriotism!"

"And you . . . ?"

"I tried to tell you," she cried. "I told you as much as you wanted to hear. I nearly said more, so many times, but I was afraid. . . . You needed to admire me. I couldn't afford to lose you."

He held up his hands in a plea for a truce. "You're right, I admired you. Maybe I didn't want to hear more. But it doesn't keep me from feeling a fool now! And what's worse—unless I'm very careful—it doesn't keep me from looking like one."

Her knees lost their strength and she sat back down on the chaise longue, very, very slowly.

"What do you mean?" she asked carefully. "Who are you afraid to have see you as a fool? It's not something that usually seems to worry you."

He crossed, uninvited, to the chaise longue and sat on the end. She pulled her legs away from him.

The chaise longue creaked under his weight; the noise was huge in the silence of the room.

"I'm afraid for both of us," he said. "If I had known the truth, I might have been able to protect you better. Now, I don't know. I don't know what damage may be done already. Or what my credibility will be when the crunch comes. You're going to have to tell me more before I know."

"Will," she said, "you're scaring me to death! Who are you?"

He exhaled as Thu had done when she found out about the chemists at Heron. "For a start, I really am a journalist. I wasn't lying to you. I really am writing that damn book and have a rough draft to prove it. But I moonlight, as they say. From time to time. The Agency is always interested in people who have good, visible reasons for poking their noses into things—journalists, photographers, teachers, engineers and surveyors, marine biologists. . . ."

A new, terrifying pattern began to form itself around him and to reach out to interlock with her own pattern.

"Right now, they're particularly interested in the growing involvement of U.S. citizens in the drug trade in Southeast Asia. It's bad for the image of the war, back home. And it's already scaring the shit out of the FDA."

A strand broke somewhere in the system of strings that were holding her together.

"I see," she said. "I see quite clearly. My God! Thu was right about you!"

"No," he said. "I don't think you see yet."

He took her arms and pulled her around to face him.

"Listen to me." He shook her gently. "It's very important for you to listen!"

She met his eyes cynically. *"J'écoute!"*

"I have no professional interest in you personally. None whatever. I am interested only in my fellow Americans. Do you understand that? And, in particular, my fellow Company employees."

She shook her head in disbelief, *"C'est fou! C'est incroyable!* You should have told me. I would have spoken more slowly tonight, to give you time to take notes!"

"You're still not listening!" He showed anger for the first time. "I'm trying to make something clear. I'm interested only

492

in Falci, and in the Americans he contacts here. Not the rest of you. Not at the moment.''

"'The rest of you!''' she repeated. "Who are you lumping me with?''

"Any other drug dealer you like!''

She flinched. There was a limit to his acceptance after all. He was right, of course.

After a moment's silence, he resumed, more gently. "I'm involved in a nasty in-house investigation. Digging out dirty linen. The SDECE may have encouraged their operatives during Operation X. But the American government feels differently about its services. The Agency isn't keen to have its people pick up where French intelligence left off. Certainly not in a visible way.''

He was after Thu's new White Devil allies.

"And what about the 'rest of us'?'' she asked. "What responsibility do you have to report on us? If you think it's relevant?''

Not only had she lost Will John, she might have lost the right to enter America again, to use the bank account she had so recently opened.

He rubbed his hands over his rough face as if washing it, then looked at her so directly that she felt it to the tops of her knees.

"I've just spent the last four hours going crazy over that question. I didn't come here until I began to see my way through.''

"You mustn't compromise yourself for the sake of a good dink lay,'' she said.

"Cut the crap, Nina. We're both too tired.... I went back over things in my mind.... I don't think that any of my reports so far can implicate you. Unless you have connections I don't know about which could damage you. I now have a very straightforward get-out, which is that I happen to consider my reporting officer here to be under suspicion. I won't be expected to report anything to him. I don't know what or how much they're going to believe when I get back to Washington, anyway. In any case, you won't count for much over there. Thank God!'' He looked at her. "And of course, there's the mitigating factor that you're getting out. If you can pull it off. I'm sure you could make up a good story about your motives to make the whole thing look positively noble.''

She gazed at him in despair. "You'd never believe how close you are to being right!'' A dreadful new thought struck her. "Did you know I would be there tonight?''

"It occurred to me as a wild possibility when I heard the venue."

"When did you hear?"

"The night before last."

"Oh, my God," she whispered, "and I didn't know it."

"We're both having to adjust to our own ignorance," he said. Then he leaned forward and his face changed. She braced herself for the question she knew was coming next.

"Nina, are you really pregnant?"

She couldn't make her first request for help when she had just destroyed his feelings for her.

"No," she said, and looked away so she wouldn't have to see the relief on his face. "I thought it would sound good. I think I was right."

"Yeah." His voice was muffled.

She looked in spite of herself. He had buried his face in his huge hands again and was rubbing the temples with his fingertips. Light gleamed on his almond-colored hair. She fought the desire to smooth the hair above his ear that he had tousled by his rubbing. Her main sensation now was grief.

"Well," he said after a while. "Well, well, well. Where does this leave us?" When he raised his face, the planes seemed disarranged. "I guess I should go before I pretend that none of it happened, because I want to take you to bed again."

"Please . . . Will."

"That wouldn't clear our heads, would it?" He gave her a shaky smile and rose quickly. He crossed to the door as if in a sudden hurry to get away. Then he paused beside it.

"The old man isn't going to beat me up, is he?" he asked, with a touch of his old humor.

"Please go!" she begged him.

When the door closed behind him, she ran into the washroom and threw up into the basin. She retched and retched until only bitter green slime was left.

I thought morning sickness was only for mornings, she said to her reflection as she wiped her face and neck with a cloth wrung out in cool water. At that moment she wanted to vomit up the child.

46

Five days later, Clinton Clay rang her doorbell.

"I hope you don't mind if I bother you at home," he said. He fanned the bulge of his belly, which sagged between his khaki-covered thighs as he sat on her formal sofa in the drawing room. His white T-shirt was dark around the neck and sweat gleamed through the bristle on the top of his head.

"I got a long-distance phone call from America this morning," he explained. "Through the military switchboard; it was a message for you! The party thought you'd understand if he didn't get in touch personally."

Her heart began to thud.

"I'm honored that you take the trouble," she began.

"Yeah!" he said. "And all that." He grinned.

She couldn't help grinning back. The man was a scoundrel, but his airy dismissal of formalities had its appeal.

"He wants you to go ahead with your plans for his holiday in 'Nam. . . . He liked it so much last time he was out!" He rolled his eyes toward the chandelier.

She exhaled sharply.

"Was it definite? Or just in principle?"

"I quote," said Clay. " 'Her figures are in the ball park. . . .' Want a translation?" He gave it.

"When is he back in town?" she asked. So Clay was their man in Saigon already! For a man of his bulk, he was fast on his feet.

"In a few weeks. He'd like to take you to dinner. Lucky man." Clay's compliment was too casual to give offense.

He tilted his head back and swallowed the second half of his beer. "I'd better be going. I expect you have a lot to do, to get ready for that dinner."

As they stood to shake hands, she saw his eyes run over her belly.

When he had gone, Eight Hand Horse appeared to tell her that Clay had offered him a bribe to be told whether or not she was really pregnant.

"Did you accept?"

"Of course!" The old man looked injured that she should doubt it.

"I hope you made him pay. He can afford it."

"Mademoiselle Nina!" He lifted his chin and wisps of whiskers. "Do you think I am completely past it?"

"Just checking." She laughed. "Old Uncle, it seems that we are in the ball park!"

"Is that a good place to be?"

"It's on our way."

The bad news was that she could no longer trust Clay to help make her travel arrangements, and her next project was another trip back north. She was ready to begin her second phase of the plans she and her father had made.

The next day she reconsidered, and asked Clay to get her a number three priority press card. He asked no questions and she offered no information on how she planned to use it. When she returned to Saigon, after being away four weeks, her pregnancy was entering its fourth month.

She felt less ill but very tired. Only a close observer would notice a slight overall filling out of her flesh; her belly was still flat, though she could feel a solidity inside it that would soon begin to nudge at her outline. As in the folklore about pregnancy, her hair was glossy, her skin smooth. The most visible hint of her condition was a lavender translucence in the skin beneath her eyes.

As soon as she was back, she contacted Hong to ask him to recruit additional assistants for one season only. She gave him the necessary funds, and a guarantee of enough money to see young Ping through university. She also began to look for a safe site for another lab.

She had Chinchook arrange two safe-deposit boxes under false names, one at the Hong Kong and Shanghai Bank, the other at the Chartered Bank. Into the one at the Chartered Bank he put a sealed envelope containing all the information for Falci and left the box in the name of Farrantino. Into the box at the Hong Kong and Shanghai he put copies of everything in Falci's box.

Then Clay stopped by again, to say that Falci was back in town and wanted to meet.

Will John had not contacted her since he had walked out of her house the night they had met Falci.

Getting north had not been as difficult as she had feared. Tiny Albert had a cousin who was an ARVN driver; there was a convoy leaving Saigon for Dalat; Nina, back in an *ao dai,* rode along as a girlfriend, a cousin, or a sister; no one asked. Using the number three priority press card she got a seat on a flight from Dalat to An Khe, in the central highlands of Annam. At An Khe she paid an extortionate price for an old 4 CV Renault, and a nearly equal amount to the former owner to drive it for her. He had refused to hire it to her because of the risk of mines and the scarcity of replacements once out of Saigon.

By night the Vietcong had closed the roads in the area to all traffic, but by day private cars were usually permitted on the

496

roads, safe as long as they avoided mines. Nina slept in An Khe and set out the next morning along Route 19 into the Mang Yang Pass, which led into North Vietnam.

In the front, the driver was nested among four sandbags; in the back, Nina was protected by used flak jackets and a heavy steel plate under the seat. Ahead of them was a narrow slice of air between two walls of rock—the Mang Yang Pass.

"Merde!" said her driver suddenly as they rounded a bend. He leaned on his horn. They had overtaken a unit of montagnard soldiers accompanied by two American Green Berets who rode a jeep at the rear of the marching column.

Horn blaring, they bumped past the line of men. Once they were clear, the driver put his foot flat to the floor. The car leaped across the scar of a mine explosion and strained forward up the step mountain road. The flak jackets rapped against the back doors of the car and Nina laid a protective hand on her belly.

The driver glanced at her in the mirror. "Sorry, madame! But VC wait for soldiers. Very dangerous near them."

Two kilometers farther on, he slowed down as suddenly as he had accelerated.

"Don't look, madame. We pass VC now. Both sides."

Nina swiveled her eyeballs, neck stiff, but could see nothing.

They drove straight down the center of the road, at a dowager's pace, in total silence. The countryside was as still as the inside of the car.

Then they heard the sound of shooting below them, back along the road. Even more faintly, a little later, they heard the buzz of helicopters coming in from the base at An Khe. Then they slipped over the top of the pass.

The first agent she met was a warlord turned local militia captain. He was suspicious, but her father's name, and the letter from him to the warlord which she had brought, convinced him to take the risk she was proposing. He was also persuaded by the potential profit of the risk. Her message to him was the same as to all the agents she met, and it was simple—hold back stock and sell it secretly to her for a higher than normal price. Blame the shortfall on a bad harvest.

Other agents were more difficult, both personally and geographically. The morning after leaving the ex-warlord, her driver had refused to go any farther. She abandoned the car in exchange for a water buffalo and cart which took her as far as a local airstrip and a private plane, flown by a pilot whose name she got from Thu.

None of the agents she met was already acting for her father;

he was speaking to his own people in his area, leaving her the unknowns. In some cases he warned her not to mention his name. She went in obliquely, smelling out reluctance or the wrong kind of greedy alertness. She never even came to the point with one tough little man—a local police chief—with eyes like bullets and a Colt revolver he wore like a ceremonial sword. He had the arrogance of a man with his finger in every known pie and a need to control. She could not trust him not to try to improve on her offer by opening the auction to a higher bidder.

She had one refusal—a wealthy widow, a hotelier and former Catholic, whose four sons did the running and whose careers she mapped out. The woman simply refused to hear any of Nina's leads. Courteously, over scented tea, she spat out every baited hook and waited for Nina to leave them in peace, insofar as that word could now be used in daily life.

She persuaded the rest that the risk was almost entirely hers. With supply lines disrupted by bombing, the problem was getting the opium to Saigon. They would be paid whether the opium got through or not. All each of them had to do was keep his or her mouth shut.

By the end of the four weeks she had spoken to nineteen agents, ranging in scale of their operations from a headman with half a dozen villages to the ex-warlord who controlled production of twenty villages over a wide and difficult terrain.

Two men on her father's list were dead, their villages wiped out in Operation Rolling Thunder. She had almost reached another man before she learned through gossip along the way that he had become a trainer of VC cadres, and wrote him off as a bad risk. She couldn't reach three others, because of fighting in their districts. When she had finished, she had recruited seventeen; with her father's people that should be just enough to present a convincing picture of two provinces and provide her with the extra amounts of raw opium she needed.

The more she saw of the countryside, the more she realized what a protected island of relative peace Saigon now was. She was shocked by huge areas of charred, jagged teeth of incinerated trees, and by the unreadable spaces filled with disorganized matter in which her eyes searched for clues—fragments of broken carts, a standing cross beam, or a black frizz of burned thatch. Then, slowly, like a lantern slide coming into focus, the ghostly image of a former village would take shape.

The Saigonese did not yet know that these ghostly images were replacing their country as they knew it. They would certainly never know what might or might not have happened in the even more remote areas, high in the mountains, where the poppies grew—unless they did as she had done, and traveled there. That was her greatest risk, one which she and her father had decided was worth taking.

She was less happy about her other main area of risk; the journey had convinced her that she would never be able alone to organize the logistics of transporting the extra opium. Reluctantly, she decided that she would have to bring in Thu. He would cooperate as long as he understood how much money would be made and did not guess what she planned to do with it. Her plan would also explain to him her need to delay her departure for Laos.

Falci invited her to dinner, as Clay had said, five days after she returned. His apartment in a new block was like a hotel suite, all ostentatious luxury without personality—raw silk, marble, a miniature refrigerator disguised as a disguised television set. The noisy air-conditioning was set so high that the room felt like a walk-in freezer at a meat-packing plant. Nina shivered in the flowing silk smock she wore over her straight skirt to exaggerate her pregnancy.

She sank into the huge beige chair, shaped like a manta ray, and arranged her alligator-shod feet and jeweled hands into careful insouciance, while Falci offered the self-consciously gallant assistance due to her condition. From the beginning, this meeting felt different from their last one; Falci had obviously been instructed to treat her as a friend and ally. Their respective lawyers joined them for liqueurs and coffee after dinner. To Nina's relief, Falci had brought his own lawyer from the U.S.A.; she would not have been happy to see a Saigon legal man there.

The only bad moment was the one she had been preparing herself for ever since their first meeting at the Happy Garden. When they had finally settled on the details both of the sale and of her unwritten but understood and highly paid agreement to advise and inform them for a set period of one year after the sale, Falci asked the question she had not yet been able to answer for herself.

"How do you want payment arranged?"

"U.S. dollars, by cable transfer," she said.

"To where?"

She hesitated. She had two choices—Hong Kong or Los Angeles. The more time went by without hearing from Will John, the more she became convinced that he was going to include her in his final report to his superiors in Washington.

Diem's sister-in-law had already been refused permission to enter America because of her political activities; Nina did not consider herself likely to be any more attractive to the U.S. immigration authorities. On the other hand, she did not want a trail of Mafia money, laundered or not, leading out of the country to her in Hong Kong. She wanted to move it herself, in her own time and her own way.

The choice was impossible. There was no way to judge; she took a deep breath and heard herself say, "Los Angeles."

Oh, buffalo calf, she reproved herself. You'll never learn!

A week later they met again to sign the deeds for Heron Confectionery, the fleet of fishing sampans, and the house in Dalat. Falci signed in the name of William Farrantino. The transfer of his company's money into her account would be confirmed by telex, to Le Thuyet.

That week she also found a second, larger, laboratory site, an old French school near a sugar refinery south of Saigon. She moved Hong there from the syrup bottling plant.

To her disquiet, the lull in bombing continued and the papers and radio were full of reports of "peace efforts," or "smoke screens," depending on the point of view. In any case, if these efforts continued they might ease Thu's transport problems out of the North but would increase the chances that her secret dealings with the agents would be discovered.

She still had heard nothing from Will John.

To keep up social appearances, she went to a USOM reception for some visiting bigwig or other. It was held in a large private house in the American sector belonging to the main USOM representative in Saigon. Guests flowed in and out of the house, to and from the long tables arranged on the lawn, holding bottles and glasses, or plates of small pieces of food skewered on slivers of bamboo. Torches stuttered in the flowerbeds. In the far corner of the garden a concrete block barbecue, supervised by the host, sent up smoke signals with news of burned pork chops and chicken. She noticed with interest that Falci was not there, either *non grata* on the official government level or not interested in being *grata*.

Will John was standing near the barbecue. Nina abandoned her glass and paper plate and fled to her car. She didn't even look for her hostess to say good-bye. She found the car but not Eight Hand Horse, who had seized the chance of free food, drink, and gossip with other chauffeurs in the servants' quarters. Tiny

Albert nodded from a farther car where he was chatting with a friend. There was no one else in the street but the youth who had been delegated to watch all the expensive American cars and their hubcaps. She collapsed into the backseat.

She wished she hadn't seen him. In the last few weeks she had tried not even to think of him. By day she had almost succeeded, but at night she felt a grief worse than death. She asked herself why she was struggling so hard to survive when she was already half dead without him. Seeing him was like regarding an amputated limb, a part of oneself now gone, belonging and lost at the same time.

Will John opened the car door. The car seat sagged toward him. He raised his hand to cut off her protest.

"I have to see you. I'm leaving tomorrow."

Shock canceled all other reactions.

"For how long?" she asked, too numb to think.

"Probably for good." He looked at her for the first time since he had made his kamikaze dive into the car. "We have to decide whether we trust each other or not."

"What does 'trust' mean in the circumstances?"

"It means whether or not we are going to try to change the circumstances. If we don't do that before I leave, we've had it. Us, I mean."

She had never heard him talk so fast or so intensely. His nervous energy made her frightened for him.

"How can I trust you," she asked, "when Falci does too?"

"That's the point you kept missing when we talked last time. And a central point that I'm going to make when I get back—as soon as he knew who I was working for, Falci took me for granted. It's pretty damning, however you look at it."

"Do you really want to change the circumstances?" she asked. "Do you really trust me?"

"I probably won't trust you at all for a long time. But I love you. That's the problem."

"Not the only one," she muttered under her breath. Dusk hid the gentle bulge of her belly.

"He touched her hand and she jumped as if he had burned her. "I won't stay long," he said, "because you shouldn't be seen with me right now. Apart from everything else, I'm beginning to make some people here a little nervous. But there are two things I have to tell you. The first is this."

He gave her a strip of paper. "It's a contact number for me in the States. Classified, so be careful how you use it. You'll have to leave a message, but it will reach me. Promise to use it if you need to."

She peered at it in the fading light, then folded it carefully. This was happening too fast; she had things to say to him but couldn't think what they were.

"The other thing is that I'm going to file for divorce when I get back. Not because of you, necessarily. It's just that I've overdosed on deceit. Where I have the choice to cut down on deceit, I have to take it . . . are you listening to me?" He bent down his large head toward her.

She nodded dumbly, still scrabbling for words. Tomorrow he would be gone, and take with him every chance that things could be put right again. She didn't believe they could, but now she realized that she had hoped.

"Will you let me know if you pull off what you're doing with Falci . . . whether you do get clear? Please!"

She nodded again.

"Do you hate me?" His question shocked her.

"I . . . hate *you*?"

"For the lies?" His earnestness almost made her smile.

"Why should I?" she asked. "They make you a little more like me."

He made an undecipherable sound in his throat and picked up her hand. She closed her fingers on the back of his hand for strength.

An American couple passed the car on the way back to their own, laughing loudly. There was an awkward silence inside Nina's car. Then he kissed the palm of her hand quickly and got out. Through the window he said, "Be careful. And let me know."

Then he disappeared through another group of departing guests.

She sent Snow Man to Tan Son Nhut the next day to see that he left safely.

47

Shortly before the Tet New Year 1966, a prominent *tay phap* did a reading for a Chiu Chao drug dealer in which he warned the man of a bad poppy harvest. "The poppies are not ripening well, the fighting in the North has upset the spirits who encourage the rising of the juices. These spirits have fled into the highest mountain peaks to sulk.''

This news was all over both Cholon and Saigon in twenty-four hours. When she heard it, Nina asked Eight Hand Horse to send a further gift of respect and thanks to the *tay phap* involved. Her second phase was well under way.

The news reached Carbone the following day. He thought about it for another two days. All the early reports had suggested a good harvest. This had happened before; sometimes the predictions had been accurate, sometimes not. Then he pinpointed what was bothering him. Though the *jaunes* dressed their predictions up in the language of spirits and magic, Carbone could usually detect a natural explanation under the flights of religious poetry. But not this time. He decided to send a man north, to see for himself, a *jaune* he could trust.

The Tet passed with media reports of renewed efforts at finding peace. High in the mountains, the poppies began once again to open. The women sharpened their double-bladed knives and cleaned their containers to be ready for the brown sap.

By the end of the second week after petal fall, Thu's men were making calls that were not on their usual collection routes. Other Meos, recruited by Luoc and Eight Hand Horse, visited other villages and other agents. They moved fast and secretly, because the regular collectors for the region were right behind them.

They called on the agents whom Nina had visited. These agents reported to the regular collectors that the harvest had been surprisingly bad, as had been predicted not only by the *tay phap* in Saigon but by other *tay phaps* closer to the poppy fields themselves. The regular agents passed the news of the shortage to the next link in the chain and the price of crude opium began to rise. The local warlords and officials put up their prices for the small quantities of gum they had been able to garner. The men who brought the gum for their labs to refine to morphine base had no choice but to pay. In any case, they would pass the price increases on to the next buyers in the chain.

Carbone's man could learn nothing that seemed out of order. Every agent he spoke to corroborated the reports of a bad harvest and a surprise shortage of crude gum. On his last night before returning to Saigon he stayed with an old friend, a district police superintendent. Though a good northern nationalist, the policeman had greatly admired the American General Patton and, like him, carried a Colt revolver at his belt.

"No. Nothing," he told his friend when asked if anything strange had happened in the last few months. "Everything is quite normal. Poppies not bad. The defoliants are dropped lower in the foothills."

Carbone's man stiffened. "Not a bad harvest, then?"

"Why do you ask? Is something funny going on?" The policeman leaned forward in interest. "I did have a visitor three months ago . . . perhaps a little less. A woman. I never learned what she wanted. She went away without saying. Seemed strange."

"Can you describe her?" The portrait meant little to Carbone's man, as his instructions were to learn about the harvest, but he filed it away to report to Carbone just in case. He also decided to stay another two days and to pay a personal visit to one of the poppy-growing villages.

In Saigon, Nina kept close tally of the quantities of crude opium that reached her. One consignment never arrived; the man responsible for transferring it on its last leg of the journey said that the caravan had never reached the rendezvous but had been attacked by VC just south of the DMZ. The rest, however, kept trickling in. More and more, until the trickle became a stream, and the stream a river. A secret river.

The next weeks would be a test of her nerve. The longer she waited, holding back her stocks, the higher the price increases would reach in the chain of sales. But the longer she waited, the greater were the chances that someone's nerve would break, or that someone would get too suspicious and she would be betrayed.

She gave Chinchook extra funds to put out a special alert for any news that was relevant—the price being paid at all levels, any movements of supplies, any rumor whatsoever about the trade. It was not Chinchook, however, but Louis who brought her the rumor that a *kaitong* who was prominent in opium dealing in Laos had been shot, for reasons that were not clear. The story couldn't be verified, but it troubled Nina; even the rumor of violence was enough to frighten the people from whom she had made her secret purchases. She could only hope that she had paid more than the possible rewards of treachery.

Both Eight Hand Horse and Chinchook separately brought her the story that a Corsican importer in Vientiane had been attacked by a Laotian general, who accused him of hiring bandits in order to attack one of the general's mule trains and to steal the consignment of raw opium it carried. Nina was relieved to have

504

attention shifted away from Saigon to Vientiane; dealers were growing jumpy as prices continued to rise. The price of Indian opium had also begun to rise. Nina began to have the familiar sensation of running over water, trying not to fall through the surface. When the price of crude opium reached thirty U.S. dollars a kilo she decided to go into final gear. First, she checked that Hong and his reinforced group of assistants were under way in the new lab. Then she summoned Daniel Jouvet.

"My dear Nina," said Jouvet, as he bent over her hand on her veranda. "Is it possible that you're *enceinte?*"

She smoothed her silk dress over the now-visible bump and recrossed her ankles, which had begun to swell. "I'm not exactly announcing it in the press."

"Well, well." Jouvet's eyes gleamed. "Enough said. I'm dumb as the grave. Is it your John Wayne's by any chance?"

"Daniel! I'm surprised at you. There are some things a gentleman waits to be told by a lady."

Lady, in a pig's eye! he thought. "Sorry," he said. *"Mea culpa."*

He accepted a gin and tonic from the *mama-san,*

"I have another buyer for you," said Nina. "I think you should broaden your scope a little, beyond Clay. It's somebody who won't toss it in along with his jukeboxes and black market whiskey deals. A serious buyer."

He leaned forward in his chair. "I'm all ears. Who?"

"The new tourist in town. Falci."

Jouvet leaned back; he had had his ear to the ground too, by the troubled expression on his face. "You're playing with *de grands fromages!"*

"Scared?"

He brushed both mustaches in turn, like a giant chipmunk smoothing its cheeks. "Why should I be scared? I'll take Falci before the Chiu Chao any day." He thought for a moment. "What about Clay?"

"There will be enough for both of them."

"You're joking. You, of all people, must know that the harvest has been lousy!" He stopped suddenly and looked at her. "How?" he asked. "How is there enough?"

"Luck," she said. "The poppy-tending spirits seem to have been a bit stauncher in my part of the mountains than elsewhere."

She ignored the skepticism in his eyes. "It would be a good introduction for you, Daniel. To be able to offer Falci something he will have trouble getting anywhere else in the same quantity. And at a reasonable price.''

He knew there was something wrong; he moved uncomfortably in his chair. She was counting on his greed.

"You *are* talking about number four?" he confirmed.

She nodded.

"How many kilos?"

She didn't want to frighten him off with the scale of the figures. Not till he bit. "I don't know. I'm still keeping track of the crude coming in. I'll let you know as soon as I have final figures myself. Meanwhile, I thought you might want to contact Falci, just to break the ice."

As soon as Jouvet had left, Chinchook arrived. In spite of her precautions to him about being seen with her, he swung up the driveway in a silver green Studebaker and sprayed gravel into the flowerbeds when he stopped under the corner of the veranda.

"Messenger boy!" he called cheerfully as his cockade of hair bounced up the steps. "What about that car, then? Number fucking one, hey?"

"Whose is it?" she asked.

"Mine!" He dropped into Jouvet's chair with an expression of uncontained delight. "I'll take you for a ride if you like, Big Sister. Listen, it has a radio too."

The instruction was unnecessary. Pat Boone's latest hit was shaking the hibiscus through the open car windows.

"Good for top-secret work," she said.

He grinned. "I make so much noise, nobody thinks it's secret. That's the best way!" He dug into the pockets of his tight American blue jeans, which had recently replaced his shorts, and gave her a crumpled telex.

"From the hotel board. Coca-Cola Boy told me it came."

It was addressed to Miss Thuyet, care of the latest big new American hotel, which received and posted international telexes as a service to its guests. It confirmed the transfer of $210,000 into account number 003 259 44761, and was signed by the manager of the Los Angeles bank. The sale was now confirmed and concluded.

She read it again, then crumpled it and tossed the ball of paper into the air. She didn't know whether to feel exhilaration or terror. She was laying mines in the road behind her.

"Good news?" asked Chinchook. He still had not learned to read.

"I think so, Little Brother. I hope it will turn out to be good

506

news. . . ." She gave him money for himself and an envelope for Coca-Cola Boy.

"Where did you get that car, Little Brother?"

"I had some good luck," he said. "Never mind!" His eyes were both smug and evasive.

The next morning she sent Falci his safe-deposit key and the name on the box. She kept the second key on the chain with her seal for the time being.

"Are you quite sure?" Carbone demanded of the man he had sent north.

"No mistake. The headman himself told me the crop was better than last year."

"Mother of God!" Carbone threw down the brass letter opener with which he had been etching grooves in his blotter and walked to his bookcase, where he stared at five volumes of *Voyages dans l'Indochine* without seeing them. Then he crossed to the window. Angelica and the gardener had their heads bent intently over some minute sprig of green. His own morning coffee stood abandoned on the white table on the lawn.

"And this woman, who visited your friend, then went away without saying what she wanted—did she visit anyone else?"

The other man looked downcast. "I do not know. I only learned of her at the end."

"It would have been useful to know. What was she like?"

As the man talked, Carbone's face began to darken in the way that terrified Angelica

"Was he absolutely sure she was a *métisse*?"

"One can always tell."

"And not over thirty?"

The other man looked sly. "He was sure of that. He said he would have liked to ask her for . . . you know . . . but she was too much of a . . . *personnage*, if you know what I mean. He didn't want to put his neck on the block just for the sake of fun. He thought she might be a VC cadre, and they can be very holy-minded. So he thought better of it."

It was enough for Carbone. He might be wrong, but he didn't think so. If the woman had been Nina, it was no coincidence that false reports of a bad harvest were pushing prices up at his expense. Carbone sent for his second gardener, whom he had hired because the boy's sister was one of Nina's maids. Just to be sure.

The day Carbone met his messenger, Nina had three important meetings. The first was with Jonathan Hong. As a result of what

507

he told her in the morning she arranged to see Daniel Jouvet later the same day at the Espresso Bongo coffee bar.

"How was your first meeting with Falci?" she asked him.

"Very cordial," said Jouvet. "Very friendly. I think he's beginning to understand how much he has to learn out here."

"How fast could you settle a deal with him?"

"Tonight, if I had the information to work on."

"Go ahead, then,"she said. "Tonight. Three hundred kilos, plus."

Jouvet's cup of coffee hovered just over its saucer. After a count of two, it clinked into place. He took a deep breath. "Three hundred . . . of number four? Where did you steal that much?"

"Some people," she said gently, "might object to that question. It's all bought and paid for. I gambled with expected profits this year . . . borrowed cash and bought some base in, from Laos."

If he had heard any rumors connecting her with Thu, they would confirm this possibility. She watched him try to find the courage to tell her she was lying.

"I thought you'd be busy calculating your percentage instead of worrying," she said. "If the scale makes you nervous, I can get someone else to handle it."

The ploy seemed obvious, but it worked.

"I'm not nervous," he said testily. "I'll admit it's big. But it doesn't make me nervous." His forehead was beaded with sweat.

"It's big," he repeated. "Yesss. . . ." At last she saw his mental calculator start to whir.

"You can see why I need someone I can trust to handle it for me."

"I can indeed." His pupils widened slightly as he finished his calculation. "Yes. I can see why!" He stretched his lips nervously.

"Don't let Falci know it comes from one source," she said, letting the gentleness slide off her voice. "Concentrate on building his faith in you . . . for the future."

He nodded. "Does he know you're involved?"

"No. And I'd like it to stay that way." It couldn't stay that way for long; Falci was no fool. She just hoped it would stay that way long enough for her to get out of the country.

"I'll try to talk to him tonight," he said.

That night, while Jouvet was meeting Falci, Nina saw Louis Wu in the drive and rushed to open the door.

"Louis!" She hadn't seen him for several weeks. "What have

you been up to? I've been wondering if you're romantically entangled somewhere . . . you've disappeared!''

He kissed her quietly and led her into the drawing room. Behind them, on the veranda, she saw Eight Hand Horse squatting with his arms over his head.

"Louis, what's wrong?" She felt the boat begin to drop down the side of the wave.

His eyes were on the silk handkerchief he was unwrapping from around a small object. "This was smuggled to me in a consignment of netsuke from an old friend in Hue."

He held out his hand. An ivory seal lay on his palm. Slowly she picked it up, numbed against its meaning. On the bottom a carved dragon curled around itself. The ivory was dark from years of use.

She found herself sitting on the settee.

"You may bury it with him, if you like. Though it would be bad for it to fall into the wrong hands."

"When did he die?" she asked softly. Her words sounded unreal.

"Four days ago. I have the exact time for the horoscope reading. They are keeping him at the villa meanwhile."

With the strange attention to irrelevancies that cushion such moments, she noticed how pale Louis looked without his usual discreet touch of rouge.

"The good men are all leaving us, Louis." Then it hit her. He had left her, alone. Without comfort. So soon after refinding each other.

"Do you want to come here and live with me?" She had been too full of her own problems to pay proper attention to his words. Her loss seemed to turn her inside out. She began to weep.

Louis sat beside her and took her hand. Then he burst into tears.

"Merde," he said. "This isn't what you need from me." He wiped his eyes on his silk handkerchief.

"What could be better?" she asked. They wept together.

"Oh, dear God!" she said suddenly.

"What?"

"I promised to bury him . . . !"

"I thought perhaps you had." Louis assumed it as a matter of course.

"But . . ." She stood up. "I don't see how . . . !"

Louis watched her, puzzled. "Like your brother, but a little more modestly, I would think."

"Oh, Louis!" She watched Louis wiping his eyes again. She couldn't burden him with the fears and uncertainties, or the danger of knowing what she was up to. She would have to rethink all her travel plans.

"Will you get the horoscope read for me, Louis? Encourage the *tay phap* to decide that sooner is better than later. In about five or six days' time."

What if he had died after she had gone? What would she have done about her promise then? It was difficult enough, even now.

The question froze her on the spot. It would have occurred to her father too.

"Do you know how he died?" She could hardly say the words.

He shook his head.

She heard her father's voice saying, "I believe it will be very easy merely to stop." Perhaps he had not done anything to hasten it after all.

It did not occur to her to break her promise to her father. It was all she had. Except the lump in her belly.

On impulse, she suddenly asked Louis, "Could you arrange access to a secure line for an international call for me?" After all, what more could she lose?

Two hours later he led her into an empty office in Cholon whose leather swivel chair still held the rump-print of the absent desk owner, off duty for the night. Louis unlocked a drawer and gave her the telephone.

"I'll wait outside," he said.

Nina asked for the number she had memorized from the strip of paper. The telephone in America was picked up after two rings.

"I have a message for Mr. Will John Haines," she said quickly before she could panic and slam the receiver down again.

"Go ahead," said the American voice on the other end.

"Please tell him that the deal was concluded successfully. If necessary, Miss Thuyet can be contacted by telex, Newhotel, Saigon." She gave the call number.

"Is that all?"

"That's all."

The voice read her words back to her and repeated the call number twice.

"Thank you," she said. She didn't want to let go of even this fragile connection to him.

"You're welcome," said the voice politely. There was a pause. "Good-bye," it said. The line was dead.

I should have left things closed, she told herself. For his sake as well as mine.

48

The next morning, while she waited to hear from Jouvet how his meeting with Falci had gone, Nina began her personal countdown. First she spent two hours with Eight Hand Horse going over their arrangements for their separate journeys out of Vietnam, and for everything that had to be done first. He also gave her a message for his sister, whom he wanted to join him now that both her son and her protector were dead.

"And the grandson?" asked Nina.

"Fortune willing." The old man sighed happily.

He was looking less tired than he had a few months before in spite of his grief. Nina was afraid that retirement would unman him, but he had become animated and excited as he had not been since the night of Thin Pig and the baby. The wisp of hair at one temple twisted upward like a silvery flame, the other downward, giving him a lopsided, tipsy air. His eyes searched the middle distance for escaped ideas and further understandings with an intensity she had not seen for months.

After he left, she began to go through the desk systematically. She put a few papers into her case, burned the rest in the washroom, and washed the ashes down the drain. She put her unused stationery and a few harmless papers back into their usual places. It felt as if she were erasing her life.

I suppose I am, she thought. She paused suddenly, almost drowned in the enormity of what she was doing. She saw herself floating away into space as her mother had done in her dream. Then she shook her head to steady it again.

Look only at the next step, she told herself.

She told her staff that she was planning to visit Dalat the day after next for a much-needed rest out of the heat, possible now that the fighting seemed to have eased. She would take Eight Hand Horse and send for the *mama-san* and others when she arrived and could see for herself if peace there seemed likely to last. She laid out some clothes to be cleaned for the supposed trip.

Jouvet arrived at lunchtime, carrying a briefcase and vibrant with nerves.

"Thank God, it's yours now!" He thrust the case into her hands as soon as they were alone in the drawing room.

"The meeting went well, I take it," said Nina, hefting the case.

"Fifty percent in advance of delivery. He came out with ready cash, planning to buy. But I don't think he expected to spend it all at one time."

Jouvet didn't sit, but paced the room as if looking for an escape route.

"I hope to God you've really got the stuff for me to deliver!"

He stopped, paralyzed by a sudden dreadful fear that perhaps for some reason she wanted to set him up. She could see the thought in his eyes.

"Sit down, Daniel. And calm down."

She opened the case. It was full of American dollars in bundles of hundred-dollar bills.

"It's all there," said Jouvet. "Less mine."

"Daniel, you're doing a splendid job. Now please sit down; you're driving me mad! How long will it take him to get the balance?"

"Two days, he said."

Nina thought. Two more days. She couldn't wait for the second installment. She had to get away from Saigon. She felt it, something oppressive in the back of her mind. She had gambled on too many things. And she felt the pattern settling around her into a final shape. Which must not include her.

"I had planned to fly to Dalat for a week or two," she said at last. "Could I trust you to handle it in my absence? As in normal cases, make the deposits for me."

"Of course you can trust me," said Jouvet. "Or else I assume you wouldn't be doing business with me at all." He looked at her with oversteady eyes.

Why do you feel you need to convince me? she wondered to herself.

"Then I'll go ahead as I had planned," she said aloud. "I'll also tell you how to contact me in Dalat, if you need to. But we'll both assume there won't be a need." She smiled sweetly at him.

* * *

"Yes, sir," said Carbone's second gardener. They were on the back veranda. "She is going to Dalat. The day after tomorrow. For one, two weeks. Depends on the fighting. She said she will send for my sister and others later."

"And your sister is certain that she was away for four weeks about five months ago?"

"Yes, sir. There was a big cleanup in the house while she was away. So as not to bother her. My sister says the *mama-san* and the old man drive her crazy with work."

"Did anyone know where she went?"

"Maybe the old man knows, but he won't say."

Carbone gave the young man several piastres. "Now, see if your sister can find out what time she's leaving the day after tomorrow. Ask her to look for a ticket or jottings of times. Anything like that."

The gardener bowed and left.

When he was alone, Carbone exhaled between closed teeth, hissing like a puncture. He dropped heavily onto the rattan settee on the veranda and let his head fall back against the rounded curve behind him.

Damn her! Damn her! Damn her!

Why wouldn't they all leave him alone? He was seventy-two. He had high blood pressure and a heart condition. He wanted to retire and enjoy life for a year or two before he popped off. He might even take Angelica back to Corsica to see his old village.

He heard his wife come out onto the veranda; her hand touched his shoulder.

"Are you all right?"

He heard the panic in her voice.

"I'm fine. Fine." He didn't want to do what he had to do, but Nina was forcing his hand. With Falci and his gang snapping at his heels already. It would restore his fading prestige if he could identify and punish the person behind the unnatural price rises, which were hitting everyone, not just himself. He needed the extra clout. Every bit he could manage.

Personally? He was angry, of course. Furious. Enraged that the Luoc clan had once again made him into a fool. At the same time it made him very sad.

"Shall I bring your coffee up here?" asked Angelica. "I'll ask to have more made; the other's gone cold."

"Don't bother," snapped Carbone. Her hand fell from his shoulder.

He would concentrate on his anger until he had settled things once and for all.

Dalat, my ass! he thought. Who was she kidding? Nina could not be allowed to leave Saigon alive. He sent a servant to bring Paul Buonaparte. I warned you, he said to her silently, I warned you!

Suddenly, in the afternoon, Nina found herself with nothing to do except wait. When she realized that she had just made a second tour of the house, touching objects in farewell, she decided she must go out. Eight Hand Horse was already out making his own arrangements. Trailed by Tiny Albert, Nina set off, wearing an *ao dai*. She had no destination; she just wanted to walk. After half an hour she knew that she was saying farewell to the city just as she had done to the house.

Abruptly, she turned in the direction of the New Yorker Hotel. She would check the telex board herself, on the chance that there might be some word from Will John. At least this action would look forward and not back. The continuing existence for her of Saigon did not depend on farewells. It was already lodged deep inside her.

There was no message for Miss Thuyet. She hadn't really expected one.

She paused on the pavement while Tiny Albert inspected a rack of girlie magazines propped against the wall of the hotel.

The milky pink globe alerted her, but not soon enough. The taxi driver still chewed bubble gum. Just as before, he turned to open the door. Just as before, someone pushed her toward the backseat. Over the man's shoulder she saw Tiny Albert lunge toward her, then disappear behind a large coolie. He did not reappear in the time it took for the door to be closed and the taxi to pull out into the traffic.

Not now! Oh God, not now!

Nina reached for the door handle. Then she stopped. If she escaped now, Thu would know for certain she was up to something. She could never avoid him for thirty-six more hours. She considered quickly whether she could change her flight plans. But it was all arranged; it would be too dangerous to call attention to any urgency on her part. She leaned back in the seat.

Thu was in an old villa on the borders where Cholon met Saigon, once a country residence until the two creeping cities met to flood around its walls.

He wore a business suit, without a tie, but he stood waiting for her in the huge plaster-walled drawing room, surrounded by packing crates and boxes, just as he had stood under the chandelier in the pavilion in the Rung Sat.

She held out her hands to him as she entered the room.

"Cousin Thu! You have saved me from the trouble of sending you a message."

"And what was the message?" He did not respond to the warmth of her greeting, but treated her to his measuring stare.

"I am going to Dalat the day after tomorrow. To rest a little. I wanted you to know, so that you might perhaps join me for a few days. It might bring back older, more peaceful times." She smiled, undeterred by his seriousness.

He smiled back at her suddenly. "I've saved you more than the trouble of a message, then."

She felt it coming and put it off as much as she could. "Aren't you going to ask me to sit down before you drag me into conversation?"

He waved her to a fringed brocade overstuffed chair.

"We are leaving for Laos tonight," he said.

She felt the blood leave her head; a great weight sucked her down. She locked her elbows to remain upright.

"Is it such a shock?" His voice had its dangerous edge. "Your American is gone. What's the problem?"

"There's no problem," she said.

"I will send people to bring what you need from your house."

"No problem except suddenness." She began to be able to lift her head again without feeling darkness edge into her brain. His people will find the money. Think, she ordered herself.

"I have not yet quite tied things up," she said. "A few more days . . . a week. I haven't concluded the last sale. And we still need the money."

Thu squatted in front of her chair and looked into her face. "I have been unsure of you, School Dragon, since I decided that you don't like having me in Saigon."

His perceptions were accurate as ever.

She decided to meet him head on. It was safest. "I don't know you in Saigon. You are the one who is changing. You are the one with mysterious new allies. You are the one with plans you tell me at the last minute. And you say that *you* are not sure of *me*!"

He took her wrists gently. She felt him judge her response, alert to the slightest pulling back from her. She made herself lean a little toward him. "Why should I trust you?"

He released one wrist and touched her face.

Gods of Heaven, forgive me for the lie, she thought. There is no other way.

"Why should I trust you when you keep so much from me? When you are so ill-mannered in your surprises? And when I most need to trust you?"

She was convincing because these questions were absolutely genuine.

"Why do you need to trust me now, more than before?"

In spite of her fear, she found it difficult to go through with.

"I am about to go away with you, to a strange place..." she stammered.

"You knew that before." He was watching her intently. Curiously.

"Yes... but, now... it's so close. And there's more."

She leaned back in her chair and smoothed the loose silk of the *ao dai* close to her belly.

He stared without breathing. Then he made a tiny noise in his throat.

"How soon?" he asked.

She made a lightning calculation, thinking back to the date of his last visit. "A few weeks."

He had begun to breathe quickly. She watched him think.

"You are very small, are you not?"

"Yes."

"Look at me, School Dragon...."

She did, hauling into her mind every good image of their times together to warm her eyes and hide the fear.

"Is it mine?"

"Yes."

He gripped her wrists again.

"Swear on your father's grave!"

It was Will John she was betraying, not Thu, she told herself. And he would have accepted the necessity for the lie.

"I swear it on my father's grave."

He held her eyes for a long time; she willed him to believe her.

"You are hurting my wrists," she said at last.

He opened his fingers and bent his head to kiss the marks of his fingers. His head remained bent for several seconds, his mouth against her skin. Then he stood suddenly and sprang away from her chair. He twisted through four kicks and turns of a martial arts exercise, finishing jubilantly with both arms held aloft.

"It will be a boy!" He swung and wove twice more. "My son!"

She laughed. She couldn't help it. He had startled her. And relief burst out, in spite of her.

His eyes swung back to her. For a moment he judged whether

she was laughing at him. Then he laughed back, offering her his jubilation. At that, tears came to her eyes.

"Forgive me," she said. "You know how it is when women are pregnant."

He seized a piece of silk from the top of a packing case and dropped it in her lap. "Please stop it at once, you silly pregnant female."

He grinned down at her while she wiped her eyes.

An hour later she was back in her own house. He had given her three days to complete the sale and get ready to leave. Even his impetuousness could see that she needed to make special arrangements for a child to be born in a villa in the mountains of Laos.

There was no sign of Tiny Albert. Nina asked to be told as soon as he returned. She considered sending someone again to see if a telex had arrived for Miss Thuyet, but decided against it. Coca-Cola Boy would let Chinchook know if one did arrive. She prepared for her last night in Saigon.

At about the same time that Nina returned to her house from Thu's Saigon villa, Carbone was having his first aperitif of the evening with a clerk working at Tan Son Nhut. He had come to report the rumor that someone had begun arrangements to fly a large shipment of smack from Saigon to Seattle, U.S.A.

When the young man had left, Carbone put out an information alert to find out who had made a large sale or purchase in the last two or three days. By one o'clock in the morning he knew it had been none of the usual dealers. He lay awake most of the night, beside the comfortable mountain range of his wife. When there was no further news by early morning, he invited William Falci to lunch.

At eleven o'clock that same night Louis arrived at Nina's house in answer to her summons. He was loose-cheeked from wine and brandy, and wearing evening clothes.

"You're looking flushed and cheerful tonight," she said. "Is there something I should know? Someone interesting in your life?"

To her amazement, Louis was evasive and slightly uncomfortable as he told her he had been dining with an American doctor who had wanted to discuss the real feelings of the peasants in South Vietnam toward Western-style medicine.

"I think you're hiding something from me," she teased. "But it makes what I'm going to say a little easier."

Louis busied himself with his stick and his scarf. "Don't be silly. You know how I hate entanglements."

She sat beside him on the sofa. "I'm afraid I'm going to burden you with a little knowledge. I'm going away...."

"You're taking my advice at last!" He was relieved by her change of subject. "A rest at last. In your condition. Where are you going?"

"I won't be back."

His mouth made a silent O and the silver willow leaves arched above his eyes. "I see," he said after a pause. "Well, thank you for burdening me. I would never have forgiven you otherwise."

"I had to say good-bye properly."

"I don't suppose I should ask where?"

"I wouldn't tell you," she said. "You'll learn why soon enough. If all goes well, I may be able to let you know how to get in touch."

She reached over and took his hand. Though the nails were buffed to a healthy pink, the skin was loose over his knuckles. With his other hand, he extracted a silk handkerchief from his pocket and snapped it like a conjurer. Then he blew his nose.

"*Merde!* Look what you've made me do. I suppose I was rather counting on my adoptive grandson."

He blew his nose again.

"Who knows," she said. "The fighting can't last forever. Or the Americans."

"Nor will any of us, my dear. Still..." He began to tuck the handkerchief back into his pocket. "Here I am worrying about how all this is going to affect me. Selfish old brute! Wondering how I shall play out my last few scenes without you."

"You're a melodramatic old brute," she said. "And I'm going to say it, even if it makes you climb under the sofa—I love you dearly and owe you much more than you can possibly imagine. I'm really a bunch of seams holding together some holes, underneath all your patches."

"The sofa is far too low for me," he said mournfully.

"I want you to have the Géricault," she said. "Come for it tomorrow; I'll leave instructions. I'm sure you can manage better than anyone else without the legal title. I've tried to find it, but I couldn't."

He threw his eyes to the ceiling. "This damned woman is trying to reduce me to helpless sobs!" Then he held out his arms. "It's never possible to say the right things at these times... forgive me.... But you must know."

She hugged him tightly.

"There's one last thing I need you to do for me." She took the second safe-deposit key off the chain around her neck. "Will you see that this is delivered for me? Make sure, personally, that it arrives?"

"Of course. Anything in exchange for a Géricault! Where would you like me to deliver it?"

She told him.

The willow leaves quivered. He opened his mouth, then closed it again.

"By what time?" he asked at last.

"Tomorrow will do." She looked at him again. "Are you going somewhere else tonight?"

To her amazement he blushed deep, mangosteen purple.

"It is an entanglement!" she cried.

"Companionship," he said quickly. "For my old age. Now that you're deserting me."

"How can I possibly leave now that you've given me something to torment you about? The gods are quite unfair!"

She walked him to the door. They embraced once more, quickly. He trotted down the steps without looking back, but just before he disappeared down the drive he twirled the jade-topped cane in a quick Fred Astaire shuffle. Then he was gone.

Before going to bed, Nina checked again about Tiny Albert. No one had seen him. Eight Hand Horse said he would put out word to look for him.

"Thu's people would have no reason to kill him," said Nina.

"He's not dead," said Eight Hand Horse sourly. "Run away, more likely. He let you get taken. He's ashamed. And piss-scared. I should have been there!"

"I need you tomorrow. And it was all right in the end."

"He doesn't know that."

Like Emile Carbone, Nina could not sleep that night.

She saw too much in the darkness. Thu changing his mind and coming for her during the night. Will John testifying against her in Washington. Falci learning, somehow, of her arrangement with the northern brokers before his meeting in the morning with Jouvet. And Carbone.

She saw her plane the next night being hit by antiaircraft artillery. She saw her father's village under air attack during his burial. In the shadowy bombardment, she saw her unborn baby flying in one direction and herself in another.

At half past five she got up and turned on the light.

At 8 A.M. Emile Carbone told Paul Buonaparte to station his

519

men at Tan Son Nhut immediately. One in the civilian departure area, two on the base. The maid had not been able to learn exactly the time of Nina's flight to "Dalat." As Carbone was sure she was not going to Dalat, flight schedules were no help whatsoever.

"Tell them to wait all day... all night if necessary. Put in relief men, if you have to. Whatever else happens, she must not leave the airport alive!"

That's that, said Carbone to himself when Buonaparte had gone. But it gave him no satisfaction. Nor did the prospect of lunch with William Falci from Tampa, Florida, U.S.A.

At half past eight that morning Chinchook honked the horn of the Studebaker as he skidded to a stop in front of the house. He wore a radioactive blue rayon suit and an open-necked sports shirt printed all over with scottie dogs. On his bare feet was a pair of American loafers. He had been up all night, at the Mother Goose Casino. Nina sent for coffee.

"You should have been with me," he said expansively. "Shared in my luck. Fucking good, I tell you! No one could stop me!" He leaned back in his chair and sipped his coffee.

Nina smiled from her own chair; she was glad of the distraction from the agony of waiting. She smoothed her dressing gown demurely.

"I'm glad you had good luck... you won't be needing what I had been going to give you."

He sat upright. "What's that?"

"Nothing much." She sipped her own coffee, then put it down. It made her feel ill.

"Don't tease, Big Sister," said Chinchook seriously. "It's not gentlemanly."

She tossed him an envelope.

He opened it and began to count the notes inside. After a few seconds his hands began to shake. When he looked up, his eyes were filled with alarm.

"What do you want me to do for this? I don't do things *this* expensive. Big Sister, don't ask so much of me!"

She regretted teasing him. "Do you remember many years ago when we first knew each other, you said you wished to be a poet, like your famous namesake?" Her voice was reassuring.

"I think it is time for you to begin now. I wish to become your first patron."

Suspicion ebbed and flowed in his eyes. "You're crazy," he said. "Loco!"

"No," she replied. "Unless it is crazy to have such faith in you. You must use that to go to some inspiring spot away from Saigon that will open the fountains of your spirit.''

He still looked at her, convinced that he had been right, back beside the water jars on the ruins, to think she was completely mad.

''I'm going to Dalat,'' she said. ''For a rest and mountain air.'' She touched her belly lightly. ''Travel is risky these days. Anything can happen to any of us at any time. I was thinking about this the other day and decided that it was foolish to wait any longer to speak to you. We have been much to each other. And I want to thank you.''

His brow wrinkled at the odd weight of finality behind her words. He looked down at the envelope in his hands. Then he decided to take her at face value.

''You are welcome, Big Sister. You are welcome!'' He began to glow with magnanimity and pleasure.

''Listen to me,'' she said seriously. ''I said it seemed foolish to wait. . . . I would also like you to think what you really wish to do. And do it now. No waiting.''

He looked puzzled. ''I will try to make a poem . . . as you wish.''

''Please think,'' she repeated.

''I do fine right now.'' With his thumb, he began to revolve one of his gold rings around its finger. ''I do number one, OK.''

''As you say.''

''Bad time for soldiers and a good time for me!'' He nodded his own confirmation. ''A very good time!''

A small sliver of despair lodged in her chest. She had given him all she could to weigh against the boom, the opportunities.

''It is also a time to be careful,'' she said. ''And to reflect on the dangers of disorder.''

''Don't worry about me!'' He was beginning to look indignant. ''Why do you worry? I'm not stupid. I'm not a baby, or a montagnard savage. You know me, Big Sister!''

''Yes, I know you. You're a man with number one luck.''

''Right on!'' He grinned at his newly acquired American phrase. ''Thank you all the same for the nice holiday.'' He held up the envelope.

As she said good-bye, she bit her tongue to keep from repeating her warning to be careful. He might well survive the next few years; his knavery had a cheerful impartiality that somehow avoided offense. And she had given him enough to buy his way out of a few situations that he couldn't talk his way out of first.

When he left, she opened the big case that her maid had already packed for Dalat and began to shift a few of the contents into another, smaller bag. In the small bag were also several large-denomination dollar bills, changed for Falci's hundreds, a few bundles of the hundreds, a thick envelope of bearer bonds, and another envelope of Laotian *kip,* Thai *baht,* Hong Kong dollars, and some gold pieces. Tucked under the leather lining of the bag was a French passport with a valid entry visa for the United States.

At twelve noon Daniel Jouvet left Falci's apartment with the second half of the payment for the three hundred kilos of number four. He went first to the Chartered Bank and made a large cash deposit. Then he went to the Banque d'Indochine where he made a second deposit. He would have to wait until after the midday break before he could make his last deposit at the Hong Kong and Shanghai. Though this was his usual procedure after making a sale for Nina, he was sweating hard inside his cream-colored jacket. The deposits were larger than any he had ever made before. He had done his best to check for surveillance after leaving Falci, but he imagined that both bank clerks had looked at him with suspicion. As he left the first two banks he visualized the clerks rushing off as soon as he had left, to pass a message to some interested paymaster.

He steadied himself with the thought of the unusually large deposit of cash he could now go and hide behind the paneling of his dressing room at home.

At the time Jouvet was heading home a small boy delivered a packet to Carbone.

"Who sent it?" asked Carbone, though he knew the inevitable answer.

"Man I never see," said the boy. He looked gloomy. "He pay me number ten."

Carbone gave him a few piastres and he scampered down the steps of the veranda and out the gate. Carbone watched him go, but saw no trace of the elderly Chinese *métis* who was waiting in the street to give the boy the rest of his delivery fee. If he had seen Louis, he would have recognized him and would undoubtedly have treated the parcel with more urgency.

As it was, he asked his *boyesse* to open it, at a slight distance for safety's sake. But it held nothing sinister, only a safe-deposit key tied to a tag giving a number and the name of the Hong Kong and Shanghai Bank.

Carbone looked at it curiously. Then examined the packet to be sure that the *boyesse* hadn't overlooked a note with an explanation. Then he set the key aside; Falci was due to arrive at any time for lunch.

An hour later, the preliminaries were over. The two men eyed each other across a cloth littered with crumbs sticky with tinned butter from Denmark, while the *boyesse* served each of them a grilled mullet.

Falci was enjoying himself. He was sure the old bastard had decided to deal with him after all, and was waiting to see what would be offered. It would give him pleasure to tell him that it was too late . . . unless he could offer very special terms indeed.

Carbone concentrated on surgery for a few minutes, then flicked the fish's spine clear of the flesh. "My friend," he said, "I consider it my painful duty to give you a little bad news."

He glanced up. Falci had a crumb stuck to the pillow of his chin; he looked curious rather than perturbed by the announcement.

"Rumor has reached me that you have been taken for a ride."

"I haven't gone anywhere with anybody that I know of," replied Falci.

"I'm glad I'm wrong," said Carbone. "I heard that you had made a very large purchase in the last day or two. Of something supposed to be in short supply."

He was gratified by the slight flicker of the puffy eyelids.

"That sounds more like a reason for congratulations," said Falci. "If it's true."

"How much did you pay?"

Falci laughed. "If you're preparing a pitch of your own, forget it, I would never pay more than the going market value. Take it from there yourself."

"That's my point," said Carbone. "The market value."

Falci's face shifted into neutral.

"It's high," explained Carbone.

"Sure it's high! Supplies are short." Falci dug at his fish. "It makes sense."

"You poor ignorant Yank," said Carbone gently. "Of course, it makes sense. *If* supplies are really short."

"What are you trying to say . . . ?"

"The harvest in Annam and Tonkin was excellent this year."

Falci sat still, with the top of his black crew cut in perfect parallel with the line of the windowsill behind him. "Why do you say that?"

"But since it wasn't you who made the purchase," continued

523

Carbone, "it's not so serious. But if I were the buyer, I would want to talk to the agent who sold him such a large amount at an artificially inflated price. Wouldn't you? It rather narrows the margin of profit at street level, where there's a natural ceiling on prices."

Carbone chewed a piece of fish. "I would want to know where this agent got his supplies. I'd like to know who was taking advantage of a stranger in town. Taking my money and making a fool of me at the same time. Word will get around."

He turned to look out the window, to give Falci time to think it over. Angelica had eaten earlier and was in the garden pointing out to the gardener which blooms to cut for the house.

Then Carbone delivered his *coup de grace*. "In his place, I would hate to have to explain to my superiors."

After Falci left, Carbone settled back to see what happened next. He decided to have a nap and called for Angelica to come and lie beside him; her presence soothed him. He did not remember the little key until late in the afternoon.

Jouvet was in the usual shower cubicle at the Cercle Sportif, recovering from an early evening session of squash. He closed his eyes to let the water break over the top of his head and twine in sensuous strands down his soapy body. Through the rushing of water, he heard the shower curtain scrape back along its track.

With his eyes still closed, he groped for his towel to clear the soap. An American voice said, "Time to put your clothes on, Mr. Jewvay."

The heavy Turkish towel hit him in the face.

When he could open his eyes, he saw the smiling face of Falci's driver.

Daniel Jouvet had never, privately, considered himself a brave man. That self-knowledge kept him relatively honest, as honesty went. When William Falci asked him who had provided the consignment of number four heroin, a combination of cowardice and honesty led Jouvet to tell him immediately.

"She's going to Dalat today," said Jouvet. "But I know where she'll be."

"I'm sure you do," said Falci grimly. He regarded Jouvet with open speculation.

Jouvet smoothed his mustaches nervously, as a frightened cat stops to lick its fur. "Why do you want to know? Is there something wrong?" He allowed a touch of indignation into his voice. "If there is, as the middleman I would like to know—I have a professional standing to protect. I have a right to know!"

"Yeah, there's something wrong!" Falci stared down from his window at the tops of the palm-leaf umbrellas that shaded the cocktail tables around the turquoise pool.

Jouvet shivered, and blamed the air-conditioning. Its high-pitched keening from the grille-covered box beneath the window was getting on his nerves. When Falci looked back at him he felt like a Tu Do whore being sized up.

"That's an interesting point you just raised," said Falci. "Professional standing. I guess it matters out here just as much as everywhere else."

Jouvet tried to misread the man's drift. But his feet went cold inside their silk socks. The palms of his hands became clammy. A feeling of pressure closed around his throat and the back of his head.

"If you ask around," he said as calmly as he could, "you'll find that I'm considered a good lawyer. Discreet. Experienced in French corporate law. If there's any way at all that I can help you out here, I'd be delighted." He smiled with lips made of stone. "You could do worse."

"Thanks," said Falci. "I might take you up on that." He continued to study Jouvet, almost absently. "Yeah, you could advise me on the way things work out here. Things like professional standing. Let's get together sometime and talk about it."

Jouvet had been dismissed. He stood up, unable to believe that he was going to leave freely after all.

Falci held out his hand to shake. "Sorry if Ricky gave you a scare in the shower."

All the way down the two flights of stairs Jouvet kept his hand on the ebony rail to steady himself. He congratulated himself on his ability to size up a new set of circumstances and adapt to them. It would be tough on Nina, but she had chosen the risk. She hadn't confided in him that she had pushed the price up; she couldn't expect him to take the heat for her. He would stay out of her way until Falci had sorted her out. It was too bad about the child.

He had begun to speculate on the advantages of being paid in dollars when he heard someone behind him on the stairs. He just managed to control his bladder when he saw Ricky again, smiling the same smile as he had in the shower room.

"Mr. Falci said I should take you home."

"I don't mind taking a taxi," said Jouvet. "Tell him thank you all the same."

"Nah!" said Ricky. "The boss don't like his people to have to rush around in the heat. I'll take you home."

Jouvet's instinct to run was outweighed by Rick's use of the words "his people." He let the driver hold the street door open for him, and followed him to the car.

At the big house Nina made one final check in her mind. She gave the small bag to Eight Hand Horse to put into the car. She also gave him the large case intended for Dalat; he loaded it with noisy grunts and groans.

She said good-bye to Snow Man and the servants and gave the *mama-san* money and instructions on how to join her when she sent for her. Tiny Albert was still absent. Then she marched quickly down the steps and into the car. She was afraid that if she paused to think about what she was doing she would become paralyzed and stand forever looking back, a statue on her own doorstep.

At Tan Son Nhut the young Vietnamese was growing both anxious and bored. He had been standing in Departures since eight o'clock that morning. The nerves of being on a job had long worn off, and this worried him. In those hours his eyes had glanced over more faces than he could count. He had begun to imagine that he had missed the face in the photograph, or to imagine that every other woman resembled her. That the photo was bad. That he had fallen asleep on his feet. Worst of all, he knew that all of these niggling worries were distracting him and could make him careless when the time finally came, if it ever did. He touched the tip of his middle finger to the long, slim blade in his sleeve. He looked once more across the concourse at the newspaper seller who would make a disturbance at the appropriate moment. The man was dozing against the wall.

The young Vietnamese blinked and straightened his shoulders. He touched the knife once more. If he did this job well, he was made. It was a big one, he knew. And he was good at the job; he knew that too. He reset himself like a clock and scanned the tide of incoming faces with renewed sharpness.

Carbone turned restlessly and yawned. It was a yawn of nerves. Beside him, Angelica had propped her glasses on her cheeks and was knitting a strip of lace. Carbone sat up against the pillow and poured a glass of water from the carafe beside the bed. The late afternoon light was filtered and cool under the leaves of the lime trees outside the window. When he replaced the glass on the tray with a tiny click, he remembered the safe-deposit key.

Forty-five minutes later, he stared down at the papers in front of him on the table in the little cubicle at the Hong Kong and Shanghai Bank. Maps. Lists of names and addresses. He knew what he was looking at, but not why.

He picked up a contract for the sale of Heron Confectionery to Cajun Inc., Tallahassee, Florida, U.S.A., and turned to the last page to see the signatures. The seller was Nina Martell, the buyer William Farrantino, for Cajun Inc. He looked at the sales documents for seven fishing junks. The seller's signature was an unfamiliar Vietnamese, on behalf of Happy Chrysanthemum Holdings; the buyer was also William Farrantino.

He looked at the little key as if demanding it to explain itself. Then he shut his eyes and sat down on the upholstered upright chair beside the table.

Don't jump to any conclusions, he told himself. Much as you might want to. Farrantino... Falci... Florida. For several minutes he looked for the trick, the trap, the way he would be made to look a fool. Finally he decided that it really was the other way around.

He shuffled together the papers from the box and went through them again, carefully. His forefinger moved over the list of names, stopping every so often. It touched that of Daniel Jouvet.

"Yes, I wondered about you, too, young man," he said aloud.

He stopped for a long time over the name of Clinton Clay and the information noted after it.

He looked for the name of the River Pirate cousin, but it was not there on any of the lists. Thu's absence did not change his growing conviction.

"Holy Mary, Mother of God!" he said aloud at last. "It's a marked deck! And I think the little bitch has deliberately left it for me."

He began to divide the papers among his various inside pockets.

He was willing to consider them quits. She had her father's sense of style, too. He nearly smiled. Then he stood up so fast he nearly knocked over his chair. He stuffed the remainder of the papers back into the box, threw the box at the bank clerk, and sprinted to his car, trailed by an alarmed bodyguard.

'Tan Son Nhut!'' he shouted to his driver. "Fast!"

Nina watched the streets of Saigon pass the car windows; she felt as if she had died and was regarding everything from somewhere else. She concentrated fiercely on a pattern of cracks

in the back of the leather seat in front of her; the lines divided
and spread like streams in the delta.

She looked back out the window. In two hours she would
leave the city. In a few days' time she would leave her country
for good. What she was leaving already looked distant and
strange. And yet the place from which she regarded it was even
more alien and unknown.

She looked at her watch nervously. Two hours to go until her
flight. Traffic was bad. She needed time at the airport to sort out any
last-minute problems . . . there were always problems with travel
these days. But she knew what she had to do before she left.

"Please stop at the New Yorker," she said to Eight Hand Horse.

The telex board was outside the coffee shop, just past the little
fountain that changed from blue to pink to saffron gold in endless
sequence. Nina leaned across a plastic rubber plant and scanned
the names. Moran. Schumacher. Billings. Chomsky. Platt. Lee
Wing On. Anderson. Texaco. BBC. *St. Louis Post Dispatch*.
Violins were playing movie themes over the public address
system. The little fountain made the sound of five men pissing
from a height onto a damp pavement. She looked again. Barnard.
The People. Kriangsak. Miller. Then she saw it. Thuyet.

She dropped the pin that held it to the board and opened the
flimsy paper with shaking hands. "Congratulations," it said, "on
the successful conclusion of deal. I repeat offer of merger this end.
Other company was already trading elsewhere. I stress merger, not
takeover. Suggest meeting here. Please consider seriously. Contact
as before. I'll stand by." It was signed "K. Kong."

She pressed it to her face in joy and relief before she
remembered that she was still in a public place. Then she also
recalled how much there was still to be done before she was safe
enough to consider the possibilities that Will John's telex offered.

On Doan Thi Diem Street, Carbone's car became jammed
behind a convoy of American transport trucks. The jam moved in
shifting currents, at different rates. While the whales idled, the
minnows darted through crevices. Meanwhile, the sharks and
remoras shouldered and twisted themselves steadily from pause
to pause. Carbone's driver, a shark, finally cut across the
oncoming traffic, drove ten meters against the tide, and turned
into a cross avenue to detour around the obstruction.

At Tan Son Nhut, Nina checked in for the evening flight to
Vientiane. At the time of check-in it was still scheduled to leave,

although there had been reports of antiaircraft artillery attacks to the west during the afternoon. She took the small bag and headed toward Passport Control. She had said good-bye to Eight Hand Horse in the car; they would meet in Tonkin, if all went well.

She did not look around; if she were being watched she would never be able to detect the watcher among the airport crowds, ground staff, cleaners, and vendors. She walked, not too fast, toward the narrow neck of her escape route, where a uniformed officer was checking passports at a desk.

The hand under her elbow was light; the fingers closed just enough to register their presence and to guide her gently off course. For three steps she let herself be led while her mind raced. She would not let herself be taken, not this close to the end. They would have to kill her, right here. She turned her head. It was not Thu's gum-chewing taxi driver, nor any of his heavies that she recognized. The young Vietnamese was clean, well barbered, anonymous. His expression was pleasant. She knew suddenly what he was. She was glad she had already decided that she preferred to die.

His free hand came up. She stared stupidly. He continued to hold out his hand with the single red rose, in a cone of cheap commercial cellophane, waiting for her to relieve him of it. She looked at him searchingly. His own eyes were blank and disclaiming. But he had tight lines around his mouth and nostrils. She was sure she was right about him. But she could not make sense of it all.

She took the rose carefully, still thinking that it held a trap. A weapon. A danger. The stem and paper still dripped from the vendor's pail. The edges of the petals had begun to crinkle like aging skin after a day on display. As soon as she took the flower, the young Vietnamese muttered an imprecation under his breath and ducked away into the crowd.

Nina stood, still dumbfounded, clutching her bag in one hand and the aging rose in the other, while people pushed past her toward Passport Control. If she risked a step, her knees would buckle. She waited for them to regain strength and for her heart to slow a little, and until her pulse began to thud a little less against her eardrums.

While she waited, she lifted her head and studied the crowd. Against the far wall a heavy, gray-haired European was buying a newspaper. He turned and looked directly into her eyes. It was Carbone. He flicked a quick finger up in greeting, then turned and left with his paper.

She couldn't put it all together for herself until after the plane for Vientiane had begun to strain upward to get above range of VC antiaircraft guns. When at last she saw the pattern she wrapped her arms around herself and began to shake.

After they had been airborne for half an hour she finally settled back in her seat. Now it was only a matter of getting from Laos across the mountains into Tonkin, a relatively short journey, though a rough one. But she had escaped from the pattern. She was moving now as randomly as one shooting star among millions of other stars.

The next morning, while Nina was beginning her journey northeast from Vientiane into Tonkin, Eight Hand Horse visited the same banks Jouvet had visited the day before, and using Nina's seal withdrew the money Jouvet had deposited. He then spent the rest of the morning buying several high-denomination bank bonds made out to the bearer, and a selection of international shares likewise made out to the bearer. He visited a German money changer who specialized in black market foreign currency. By the end of the afternoon he had reduced paper which would once have filled a large suitcase to one plump envelope and several large-denomination U.S. and HK dollar bills. If he couldn't smuggle that out of the country, he told himself, he would admit that he was past it after all.

By evening an elderly peasant, surrounded by bundles and baskets of his possessions, squatted humbly on a small quay at the U.S. naval docks. He smoked a cheroot as he waited for his unofficial lift downstream on a river patrol boat. His presence would buy the crew a few drinks when they got back to port.

Carbone knew before he opened it that the parcel was not nice; it had a bad feel to it. As he peered into the box, at the plastic sandwich bag secured with twisted wire, he congratulated himself on not having lost his instincts with old age. Inside the sandwich bag were a man's testicles and penis.

He guessed that Falci had taken his advice and had a word or two with the heroin broker. He covered the box again and took it to his study. He put it, covered, on his desk and paced the room, looking at the box from time to time.

Falci hadn't been grateful for Carbone's tip-off.

Not that I would have been either, he reflected grimly.

But to dare to send him a warning.

Carbone felt as if he were getting a migraine. He did not usually suffer from them, but felt one now, shooting through the side of his head and veiling his eyes with a haze of pain.

"Angelica!" he shouted out the open window into the garden where his wife was tending some tomato plants she had raised from seed.

She raised her head in alarm and began to run toward the house, her heavy figure suddenly light-footed.

"It's nothing," he said irritably as she panted wide-eyed into the room. "I just want you to sit with me for a while."

49

Her father's village was one of the landscape ghosts that Nina had seen on her last trip north. Her eyes now knew what to look for—parallel lines, flat-sided timbers, X's of lashed joints rather than Y's of natural branching. With her guide, a farmer from a village farther south, she pondered the remains of the huts. They were deserted, but Nina had seen a patch of yams a short way back along the track, which was still being tended.

"Wait," said the farmer. "Maybe they think we are VC." He disappeared around a small raw mountain kicked up by a shell from the crater beyond. The head of a water buffalo twisted up from the irrigation ditch on Nina's right. Flies crawled in the empty eye sockets and the hide shivered and twitched. Nina looked away.

The farmer was gone a long time. When he returned, he walked very slowly, leading an old, old woman.

She was older than anyone Nina had ever seen, bent nearly double so that she was no taller than Titi had been, and fleshless as a dried leaf. Bare scalp showed through the sparse strands of gray hair scraped back into a meager knot at her nape. The parchment of her arms and legs clung to the knobs and ridges of bone and stringy sinew.

She pushed her feet forward in turn, with painful effort, each sandal heavy as a tombstone; her nails curled around the end of her toes. As the farmer led her closer, Nina saw the fogging of cataracts over the old woman's eyes.

"She is Number One Wife of the headman who was killed," he explained.

Nina dropped to her haunches to look into the old woman's face. She searched the corded flesh around the nose, mouth, and veiled eyes for the face it had once been.

"Did she have two sons, one of whom went away?"

The old woman shook her head in bewilderment. "Who wants

531

to know about my sons?'' She held out an exploratory hand. ''Who is it?''

Nina took the hand in hers and felt a fragile dryness like cast-off snakeskin. In all her imaginings she had not thought of this possibility. A lump blocked her throat.

She swallowed and said, ''Grandmother. . . .'' The word made tears come. ''It is the daughter of your eldest son.'' She paused.

The old woman went very still.

''I am bringing my father back to lie with his ancestors,'' said Nina.

The woman gave a small moan. For a minute Nina was afraid the shock had been too great. Then the old woman fastened both fragile claws on Nina's hand in a ferocious grip. She pulled as if she were reeling herself to shore. One of her hands reached for Nina's face. The clouded eyes strained to see detail in the shadowed form of her granddaughter.

Nina knelt, to stop the trembling of her legs. The dry little hands explored her face, felt the tears, then fastened in her hair.

The old woman began to weep.

''I thought it had ended,'' she said. ''That I was the last.'' Tears raced down the channels between wrinkles and fell from the sharp edges of her jawbone. Nina folded her in her arms, as gently as a trapped bird. The woman placed her damp cheek against Nina's face again and again as if to confirm her living warmth.

''So my eldest son is dead too.'' The old woman had recovered her calm.

They sat under a thatched shelter outside the circumference of the old village, near the opening into the tunnels. Nina was eating rice gruel prepared by a curious younger woman whom the old woman had called out of the tunnel. A circle of women and children watched her.

''He sent me messages,'' her grandmother continued. ''And money for myself and to tend the graves. But it has been difficult. He said it would be dangerous for us if he came here.'' She paused and looked toward the ruins of the village. ''Hee, hee, hee.'' Her mirth was high-pitched and abrupt. ''What did he think we had left to fear?'' She rocked on her heels for a moment. ''Well, he's gone.'' She suddenly grasped Nina's arm. ''Are you married? Do you have a son?''

Nina moved the dry claw to the hard eight-month swelling of her belly.

''Ahhh.'' The old woman sighed a deep gust of pleasure.

"That's good! That's very good! My husband will be happy too."

She paused, as if conducting an unheard conversation with him. Her hand stroked Nina's belly absently.

"I don't suppose you could live here ... ?" Her voice trailed away. "Why would you want to ... ?"

"I will come back," said Nina, and bit her tongue. In spite of herself, she continued. "I will bring my child to honor its ancestors."

"That's good. That's good," said the old woman once more. She rocked on her heels and sank into private meditation. Every so often she repeated, "That's good."

The young woman took Nina to the tombs. She was a cousin of some sort; Nina had not quite followed her grandmother's explanations of family lines. Two small boys trailed after them, also family.

They detoured through some dry rice, around a crater that had filled with muddy water. Beyond the crater, burned, broken tree trunks rising through scrub were all that remained of a former grove. The fallen tops had been cleared for firewood. In a stand of long grass beyond the broken grove were the burial mounds, overgrown and crumbling. Traces of color were caught in the rough stone of the markers. A chipped enamel plate and a few burned ends of joss lay on the grass in front of the nearest grave.

Nina was suddenly overwhelmed by a sense of death. It was not the graves but the country around her. Its wounds gaped open and muddy, like a rotting corpse. The mountains seemed to be drawing themselves up, away from the desolation at their feet. The *paddi* fields were silent. Breezes could not stir the black splinters of the trees of the grove.

The woman dropped to her knees in the long grass. Nina wondered if she too felt the emptiness. When the land had still lived, the men buried in the tombs still lived, released from their bodies but part of the rich sea that washed the villagers. Good and bad, helpful and malicious, all the spirits had helped shape the forces that worked on man. Life was made up equally of the seen and unseen, balanced in careful harmony; the dead demanded care from the living but also gave help and guidance.

She remembered, suddenly, the night she had stayed awake to watch the offerings she and Simpoh Flower had placed in the garden of the big house. Her mother had discovered her and sent her to bed before the spirits came, but in the morning the offerings were gone. More than twenty years later, she could still recall the deep joy that had filled her at the sight of the clean plates on the altar, even though her mother had said that rats and mice had eaten it all.

Here, in the mountains, the tree trunks had released their spirits; the homes of the Water Goddess had been filled with putrefying flesh. There was no longer food for the ghosts of dead cats, or dogs, or pigs. The spine of the Dragon was being broken, his tail cut off, his eye put out, his veins broken and dammed.

She dropped to her knees beside her cousin.

She would go back to An Khe. She would bribe cement from the clerk at the supply depot. She would pay someone to make the bamboo horses and paper money and paper house. She would find a priest to site the grave properly. She would pay to have a body bag smuggled on board a night run from the base. She would make a tomb over her father and cut the grass from around the others.

She looked around her. It would be like pouring a cup of water into a dry *paddi* field. But it would also be a tying up of broken ends. A promise.

The mountains might be persuaded to put down their roots again and link this place with the Heavens once more. She did not know if the Dragon would heal; it received more wounds every day and more seemed doomed to come. But it might yet coil into a flower of flames and be reborn.

She had a curious sensation of being distanced from herself. She watched herself as if she were a bird flying overhead. Then the bird swooped and settled into the stillness that was even greater than the stillness of death in the land. Ghostly fingers stirred her hair. She shook her head against the breeze like a young mare, but the sense of stillness remained.

"Grandfather," she said silently, "so soon after coming to you, I am going away again. I am taking your great-grandchild over the mountains into Laos, all the way to America. To its Round Eye father.

"When I first decided to do that," she said, "I thought I was running away. But it is more than that. To survive with honor is all there is for us . . . and to continue. I wish that I believed enough to ask for your blessing. But I promise myself and you, if you are there, that I will one day bring my half-Round Eye child to do honor to its ancestors here."

She stayed on her knees in the grass a few moments longer, wanting to believe that it was her grandfather who lifted and dropped the short strand of hair that had fallen beside her temple. Even if it were not, the breeze filled her with the peace of a caress.

ABOUT THE AUTHOR

Born in Indianapolis, Indiana, CHRISTIE DICKASON grew up in Southeast Asia, Mexico, and Switzerland. Her father, an English professor, served in U.S. Intelligence for Southeast Asia during World War II. In 1954, he returned to Thailand with his family, where he set up an English-language teaching program for a Thai university. The extraordinary sense of place in this novel comes from the author's own experience of Southeast Asia before the Vietnam War. Christie Dickason went on to graduate Phi Beta Kappa from Radcliffe and received a master's in fine arts from Yale Drama School. She has worked as a theater director and choreographer for fourteen years in England, including three years with the Royal Shakespeare Company. She served as drama officer for the Arts Council of Great Britain for three years. She lives in London with her husband and two sons.

OFFICIAL RULES

NO PURCHASE NECESSARY.

To enter identify this month's Bantam Book titles by placing a circle around each word forming each title. There are three titles shown on previous page to be found in this month's puzzle. Mail your entry to: Grand Slam Sweepstakes, P.O. Box 18, New York, N.Y. 10046.

This is a monthly sweepstakes starting February 1, 1988 and ending January 31, 1989. During this sweepstakes period, one automobile winner will be selected each month from all entries that have correctly solved the puzzle. To participate in a particular month's drawing, your entry must be received by the last day of that month. The Grand Slam prize drawing will be held on February 14, 1989 from all entries received during all twelve months of the sweepstakes.

To obtain a free entry blank/puzzle/rules, send a self-addressed stamped envelope to: Winning Titles, P.O. Box 650, Sayreville, N.J. 08872. Residents of Vermont and Washington need not include return postage.

PRIZES: Each month for twelve months a Chevrolet automobile will be awarded with an approximate retail value of $12,000 each.

The Grand Slam Prize Winner will receive 2 Chevrolet automobiles plus $10,000 cash (ARV $34,000).

Winners will be selected under the supervision of Marden-Kane, Inc., an independent judging organization. By entering this sweepstakes each entrant accepts and agrees to be bound by these rules and the decisions of the judges which shall final and binding. Winners may be required to sign an affidavit of eligibility and release which must be returned within 14 days of receipt. All prizes will be awarded. No substitution or transfer of prizes permitted. Winners will be notified by mail. Odds of winning depend on the total number of eligible entries received.

Sweepstakes open to residents of the U.S. and Canada except employees of Bantam Books, its affiliates, subsidiaries, advertising agencies and Marden-Kane, Inc. Void in the Province of Quebec and wherever else prohibited or restricted by law. Not responsible for lost or misdirected mail or printing errors. Taxes and licensing fees are the sole responsibility of the winners. All cars are standard equipped. Canadian winners will be required to answer a skill testing question.

For a list of winners, send a self-addressed, stamped envelope to: Bantam Winners, P.O. Box 711, Sayreville, N.J. 08872.

THE LATEST BOOKS
IN THE BANTAM
BESTSELLING TRADITION